the

summer

i

turned

pretty

trilogy

Also by Jenny Han

Shug

Also by Jenny Han & Siobhan Vivian

Burn for Burn

the

summer

i

turned

pretty

trilogy

JENNY HAN

SIMON & SCHUSTER BFYR

New York   London   Toronto   Sydney   New Delhi

the
summer
i
turned
pretty

JENNY HAN

SIMON & SCHUSTER BFYR

An imprint of Simon & Schuster Children's Publishing Division
1230 Avenue of the Americas, New York, New York 10020
This book is a work of fiction. Any references to historical events,
real people, or real places are used fictitiously. Other names, characters,
places, and events are the product of the author's imagination, and any
resemblance to actual events or places or persons, living or dead,
is entirely coincidental.
First SIMON & SCHUSTER BFYR bind-up edition May 2013
THE SUMMER I TURNED PRETTY © 2009 by Jenny Han
IT'S NOT SUMMER WITHOUT YOU © 2010 by Jenny Han
WE'LL ALWAYS HAVE SUMMER © 2011 by Jenny Han
These titles were previously published individually.
All rights reserved , including the right of reproduction
in whole or in part in any form.
SIMON & SCHUSTER BFYR is a trademark of Simon & Schuster, Inc.
Also available in SIMON & SCHUSTER BFYR hardcover editions.
For information about special discounts for bulk purchases,
please contact Simon & Schuster Special Sales at 1-866-506-1949
or business@simonandschuster.com.
The Simon & Schuster Speakers Bureau can bring authors to your live event.
For more information or to book an event, contact the Simon & Schuster Speakers
Bureau at 1-866-248-3049 or visit our website at www.simonspeakers.com.
Book design by Lucy Ruth Cummins
The text of this book is set in Bembo
Manufactured in the United States of America
10 9 8 7 6 5 4 3
Library of Congress Control Number: 2013936650
ISBN 978-1-4424-9971-3

*To all the important sister women in my life
and most especially Claire*

❧ ❧ ❧

Acknowledgments

First and always, thank you to the Pippin women: Emily van Beek, Holly McGhee, and Samantha Cosentino. Thank you to my editor extraordinaire Emily Meehan, who supports me like no other, as well as Courtney Bongiolatti, Lucy Ruth Cummins, and everyone at S&S. Many thanks to Jenna and Beverly and the Calhoun School for their continuous support of my writing life. Thanks to my writing group the Longstockings, and one Longstocking in particular, who has sat across from me every Monday and cheered me on—Siobhan, I'm looking at you. And thank you to Aram, who inspired me to write about the forever kind of friendship, the kind that spans over boyfriends and beaches and children and lifetimes.

I say, "I can't believe you're really here."

He sounds almost shy when he says, "Me neither."
And then he hesitates. "Are you still coming with me?"

I can't believe he even has to ask. I would go
anywhere. "Yes," I tell him. It feels like nothing else
exists outside of that word, this moment. There's
just us. Everything that happened this past summer,
and every summer before it, has all led up to this.
To now.

chapter *one*

We'd been driving for about seven thousand years. Or at least that's how it felt. My brother, Steven, drove slower than our Granna. I sat next to him in the passenger seat with my feet up on the dashboard. Meanwhile, my mother was passed out in the backseat. Even when she slept, she looked alert, like at any second she could wake up and direct traffic.

"Go faster," I urged Steven, poking him in the shoulder. "Let's pass that kid on the bike."

Steven shrugged me off. "Never touch the driver," he said. "And take your dirty feet off my dashboard."

I wiggled my toes back and forth. They looked pretty clean to me. "It's not your dashboard. It's gonna be my car soon, you know."

"If you ever get your license," he scoffed. "People like you shouldn't even be allowed to drive."

"Hey, look," I said, pointing out the window. "That guy in a wheelchair just lapped us!"

Steven ignored me, and so I started to fiddle with the radio. One of my favorite things about going to the beach was the radio stations. I was as familiar with them as I was with the ones back home, and listening to Q94 made me just really know inside that I was there, at the beach.

I found my favorite station, the one that played everything from pop to oldies to hip-hop. Tom Petty was singing "Free Fallin'." I sang right along with him. "She's a good girl, crazy 'bout Elvis. Loves horses and her boyfriend too."

Steven reached over to switch stations, and I slapped his hand away. "Belly, your voice makes me want to run this car into the ocean." He pretended to swerve right.

I sang even louder, which woke up my mother, and she started to sing too. We both had terrible voices, and Steven shook his head in his disgusted Steven way. He hated being outnumbered. It was what bothered him most about our parents being divorced, being the lone guy, without our dad to take his side.

We drove through town slowly, and even though I'd just teased Steven about it, I didn't really mind. I loved this drive, this moment. Seeing the town again, Jimmy's Crab Shack, the Putt Putt, all the surf shops. It was like coming home after you'd been gone a long, long time. It held a million promises of summer and of what just might be.

As we got closer and closer to the house, I could feel that familiar flutter in my chest. We were almost there.

I rolled down the window and took it all in. The air tasted just the same, smelled just the same. The wind making my hair feel sticky, the salty sea breeze, all of it felt just right. Like it had been waiting for me to get there.

Steven elbowed me. "Are you thinking about Conrad?" he asked mockingly.

For once the answer was no. "No," I snapped.

My mother stuck her head in between our two seats. "Belly, do you still like Conrad? From the looks of things last summer, I thought there might be something between you and Jeremiah."

"WHAT? You and Jeremiah?" Steven looked sickened. "What happened with you and Jeremiah?"

"Nothing," I told them both. I could feel the flush rising up from my chest. I wished I had a tan already to cover it up. "Mom, just because two people are good friends, it doesn't mean there's anything going on. Please never bring that up again."

My mother leaned back into the backseat. "Done," she said. Her voice had that note of finality that I knew Steven wouldn't be able to break through.

Because he was Steven, he tried anyway. "What happened with you and Jeremiah? You can't say something like that and not explain."

"Get over it," I told him. Telling Steven anything

would only give him ammunition to make fun of me. And anyway, there was nothing to tell. There had never been anything to tell, not really.

Conrad and Jeremiah were Beck's boys. Beck was Susannah Fisher, formerly Susannah Beck. My mother was the only one who called her Beck. They'd known each other since they were nine—blood sisters, they called each other. And they had the scars to prove it—identical marks on their wrists that looked like hearts.

Susannah told me that when I was born, she knew I was destined for one of her boys. She said it was fate. My mother, who didn't normally go in for that kind of thing, said it would be perfect, as long as I'd had at least a few loves before I settled down. Actually, she said "lovers," but that word made me cringe. Susannah put her hands on my cheeks and said, "Belly, you have my unequivocal blessing. I'd hate to lose my boys to anyone else."

We'd been going to Susannah's beach house in Cousins Beach every summer since I was a baby, since before I was born even. For me, Cousins was less about the town and more about the house. The house was my world. We had our own stretch of beach, all to ourselves. The summer house was made up of lots of things. The wraparound porch we used to run around on, jugs of sun tea, the swimming pool at night—but the boys, the boys most of all.

I always wondered what the boys looked like in

December. I tried to picture them in cranberry-colored scarves and turtleneck sweaters, rosy-cheeked and standing beside a Christmas tree, but the image always seemed false. I did not know the winter Jeremiah or the winter Conrad, and I was jealous of everyone who did. I got flip-flops and sunburned noses and swim trunks and sand. But what about those New England girls who had snowball fights with them in the woods? The ones who snuggled up to them while they waited for the car to heat up, the ones they gave their coats to when it was chilly outside. Well, Jeremiah, maybe. Not Conrad. Conrad would never; it wasn't his style. Either way, it didn't seem fair.

I'd sit next to the radiator in history class and wonder what they were doing, if they were warming their feet along the bottom of a radiator somewhere too. Counting the days until summer again. For me, it was almost like winter didn't count. Summer was what mattered. My whole life was measured in summers. Like I don't really begin living until June, until I'm at that beach, in that house.

Conrad was the older one, by a year and a half. He was dark, dark, dark. Completely unattainable, unavailable. He had a smirky kind of mouth, and I always found myself staring at it. Smirky mouths make you want to kiss them, to smooth them out and kiss the smirkiness away. Or maybe not away . . . but you want to control it somehow. Make it yours. It was exactly what I wanted to do with Conrad. Make him mine.

Jeremiah, though—he was my friend. He was nice to me. He was the kind of boy who still hugged his mother, still wanted to hold her hand even when he was technically too old for it. He wasn't embarrassed either. Jeremiah Fisher was too busy having fun to ever be embarrassed.

I bet Jeremiah was more popular than Conrad at school. I bet the girls liked him better. I bet that if it weren't for football, Conrad wouldn't be some big deal. He would just be quiet, moody Conrad, not a football god. And I liked that. I liked that Conrad preferred to be alone, playing his guitar. Like he was above all the stupid high school stuff. I liked to think that if Conrad went to my school, he wouldn't play football, he'd be on the lit mag, and he'd notice someone like me.

When we finally pulled up to the house, Jeremiah and Conrad were sitting out on the front porch. I leaned over Steven and honked the horn twice, which in our summer language meant, *Come help with the bags, stat.*

Conrad was eighteen now. He'd just had a birthday. He was taller than last summer, if you can believe it. His hair was cut short around his ears and was as dark as ever. Unlike Jeremiah's, whose hair had gotten longer, so he looked a little shaggy but in a good way—like a 1970s tennis player. When he was younger, it was curly yellow, almost platinum in the summer. Jeremiah hated his curls. For a while, Conrad had him convinced that crusts made your hair curly, so Jeremiah had stopped eating sandwich crusts, and Conrad would polish them off. As Jeremiah got older, though, his hair was less and less curly and more wavy. I missed his curls. Susannah called him her little angel, and he used to look like one, with his rosy cheeks and yellow curls. He still had the rosy cheeks.

Jeremiah made a megaphone with his hands and yelled, "Steve-o!"

I sat in the car and watched Steven amble up to them and hug the way guys do. The air smelled salty and wet, like it might rain seawater any second. I pretended to be tying the laces on my sneakers, but really I just wanted a moment to look at them, at the house for a little while, in private. The house was large and gray and white, and it looked like most every other house on the road, but better. It looked just the way I thought a beach house should look. It looked like home.

My mother got out of the car then too. "Hey, boys. Where's your mother?" she called out.

"Hey, Laurel. She's taking a nap," Jeremiah called back. Usually she came flying out of the house the second our car pulled up.

My mother walked over to them in about three strides, and she hugged them both, tightly. My mother's hug was as firm and solid as her handshake. She disappeared into the house with her sunglasses perched on the top of her head.

I got out of the car and slung my bag over my shoulder. They didn't even notice me walk up at first. But then they did. They really did. Conrad gave me a quick glanceover the way boys do at the mall. He had never looked at me like that before in my whole life. Not once. I could feel my flush from the car return. Jeremiah, on the other hand, did a double take. He looked at me like he didn't even recognize me. All of this happened in the span of about three seconds, but it felt much, much longer.

Conrad hugged me first, but a faraway kind of hug, careful not to get too close. He'd just gotten a haircut, and the skin around the nape of his neck looked pink and new, like a baby's. He smelled like the ocean. He smelled like Conrad. "I liked you better with glasses," he said, his lips close to my ear.

That stung. I shoved him away and said, "Well, too bad. My contacts are here to stay."

He smiled at me, and that smile—he just gets in. His smile did it every time. "I think you got a few new ones," he said, tapping me on the nose. He knew how self-conscious I was about my freckles and he still teased me every time.

Then Jeremiah grabbed me next, and he almost lifted me into the air. "Belly Button's all growed up," he crowed.

I laughed. "Put me down," I told him. "You smell like BO."

Jeremiah laughed loudly. "Same old Belly," he said, but he was staring at me like he wasn't quite sure who I was.

He cocked his head and said, "Something looks different about you, Belly."

I braced myself for the punch line. "What? I got contacts." I wasn't completely used to myself without glasses either. My best friend Taylor had been trying to convince me to get contacts since the sixth grade, and I'd finally listened.

He smiled. "It's not that. You just look different."

I went back to the car then, and the boys followed me. We unloaded the car quickly, and as soon as we were done, I picked up my suitcase and my book bag and headed straight for my old bedroom. My room was Susannah's from when she was a child. It had faded calico wallpaper and a white bedroom set. There was a music box I loved. When you opened it, there was a twirling ballerina that danced to the theme song from *Romeo and Juliet*, the old-timey version. I kept my jewelry in it. Everything about my room was old and faded, but I loved that about it. It felt like there might be secrets in the walls, in the four-poster bed, especially in that music box.

Seeing Conrad again, having him look at me that way, I felt like I needed a second to breathe. I grabbed the stuffed polar bear on my dresser and hugged him close to my chest—his name was Junior Mint, Junior for short. I sat down with Junior on my twin bed. My heart was beating so loudly I could hear it. Everything was the same but not. They had looked at me like I was a real girl, not just somebody's little sister.

chapter *two*
AGE 12

The first time I ever had my heart broken was at this house. I was twelve.

It was one of those really rare nights when the boys weren't all together—Steven and Jeremiah went on an overnight fishing trip with some boys they'd met at the arcade. Conrad said he didn't feel like going, and of course I wasn't invited, so it was just me and him.

Well, not together, but in the same house.

I was reading a romance novel in my room with my feet on the wall when Conrad walked by. He stopped and said, "Belly, what are you doing tonight?"

I folded the cover of my book over quickly. "Nothing," I said. I tried to keep my voice even, not too excited or eager. I had left my door open on purpose, hoping he'd stop by.

"Want to go to the boardwalk with me?" he asked. He sounded casual, almost too casual.

This was the moment I had been waiting for. This was it. I was finally old enough. Some part of me knew it too, it was ready. I glanced over at him, just as casual as he'd been. "Maybe. I have been craving a caramel apple."

"I'll buy one for you," he offered. "Just hurry up and put some clothes on and we'll go. Our moms are going to the movies; they'll drop us off on the way."

I sat up and said, "Okay."

As soon as Conrad left, I closed my door and ran over to my mirror. I took my hair out of its braids and brushed it. It was long that summer, almost to my waist. Then I changed out of my bathing suit and put on white shorts and my favorite gray shirt. My dad said it matched my eyes. I smeared some strawberry frosting lip gloss on my lips and tucked the tube into my pocket, for later. In case I needed to reapply.

In the car Susannah kept smiling at me in the rearview mirror. I gave her a look like, *Quit, please*—but I wanted to smile back. Conrad wasn't paying attention anyway. He was looking out the window the whole ride there.

"Have fun, kids," said Susannah, winking at me as I closed my door.

Conrad bought me a caramel apple first. He bought himself a soda, but that was it—usually he ate at least an apple or two, or a funnel cake. He seemed nervous, which made me feel less nervous.

As we walked down the boardwalk, I let my arm hang loose—*in case*. But he didn't reach for it. It was one of those perfect summer nights, the kind where there's a cool breeze and not one drop of rain. There would be rain tomorrow, but that night there were cool breezes and that was it.

I said, "Let's sit down so I can eat my apple," so we did. We sat on a bench that faced the beach.

I bit into my apple, carefully; I was worried I might get caramel all stuck in my teeth, and then how would he kiss me?

He sipped his Coke noisily, and then glanced down at his watch. "When you finish that, let's go to the ring-toss."

He wanted to win me a stuffed animal! I already knew which one I'd pick too—the polar bear with wire-frame glasses and a scarf. I'd had my eye on it all summer. I could already picture myself showing it off to Taylor. Oh, that? Conrad Fisher won it for me.

I wolfed down the rest of my apple in about two bites. "'Kay," I said, wiping my mouth with the back of my hand. "Let's go."

Conrad walked straight over to the ringtoss, and I had to walk superquick to keep up. As usual, he wasn't talking much, so I talked even more to make up for it. "I think when we get back, my mom might finally get cable. Steven and I have been trying to convince her for forever. She claims to be so against TV, but then she watches movies on A&E, like, the whole time we're here. It's so hypocritical," I said, and my voice trailed off when I saw that Conrad wasn't even listening. He was watching the girl who worked the ringtoss.

She looked about fourteen or fifteen. The first thing I noticed about her was her shorts. They were canary yellow, and they were really, really short. The exact same kind of shorts that the boys had made fun of me for wearing two days before. I felt so good about buying those shorts with Susannah, and then the boys had laughed at me for it. The shorts looked a whole lot better on her.

Her legs were skinny and freckled, and so were her arms. Everything about her was skinny, even her lips. Her hair was long and wavy. It was red, but it was so light it was almost peach. I think it might have been the prettiest hair I'd ever seen. She had it pulled over to the side, and it was so long that she had to keep flicking it away as she handed people rings.

Conrad had come to the boardwalk for her. He'd brought me because he hadn't wanted to come alone and he hadn't wanted Steven and Jeremiah to give him a hard time. That was it. That was the whole reason. I could see it all in the way he looked at her, the way he almost seemed to hold his breath.

"Do you know her?" I asked.

He looked startled, like he'd forgotten I was there. "Her? No, not really."

I bit my lip. "Well, do you want to?"

"Do I want to what?" Conrad was confused, which was annoying.

"Do you want to know her?" I asked impatiently.

"I guess."

I grabbed him by his shirt sleeve and walked right up to the booth. The girl smiled at us, and I smiled back, but it was just for show. I was playing a part. "How many rings?" she asked. She had braces, but on her they looked interesting, like teeth jewelry and not like orthodontics.

"We'll take three," I told her. "I like your shorts."

"Thanks," she said.

Conrad cleared his throat. "They're nice."

"I thought you said they were too short when I wore the exact same pair two days ago." I turned to the girl and said, "Conrad is so overprotective. Do you have a big brother?"

She laughed. "No." To Conrad she said, "You think they're too short?"

He blushed. I'd never seen him blush before, not in the whole time I'd known him. I had a feeling it might be the last time. I made a big show of looking at my watch and said, "Con, I'm gonna go ride the Ferris wheel before we leave. Win me a prize, okay?"

Conrad nodded quickly, and I said bye to the girl and

left. I walked over to the Ferris wheel as fast as I could so they wouldn't see me cry.

Later on, I found out the girl's name was Angie. Conrad ended up winning me the polar bear with the wire-frame glasses and scarf. He said Angie told him it was the best prize they had. He said he thought I'd like it too. I told him I'd rather have had the giraffe, but thanks anyway. I named him Junior Mint, and I left him where he belonged, at the summer house.

chapter *three*

After I unpacked, I went straight down to the pool,
where I knew the boys would be. They were lying
around on the deck chairs, their dirty bare feet hanging
off the edges.

As soon as Jeremiah saw me, he sprang up. "Ladies
and Gentlemen-men-men," he began, bowing like a
circus ringmaster. "I do believe it is time . . . for our first
belly flop of the summer."

I inched away from them uneasily. Too fast a move-
ment, and it would be all over—they'd chase me then.
"No way," I said.

Then Conrad and Steven stood up, circling me. "You
can't fight tradition," Steven said. Conrad just grinned
evilly.

"I'm too old for this," I said desperately. I walked

backward, and that's when they grabbed me. Steven and Jeremiah each took a wrist.

"Come on, guys," I said, trying to wriggle out of their grasp. I dragged my feet, but they pulled me along. I knew it was futile to resist, but I always tried, even though the bottoms of my feet got burned along the pavement in the process.

"Ready?" Jeremiah said, lifting me up under my armpits.

Conrad grabbed my feet, and then Steven took my right arm while Jeremiah hung on to my left. They swung me back and forth like I was a sack of flour. "I hate you guys," I yelled over their laughter.

"One," Jeremiah began.

"Two," Steven said.

"And three," Conrad finished. Then they launched me into the pool, clothes and all. I hit the water with a loud smack. Underwater, I could hear them busting up.

The Belly Flop was something they'd started about a million summers ago. Probably it had been Steven. I hated it. Even though it was one of the only times I was included in their fun, I hated being the brunt of it. It made me feel utterly powerless, and it was a reminder that I was an outsider, too weak to fight them, all because I was a girl. Somebody's little sister.

I used to cry about it, run to Susannah and my mother, but it didn't do any good. The boys just accused me of being a tattletale. Not this time, though. This time I was going to be a good sport. If I was a good sport, maybe that would take away some of their joy.

When I came up to the surface, I smiled and said, "You guys are ten-year-olds."

"For life," Steven said smugly. His smuggy face made me want to splash him and soak him and his precious Hugo Boss sunglasses that he worked for three weeks to pay for.

Then I said, "I think you twisted my ankle, Conrad." I pretended to have trouble swimming over to them.

He walked over to the edge of the pool. "I'm pretty sure you'll live," he said, smirking.

"At least help me out," I demanded.

He squatted and gave me his hand, which I took.

"Thanks," I said giddily. Then I gripped tight and pulled his arm as hard as I could. He stumbled, fell forward, and landed in the pool with a splash even bigger than mine. I think I laughed harder right then than I've laughed in my whole life. So did Jeremiah and Steven. I think maybe all of Cousins Beach heard us laughing.

Conrad's head bobbed up quickly, and he swam over to me in about two strokes. I worried he might be mad, but he wasn't, not completely. He was smiling but in a threatening kind of way. I dodged away from him. "Can't catch me," I said gleefully. "Too slow!"

Every time he came close, I swam away. "Marco," I called out, giggling.

Jeremiah and Steven, who were headed back to the house, said, "Polo!"

Which made me laugh, which made me slow to swim away, and Conrad caught my foot. "Let go," I gasped, still laughing.

Conrad shook his head. "I thought I was too slow," he said, treading water closer to me. We were in the diving well. His white T-shirt was soaked through, and I could see the pinky gold of his skin.

There was this weird stillness between us all of a sudden. He still held on to my foot, and I was trying to stay afloat. For a second I wished Jeremiah and Steven were still there. I didn't know why.

"Let go," I said again.

He pulled on my foot, drawing me closer. Being this close to him was making me feel dizzy and nervous. I said it again, one last time, even though I didn't mean it. "Conrad, let go of me."

He did. And then he dunked me. It didn't matter. I was already holding my breath.

chapter *four*

Susannah came down from her nap a little while after
we put on dry clothes, apologizing for missing our big
homecoming. She still looked sleepy and her hair was
all feathery on one side like a kid's. She and my mother
hugged first, fierce and long. My mother looked so happy
to see her that she was teary, and my mother was never
teary.

Then it was my turn. Susannah swept me in for a hug,
the close kind that's long enough to make you wonder
how long it's going to last, who'll pull away first.

"You look thin," I told her, partly because it was true
and partly because I knew she loved to hear it. She was
always on a diet, always watching what she ate. To me, she
was perfect.

"Thanks, honey," Susannah said, finally letting me go,

looking at me from arm's length. She shook her head and said, "When did you go and grow up? When did you turn into this phenomenal woman?"

I smiled self-consciously, glad that the boys were upstairs and not around to hear this. "I look pretty much the same."

"You've always been lovely, but oh honey, look at you." She shook her head like she was in awe of me. "You're so pretty. So pretty. You're going to have an amazing, amazing summer. It'll be a summer you'll never forget." Susannah always spoke in absolutes like that—and when she did, it sounded like a proclamation, like it would come true because she said so.

The thing is, Susannah was right. It was a summer I'd never, ever forget. It was the summer everything began. It was the summer I turned pretty. Because for the first time, I felt it. Pretty, I mean. Every summer up to this one, I believed it'd be different. Life would be different. And that summer, it finally was. I was.

chapter *five*

Dinner the first night was always the same: a big pot of spicy bouillabaisse that Susannah cooked up while she waited for us to arrive. Lots of shrimp and crab legs and squid—she knew I loved squid. Even when I was little, I would pick out the squid and save it for last. Susannah put the pot in the middle of the table, along with a few crusty loaves of French bread from the bakery nearby. Each of us would get a bowl, and we'd help ourselves to the pot all throughout dinner, dipping the ladle back into the pot. Susannah and my mother always had red wine, and us kids had grape Fanta, but on that night there were wineglasses for everyone.

"I think we're all old enough to partake now, don't you, Laur?" Susannah said as we sat down.

"I don't know about that," my mother began, but then

she stopped. "Oh, all right. Fine. I'm being provincial, isn't that right, Beck?"

Susannah laughed and uncorked the bottle. "You? Never," she said, pouring a little wine for each of us. "It's a special night. It's the first night of summer."

Conrad drank his wine in about two gulps. He drank it like he was used to drinking it. I guess a lot can happen over the course of a year. He said, "It's not the first night of summer, Mom."

"Oh, yes it is. Summer doesn't start until our friends get here," Susannah said, reaching across the table and touching my hand, and Conrad's, too.

He jerked away from her, almost by accident. Susannah didn't seem to notice, but I did. I always noticed Conrad.

Jeremiah must have seen it too, because he changed the subject. "Belly, check out my latest scar," he said, pulling up his shirt. "I scored three field goals that night." Jeremiah played football. He was proud of all of his battle scars.

I leaned in next to him to get a good look. It was a long scar that was just beginning to fade, right across the bottom of his stomach. Clearly, he'd been working out. His stomach was flat and hard, and it hadn't looked like that last summer even. He looked bigger than Conrad now. "Wow," I said.

Conrad snorted. "Jere just wants to show off his two-pack," he said, breaking off a piece of bread and dipping it into his bowl. "Why don't you show all of us, and not just Belly?"

"Yeah, show us, Jere," Steven said, grinning.

Jeremiah grinned right back. To Conrad he said, "You're just jealous because you quit." Conrad had quit football? That was news to me.

"Conrad, you quit, man?" Steven asked. I guessed it was news to him, too. Conrad was really good; Susannah used to mail us his newspaper clippings. He and Jeremiah had been on the team together these last two years, but it was Conrad who'd been the star.

Conrad shrugged indifferently. His hair was still wet from the pool, and so was mine. "It got boring," he said.

"What he means is, he got boring," Jeremiah said. Then he stood up and pulled off his shirt. "Pretty nice, huh?"

Susannah threw her head back and laughed, and my mother did too. "Sit down, Jeremiah," she said, shaking the loaf of bread at him like a sword.

"What do you think, Belly?" he asked me. He looked like he was winking even though he wasn't.

"Pretty nice," I agreed, trying not to smile.

"Now it's Belly's turn to show off," Conrad said mockingly.

"Belly doesn't need to show off. We can all see how lovely she is just looking at her," Susannah said, sipping her wine and smiling at me.

"Lovely? Yeah, right," said Steven. "She's a lovely pain in my ass."

"Steven," my mother warned.

"What? What'd I say?" he asked.

"Steven's too much of a pig to understand the concept of lovely," I said sweetly. I pushed the bread to him. "Oink, oink, Steven. Have some more bread."

"Don't mind if I do," he said, breaking off a crusty chunk.

"Belly, tell us about all the hot friends you're gonna set me up with," Jeremiah said.

"Didn't we already try that once?" I said. "Don't tell me you've forgotten about Taylor Jewel already."

Everyone busted up laughing then, even Conrad.

Jeremiah's cheeks turned pink, but he was laughing too, and shaking his head. "You're not a nice girl, Belly," he said. "There's plenty of cute girls at the country club, so don't worry about me. Worry about Con. He's the one missing out."

The original plan was for both Jeremiah and Conrad to work at the country club as lifeguards. Conrad had done it the summer before. This summer Jeremiah was old enough to do it with him, but Conrad changed his mind at the last minute and decided to bus tables at the fancy seafood buffet instead.

We used to go there all the time. Kids twelve and younger could eat there for twenty dollars. There was a time when I was the only one twelve or younger. My mother always made sure to tell the waiter that I was younger than twelve. As, like, principle. Every time she did it, I felt like disappearing. I wished I was invisible. It wasn't that the boys even made a big deal out of it, which they easily could have, but it was the feeling different, like an outsider, that I hated. I hated it being pointed out. I just wanted to be like them.

chapter *six*
AGE 10

Right off the bat, the boys were a unit. Conrad was the leader. His word was pretty much law. Steven was his second in command, and Jeremiah was the jester. That first night, Conrad decided that the boys were going to sleep on the beach in sleeping bags and make a fire. He was a Boy Scout; he knew all about that kind of stuff.

Jealously, I watched them plan. Especially when they packed the graham crackers and marshmallows. Don't take the whole box, I wanted to tell them. I didn't, though—it wasn't my place. It wasn't even my house.

"Steven, make sure you bring the flashlight," Conrad directed. Steven nodded quickly. I had never seen him follow orders before. He looked up to Conrad, who was eight months older; it had always been that way.

Everybody had somebody but me. I wished I was at home, making butterscotch sundaes with my dad and eating them on our living room floor.

"Jeremiah, don't forget the cards," Conrad added, rolling up a sleeping bag.

Jeremiah saluted him and danced a little jig, which made me giggle. "Sir, yes, sir." He turned to me on the couch and said, "Conrad is bossy like our dad. Don't feel like you have to listen to him or anything."

Jeremiah talking to me made me feel brave enough to say, "Can I come too?"

Right away Steven said, "No. Guys only. Right, Con?"

Conrad hesitated. "Sorry, Belly," he said, and he really did look sorry for a second. Two seconds, even. Then he went back to rolling his sleeping bag.

I turned away from them and faced the TV. "That's okay. I don't really care anyway."

"Ooh, watch out, Belly's gonna cry," Steven said joyously. To Jeremiah and Conrad he said, "When she doesn't get her way, she cries. Our dad always falls for it."

"Shut up, Steven!" I yelled. I was worried I really might cry. The last thing I needed was to be a crybaby our first night. Then they'd never take me along for real.

"Belly's gonna cry," Steven said in a singsong voice. Then he and Jeremiah started to dance a jig together.

"Leave her alone," Conrad said.

Steven stopped dancing. "What?" he said, confused.

"You guys are so immature," Conrad said, shaking his head.

I watched them pick up their gear and get ready to leave. I was about to lose my chance to camp, to be a part of the gang. Quickly I said, "Steven, if you don't let me go, I'll tell Mom."

Steven's face twisted. "No, you won't. Mom hates it when you tattletale."

It was true, my mother hated it when I told on Steven for things like this. She'd say he needed his own time, that I could go the next time around, that it would be more fun at the house with her and Beck anyway. I sank into the couch, arms crossed. I'd lost my chance. Now I just looked like a tattletale, a baby.

On the way out Jeremiah turned around and danced a quick jig for me, and I couldn't help it, I laughed. Over his shoulder Conrad said, "Good night, Belly."

And that was it. I was in love.

chapter *seven*

I didn't notice right away that their family had more money than ours. The beach house wasn't some fancy kind of place. It was a real honest-to-God beach house, the kind that's lived in and comfortable. It had faded old seersucker couches and a creaking La-Z-Boy us kids always fought over, and peeling white paint and hard-wood floors that had been bleached by the sun.

But it was a big house, room enough for all of us and more. They'd built an addition years ago. On one end there was my mother's room, Susannah and Mr. Fisher's room, and an empty guest room. On the other end was my room, another guest room, and the room the boys shared, which I was jealous of. There used to be bunk beds and a twin in that room, and I hated that I had to sleep all alone in mine when I could hear them giggling and whispering all night through the wall. A couple of times the boys let me sleep in there too, but only when they had some especially gruesome story they wanted to tell. I was a good audience. I always screamed at all the right places.

Since we've gotten older, the boys have stopped sharing a room. Steven started staying over on the parents' end, and Jeremiah and Conrad both had their rooms on my end. The boys and I have shared a bathroom since the beginning. Ours is on our end of the house, and then my mother has her own, and Susannah's is connected to the master bedroom. There are two sinks—Jeremiah and Conrad shared one, and Steven and I shared the other.

When we were little, the boys never put the seat down, and they still didn't. It was a constant reminder that I was different, that I wasn't one of them. Little things have changed, though. It used to be that they left water all over the place, either from splash fights or from just being careless. Now that they shaved, they left their little chin hairs all over the sink. The counter was crowded with their different deodorants and shaving cream and cologne.

They had more cologne than I had perfume—one pink French bottle my dad bought me for Christmas when I was thirteen. It smelled like vanilla and burnt sugar and lemon. I think his grad student girlfriend picked it out. He wasn't good at that sort of thing. Anyway, I didn't leave my perfume in the bathroom mixed in with all their stuff. I kept it on the dresser in my room, and I never wore it anyway. I didn't know why I even brought it with me.

chapter *eight*

After dinner I stayed downstairs on the couch and so did Conrad. He sat there across from me, strumming chords on his guitar with his head bent.

"So I heard you have a girlfriend," I said. "I heard it's pretty serious."

"My brother has a big mouth." About a month before we'd left for Cousins, Jeremiah had called Steven. They were on the phone for a while, and I hid outside Steven's bedroom door listening. Steven didn't say a whole lot on his end, but it seemed like a serious conversation. I burst into his room and asked him what they were talking about, and Steven accused me of being a nosy little spy, and then he finally told me that Conrad had a girlfriend.

"So what's she like?" I didn't look at him when I said

this. I was afraid he'd be able to see how much I cared.

Conrad cleared his throat. "We broke up," he said.

I almost gasped. My heart did a little ping. "Your mom is right, you are a heartbreaker." I meant it to come out as a joke, but the words rang in my head and in the air like some kind of declaration.

He flinched. "She dumped me," he said flatly.

I couldn't imagine anyone breaking up with Conrad. I wondered what she was like. Suddenly she was this compelling, actual person in my mind. "What was her name?"

"What does it matter?" he said, his voice rough. Then, "Aubrey. Her name is Aubrey."

"Why did she break up with you?" I couldn't help myself. I was too curious. Who was this girl? I pictured someone with pale white blond hair and turquoise eyes, someone with perfect cuticles and oval-shaped nails. I'd always had to keep mine short for piano, and then after I quit, I still kept them short, because I was used to them that way.

Conrad put down the guitar and stared off into space moodily. "She said I changed."

"And did you?"

"I don't know. Everybody changes. You did."

"How did I change?"

He shrugged and picked up his guitar again. "Like I said, everybody changes."

Conrad started playing the guitar in middle school. I hated it when he played the guitar. He'd sit there, strumming, halfway paying attention, only halfway present. He'd hum to himself, and he was someplace else. We'd be watching TV, or playing cards, and he'd be strumming the guitar. Or he'd be in his room, practicing. For what, I didn't know. All I knew was that it took time away from us.

"Listen to this," he'd said once, stretching out his headphones so I had one and he had the other. Our heads touched. "Isn't it amazing?"

"It" was Pearl Jam. Conrad was as happy and enthralled as if he had discovered them himself. I'd never heard of them, but at that moment, it was the best song I'd ever heard. I went out and bought *Ten* and listened to it on repeat. When I listened to track five, "Black," it was like I was there, in that moment all over again.

After the summer was over, when I got back home, I went to the music store and bought the sheet music and learned to play it on the piano. I thought one day I could accompany Conrad and we could be, like, a band. Which was so stupid, the summer house didn't even have a piano. Susannah tried to get one for the summer house, so I could practice, but my mother wouldn't let her.

chapter *nine*

At night when I couldn't sleep, I'd sneak downstairs and go for a swim in the pool. I'd start doing laps, and I'd keep going until I felt tired. When I went to bed, my muscles felt nice and sore but also shivery and relaxed. I loved bundling myself up after a swim in one of Susannah's cornflower blue bath sheets—I'd never even heard of bath sheets before Susannah. And then, tiptoeing back upstairs, falling asleep with my hair still wet. You sleep so well after you've been in the water. It's like no other feeling.

Two summers ago Susannah found me down there, and some nights she'd swim with me. I'd be underwater, doing my laps, and I'd feel her dive in and start to swim on the other side of the pool. We wouldn't talk; we'd just swim, but it was comforting to have her there. It was the only time that summer that I ever saw her without her wig.

Back then, because of the chemo, Susannah wore her wig all the time. No one saw her without it, not even my mother. Susannah had had the prettiest hair. Long, caramel-colored, soft as cotton candy. Her wig didn't even compare, and it was real human hair and everything, the best money could buy. After the chemo, after her hair grew back, she kept it short, cut right below her chin. It was pretty, but it wasn't the same. Looking at her now, you'd never know who she used to be, with her hair long like a teenager, like mine.

That first night of the summer, I couldn't sleep. It always took me a night or two to get used to my bed again, even though I'd slept in it pretty much every summer of my life. I tossed and turned for a while, and then I couldn't stand it anymore. I put on my bathing suit, my old swim team one that barely fit anymore, with the gold stripes and the racerback. It was my first night swim of the summer.

When I swam alone at night, everything felt so much clearer. Listening to myself breathe in and out, it made me feel calm and steady and strong. Like I could swim forever.

I swam back and forth a few times, and on the fourth lap, I started to flip turn, but I kicked something solid. I came up for air and saw it was Conrad's leg. He was sitting on the edge of the pool with his feet dangling in.

He'd been watching me that whole time. And he was smoking a cigarette.

I stayed underwater up to my chin—I was suddenly aware of how my bathing suit was too small for me now. There was no way I was getting out of the water with him still there.

"Since when did you start smoking?" I asked accusingly. "And what are you doing down here anyway?"

"Which do you want me to answer first?" He had that amused, condescending Conrad look on his face, the one that drove me crazy.

I swam over to the wall and rested my arms on the edge. "The second."

"I couldn't sleep so I went for a walk," he said, shrugging. He was lying. He'd only come outside to smoke.

"How did you know I was out here?" I demanded.

"You always swim out here at night, Belly. Come on." He took a drag of his cigarette.

He knew I swam at night? I'd thought it was my special secret, mine and Susannah's. I wondered how long he had known. I wondered if everyone knew. I didn't even know why it mattered, but it did. To me, it did. "Okay, fine. Then when did you start smoking?"

"I don't know. Last year, maybe." He was being vague on purpose. It was maddening.

"Well, you shouldn't. You should quit right now. Are you addicted?"

He laughed. "No."

"Then quit. If you put your mind to it, I know you can." If he put his mind to it, I knew he could do anything.

"Maybe I don't want to."

"You should, Conrad. Smoking is so bad for you."

"What will you give me if I do?" he asked teasingly. He held the cigarette in the air, above his beer can.

The air felt different all of a sudden. It felt charged, electric, like I had been zapped by a thunderbolt. I let go of the edge and started to tread water, away from him. It felt like forever before I spoke. "Nothing," I said. "You should quit for yourself."

"You're right," he said, and the moment was over. He stood up and ground his cigarette out on the top of the can. "Good night, Belly. Don't stay out here too late. You never know what kind of monsters come out at night."

Everything felt normal again. I splashed water at his legs as he walked away. "Screw you," I said to his back. A long time ago Conrad and Jeremiah and Steven convinced me that there was a child killer on the loose, the kind who liked chubby little girls with brown hair and grayish-blue eyes.

"Wait! Are you quitting or not?" I yelled.

He didn't answer me. He just laughed. I could tell by the way his shoulders shook as he closed the gate.

After he left, I fell back into the water and floated. I

could feel my heart beating through my ears. It thudded quick-quick-quick like a metronome. Conrad was different. I'd sensed something even at dinner, before he'd told me about Aubrey. He had changed. And yet, the way he affected me was still the same. It felt just exactly the same. It felt like I was at the top of the Grizzly at Kings Dominion, right about to go down the first hill.

chapter *ten*

"Belly, have you called your dad yet?" my mother asked me.

"No."

"I think you should call him and tell him how you're doing."

I rolled my eyes. "I doubt he's sitting at home worrying about it."

"Still."

"Well, have you made Steven call him?" I countered.

"No, I haven't," she said, her tone level. "Your dad and Steven are about to spend two weeks together looking at colleges. You, on the other hand, won't get to see him until the end of summer."

Why did she have to be so reasonable? Everything was that way with her. My mother was the only person I knew who could have a reasonable divorce.

My mother got up and handed me the phone. "Call your father," she said, leaving the room. She always left the room when I called my father, like she was giving me privacy. As if there were some secrets I needed to tell my father that I couldn't tell him in front of her.

I didn't call him. I put the phone back in its cradle. He should be the one calling me; not the other way around. He was the father; I was just the kid. And anyway, dads didn't belong in the summer house. Not my father and not Mr. Fisher. Sure, they'd come to visit, but it wasn't their place. They didn't belong to it. Not the way we all did, the mothers and us kids.

chapter *eleven*
AGE 9

We were playing cards outside on the porch, and my mother and Susannah were drinking margaritas and playing their own card game. The sun was starting to go down, and soon the mothers would have to go inside and boil corn and hot dogs. But not yet. First they played cards.

"Laurel, why do you call my mom Beck when everyone else calls her Susannah?" Jeremiah wanted to know. He and my brother, Steven, were a team, and they were losing. Card games bored Jeremiah, and he was always looking for something more interesting to do, to talk about.

"Because her maiden name is Beck," my mother explained, grinding out a cigarette. They only smoked when they were together, so it was a special occasion. My mother said smoking with Susannah made her feel young again. I said it would shorten her life span by years but she waved off my worries and called me a doomsdayer.

"What's a maiden name?" Jeremiah asked. My brother tapped Jeremiah's hand of cards to get him back into the game, but Jeremiah ignored him.

"It's a lady's name before she gets married, dipwad," said Conrad.

"Don't call him dipwad, Conrad," Susannah said automatically, sorting through her hand.

"But why does she have to change her name at all?" Jeremiah wondered.

"She doesn't. I didn't. My name is Laurel Dunne, same as the day I was born. Nice, huh?" My mother liked to feel superior to Susannah for not changing her name. "After all, why should a woman have to change her name for a man? She shouldn't."

"Laurel, please shut up," said Susannah, throwing a few cards down onto the table. "Gin."

My mother sighed, and threw her cards down too. "I don't want to play gin anymore. Let's play something else. Let's play go fish with these guys."

"Sore loser," Susannah said.

"Mom, we're not playing go fish. We're playing hearts, and you can't play because you always try to cheat," I said. Conrad was my partner, and I was pretty sure we were going to win. I had picked him on purpose. Conrad was good at winning. He was the fastest swimmer, the best boogie boarder, and he always, always won at cards.

Susannah clapped her hands together and laughed. "Laur, this girl is you all over again."

My mother said, "No, Belly's her father's daughter," and they exchanged this secret look that made me want to say, "What, what?" But I knew my mother would never say. She was a secret-keeper, always had been. And I guessed I did look like my father: I had his eyes that turned up at the corners, a little girl version of his nose, his chin that jutted out. All I had of my mother was her hands.

Then the moment was over and Susannah smiled at me and said, "You're absolutely right, Belly. Your mother does cheat. She's always cheated at hearts. Cheaters never prosper, children."

Susannah was always calling us children, but the thing was, I didn't even mind. Normally I would. But the way Susannah said it, it didn't seem like a bad thing, not like we were small and babyish. Instead it sounded like we had our whole lives in front of us.

chapter *twelve*

Mr. Fisher would pop in throughout the summer, an occasional weekend and always the first week of August. He was a banker, and getting away for any real length of time was, according to him, simply impossible. And anyway, it was better without him there, when it was just us. When Mr. Fisher came to town, which wasn't very often, I stood up a little straighter. Everyone did. Well, except Susannah and my mother, of course. The funny thing was, my mother had known Mr. Fisher for as long as Susannah had—the three of them had gone to college together, and their school was small.

Susannah always told me to call Mr. Fisher "Adam," but I could never do it. It just didn't sound right. Mr. Fisher was what sounded right, so that's what I called him, and that's what Steven called him too. I think something about him inspired people to call him that, and not just kids, either. I think he preferred it that way.

He'd arrive at dinnertime on Friday night, and we'd wait for him. Susannah would fix his favorite drink and have it ready, ginger and Maker's Mark. My mother teased her for waiting on him, but Susannah didn't mind. My mother teased Mr. Fisher, too, in fact. He teased her right back. Maybe teasing isn't the right word. It was more like bickering. They bickered a lot, but they smiled, too. It was funny: My mother and father had rarely argued, but they hadn't smiled that much either.

I guess Mr. Fisher was good-looking, for a dad. He was better-looking than my father anyway, but he was also vainer than him. I don't know that he was as good-looking as Susannah was beautiful, but that might've just been because I loved Susannah more than almost anyone, and who could ever measure up to a person like that? Sometimes it's like people are a million times more beautiful to you in your mind. It's like you see them through a special lens—but maybe if it's how you see them, that's how they really are. It's like the whole tree falling in the forest thing.

Mr. Fisher gave us kids a twenty anytime we went anywhere. Conrad was always in charge of it. "For ice cream," he'd say. "Buy yourselves something sweet." Something sweet. It was always something sweet. Conrad worshipped him. His dad was his hero. For a long time, anyway. Longer than most people. I think my dad stopped being my hero when I saw him with one of his PhD students after he and my mother separated. She wasn't even pretty.

It would be easy to blame my dad for the whole thing—the divorce, the new apartment. But if I blamed anyone, it was my mother. Why did she have to be so calm, so placid? At least my father cried. At least he was in pain. My mother said nothing, revealed nothing. Our family broke up, and she just went on. It wasn't right.

When we got home from the beach that summer, my dad had already moved out—his first-edition Hemingways, his chess set, his Billy Joel CDs, Claude. Claude was his cat, and he belonged to my dad in a way that he didn't to anyone else. It was only right that he took Claude. Still, I was sad. In a way, Claude being gone was almost worse than my dad, because Claude was so permanent in the way he lived in our house, the way he inhabited every single space. It was like he owned the place.

My dad took me out for lunch to Applebee's, and he said, apologetically, "I'm sorry I took Claude. Do you miss him?" He had Russian dressing on his beard, newly grown out, for most of the lunch. It was annoying. The beard was annoying; the lunch was annoying.

"No," I said. I couldn't look up from my French onion soup. "He's yours anyway."

So my father got Claude, and my mother got Steven and me. It worked out for everyone. We saw my father most weekends. We'd stay at his new apartment that smelled like mildew, no matter how much incense he lit.

I hated incense, and so did my mother. It made me sneeze. I think it made my father feel independent and exotic to light all the incense he wanted, in his new pad, as he called it. As soon as I walked into the apartment, I said accusingly, "Have you been lighting incense in here?" Had he forgotten about my allergy already?

Guiltily, my father admitted that yes, he had lit some incense, but he wouldn't do it anymore. He still did, though. He did it when I wasn't there, out the window, but I could still smell the stuff.

It was a two-bedroom apartment; he slept in the master bedroom, and I slept in the other one in a little twin bed with pink sheets. My brother slept on the pullout couch. Which, I was actually jealous of, because he got to stay up watching TV. All my room had was a bed and a white dresser set that I barely even used. Only one drawer had clothes in it. The rest were empty. There was a bookshelf too, with books my father had bought for me. My father was always buying me books. He kept hoping I'd turn out smart like him, someone who loved words, loved to read. I did like to read, but not the way he wanted me to. Not in the way of being, like, a scholar. I liked novels, not nonfiction. And I hated those scratchy pink sheets. If he had asked me, I would have told him yellow, not pink.

He did try, though. In his own way, he tried. He bought a secondhand piano and crammed it into the dining room, just for me. So I could still practice even when I stayed over there, he said. I hardly did, though— the piano was out of tune, and I never had the heart to tell him.

It's part of why I longed for summer. It meant I didn't have to stay at my father's sad little apartment. It wasn't that I didn't like seeing him: I did. I missed him so much. But that apartment, it was depressing. I wished I could see him at our house. Our real house. I wished it could be like it used to be. And since my mother had us most of the summer, he took Steven and me on a trip when we got back. Usually it was to Florida to see our grandmother. We called her Granna. It was a depressing trip too—Granna spent the whole time trying to convince him to get back together with my mother, whom she adored. "Have you talked with Laurel lately?" she'd ask, even way long after the divorce.

I hated hearing her nag him about it; it wasn't like it was in his control anyway. It was humiliating, because it was my mother who had split up with him. It was she who had precipitated the divorce, had pushed the whole thing, I knew that much for sure. My father would have been perfectly content carrying on, living in our blue two-story with Claude and all his books.

My dad once told me that Winston Churchill said that Russia was a riddle, wrapped in a mystery, inside an enigma. According to my dad, Churchill had been talking about my mother. This was before the divorce, and he said it half-bitterly, half-respectfully. Because even when he hated her, he admired her.

I think he would have stayed with her forever, trying to figure out the mystery. He was a puzzle solver, the kind of person who likes theorems, theories. X always had to equal something. It couldn't just be X.

To me, my mother wasn't that mysterious. She was my mother. Always reasonable, always sure of herself. To me, she was about as mysterious as a glass of water. She knew what she wanted; she knew what she didn't want. And that was to be married to my father. I wasn't sure if it was that she fell out of love or if it was that she just never was. In love, I mean.

When we were at Granna's, my mother took off on one of her trips. She'd go to far-off places like Hungary or Alaska. She always went alone. She took pictures, but I never asked to look at them, and she never asked if I wanted to.

chapter *thirteen*

I was sitting in an Adirondack chair eating toast and reading a magazine when my mother came out and joined me. She had that serious look on her face, her look of purpose, the one she got when she wanted to have one of her mother-daughter talks. I dreaded those talks the same way I dreaded my period.

"What are you doing today?" she asked me casually.

I stuffed the rest of my toast into my mouth. "This?"

"Maybe you could get started on your summer reading for AP English," she said, reaching over and brushing some crumbs off my chin.

"Yeah, I was planning on it," I said, even though I hadn't been.

My mother cleared her throat. "Is Conrad doing drugs?" she asked me.

"What?"

"Is Conrad doing drugs?"

I almost choked. "No! Why are you asking me anyway? Conrad doesn't talk to me. Ask Steven."

"I already did. He doesn't know. He wouldn't lie," she said, peering at me.

"Well, I wouldn't either!"

My mother sighed. "I know. Beck's worried. He's been acting differently. He quit football . . ."

"I quit dance," I said, rolling my eyes. "And you don't see me running around with a crack pipe."

She pursed her lips. "Will you promise to tell me if you hear something?"

"I don't know . . . ," I said teasingly. I didn't need to promise her. I knew Conrad wasn't doing drugs. A beer was one thing, but he would never do drugs. I would bet my life on it.

"Belly, this is serious."

"Mom, chill. He's not doing drugs. When'd you turn into such a narc, anyway? You're one to talk." I elbowed her playfully.

She bit back a smile and shook her head. "Don't start."

chapter *fourteen*
AGE 13

The first time they did it, they thought we didn't know. It was actually pretty stupid of them, because it was one of those rare nights when we were all at home. We were in the living room. Conrad was listening to music with his headphones on, and Jeremiah and Steven were playing a video game. I was sitting on the La-Z-Boy reading *Emma*—mostly because I thought it made me look smart, not really because I enjoyed it. If I was reading for real, I would be locked in my room with *Flowers in the Attic* or something and not Jane Austen.

I think Steven smelled it first. He looked around, sniffed like a dog, and then said, "Do you guys smell that?"

"I told you not to eat all those baked beans, Steven," Jeremiah said, his eyes focused on the TV screen.

I snickered. But it wasn't gas; I smelled it too. It was pot. "It's pot," I said, loudly. I wanted to be the one who said it first, to prove how sophisticated and knowledgeable I was.

"No way," said Jeremiah.

Conrad took off his headphones and said, "Belly's right. It's pot."

Steven paused the game and turned to look at me. "How do you know what pot smells like, Belly?" he asked me suspiciously.

"Because, Steven, I get high all the time. I'm a burnout. You didn't know?" I hated it when Steven pulled the big brother routine, especially in front of Conrad and Jeremiah. It was like he was trying to make me feel small on purpose.

He ignored me. "Is that coming from upstairs?"

"It's my mom's," Conrad said, putting his headphones back on again. "For her chemo."

Jeremiah didn't know, I could tell. He didn't say anything, but he looked confused and even hurt, the way he scratched the back of his neck and looked off into space for a minute. Steven and I exchanged a look. It was awkward, whenever Susannah's cancer came up, the two of us being outsiders and all. We never knew what to say, so we didn't say anything. We mostly pretended it wasn't happening, the way Jeremiah did.

My mother didn't, though. She was matter-of-fact,

calm, the way she is about everything. Susannah said my mother made her feel normal. My mother was good at that, making people feel normal. Safe. Like as long as she was there, nothing truly bad could happen.

When they came downstairs a little while later, they were giggling like two teenagers who had snuck into their parents' liquor cabinet. Clearly my mother had partaken in Susannah's stash as well.

Steven and I exchanged another look, this time a horrified one. My mother was probably the last person on earth who would smoke pot, with the exception of our grandmother Gran, her mother.

"Did you kids eat all the Cheetos?" my mother asked, rummaging through a cabinet. "I'm starving."

"Yes," Steven said. He couldn't even look at her.

"What about that bag of Fritos? Get those," Susannah ordered, coming up behind my La-Z-Boy. She touched my hair lightly, which I loved. Susannah was much more affectionate than my mother in those kinds of ways, and she was always calling me the daughter she never had. She loved sharing me with my mother, and my mother didn't mind. Neither did I.

"How are you liking *Emma* so far?" she asked me. Susannah had a way of focusing on you that made you feel like the most interesting person in the room.

I opened my mouth to lie and tell her how great

I thought it was, but before I could, Conrad said very loudly, "She hasn't turned a page in over an hour." He was still wearing his headphones.

I glared at him, but inside I was thrilled that he had noticed. For once, *he* had been watching *me*. But of course he'd noticed—Conrad noticed everything. Conrad would notice if the neighbor's dog had more crust in its right eye than its left, or if the pizza delivery guy was driving a different car. It wasn't really a compliment to be noticed by Conrad. It was a matter of fact.

"You'll love it once it gets going," Susannah assured me, sweeping my bangs across my forehead.

"It always takes me a while to get into a book," I said, in a way that sounded like I was saying sorry. I didn't want her to feel bad, seeing as how she was the one who'd recommended it to me.

Then my mother came into the room with a bag of Twizzlers and the half-eaten bag of Fritos. She tossed a Twizzler at Susannah and said, belatedly, "Catch!"

Susannah reached for it, but it fell on the floor, and she giggled as she picked it up. "Clumsy me," she said, chewing on one end like it was straw and she was a hick. "Whatever has gotten into me?"

"Mom, everyone knows you guys were smoking pot upstairs," Conrad said, just barely bobbing his head to the music that only he could hear.

Susannah covered her mouth with her hand. She didn't say anything, but she looked genuinely upset.

"Whoops," my mother said. "I guess the cat's out of the bag, Beck. Boys, your mother's been taking medicinal marijuana to help with the nausea from her chemo."

Steven didn't look away from the TV when he said, "What about you, Mom? Are you toking up because of your chemo too?"

I knew he was trying to lighten the mood, and it worked. Steven was good at that.

Susannah choked out a laugh, and my mother threw a Twizzler at the back of Steven's head. "Smart-ass. I'm offering up moral support to my best friend in the world. There are worse things."

Steven picked the Twizzler up and dusted it off before popping it into his mouth. "So I guess it's okay with you if I smoke up too?"

"When you get breast cancer," my mother told him, exchanging a smile with Susannah, her best friend in the world.

"Or when your best friend does," Susannah said.

Throughout all of this, Jeremiah wasn't saying anything. He just kept looking at Susannah and then back at the TV, like he was worried she would vanish into thin air while his back was turned.

Our mothers thought we were all at the beach that afternoon. They didn't know that Jeremiah and I had gotten bored and decided to come back to the house for a snack. As we walked up the porch steps, we heard them talking through the window screen.

Jeremiah stopped when he heard Susannah say, "Laur, I hate myself for even thinking this, but I almost think I'd rather die than lose my breast." Jeremiah stopped breathing as he stood there, listening. Then he sat down, and I did too.

My mother said, "I know you don't mean that."

I hated it when my mother said that, and I guessed Susannah did too because she said, "Don't tell me what I mean," and I'd never heard her voice like that before— harsh, angry.

"Okay. Okay. I won't."

Susannah started to cry then. And even though we couldn't see them, I knew that my mother was rubbing Susannah's back in wide circles, the same way she did mine when I was upset.

I wished I could do that for Jeremiah. I knew it would make him feel better, but I couldn't. Instead, I reached over and grabbed his hand and squeezed it tight. He didn't look at me, but he didn't let go either. This was the moment when we became true, real friends.

Then my mother said in her most serious, most deadpan voice, "Your boobs really are pretty goddamn amazing."

Susannah burst out into laughter that sounded like a seal barking, and then she was laughing and crying at the same time. Everything was going to be okay. If my mother was cussing, if Susannah was laughing, it would all be fine.

I let go of Jeremiah's hand and stood up. He did too. We walked back to the beach, neither of us saying anything. What was there to say? "Sorry your mom has cancer"? "I hope she doesn't lose a boob"?

When we got back to our stretch of beach, Conrad and Steven had just come out of the water with their boogie boards. We still weren't saying anything, and Steven noticed. I guessed Conrad did too, but he didn't say anything. It was Steven who said, "What's with you guys?"

"Nothing," I said, pulling my knees to my chest.

"Did you guys just have your first kiss or something?" he said, shaking water off his trunks and onto my knees.

"Shut up," I told him. I was tempted to pants him just to change the subject. The summer before, the boys had gone through an obsession with pantsing one another in public. I had never participated, but at that moment I really wanted to.

"Aww, I knew it!" he said, jabbing me in the shoulder. I shrugged him off and told him to shut up again. He started to sing, "Summer lovin', had me a blast, summer lovin', happened so fast . . ."

"Steven, quit being dumb," I said, turning to shake my head and roll my eyes with Jeremiah.

But then Jeremiah stood up, brushed sand off his shorts, and started walking toward the water and away from us, away from the house.

"Jeremiah, are you on your period or something? I was just kidding, man!" Steven called to him. Jeremiah didn't turn around; he just kept walking down the shore. "Come on!"

"Just leave him alone," Conrad said. The two of them never seemed particularly close, but there were times when I saw how well they understood each other, and this was one of them. Seeing Conrad protective of Jeremiah made me feel this huge surge of love for him—it felt like a wave in my chest washing over me. Which then made me feel guilty, because why should I be feeding into a crush when Susannah had cancer?

I could tell Steven felt bad, and also confused. It was unlike Jeremiah to walk away. He was always the first to laugh, to joke right back.

And because I felt like rubbing salt in the wound, I said, "You're such an asshole, Steven."

Steven gaped at me. "Geez, what did I do?"

I ignored him and fell back onto the towel and closed my eyes. I wished I had Conrad's earphones. I kind of wanted to forget this day ever happened.

Later, when Conrad and Steven decided to go night fishing, Jeremiah declined, even though night fishing was his favorite. He was always trying to get people to go night fishing with him. That night he said he wasn't in the mood. So they left, and Jeremiah stayed behind, with me. We watched TV and played cards. We spent most of the summer doing that, just us. We cemented things between us that summer. He'd wake me up early some mornings, and we would go collect shells or sand crabs, or ride our bikes to the ice cream place three miles away. When it was just us two, he didn't joke around as much, but he was still Jeremiah.

From that summer on I felt closer to Jeremiah than I did to my own brother. Jeremiah was nicer. Maybe because he was somebody's little sibling too, or maybe just because he was that kind of person. He was nice to everybody. He had a talent for making people feel comfortable.

chapter *fifteen*

It had been raining for three days. By four o'clock the third day, Jeremiah was stir-crazy. He wasn't the kind of person to stay inside; he was always moving. Always on his way somewhere new. He said he couldn't take it anymore and asked who wanted to go to the movies. There was only one movie theater in Cousins besides the drive-in, and it was in a mall.

Conrad was in his room, and when Jeremiah went up and asked him to come, he said no. He'd been spending an awful lot of time alone, in his room, and I could tell it hurt Steven's feelings. He'd be leaving soon for a college road trip with our dad, and Conrad didn't seem to care. When Conrad wasn't at work, he was too busy strumming his guitar and listening to music.

So it was just Jeremiah, Steven, and me. I convinced

them to watch a romantic comedy about two dog walkers who walk the same route and fall in love. It was the only thing playing. The next movie wouldn't start for another hour. About five minutes in, Steven stood up, disgusted. "I can't watch this," he said. "You coming, Jere?"

Jeremiah said, "Nah, I'll stay with Belly."

Steven looked surprised. He shrugged and said, "I'll meet you guys when it's over."

I was surprised too. It *was* pretty awful.

Not long after Steven left, a big burly guy sat in the seat right in front of me. "I'll trade you," Jeremiah whispered.

I thought about doing the fake "That's okay" thing but decided against it. This was Jeremiah, after all. I didn't have to be polite. So instead I said thanks and we traded. To see the screen Jeremiah had to keep craning his neck to the right and lean toward me. His hair smelled like Asian pears, this expensive shampoo Susannah used. It was funny. He was this big tall football guy now, and he smelled so sweet. Every time he leaned in, I breathed in the sweet smell of his hair. I wished my hair smelled like that.

Halfway through the movie, Jeremiah got up suddenly. He was gone a few minutes. When he came back, he had a large soda and a pack of Twizzlers. I reached for the soda to take a sip, but there were no straws. "You forgot the straws," I told him.

He ripped the plastic off of the Twizzler box and bit the ends off of two Twizzlers. Then he put them in the cup. He grinned broadly. He looked so proud of himself. I'd forgotten all about our Twizzler straws. We used to do it all the time.

We sipped out of the straws at the same time, like in a 1950s Coke commercial—heads bent, foreheads almost touching. I wondered if people thought we were on a date.

Jeremiah looked at me, and he smiled in this familiar way, and suddenly I had this crazy thought. I thought, *Jeremiah Fisher wants to kiss me.*

Which, was crazy. This was Jeremiah. He'd never looked at me like that, and as for me, Conrad was the one I liked, even when he was moody and inaccessible the way he was now. It had always been Conrad. I'd never seriously considered Jeremiah, not with Conrad standing there. And of course Jeremiah had never looked at me that way before either. I was his pal. His movie-watching partner, the girl he shared a bathroom with, shared secrets with. I wasn't the girl he kissed.

chapter *sixteen*
AGE 14

I knew bringing Taylor was a mistake. I knew it. I knew
it and I did it anyway. Taylor Jewel, my best friend. The
boys in our grade called her Jewel, which she pretended
to hate but secretly loved.

Taylor used to say that every time I came back from
the summer house, she had to win me over again. She had
to make me want to be there, in my real life with school
and school boys and school friends. She'd try to pair me
up with the cutest friend of the guy she was obsessed
with at the time. I'd go along with it, and maybe we'd go
to the movies or to the Waffle House, but I'd never really
be there, not completely. Those boys didn't compare to
Conrad or Jeremiah, so what was the point?

Taylor was always the pretty one, the one the boys

looked at for that extra beat. I was the funny one, the one who made the boys laugh. I thought that by bringing her I'd be proving that I was a pretty one too. See? See, I'm like her; we are the same. But we weren't, and everybody knew it. I thought that bringing Taylor would guarantee me an invitation to the boys' late-night walks on the boardwalk and their nights on the beach in sleeping bags. I thought it would open up my whole social world that summer, that I would finally, finally be in the thick of things.

I was right about that part at least.

Taylor had been begging me to bring her for forever. I'd resisted her, saying it'd be too crowded, but she was very persuasive. It was my own fault. I'd bragged about the boys too much. And deep down, I did want her there. She was my best friend, after all. She hated that we didn't share everything—every moment, every experience. When she joined the Spanish club, she insisted I join too, even though I didn't take Spanish. "For when we go to Cabo after graduation," she said. I wanted to go to the Galápagos Islands for graduation, that was my dream. I wanted to see a blue-footed booby. My dad said he'd take me too. I didn't tell Taylor, though. She wouldn't like it.

My mother and I picked Taylor up at the airport. She walked off the plane in a pair of short shorts and a tank top I'd never seen before. Hugging her, I tried not to sound jealous when I said, "When'd you get that?"

"My mom took me shopping for beach stuff right before I left," she said, handing me one of her duffel bags. "Cute, right?"

"Yeah, cute." Her bag was heavy. I wondered if she'd forgotten she was only staying a week.

"She feels bad she and Daddy are getting a divorce so she's buying me all kinds of stuff," Taylor continued, rolling her eyes. "We even got mani-pedis together. Look!" Taylor lifted up her right hand. Her nails were painted a raspberry color, and they were long and square.

"Are those real?"

"Yeah! Duh. I don't wear fake, Belly."

"But I thought you had to keep your nails short for violin."

"Oh, that. Mommy finally let me quit violin. Divorce guilt," she said knowingly. "You know how it is."

Taylor was the only girl I knew our age who still called her mother Mommy. She was the only one who could get away with it too.

The boys came to attention right away. Right away they looked at her, checked out her smallish B-cups and her blond hair. It's a Miracle Bra, I wanted to tell them. That's half a bottle of Sun-In. Her hair isn't usually that yellow. Not that they would've cared either way.

My brother, on the other hand, barely looked up from the TV. Taylor irritated him, always had. I wondered if he'd already warned Conrad and Jeremiah about her.

"Hi, Ste-ven," she said in a singsong voice.

"Hey," he mumbled.

Taylor looked at me and crossed her eyes. *Grump*, she mouthed, emphasis on the *p*.

I laughed. "Taylor, this is Conrad and Jeremiah. Steven you know." I was curious about who she'd pick, who she'd think was cuter, funnier. Better.

"Hey," she said, sizing them up, and right away I could tell Conrad was the one. And I was glad. Because I knew that Conrad would never, ever go for her.

"Hey," they said.

Then Conrad turned back to the TV just like I knew he would. Jeremiah treated her to one of his lopsided smiles and said, "So you're Belly's friend, huh? We thought she didn't have any friends."

I waited for him to grin at me to show he was just joking, but he didn't even look my way. "Shut up, Jeremiah," I said, and he grinned at me then, but it was a quick cursory one, and he went right back to looking at Taylor.

"Belly has tons of friends," Taylor informed him in her breezy way. "Do I look like someone who would hang with a loser?"

"Yes," my brother said from the couch. His head popped up. "You do."

Taylor glared at him. "Go back to jacking off, Steven." She turned to me and said, "Why don't you show me our room?"

"Yes, why don't you do that, Belly? Why don't you go be Tay-Tay's slave?" Steven said. Then he lay back down again.

I ignored him. "Come on, Taylor."

As soon as we got to my room, Taylor flung herself onto the bed by the window, my bed, the one I always slept in. "Oh my God, he is so cute."

"Which one?" I said, even though I knew.

"The dark one, of course. I love my men dark."

Inwardly I rolled my eyes. Men? Taylor had only ever gone out with two boys, neither of them anything close to being men.

"I doubt it will happen," I told her. "Conrad doesn't care about girls." I knew that wasn't true; he did care about girls. He'd cared enough about that girl Angie from last summer to go to second with her, hadn't he?

Taylor's brown eyes gleamed. "I love a challenge. Didn't I win class president last year? And class secretary the year before that?"

"Of course I remember. I was your campaign manager. But Conrad's different. He's . . ." I hesitated, searching for just the right word to scare Taylor off. "Almost, like, disturbed."

"What?" she shrieked.

Quickly I backtracked. Maybe "disturbed" had been too strong a word. "I don't mean "disturbed," exactly, but he can be really intense. Serious. You should go for

Jeremiah. I think he's more your type."

"And just what does that mean, Belly?" Taylor demanded. "That I'm not deep?"

"Well—" She was about as deep as an inflatable kiddie pool.

"Don't answer that." Taylor opened up her duffel bag and started pulling things out. "Jeremiah is cute, but Conrad's the one I want. I am gonna make that boy's head spin."

"Don't say I didn't warn you." I was already looking forward to saying I told you so, whenever that moment should arrive. Hopefully sooner than later.

She lifted up a yellow polka-dot bikini. "Itsy-bitsy enough for Conrad, do you think?"

"That bikini wouldn't fit Bridget," I said. Her little sister Bridget was seven, and she was small for her age.

"Exactly."

I rolled my eyes. "Don't say I didn't warn you. And that's my bed you're sitting on."

The two of us changed into our suits right away—Taylor into her tiny yellow bikini and me into my black tankini with the support bra and the really high neckline. As we changed, she looked me over and said, "Belly, your boobs have really gotten big!"

I threw my T-shirt over my head and said, "Not really."

But it was true, they had. Overnight, almost. I didn't

have them the summer before, that was for sure. I hated them. They slowed me down: I couldn't run fast anymore—it was too embarrassing. It was why I wore baggy T-shirts and one-pieces. I couldn't stand to hear what the boys would say about it. They would tease me for sure, and Steven would tell me to go put some clothes on, which would make me want to die.

"What size are you now?" she asked accusingly.

"B," I lied. It was more like a C.

Taylor looked relieved. "Oh, well we're still the same, then, because I'm practically a B. Why don't you wear one of my bikinis? You look like you're trying out for the swim team in that one-piece." She lifted up a blue-and-white striped one with red bows on the sides.

"I *am* on the swim team," I reminded her. I'd done winter swim with my neighborhood swim team. I couldn't compete in summer because I was always at Cousins. Being on the swim team made me feel connected to my summer life, like it was just a matter of time before I was at the beach again.

"Ugh, don't remind me," Taylor said. She dangled the bikini from side to side. "This would be *so* cute on you, with your brown hair and your new boobs."

I made a face and pushed the bikini away.

Part of me did want to show off and wow them with how much I had grown, how I was a real girl now, but the other more sane part knew it would be a death wish.

Steven would throw a towel over my head, and I would feel ten years old again instead of thirteen.

"But why?"

"I like to do laps in the pool," I said. Which was true. I did.

She shrugged. "Okay, but don't blame me when the guys don't talk to you."

I shrugged right back at her. "I don't care if they talk to me or not, I don't think of them that way."

"Yeah, right! You've been, like, obsessed with Conrad for as long as I've known you! You wouldn't even talk to any of the guys at school last year."

"Taylor, that was a really long time ago. They're like brothers to me, just like Steven," I said, pulling on a pair of gym shorts. "Talk to them all you want."

The truth was, I liked both of them in different ways and I didn't want her to know, because whichever guy she picked would feel like a leftover. And it wasn't like it would sway Taylor. She was going for Conrad either way. I wanted to tell her, Anyone but Conrad, but it wouldn't be true, not completely. I would be jealous if she picked Jeremiah, too, because he was *my* friend, not hers.

It took Taylor forever to pick out a pair of sunglasses that matched her bikini (she'd brought four pairs), plus two magazines and her suntan oil. By the time we got outside, the boys were already in the pool.

I threw my clothes off right away, ready to jump in,

but Taylor hesitated, her Polo towel tight around her shoulders. I could tell she was suddenly nervous about her itsy-bitsy bikini, and I was glad. I was getting a little bit sick of her showing off.

The boys didn't even look over. I had been worried that with Taylor there they might not want to do all the usual stuff, that they might act differently. But there they were, dunking one another for all it was worth.

Kicking off my flip-flops, I said, "Let's get in the pool."

"I might lay out for a little bit first," Taylor said. She finally dropped her towel and spread it out on a lounge chair. "Don't you want to lay out too?"

"No. It's hot and I want to swim. Besides, I'm already tan." And I was. I was turning the color of dark toffee. I looked like a whole different person in the summer, which might have been the best part of it.

Taylor on the other hand was pasty and bright like biscuit dough. I had a feeling she'd catch up with me fast, though. She was good at that.

I took off my glasses and set them on top of my clothes. Then I walked over to the deep end and jumped right in. The water felt like a shock to the system, in the best way possible. When I came up for air, I treaded water over to the boys. "Let's play Marco Polo," I said.

Steven, who was busy trying to dunk Conrad, stopped and said, "Marco Polo's boring."

"Let's play chicken," Jeremiah suggested.

"What's that?" I said.

"It's when two teams of people climb up on each other's shoulders and you try to push the other person down," my brother explained.

"It's fun, I swear," Jeremiah assured me. Then he called over to Taylor, "Tyler, you wanna play chicken with us? Or are you too chicken?"

Taylor looked up from her magazine. I couldn't see her eyes because of her sunglasses, but I knew she was annoyed. "It's Tay-lor, not Tyler, Jeremy. And no, I don't want to play."

Steven and Conrad exchanged a look. I knew what they were thinking. "Come on, Taylor, it'll be fun," I said, rolling my eyes. "Don't be a chicken."

She made a big show of sighing, and then she put her magazine down and stood up, smoothing down her bikini in the back. "Do I have to take my sunglasses off?"

Jeremiah grinned at her. "Not if you're on my team. You won't be falling off."

Taylor took them off anyway, and I realized then that the teams were uneven, and someone would have to sit out. "I'll watch," I offered, even though I wanted to play.

"That's okay. I won't play," Conrad said.

"We'll play two rounds," said Steven.

Conrad shrugged. "That's all right." He swam over to the side of the pool.

"I call Tay-lor," Jeremiah announced.

"No fair; she's lighter," Steven argued. Then he looked over and saw the expression on my face. "It's just that you're taller than her is all."

I didn't want to play anymore. "Why don't I just sit out, then? I'd hate to break your back, Steven."

Jeremiah said, "Aw, I'll take you, Belly. We'll take those guys down. I think you're probably a lot tougher than little Tay-lor."

Taylor walked down the steps and into the pool slowly, cringing at the temperature. "I'm very tough, Jeremy," she said.

Then Jeremiah crouched down in the water, and I scrambled to get onto his shoulders. He was slippery, so it was hard to stay on at first. Then he stood up and righted himself.

I shifted and balanced my hands on his head. "Am I too heavy?" I asked him quietly. He was so wiry and thin, I was afraid I'd break him.

"You weigh, like, nothing," he lied, breathing hard and gripping on to my legs.

I wanted to kiss the top of his head right then.

Across from us Taylor was perched on top of Steven's shoulders giggling and pulling his hair to hold herself steady. Steven looked like he was ready to pitch her off of him and across the pool.

"Ready?" Jeremiah asked. In a low voice he said to me, "The trick is to just keep steady."

Steven nodded, and we waddled over to the middle of the pool.

Conrad, who was treading over by the side, said, "Ready, set, go."

Taylor and I stretched our arms out to each other, pushing and shoving. She couldn't stop giggling, and when I gave her one strong push, she said, "Oh, shit!" and they both fell backward.

Jeremiah and I burst out laughing and high-fived each other. When they resurfaced, Steven glared at Taylor and said, "I told you to hold on tight."

She splashed him right in the face and said, "I was!" Her eyeliner was smudged and her mascara was starting to run. She still looked pretty, though.

Jeremiah said, "Belly?"

I said, "Hmm?" I was starting to get pretty comfortable up there, so high.

"Watch out." Then he lurched forward, and I was flying into the water, and so was he. I couldn't stop laughing, and I swallowed about a jugful of water, but I didn't care.

When both of our heads popped up, I went straight for his and took him by surprise with a good dunk.

Then Taylor said, "Let's play again. I'll be with Jeremy this time. Steven, you can be Belly's partner."

Steven still looked grumpy, and he said, "Con, take my spot."

"All right," Conrad said, but his voice said he didn't want to at all.

When he swam over to me, I said defensively, "I'm not that heavy."

"I never said you were." Then he stooped in front of me, and I climbed on top. His shoulders were more muscular than Jeremiah's, more weighty. "You okay up there?"

"Yeah."

Across from us Taylor was having trouble getting onto Jeremiah's shoulders. She kept slipping right off and laughing. They were having a lot of fun. Too much fun. I watched them jealously, and I almost forgot to be aware of the fact that Conrad was holding on to my legs, and as far as I could remember, he had never so much as accidentally grazed my knee before.

"Let's hurry up and play," I said. My voice sounded jealous even to my own ears. I hated that.

Conrad had less trouble moving into the center of the pool. I was kind of surprised by how easily he moved around with my extra weight around his shoulders.

"Ready?" Conrad said to Jeremiah and Taylor, who had finally managed to stay put.

"Yes!" Taylor shouted.

In my head I said, *You're going down, Jewel.* "Yes," I said out loud.

I leaned forward and used both of my hands to give

her a hard push. She swayed to the side but stayed on, and said, "Hey!"

I smiled. "Hey," I said, and pushed her again.

Taylor narrowed her eyes and pushed me back, hard but not hard enough.

Then we were both pushing at each other, only this time it was so much easier because I felt steady. I pushed her once, firmly, and she tipped forward, but Jeremiah was still standing. I clapped loudly. This was pretty fun.

I was surprised when Conrad held out his hand for a high five. He wasn't a high five kind of person.

When Taylor resurfaced this time, she wasn't laughing. Her blond hair was matted to her head, and she said, "This game sucks. I don't want to play anymore."

"Sore loser," I said, and Conrad lowered me into the water.

"Nice job," he said, giving me one of his rare smiles. I felt like I had won the lottery from that one smile.

"I play to win," I told him. I knew he did too.

chapter *seventeen*

A few days after we shared Twizzlers at the movies, Jeremiah announced, "I'm gonna teach Belly how to drive stick shift today."

"Do you mean it?" I said eagerly. It was a clear day; the first all week. A perfect day for driving. It was Jeremiah's day off, and I couldn't believe he was willing to spend it teaching me how to drive stick. I'd been begging him since last year to teach me—Steven had tried and had given up after our third lesson.

Steven shook his head and took a swig of orange juice from the carton on the table. "Do you want to die, man? Because Belly will kill you both, not to mention your clutch. Don't do it. I'm telling you this as your friend."

"Shut up, Steven!" I yelled, kicking him under the

table. "Just 'cause you're a terrible teacher . . ." Steven had refused to get into a car with me again after I'd accidentally gotten a teeny-tiny dent in his fender when he was teaching me how to parallel park.

"I'm confident in my teaching skills," Jeremiah said. "By the time I'm finished with her, she'll be better than you."

Steven snorted. "Good luck." Then he frowned. "How long are you gonna be gone? I thought we were going to the driving range."

"You could come with us," I offered.

Steven ignored me and said to Jeremiah, "You need to practice your swing, dude."

I glanced at Jeremiah, who looked at me and hesitated. "I'll be back by lunch. We can go after," he said.

Steven rolled his eyes. "Fine." I could tell he was annoyed and a little hurt, which made me feel both smug and sorry for him. He wasn't used to being left out of things the way I was.

We went out to practice on the road that led down to the other side of the beach. It was quiet. There was no one else out on the road, just us. We listened to Jeremiah's old *Nevermind* CD from a million years ago.

"It's hot when a girl can drive stick," Jeremiah explained above Kurt Cobain. "It shows she's confident, she knows what she's doing."

I put the car into first gear and eased my foot off the

clutch. "I thought boys liked it when girls were help-less."

"They like that too. But I just happen to prefer smart, confident girls."

"Bull. You liked Taylor, and she's not like that."

He groaned and stuck his arm out the window. "Do you have to bring that up again?"

"I'm just saying. She wasn't that smart and confi-dent."

"Maybe not, but she definitely knew what she was doing," he said, before exploding into laughter.

I hit him on the arm, hard. "You're so gross," I said. "And you're also a liar. I know for a fact that you guys didn't even get to second."

He stopped laughing. "Okay, fine. We didn't. But she was a good kisser. She tasted like Skittles."

Taylor loved Skittles. She was always popping them into her mouth, like vitamins, like they were good for her. I wondered how I'd stacked up against Taylor, if he thought I'd been a good kisser too.

I sneaked a peek at him, and he must have seen it on my face, because he laughed and said, "But you, you were the best, Bells."

I punched him on the arm, and even then he didn't stop laughing. He just laughed harder. "Don't take your foot off the clutch," he said, gasping with laughter.

I was kind of surprised he even remembered. I mean,

it had been memorable for me, but it had been my first kiss and it had been *Jeremiah*. But the fact that he remembered, that sort of made his laughing okay.

"You were my first kiss," I said. I felt like I could say anything to him at that moment. It felt like how it used to be with us before we grew up and things got complicated. It felt easy and friendly and normal.

He looked away, embarrassed. "Yeah, I know."

"How did you know?" I demanded. Had I been that awful at kissing that he'd suspected? How humiliating.

"Um, Taylor told me. Afterward."

"What! I can't believe she did that. That Judas!" I almost stopped the car. Actually, I could believe it. But it still felt like a betrayal.

"It's no big deal." But his cheeks were patchy and pink. "I mean, the first time I kissed a girl was a joke. She kept telling me I was doing it wrong."

"Who? Who was your first kiss?"

"You don't know her. It doesn't matter."

"Come on," I wheedled. "Tell me."

We stalled out then, and Jeremiah said, "Just put your foot on the clutch and put it in neutral."

"Not until you tell me."

"Fine. It was Christi Turnduck," he said, ducking his head.

"You kissed Turducken?" Now I was laughing. I did so know Christi Turnduck. She used to be a Cousins Beach regular just like us, only she lived there year round.

"She had a big crush on me," Jeremiah said, shrugging his shoulders.

"Did you tell Con and Steven?"

"Hell, no, I didn't tell them I kissed Turducken!" he said. "And you better not either! Pinky promise."

I offered him my pinky, and we shook on it.

"Christi Turnduck. She did kiss nice. She taught me everything I know. I wonder what ever happened to her."

I wondered if Turducken had been a better kisser than me too. She must have been, if she had taught Jeremiah.

We stalled out again. "This sucks. I quit."

"There's no quitting in driving," Jeremiah ordered. "Come on."

I sighed and started the car up again. Two hours later, I had it. Sort of. I still stalled out, but I was getting somewhere. I was driving. Jeremiah said I was a natural.

By the time we got back to the house, it was after four and Steven had left. I guessed he'd gotten tired of waiting and had gone to the driving range by himself. My mother and Susannah were watching old movies in Susannah's room. It was dark, and they had the curtains drawn.

I stood outside their door a minute, listening to them laugh. I felt left out. I envied their relationship. They were exactly like copilots, in perfect balance. I didn't have that kind of friendship, the forever kind of friendship that will last your whole life through, no matter what.

I walked into the room, and Susannah said, "Belly! Come watch movies with us."

I crawled into bed in between the two of them. Lying on the bed in the semi-dark, it felt cozy, like we were in a cave. "Jeremiah's been teaching me how to drive," I told them.

"Darling boy," Susannah said, smiling faintly.

"Brave, too," my mother said. She tweaked my nose.

I snuggled under the comforter. He *was* pretty great. It had been nice of him to take me out driving when no one else would. Just because I'd banged up the car a few times, it didn't mean that I wasn't going to end up being an excellent driver like everyone else. Thanks to him, I could drive stick now. I was going to be one of those confident girls, the kind who knows what she's doing. When I got my license, I would drive up to Susannah's house and take Jeremiah for a drive, to thank him.

chapter *eighteen*
AGE 14

After Taylor got out of the shower, she started rummaging through her duffel bag and I lay on my bed and watched her. She pulled out three different sundresses—one white eyelet, one Hawaiian print, and one black linen. "Which one should I wear tonight?" she asked me. She asked the question like it was a test.

I was tired of her tests and having to prove myself all the time. I said, "We're just eating dinner, Taylor. We're not going anywhere special."

She shook her head at me, and the towel on her head bounced back and forth. "We're going to the boardwalk tonight, though, remember? We have to look cute for that. There'll be boys there. Let me pick out your outfit, okay?"

It used to be that when Taylor picked out my clothes, I felt like the nerdy girl transformed at the prom, in a good way. Now it felt like I was her clueless mom who didn't know how to dress right.

I hadn't brought any dresses with me. In fact, I never had. I never even thought to. I only had two dresses at home—one my grandmother bought me for Easter and one I had to buy for eighth-grade graduation. Nothing seemed to fit me right lately. Things were either too long in the crotch or too tight in the waist. I had never thought much about dresses, but looking at hers all laid out on the bed like that, I was jealous.

"I'm not getting dressed up for the boardwalk," I told her.

"Let me just see what you have," she said, walking over to my closet.

"Taylor, I said no! This is what I'm wearing." I gestured at my cutoff shorts and Cousins Beach T-shirt.

Taylor made a face, but she backed away from my closet and went back to her three sundresses. "Fine. Have it your way, grumpy. Now, which one should I wear?"

I sighed. "The black one," I said, closing my eyes. "Now hurry up and put some clothes on."

Dinner that night was scallops and asparagus. When my mother cooked, it was always some sort of seafood with lemon and olive oil and a vegetable. Every time. Susannah only cooked every once in a while, so besides the first night, which was always bouillabaisse, you never knew what you were going to get. She might spend the whole afternoon puttering around the kitchen, making something I'd never had before, like Moroccan chicken with figs. She'd pull out her spiral bound Junior League cookbook that had buttery pages and notes in the margins, the one my mother made fun of. Or she might make American cheese omelets with ketchup and toast. Us kids were supposedly in charge of one night a week too, and that usually meant hamburgers or frozen pizza. But most nights, we ate whatever we wanted, whenever we felt like eating. I loved that about the summer house. At home, we had dinner every night at six thirty, like clockwork. Here, it was like everything just kind of relaxed, even my mother.

Taylor leaned forward and said, "Laurel, what's the craziest thing you and Susannah did when you were our age?" Taylor talked to people like she was at a slumber party, always. Adults, boys, the cafeteria lady, everyone.

My mother and Susannah looked at each other and smiled. They knew, but they weren't telling. My mother wiped her mouth with her napkin and said, "We snuck onto the golf course one night and planted daisies."

I knew that wasn't the truth, but Steven and Jeremiah laughed. Steven said in his annoying know-it-all kind of way, "You guys were boring even when you were teenagers."

"*I* think it's really sweet," Taylor said, squirting a glob of ketchup onto her plate. Taylor ate everything with ketchup—eggs, pizza, pasta, everything.

Conrad, who I thought hadn't even been listening, said, "You guys are lying. That wasn't the craziest thing you ever did."

Susannah put her hands up, like, *I surrender.* "Mothers get to have secrets too," she said. "I don't ask you boys about your secrets, now, do I?"

"Yes, you do," said Jeremiah. He pointed his fork at her. "You ask all the time. If I had a journal, you would read it."

"No, I wouldn't," she protested.

My mother said, "Yes, you would."

Susannah glared at my mother. "I would never." Then she looked at Conrad and Jeremiah sitting next to each other. "Fine, I might, but only Conrad's. He's so good at keeping everything locked inside, I never know what he's thinking. But not you, Jeremiah. You, my baby boy, wear your heart right here." She reached over and touched his sweatshirt sleeve.

"No, I don't," he protested, stabbing a scallop on his plate. "I have secrets."

That's when Taylor said, "Sure you do, Jeremy," in this really sickeningly flirtatious way.

He grinned at her, which made me want to choke on my asparagus.

That's when *I* said, "Taylor and I are going to go to the boardwalk tonight. Will one of you guys drop us off?"

Before my mother or Susannah could answer, Jeremiah said, "Ooh, the boardwalk. I think we should go to the boardwalk too." Turning to Conrad and Steven, he added, "Right, guys?" Normally I would have been thrilled that any of them wanted to go somewhere I was going, but not this time. I knew it wasn't for me.

I looked at Taylor, who was suddenly busy cutting up her scallops into tiny bite-size pieces. She knew it was for her too.

"The boardwalk sucks," said Steven.

Conrad said, "Not interested."

"Who invited you guys anyway?" I said.

Steven rolled his eyes. "No one invites anyone to the boardwalk. You just go. It's a free country."

"Is it a free country?" my mother mused. "I want you to really think about that statement, Steven. What about our civil liberties? Are we really free if—"

"Laurel, please," Susannah said, shaking her head. "Let's not talk politics at the dinner table."

"I don't know of a better time for political discourse," my mother said calmly. Then she looked at me. I mouthed, *Please stop*, and she sighed. It was better to stop her right away before she really got going. "Okay, fine. Fine. No more politics. I'm going to the bookstore downtown. I'll drop you guys off on the way."

"Thanks, Mom," I said. "It'll be just Taylor and me."

Jeremiah ignored me and turned to Steven and Conrad. "Come on, guys," he said. "It'll be *amazing*." Taylor had been calling everything amazing all day.

"Fine, but I'm going to the arcade," said Steven.

"Con?" Jeremiah looked at Conrad, who shook his head.

"Come on, *Con*," Taylor said, poking at him with her fork. "Come with us."

He shook his head, and Taylor made a face. "Fine. We'll be sure to have lots of fun without you."

Jeremiah said, "Don't worry about him. He's gonna have lots of fun here, reading the Encyclopaedia Britannica." Conrad ignored this, but Taylor giggled and tucked her hair behind her ears, which is when I knew that she liked Jeremiah now.

Then Susannah said, "Don't leave without some money for ice cream." I could tell she was happy we were all hanging out, except for Conrad, who seemed to prefer hanging out by himself this summer. Nothing made Susannah happier than thinking up activities for us kids to do. I think that she would have made a really good camp director.

In the car we waited for my mother and the boys to come out, and I whispered, "I thought you liked Conrad."

Taylor rolled her eyes. "Blah. He's boring. I think I'll like Jeremy instead."

"His name is Jeremiah," I said sourly.

"I *know* that." Then she looked at me, and her eyes widened. "Why, do you like him now?"

"No!"

She let out an impatient breath of air. "Belly, you've got to pick one. You can't have them both."

"I know that," I snapped. "And for your information, I don't want either of them. It's not like they look at me like that anyway. They look at me like Steven does. Like a little sister."

Taylor tugged at my T-shirt collar. "Well, maybe if you showed a little cleave . . ."

I shrugged her hand away. "I'm not showing any 'cleave.' And I told you I don't like either of them. Not anymore."

"So you don't care that I'm going after Jeremy?" she asked. I could tell the only reason she was asking was so she could absolve herself of any future guilt. Not that she would even feel guilty.

So I said, "If I told you I cared, would you stop?"

She thought for, like, a second. "Probably. If you really, really cared. But then I would just go after Conrad. I'm here to have fun, Belly."

I sighed. At least she was honest. I wanted to say, I thought you were here to have fun with *me*. But I didn't.

"Go after him," I told her. "I don't care."

Taylor wiggled her eyebrows at me, her old trademark move. "Yay! It is *so* on."

"Wait." I grabbed her wrist. "Promise me you'll be nice to him."

"Of course I'll be nice. I'm always nice." She patted me on the shoulder. "You're such a worrier, Belly. I told you, I just want to have fun."

That's when my mother and the boys came out, and for the first time there was no fight over shotgun. Jeremiah gave it over to Steven easily.

When we got to the boardwalk, Steven headed straight for the arcade and spent the whole night there. Jeremiah walked around with us, and he even rode the carousel, even though I knew he thought it was lame. He got all stretched out on the sleigh and pretended to take a nap while Taylor and I bounced up and down on horses, mine a blond palomino and hers a black stallion. (*Black Beauty* was still her favorite book, although she'd never admit it.) Then Taylor made him win her a stuffed Tweety Bird with the quarter toss. Jeremiah was a pro at the quarter toss. The Tweety Bird was huge, almost as tall as she was. He carried it for her.

I should never have gone along. I could have predicted the whole night, right down to how invisible I'd feel. All the time I wished I was at home, listening to Conrad play the guitar through my bedroom wall, or watching Woody Allen movies with Susannah and my mother. And I didn't even like Woody Allen. I wondered if this was how the rest of the week was going to be. I'd forgotten that about Taylor, the way she got when she wanted something—driven, single-minded, and determined as all get-out. She'd just arrived, and already she'd forgotten about me.

chapter *nineteen*

We'd only just gotten there, and it was already time for Steven to go. He and our dad were going on their college road trip, and instead of coming back to Cousins after, he was going home. Supposedly to start studying for the SATs, but more likely, to hang out with his new girlfriend.

I went to his room to watch him pack up. He hadn't brought much, just a duffel bag. I was suddenly sad to see him leave. Without Steven everything would be off balance—he was the buffer, the real life reminder that nothing really changes, that everything can stay the same. Because, Steven never changed. He was just obnoxious, insufferable Steven, my big brother, the bane of my existence. He was like our old flannel blanket that smelled like wet dog—smelly, comforting, a part of the infrastructure that made up my world. And with him there, everything would still be the same, three against one, boys against girls.

"I wish you weren't leaving," I said, tucking my knees into my chest.

"I'll see you in a month," he reminded me.

"A month and a half," I corrected him sullenly. "You're missing my birthday, you know."

"I'll give you your present when I see you at home."

"Not the same." I knew I was being a baby, but I couldn't help it. "Will you at least send me a postcard?"

Steven zipped up his duffel bag. "I doubt I'll have time. I'll send you a text, though."

"Will you bring me back a Princeton sweatshirt?" I couldn't wait to wear a college sweatshirt. They were like a badge that said you were mature, practically college age if not already. I wished I had a whole drawer full of them.

"If I remember," he said.

"I'll remind you," I said. "I'll text you."

"Okay. It'll be your birthday present."

"Deal." I fell back onto his bed and pushed my feet up against his wall. He hated it when I did that. "I'll probably miss you, a little bit."

"You'll be too busy drooling over Conrad to notice I'm gone," Steven said.

I stuck my tongue out at him.

Steven left really early the next morning. Conrad and Jeremiah were going to drive him to the airport. I went down to say good-bye, but I didn't try to go along because I knew he wouldn't want me to. He wanted some time, just them, and for once I was going to let him have it without a fight.

When he hugged me good-bye, he gave me his trademark condescending look—sad eyes and a half grimace—and said, "Don't do anything stupid, all right?" He said it in this really meaningful way, like he was trying to tell me something important, like I was supposed to understand.

But I didn't. I said, "Don't you do anything stupid either, butthead."

He sighed and shook his head at me like I was a child.

I tried not to let it bother me. After all, he was leaving, and things wouldn't be the same without him. At the very least I could send him off without getting into a petty argument. "Tell Dad I said hi," I said.

I didn't go back to bed right away. I stayed on the front porch awhile, feeling blue and a little teary—not that I would ever admit it to Steven.

In a lot of ways it was like the last summer. That fall, Conrad would start college. He was going to Brown. He might not come back next summer. He might have an internship, or summer school, or he might backpack across Europe with all his new dorm buddies. And Jeremiah, he might go to the football camp he was always talking about. There were a lot of things that could happen between now and then. It occurred to me that I was going to have to make the most of this summer, really make it count, in case there wasn't another one quite like it. After all, I would be sixteen soon. I was getting older too. Things couldn't stay the same forever.

chapter *twenty*
AGE 11

The four of us were lying on a big blanket in the sand. Conrad, Steven, Jeremiah, and then me on the edge. That was my spot. When they let me come along. This was one of those rare days.

It was already midafternoon, so hot my hair felt like it was on fire, and they were playing cards while I listened in.

Jeremiah said, "Would you rather be boiled in olive oil or skinned alive with a burning hot butter knife?"

"Olive oil," said Conrad confidently. "It's over quicker."

"Olive oil," I echoed.

"Butter knife," said Steven. "There's more of a chance I can turn the tables on the guy and skin *him*."

"That wasn't an option," Conrad told him. "It's a question about death, not turning the tables on somebody."

"Fine. Olive oil," Steven said grumpily. "What about you, Jeremiah?"

"Olive oil," Jeremiah said. "Now you go, Con."

Conrad squinted his eyes up at the sun and said, "Would you rather live one perfect day over and over or live your life with no perfect days but just decent ones?"

Jeremiah didn't say anything for a minute. He loved this game. He loved to mull over the different possibilities. "With that one perfect day, would I know I was reliving it, like *Groundhog Day?*"

"No."

"Then I'll take the perfect day," he decided.

"Well, if the perfect day involves—," Steven began, but then he looked over at me and stopped speaking, which I hated. "I'll take the perfect day too."

"Belly?" Conrad looked at me. "What would you pick?"

My mind raced around in circles as I tried to find the right answer. "Um. I'd take living my life with decent days. That way I could still hope for that one perfect day," I said. "I wouldn't want to have a life that's just one day over and over."

"Yeah, but you wouldn't know it," Jeremiah argued.

I shrugged. "But you might, deep down."

"That's stupid," Steven said.

"I don't think it's stupid. I think I agree with her." Conrad gave me this look, the kind of look I bet soldiers give each other when they're teaming up against some-body else. It was like we were in it together.

I gave Steven a little shimmy. I couldn't help myself. "See?" I said. "Conrad agrees with me."

Steven mimicked, "Conrad agrees with me. Conrad loves me. Conrad's *awesome*—"

"Shut up, Steven!" I yelled.

He grinned and said, "My turn to ask a question. Belly, would you rather eat mayonnaise every day, or be flat-chested for the rest of your life?"

I turned on my side, grabbed a handful of sand, and threw it at Steven. He was in the middle of laughing, and a bunch got in his mouth and stuck to his wet cheeks. He screamed, "You're dead, Belly!"

Then he lunged at me, and I rolled away from him. "Leave me alone," I said defiantly. "You can't hurt me or I'll tell Mom."

"You're such a pain in the ass," he spat out, grabbing my leg roughly. "I'm throwing you in the water."

I tried to shake him off, but I only succeeded in kick-ing more sand into his face. Which of course only made him madder.

Conrad said, "Leave her alone, Steven. Let's go swim."

"Yeah, come on," said Jeremiah.

Steven hesitated. "Fine," he said, spitting out sand. "But you're still dead, Belly." He pointed at me, and then made a cutting motion with his finger.

I gave him the finger and flipped over, but inside I was shaking. Conrad had defended me. Conrad cared whether or not I was dead.

Steven was mad at me the whole rest of the day, but it was worth it. It was also ironic, Steven teasing me about being flat-chested, because two summers later I had to wear a bra, but, like, for real.

chapter *twenty-one*

The night Steven left, I headed down to the pool for one of my midnight swims, and Conrad and Jeremiah and this neighbor guy Clay Bertolet were sitting on the lounge chairs drinking beer. Clay lived way down the street, and he'd been coming to Cousins Beach for almost as long as we had. He was a year older than Conrad. No one had even liked him much. He was just a person to hang out with, I guess.

Right away I stiffened and held my beach towel closer to my chest. I wondered if I should turn back. Clay had always made me nervous. I didn't have to swim that night. I could do it the next night. But no, I had as much right to be out there as they did. More, even.

I walked over to them, pretend-confident. "Hey, guys," I said. I didn't let go of my towel. It felt funny to be standing there in a towel and a bikini when they were all wearing clothes.

Clay looked up at me, his eyes narrow. "Hey, Belly. Long time no see." He patted the lounge chair. "Sit down."

I hated when people said "long time no see." It was such a dumb way to say hello. But I sat down anyway.

He leaned in and gave me a hug. He smelled like beer and Polo Sport. "So how've you been?" he asked.

Before I could answer, Conrad said, "She's fine, and now it's time for bed. Good night, Belly."

I tried not to sound like a five-year-old when I said, "I'm not going to sleep yet, I'm swimming."

"You should head back up," Jeremiah said, putting his beer down. "Your mom will kill you for drinking."

"Hello. I'm not drinking," I reminded him.

Clay offered me his Corona. "Here," he said, winking. He seemed drunk.

I hesitated, and Conrad snapped irritably, "Don't give her that. She's a kid, for God's sake."

I glared at him. "Quit acting like Steven." For a second or two I considered taking Clay's beer. It would be my first. But then I'd only be doing it to spite Conrad, and I wasn't going to let him control what I did.

"No, thanks," I told him.

Conrad nodded imperceptibly. "Now go back to bed like a good girl."

It felt just like when he and Steven and Jeremiah used to leave me out of things on purpose. I could feel my cheeks burning as I said, "I'm only two years younger than you."

"Two and a quarter," he corrected automatically.

Clay laughed, and I could smell his yeasty breath. "Shit, my girlfriend was fifteen." Then he looked at me. "Ex-girlfriend."

I smiled weakly. Inside, I was shrinking away from him and his breath. But the way Conrad was watching us, well, I liked it. I liked taking his friend away from him, even if it was just for five minutes. "Isn't that, like, illegal?" I asked Clay.

He laughed again. "You're cute, Belly."

I could feel myself blush. "So, um, why did you break up?" I asked, like I didn't already know. They broke up because Clay's a jerk, that was why. Clay had always been a jerk. He used to try to feed the seagulls Alka-Seltzer because he heard it made their stomachs blow up.

Clay scratched the back of his neck. "I don't know. She had to go to horse camp or something. Long distance relationships are BS."

"But it would just be for the summer," I protested. "It's dumb to break up over a summer." I'd nursed a crush on Conrad for whole school years. I could survive for months, years, on a crush. It was like food. It could sustain me. If Conrad was mine, there was no way I'd break up with him over a summer—or a school year, for that matter.

Clay looked at me with his heavy-lidded, sleepy eyes and said, "Do you have a boyfriend?"

"Yes," I said, and I couldn't help myself—I looked at Conrad when I said it. *See,* I was saying, *I'm not a stupid twelve-year-old girl with a crush anymore. I'm a real person.* With an actual boyfriend. Who cared if it wasn't true? Conrad's eyes flickered, but his face was the same, expressionless. Jeremiah, though, he looked surprised.

"Belly, you have a boyfriend?" He frowned. "You never mentioned him."

"It's not that serious." I picked at an unraveling thread on the seat cushion. I was already regretting making it up. "In fact, we're really, really casual."

"See? Then what's the point of a relationship during summer? What if you meet people?" Clay winked at me in a jokey way. "Like right now?"

"We've already met, Clay. Like, ten years ago." Not that he'd ever actually paid me any attention.

He nudged me with his knee. "Nice to meet you. I'm Clay."

I laughed, even though it wasn't funny. It just felt like the right thing to do. "Hi, I'm Belly."

"So, Belly, are you gonna come to my bonfire tomorrow night?" he asked me.

"Um, sure," I said, trying not to sound too excited.

Conrad and Steven and Jeremiah went to the big Fourth of July bonfire every year. Clay had it at his house because there were a ton of fireworks on that end of the beach. His mom always put out stuff for s'mores. I once made Jeremiah bring one back for me, and he did. It was rubbery and burnt, but I still ate it, and I was still grateful to Jeremiah for it. It was like a little piece of the party. They never let me go with them, and I never tried to make them. I watched the show from our back porch, in my pajamas, with Susannah and my mother. They drank champagne and I drank Martinelli's Sparkling Cider.

"I thought you came down here to swim," Conrad said abruptly.

"Geez, give her a break, Con," Jeremiah said. "If she wants to swim, she'll swim."

We exchanged a look, our look that meant, *Why is Conrad such a freaking dad?* Conrad flicked his cigarette into his half-empty can. "Do what you want," he said.

"I will," I said, sticking my tongue out at Conrad and standing up. I threw off my towel and dove into the water, a perfect swan dive. I stayed underwater for a minute. Then I started doing the backstroke so I could eavesdrop on their conversation.

In a low voice I heard Clay say, "Man, Cousins is starting to get old. I want to hurry up and get back."

"Yeah, me too," Conrad said.

So Conrad was ready to leave. Even though a little

part of me knew that already, it still hurt. I wanted to say, Then leave already. If you don't want to be here, don't be here. Just leave. But I wasn't going to let Conrad bother me, not when things were finally looking up.

At last I was invited to Clay Bertolet's Fourth of July bonfire. I was one of the big kids now. Life was good. Or it was getting there, anyway.

I thought about what I was going to wear all day. Since I'd never been, I had no idea what to wear. Probably it would get cold, but who wanted to bundle up at a bonfire? Not for my first one. I also didn't want Conrad and Jeremiah to give me a hard time if I was too dressed up. I figured shorts, a tank top, and no shoes were the safe way to go.

When we got there, I saw that I had chosen wrong. The other girls were wearing sundresses and little skirts and Uggs. If I'd had girl friends at Cousins, I might have known that. "You didn't tell me that girls got dressed up," I hissed at Jeremiah.

"You look fine. Don't be dumb," he said, walking straight over to the keg. There was a keg. There were no graham crackers or marshmallows anywhere I could see.

I'd actually never seen a keg before in real life. Just in movies. I started to follow him, but Conrad grabbed my arm. "Don't drink tonight," he warned. "My mom will kill me if I let you drink."

I shook him off. "You're not 'letting' me do anything."

"Come on. Please?"

"We'll see," I said, walking away from him and toward the fire. I wasn't sure if I even wanted to drink. Even though I'd seen Clay drinking the night before, I'd still been expecting s'mores.

Going to the bonfire was nice in theory, but actually being there was something else. Jeremiah was chatting up some girl in a red, white, and blue bikini top and a jean skirt, and Conrad was talking to Clay and some other guys I didn't recognize. I thought after the way Clay had been flirty last night, he might at least come over to say hi. But he didn't. He had his hand on some girl's back.

I stood by the fire alone and pretended to warm my hands even though they weren't cold. That's when I saw him. He was standing alone too, drinking a bottle of water. It didn't seem like he knew anybody either, since he was standing all by himself. He looked like he was my age. But there was something about him that seemed safe and comfortable, like he was younger than me even though he wasn't. It took me a few glances to figure out what it was. When I finally figured it out, it was like, Aha!

It was his eyelashes. They were so long they practically hit his cheekbones. Granted, his cheekbones were high, but still. Also, he had a slight underbite, and his skin was clear and smooth, the color of toasted coconut flakes, the kind you put on ice cream. I touched my cheek and felt relieved that the sun had dried out the pimple from two days before. His skin was perfect. To my eyes, everything about him was pretty perfect.

He was tall, taller than Steven or Jeremiah, maybe even Conrad. He looked like he was maybe half-white, half-Japanese, or Korean maybe. He was so pretty I felt like I could draw his face, and I didn't even know how to draw.

He caught me looking at him, and I looked away. Then I looked back over and he caught me again. He raised his hand and waved it, just slightly.

I could feel my cheeks flaming. There was nothing for me to say but, "Hi." I walked over, stuck out my hand, and immediately regretted it. Who shook hands anymore?

He took my hand and shook it. He didn't say anything at first. He just stared at me, like he was trying to figure something out. "You look familiar," he said at last.

I tried not to smile. Wasn't that what boys said to girls when they came on to them at bars? I wondered if he'd seen me on the beach in my new polka-dot bikini. I'd only had the nerve to wear it the one time, but maybe that was what had gotten me noticed by this guy. "Maybe you've seen me on the beach?"

He shook his head. "No. . . . That's not it."

So it hadn't been the bikini, then. I tried again. "Maybe over at Scoops, the ice cream place?"

"No, that's not it either," he said. Then it was like the little light went on in his head, because he grinned suddenly. "Did you take Latin?"

What in the world? "Um . . . yes."

"Did you ever go to Latin Convention in Washington, DC?" he asked.

"Yes," I said. Who was this boy anyway?

He nodded, satisfied. "So did I. In eighth grade, right?"

"Yeah . . ." In eighth grade I had a retainer and I still wore glasses. I hated, hated that he knew me from back then. Why couldn't he know me from now, in my polka-dot bikini?

"That's how I know you. I've been standing here trying to figure it out." He grinned. "I'm Cam, but my Latin name was Sextus. Salve."

Suddenly giggles rose up in my chest like soda bubbles. It was kind of funny. "Salve. I'm Flavia. I mean, Belly. I mean, my name is Isabel, but everyone calls me Belly."

"Why?" He looked at me like he really wondered why.

"It's my dad's nickname for me from when I was little. He thought Isabel was too long a name," I explained. "Everyone just still calls me that. It's dumb."

He ignored the last part and said, "Why not Izzy, then? Or Belle?"

"I don't know. It's partly because Jelly Bellys are my

favorite, and my dad and I used to play this game. He'd ask me what kind of mood I was in, but I would answer him in Jelly Belly flavors. Like plum if I was in a good mood . . ." My voice trailed off. I babbled when I was nervous, and I was definitely nervous. I'd always hated the name Belly—partly because it wasn't even a real name. It was a child's nickname, not a real name at all. Isabel, on the other hand, was the name of an exotic kind of girl, the kind of girl who went to places like Morocco and Mozambique, who wore red nail polish year round and had dark bangs. Belly was the kind of name that conjured up images of plump children or men in wifebeaters. "Anyway, I hate the name Izzy, but I do wish people called me Belle. It's prettier."

He nodded. "That's what it means too. Beautiful."

"I know," I said. "I'm in AP French."

Cam said something in French, so fast I couldn't understand him.

"What?" I said. I felt stupid. It's embarrassing to speak French when it's not in a classroom. It's like, conjugating verbs is one thing, but actually speaking it, to an actual French person, is a whole different thing.

"My grandmother's French," he said. "I grew up speaking it."

"Oh." Now I felt stupid for bragging about being in AP French.

"You know, the *v* is supposed to be pronounced *w*."

"What?"

"In Flavia. It's supposed to be pronounced Fla-wia."

"Of course I know that," I snapped. "I took second prize in oration. But Flawia sounds dumb."

"I took first prize," he said, trying not to sound smug. I had a sudden memory of a boy in a black T-shirt and a striped tie, blowing everyone away with his Catullus speech, taking first place. It was him. "Why did you pick it if you thought it sounded dumb?"

I sighed. "Because Cornelia was taken. Everyone wanted to be Cornelia."

"Yeah, everyone wanted to be Sextus too."

"Why?" I said. Immediately I regretted it. "Oh. Never mind."

Cam laughed. "Eighth-grade boy humor isn't very developed."

I laughed too. Then I said, "So do you stay in a house around here?"

"We're renting the house two blocks down. My mom sort of made me come," Cam said, rubbing the top of his head self-consciously.

"Oh." I wished I would stop saying "oh," but I couldn't think of anything else.

"What about you? Why'd you come, Isabel?"

I was startled when he used my real name. It just rolled right off his tongue. It felt like the first day of school. But I liked it. "I don't know," I said. "I guess because Clay invited me."

Everything that came out of my mouth sounded so generic. For some reason I wanted to impress this boy. I wanted him to like me. I could feel him judging me, judging the dumb things I said. I'm smart too, I wanted to tell him. I told myself it was fine, it didn't matter if he thought I was smart or not. But it did.

"I think I'm going to leave soon," he said, finishing his water. He didn't look at me when he said, "Do you need a ride?"

"No," I said. I tried to swallow my disappointment that he was leaving already. "I came with those guys over there." I pointed at Conrad and Jeremiah.

He nodded. "I figured, the way your brother kept looking over here."

I almost choked. "My brother? Who? Him?" I pointed at Conrad. He wasn't looking at us. He was looking at a blond girl in a Red Sox cap, and she was looking right back. He was laughing, and he never laughed.

"Yeah."

"He's not my brother. He tries to act like he is, but he's not," I said. "He thinks he's everybody's big brother. It's so patronizing. . . . Why are you leaving already anyway? You're gonna miss the fireworks."

He cleared his throat like he was embarrassed. "Um, I was actually gonna go home and study."

"Latin?" I covered my mouth with my hand to keep from giggling.

"No. I'm studying whales. I want to intern on a whale watching boat, and I have to take this whaling exam next month," he said, rubbing the top of his head again.

"Oh. That's cool," I said. I wished he wasn't leaving already. I didn't want him to go. He was nice. Standing next to him, I felt like Thumbelina, little and precious. He was that tall. If he left, I'd be all alone. "You know what, maybe I will get a ride. Wait here. I'll be right back."

I hurried over to Conrad, walking so fast I kicked up sand behind me. "Hey, I'm gonna get a ride," I said breathlessly.

The blond Red Sox girl looked me up and down. "Hello," she said.

Conrad said, "With who?"

I pointed at Cam. "Him."

"You're not riding with someone you don't even know," he said flatly.

"I do so know him. He's Sextus."

He narrowed his eyes. "Sex what?"

"Never mind. His name is Cam, he's studying whales, and you don't get to decide who I ride home with. I was just letting you know, as a courtesy. I wasn't asking for your permission." I started to walk away, but he grabbed my elbow.

"I don't care what he's studying. It's not gonna happen," he said casually, but his grip was tight. "If you want to go, I'll take you."

I took a deep breath. I had to keep cool. I wasn't going to let him goad me into being a baby, not in front of all these people. "No, thanks," I said, trying to walk away again. But he didn't let go.

"I thought you already had a boyfriend?" His tone was mocking, and I knew he'd seen through my lie the night before.

I wanted so badly to throw a handful of sand in his face. I tried to twist out of his grip. "Let go of me! That hurts!"

He let go immediately, his face red. It didn't really hurt, but I wanted to embarrass him the way he was embarrassing me. I said loudly, "I'd rather ride with a stranger than with someone who's been drinking!"

"I've had one beer," he snapped. "I weigh a hundred and seventy-five pounds. Wait half an hour and I'll take you. Stop being such a brat."

I could feel tears starting to spark my eyelids. I looked over my shoulder to see if Cam was watching. He was. "You're an asshole," I said.

He looked me dead in the eyes and said, "And you're a four-year-old."

As I walked away, I heard the girl ask, "Is she your girlfriend?"

I whirled around, and we both said "No!" at the same time.

Confused, she said, "Well, is she your little sister?" like I wasn't standing right there. Her perfume was heavy. It felt like it filled all the air around us, like we were breathing her in.

"No, I'm not his little sister." I hated this girl for being a witness to all this. It was humiliating. And she was pretty, in the same kind of way Taylor was pretty, which somehow made things worse.

Conrad said, "Her mom is best friends with my mom." So that was all I was to him? His mom's friend's daughter?

I took a deep breath, and without even thinking, I said to the girl, "I've known Conrad my whole life. So let me be the one to tell you you're barking up the wrong tree. Conrad will never love anyone as much as he loves himself, if you know what I mean—" I lifted up my hand and wiggled my fingers.

"Shut up, Belly," Conrad warned. The tops of his ears were turning bright red. It was a low blow, but I didn't care. He deserved it.

Red Sox girl frowned. "What is she talking about, Conrad?"

To her I blurted out, "Oh, I'm sorry, do you not know what the idiom 'barking up the wrong tree' means?"

Her pretty face twisted. "You little skank," she hissed.

I could feel myself shrinking. I wished I could take it back. I'd never gotten into a fight with a girl before, or with anyone for that matter.

Thankfully, Conrad broke in then and pointed to the

bonfire. "Belly, go back over there, and wait for me to come get you," he said harshly.

That's when Jeremiah ambled over. "Hey, hey, what's going on?" he asked, smiling in his easy, goofy way.

"Your brother is a jerk," I said. "That's what's going on."

Jeremiah put his arm around me. He smelled like beer. "You guys play nice, you hear?"

I shrugged out of his hold and said, "I *am* playing nice. Tell your brother to play nice."

"Wait, are you guys brother and sister too?" the girl asked.

Conrad said, "Don't even think about leaving with that guy."

"Con, chill out," Jeremiah said. "She's not leaving. Right, Belly?"

He looked at me, and I pursed my lips and nodded. Then I gave Conrad the dirtiest look I could muster, and I shot one at the girl, too, when I was far enough away that she wouldn't be able to reach out and grab me by the hair. I walked back to the bonfire, trying to keep my shoulders straight and high, when inside I felt like a kid who'd gotten yelled at at her own birthday party. It wasn't fair, to be treated like I was a kid when I wasn't. I bet me and that girl were the same age.

Cam said, "What was that all about?"

I was choking back tears as I said, "Let's just go."

He hesitated, glancing back over at Conrad. "I don't think that's such a good idea, Flavia. But I'll stay here with you and hang out for a while. The whales can wait."

I wanted to kiss him then. I wanted to forget I ever knew Conrad and just be there, existing in the bubble of that moment. The first firework went off, somewhere high above us. It sounded like a teakettle whistling loud and proud. It was gold, and it exploded into millions of gold flecks, like confetti over our heads.

We sat by the fire and he told me about whales and I told him about stupid things, like being secretary of French Club, and how my favorite food was pulled pork sandwiches. He said he was a vegetarian. We must have sat there for an hour. I could feel Conrad watching us the whole time, and I was so tempted to give him the finger—I hated it when he won.

When it started to get cold, I rubbed my arms, and Cam took off his hoodie and gave it to me. Which, was sort of my dream come true—getting cold and having a guy actually give you his hoodie instead of gloating over how smart he'd been to bring one.

Underneath, his T-shirt said STRAIGHT EDGE, with a picture of a razor blade, the kind a guy shaves with. "What does that mean?" I asked, zipping up his hoodie. It was warm and it smelled like boy, but in a good way.

"I'm straight edge," he said. "I don't drink or do drugs. I used to be hardcore, where you don't take over-the-counter medicine or drink caffeine, but I quit that."

"Why?"

"Why was I hardcore straight edge or why did I quit?"

"Both."

"I don't believe in polluting your body with unnatural stuff," he said. "I quit because it was making my mom crazy. And I also just really missed Dr Pepper."

I liked Dr Pepper too. I was glad I hadn't been drinking. I didn't want him to think badly of me. I wanted him to think I was cool, like the kind of girl who didn't care what people thought, the kind of person he obviously was. I wanted to be his friend. I also wanted to kiss him.

Cam left when we left. He got up as soon as he saw Jeremiah coming over to get me. "So long, Flavia," he said.

I started to unzip his hoodie, and he said, "That's all right. You can give it to me later."

"Here, I'll give you my number," I said, holding my hand out for his phone. I'd never given a boy my phone number before. As I punched in my number, I felt really proud of myself for offering it to him.

Backing away, he put the phone into his pocket and said, "I would have found a way to get it back without your number. I'm smart, remember? First prize in oration."

I tried not to smile as he walked away. "You're not that smart," I called out. It felt like fate that we'd met. It felt like the most romantic thing that had ever happened to me, and it was.

I watched Conrad say good-bye to Red Sox girl. She gave him a hug, and he hugged her back, but not really. I was glad I had ruined his night, if only a little bit.

On the way to the car a girl stopped me. She wore her blondish-brown hair in two pigtails, and she had on a pink low-cut shirt. "Do you like Cam?" the girl asked me casually. I wondered how she knew him—I thought he'd been a nobody just like me.

"I barely even know him," I told her, and her face relaxed. She was relieved. I recognized that look in her eyes—dreamy and hopeful. It must have been the way I looked when I used to talk about Conrad, used to try to think of ways to insert his name into conversation. It made me sad for her, for me.

"I saw the way Nicole talked to you," she said abruptly. "Don't worry about her. She sucks as a person."

"Red Sox girl? Yeah, she kind of does suck at being a person," I agreed. Then I waved good-bye to her as Jeremiah and Conrad and I made our way to the car.

Conrad drove. He was completely sober, and I knew he had been all along. He checked out Cam's hoodie, but he didn't say anything. We didn't speak to each other once. Jeremiah and I both sat in the backseat, and he tried to joke around, but nobody laughed. I was too busy thinking, remembering everything that had happened that night. I thought to myself, *That might have been the best night of my life.*

In my yearbook the year before, Sean Kirkpatrick wrote that I had "eyes so clear" he could "see right into my soul." Sean was a drama geek, but so what. It still made me feel good. Taylor snickered when I showed it to her. She said only Sean Kirkpatrick would notice the color of my eyes when the rest of the guys were too busy looking at my chest. But this wasn't Sean Kirkpatrick. This was Cam, a real guy who had noticed me even before I was pretty.

I was brushing my teeth in the upstairs bathroom when Jeremiah came in, shutting the door behind him. Reaching for his toothbrush, he said, "What's going on with you and Con? Why are you guys so mad at each other?" He hopped up onto the sink.

Jeremiah hated it when people fought. It was part of why he always played the clown. He took it upon himself to bring levity to any situation. It was sweet but also kind of annoying.

Through a mouthful of toothpaste I said, "Um, because he's a self-righteous neo-maxi-zoom-dweebie?"

We both laughed at that. It was one of our little inside jokes, a line from *The Breakfast Club* that we spent repeating to each other the summer I was eight and he was nine.

He cleared his throat. "Seriously, though, don't be so hard on him. He's going through some stuff."

This was news to me. "What? What stuff?" I demanded.

Jeremiah hesitated. "It's not up to me to tell you."

"Come on. We tell each other everything, Jere. No secrets, remember?"

He smiled. "I remember. But I still can't tell you. It's not my secret."

Frowning, I turned the faucet on and said, "You always take his side."

"I'm not taking his side. I'm just telling his side."

"Same thing."

He reached out and turned the corners of my mouth up. It was one of his oldest tricks; no matter what, it made me smile. "No pouting, Bells, remember?"

No Pouting was a rule Conrad and Steven had made up one summer. I think I was eight or nine. The thing was, it only applied to me. They even put a sign up on my bedroom door. I tore it down, of course, and I ran and told Susannah and my mother. That night I got seconds on dessert, I remember. Anytime I acted the slightest bit sad or unhappy, one of the boys would start yelling, "No pouting. No pouting." And, okay, maybe I did pout a lot, but it was the only way I could ever get my way. In some ways it was even harder being the only girl back then. In some ways not.

chapter *twenty-two*

That night I slept in Cam's hoodie. It was stupid and kind of sappy, but I didn't care. And the next day I wore it outside, even though it was blazing hot out. I loved how the sleeves were frayed, the way it felt lived in. It felt like a boy's.

Cam was the first boy to pay attention to me like that, to be up front about the fact that he actually wanted to hang out with me. And not be, like, embarrassed about it.

When I woke up, I realized that I had given him the house number. I didn't know why. I could have given him my cell phone number just as easily.

I kept waiting for the phone to ring. The phone never rang at the summer house. The only people who called the house phone were Susannah, trying to figure out what kind of fish we wanted for dinner, or my mother, calling to tell Steven to put the towels in the dryer, or to get the grill going.

I stayed on the deck, sunning and reading magazines with Cam's hoodie balled up in my lap like a stuffed animal. Since we kept the windows open, I knew I'd hear if the phone rang.

I slathered myself with sunscreen first, and then two layers of tanning oil. I didn't know if it was an oxymoron or what, but better safe than sorry was how I figured it. I set myself up with a little station of cherry Kool-Aid in an old water bottle, plus a radio, plus sunglasses, and magazines. The sunglasses were a pair that Susannah had bought me years ago. Susannah loved to buy presents. When she went off for errands, she'd come home with presents. Little things, like this pair of red heart sunglasses she said I just had to have. She knew just what I'd love, things I hadn't even thought of, had certainly never thought of buying. Things like lavender foot lotion, or a silk quilted pouch for tissues.

My mother and Susannah had left early that morning for one of their art gallery trips to Dyerstown, and Conrad, thank God, had left for work already. Jeremiah was still asleep. The house was mine.

The idea of tanning sounds so fun in theory. Laying out, soaking up sun and sipping on soda, falling asleep like a fat cat. But then the actual act of it is kind of tedious and boring. And hot. I would always rather be floating in an ocean, catching sun that way, than lying down sweating in the sun. They say you get tanner faster when you're wet, anyhow.

But that morning I had no choice. In case Cam called, I mean. So I lay there, sweating and sizzling like a piece of chicken on a grill. It was boring, but it was a necessity.

Just after ten, the phone rang. I sprang up and ran into the kitchen. "Hello?" I said breathlessly.

"Hi, Belly. It's Mr. Fisher."

"Oh, hi, Mr. Fisher," I said. I tried not to sound too disappointed.

He cleared his throat. "So, how's it going down there?"

"Pretty good. Susannah's not home, though. She and my mom went to Dyerstown to visit some galleries."

"I see. . . . How are the boys?"

"Good . . ." I never knew what to say to Mr. Fisher. "Conrad's at work and Jeremiah's still asleep. Do you want me to wake him up?"

"No, no, that's all right."

There was this long pause, and I scrambled to think of something to say.

"Are you, um, coming down this weekend?" I asked.

"No, not this weekend," he said. His voice sounded really far away. "I'll just call back later. You have fun, Belly."

I hung up the phone. Mr. Fisher hadn't been down to Cousins once yet. He used to come the weekend after the Fourth, because it was easier getting away from work after the holiday. When he came, he'd fire up the barbecue all weekend long, and he'd wear his apron that said CHEF KNOWS BEST. I wondered if Susannah would be sad he wasn't coming, if the boys would care.

I trudged back to my lounge chair, back to the sun. I fell asleep on my lounge chair, and I woke up to Jeremiah sprinkling Kool-Aid onto my stomach. "Quit it," I said grouchily, sitting up. I was thirsty from my extra sweet Kool-Aid (I always made it with double sugar), and I felt dehydrated and sweaty.

He laughed and sat down on my lounge chair. "Is this what you're doing all day?"

"Yes," I said, wiping off my stomach and then wiping my hand on his shorts.

"Don't be boring. Come do something with me," he ordered. "I don't have to work until tonight."

"I'm working on my tan," I told him.

"You're tan enough."

"Will you let me drive?"

He hesitated. "Fine," he said. "But you have to rinse off first. I don't want you getting my seat all oily."

I stood up, throwing my limp greasy hair into a high ponytail. "I'll go right now. Just wait," I said.

Jeremiah waited for me in the car, with the AC on full

blast. He sat in the passenger seat. "Where are we going?" I asked, getting into the driver's seat. I felt like an old pro. "Tennessee? New Mexico? We have to go far so I can get good practice."

He closed his eyes and laid his head back. "Just take a left out of the driveway," he told me.

"Yessir," I said, turning off the AC and opening all four windows. It was so much better driving with the windows down. It felt like you were actually going somewhere.

He continued giving me directions, and then we pulled up to Go Kart City. "Are you serious?"

"We're gonna get you some driving practice," he said, grinning like crazy.

We waited in line for the cars, and when it was our turn, the guy told me to get in the blue one. I said, "Can I drive the red one instead?"

He winked at me and said, "You're so pretty, I'd let you drive *my* car."

I could feel myself blush, but I liked it. The guy was older than me, and he was actually paying me attention. It was kind of amazing. I'd seen him there the summer before, and he hadn't looked at me once.

Getting into the car next to me, Jeremiah muttered, "What a freaking cheeseball. He needs to get a real job."

"Like lifeguarding is a real job?" I countered.

Jeremiah scowled. "Just drive."

Every time my car came back around the track, the guy waved at me. The third time he did it, I waved back.

We rode around the track a bunch of times, until it was time for Jeremiah to go to work.

"I think you've had enough driving for today," Jeremiah said, rubbing his neck. "I'll drive us home."

I didn't argue with him. He drove home fast, and dropped me off at the curb and headed to work. I stepped back into the house feeling very tired and tan. And also satisfied.

"Someone named Cam called for you," my mother said. She was sitting at the kitchen table, reading the paper with her horn-rimmed reading glasses on. She didn't look up.

"He did?" I asked, covering my smile with the back of my hand. "Well, did he leave a number?"

"No," she said. "He said he'd call back."

"Why didn't you ask for it?" I said, and I hated the whininess in my voice, but when it came to my mother, it was like I couldn't help it.

That's when she looked at me, perplexed. "I don't know. He wasn't offering it. Who is he anyway?"

"Forget it," I told her, walking over to the refrigerator for some lemonade.

"Suit yourself," my mother said, going back to her paper.

She didn't press the issue. She never did. She at least could have gotten his number. If Susannah had been down here instead of her, she would have been singsongy and she would have teased and snooped until I told her everything. Which I would have, gladly.

"Mr. Fisher called this morning," I said.

My mother looked up again. "What did he say?"

"Nothing much. Just that he can't come this weekend."

She pursed her lips, but she didn't say anything.

"Where's Susannah?" I asked. "Is she in her room?"

"Yes, but she doesn't feel well. She's taking a nap," my mother said. In other words, Don't go up and bother her.

"What's wrong with her?"

"She has a summer cold," my mother said automatically.

My mother was a terrible liar. Susannah had been spending a lot of time in her room, and there was a sadness to her that hadn't been there before. I knew something was up. I just wasn't completely sure what.

chapter *twenty-three*

Cam called again the next night, and the night after that. We talked on the phone twice before we met up again, for, like, four or five hours at a time. When we talked, I lay on one of the lounge chairs on the porch and stared up at the moon with my toes pointed toward the sky. I laughed so hard that Jeremiah yelled out his window for me to keep it down. We talked about everything, and I loved it, but the whole time I wondered when he was going to ask to see me again. He didn't.

So I had to take matters into my own hands. I invited Cam to come over and play video games and maybe swim. I felt like some kind of liberated woman calling him up and inviting him over, like it was the kind of thing I did all the time. When really, I was only doing it because I knew no one was going to be at home. I didn't want Jeremiah or Conrad or my mother or even Susannah to see him just yet. For now, he was just mine.

"I'm a really good swimmer, so don't be mad when we race and I beat you," I said over the phone.

He laughed and said, "At freestyle?"

"At any style."

"Why do you like to win so much?"

I didn't have an answer for that, except to say that winning was fun, and anyway, who didn't like to win? Growing up with Steven and spending my summers with Jeremiah and Conrad, winning was always important, and doubly so because I was a girl and was never expected to win anything. Victory is a thousand times sweeter when you're the underdog.

Cam came over, and I watched from my bedroom window as he drove up. His car was navy blue and old and beat-up looking, like his hoodie that I was already planning on keeping. It looked like exactly the kind of car he'd drive.

He rang the doorbell, and I flew down the stairs to open the door. "Hi," I said. I was wearing his hoodie.

"You're wearing my hoodie," he said, smiling down at me. He was even taller than I'd remembered.

"You know, I was thinking that I want to keep it," I told him, letting him in and closing the door behind me. "But I don't expect to get it for free. I'll race you for it."

"But if we race, you can't be mad if I beat you," he

said, raising an eyebrow at me. "It's my favorite hoodie, and if I win, I'm taking it."

"No problem," I told him.

We went out to the pool through the back screen door, down the porch steps. I threw off my shorts and T-shirt and his hoodie quickly, without even thinking— Jeremiah and I raced all the time in the pool. It didn't occur to me to be self-conscious to be in a bikini in front of Cam. After all, we spent the whole summer in bathing suits in that house.

But he looked away quickly and took off his T-shirt. "Ready?" he said, standing by the edge.

I walked over next to him. "One full lap?" I asked, dipping my toe into the water.

"Sure," he said. "You want a head start?"

I snorted. "Do *you* want a head start?"

"Touché," he said, grinning.

I'd never heard a boy say "touché" before. Or anyone else, for that matter. Maybe my mother. But on him it looked good. It was different.

I won the first race easily. "You let me win," I accused.

"No, I didn't," he said, but I knew it wasn't true. In all the summers and all of the races, no boy, not Conrad or Jeremiah or certainly not Steven, had ever let me win.

"You better give it your all this time," I warned. "Or I'm keeping the hoodie."

"Best two out of three," Cam said, wiping the hair out of his eyes.

He won the next heat, and I won the last one. I wasn't fully convinced that he didn't just let me win—after all, he was so tall and long, his one stroke was worth two of mine. But I wanted to keep the hoodie, so I didn't challenge the win. After all, a win was a win.

When he had to leave, I walked him to his car. He didn't get in right away. There was this long pause, the first we'd had, if you can believe it. Cam cleared his throat and said, "So this guy I know, Kinsey, is having a party tomorrow night. Do you maybe want to come?"

"Yeah," I said right away. "I do."

I made the mistake of mentioning it at breakfast the next morning. My mother and Susannah were grocery shopping. It was just me and the boys, the way it had been for the most part this summer. "I'm going to a party tonight," I said, partly just to say it out loud and partly to brag.

Conrad raised his eyebrows. "You?"

"Whose party?" Jeremiah demanded. "Kinsey's?"

I put down my juice. "How'd you know?"

Jeremiah laughed and wagged his finger at me. "I know everybody in Cousins, Belly. I'm a lifeguard. That's like being the mayor. Greg Kinsey works at that surf shop over by the mall."

Frowning, Conrad said, "Doesn't Greg Kinsey sell crystal meth out of his trunk?"

"What? No. Cam wouldn't be friends with someone like that," I said defensively.

"Who's Cam?" Jeremiah asked me.

"That guy I met at Clay's bonfire. He asked me to go to this party with him, and I said yes."

"Sorry. You aren't going to some meth addict's party," Conrad said.

This was the second time Conrad was trying to tell me what to do, and I was sick of it. Who did he think he was? I had to go to this party. I didn't care if there was crystal meth or not, I was going. "I'm telling you, Cam wouldn't be friends with someone like that! He's straight edge."

Conrad and Jeremiah both snorted. In moments like these, they were a team. "He's straight edge?" Jeremiah said, trying not to smile. "Neat."

"Very cool," agreed Conrad.

I glared at the both of them. First they didn't want me hanging out with meth addicts, and then being straight edge wasn't cool either. "He doesn't do drugs, all right? Which is why I highly doubt he'd be friends with a drug dealer."

Jeremiah scratched his cheek and said, "You know what, it might be Greg Rosenberg who's the meth dealer. Greg Kinsey's pretty cool. He has a pool table. I think I'll check this party out too."

"Wait, what?" I was starting to panic.

"I think I'll go too," Conrad said. "I like pool."

I stood up. "You guys can't come. You weren't invited."

Conrad leaned back in his chair and put his arms behind his head. "Don't worry, Belly. We won't bother you on your big date."

"Unless he puts his hands on you." Jeremiah ground his fist into his hand threateningly, his blue eyes narrow. "Then his ass is grass."

"This isn't happening," I moaned. "You guys, I'm begging you. Don't come. Please, please don't come."

Jeremiah ignored me. "Con, what are you gonna wear?"

"I haven't thought about it. Maybe my khaki shorts? What are *you* gonna wear?"

"I hate you guys," I said.

Things had been weird with me and Conrad and also with me and Jeremiah—an impossible thought crept its way into my head. Was it possible they didn't want me with Cam? Because *they*, like, had feelings for me? Could that even be? I doubted it. I was like a little sister to them. Only, I wasn't.

When I finished getting ready and it was almost time to go, I stopped by Susannah's room to say good-bye. She and my mother were holed up in there sorting through old pictures. Susannah was all ready for bed, even though it was still pretty early. She had her pillows propped up around her, and she was wearing one of her silk robes that Mr. Fisher had bought her on a business trip to Hong Kong. It was poppy and cream, and when I got married, I wanted one just like it.

"Come sit down and help us put this album together," my mother said, rifling through an old striped hatbox.

"Laurel, can't you see she's all dressed up? She's got better things to do than look at dusty old pictures." Susannah winked at me. "Belly, you look fresh as a daisy. I love you in white with your tan. It sets you off like a picture frame."

"Thanks, Susannah," I said.

I wasn't all that dressed up, but I wasn't in shorts like the night of the bonfire. I was wearing a white sundress and flip-flops, and I'd put my hair in braids while it was still wet. I knew I'd probably take them out in about half an hour because they were so tight, but I didn't care. They were cute.

"You do look lovely. Where are you headed?" my mother asked me.

"Just to a party," I said.

My mother frowned and said, "Are Conrad and Jeremiah going to this party too?"

"They're not my bodyguards," I said, rolling my eyes.

"I didn't say they were," my mother said.

Susannah waved me off and said, "Have fun, Belly!"

"I will," I said, shutting the door before my mother could ask me any more questions.

I'd hoped that Conrad and Jeremiah had just been kidding around, that they weren't really gonna try to come. But when I ran down the stairs to meet Cam's car, Jeremiah called out, "Hey, Belly?"

He and Conrad were watching TV in the family room. I poked my head in the doorway. "What?" I snapped. "I'm kind of in a hurry."

Jeremiah turned his head toward me and winked lazily. "See you soon."

Conrad looked at me and said, "What's with the perfume? It's giving me a headache. And why are you wearing all that makeup?"

I wasn't wearing that much makeup. I had some blush and mascara and a little lip gloss, that was it. It was just that he wasn't used to me wearing any. And I'd sprayed my neck and wrists, that was all. Conrad sure hadn't minded Red Sox girl's perfume. He'd loved *her* perfume. Still, I took one last look at myself in the mirror in the hallway—and I rubbed a little of the blush off, also the perfume.

Then I slammed the door shut and ran down the driveway, where Cam was turning in. I'd been watching from my bedroom window so I'd know the exact moment he drove up, so he wouldn't have to come inside and meet my mother.

I hopped into Cam's car. "Hi," I said.

"Hi. I would've rung the doorbell," he told me.

"Trust me, it's better this way," I said, suddenly feeling very shy. How is it possible to talk to someone on the phone for hours and hours, to even swim with this person, and then feel like you don't know them?

"So this guy Kinsey, he's kind of weird, but he's a good person," Cam told me as he backed out of the driveway. He was a good driver, careful.

Casually I asked, "Does he by any chance sell crystal meth?"

"Um, not that I know of," he told me, smiling. His right cheek had a dimple in it that I hadn't noticed the other night. It was nice.

I relaxed. Now that the crystal meth stuff was out of the way, there was only one more thing. I twisted the charm bracelet on my wrist over and over and said, "So, you know those guys I was with at the bonfire? Jeremiah and Conrad?"

"Your fake brothers?"

"Yeah. I think they might be stopping by the party too. They know, um, Kinsey," I said.

"Oh, really?" he said. "Cool. Maybe they'll see that I'm not some kind of creep."

"They don't think you're a creep," I told him. "Well, they kind of do, but they'd think any guy I talk to is a creep, so it's nothing personal."

"They must really care about you a lot to be so protective," he said.

Did they?

"Um, not really. Well, Jeremiah does, but Conrad is all about duty. Or he used to be anyway. He should've been one of those samurais." I glanced over at him. "I'm sorry. Is this boring?"

"No, keep talking," Cam said. "How do you know about samurais?"

Tucking my legs under my butt, I said, "Ms. Baskerville's global studies class in ninth grade. We did a whole unit on Japan and Bushido. I was, like, obsessed with the idea of seppuku."

"My dad's half-Japanese," he said. "My grandmother lives there, so we go out and visit her once a year."

"Wow." I'd never been to Japan, or anywhere in Asia for that matter. My mother's travels hadn't taken her there yet either, though I knew she wanted to go. "Do you speak Japanese?"

"A little," he said, rubbing the top of his head. "I get by okay."

I whistled—my whistle was something I was proud of. My brother, Steven, had taught me. "So you speak English, French, and Japanese? That's pretty amazing. You're like some kind of genius, huh," I teased.

"I speak Latin, too," he reminded me, grinning.

"Latin's not spoken. It's a dead language," I said, just to be contrary.

"It's not dead. It's in every Western language." He sounded like my seventh-grade Latin teacher, Mr. Coney.

When we pulled up to this guy Kinsey's house, I kind of didn't want to get out of the car. I loved the feeling of talking and having somebody really listen to what I had to say. It was like a high or something. In this weird way, I felt powerful.

We parked in the cul-de-sac—there were a ton of cars. Some were halfway on the lawn. Cam walked quickly. His legs were so long that I had to hurry to keep up. "So how do you know this guy?" I asked him.

"He's my supplier." He laughed at the expression on my face. "You're really gullible, Flavia. His parents have a boat. I've seen him down at the marina. He's a nice guy."

We walked right in without knocking. The music was so loud I could hear it from the driveway. It was karaoke music—there was a girl singing "Like a Virgin" at the top of her lungs and rolling around on the ground, her mike getting twisted up in her jeans. There were ten or so people in the living room, drinking beer and passing around a songbook. "Sing 'Livin' on a Prayer' next," some guy urged the girl on the floor.

A couple of guys I didn't recognize were checking me out—I could feel their eyes on me, and I wondered if I really had worn too much makeup. It was a new thing to have guys looking at me, much less asking me on dates. It felt equal parts amazing and scary. I spotted the girl from the bonfire, the one who liked Cam. She looked at us, and then she looked away, sneaking glances every once in a while. I felt bad for her; I knew how that felt.

I also recognized our neighbor Jill, who spent weekends at Cousins—she waved at me, and it occurred to me that I'd never seen her outside of the neighborhood, our front yards. She was sitting next to the guy from the video store, the one who worked on Tuesdays and wore his name tag upside down. I'd never seen the lower half of his body before, he was always standing behind the counter. And then there was the waitress Katie from Jimmy's Crab Shack without her red-and-white striped uniform. These were people I'd been seeing every summer for my whole life. So this is where they'd been all this time. Out, at parties, while I'd been left out, locked away in the summer house like Rapunzel, watching old movies with my mother and Susannah.

Cam seemed to know everybody. He said hi, shoulder-bumping guys and hugging girls. He introduced me. He called me his friend Flavia. "Meet my friend Flavia," he said. "This is Kinsey. This is his house."

"Hi, Kinsey," I said.

Kinsey was sprawled out on the couch, and he wasn't wearing a shirt. He had a scrawny bird chest. He didn't look like a meth dealer. He looked like a paperboy.

He took a gulp of beer and said, "My name's not really Kinsey. It's Greg. Everybody just calls me Kinsey."

"My name's not really Flavia. It's Belly. Only Cam calls me Flavia."

Kinsey nodded like that actually made sense. "You guys want something to drink, there's a cooler in the kitchen."

Cam said, "Do you want something to drink?"

I wasn't sure if I should say yes or not. On the one hand, yeah, I kind of did. I never drank. It would be, like, an experience. Further proof that this summer was special, important. On the other hand, would he be grossed out by me if I did? Would he judge me for it? I didn't know what the straight edge rules were.

I decided against it. The last thing I needed was to smell like Clay had the other night. "I'll have a Coke," I told him.

Cam nodded, and I could tell he approved. We headed over to the kitchen. As we walked, I heard little snatches of conversation—"I heard Kelly got a DUI and that's why she isn't here this summer." "I heard she got kicked out of school." I wondered who Kelly was. I wondered if I'd recognize her if I saw her. It was all Steven and Jeremiah and Conrad's fault—they never took me anywhere. That was why I didn't know anybody.

All of the chairs in the kitchen had purses and jackets

on them, so Cam moved over some empty beer bottles and made an empty space on the counter. I hopped up and sat on it.

"Do you know all these people?" I asked Cam.

"Not really," he said. "I just wanted you to think I was cool."

"I already do," I said, and I blushed almost immediately.

He laughed like I had made a joke, which made me feel better. He opened up the cooler and pulled out a Coke. He opened it and handed it to me.

Cam said, "Just because I'm straight edge doesn't mean you can't drink. I mean, I'll judge you for it, but you can still drink if you want to. That was a joke, by the way."

"I know," I said. "But I'm good with this Coke." Which was true.

I took a long sip of my Coke and burped. "Scuse me," I said, unraveling one of my braids. They were already too tight, and my head felt sore.

"You burp, like, baby burps," he said. "It's kind of gross but also kind of cute."

I unraveled the other braid and hit him on the shoulder. In my head I heard Conrad go, *Ooh, you're hitting him now. Way to flirt, Belly, way to flirt.* Even when he wasn't there, he was there. And then he really was.

Out of nowhere, I heard Jeremiah's signature yodel on the karaoke machine. I bit my lip. "They're here," I said.

"You want to go out and say hi?"

"Not really," I said, but I hopped down from the counter.

We went back to the living room, and Jeremiah was center stage, falsetto and singing some song I'd never heard of. The girls were laughing and watching him, all googly-eyed. And Conrad, he was on the couch with a beer in his hand. Red Sox girl was perched on the armrest next to him, leaning in close and letting her hair fall in his face like a curtain that encased the two of them. I wondered if they'd picked her up, if he'd let her sit shotgun.

"He's a good singer," Cam said. Then he looked where I was looking and said, "Are he and Nicole together?"

"Who knows?" I said. "Who cares?"

Jeremiah spotted me then, as he bowed at the end of his song. "Belly! This next song goes out to you." He pointed at Cam. "What's your name?"

Cam cleared his throat. "Cam. Cameron."

Jeremiah said right into the mike, "Your name is Cam Cameron? Damn, that sucks, dude." Everyone laughed, especially Conrad, when just a second ago he'd looked so bored.

"It's just Cam," Cam said quietly. He looked at me then, and I was embarrassed. Not for him, but of him. I hated them for that.

It was like Conrad and Jeremiah had deemed him

unworthy and so I had to too. It was funny how I'd felt so close to him just a few minutes before.

"Okay, Cam Cameron. This song goes out to you and our favorite little Belly Button. Hit it, ladies." Some girl pushed the play button on the remote. "Summer lovin', had me a blast . . ."

I wanted to kill him, but all I could do was shake my head at him and glare. It wasn't like I could grab the mike out of his hand in front of all these people. Jeremiah just grinned at me and started to dance. One of the girls sitting on the floor jumped up and started dancing with him. She sang the Olivia Newton-John part, off-key. Conrad watched in his amused, condescending way. I heard someone say, "Who is that girl anyway?" She was looking right at me as she said it.

Next to me, Cam was laughing. I couldn't believe it. I was dying of embarrassment and he was laughing. "Smile, Flavia," he said, poking me in the side.

When someone tells me to smile, I can't help it. I always do.

Midway through Jeremiah's song, Cam and I walked out—without even looking, I knew Conrad was watching us.

Cam and I sat on the staircase and talked. He sat on the step above me. He was nice to talk to, not intimidating at all. I loved the way he laughed so easily—not like with Conrad. With Conrad you had to work hard for every smile. Nothing ever came easy with Conrad.

The way Cam was leaning into me, I thought he might try to kiss me. I was pretty sure I'd let him. But he'd lean in and scratch his ankle, or tug at his sock, and then shift away, and then he'd do it again.

When he was in the middle of a lean in, I heard pissed off, belligerent voices coming from the deck outside. One of them was definitely Conrad's pissed off, belligerent voice. I jumped up. "Something's going on out there."

"Let's check it out," said Cam, leading the way.

Conrad and some guy with a barbed wire tattoo on his forearm were arguing. The guy was shorter than Conrad, but stockier. He was packing some serious muscle, and he looked like he was, like, twenty-five. Jeremiah watched, bemused, but I could tell he was alert, ready to jump in if he needed to.

To Jeremiah I whispered, "What are they fighting about?"

He shrugged. "Conrad's wasted. Don't worry about it. They're just showing off."

"They look like they might kill each other," I said uneasily.

"They're fine," Cam said. "But we should probably get out of here. It's late."

I glanced at him. I'd almost forgotten he was standing next to me. "I'm not leaving," I said. Not that I could do anything to stop a fight from happening. But it wouldn't be right to just leave him there.

Conrad stepped up close to the tattoo guy, who

shoved him away easily, and Conrad laughed. I could feel an actual fight brewing, like a thunderstorm. Just like the way the water got really still before the sky broke open.

"Are you gonna do something?" I hissed.

"He's a big boy," Jeremiah said, his eyes close on Conrad. "He'll be fine."

But he didn't believe it, and neither did I. Conrad didn't seem fine at all. He didn't seem like the Conrad Fisher I knew, all wild and out of control. What if he got himself hurt? What then? I had to help, I just had to.

I started walking over to them, and I waved off Jeremiah when he tried to stop me. When I got there, I realized I had no idea what to say. I had never tried to break up a fight before.

"Um, hi," I said, standing between the two of them. "We have to leave."

Conrad pushed me out of the way. "Get the hell out of here, Belly."

"Who is this? Your baby sister?" The guy looked me up and down.

"No. I'm Belly," I told him. Only, I was nervous, and I stuttered when I said my name.

"Belly?" The guy busted out laughing, and I grabbed Conrad's arm.

"We're gonna leave now," I said.

I realized how drunk he was when he swayed a little as he tried to swat me off. "Don't leave. Things are just getting fun. See, I'm about to kick this guy's ass." I'd never seen him like this before. His intensity scared me. I wondered where Red Sox girl had gone. I kind of wished she was here to handle Conrad and not me. I didn't know what I was supposed to do.

The guy laughed, but I could tell he wanted a fight just about as much as I did. He looked tired, like all he wanted was to head home and watch TV in his boxers. Whereas Conrad was running on all cylinders. Conrad was like a soda bottle that had been shaken up; he was about to explode on somebody. It didn't matter who it was. It didn't matter that this guy was bigger than him. It wouldn't have mattered if he was twenty feet tall and built like a brick. Conrad was looking for a fight. He wouldn't be satisfied until he got one. And this guy, he could kill Conrad.

The guy kept looking at Conrad and then back at me. Shaking his head, he said, "Belly, you better get this little boy home."

"Don't talk to her," Conrad warned.

I put my hand on Conrad's chest. I had never done that before. It felt solid and warm; I could feel his heart beating fast and out of control. "Can we please just go home," I pleaded. But it was like Conrad didn't even see me standing there, or feel my hand on his chest.

"Listen to your girlfriend, kid," the guy said.

"I'm not his girlfriend," I said, glancing over at Cam, who had no expression on his face.

Then I looked back at Jeremiah helplessly, and he ambled over. He whispered something in Conrad's ear, and Conrad shook him off. But Jeremiah kept talking to him in his low voice, and when they looked at me, I realized it was about me. Conrad hesitated, and then he finally nodded. Then he half jokingly made like he was going to hit the guy, and the guy rolled his eyes. "Good night, douche," he said to the guy.

The guy waved him off with one hand. I let out a big breath.

As we walked back to the car, Cam grabbed my arm. "Are you okay to go home with these guys?" he asked me.

Conrad whirled around and said, "Who is this guy?"

I shook my head at Cam and said, "I'll be fine. Don't worry. I'll call you."

He looked worried. "Who's driving?"

"I am," Jeremiah said, and Conrad didn't argue. "Don't worry, Straight Edge, I don't drink and drive."

I was embarrassed, and I could tell Cam was bothered, but he just nodded. Quickly I hugged him, and he felt stiff. I wanted to make things okay. "Thanks for tonight," I said.

I watched him walk away, and I felt a stab of resentment—Conrad and his stupid temper had ruined my first real date. It wasn't fair.

Jeremiah said, "You guys get in the car; I left my hat inside. I'll be right back."

"Just hurry," I told him.

Conrad and I got in the car silently. It felt eerily quiet, and even though it was only just past one, it felt like it was four in the morning and the whole world had gone to sleep. He lay down in the backseat, all of his energy from before gone. I sat in the front seat with my bare feet on the dashboard, leaning back far in the seat. Neither of us spoke. It had been frightening back there. I didn't recognize him, the way he'd acted. I suddenly felt very tired.

My hair was hanging low, and from the backseat, all of a sudden, I felt Conrad touching it, running his fingers through the bottom. I think I stopped breathing. We were sitting in perfect silence, and Conrad Fisher was playing with my hair.

"Your hair is like a little kid's, the way it's always so messy," he said softly. His voice made me shiver, it was like the sound of water when it pulls off the sand.

I didn't say anything. I didn't even look at him. I didn't want to scare him off. It was like the time I had a really high fever, and everything felt gauzy and dizzy and unreal, it felt just like that. All I knew was, I didn't want him to stop.

But he finally did. I watched him in the visor mirror. He closed his eyes and sighed. I did too.

"Belly," he began.

Just as suddenly, everything in me was alert. The sleepy feeling was gone; every part of my body was awake now. I was holding my breath, waiting for what he would say. I didn't answer him. I didn't want to break the spell.

That's when Jeremiah came back, opened the door, slammed it shut. This moment between us, fragile and tenuous, snapped in half. It was over. It would do no good to wonder what he was going to say. Moments, when lost, can't be found again. They're just gone.

Jeremiah looked at me funny. I could tell he knew that he'd walked in on something. I shrugged at him, and he turned away and started the car.

I reached over to the radio and turned it on, loud.

The whole way home, there was this strange tension, everyone keeping quiet—Conrad passed out in the backseat, Jeremiah and me not looking at each other in the front seat. Until we pulled up the driveway, when Jeremiah said to Conrad, in what was a harsh tone for him, "Don't let Mom see you like this."

Which was when I realized, remembered, that Conrad really had been drunk, that he couldn't really have been responsible for anything he'd said or done that night. He probably wouldn't remember it tomorrow. It would be like it had never happened.

As soon as we got inside, I ran up to my room. I wanted to forget what had happened in the car and only remember the way Cam had looked at me, on the stairs with his arm touching my shoulder.

chapter *twenty-four*

The next day, nothing. It wasn't that he ignored me, because that would have been something. Some kind of proof that it had happened, that something had changed. But no, he treated me the same. Like I was still little Belly, the girl with the messy flyaway ponytail and the bony knees, running after them on the beach. I should have known better.

The thing was, whether he was pushing me away or pulling me toward him, I was still going in the same direction. Toward Conrad.

Cam didn't call me for a few days. Not that I blamed him. I didn't call him either—although I thought about it. I just didn't know what to say.

When he finally called, he didn't bring up the party. He asked me to go to the drive-in. I said yes. Right away

I worried, though—did going to the drive-in mean we were going to have to make out? Like, crazy make out, steamed windows and seats all the way back?

Because that was what people did at the drive-in. There were the families, and then there were the hot and heavy couples toward the back of the lot. I'd never been part of a couple before. I'd gone as a family, with Susannah and my mother and everyone, and I'd gone with the boys, but never as a couple, like on a date.

Once, Jeremiah and Steven and I went and spied on Conrad on one of his dates. Susannah let Jeremiah drive us, even though he only had a permit. The drive-in was three miles away, and at Cousins, everyone drove, even kids on their parents' laps. Conrad had been furious when he'd caught us spying on him. He'd been on his way to the concession stand when he saw us. It had been pretty funny—his hair was all messed up as he yelled at us, and his lips were rosy and they had a glossy sheen. Jeremiah cracked up the whole time.

I wished Steven and Jeremiah were out there in the dark somewhere, spying on us and cracking up. It would make me feel comforted somehow. Safer.

I was wearing Cam's hoodie, and I kept it zipped all the way to my neck. I sat with my arms crossed, like I was shivering. Even though I liked Cam, even though I wanted to be there, I had the sudden urge to jump out of the car and walk home. I'd only ever kissed one boy, and that hadn't been for real. Taylor called me the nun. Maybe I was one, at heart. Maybe I should have joined a convent. I didn't even know if this was an actual date. Maybe he'd been so turned off by me the other night that all he wanted was to be my friend.

Cam tuned the radio until he found the right station. Drumming his hands on the steering wheel, he said, "Do you want any popcorn or anything?"

I kind of did, but I didn't want it to get stuck in my teeth, so I said no, thanks.

He was pretty into the movie, the way he leaned up close to the windshield to get a closer look sometimes. It was an old horror movie, one that Cam told me was really famous, but I'd never heard of it. I was barely paying attention anyway—I felt like I was watching him way more than I was watching the movie. He licked his lips a lot. He didn't look over and laugh with me during the funny parts the way Jeremiah did. He just sat on his side of the car, leaned up against the door, as far away from me as possible.

When the movie was over, he started the car up. "Ready?" he said.

I felt a wave of disappointment. He was taking me home already. He wasn't going to take me to Scoops for an ice cream cone, or a hot fudge sundae to share. The date, if you could even call it that, had been a failure. He didn't try to make out with me once. Not that I knew if I'd even have let him, but still. He could've at least tried.

"Um-hmm," I said. I felt like I might cry, and I wasn't quite sure why, when I hadn't even been sure if I wanted to kiss him in the first place.

We drove home in silence. He parked the car in front of the house—I held my breath a little, my hand on the door handle, waiting to see if he'd turn off the ignition or if I should hop out. But he turned it off and leaned his head back against the headrest a second.

"Do you know why I remembered you?" he asked me suddenly.

It was a question so out of nowhere that it took me a little while to figure out what he was talking about.

"You mean from Latin Convention?"

"Yeah."

"Was it my Coliseum model?" I was only half-joking. Steven had helped me build it; it had been pretty impressive.

"No." Cam ran his hand through his hair. He wouldn't look at me. "It's because I thought you were really pretty. Like, maybe the prettiest girl I'd ever seen."

I laughed. In the car, it sounded really loud. "Yeah, right. Nice try, Sextus."

"I mean it," he insisted, his voice rising.

"You're making that up." I didn't believe it could be true. I didn't want to let myself believe it. With the boys any compliment like this would always be the first part of a joke.

He shook his head, lips tight. He was offended that I didn't believe him. I hadn't meant to hurt his feelings. I just didn't see how it could be true. It was almost mean of him to lie about it. I knew what I looked like back then, and I wasn't the prettiest girl *anybody* had ever seen, not with my thick glasses and chubby cheeks and little-girl body.

Cam looked me in the eyes then. "The first day, you wore a blue dress. It was, like, corduroy or something. It made your eyes look really blue."

"My eyes are gray," I said.

"Yes, but that dress made them look blue."

Which was why I wore it. It was my favorite. I wondered where it was now. Probably packed up in the attic back home, with all my winter clothes. It was too small now anyway.

He looked so sweet, the way he watched me, waiting for my reaction. His cheeks were flushed peach. I swallowed hard and said, "Why didn't you come up to me?"

He shrugged. "You were always with your friends. I watched you that whole week, trying to get up the nerve. I couldn't believe it when I saw you at the bonfire that night. Pretty bizarre, huh?" Cam laughed, but he sounded embarrassed.

"Pretty bizarre," I echoed. I couldn't believe he'd noticed me. With Taylor by my side, who would have even bothered to look at me?

"I almost messed up my Catullus speech on purpose, so you'd win," he said, remembering. He inched a little closer to me.

"I'm glad you didn't," I said. I reached out and touched his arm. My hand shook. "I wish you had come up to me."

That's when he dipped his head low and kissed me. I didn't let go of the door handle. All I could think was, *I wish this had been my first kiss.*

chapter *twenty-five*

When I went into the house, I was walking on cotton candy and clouds, replaying everything that had just happened—until I heard my mother and Susannah arguing in the living room. Fear seized up inside of me; it felt like a fist clenched tight around my heart. They never fought, not really. I'd only ever seen them fight one time. It was last summer. The three of us had gone shopping to this fancy mall an hour away from Cousins. It was an outdoor mall, the kind where people bring their pocket-size dogs on fancy leashes. I saw this dress—it was a purpley plum chiffon, with little off the shoulder straps, way too old for me. I loved it. Susannah said I should try it on, just for fun, so I did. She took one look at me and said I had to have it. My mother shook her head right away. She said, "She's fourteen. Where will she wear a dress like that?" Susannah said it didn't matter, that it was made for me. I knew we couldn't afford it, my mother was newly divorced, after all, but I still pleaded with her. I begged. They got into an argument right there in the boutique, in front of people. Susannah wanted to buy it for me, and my mother wouldn't let her. I told them never mind, I didn't want it, even though I did. I knew my mother was right, I'd never wear it.

When we got back from Cousins at the end of summer, I found the dress in my suitcase, wrapped in paper and packed neatly on top like it had always been there. Susannah had gone back and bought it for me. It was so like her to do that. Later, my mother must have seen it hanging up in my closet, but she never said anything.

Standing there in the foyer, listening, I felt like the spy Steven was always accusing me of being. But I couldn't help it.

I heard Susannah say, "Laurel, I'm a big girl now. I need you to stop trying to manage my life. I'm the one who gets to decide how I want to live it."

I didn't wait for my mother's response. I walked right in and said, "What's going on?" I looked at my mother when I said it, and I knew I sounded like I was blaming her, but I didn't care.

"Nothing. Everything's fine," my mother said, but her eyes looked red and tired.

"Then why were you fighting?"

"We weren't fighting, hon," Susannah assured me. She reached out and smoothed my shoulder, like she was ironing out wrinkled silk. "Everything really is fine."

"It didn't sound like it."

"Well, it is," Susannah told me.

"Promise?" I asked. I wanted to believe her.

"Promise," she said without hesitation.

My mother walked away from us, and I could see from the stiffness of her shoulders that everything was not fine, that she was still upset. But because I wanted to stay with Susannah, where everything really was fine, I didn't follow her. My mother was the kind of person who would rather be alone anyway. Just ask my father.

"What's the matter with her?" I whispered to Susannah.

"It's nothing. Tell me about your date with Cam," she said, leading me to the wicker couch in the sunroom.

I should have kept pressing her, should have tried to figure out what had really happened between the two of them, but my worry was already fading away. I wanted to tell her everything about Cam, everything. Susannah had that way about her, where you wanted to tell her all your secrets and everything in between.

She sat on the couch and patted her lap. I sat down next to her and put my head in her lap and she smoothed my hair away from my forehead. Everything felt safe and cozy, like that fight hadn't happened. And maybe it hadn't even been a fight, maybe I'd misread the whole thing. "Well, he's different from anyone I've ever met," I began.

"How so?"

"He's just so smart, and he doesn't care what people think. And he's so good-looking. I can't even believe he pays me any attention."

Susannah shook her head. "Oh, please. Of course he should pay you attention. You're so lovely, darling. You've really blossomed this summer. People can't *help* but pay you attention."

"Ha," I said, but I felt flattered. She was so good at making people feel special. "I'm glad I have you to talk to about this kind of stuff."

"I am too. But you know, you could talk to your mother."

"She wouldn't be interested in any of it, not really. She'd pretend to care, but she wouldn't."

"Oh, Belly. That's not true. She would care. She does care." Susannah cradled my face in her hands. "Your mother is your biggest fan, next to me. She cares about everything you do. Don't shut her out."

I didn't want to talk about my mother anymore. I wanted to talk about Cam. "You'll never believe what Cam said to me tonight," I began.

chapter *twenty-six*

Just like that, July turned into August. I guessed summer went by a lot faster when you had someone to spend it with. For me, that someone was Cam. Cam Cameron.

Mr. Fisher always came the first week of August. He'd bring Susannah's favorites from the city, almond croissants and lavender chocolates. And flowers, he always brought flowers. Susannah loved flowers. She said she needed them like air, to breathe. She had more vases than I could count, tall ones and fat ones and glass ones. They were all over the house, flowers in vases in every room. Her favorites were peonies. She kept them on her nightstand in her bedroom, so they were the first thing she saw in the morning.

Shells, too. She loved shells. She kept them in hurricane glasses. When she'd come back from a walk on the beach, she'd always come back with a handful of shells. She'd arrange them on the kitchen table, admire them first, say things like, "Doesn't this one look just like an ear?" Or, "Isn't this one the perfect shade of pink?" Then she'd put them in order from biggest to smallest. It was one of her rituals, something I loved to watch her do.

That week, right around when Mr. Fisher usually came, Susannah mentioned that he couldn't get away from work. There had been some sort of emergency at the bank. It would just be the five of us finishing out the summer. It would be the first year without Mr. Fisher and my brother.

After she went to bed, early, Conrad said to me, conversationally, "They're getting a divorce."

"Who?" I said.

"My parents. It's about time."

Jeremiah glared at him. "Shut up, Conrad."

Conrad shrugged. "Why? You know it's true. Belly's not surprised, are you, Belly?"

I was. I was really surprised. I said, to both of them, "I thought they seemed like they were really in love."

Whatever love was, I was sure they had it. I thought they had it a million times over. The way they gazed at each other at the dinner table, how excited Susannah got when he came to the summer house. I didn't think people like that got divorced. People like my parents got divorced. Not Susannah and Mr. Fisher.

"They *were* in love," Jeremiah told me. "I don't really know what happened."

"Dad's a dick. That's what happened," Conrad said, getting up. He sounded so blasé and matter-of-fact, but that didn't seem right. Not when I knew he adored his dad. I wondered if Mr. Fisher had a new girlfriend the way my father did. I wondered if he'd cheated on Susannah. But who would ever cheat on Susannah? It was impossible.

"Don't tell your mom you know," Jeremiah said suddenly. "Mom doesn't know we know."

"I won't," I said. I wondered how they'd found out. My parents had sat Steven and me down and told us everything, explained it all in detail.

As Conrad left, Jeremiah said to me, "Before we left, our dad had been sleeping in the guest room for weeks. He's already moved out most of his clothes. They think we're retarded or something, for us not to notice." His voice cracked at the last part.

I grabbed his hand and squeezed it. He was really hurting. I guessed maybe Conrad was too, even if he didn't show it. It all made sense, when I thought about it. The way Conrad had been acting, so different, so lost. So un-Conrad-like. He was suffering. And then there was Susannah. The way she'd been spending so much time in bed, the way she seemed so sad. She was hurting too.

chapter *twenty-seven*

"You and Cam have been spending a lot of time together," my mother said, looking at me over her newspaper.

"Not really," I said, even though we had been. At the summer house one day just kind of melted into the next; you didn't notice time passing. Cam and I had been hanging out for two weeks before I realized it: He was kind of my boyfriend. We'd spent practically every day together. I didn't know what I'd done before I'd met him. My life must have been really boring.

My mother said, "We miss you around the house." If Susannah had said it, I'd have been flattered, but from my mother it was just really annoying. It felt like recrimination. And anyway, it wasn't like they'd been around so much either. They were always off doing things, just the two of them.

"Belly, will you bring this boy of yours to dinner tomorrow night?" Susannah asked me sweetly.

I wanted to say no, but for me, saying no to Susannah was impossible. Especially with her going through a divorce. I couldn't say no. So instead I said, "Um . . . maybe . . ."

"Please, honey? I'd really like to meet him."

I caved. "All right, I'll ask. I can't promise he doesn't have plans, though."

Susannah nodded serenely. "As long as you ask."

Unfortunately for me, Cam didn't have plans.

Susannah cooked; she made a tofu stir-fry because Cam was a vegetarian. Again, it was something I'd admired about him, but when I saw the look Jeremiah gave me, it made me shrink a little. Jeremiah cooked hamburgers that night—he liked any excuse to use the grill, just like his dad. He asked me if I wanted one too, and I said no even though I did.

Conrad had already eaten and was upstairs playing his guitar. He couldn't even be bothered to eat with us. He came down to get a bottled water, and he didn't even say hello to Cam.

"So why don't you eat meat, Cam?" Jeremiah asked, stuffing half his burger into his mouth.

Cam swallowed his water and said, "I'm morally opposed to eating animals."

Jeremiah nodded seriously. "But Belly eats meat. You let her kiss you with those lips?" Then he cracked up. Susannah and my mother exchanged a knowing kind of smile.

I could feel my face getting hot, and I could feel how tense Cam was beside me. "Shut up, Jeremiah."

Cam glanced at my mother and laughed uneasily. "I don't judge people who choose to eat meat. It's a personal choice."

Jeremiah continued, "So you don't mind when her lips touch dead animal and then they touch your, um, lips?"

Susannah chuckled lightly and said, "Jere, give the guy a break."

"Yeah, Jere, give the guy a break," I said, glaring at him. I kicked him under the table, hard. Hard enough to make him flinch.

"No, it's fine," Cam said. "I don't mind at all. In fact—" Then he pulled me to him and kissed me quickly, right in front of everyone. It was only a peck, but it was embarrassing.

"Please don't kiss Belly at the dinner table," said Jeremiah, gagging a little for effect. "You're making me nauseous."

My mother shook her head at him and said, "Belly's allowed to kiss." Then she pointed her fork at Cam. "But that's it."

She burst out laughing like it was the funniest thing

she'd ever said, and Susannah tried not to smile and told her to hush. I wanted to kill my mother and then myself. "Mom, please. You're so not funny," I said. "No more wine for Mom." I refused to look anywhere near Jeremiah's direction, or Cam's, for that matter.

The truth was, Cam and I hadn't done much else besides kiss. He didn't seem to be in any big hurry. He was careful with me, sweet—nervous even. It was completely different from the way I'd seen other guys behave with girls. Last summer I caught Jeremiah with a girl on the beach, right outside of the house. They were frantic, like if they hadn't been wearing clothes, they'd already have been having sex. I gave him hell for it the whole rest of the summer, but he didn't really care. I wished Cam would care a little more.

"Belly, I'm kidding. You know I'm open to you exploring yourself," my mother said, taking a long sip of chardonnay.

Jeremiah busted out laughing. I stood up and said, "That's it. Cam and I are eating our dinner on the porch." I grabbed my plate and waited for Cam to stand up too.

But he didn't. "Belly, calm down. Everybody's just joking around," he said, loading up his fork with rice and bok choy and shoveling it into his mouth.

"Way to keep her in check, Cam," Jeremiah said, nodding at him. He really did look kind of impressed.

I sat back down, although it killed me to do it. I hated

losing face in front of everyone, but if I did walk out by myself, I knew no one would come after me. I would just be little Belly Button, off pouting again. That was my name when I was being a baby, Belly Button—Steven thought he was such a genius for thinking that one up. "No one keeps me in check, Jeremiah. Least of all Cam Cameron."

Everyone hooted and hollered then, even Cam, and all of a sudden, it was all very normal, like he really belonged there. I could feel myself start to relax. It was all going to be okay. Great, in fact. Amazing, just like Susannah had promised.

After dinner, Cam and I took a walk on the beach. For me there was—is—nothing better than walking on the beach late at night. It feels like you could walk forever, like the whole night is yours and so is the ocean. When you walk on the beach at night, you can say things you can't say in real life. In the dark you can feel really close to a person. You can say whatever you want.

"I'm really glad you came," I told him.

He took my hand and said, "Me too. I'm glad you're glad."

"Of course I'm glad."

I let go of his hand to roll up the bottoms of my jeans, and he said, quietly, "It didn't seem like you were that glad."

"Well, I am." I looked up at him and gave him a quick kiss. "See? This is me, being glad."

He smiled and we started walking again. "Good. So which one of those guys was your first kiss?"

"I told you that?"

"Yup. You said your first kiss was a boy at the beach when you were thirteen."

"Oh." I looked up at his face in the moonlight, and he was still smiling. "Guess."

Immediately he said, "The older one, Conrad."

"Why'd you guess him?"

He shrugged. "Just a feeling, the way he looks at you."

"He hardly looks at me at all," I told him. "And you're wrong, Sextus. It was Jeremiah."

chapter *twenty-eight*

AGE 14

"Truth or dare?" Taylor asked Conrad.

"I'm not playing," he said.

Taylor pouted. "Don't be so gay," she said.

Jeremiah said, "You shouldn't use the word 'gay' like that."

Taylor opened her mouth and closed it. Then she said, "I didn't mean anything by it, Jeremy. I just meant he's being lame."

"Well, 'gay' doesn't mean 'lame,' Taylor, now does it?" Jeremiah said. He spoke in a sarcastic tone, but even mean attention was better than no attention. Probably he was just mad about all the attention she'd been giving Conrad that day.

Taylor heaved a great big sigh and turned to Conrad.

"Conrad, you're being very lame. Play truth or dare with us."

He ignored her and turned the volume on the TV up louder. Then he pretended to mute her with the remote, which made me laugh out loud.

"Fine, he's out. Steven, truth or dare."

Steven rolled his eyes. "Truth."

Taylor's eyes lit up. "Okay. How far did you go with Claire Cho?" I knew she'd been saving that one up for a long time, waiting for the exact moment she could ask. Claire Cho was a girl that Steven had dated for most of freshman year. Taylor swore Claire had cankles, but I thought Claire's ankles were perfectly slim. I thought Claire Cho was kind of perfect.

Steven actually blushed. "I'm not answering that."

"You have to. It's truth or dare. You can't sit here and listen to other people tell secrets if you're not going to," I said. I had been wondering about him and Claire too.

"Nobody's even told any secrets yet!" he protested.

"We're about to, Steven," Taylor said. "Now man up and tell us."

"Yeah, Steven, man up," Jeremiah chimed in.

We all started to chant, "Man up! Man up!" Even Conrad turned the TV on mute to hear the answer.

"Fine," Steven said. "If you shut up, I'll tell you."

We shut right up and waited. "Well?" I said.

"Third," he said at last.

I relaxed back into the couch. Third base. Wow. Interesting. My brother had been to third base. Weird. Gross.

Taylor looked pink with satisfaction. "Well done, Stevie."

He shook his head at her and said, "Now it's my turn." He looked around the room, and I sank deep into the couch cushions. I really, really hoped he wasn't going to pick me and make me say it out loud—how I hadn't even so much as kissed a boy yet. Knowing Steven, he would.

He surprised me when he said, "Taylor. Truth or dare?" He was actually playing along.

Automatically she said, "You can't pick me because I just asked you. You have to pick someone else." Which was true, that was the rule.

"Are you scared, Tay-Tay? Why don't you man up?"

Taylor hesitated. "Fine. Truth."

Steven grinned evilly. "Who would you kiss in this room?"

Taylor considered it for a few seconds, and then she got that cat-that-ate-the-canary look on her face. It was the same look she'd had on her face when she'd dyed her little sister's hair blue when we were eight. She waited until she had everyone's attention, and then she said, triumphantly, "Belly."

There was a stunned kind of silence for a minute, and then everyone started to laugh, Conrad loudest. I threw a pillow at Taylor, hard.

"That's not fair. You didn't answer for real," Jeremiah said, shaking his finger at her.

"Yes, I did," Taylor said smugly. "I pick Belly. Take a closer look at everybody's favorite little sister, Jeremy. She's turning hot before your very eyes."

I hid my face behind a pillow. I knew I was blushing even harder than Steven had. Mostly because it wasn't true, I wasn't turning hot before anyone's eyes, and we all knew it. "Taylor, shut up. Please shut up."

"Yes, please shut up, Tay-Tay," Steven said. He looked kind of red too.

"If you're so serious, then kiss her," said Conrad, his eyes still on the TV.

"Hey," I said, glaring at him. "I'm a person. You can't just kiss me without my permission."

He looked at me and said, "I'm not the one who wants to kiss you."

Hotly, I said, "Either way, permission not granted. To either of you." I wished I could stick my tongue out at him without being accused of being a big baby.

Taylor broke in quickly. She said, "I picked truth, not dare. That's why we're not kissing right now."

"We're not kissing right now because I don't want to kiss you," I told her. I felt flushed, partly because I was mad, and partly because I was flattered. "Now let's stop talking about it. It's your turn to ask."

"Fine. Jeremiah. Truth or dare."

"Dare," he said, leaning against the couch lazily.

"Okay. Kiss somebody in this room, right now." Taylor looked at him confidently and waited.

It felt like the whole room was sitting on the edge of its seat while we waited for Jeremiah to say something. Would he actually do it? He was not the kind of guy to pass up a dare. I, for one, was curious about what kind of kisser he'd be, if he'd go for a French or if he'd give her a quick peck. I also wondered if it would be their first kiss, or if they'd kissed sometime earlier in the week, like at the arcade when I wasn't looking, maybe. I was pretty sure they had.

Jeremiah sat up straight. "Easy," he said, rubbing his hands together with a smile. Taylor smiled back and tilted her head to the side so her hair fell in her eyes just a little bit.

Then he leaned over to me and said, "Ready?" and before I could answer, he kissed me right on the lips. His mouth was a little bit open, but it wasn't a French kiss or anything. I tried to push him off, but he kept on kissing me, for a few more seconds.

I pushed him off again, and he leaned back into the couch, as casual as can be. Everyone else was sitting there with their mouths hanging open, except for Conrad, who didn't even look surprised. But then, he never looked surprised. I, on the other hand, was finding it kind of hard to breathe. I had just had my first kiss. In front of people. In front of my brother.

I couldn't believe that Jeremiah had stolen my first kiss like that. I had been waiting, wanting it to be special, and it had happened during a game of truth or dare. How unspecial could you get? And to top it all off, he had only done it to make Taylor jealous, not because he liked me.

It had worked. Her eyes were narrowed, and she was staring at Jeremiah like he had thrown down some kind of gauntlet. Which, I guess he kind of had.

"Gross," Steven said. "This game is gross. I'm outta here." Then he looked at all of us disgustedly and left.

I got up too, and so did Conrad. "See ya," I said. "And, Jeremiah, I'm getting you back for that."

He winked and said, "A back rub should make us about even," and I threw a pillow directly at his head and slammed the door behind me. The fact that he was being fake-flirty was the worst part. It was so patronizing, so demeaning.

It took me about three seconds before I realized that Taylor wasn't coming after me. She was inside, laughing at Jeremiah's dumb jokes.

In the hallway, Conrad gave me his trademark knowing look and said, "You know you loved it."

I glared at him. "How would you know? You're too obsessed with yourself to notice anybody else."

He walked away from me and said over his shoulder, "Oh, I notice everything, Belly. Even poor little you."

"Screw you!" I said, because that was all I could think

of. I could hear him chuckling as he shut his bedroom door.

I went back to my room and got under the covers. I closed my eyes and replayed and replayed what had just happened. Jeremiah's lips had touched my lips. My lips were no longer my own. They had been touched. By *Jeremiah*. I had finally been kissed, and it was my friend Jeremiah who'd been the one to do it. My friend Jeremiah who had been ignoring me that whole week.

I wished I could talk to Taylor. I wished we could talk about my first kiss, but we couldn't, because right this minute she was downstairs kissing the same boy who had just kissed me. I was sure of it.

When she came back upstairs an hour later, I pretended I was sleeping.

"Belly?" she whispered across the room.

I didn't say anything, but I stirred a little, for effect.

"I know you're still awake, Belly," she said. "And I forgive you."

I wanted to sit right up and say, "You forgive me? Well, I don't forgive you, for coming here and ruining my whole summer." But I didn't say any of it. I just kept fake-sleeping.

The next morning I woke up early, just after seven, and Taylor was already gone. I knew where she was. She'd gone to watch the sunrise with Jeremiah. We'd been planning to go watch the sunrise on the beach one morning before she left, but we always overslept. It was her second to last morning, and she'd chosen Jeremiah. Figured.

I changed into my bathing suit and headed for the pool. In the mornings it was always a little cold outside, just a little bit of bite to the air, but I didn't mind. Swimming in the mornings made me feel like I was swimming in the ocean even when I wasn't. In theory swimming in the ocean sounds great and all, but the salt water burned my eyes too much to do it every day. Plus, the pool was more private, more my own. Even though everyone else swam in it too, in the mornings and at night I had it pretty much to myself, besides Susannah.

When I opened the gate to the pool, I saw my mother sitting in one of the lounge chairs reading a book. Except she wasn't really reading it. She was more just holding it and staring off into space.

"Hi, Mom," I said, more to break her out of her spell than anything else.

She looked up, startled. "Good morning," she said, clearing her throat. "Did you sleep well?"

I shrugged and dropped my towel onto the chair next to hers. "I guess," I said.

My mother shaded her eyes with her hand and looked up at me. "Are you and Taylor having fun?"

"Tons," I said. "Buckets full."

"Where is Taylor?"

"Who knows?" I said. "Who cares?"

"Are you two fighting?" my mother asked casually.

"No. I'm just starting to wish I hadn't brung her, is all."

"Best friends are important. They're the closest thing to a sister you'll ever have," she told me. "Don't squander it."

Irritably I said, "I haven't squandered anything. Why do you always have to put the blame on me for everything?"

"I'm not blaming you. Why must you always make things about you, dear?" My mother smiled at me in her infuriatingly calm way.

I rolled my eyes and jumped backward into the pool. It was freezing cold. When I came up to the surface, I yelled, "I don't!"

Then I started my laps, and whenever I thought about Taylor and Jeremiah, I got madder and pushed harder. By the time I was done, my shoulders burned.

My mother had left, but Taylor and Jeremiah and Steven were just coming in.

"Belly, if you swim too much, you'll get those broad swimmer's shoulders," Taylor warned, dipping her foot in the water.

I ignored her. What did Taylor know about exercise? She thought walking around the mall in high heels was exercise. "Where were you guys?" I asked, floating on my back.

"Just hanging out," Jeremiah said vaguely.

Judas, I thought. A bunch of Benedict Arnolds. "Where's Conrad?"

"Who knows? He's too cool to hang out," Jeremiah said, falling onto a lounge chair.

"He went running," Steven said, a tad defensively. "He has to get in shape for football season. He has to leave for practice next week, remember?"

I remembered. That year Conrad had to leave early so he could get back in time for tryouts. He'd never seemed like the football type to me, but there he was, trying out for the team. I guessed Mr. Fisher had a lot to do with it; he was exactly the type. So was Jeremiah. Although he'd never take it seriously. He never took anything seriously.

"I'll probably play for the team next year too," Jeremiah said casually. He sneaked a peek at Taylor to see if she looked impressed. She didn't. She wasn't even looking at him.

His shoulders sagged a little, and I felt sorry for him despite myself.

I said, "Jere, race me, okay?"

He shrugged and stood up, taking off his shirt. Then he walked over to the deep end and dove in. "You want a handicap?" he asked when he emerged up top.

"No. I think I can beat you without one," I said, paddling over. "Whoo-hoo! Let's see."

We raced across the length of the pool, freestyle, and

he beat me the first time, and then the second. But I wore him down by the third and fourth and beat him too. Taylor cheered me on, which only annoyed me more.

The next morning she was gone again. This time, though, I was gonna join them. It wasn't like she and Jeremiah owned the beach. I had just as much right as they did to watch the sunrise. I got up, put my clothes on, and headed outside.

I didn't see them at first. They were farther down than usual, and they had their backs to me. He had his arms around her, and they were kissing. They weren't even watching the sunrise. And . . . it wasn't Jeremiah, either. It was Steven. My brother.

It was just like in those movies with the surprise ending, where everything falls into place and clicks. Suddenly my life had become *The Usual Suspects*, and Taylor, Taylor was Keyser Soze. The scenes ran through the mind— Taylor and Steven bickering, the way he had come to the boardwalk that night, Taylor claiming that Claire Cho had cankles, all the afternoons she'd spent at my house.

They didn't hear me walk up. But then I said, loudly, "Wow, so first Conrad, then Jeremiah, and now my brother."

She turned around, surprised, and Steven looked surprised too. "Belly—," she started.

"Shut up." I looked at my brother then, and he squirmed.

"You're a hypocrite. You don't even like her! You said she bleached out all her brain cells with her Sun-In!"

He cleared his throat. "I never said that," he said, glancing back and forth between Taylor and me. Her eyes had welled up, and she was wiping her left eye with the back of her sweatshirt sleeve. *Steven's* sweatshirt sleeve. I was too angry to cry.

"I'm telling Jeremiah."

"Belly, just freakin' calm down. You're too old for your temper tantrums," Steven said, shaking his head in his brotherly way.

The words came out of me, hot and fast and sure. "Go to hell." I had never talked like that to my brother before. I don't think I'd ever talked like that to *anyone* before. Steven blinked.

That's when I started to walk away, and Taylor chased after me. She had to run to catch up, that's how fast I was walking. I guess anger gives you speed.

"Belly, I'm so sorry," she began. "I was going to tell you. Things just happened really fast."

I stopped walking and spun around. "When? When did they happen? Because from what I saw, things were happening so fast with *Jeremy*, not with my older brother."

She shrugged helplessly, which only made me madder. Poor helpless little Taylor. "I've always had a crush on Steven. You know that, Belly."

"Actually, I didn't. Thanks for telling me."

"When he liked me back, it was like, I couldn't believe it. I didn't think."

"That's the thing. He doesn't like you. He's just using you because you're around," I said. I knew it was cruel, but I also knew it was true. Then I walked into the house and left her standing outside.

She chased after me and grabbed my arm, but I shrugged her off.

"Please don't be mad, Belly. I want things to stay the same with us forever," Taylor said, brown eyes brimming with tears. What she really meant was, I want you to stay the same forever while I grow bigger breasts and quit violin and kiss your brother.

"Things can't stay the same forever," I said. I was saying it to hurt her because I knew it would.

"Don't be mad at me, okay, Belly?" she pleaded. Taylor hated it when people were mad at her.

"I'm not mad at you," I said. "I just don't think we really know each other anymore."

"Don't say that, Belly."

"I'm only saying it because it's true."

She said, "I'm sorry, okay?"

I looked away for a second. "You promised you'd be nice to him."

"Who? Steven?" Taylor looked genuinely confused.

"No. Jeremiah. You said you'd be nice."

She waved her hand in the air. "Oh, he doesn't care."

"Yeah, he does. It's just that you don't know him." Like I do, I wanted to add. "I didn't think you'd ever act so—so . . ." I searched for the perfect word, to cut her the way she'd cut me. "Slutty."

"I'm not a slut," she said in a tiny voice.

So this was my power over her, my supposed innocence over her supposed sluttiness. It was all such BS. I would've traded my spot for hers in a second.

Later, Jeremiah asked me if I wanted to play spit. We hadn't played once all summer. It used to be our thing, our tradition. I was grateful to have it back. Even if it was a consolation prize.

He dealt me my hand, and we began to play, but both of us were just going through the motions. We had other things on our minds. I thought that we had this unspoken agreement not to talk about her, that maybe he didn't even know what had happened, but then he said, "I wish you never brought her."

"Me too."

"It's better when it's just us," he said, shuffling his stack.

"Yeah," I agreed.

After she left, after that summer, things were the same and they weren't. She and I were still friends, but not best friends, not like we used to be. But we were still friends. She'd known me my whole life. It's hard to throw away history. It was like you were throwing away a part of yourself.

Steven went right back to ignoring Taylor and obsessing over Claire Cho. We just pretended like none of it had ever happened. But it did.

chapter *twenty-nine*

I heard him come home. I think the whole house must have—except for Jeremiah, who could sleep through a tidal wave. Conrad made his way up the stairs, tripping and cursing, and then he shut his door and turned on his stereo, loud. It was three in the morning.

I lay in bed for about three seconds before I leapt up and ran down the hallway to his room. I knocked, twice, but the music was so loud I doubted he could hear anything. I opened the door. He was sitting on the edge of his bed, taking his shoes off. He looked up and saw me standing there. "Didn't your mom teach you to knock?" he asked, getting up and turning down the stereo.

"I did, but your music was so loud you couldn't hear me. You probably woke up the whole house, Conrad." I stepped inside and closed the door behind me. I hadn't been in his room in a long time. It was the same as I remembered, perfectly neat. Jeremiah's looked like hurricane season, but not Conrad's. In Conrad's room there was a place for everything, and everything was in its place. His pencil drawings, still tacked onto the bulletin board, his model cars still lined up on the dresser. It was comforting to see that at least that was still the same.

His hair was messed up, like someone had been running their hands through it. Probably Red Sox girl. "Are you going to tell on me, Belly? Are you still a tattletale?"

I ignored him and walked over to his desk. Hanging right above it there was a framed picture of him in his football uniform, the football tucked under his arm. "Why'd you quit, anyway?"

"It wasn't fun anymore."

"I thought you loved it."

"No, it was my dad who loved it," he said.

"It seemed like you did too." In the picture he looked tough, but I could tell he was trying not to smile.

"Why'd you quit dance?"

I turned around and looked at him. He was unbuttoning his work shirt, a white button-down, and he had on a T-shirt underneath.

"You remember that?"

"You used to dance all around the house like a little gnome."

I narrowed my eyes at him. "Gnomes don't dance. I was a ballerina, for your information."

He smirked. "So why'd you quit, then?"

It had been around the time my parents got divorced. My mom couldn't pick me up and drop me off twice a week all on her own. She had a job. It just didn't seem worth it anymore. I was bored of it by then anyway, and Taylor wasn't doing it anymore either. Also, I hated the way I looked in my leotard. I got boobs before the whole rest of the class, and in our class picture I looked like I could be the teacher. It was embarrassing.

I didn't answer his question. Instead I said, "I was really good! I could have been dancing in a company by now!" I couldn't have. I wasn't that good, not by any stretch of the imagination.

"Right," he said mockingly. He looked so smug sitting there on the bed.

"At least I can dance."

"Hey, I can dance," he protested.

I crossed my arms. "Prove it."

"I don't have to prove it. I taught you some moves, remember? How quickly we forget." Conrad jumped up off the bed and grabbed my hand and twirled me around. "See? We're dancing."

His arm was slung around my waist, and he laughed before he let me go. "I'm a better dancer than you, Belly," he said, collapsing onto his bed.

I stared at him. I didn't get him at all. One minute he was broody and withdrawn, and the next he was laughing and twirling me around the room. "I don't consider that dancing," I said. I backed out of the room. "And can you keep your music down? You already woke up the whole house."

He smiled. Conrad had a way of looking at me, at you, at anybody, that made everything unravel and want to fall at his feet. He said, "Sure. Good night, Bells." Bells, my nickname from a thousand years ago.

He made it so hard not to love him. When he was sweet like this, I remembered why I did. Used to love him, I mean.

I remembered everything.

chapter *thirty*
AGE 11

The summer house had a stack of CDs that we listened to, and that was pretty much it. We spent the whole summer listening to the same CDs. There was the Police, which Susannah put on in the morning; there was Bob Dylan, which she put on in the afternoon; and there was Billie Holiday, which she put on at dinner. The nights were a free-for-all. It was the funniest thing. Jeremiah would put on his Chronic CD, and my mother would be doing laundry, humming along. Even though she hated gangster rap. And then my mother might put on her Aretha Franklin CD, and Jeremiah would sing all the words, because we all knew them by that time, we'd heard it so much.

My favorite music was the Motown and the beach

music. I would listen to it on Susannah's old Walkman when I tanned. That night I put the *Boogie Beach Shag* CD on the big stereo in the living room, and Susannah grabbed Jeremiah and started to dance. He'd been playing poker with Steven and Conrad and my mother, who was very, very good at poker.

At first Jeremiah protested, but then he was dancing too. It was called the shag, and it was a 1960s kind of beach dance. I watched them, Susannah throwing her head back and laughing, and Jeremiah twirling her around, and I wanted to dance too. My feet positively itched to dance. I did dance ballet and modern, after all. I could show off how good I was.

"Stevie, dance with me," I demanded, poking him with my big toe. I was lying down on the floor, on my stomach, looking up at them.

"Yeah, right," he said. Not that he even knew how.

"Connie, dance with Belly," Susannah urged, her face flushed as Jeremiah twirled her again.

I didn't dare look at Conrad. I was afraid my love for him and my need for him to say yes would be written on my face like a poem.

Conrad sighed. He was still big on doing the right thing then. So he gave me his hand and pulled me up. I got to my feet shakily. He didn't let go of my hand. "This is how you shag," he said, shuffling his feet from side to side. "One-two-three, one-two-three, rock step."

It took me a few tries to get it. It was harder than it looked, and I was nervous. "Get on the beat," Steven said from the sidelines.

"Don't look so uptight, Belly. It's a relaxed kind of dance," my mother said from the couch.

I tried to ignore them and look only at Conrad. "How did you learn this?" I asked him.

"My mom taught both of us," Conrad said simply. Then he brought me in close and positioned my arms around his so we stepped together, side by side. "This is called the cuddle."

The cuddle was my favorite part. It was the closest I had ever been to him. "Let's do it again," I said, pretending to be confused.

He showed me again, putting his arm over mine. "See? You're getting it now."

He spun me around, and I felt dizzy. With pure, absolute joy.

chapter *thirty-one*

I spent the whole next day in the ocean with Cam. We packed a picnic. Cam made avocado and sprout sandwiches with Susannah's homemade mayonnaise and whole wheat bread. They were good, too. We stayed in the ocean for what felt like hours at a time. Every time a wave began to crest, one of us would start to laugh, and then we'd get overtaken by the wave and water. My eyes burned from the salty seawater, and my skin felt raw from scraping against the sand so many times, like I'd scrubbed my whole body with my mother's St. Ives Apricot Scrub. It was pretty great.

After, we stumbled back to our towels. I loved getting cold and wet in the ocean and then running back to the towels and letting the sun bake the sand off. I could do it all day—ocean, sand, ocean, sand.

I'd packed strawberry Fruit Roll-Ups, and we ate them so quick my teeth hurt. "I love Fruit Roll-Ups," I said, reaching for the last one.

He snatched it away. "So do I, and you already had three and I only had two," he said, peeling away the plastic sheet. He grinned and dangled it above my mouth.

"You have three seconds to hand it over," I warned. "I don't care if you had two Fruit Roll-Ups and I had twenty. It's my house."

Cam laughed and popped the whole thing into his mouth. Chewing loudly, he said, "It's not your house. It's Susannah's house."

"Shows how much you know. It's *all* of our house," I said, falling back on my towel. I was suddenly really thirsty. Fruit Roll-Ups will do that. Especially when you have three in about three minutes. Squinting up at him, I said, "Will you go back to *our* house and get some Kool-Aid? Pretty please?"

"I don't know anyone who consumes more sugar than you do in one day," Cam said, shaking his head at me sadly. "White sugar is evil."

"Says the guy who just ate the last Fruit Roll-Up," I countered.

"Waste not, want not," he said. He stood up and brushed the sand off his shorts. "I'll bring you water, not Kool-Aid."

I stuck my tongue out at him and rolled over. "Just be quick about it," I said.

He wasn't. He was gone forty-five minutes before I headed back to the house, loaded up with our towels and sunscreen and trash, breathing hard and sweating like a camel in the desert. He was in the living room, playing video games with the boys. They were all lying around in their swimming trunks. We pretty much stayed suited up all summer.

"Thanks for never coming back with my Kool-Aid," I said, tossing my beach bag onto the ground.

Cam looked up from his game guiltily. "Whoops! My bad. The guys asked me to play, so . . ." He trailed off.

"Don't apologize," Conrad advised him.

"Yeah, what are you, her slave? Now she's got you making her Kool-Aid?" Jeremiah said, jamming his thumb into the controller. He turned around and grinned at me to show me he was kidding, but I didn't grin back to show him it was okay.

Conrad didn't say anything, and I didn't even look at him. I could feel him looking at me, though. I wished he'd stop.

Why was it that even when I had my own friend I still felt left out of their club? It wasn't fair. It wasn't fair that Cam was so grateful to be a part of it all. The day had been so good, too.

"Where's my mom and Susannah?" I snapped.

"They went off somewhere," Jeremiah said vaguely. "Shopping, maybe?"

My mother hated shopping. Susannah must have dragged her.

I stalked off to the kitchen for my Kool-Aid. Conrad got up and followed me. I didn't have to turn around to know it was him.

I went about my business, pouring myself a tall glass of grape Kool-Aid and pretending he wasn't standing there watching me. "Are you just going to ignore me?" he finally said.

"No," I said. "What do you want?"

He sighed and came closer. "Why do you have to be like that?" Then he leaned forward, close, too close. "Can I have some?"

I put the glass on the counter and started to walk away, but he grabbed my wrist. I think I might have gasped. He said, "Come on, Bells."

His fingers felt cool, the way he always was. Suddenly I felt hot and feverish. I snatched my hand away. "Leave me alone."

"Why are you mad at me?" He had the nerve to look genuinely confused and also anxious. Because for him, the two things were connected—if he was confused, he was anxious. And he was hardly ever confused, so then he was hardly ever anxious. He'd certainly never been anxious over me. I was inconsequential to him. Always had been.

"Do you honestly care?" I could feel my heart thudding hard in my chest. I felt prickly and strange, waiting for his answer.

"Yes." Conrad looked surprised, like he couldn't believe he cared either.

The problem was, I didn't entirely know. I guessed it was mostly the way he was making me feel all mixed-up inside. Being nice to me one minute and cold the next. He made me remember things I didn't want to remember. Not now. Things were really going well with Cam, but every time I thought I was sure about him, Conrad would look at me a certain way, or twirl me, or call me Bells, and it all went to crap.

"Oh, why don't you go smoke a cigarette," I said.

The muscle in his jaw twitched. "Okay," he said.

I felt a mixture of guilt and satisfaction that I had finally gotten to him. And then he said, "Why don't you go look at yourself in the mirror some more?"

It was like he had slapped me. It was mortifying, being caught out and having someone see the bad things about you. Had he caught me looking at myself in the mirror, checking myself out, admiring myself? Did everyone think I was vain and shallow now?

I closed my lips tight and backed away from him, shaking my head slowly.

"Belly—," he started. He was sorry. It was written all over his face.

I walked into the living room and left him standing there. Cam and Jeremiah stared at me like they knew something was up. Had they heard us? Did it even matter?

"I get next game," I said. I wondered if this was the way old crushes died, with a whimper, slowly, and then, just like that—gone.

chapter *thirty-two*

Cam came over again, and he stayed till late. Around midnight I asked him if he wanted to go for a walk on the beach. So we did, and we held hands, too. The ocean looked silver and bottomless, like it was a million years old. Which I guessed it was.

"Truth or dare?" he asked me.

I wasn't in the mood for real truths. An idea came to me, from out of nowhere. The idea was this: I wanted to go skinny-dipping. With Cam. That was what older kids did at the beach, just like hooking up at the drive-in. If we went skinny-dipping, it would be like proof. That I had grown up.

So I said, "Cam, let's play Would You Rather. Would you rather go skinny-dipping right this second, or . . ." I was having trouble thinking of an "or."

"The first one, the first one," he said, grinning. "Or both, whatever the second one is."

Suddenly I felt giddy, almost drunk. I ran away from him, toward the water, and threw my sweatshirt into the sand. I had on my bikini underneath my clothes. "Here are the rules," I called out, unbuttoning my shorts. "No nakedness until we're fully submerged! And no peeking!"

"Wait," he said, running up to me, sand flying everywhere. "Are we really doing this?"

"Well, yeah. Don't you want to?"

"Yeah, but what if your mom sees us?" Cam glanced back toward the house.

"She won't. You can't see anything from the house; it's too dark."

He glanced at me and then back at the house again. "Maybe later," he said doubtfully.

I stared at him. Wasn't he the one who was supposed to be convincing me? "Are you serious?" What I really wanted to say was, Are you gay?

"Yeah. It's not late enough. What if people are still awake?" He picked up my sweatshirt and handed it to me. "Maybe we can come back later."

I knew he didn't mean it.

Part of me was mad, and part of me was relieved. It was like craving a fried peanut butter and banana sandwich and then realizing two bites in that you didn't want it after all.

I snatched my sweatshirt from him and said, "Don't do me any favors, Cam." Then I walked away as fast as I could, and sand kicked up behind me. I thought he might follow me, but he didn't. I didn't look back to see what he was doing either. He was probably sitting in the sand writing one of his stupid poems by the light of the moon.

As soon as I got back inside, I stormed into the kitchen. There was one light on; Conrad was sitting at the table spooning into a watermelon. "Where's Cam Cameron?" he asked wryly.

I had to think for a second about whether he was being nice or making fun of me. His expression looked normal and bland, so I took it as a little of both. If he was going to pretend our fight from before hadn't happened, then so would I.

"Who knows," I said, rummaging around the fridge and pulling out a yogurt. "Who cares?"

"Lover's spat?"

The smug look on his face made me want to slap him. "Mind your own business," I said, sitting down next to him with a spoon and a container of strawberry yogurt. It was Susannah's fat-free stuff, and the top looked watery and solid. I closed the foil flap on the yogurt and pushed it away.

Conrad pushed the watermelon over to me. "You shouldn't be so hard on people, Belly." Then he stood up and said, "And put your shirt on."

I scooped out a chunk of watermelon and stuck my tongue out at his retreating figure. Why did he make me feel like I was still thirteen? In my head I heard my mother's voice—"Nobody can make you feel like anything, Belly. Not without your permission. Eleanor Roosevelt said that. I almost named you after her." Blah, blah, blah. But she was kind of right. I wasn't giving him permission to make me feel bad, not anymore. I just wished my hair had at least been wet, or I'd had sand in my clothes, so he could have thought we'd been up to something, even if we hadn't been.

I sat at the table and ate watermelon. I ate it until I had scooped out half of the middle. I was waiting for Cam to come back inside, and when he didn't, I only felt madder. Part of me was tempted to lock the door on him. He'd probably meet some random homeless guy and become best friends with him, and then he'd tell me the man's life story the next day. Not that there were any homeless guys on our end of the beach. Not that I'd ever seen a homeless person in Cousins, for that matter. But if there was, Cam would find him.

Only, Cam didn't come back to the house. He just left. I heard his car start, watched from the downstairs hallway as he backed down the driveway. I wanted to run after his car and yell at him. He was supposed to come back. What if I'd ruined things and he didn't like me anymore? What if I never saw him again?

That night I lay in bed, thinking about how summer romances really do happen so fast, and then they're over so fast.

But the next morning, when I went to the deck to eat my toast, I found an empty water bottle on the steps that led down to the beach. Poland Spring, the kind Cam was always drinking. There was a piece of paper inside, a note. A message in a bottle. The ink was a little smeared, but I could still read what it said. It said, "IOU one skinny-dip."

chapter *thirty-three*

Jeremiah told me I could come hang by the pool while he lifeguarded. I'd never been inside the country club pool. It was huge and fancy, so I jumped at the chance. The country club seemed like a mysterious place. Conrad hadn't let us come the summer before; he'd said it would be embarrassing.

Midafternoon, I rode my bike over. Everything there was lush and green; it was surrounded by a golf course. There was a girl at a table with a clipboard, and I went over and told her I was there to see Jeremiah, and she waved me in.

I spotted Jeremiah before he saw me. He was sitting in the lifeguard chair, talking to a dark-haired girl in a white bikini. He was laughing, and so was she. He looked so important in the chair. I'd never seen him at an actual job before.

Suddenly I felt shy. I walked over slowly, my flip-flops slapping along the pavement. "Hey," I said when I was a few feet away.

Jeremiah looked down from his chair and grinned at me. "You came," he said, squinting at me and shielding his eyes with his hands like a visor.

"Yup." I swung my canvas bag back and forth, like a pendulum. The bag had my name on it in cursive. It was from L.L.Bean, a gift from Susannah.

"Belly, this is Yolie. She's my co-lifeguard."

Yolie reached over and shook my hand. It struck me as a businessy thing to do for someone in a bikini. She had a firm handshake, a nice grip, something my mother would have appreciated. "Hi, Belly," she said. "I've heard a lot about you."

"You have?" I looked up at Jeremiah.

He smirked. "Yeah. I told her all about the way you snore so loud that I can hear you down the hall."

I smacked his foot. "Shut up." Turning to Yolie, I said, "It's nice to meet you."

She smiled at me. She had dimples in both cheeks and a crooked bottom tooth. "You too. Jere, do you want to take your break now?"

"In a little bit," he said. "Belly, go work on your sun damage."

I stuck my tongue out at him and spread out my towel on a lounge chair not too far away. The pool was a perfect turquoise, and there were two diving boards, one high and one low. There were a ton of kids splashing around inside, and I figured I'd swim too when I got too hot to stand it. I just lay there with my sunglasses on and my eyes closed, tanning and listening to my music.

Jeremiah came over after a while. He sat on the edge of my chair and drank from my thermos of Kool-Aid. "She's pretty," I said.

"Who? Yolie?" He shrugged. "She's nice. One of my many admirers."

"Ha!"

"So what about you? Cam Cameron, huh? Cam the vegetarian. Cam the straight edge."

I tried not to smile. "So what? I like him."

"He's kind of a dork."

"That's what I like about him. He's . . . different."

He frowned slightly. "Different from who?"

"I don't know." But I did know. I knew exactly who he was different from.

"You mean he's not a dick like Conrad?"

I laughed, and so did he. "Yeah, exactly. He's nice."

"Just nice, huh?"

"More than nice."

"So you're over him, then? For real?" We both knew the "him" he was talking about.

"Yes," I told him.

"I don't believe you," Jeremiah said, watching me

closely—just like when he was trying to figure out what kind of hand I had in Uno.

I took off my sunglasses and looked him in the eye. "It's true. I'm over him."

"We'll see," Jeremiah said, standing up. "My break's over. Are you okay over here? Wait around and I'll drive us home. I can put your bike in the back."

I nodded, and watched him walk back to the lifeguard chair. Jeremiah was a good friend. He'd always been good to me, watched out for me.

chapter *thirty-four*

My mother and Susannah sat in beach chairs, and I lay on an old Ralph Lauren teddy bear towel. It was my favorite one because it was extra long, and soft from so many washings.

"What are you up to tonight, bean?" my mother asked me. I loved it when she called me bean. It reminded me of being six years old and falling asleep in her bed.

Proudly I told them, "Me and Cam are going to Putt Putt."

We used to go all the time as kids. Mr. Fisher would take us, and he was always pitting the boys against one another. "Twenty dollars for the first one to get a hole in one." "Twenty dollars for the winner." Steven loved it. I think he wished Mr. Fisher was our dad. He actually could've been. Susannah told me my mother had dated him first, but my mother had handed him over to Susannah because she knew they'd be perfect together.

Mr. Fisher included me in the mini golf competitions, but he never expected me to win. Of course I never did. I hated mini golf anyway. I hated the little pencils and the fake turf. It was all so annoyingly perfect. Kind of like Mr. Fisher. Conrad wanted so badly to be like him, and I used to hope he never would. Be like him, I mean.

The last time I had been to Putt Putt was when I was thirteen and I'd gotten my period for the first time. I was wearing white cutoffs, and Steven had been scared. He'd thought I had cut myself or something—for a second, I'd thought so too. After that, after getting my period by the fourth hole, I never wanted to go back. Not even when the boys invited me. So going with Cam felt like I was reclaiming Putt Putt, taking it back for my twelve-year-old self. It had even been my idea to go.

My mother said, "Can you be home early? I want us to spend a little time together, maybe watch a movie."

"How early? You guys go to bed at, like, nine."

My mother took her sunglasses off and looked at me. She had two indentations on her nose where her glasses had been. "I wish you'd spend more time at the house."

"I'm at the house right now," I reminded her.

She acted like she didn't hear me. "You've been spending so much time with this person—"

"You said you liked him!" I looked at Susannah for

support, and she looked back at me sympathetically.

My mother sighed, and Susannah broke in then, saying, "We do like Cam. We just miss you, Belly. We completely accept the fact that you have an actual life." She adjusted her floppy straw hat and winked at me. "We just want you to include us a little bit!"

I smiled in spite of myself. "Okay," I said, lying back down on the towel. "I'll come home early. We'll watch a movie."

"Done," my mother said.

I closed my eyes and put my headphones on. Maybe she had a point. I had been spending all my time with Cam. Maybe she really did miss me. It was just, she couldn't take for granted that I was going to spend every night at home like I had every other summer. I was almost sixteen, practically an adult. My mother had to accept that I couldn't be her bean forever.

They thought I was asleep when they started talking. But I wasn't. I could hear what they were saying, even over the music.

"Conrad's been behaving like a little shit," my mother said in a low voice. "He left all these beer bottles out on the deck this morning for me to clean up. It's getting out of hand."

Susannah sighed. "I think he knows something's up. He's been like this for months now. He's so sensitive, I know it's going to hit him harder."

"Don't you think it's time you told the boys?" Whenever my mother said "Don't you think," all she really meant was, "I think. So you should too."

"When the summer's over. That's soon enough."

"Beck," my mother began, "I think it might be time."

"I'll know when it's time," Susannah said. "Don't push me, Laur."

I knew there was nothing my mother could say that would change her mind. Susannah was soft, but she was resolute, stubborn as a mule when she wanted to be. She was pure steel underneath all her softness.

I wanted to tell them both, Conrad knows already and so does Jeremiah, but I couldn't. It wouldn't be right. It wasn't my business to tell.

Susannah wanted it to be some kind of perfect summer, where the parents were still together and everything was the way it had always been. Those kinds of summers don't exist anymore, I wanted to tell her.

chapter *thirty-five*

Around sunset, Cam came and picked me up for mini golf. I waited for him on the front porch, and when he pulled into the driveway, I ran up to his car. Instead of going to the passenger side, I walked right around to the driver's side. "Can I drive?" I asked. I knew he'd say yes.

He shook his head at me and said, dryly, "How does anybody ever say no to you?"

I batted my eyelashes at him. "No one ever does," I said, even though it wasn't true, not even a little bit.

I opened the car door, and he scooted over.

Backing out of the driveway, I told him, "I have to be home early tonight."

"No problem." He cleared his throat. "And, um, can you slow down a little? The speed limit is thirty-five on this road."

As I drove, he kept looking over at me and smiling. "What? Why are you smiling?" I asked. I felt like covering my face up with my T-shirt.

"Instead of a ski-slope nose, you have, like, a little bunny slope." He reached over and tapped it. I slapped his hand away.

"I hate my nose," I told him.

Cam looked perplexed. "Why? Your nose is cute. It's the imperfections that make things beautiful."

I wondered if that meant he thought I was beautiful. I wondered if that was why he liked me, my imperfections.

We ended up staying out later than I'd planned. The people in front of us took forever on each hole; they were a couple, and they kept stopping to kiss. It was annoying. I wanted to tell them, Mini golf is not where you go to hook up. That's what the drive-in's for. And then after, Cam was hungry, so we stopped for fried clams, and by that time it was after ten, and I knew my mother and Susannah would already be asleep.

He let me drive home. I didn't even have to ask; he just handed me the keys. In the driveway when we got home, I turned off the ignition. All of the lights in the house were off except for Conrad's. "I don't want to go inside yet," I told Cam.

"I thought you had to be home early."

"I did. I do. I'm just not ready to go inside yet." I turned on the radio, and we sat there for five minutes listening.

Then Cam cleared his throat and said, "Can I kiss you?"

I wished he hadn't asked. I wished he'd just done it. Asking made everything feel awkward; it put me in a position where I had to say yes. I wanted to roll my eyes at him but instead I said, "Um, okay. But next time, please don't ask. Asking someone if they want to kiss you is weird. You're supposed to just do it."

I regretted saying it right away, as soon as I saw the look on Cam's face. "Never mind," he said, red-faced. "Forget I asked."

"Cam, I'm sorr—" Before I could finish, he leaned over and kissed me. His cheek was stubbly and it felt kind of rough but nice.

When it was over, he said, "Okay?"

I smiled and said, "Okay." I unbuckled my seat belt. "Good night."

Then I got out of the car, and he came around and took the driver's seat. We hugged, and I found myself wishing that Conrad was watching. Even though it didn't matter, even though I didn't even like him anymore. I just wanted him to know I didn't like him anymore, to really know it. To see it with his own two eyes.

I ran up to the front door, and I didn't have to turn around to know that Cam would wait until I was inside before he drove away.

The next day my mother didn't mention anything, but she didn't have to. She could make me feel guilty without saying a word.

chapter *thirty-six*

My birthday always marked the beginning of the end of summer. It was my final thing to look forward to. And this summer I was turning sixteen. Sweet sixteen was supposed to be special, a really big deal—Taylor was renting out a reception hall for hers, and her cousin was DJ-ing and she was inviting the whole school. She'd had it planned for ages. My birthdays here were always the same: cake; gag gifts from the boys; and looking through all the old photo albums, with me sandwiched between Susannah and my mom on the couch. Every birthday I've ever had has been here, in this house. There are pictures of my mother sitting on the porch pregnant, with a glass of iced tea and a wide brimmed hat, and there's me, inside her belly. There are pictures of the four of us, Conrad, Steven, Jeremiah, and me, running around on the beach—I was naked except for my birthday hat, chasing after them. My mother didn't put me in a bathing suit until I was four years old. She just let me run around wild.

I didn't expect this birthday to be any different. Which, was comforting and also kind of depressing. Except, Steven wouldn't be there—my first birthday without him trying to elbow in and blow out my candles before I could.

I already knew what my parents were giving me: Steven's old car; they were getting it detailed with a new paint job and everything. When I got back to school, I would take driver's ed, and soon I wouldn't have to ask for a ride ever again.

I couldn't help but wonder if anyone back home remembered it was my birthday. Besides Taylor. She remembered; she always did. She called me at exactly 9:02 in the morning to sing happy birthday, every year. That was nice and all, but the trouble with having a summer birthday and being away was you couldn't have a party with all your school friends. You didn't get the balloons taped to your locker or any of it. I'd never really minded, but just then I did, a little.

My mother told me I could invite Cam over. But I didn't. I didn't even tell him it was my birthday. I didn't want him to feel like he had to do something. But it was more than that. I figured that if this birthday was going to be like every other one, I might as well really have it be like every other one. It should just be us, my summer family.

When I woke up that morning, the house smelled like butter and sugar. Susannah had baked a birthday cake. It was three layers and it was pink with a white border. She wrote in loopy white frosting HAPPY BIRTH-DAY, BELLS. She'd lit a few sparkler candles on top, and they sizzled and sparked like mad fireflies. She and my mother started to sing, and Susannah gestured for Conrad and Jeremiah to join in. They both did, off-key and obnoxious.

"Make a wish, Belly," my mother said.

I was still in my pajamas, and I couldn't stop smiling. The past four birthdays I had wished for the same thing. Not this year. This year I would wish for something else. I watched the sparklers die down, and then I closed my eyes and blew.

"Open my present first," Susannah urged. She thrust a small box wrapped in pink paper into my hands.

My mother looked at her questioningly. "What did you do, Beck?"

She smiled a mysterious smile and squeezed my wrist. "Open it, honey."

I ripped the paper off and opened the box. It was a pearl necklace, a whole strand of tiny creamy white pearls with a shiny gold clasp. It looked old, not like something you could buy today. It was like my father's Swiss grand-father clock, beautifully crafted, right down to the clasp. It was the prettiest thing I'd ever seen.

"Oh my gosh," I breathed, lifting it up.

I looked at Susannah, who was beaming, and then at my mother, who I thought would say it was much too extravagant, but she didn't. She smiled and said, "Are those—"

"Yes." Susannah turned to me and said, "My father gave me those for my sixteenth birthday. I want you to have them."

"Really?" I looked back at my mother, to make sure it was okay. She nodded. "Wow, thank you, Susannah. They're beautiful."

She took them from me and fastened them around my neck. I'd never worn pearls before. I couldn't stop touching them.

Susannah clapped her hands. She didn't like to linger too much after she'd given a gift; she just enjoyed the giv-ing of it. "Okay, what's next? Jeremiah? Con?"

Conrad shifted uncomfortably. "I forgot. Sorry, Belly."

I blinked. He'd never forgotten my birthday before. "That's okay," I said. I couldn't even look at him.

"Open mine next," Jeremiah said. "Although, after that, mine kind of sucks in comparison. Thanks a lot, Mom." He handed me a small box and leaned back in his chair.

I shook the box. "Okay, what could it be? Plastic poop? A license plate key chain?"

He smiled. "You'll see. Yolie helped me pick it out."

"Who's Yolie?" Susannah asked.

"A girl who's in love with Jeremiah," I said, opening the box.

Inside, nestled on a bed of cotton, was a small charm, a tiny silver key.

chapter *thirty-seven*
AGE 11

"Happy birthday, butthead," Steven sang, dumping a pail full of sand into my lap. A sand crab wriggled out of the sand and crawled onto my thigh. I let out a shriek and jumped up. I chased Steven down the beach, white hot fury pumping through my veins. I wasn't fast enough to catch him; I never was. He ran circles around me.

"Come and blow out your candles," my mother called.

As soon as Steven turned around to head back to the towel, I leapt onto his back and with one arm around his neck, I pulled his hair as hard as I could.

"Ow!" he howled, stumbling. I clung to his back like a monkey, even with Jeremiah grabbing my foot and trying to pull me off. Conrad fell to his knees, laughing.

"Children," Susannah called. "There's cake!"

I hopped off of Steven's back and scrambled over to the blanket.

"I'm gonna get you!" he yelled, chasing after me.

I hid behind my mother. "You can't. It's my birthday." I stuck my tongue out at him. The boys fell onto the blanket, wet and sandy.

"Mom," Steven complained. "She pulled out a hunk of my hair."

"Steven, you have a whole head full. I wouldn't worry about it." My mother lit the candles on the cake she'd baked that morning. It was a lopsided Duncan Hines yellow cake with chocolate frosting. She had messy handwriting, so "Happy Birthday" looked like "Happy Bimday."

I blew out the candles before Steven could try to "help" me. I didn't want him stealing my wish. I wished for Conrad, of course.

"Open your presents, Smelly," Steven said sullenly. I already knew what he'd gotten me. A stick of deodorant. He'd wrapped it in Kleenex; I could see right through the tissue.

I ignored him and reached for a small flat box wrapped in seashell paper. It was from Susannah, so I knew it would be good. I tore off the wrapping paper, and inside there was a silver charm bracelet, from the store Susannah loved, Rheingold's, where they sold fancy china and crystal candy dishes. On the bracelet there were five charms: a conch shell, a bathing suit, a sand castle, a pair of sunglasses, and a horseshoe.

"For how lucky we are to have you in our lives," Susannah said, touching the horseshoe.

I lifted it up, and the charms glinted and sparkled in the sunlight. "I love it."

My mother was silent. I knew what she was thinking. She was thinking that Susannah had overdone it, that she'd spent too much money. I felt guilty for loving the bracelet so much. My mother had bought me sheet music and CDs. We didn't have as much money as they did, and in that moment I finally understood what that meant.

chapter *thirty-eight*

"I love it," I said.

I ran upstairs to my room and went straight for
the music box on my dresser, where I kept my charm
bracelet. I grabbed the bracelet and ran back downstairs.

"See?" I said, putting the key charm on and fastening
it onto my wrist.

"It's a key, because you'll be driving soon. Get it?"
Jeremiah said, leaning back in his chair and clasping his
hands behind his head.

I got it. I smiled to show him I did.

Conrad leaned in for a closer look. "Nice," he said.

I held it in the palm of my other hand. I couldn't
stop looking at it. "I love it," I said again. "But it's from
Rheingold's. It must have been really expensive."

"I saved up all summer to buy it," he said solemnly.

I stared at him. "No, you didn't!"

He broke into a smile. "Fooled ya. Gullible as ever, aren't you?"

Punching him on the arm, I said, "I didn't believe you anyway, jerk." Even though I had, for a second.

Jeremiah rubbed his arm where I'd punched it. "It wasn't that expensive. Anyway, I'm big-time now, remember? Don't worry about me. I'm just glad you like it. Yolie said you would."

I hugged him fiercely. "It's perfect."

"What a wonderful gift, Jere," Susannah said. "It's better than my old necklace, that's for sure."

He laughed. "Yeah, right," he said, but I could tell he was pleased.

My mother got up and started cutting the cake. She wasn't a very good cake cutter: The pieces were too big, and they fell apart on the sides. "Who wants cake?" she said, licking her finger.

"I'm not hungry," Conrad said abruptly. He stood up, looking at his watch. "I've gotta get dressed for work. Happy birthday, Belly."

He went upstairs, and nobody said anything for a minute. Then my mother said, loudly, "This cake is delicious. Have some, Beck." She pushed a piece in front of her.

Smiling faintly, Susannah said, "I'm not hungry either.

You know what they say about the cook not having a taste for her own cooking. But you guys eat."

I took a big bite. "Mmm. Yellow cake, my favorite."

"From scratch," my mother said.

chapter *thirty-nine*

Conrad invited Nicole, Red Sox girl, over to the house.
Our house. I couldn't believe Red Sox girl was at our
house. It was bizarre to have a girl there other than
me.

It was midafternoon. I was out on the deck, sitting
at the patio table, eating a Doritos sandwich when they
drove up. She was wearing short shorts and a white
T-shirt, and a pair of sunglasses on top of her head. The
Red Sox hat was nowhere in sight. She looked chic. She
looked like she belonged. Unlike me, in my old Cuz
Beach shirt that doubled as a pajama dress. I thought he'd
at least bring her inside the house, but they hung out on
the other side of the deck, lying on the lounge chairs. I
couldn't hear what they were saying, but I could hear her
giggling like crazy.

After about five minutes I couldn't take it anymore. I got on the phone and called Cam. He said he'd be over in half an hour, but it was more like fifteen minutes.

They walked back into the house when Cam and I were arguing over which movie to watch. "What are you guys gonna watch?" Conrad asked, sitting on the couch opposite us. Red Sox girl sat next to him. She was practically in his lap.

I didn't look at him when I said, "We're trying to decide." Emphasis on the "we're."

"Can we watch too?" Conrad asked. "You guys know Nicole, right?"

So, suddenly Conrad felt like being social when he'd spent the whole summer locked up in his room?

"Hey," she said in a bored tone.

"Hey," I said, matching her tone as best I could.

"Hey, Nicole," Cam said. I wanted to tell him not to be so friendly, but I knew he wouldn't have listened anyway. "I want to watch *Reservoir Dogs*, but Belly wants to watch *Titanic*."

"Seriously?" the girl said, and Conrad laughed.

"Belly loves *Titanic*," he said mockingly.

"I loved it when I was, like, nine," I said. "I want to watch right now so I can laugh at it, for your information."

I was as cool as a cucumber. I wasn't going to let him

goad me in front of Cam again. And actually, I still loved *Titanic*. What wasn't to love about a doomed romance on a doomed ship? I knew for a fact that Conrad had liked it too, even though he'd pretended not to.

"I vote for *Reservoir Dogs*," Nicole said, examining her fingernails.

Did she even get a vote? What was she doing there anyway?

"Two votes for *Reservoir Dogs*," Cam said. "What about you, Conrad?"

"I think I'll vote for *Titanic*," he said blandly. "*Reservoir Dogs* sucks even harder than *Titanic*. It's overrated."

I narrowed my eyes at him. "You know what? I think I'll change my vote to *Reservoir Dogs*. So it looks like you're outnumbered, Conrad," I said.

Nicole looked up from her fingernails and said, "Well, then, I change my vote to *Titanic*."

"Who are you?" I muttered under my breath. "Does she even get voting privileges here?"

"Does he?" Conrad jerked his elbow at Cam, who looked startled. "Just kidding, man."

"Let's just watch *Titanic*," Cam said, taking the DVD out of its case.

We sat and watched stiffly. Everyone else busted up laughing at the part when Jack stands at the helm and says, "I'm the king of the world." I was silent. About midway through, Nicole whispered something into Conrad's ear, and the two of them stood up. "See you guys later," Conrad said.

As soon as they were gone, I hissed, "They're so disgusting. They probably went upstairs to go at it."

"Go at it? Who says 'go at it'?" Cam said, bemused.

"Shut up. Don't you think she was gross?"

"Gross? No. I think she's cute. A little too much bronzer, maybe."

I laughed in spite of myself. "Bronzer? What do you know about bronzer?"

"I have an older sister, remember," he said, smiling self-consciously. "She likes makeup. We share a bathroom."

I didn't remember Cam saying he had a sister.

"Well, anyway, she does wear too much bronzer. She's bright orange! I wonder where her Red Sox hat is," I mused.

Cam picked up the remote control and paused the movie. "Why are you so obsessed with her?"

"I'm not obsessed with her. Why would I be obsessed with her? She has no personality. She's like one of those pod people. She looks at Conrad like he's God." I knew he was judging me for being so mean, but I couldn't stop talking.

He looked at me like he wanted to say something, but he didn't. Instead he turned the movie back on.

We sat there on the couch and finished watching the movie in silence. Toward the end I heard Conrad's voice on the stairs, and without even thinking I snuggled closer to Cam. I rested my head on his shoulder.

Conrad and Nicole came back downstairs, and Conrad looked at the two of us for a second before saying, "Tell my mom I took Nicole home."

I barely looked up. "Okay."

As soon as they were gone, Cam sat straight up, and I did too. He took a breath. "Did you invite me over here to make him jealous?"

"Who?" I said.

"You know who. Conrad."

I could feel a flush rising up my chest and all the way to my cheeks. "No." It seemed like everybody was wanting to know where things stood with Conrad and me.

"Do you still like him?"

"No."

He let out a breath of air. "See, you hesitated."

"No, I didn't!"

Did I? Had I? I was sure I hadn't. To Cam I said, "When I look at Conrad, all I feel is disgust."

I could tell he didn't believe it. I didn't either. Because the truth was, when I looked at Conrad, all I felt was a yearning that never went away. It was the same as it had always been. Here I had this really great guy who actually liked me, and deep down inside I was still hung up on Conrad. There, that was the real truth. I had never really let go. I was just like Rose on that stupid makeshift raft.

Cam cleared his throat and said, "You're leaving soon. Do you want to keep in touch?"

I hadn't thought about that. He was right, the summer was almost over. Pretty soon I would be home again. "Um . . . do you?"

"Well, yeah. I do."

He looked at me like he was expecting something, and I couldn't figure out what it was for a few seconds. Then I said, "Me too. I do too." But it came too late. Cam took his cell phone out of his pocket and said he'd better get going. I didn't argue.

chapter *forty*

We finally had our movie night. My mother, Susannah, Jeremiah, and I watched Susannah's favorite Alfred Hitchcock movies in the rec room with all the lights off. My mother made kettle corn in the big cast-iron pot, and she went out and bought Milk Duds and gummy bears and saltwater taffy. Susannah loved saltwater taffy. It was classic, like old times, only without Steven and Conrad, who was working a dinner shift.

Halfway through *Notorious*, her most favorite of all, Susannah fell asleep. My mother covered her with a blanket, and when the movie was over, she whispered, "Jeremiah, will you carry her upstairs?"

Jeremiah nodded quickly, and Susannah didn't even wake up when he lifted her in his arms and carried her up the rec room stairs. He picked her up like she was weightless, a feather. I'd never seen him do that before. Even though we were almost the same age, in that moment he almost seemed grown-up.

My mother got up too, stretching. "I'm exhausted. Are you going to bed, too, Belly?"

"Not yet. I think I'll clean up down here first," I said.

"Good girl," she said, winking at me, and then she headed upstairs.

I started picking up the taffy wrappers and a few kernels that had fallen onto the carpet.

Jeremiah came back down when I was putting the movie into its case. He sank into the couch cushions. "Let's not go to sleep yet," he said, looking up at me.

"Okay. Do you wanna watch another movie?"

"Nah. Let's just watch TV." He picked up the remote and started flipping through channels randomly. "Where's Cam Cameron been lately?"

Sitting back down, I sighed a little. "I don't know. He hasn't called, and I haven't called him. The summer's almost over. I'll probably never see him again."

He didn't look at me when he said, "Do you want to? See him again?"

"I don't know. . . . I'm not sure. Maybe. Maybe not."

Jeremiah put the TV on mute. He turned and looked at me then. "I don't think he's the guy for you." His eyes looked somber. I'd never seen him look so somber.

Lightly I said, "Yeah, I doubt it too."

"Belly . . . ," he began. He took a deep breath of air and puffed up his cheeks, and then he blew it out so hard the hair on his forehead fluttered. I could feel my heart start to pound—something was going to happen. He was going to say something I didn't want to hear. He was going to go and change everything.

I opened my mouth to speak, to interrupt him before he said something he couldn't take back, and he shook his head. "Just let me get this out."

He took another deep breath. "You've always been my best friend. But now it's more. I see you as more than that." He continued, scooting closer to me. "You're cooler than any other girl I've ever met, and you're there for me. You've always been there for me. I . . . I can count on you. And you can count on me too. You know that."

I nodded. I could hear him talking, see his lips moving, but my mind was working a million miles a minute. This was Jeremiah. My buddy, my best pal. Practically my brother. The hugeness of it all made it hard to breathe. I could barely look at him. Because I didn't. I didn't see him that way. There was only one person. For me that person was Conrad.

"And I know you've always liked Conrad, but you're over him now, right?" His eyes looked so hopeful, it killed me, killed me to not answer him the way he wanted me to.

"I . . . I don't know," I whispered.

He sucked in his breath, the way he did when he was frustrated. "But why? He doesn't see you that way. I do."

I could feel my eyes starting to tear up, which wasn't fair. I couldn't cry. It was just that he was right. Conrad didn't see me that way. I only wished I could see Jeremiah the way he saw me. "I know. I wish I didn't. But I do. I still do."

Jeremiah moved away from me. He wouldn't look at me; his eyes looked everywhere but at mine. "He'll only end up hurting you," he said, and his voice cracked.

"I'm so, so sorry. Please don't be mad at me. I couldn't take it if you were mad at me."

He sighed. "I'm not mad at you. I'm just—why does it always have to be Conrad?"

Then he got up, and left me sitting there.

chapter *forty-one*
AGE 12

Mr. Fisher had taken the boys on one of their overnight deep-sea fishing trips. Jeremiah couldn't go; he'd been sick earlier that day so Susannah made him stay home. The two of us spent the night on the old plaid couch in the basement eating chips and dip and watching movies.

In between *The Terminator* and *Terminator 2*, Jeremiah said bitterly, "He likes Con better than me, you know."

I had gotten up to change the DVDs, and I turned around and said, "Huh?"

"It's true. I don't really care anyway. I think he's a dick," Jeremiah said, picking at a thread on the flannel blanket in his lap.

I thought he was kind of a dick too, but I didn't say so. You're not supposed to join in when someone is bashing his father. I just put the DVD in and sat back down. Taking a corner of the blanket, I said, "He's not so bad."

Jeremiah gave me a look. "He is, and you know it. Con thinks he's God or something. So does your brother."

"It's just that your dad is so different from our dad," I said defensively. "Your dad takes you guys fishing and, like, plays football with you. Our dad doesn't do that kind of stuff. He likes chess."

He shrugged. "I like chess."

I hadn't known that about him. I liked it too. My dad had taught me to play when I was seven. I wasn't bad either. I had never joined chess club, even though I'd kind of wanted to. Chess club was for the nose-pickers. That's what Taylor called them.

"And Conrad likes chess too," Jeremiah said. "He just tries to be what our dad wants. And the thing is, I don't even think he likes football, not like I do. He's just good at it like he is at everything."

There was nothing I could say to that. Conrad *was* good at everything. I grabbed a handful of chips and stuffed them into my mouth so I wouldn't have to say anything.

"One day I'm gonna be better than him," Jeremiah said.

I didn't see that happening. Conrad was too good.

"I know you like Conrad," Jeremiah said suddenly.

I swallowed the chips. They tasted like rabbit feed all of a sudden. "No, I don't," I said. "I don't like Conrad."

"Yes, you do," he said, and his eyes looked so knowing and wise. "Tell the truth. No secrets, remember?" No secrets was something Jeremiah and I had been saying for pretty much forever. It was a tradition, the same way Jeremiah's drinking my sweet cereal milk was tradition—just one of those things we said to each other when it was just the two of us.

"No, I really don't like him," I insisted. "I like him like a friend. I don't look at him like that."

"Yes, you do. You look at him like you love him."

I couldn't take those knowing eyes looking at me for one more second. Hotly I said, "You just think that because you're jealous of anything Conrad does."

"I'm not jealous. I just wish I could be as good as him," he said softly. Then he burped and turned the movie on.

The thing was, Jeremiah was right. I did love him. I knew the exact moment it became real too. Conrad got up early to make a special belated Father's Day breakfast, only Mr. Fisher hadn't been able to come down the night before. He wasn't there the next morning the way he was supposed to be. Conrad cooked anyway, and he was thirteen and a terrible cook, but we all ate it. Watching him serving rubbery eggs and pretending not to be sad, I thought to myself, *I will love this boy forever.*

chapter *forty-two*

He'd gone running on the beach, something he'd started doing recently—I knew because I'd watched him from my window two mornings in a row. He was wearing gym shorts and a T-shirt; sweat had formed in a circle in the middle of his back. He'd left about an hour before, I'd seen him take off, and he was running back to the house now.

I walked out there, to the porch, without a real plan in my mind. All I knew was that the summer was almost over. Soon it would be too late. We would drive away, and I would never have told him. Jeremiah had laid it all out on the line. Now it was my turn. I couldn't go another whole year not having told him. I'd been so afraid of change, of anything tipping our little summer sailboat—but Jeremiah had already done that, and look, we were still alive. We were still Belly and Jeremiah.

I had to, I had to do it, because to not do it would kill me. I couldn't keep yearning for something, for someone who might or might not like me back. I had to know for sure. Now or never.

He didn't hear me coming up behind him. He was bent down loosening the laces of his sneakers.

"Conrad," I said. He didn't hear me, so I said it again, louder. "Conrad."

He looked up, startled. Then he stood up straight. "Hey."

Catching him off guard felt like a good sign. He had a million walls. Maybe if I just started talking, he wouldn't have time to build up a new one.

I sucked in my lips and began to speak. I said the first words I thought of, the ones that had been on my heart since the beginning. I said, "I've loved you since I was ten years old."

He blinked.

"You're the only boy I've ever thought about. My whole life, it's always been you. You taught me how to dance, you came out and got me the time I swam out too far. Do you remember that? You stayed with me and you pushed me back to shore, and the whole time, you kept saying, 'We're almost there,' and I believed it. I believed it because you were the one who was saying it, and I believed everything you ever said. Compared to you, everyone else is saltines, even Cam. And I hate saltines. You know that. You know everything about me, even this, which is that I really love you."

I waited, standing in front of him. I was out of breath. I felt like my heart would explode, it was so full. I pulled my hair into a ponytail with my hand and held it like that, still waiting for him to say something, anything.

It felt like a thousand years before he spoke.

"Well you shouldn't. I'm not the one. Sorry."

And that was all he said. I let out a big breath of air and stared at him. "I don't believe you," I said. "You like me too; I know it." I'd seen the way he'd looked at me when I was with Cam, I'd seen it with my own two eyes.

"Not the way you want me to," he said. He sighed, and in this sad way, like he felt sorry for me, he said, "You're still such a kid, Belly."

"I'm not a kid anymore! You just wish I was, so that way you wouldn't have to deal with any of it. That's why you've been mad at me this whole summer," I said, my voice getting louder. "You do like me. Admit it."

"You're crazy," he said, laughing a little as he walked away from me.

But not this time. I wasn't going to let him off the hook that easily. I was sick and tired of his brooding James

Dean routine. He had feelings for me. I knew it. I was going to make him say it.

I grabbed his shirt sleeve. "Admit it. You were mad when I started hanging out with Cam. You wanted me to still be your little admirer."

"What?" He shook me off. "Get your head out of your ass, Belly. The world doesn't revolve around you."

My cheeks flamed bright red; I could feel the heat beneath my skin. It was like a sunburn times a million. "Yes, exactly, because the world revolves around *you*, right?"

"You have no idea what you're talking about." There was a warning in his voice, but I didn't stop to listen. I was too mad. I was finally saying what I really thought, and there was no turning back now.

I kept getting in his face. I wasn't going to let him walk away from me, not this time. "You just want to keep me on this hook, right? So I'll keep chasing after you and you can feel good about yourself. As soon as I start to get over you, you just reel me back in. You're so screwed up in the head. But I'm telling you, Conrad, this is it."

He snapped, "What are you talking about?"

My hair whipped around my face as I spun around to walk backward, facing him. "This is it. You don't get to have me anymore. Not as your friend or your admirer or anything. I'm through."

His mouth twisted. "What do you want from me?

You have your little boyfriend to play with now, remember?"

I shook my head and backed away from him. "It's not like that," I said. He'd gotten it all wrong. That wasn't what I was trying to do. He'd been the one stringing *me* along, like, my whole life. He knew how I felt, and he let me love him. He *wanted* me to.

He stepped closer to me. "One minute you like me. Then Cam . . ." Conrad paused. "And then Jeremiah. Isn't that right? You want to have your cake and eat it too, but you also want your cookies, and your ice cream . . ."

"Shut up!" I yelled.

"You're the one who's been playing games, Belly." He was trying to sound casual, offhand, but his body was tense, like every muscle was as tight as his stupid guitar strings.

"You've been an ass all summer. All you think about is yourself. So your parents are getting divorced! So what? People's parents get divorced. It's not an excuse to treat people like crap!"

He snapped his head away from me. "Shut your mouth," he said, and his jaw twitched. I had finally done it. I was getting to him.

"Susannah was crying the other day because of you—she could barely get out of bed! Do you even care? Do you even know how selfish you are?"

Conrad stepped up close to me, so close our faces

were nearly touching, like he might either hit me or kiss me. I could hear my heart pounding in my ears. I was so mad I almost wished he'd hit me. I knew he'd never do it, not in a million years. He grabbed my arms and shook me, and then he let go just as suddenly. I could feel tears building up, because for a second there, I thought he might.

Kiss me.

I was crying when Jeremiah walked up. He'd been at work lifeguarding; his hair was still wet. I didn't even hear his car pull up. He took one look at the two of us, and he knew something bad was happening. He almost looked scared. And then he just looked furious. He said, "What the hell is going on? Conrad, what's your problem?"

Conrad glared at him. "Just keep her away from me. I'm not in the mood to deal with any of this."

I flinched. It was like he really had hit me. It was worse than that.

He started to walk away, and Jeremiah grabbed his arm. "You need to start dealing with this, man. You're acting like a jerk. Quit taking your anger out on everybody else. Leave Belly alone."

I shivered. Was this because of me? All summer, Conrad's moodiness, locking himself up in his room— had it really been because of me? Was it more than just his parents divorcing? Had he been that upset over seeing me with someone else?

Conrad tried to shrug him off. "Why don't *you* leave *me* alone? How about we try that instead?"

But Jeremiah wouldn't let go. He said, "We've been leaving you alone. We've left you alone this whole summer, getting drunk and sulking like a little kid. You're supposed to be the older one, right? The big brother? Act like it, dumbass. Freaking man up and handle your business."

"Get out of my face," Conrad growled.

"No." Jeremiah stepped closer, until their faces were inches apart, just like ours had been not fifteen minutes before.

In a dangerous voice Conrad said, "I'm warning you, Jeremiah."

The two of them were like two angry dogs, growling and spitting and circling each other. They'd forgotten I was there. I felt like I was watching something I shouldn't, like I was spying. I wanted to put my hands over my ears. They'd never been like this with each other in all the time I'd known them. They might have argued, but it had never been like this, not once. I knew I should leave, but I couldn't bring myself to do it. I just stood there on the periphery, holding my arms close to my chest.

"You're just like Dad, you know that?" Jeremiah shouted.

That's when I knew it had nothing to do with me. This was bigger than anything I could be a part of.

This was something I knew nothing about.

Conrad pushed Jeremiah away roughly, and Jeremiah pushed him back. Conrad stumbled and nearly fell, and when he rose up, he punched Jeremiah right in the face. I think I screamed. Then they were wrestling around, grabbing at each other, hitting and cursing and breathing heavy. They knocked over Susannah's big glass jar of sun tea, and it cracked open. Tea spilled out all over the porch. There was blood on the sand. I didn't know whose it was.

They kept fighting, fighting over the broken glass, even though Jeremiah was about to lose his flip-flops. A few times I said, "Stop!" but they couldn't hear me. They looked alike. I'd never noticed how alike they looked. But right then they looked like brothers. They kept struggling until suddenly, in the midst of it all, my mother was there. I guessed she'd come through the other screen door. I don't know—she was just there. She broke the two of them apart with this incredible kind of brute strength, the kind only mothers have.

She held them apart with a hand on each of their chests. "You two need to stop," she said, and instead of sounding mad, she sounded so sad. She sounded like she might cry, and my mother never cried.

They were breathing hard, not looking at each other, but they were connected, the three of them. They understood something I didn't. I was just standing there on the periphery, bearing witness to it all. It was like the time I went to church with Taylor, and everyone else knew all the words to the songs, but I didn't. They lifted their arms in the air and swayed and knew every word by heart, and I felt like an intruder.

"You know, don't you?" my mother said, her hands crumpling away from them.

Jeremiah sucked in his breath, and I knew he was holding it in, trying not to cry. His face was already starting to bruise. Conrad, though, his face was indifferent, detached. Like he wasn't there.

Until his face sort of opened up, and suddenly he looked about eight years old. I looked behind me, and there was Susannah standing in the doorway. She was wearing her white cotton housedress, and she looked so frail standing there. "I'm sorry," she said, lifting her hands up helplessly.

She stepped toward the boys, hesitant, and my mother backed away. Susannah held out her arms and Jeremiah fell right in, and even though he was so much bigger than she was, he looked small. Blood from his face smeared over the front of her dress, but they didn't pull away. He cried like I hadn't heard him cry since Conrad had accidentally closed the car door on his hand years and years ago. Conrad had cried just as hard as Jeremiah had that day, but this day he didn't. He let Susannah touch his hair, but he didn't cry.

"Belly, let's go," my mother said, taking my hand. She

hadn't done that in a very long time. Like a little kid, I followed her inside. We went upstairs, to her room. She closed the door and sat down on the bed. I sat down next to her.

"What's happening?" I asked her, faltering, searching her face for some kind of answer.

She took my hands and put them in hers. She held them tight, like she was the one holding on to me and not the other way around. She said, "Belly, Susannah's sick again."

I closed my eyes. I could hear the ocean roaring all around me; it was like holding a conch shell up to my ear really close. It wasn't true. It wasn't true. I was anywhere but there, in that moment. I was swimming under a canopy of stars; I was at school, sitting in math class; on my bike, on the trail behind our house. I wasn't there. This wasn't happening.

"Oh, bean," my mother sighed. "I need you to open your eyes. I need you to hear me."

I wouldn't open them; I wouldn't listen. I wasn't even there.

"She's sick. She has been for a long time. The cancer came back. And it's—it's aggressive. It's spread to her liver."

I opened my eyes and snatched my hands away from her. "Stop talking. She's not sick. She's fine. She's still Susannah." My face was wet and I didn't even know when I had started to cry.

My mother nodded, wet her lips. "You're right. She's still Susannah. She does things her way. She didn't want you kids to know. She wanted this summer to be—perfect." Her voice caught on the word "perfect." Like a run in a stocking, it caught, and she had tears in her eyes too.

She pulled me to her, held me against her chest and rocked me. And I let her.

"But they did know," I whimpered. "Everybody knew but me. I'm the only one who didn't know, and I love Susannah more than anybody."

Which wasn't true, I knew that. Jeremiah and Conrad, they loved her best of all. But it felt true. I wanted to tell my mother that it didn't matter anyway, Susannah had had cancer last time and she'd been fine. She'd be fine again. But if I said it out loud, it would be like admitting that she really did have cancer, that this really was happening. And I couldn't.

That night I lay in bed and cried. My whole body ached. I opened all the windows in my room and lay in the dark, just listening to the ocean. I wished the tide would carry me out and never bring me back. I wondered if that was how Conrad felt, how Jeremiah felt. How my mother felt.

It felt like the world was ending and nothing would ever be the same again. It was, and it wouldn't.

chapter *forty-three*

When we were little and the house was full, full of people like my father and Mr. Fisher and other friends, Jeremiah and I would share a bed and so would Conrad and Steven. My mother would come and tuck us in. The boys would pretend they were too old for it, but I knew they liked it just as much as I did. It was that feeling of being snug as a bug in a rug, cuddly as a burrito. I'd lie in bed and listen to the music drifting up the steps from downstairs, and Jeremiah and I would whisper scary stories to each other till we fell asleep. He always fell asleep first. I'd try to pinch him awake, but it never worked. The last time that happened might have been the last time I ever felt really, really safe in the world. Like all was right and sound.

The night of the boys' fight, I knocked on Jeremiah's door. "Come in," he said.

He was lying in bed staring at the ceiling with his hands clasped behind his head. His cheeks were wet and his eyes looked wet and red. His right eye was purpley gray, and it was already swelling up. As soon as he saw me, he rubbed his eyes with the back of his hand.

"Hey," I said. "Can I come in?"

He sat up. "Yeah, okay."

I walked over to him and sat on the edge of the bed with my back pushed up against the wall. "I'm sorry," I began. I'd been practicing what I would say, how I would say it, so he would know how sorry I was. For everything. But then I started to cry and ruined it.

He reached over and kneaded my shoulder awkwardly. He could not look at me, which in a way was easier. "It's not fair," I said, and then I began to weep.

Jeremiah said, "I've been thinking about it all summer, how this is probably the last one. This is her favorite place, you know. I wanted it to be perfect for her, but Conrad went and ruined everything. He took off. My mom's so worried, and that's the last thing she needs, to be worrying about Conrad. He's the most selfish person I know, besides my dad."

He's hurting too, I thought, but I didn't say it out loud because it wouldn't help anything. So I just said, "I wish I had known. If I had been paying attention, it would have been different."

Jeremiah shook his head. "She didn't want you to know.

She didn't want any of us to know. She wanted it to be like this, so we pretended. For her. But I wish I could have told you. It might have been easier or something." He wiped his eyes with his T-shirt collar, and I could see him trying so hard to keep it together, to be the strong one.

I reached for him, to hug him, and he shuddered, and something seemed to break inside of him. He began to cry, really cry, but quietly. We cried together, our shoulders shaking and shuddering with the weight of all of it. We cried like that for a long time. When we stopped, he let go of me and wiped his nose.

"Scoot over," I said.

He scooted closer to the wall, and I stretched my legs out next to him. "I'm sleeping in here, okay," I said, but it wasn't a question.

Jeremiah nodded and we slept like that, in our clothes on top of the comforter. Even though we were older, it felt just the same. We slept face-to-face, the way we used to.

I woke up early the next morning clinging to the side of the bed. Jeremiah was sprawled out and snoring. I covered him with my side of the comforter, so he was tucked in like with a sleeping bag. Then I left.

I headed back to my room, and I had my hand on the doorknob when I heard Conrad's voice. "Goood morning," he said. I knew right away he'd seen me leave Jeremiah's room.

Slowly I turned around. And there he was. He was standing there in last night's clothes, just like me. He looked rumpled, and he swayed just slightly. He looked like he was going to throw up.

"Are you drunk?"

He shrugged like he couldn't care less, but his shoulders were tense and rigid. Snidely he said, "Aren't you supposed to be nice to me now? Like the way you were for Jere last night?"

I opened my mouth to defend myself, to say that nothing had happened, that all we'd done was cry ourselves to sleep. But I didn't want to. Conrad didn't deserve to know anything. "You're the most selfish person I ever met," I said slowly and deliberately. I let each word puncture the air. I had never wanted to hurt somebody so bad in my whole life. "I can't believe I ever thought I loved you."

His face turned white. He opened and then closed his mouth. And then he did it again. I'd never seen him at a loss for words before.

I walked back to my room. It was the first time I'd ever gotten the last word with Conrad. I had done it. I had finally let him go. It felt like freedom, but freedom bought at some bloody, terrible price. It didn't feel good. Did I even have a right to say those things to him, with him hurting the way he was? Did I have any rights to him at all? He was in pain, and so was I.

When I got back into bed, I got under the covers and

cried some more, and here I was thinking I didn't have any more tears left. Everything was wrong.

How could it be that I had spent this whole summer worrying about boys, swimming, and getting tan, while Susannah was sick? How could that be? The thought of life without Susannah felt impossible. It was inconceivable; I couldn't even picture it. I couldn't imagine what it would be like for Jeremiah and Conrad. She was their mother.

Later that morning I didn't get out of bed. I slept until eleven, and then I just stayed there. I was afraid to go downstairs and face Susannah and have her see that I knew.

Around noon my mother bustled into my room without even knocking. "Rise and shine," she said, surveying my mess. She picked up a pair of shorts and a T-shirt and folded them against her chest.

"I'm not ready to get out of bed yet," I told her, turning over. I felt mad at her, like I had been tricked. She should have told me. She should have warned me. My whole life, I had never known my mother to lie. But she had. All those times when they'd supposedly been shopping, or at the museum, on day trips—they hadn't been any of those places. They'd been at hospitals, with doctors. I saw that now. I just wished I had seen it before.

My mother walked over to me and sat on the edge of my bed. She scratched my back, and her fingernails felt good against my skin. "You have to get out of bed, Belly," she said softly. "You're still alive and so is Susannah. You have to be strong for her. She needs you."

Her words made sense. If Susannah needed me, then that was something I could do. "I can do that," I said, turning around to look at her. "I just don't get how Mr. Fisher can leave her all alone like this when she needs him most."

She looked away, out the window, and then back down at me. "This is the way Beck wants things to be. And Adam is who he is." She cradled my cheek in her hand. "It's not up to us to decide."

Susannah was in the kitchen making blueberry muffins. She was leaning up against the counter, stirring batter in a big metal mixing bowl. She was wearing another one of her cotton housedresses, and I realized she'd been wearing them all summer, because they were loose. They hid how thin her arms were, the way her collarbone jutted up against her skin.

She hadn't seen me yet, and I was tempted to run away before she did. But I didn't. I couldn't.

"Good morning, Susannah," I said, and my voice sounded high and false, not like my own.

She looked up at me and smiled. "It's past noon. I don't think it counts as morning anymore."

"Good afternoon, then." I lingered by the door.

"Are you mad at me too?" she asked me lightly. Her eyes were worried, though.

"I could never be mad at you," I told her, coming up behind her and putting my arms around her stomach. I tucked my head in the space between her neck and her shoulder. She smelled like flowers.

She said, still in her light voice, "You'll look after him, won't you?"

"Who?"

I could feel her cheeks form into a smile. "You know who."

"Yes," I whispered, still holding on tight.

"Good," she said, sighing. "He needs you."

I didn't ask who "he" was. I didn't need to.

"Susannah?"

"Hmm?"

"Promise me something."

"Anything."

"Promise me you'll never leave."

"I promise," she said without hesitation.

I let out a breath, and then I let go. "Can I help you with the muffins?"

"Yes, please."

I helped her make a streusel topping with brown sugar and butter and oats. We took the muffins out of the oven too early, because we couldn't stand to wait, and we ate them while they were still steaming hot and gooey in the middle. I ate three. Sitting with her, watching her butter her muffin, it felt like she'd be there forever.

Somehow we got around to talking about proms and dances. Susannah loved to talk about anything girly; she said I was the only person she could talk to about those kinds of things. My mother certainly wouldn't, and neither would Conrad and Jeremiah. Only me, her pretend-daughter.

She said, "Make sure you send me pictures of you at your first big dance."

I hadn't gone to any of my school's homecomings or proms yet. No one had asked me, and I hadn't really felt like it. The one person I wanted to go with didn't go to my school. I told her, "I will. I'll wear that dress you bought me last summer."

"What dress?"

"The one from that mall, the purple one that you and Mom fought over that time. Remember, you put it in my suitcase?"

She frowned, confused. "I didn't buy you that dress. Laurel would've had a fit." Then her face cleared, and she smiled. "Your mother must have gone back and bought it for you."

"My mother?" My mother would never.

"That's your mother. So like her."

"But she never said . . ." My voice trailed off. I hadn't even considered the possibility that it had been my mother who'd bought it for me.

"She wouldn't. She's not like that." Susannah reached across the table and grabbed my hand. "You're the luckiest girl in the world to have her for a mother. Know that."

The sky was gray, and there was a chill in the air. It would rain soon.

It was so misty out that it took me a minute to find him. I finally did, about half a mile down. It always came back to the beach. He was sitting, his knees close to his chest. He didn't look at me when I sat down next to him. He just stared out at the ocean.

His eyes were these bleak and empty abysses, like sockets. There was nothing there. The boy I thought I knew so well was gone. He looked so lost sitting there. I felt that old lurch, that gravitational pull, that desire to inhabit him—like wherever he was in this world, I would know where to find him, and I would do it. I would find him and take him home. I would take care of him, just like Susannah wanted.

I spoke first. "I'm sorry. I'm really, really sorry. I wish I had known—"

"Please stop talking," he said.

"I'm sorry," I whispered, starting to get up. I was always saying the wrong thing.

"Don't leave," Conrad said, and his shoulders collapsed. His face did too. He hid it in his hands, and he was five years old again, we both were.

"I'm so pissed at her," he said, each word coming out of him like a gust of concentrated air. He bowed his head, his shoulders broken and bent. He was finally crying.

I watched him silently. I felt like I was intruding on a private moment, one he'd never let me see if he weren't grieving. The old Conrad liked to be in control.

The old pull, the tide drawing me back in. I kept getting caught in this current—first love, I mean. First love kept making me come back to this, to him. He still took my breath away, just being near him. I had been lying to myself the night before, thinking I was free, thinking I had let him go. It didn't matter what he said or did, I'd never let him go.

I wondered if it was possible to take someone's pain away with a kiss. Because that was what I wanted to do, take all of his sadness and pour it out of him, comfort him, make the boy I knew come back. I reached out and touched the back of his neck. He jerked forward, the slightest motion, but I didn't take my hand away. I let it rest there, stroking the back of his hair, and then I cupped the back of his head, moved it toward me, and kissed him. Tentatively at first, and then he started kissing me back, and we were kissing each other. His lips were warm and needy. He needed me. My mind went pure blinding white, and the only thought I had was, *I'm kissing Conrad Fisher, and he's kissing me back.* Susannah was dying, and I was kissing Conrad.

He was the one to break away. "I'm sorry," he said, his voice raw and scratchy.

I touched my lips with the backs of my fingers. "For what?" I couldn't seem to catch my breath.

"It can't happen like this." He stopped, then started again. "I do think about you. You know that. I just can't . . . Can you . . . Can you just be here with me?"

I nodded. I was afraid to open my mouth.

I took his hand and squeezed it, and it felt like the most right thing I had done in a long time. We sat there in the sand, holding hands like it was something we'd been doing all along. It started to rain, soft at first. The first raindrops hit the sand, and the grains beaded up, rolled away.

It started to come down harder, and I wanted to get up and go back to the house, but I could tell Conrad didn't. So I sat there with him, holding his hand and saying nothing. Everything else felt really far away; it was just us.

chapter *forty-four*

Toward the end of summer everything slowed down, and it started to feel ready to be done. It was like with snow days. We once had this great big blizzard, and we didn't go to school for two whole weeks. After a while you just wanted to get out of the house, even if that meant school. Being at the summer house felt like that. Even paradise could be suffocating. You could only sit on the beach doing nothing so many times before you felt ready to go. I felt it a week before we left, every time. And then of course, when the time came, I was never ready to leave. I wanted to stay forever. It was a total catch-22, like a contradiction in terms. Because as soon as we were in the car, driving away, all I wanted to do was jump out and run back to the house.

Cam called me twice. Both times I didn't answer. I let it go to voice mail. The first time he called, he didn't leave a message. The second time he said, "Hey, it's Cam. . . . I hope I get to see you before we both leave. But if not, then, well, it was really nice hanging out with you. So, yeah. Call me back, if you want."

I didn't know what to say to him. I loved Conrad and I probably always would. I would spend my whole life loving him one way or another. Maybe I would get married, maybe I would have a family, but it wouldn't matter, because a piece of my heart, the piece where summer lived, would always be Conrad's. How did I say those things to Cam? How did I tell him that there was a piece saved for him, too? He was the first boy to tell me I was beautiful. That had to count for something. But there was no way for me to say any of those things to him. So I did the only thing I could think to do. I just left it alone. I didn't call him back.

With Jeremiah it was easier. And by that I mean he went easy on me. He let me off the hook. He pretended like it hadn't happened, like we hadn't said any of those things down in the rec room. He went on telling jokes and calling me Belly Button and just being Jeremiah.

I finally understood Conrad. I mean, I understood what he meant when he said he couldn't deal with any of it—with me. I couldn't either. All I wanted to do was spend every single second at the house, with Susannah. To soak up the last drop of summer and pretend it was like all the summers that had come before it. That was all I wanted.

chapter *forty-five*

I hated the last day before we left, because it was cleanup day, and when we were kids, we weren't allowed to go to the beach at all, in case we brought in more sand. We washed all the sheets and swept up the sand, made sure all the boogie boards and floats were in the basement, cleaned out the fridge and packed sandwiches for the drive home. My mother was at the helm of this day. She was the one who insisted everything be just so. "So it's all ready for next summer," she'd say. What she didn't know was that Susannah had cleaners come in after we left and before we came back.

I caught Susannah calling them once, scheduling an appointment. She covered the phone with one hand and whispered guiltily, "Don't tell your mom, okay, Belly?"

I nodded. It was like a secret between us, and I liked

that. My mother actually liked to clean and didn't believe in housekeepers or maids or in other people doing what she considered our work. She'd say, "Would you ask someone else to brush your teeth for you, or lace up your shoes, just because you could?" The answer was no.

"Don't worry too much about the sand," Susannah would whisper when she'd see me going over the kitchen floor with a broom for the third time. I would keep sweeping anyway. I knew what my mother would say if she felt any grains on her feet.

That night for dinner we ate everything that was left in the fridge. That was the tradition. My mother heated up two frozen pizzas, reheated lo mein and fried rice, made a salad out of pale celery and tomatoes. There was clam chowder too, and half a rack of ribs, plus Susannah's potato salad from more than a week before. It was a smorgasbord of old food that no one felt like eating.

But we did. We sat around the kitchen table picking off of foil-covered plates. Conrad kept sneaking looks at me, and every time I looked back, he looked away. I'm right here, I wanted to tell him. I'm still here.

We were all pretty quiet until Jeremiah broke the silence like breaking the top of a crème brûlée. He said, "This potato salad tastes like bad breath."

"I think that would be your upper lip," Conrad said.

We all laughed, and it felt like a relief. For it to be okay to laugh. To be something other than sad.

Then Conrad said, "This rib has mold on it," and we all started to laugh again. It felt like I hadn't laughed in a long time.

My mother rolled her eyes. "Would it kill you to eat a little mold? Just scrape it off. Give it to me. I'll eat it."

Conrad put his hands up in surrender, and then he stabbed the rib with his fork and dropped it on my mother's plate ceremoniously. "Enjoy it, Laurel."

"I swear, you spoil these boys, Beck," my mother said, and everything felt normal, like any other last night. "Belly was raised on leftovers, weren't you, bean?"

"I was," I agreed. "I was a neglected child who was fed only old food that nobody else wanted."

My mother suppressed a smile and pushed the potato salad toward me.

"I do spoil them," Susannah said, touching Conrad's shoulder, Jeremiah's cheek. "They're angels. Why shouldn't I?"

The two boys looked at each other from across the table for a second. Then Conrad said, "I'm an angel. I would say Jere's more of a cherub." He reached out and tousled Jeremiah's hair roughly.

Jeremiah swatted his hand away. "He's no angel. He's the devil," he said. It was like the fight had been erased. With boys it was like that; they fought and then it was over.

My mother picked up Conrad's rib, looked down at it, and then put it down again. "I can't eat this," she said, sighing.

"Mold won't kill you," Susannah declared, laughing and pushing her hair out of her eyes. She lifted her fork in the air. "You know what will?"

We all stared at her.

"Cancer," she said triumphantly. She had the best poker face known to man. She held a straight face for four whole seconds before erupting into a fit of giggles. She rustled her hand through Conrad's hair until he finally wore a smile. I could tell he didn't want to, but he did it. For her.

"Listen up," she said. "Here's what's going to happen. I'm seeing my acupuncturist, I'm taking medicine, I'm still fighting this the best I can. My doctor says that at this point that's the most I can do. I refuse to put any more poison into my body or spend any more time in hospitals. This is where I want to be. With the people who matter most to me. Okay?" She looked around at us.

"Okay." We all said it, even though it was in no way, shape, or form okay. Nor would it ever be.

Susannah continued. "If and when I go off slow dancing in the ever after, I don't want to look like I've been stuck in a hospital room my whole life. I at least want to be tan. I want to be as tan as Belly." She pointed at me with her fork.

"Beck, if you want to be as tan as Belly, you'll need more time. That's not something you can achieve in one summer. My girl wasn't born tan; it takes years. And you're not ready yet," my mother said. She said it simply, logically.

Susannah wasn't ready yet. None of us were.

After dinner we all went our separate ways to pack. The house was quiet, too quiet. I stayed in my bedroom, packing up clothes, my shoes, my books. Until it was time to pack my bathing suit. I wasn't ready to do that yet. I wanted one more swim.

I changed into my one-piece and wrote two notes, one for Jeremiah and one for Conrad. On each of them I wrote, "Midnight swim. Meet me in ten minutes." I slid a note under each door and then ran downstairs as quick as I could with my towel streaming behind me like a flag. I couldn't let the summer end like this. We couldn't leave this house until we had one good moment, for all of us.

The house was dark, and I made my way outside without turning on the lights. I didn't need to. I knew it by heart.

As soon as I got outside, I dove into the pool. I didn't dive so much as belly flop. The last one of the summer, maybe ever—in this house, anyway. The moon was bright and white, and as I waited for the boys, I floated on my back counting stars and listening to the ocean. When the tide was low like this, it whispered and gurgled and it sounded like a lullaby. I wished I could stay forever, in this moment. Like in one of those plastic snowballs, one little moment frozen in time.

They came out together, Beck's boys. I guessed they'd run into each other on the stairs. They were both wearing their swimming trunks. It occurred to me that I hadn't seen Conrad in his trunks all summer, that we hadn't swum in this pool since that first day. And Jeremiah, we'd only swum in the ocean once or twice. It had been a summer with hardly any swim time, except for when I swam with Cam or when I swam alone. The thought made me feel unspeakably sad, that this could be the last summer and we'd hardly swum together at all.

"Hello," I said, still floating on my back.

Conrad dipped his toe in. "It's kind of cold to swim, isn't it?"

"Chicken," I said, squawking loudly. "Just jump in and get it over with."

They looked at each other. Then Jeremiah made a running leap and cannonballed in, and Conrad followed right behind him. They made two big splashes, and I swallowed a ton of water because I was smiling, but I didn't care.

We swam over to the deep end, and I treaded water to stay afloat. Conrad reached over and pushed my bangs out of my eyes. It was a tiny gesture, but Jeremiah saw, and he turned away, swam closer to the edge of the pool.

For a second I felt sad, and then suddenly, out of nowhere, it came to me. A memory, pressed in my heart like a leaf in a book. I lifted my arms in the air and twirled around in circles, like a water ballerina.

Spinning, I began to recite, "maggie and milly and molly and may."

Jeremiah took the next line, then me, then him.

And then together, Conrad too, we all said, "for whatever we lose (like a you or a me) / it's always ourselves we find in the sea."

It was Susannah's favorite poem; she'd taught it to us kids a long time ago—we were on one of her guided nature walks where she pointed out shells and jellyfish. That day we marched down the beach, arms linked, and we recited it so loudly that I think we woke up the fish. We knew it like we knew the Pledge of Allegiance, by heart.

"This might be our last summer here," I said suddenly.

"No way," Jeremiah said, floating up next to me.

"Conrad's going to college this fall, and you have football camp," I reminded him. Even though Conrad going to college and Jeremiah going to football camp for two weeks didn't really have anything to do with us not coming back next summer. I didn't say what we were all thinking, that Susannah was sick, that she might never get better, that she was the string that tied us all together.

Conrad shook his head. "It doesn't matter. We'll always come back."

Briefly I wondered if he meant just him and Jeremiah, and then he said, "All of us."

It got quiet again, and then I had an idea. "Let's make a whirlpool!" I said, clapping my hands together.

"You're such a kid," Conrad said, smiling at me and shaking his head. For the first time, it didn't bother me when he called me a kid. It felt like a compliment.

I floated out to the middle of the pool. "Come on, guys!"

They swam over to me, and we made a circle and started to run as fast as we could. "Faster!" Jeremiah yelled, laughing.

Then we stopped, let our bodies go limp and get caught in the whirlpool we'd just made. I leaned my head back and let the current carry me.

chapter *forty-six*

When he called, I didn't recognize his voice, partly because I wasn't expecting it and partly because I was still half-asleep. He said, "I'm in my car on my way to your house. Can I see you?"

It was twelve thirty in the morning. Boston was five and a half hours away. He had driven all night. He wanted to see me.

I told him to park down the street and I would meet him on the corner, after my mother had gone to bed. He said he'd wait.

I turned the lights off and waited by the window, watching for the taillights. As soon as I saw his car, I wanted to run outside, but I had to wait. I could hear my mother rustling around in her room, and I knew she would read in bed for at least half an hour before she fell asleep. It felt like torture, knowing he was out there waiting for me, not being able to go to him.

In the dark I put on my scarf and hat that Granna knit me for Christmas. Then I shut my bedroom door and tiptoe down the hallway to my mother's room, pressing my ear against the door. The light is off and I can hear her snoring softly. Steven's not even home yet, which is lucky for me, because he's a light sleeper just like our dad.

My mother is finally asleep; the house is still and silent. Our Christmas tree is still up. We keep the lights on all night because it makes it still feel like Christmas, like any minute, Santa could show up with gifts. I don't bother leaving her a note. I'll call her in the morning, when she wakes up and wonders where I am.

I creep down the stairs, careful on the creaky step in the middle, but once I'm out of the house, I'm flying down the front steps, across the frosty lawn. It crunches along the bottoms of my sneakers. I forgot to put on my coat. I remembered the scarf and hat, but no coat.

His car is on the corner, right where it's supposed to be. The car is dark, no lights, and I open the passenger side door like I've done it a million times before. But I haven't. I've never even been inside. I haven't seen him since August.

I poke my head inside, but I don't go in, not yet. I want to look at him first. I have to. It's winter, and he's wearing a gray fleece. His cheeks are pink from the cold, his tan has faded, but he still looks the same. "Hey," I say, and then I climb inside.

"You're not wearing a coat," he says.

"It's not that cold," I say, even though it is, even though I'm shivering as I say it.

"Here," he says, shrugging out of his fleece and handing it to me.

I put it on. It's warm, and it doesn't smell like cigarettes. It just smells like him. So Conrad quit smoking after all. The thought makes me smile.

He starts the engine.

I say, "I can't believe you're really here."

He sounds almost shy when he says, "Me neither." And then he hesitates. "Are you still coming with me?"

I can't believe he even has to ask. I would go anywhere. "Yes," I tell him. It feels like nothing else exists outside of that word, this moment. There's just us. Everything that happened this past summer, and every summer before it, has all led up to this. To now.

it's
not
summer
without
you

JENNY HAN

J + S forever

Acknowledgments

My heartfelt gratitude to Emily van Beek, Holly McGhee, and Elena Mechlin at Pippin Properties, and to Emily Meehan and Julia Maguire at S&S. Thanks also to my first readers—Caroline, Lisa, Emmy, Julie, and Siobhan. I'm so fortunate to know you all.

chapter *one*
JULY 2

It was a hot summer day in Cousins. I was lying by the pool with a magazine on my face. My mother was playing solitaire on the front porch, Susannah was inside puttering around the kitchen. She'd probably come out soon with a glass of sun tea and a book I should read. Something romantic.

Conrad and Jeremiah and Steven had been surfing all morning. There'd been a storm the night before. Conrad and Jeremiah came back to the house first. I heard them before I saw them. They walked up the steps, cracking up over how Steven had lost his shorts after a particularly ferocious wave. Conrad strode over to me, lifted the sweaty magazine from my face, and grinned. He said, "You have words on your cheeks."

I squinted up at him. "What do they say?"

He squatted next to me and said, "I can't tell. Let me see." And then he peered at my face in his serious Conrad way. He leaned in, and he kissed me, and his lips were cold and salty from the ocean.

Then Jeremiah said, "You guys need to get a room," but I knew he was joking. He winked at me as he came from behind, lifted Conrad up, and launched him into the pool.

Jeremiah jumped in too, and he yelled, "Come on, Belly!"

So of course I jumped too. The water felt fine. Better than fine. Just like always, Cousins was the only place I wanted to be.

"Hello? Did you hear anything I just said?"

I opened my eyes. Taylor was snapping her fingers in my face. "Sorry," I said. "What were you saying?"

I wasn't in Cousins. Conrad and I weren't together, and Susannah was dead. Nothing would ever be the same again. It had been—*How many days had it been? How many days exactly?*—two months since Susannah had died and I still couldn't believe it. I couldn't let myself believe it. When a person you love dies, it doesn't feel real. It's like it's happening to someone else. It's someone else's life. I've never been good with the abstract. What does it mean when someone is really and truly gone?

Sometimes I closed my eyes and in my head, I said over and over again, *It isn't true, it isn't true, this isn't real.* This wasn't my life. But it was my life; it was my life now. After.

I was in Marcy Yoo's backyard. The boys were messing around in the pool and us girls were lying on beach towels, all lined up in a row. I was friends with Marcy, but the rest, Katie and Evelyn and those girls, they were more Taylor's friends.

It was eighty-seven degrees already, and it was just after noon. It was going to be a hot one. I was on my stomach, and I could feel sweat pooling in the small of my back. I was starting to feel sun-sick. It was only the second day of July, and already, I was counting the days until summer was over.

"I *said*, what are you going to wear to Justin's party?" Taylor repeated. She'd lined our towels up close, so it was like we were on one big towel.

"I don't know," I said, turning my head so we were face-to-face.

She had tiny sweat beads on her nose. Taylor always sweated first on her nose. She said, "I'm going to wear that new sundress I bought with my mom at the outlet mall."

I closed my eyes again. I was wearing sunglasses, so she couldn't tell if my eyes were open or not anyway. "Which one?"

"You know, the one with the little polka dots that ties around the neck. I showed it to you, like, two days ago." Taylor let out an impatient little sigh.

"Oh, yeah," I said, but I still didn't remember and I knew Taylor could tell.

I started to say something else, something nice about the dress, but suddenly I felt ice-cold aluminum sticking to the back of my neck. I shrieked and there was Cory Wheeler, crouched down next to me with a dripping Coke can in his hand, laughing his head off.

I sat up and glared at him, wiping off my neck. I was so sick of today. I just wanted to go home. "What the *crap*, Cory!"

He was still laughing, which made me madder.

I said, "God, you're so immature."

"But you looked really hot," he protested. "I was trying to cool you off."

I didn't answer him, I just kept my hand on the back of my neck. My jaw felt really tight, and I could feel all the other girls staring at me. And then Cory's smile sort of slipped away and he said, "Sorry. You want this Coke?"

I shook my head, and he shrugged and retreated back over to the pool. I looked over and saw Katie and Evelyn making *what's-her-problem* faces, and I felt embarrassed. Being mean to Cory was like being mean to a German shepherd puppy. There was just no sense in it. Too late, I tried to catch Cory's eye, but he didn't look back at me.

In a low voice Taylor said, "It was just a joke, Belly."

I lay back down on my towel, this time faceup. I took a deep breath and let it out, slowly. The music from Marcy's iPod deck was giving me a headache. It was too loud. And I actually *was* thirsty. I should have taken that Coke from Cory.

Taylor leaned over and pushed up my sunglasses so she could see my eyes. She peered at me. "Are you mad?"

"No. It's just too hot out here." I wiped sweat off my forehead with the back of my arm.

"Don't be mad. Cory can't help being an idiot around you. He likes you."

"Cory doesn't like me," I said, looking away from her. But he sort of did like me, and I knew it. I just wished he didn't.

"Whatever, he's totally into you. I still think you should give him a chance. It'll take your mind off of you-know-who."

I turned my head away from her and she said, "How about I French braid your hair for the party tonight? I can do the front section and pin it to the side like I did last time."

"Okay."

"What are you going to wear?"

"I'm not sure."

"Well, you have to look cute because everybody's gonna be there," Taylor said. "I'll come over early and we can get ready together."

Justin Ettelbrick had thrown a big blowout birthday party every July first since the eighth grade. By July, I was already at Cousins Beach, and home and school and school friends were a million miles away. I'd never once minded missing out, not even when Taylor told me about the cotton candy machine his parents had rented one year, or the fancy fireworks they shot off over the lake at midnight.

It was the first summer I would be at home for Justin's party and it was the first summer I wasn't going back to Cousins. And that, I minded. That, I mourned. I'd thought I'd be in Cousins every summer of my life. The summer house was the only place I wanted to be. It was the only place I ever wanted to be.

"You're still coming, right?" Taylor asked me.

"Yeah. I told you I was."

Her nose wrinkled. "I know, but—" Taylor's voice broke off. "Never mind."

I knew Taylor was waiting for things to go back to normal again, to be like before. But they could never be like before. I was never going to be like before.

I used to believe. I used to think that if I wanted it bad enough, wished hard enough, everything would work out the way it was supposed to. Destiny, like Susannah said. I wished for Conrad on every birthday, every shooting star, every lost eyelash, every penny in a fountain was dedicated to the one I loved. I thought it would always be that way.

Taylor wanted me to forget about Conrad, to just erase him from my mind and memory. She kept saying things like, "Everybody has to get over a first love, it's a rite of passage." But Conrad wasn't just my first love. He wasn't some rite of passage. He was so much more than that. He and Jeremiah and Susannah were my family. In my memory, the three of them would always be entwined, forever linked. There couldn't be one without the others.

If I forgot Conrad, if I evicted him from my heart, pretended like he was never there, it would be like doing those things to Susannah. And that, I couldn't do.

chapter two

It used to be that the week school let out in June, we'd pack up the car and head straight to Cousins. My mother would go to Costco the day before and buy jugs of apple juice and economy-size boxes of granola bars, sunscreen, and whole grain cereal. When I begged for Lucky Charms or Cap'n Crunch, my mother would say, "Beck will have plenty of cereal that'll rot your teeth out, don't you worry." Of course she'd be right. Susannah—Beck to my mother—loved her kid cereal, just like me. We went through a lot of cereal at the summer house. It never even had a chance to go stale. There was one summer when the boys ate cereal for breakfast, lunch, and dinner. My brother, Steven, was Frosted Flakes, Jeremiah was Cap'n Crunch, and Conrad was Corn Pops. Jeremiah and Conrad were Beck's boys, and they loved their cereal. Me, I ate whatever was left over with sugar on top.

I'd been going to Cousins my whole life. We'd never skipped a summer, not once. Almost seventeen years of me playing catch-up to the boys, of hoping and wishing that one day I would be old enough to be a part of their crew. The summer boys crew. I finally made it, and now it was too late. In the pool, on the last night of the last summer, we said we'd always come back. It's scary how easy promises were broken. Just like that.

When I got home last summer, I waited. August turned into September, school started, and still I waited. It wasn't like Conrad and I had made any declarations. It wasn't like he was my boyfriend. All we'd done was kiss. He was going to college, where there would be a million other girls. Girls without curfews, girls on his hall, all smarter and prettier than me, all mysterious and brand-new in a way that I could never be.

I thought about him constantly—what it all meant, what we were to each other now. Because we couldn't go back. I knew *I* couldn't. What happened between us— between me and Conrad, between me and Jeremiah— it changed everything. And so when August and September began and still the phone didn't ring, all I had to do was think back to the way he'd looked at me that last night, and I knew there was still hope. I knew that I hadn't imagined it all. I couldn't have.

According to my mother, Conrad was all moved into

his dorm room, he had an annoying roommate from New Jersey, and Susannah worried he wasn't getting enough to eat. My mother told me these things casually, offhandedly, so as not to injure my pride. I never pressed her for more information. The thing is, I knew he'd call. I *knew* it. All I had to do was wait.

The call came the second week of September, three weeks since the last time I'd seen him. I was eating strawberry ice cream in the living room, and Steven and I were fighting over the remote control. It was a Monday night, nine p.m., prime TV-watching time. The phone rang, and neither Steven nor I made a move to grab it. Whoever got up would lose the battle for the TV.

My mother picked it up in her office. She brought the phone into the living room and she said, "Belly, it's for you. It's Conrad." Then she winked.

Everything in me went abuzz. I could hear the ocean in my ears. The rush, the roar in my eardrums. It was like a high. It was golden. I had waited, and this was my reward! Being right, being patient, never felt so good.

Steven was the one to break me out of my reverie. Frowning, he said, "Why would Conrad be calling *you*?"

I ignored him and took the phone from my mother. I walked away from Steven, from the remote, from my melting dish of ice cream. None of it mattered.

I made Conrad wait until I was on the staircase before I said anything. I sat down on the steps and I said, "Hey."

I tried to keep the smile off my face; I knew he would hear it over the phone.

"Hey," he said. "What's up?"

"Nothing much."

"So guess what," he said. "My roommate snores even louder than you do."

He called again the next night, and the night after. We talked for hours at a time. When the phone rang, and it was for me and not Steven, he'd been confused at first. "Why does Conrad keep calling you?" he'd demanded.

"Why do you think? He likes me. We like each other."

Steven had nearly gagged. "He's lost his mind," he said, shaking his head.

"Is it so impossible that Conrad Fisher would like me?" I asked him, crossing my arms defiantly.

He didn't even have to think about his answer. "Yes," he said. "It is so impossible."

And honestly, it was.

It was like a dream. Unreal. After all that pining and longing and wishing, years and years of it, whole summers' worth, *he* was calling *me*. He liked talking to me. I made him laugh even when he didn't want to. I understood what he was going through, because I was sort of going through it too. There were only a few people in the world who loved Susannah the way we did. I thought that would be enough.

We became something. Something that was never exactly

defined, but it was something. It was really something.

A few times, he drove the three and a half hours from school to my house. Once, he spent the night because it got so late my mother didn't want him to drive back. Conrad stayed in the guest room, and I lay in my bed awake for hours, thinking about how he was asleep just a few feet away, in *my* house of all places.

If Steven hadn't hung around us like some kind of disease, I know Conrad would have at least tried to kiss me. But with my brother around it was pretty much impossible. Conrad and I would be watching TV, and Steven would plop right down between us. He'd talk to Conrad about stuff I didn't know or care about, like football. One time, after dinner, I asked Conrad if he wanted to go get frozen custard at Brusters, and Steven chimed right in and said, "Sounds good to me." I glared at him, but he just grinned back at me. And then Conrad took my hand, right in front of Steven, and he said, "Let's all go." So we all went, my mother too. I couldn't believe I was going on dates with my mother and my brother in the backseat.

But really, it all just made that one amazing night in December all the sweeter. Conrad and I went back to Cousins, just the two of us. Perfect nights come so rarely, but that one was. Perfect, I mean. It was the kind of night worth waiting for.

I'm glad we had that night.

Because by May, it was all over.

chapter *three*

I left Marcy's house early. I told Taylor it was so I could rest up for Justin's party that night. It was partly true. I did want to rest, but I didn't care about the party. As soon as I got home, I put on my big Cousins T-shirt, filled a water bottle with grape soda and crushed ice, and I watched TV until my head hurt.

It was peacefully, blissfully silent. Just the sounds of the TV and the air conditioning kicking off and on. I had the house to myself. Steven had a summer job at Best Buy. He was saving up for a fifty-inch flat screen he'd take to college with him in the fall. My mother was home, but she spent all day locked away in her office, catching up on work, she said.

I understood. If I were her, I'd want to be alone too.

Taylor came over around six, armed with her hot pink

Victoria's Secret makeup bag. She walked into the living room and saw me lying on the couch in my Cousins T-shirt and frowned. "Belly, you haven't even showered yet?"

"I took a shower this morning," I said, not getting up.

"Yeah, and you laid out in the sun all day." She grabbed my arms and I let her lift me into a sitting position. "Hurry up and get into the shower."

I followed her upstairs and she went to my bedroom while I went to the hall bathroom. I took the fastest shower of my life. Left to her own devices, Taylor was a big snoop and would poke around my room like it was hers.

When I came out Taylor was sitting on my floor in front of my mirror. Briskly, she blended bronzer onto her cheeks. "Want me to do your makeup too?"

"No thanks," I told her. "Close your eyes while I put on my clothes, okay?"

She rolled her eyes and then closed them. "Belly, you're such a prude."

"I don't care if I am," I said, putting on my underwear and my bra. Then I put my Cousins T-shirt on again. "Okay, you can look."

Taylor opened her eyes up superwide and she applied her mascara. "I could do your nails," she offered. "I have three new colors."

"Nah, there's no point." I held up my hands. My nails were bitten down to the quick.

Taylor grimaced. "Well, what are you wearing?"

"This," I said, hiding my smile. I pointed down at my Cousins T-shirt. I'd worn it so many times it had tiny holes around the neck and it was soft as a blankie. I wished I could wear it to the party.

"Very funny," she said, shimmying over to my closet on her knees. She stood up and started rifling around, pushing hangers over to the side, like she didn't already know every article of clothing I owned by heart. Usually I didn't mind, but today I felt sort of itchy and bothered by everything.

I told her, "Don't worry about it. I'm just going to wear my cutoffs and a tank top."

"Belly, people get dressed up for Justin's parties. You've never been so you wouldn't know, but you can't just wear your old cutoffs." Taylor pulled out my white sundress. The last time I'd worn it had been last summer, at that party with Cam. Susannah had told me the dress set me off like a picture frame.

I got up and took the dress from Taylor and put it back into my closet. "That's stained," I said. "I'll find something else."

Taylor sat back down in front of the mirror and said, "Well, then wear that black dress with the little flowers. It makes your boobs look amazing."

"It's uncomfortable; it's too tight," I told her.

"Pretty please?"

Sighing, I took it off the hanger and put it on. Sometimes it was easier to just give in with Taylor. We'd been friends, best friends, since we were little kids. We'd been best friends so long it was more like a habit, the kind of thing you didn't really have a say in anymore.

"See, that looks hot." She came over and zipped me up. "Now, let's talk about our plan of action."

"What plan of action?"

"I think you and Cory Wheeler should make out at the party."

"Taylor—"

She lifted her hand. "Just hear me out. Cory's super-nice *and* he's supercute. If he worked on his body and got a little definition, he could be, like, Abercrombie hot."

I snorted. "Please."

"Well, he's at least as cute as C-word." She never called him by his name anymore. Now he was just "you-know-who," or "C-word."

"Taylor, quit pushing me. I can't be over him just because you want me to."

"Can't you at least try?" she wheedled. "Cory could be your rebound. He wouldn't mind."

"If you bring up Cory one more time, I'm not going to the party," I told her, and I meant it. In fact, I kind of hoped she would bring him up again so I'd have an excuse not to go.

Her eyes widened. "Okay, okay. Sorry. My lips are sealed."

Then she grabbed her makeup bag and sat down on the edge of my bed, and I sat down at her feet. She pulled out a comb and sectioned off my hair. She braided quickly, with fast and sure fingers, and when she was done, she pinned the braid over the crown of my head, to the side. Neither of us spoke while she worked until she said, "I love your hair like this. You look sort of Native American, like a Cherokee princess or something."

I started to laugh, but then I stopped myself. Taylor caught my eye in the mirror and said, "It's okay to laugh, you know. It's okay for you to have fun."

"I know," I said, but I didn't.

Before we left I stopped by my mother's office. She was sitting at her desk with folders and stacks of papers. Susannah had made my mother executor of her will, and there was a lot of paperwork involved with that, I guessed. My mother was on the phone with Susannah's lawyer a lot, going over things. She wanted it to go perfect, Beck's last wishes.

Susannah had left both Steven and me some college money. She'd also left me jewelry. A sapphire tennis bracelet I couldn't picture myself ever wearing. A diamond necklace for my wedding day—she'd written that specifically. Opal earrings and an opal ring. Those were my favorite.

"Mom?"

She looked up at me. "Yes?"

"Have you had dinner?" I knew she hadn't. She hadn't left her office since I'd been home.

"I'm not hungry," she said. "If there isn't any food in the fridge, you can call for a pizza if you want."

"I can fix you a sandwich," I offered. I'd gone to the store earlier that week. Steven and I had been taking turns. I doubted she even knew it was Fourth of July weekend.

"No, that's all right. I'll come down and fix myself something later."

"Okay." I hesitated. "Taylor and I are going to a party. I won't be home too late."

Part of me hoped she'd tell me to stay home. Part of me wanted to offer to stay and keep her company, to see if she maybe wanted to see what was on Turner Classic Movies, pop some popcorn.

She'd already gone back to her paperwork. She was chewing on her ballpoint pen. "Sounds good," she said. "Be careful."

I closed the door behind me.

Taylor was waiting for me in the kitchen, texting on her phone. "Let's hurry up and go already."

"Hold on, I just have to do one last thing." I went over to the fridge and pulled out stuff for a turkey sandwich. Mustard, cheese, white bread.

"Belly, there's gonna be food at the party. Don't eat that now."

"It's for my mom," I said.

I made the sandwich, put it on a plate, covered it with plastic wrap, and left it on the counter where she'd see it.

Justin's party was everything Taylor said it would be. Half our class was there, and Justin's parents were nowhere in sight. Tiki lamps lined the yard, and his speakers were practically vibrating, the music was so loud. Girls were dancing already.

There was a big keg and a big red cooler. Justin was manning the grill, flipping steaks and bratwurst. He had a Kiss the Chef apron on.

"As if anybody would make out with him." Taylor sniffed. Taylor had made a play for Justin at the beginning of the year, before she'd settled on her boyfriend, Davis. She and Justin had gone out a few times before he'd blown her off for a senior.

I'd forgotten to put on bug spray, and the mosquitoes were eating me for dinner. I kept bending down to scratch my legs, and I was glad to do it. Glad to have something to do. I was afraid of accidentally making eye contact with Cory. He was hanging out by the pool.

People were drinking beer out of red plastic cups. Taylor got us both wine coolers. Mine was Fuzzy Navel. It was syrupy and it tasted like chemicals. I took two sips before I threw it away.

Then Taylor spotted Davis over by the beer pong table

and she put her finger to her lips and grabbed my hand. We walked up behind him and Taylor slipped her arms around his back. "Gotcha!" she said.

He turned around and they kissed like they hadn't just seen each other a few hours ago. I stood there for a minute, awkwardly holding on to my purse, looking everywhere but at them. His name was actually Ben Davis, but everyone called him Davis. Davis was really cute; he had dimples and green eyes like sea glass. And he was short, which at first Taylor said was a dealbreaker but now claimed not to mind so much. I hated riding to school with them because they held hands the entire time while I sat in the back like the kid. They broke up at least once a month, and they'd only been dating since April. During one breakup, he'd called her, crying, trying to get back together, and Taylor had put him on speaker. I'd felt guilty for listening but at the same time envious and sort of awestruck that he cared that much, enough to cry.

"Pete's gonna go take a piss," Davis said, hooking his arm around Taylor's waist. "Will you stay and be my partner until he comes back?"

She looked over at me and shook her head. She stepped out of his grasp. "I can't leave Belly."

I shot her a look. "Taylor, you don't need to babysit me. You should play."

"Are you sure?"

"Sure, I'm sure."

I walked away before she could argue with me. I said hi to Marcy, to Frankie who I used to ride the bus with in middle school, to Alice who was my best friend in kindergarten, to Simon who I was on yearbook with. I'd known most of these kids my whole life and yet I'd never felt more homesick for Cousins.

Out of the corner of my eye I saw Taylor chatting it up with Cory, and I made a run for it before she could call me over. I grabbed a soda and I made my way over to the trampoline. There was no one on it yet so I kicked off my flip-flops and climbed on. I laid down right in the middle, careful to hold my skirt close to me. The stars were out, little bright diamond flecks in the sky. I gulped down my Coke, burped a few times, looked around to see if anyone had heard me. But no, everyone was back by the house. Then I tried to count stars, which is pretty much as silly as trying to count grains of sand, but I did it anyway because it was something to do. I wondered when I'd be able to sneak away and go back home. We'd taken my car, and Taylor could get a ride home with Davis. Then I wondered if it would look weird if I wrapped up a few hot dogs to take with me for later.

I hadn't thought about Susannah in two hours, at least. Maybe Taylor was right, maybe this was where I was supposed to be. If I kept wishing for Cousins, kept looking back, I would be doomed forever.

As I was thinking this over, Cory Wheeler climbed

up onto the trampoline and made his way to the middle, to where I was. He laid down right next to me and said, "Hey, Conklin."

Since when were Cory and I on a last-name basis? Since never.

And then I went ahead and said, "Hey, Wheeler." I tried not to look at him. I tried to concentrate on counting stars and not on how close he was to me.

Cory propped himself up on one elbow and said, "Having fun?"

"Sure." My stomach was starting to hurt. Running away from Cory was giving me an ulcer.

"Seen any shooting stars yet?"

"Not yet."

Cory smelled like cologne and beer and sweat, and oddly enough, it wasn't a bad combination. The crickets were so loud and the party seemed really far away.

"So, Conklin."

"Yeah?"

"Are you still seeing that guy you brought to prom? The one with the unibrow?"

I smiled. I couldn't help it. "Conrad doesn't have a unibrow. And no. We, um, broke up."

"Cool," he said, and the word hung in the air.

This was one of those fork-in-the-road kind of moments. The night could go either way. If I leaned in just a little to my left, I could kiss him. I could close my eyes and let myself get lost in Cory Wheeler. I could go right on forgetting. Pretending.

But even though Cory was cute, and he was nice, he was no Conrad. Not even close. Cory was simple, he was like a crew cut, all clean lines and everything going in the same direction. Not Conrad. Conrad could turn my insides out with one look, one smile.

Cory reached over and flicked my arm playfully. "So, Conklin . . . maybe we—"

I sat up. I said the first thing I could think of. "Shoot, I've gotta pee. I'll see you later, Cory!"

I scrambled off the trampoline as fast I could, found my flip-flops, and headed back toward the house. I spotted Taylor by the pool and made a beeline for her. "I need to talk to you," I hissed.

I grabbed her hand and pulled her over by the snack table. "Like, five seconds ago, Cory Wheeler almost asked me out."

"And? What did you say?" Taylor's eyes were gleaming, and I hated how smug she looked, like everything was going according to plan.

"I said I had to pee," I told her.

"Belly! Get your butt back over to that trampoline and make out with him!"

"Taylor, would you stop? I told you I wasn't interested in Cory. I saw you talking to him earlier. Did you make him ask me out?"

She gave a little shrug. "Well . . . he's been into you all year and he's been taking his sweet time asking you out. I might have *gently* pushed him in the right direction. You guys looked so cute on the trampoline together."

I shook my head. "I really wish you hadn't done that."

"I was just trying to take your mind off things!"

"Well, I don't need you to do that," I said.

"Yes, you do so."

We stared at each other for a minute. Some days, days like this, I wanted to wring her neck. She was just so bossy all the time. I was getting pretty sick of Taylor pushing me in this direction and that direction, dressing me up like one of her shabbier, less fortunate dolls. It had always been like this with us.

But the thing was, I finally had a real excuse to leave, and I was relieved. I said, "I think I'm gonna go home."

"What are you talking about? We just got here."

"I'm just not in the mood to be here, okay?"

I guess she was getting sick of me too, because she said, "This is starting to get old, Belly. You've been moping around for months. It's not healthy. . . . My mom thinks you should see someone."

"What? You've been talking to your mom about me?" I glared at her. "Tell your mom to save her psychiatric advice for Ellen."

Taylor gasped. "I can't believe you just said that to me."

Their cat, Ellen, had seasonal affective disorder,

according to Taylor's mother. They had her on antidepressants all winter, and when she was still moody in the spring, they sent Ellen to a cat whisperer. It didn't do any good. In my opinion, Ellen was just plain mean.

I took a breath. "I listened to you cry about Ellen for months, and then Susannah dies and you want me to just make out with Cory and play beer pong and forget about her? Well, I'm sorry, but I can't."

Taylor looked around quickly before she leaned closer and said, "Don't act like Susannah's the only thing you're sad about, Belly. You're sad about Conrad, too, and you know it."

I couldn't believe she said that to me. It stung. It stung because it was true. But it was still a low blow. My father used to call Taylor indomitable. She was. But for better or for worse, Taylor Jewel was a part of me, and I was a part of her.

Not altogether meanly, I said. "We can't all be like you, Taylor."

"You can try," she suggested, smiling a little. "Listen, I'm sorry about the Cory thing. I just want you to be happy."

"I know."

She put her arm around me, and I let her. "It's going to be an amazing summer, you'll see."

"Amazing," I echoed. I wasn't looking for amazing. I just wanted to get by. To keep moving. If I made it through this summer, the next one would be easier. It had to be.

So I stayed a little while longer. I sat on the porch with Davis and Taylor and I watched Cory flirt with a sophomore girl. I ate a hot dog. Then I went home.

At home the sandwich was still on the counter, still wrapped in plastic. I put it in the fridge and I headed upstairs. My mother's bedroom light was on, but I didn't go in to say good night. I went straight to my room and got back into my big Cousins T-shirt and undid my braid, brushed my teeth, and washed my face. Then I got under the covers and lay in bed, just thinking. I thought, *So this is what life is like now.* Without Susannah, without the boys.

It had been two months. I'd survived June. I thought to myself, *I can do this.* I can go to the movies with Taylor and Davis, I can swim in Marcy's pool, maybe I can even go out with Cory Wheeler. If I do those things, it will be all right. Maybe letting myself forget how good it used to be will make things easier.

But when I slept that night, I dreamed of Susannah and the summer house, and even in my sleep I knew exactly how good it used to be. How right it was. And no matter what you do or how hard you try, you can't stop yourself from dreaming.

chapter *four*
JEREMIAH

Seeing your dad cry really messes with your mind. Maybe not for some people. Maybe some people have dads who are cool with crying and are in touch with their emotions. Not my dad. He's not a crier, and he for sure never encouraged us to cry either. But at the hospital, and then at the funeral home, he cried like a lost little kid.

My mom died early in the morning. Everything happened so fast, it took me a minute to catch up and realize it was all really happening. It doesn't hit you right away. But later that night, the first night without her, it was just me and Conrad at the house. The first time we'd been alone in days.

The house was so quiet. Our dad was at the funeral home with Laurel. The relatives were at a hotel. It was just me and Con. All day, people had been in and out of the house, and now it was just us.

We were sitting at the kitchen table. People had sent over all kinds of stuff. Fruit baskets, sandwich platters, a coffee cake. A big tin of butter cookies from Costco.

I tore off a chunk of the coffee cake and stuffed it into my mouth. It was dry. I tore off another chunk and ate that too. "You want some?" I asked Conrad.

"Nah," he said. He was drinking milk. I wondered it if was old. I couldn't remember the last time anybody had been to the store.

"What's happening tomorrow?" I asked. "Is everyone coming over here?"

Conrad shrugged. "Probably," he said. He had a milk mustache.

That was all we said to each other. He went upstairs to his room, and I cleaned up the kitchen. And then I was tired, and I went up too. I thought about going to Conrad's room, because even though we weren't saying anything, it was better when we were together, less lonely. I stood in the hallway for a second, about to knock, and then I heard him crying. Choked sobs. I didn't go inside. I left him alone. I knew that's the way he would want it. I went to my own room and I got into bed. I cried too.

chapter *five*

I wore my old glasses to the funeral, the ones with the red plastic frames. They were like putting on a too-tight coat from a long time ago. They made me dizzy, but I didn't care. Susannah always liked me in those glasses. She said I looked like the smartest girl in the room, the kind of girl who was going somewhere and knew exactly how she was going to get there. I wore my hair halfway up, because that was the way she liked it. She said it showed my face off.

It felt like the right thing to do, to look the way she liked me best. Even though I knew she only said those things to make me feel better, they still felt true. I believed everything Susannah said. I even believed her when she said she'd never leave. I think we all did, even my mother. We were all surprised when it happened, and even when it became inevitable, a fact, we never really believed it. It seemed impossible. Not our Susannah, not Beck. You always hear about people getting better, beating the odds. I was sure Susannah would be one of them. Even if it was only a one in a million chance. She was one in a million.

Things got bad fast. So bad that my mother was shuttling between Susannah's house in Boston and ours, every other weekend at first and then more frequently. She had to take a leave of absence from work. She had a room at Susannah's house.

The call came early in the morning. It was still dark out. It was bad news, of course; bad news is the only kind that really can't wait. As soon as I heard the phone ring, even in my sleep, I knew. Susannah was gone. I lay there in my bed, waiting for my mother to come and tell me. I could hear her moving around in her room, heard the shower running.

When she didn't come, I went to her room. She was packing, her hair still wet. She looked over at me, her eyes tired and empty. "Beck's gone," she said. And that was it.

I could feel my insides sink. My knees too. So I sat on the ground, against the wall, letting it support me. I thought I knew what heartbreak felt like. I thought heartbreak was me, standing alone at the prom. That was nothing. This, this was heartbreak. The pain in your chest, the ache behind your eyes. The knowing that things will never be the same again. It's all relative, I suppose. You think you know love, you think you know real pain, but you don't. You don't know anything.

I'm not sure when I started crying. When I got started, I couldn't stop. I couldn't breathe.

My mother crossed the room and knelt down on the floor with me, hugging me, rocking me back and forth. But she didn't cry. She wasn't even there. She was an upright reed, an empty harbor.

My mother drove up to Boston that same day. The only reason she'd even been at home that day had been to check on me and get a change of clothes. She'd thought there'd be more time. She should've been there, when Susannah died. If only for the boys. I was sure she was thinking the same thoughts.

In her best professor voice, she told Steven and me that we would drive ourselves up in two days, the day of the funeral. She didn't want us in the way of funeral preparations; there was a lot of work to be done. Ends in need of tying up.

My mother had been named executor of the will, and of course Susannah had known exactly what she was doing when she'd picked her. It was true that there was no one better for the job, that they'd been going over things even before Susannah died. But even more than that, my mother was at her best when she was busy, doing things. She did not fall apart, not when she was needed. No, my mother rose to the occasion. I wished that was a gene I'd inherited. Because I was at a loss. I didn't know what to do with myself.

I thought about calling Conrad. I even dialed his number a few times. But I couldn't do it. I didn't know what to say. I was afraid of saying the wrong things, of making things worse. And then I thought about calling Jeremiah. But it was the fear that kept me back. I knew that the moment I called, the moment I said it out loud, it would be true. She would really be gone.

On the drive up, we were mostly quiet. Steven's only suit, the one he'd just worn to prom, was wrapped in plastic and hung in the backseat. I hadn't bothered to hang up my dress. "What will we say to them?" I asked at last.

"I don't know," he admitted. "The only funeral I've ever been to is Aunt Shirle's, and she was really old." I was too young to remember that funeral.

"Where will we stay tonight? Susannah's house?"

"No idea."

"How do you suppose Mr. Fisher's handling it?" I couldn't bring myself to picture Conrad or Jeremiah, not yet.

"Whiskey," was Steven's answer.

After that I stopped asking questions.

We changed into our clothes at a gas station thirty miles from the funeral home. As soon as I saw how neat and pressed Steven's suit was, I regretted not hanging up my dress. Back in the car, I kept smoothing down the skirt with my palms, but it didn't help. My mother had told me that rayon was pointless; I should have listened. I also should have tried it on before I packed it. The last time I wore it was to a reception at my mother's university three years ago, and now it was too small.

We got there early, early enough to find my mother bustling around, arranging flowers and talking to Mr. Browne, the funeral director. As soon as she saw me, she frowned. "You should have ironed that dress, Belly," she said.

I bit my bottom lip to keep from saying something I knew I would regret. "There wasn't any time," I said, even though there had been. There had been plenty of time. I tugged down the skirt so it didn't look so short.

She nodded tersely. "Go find the boys, will you? Belly, talk to Conrad."

Steven and I exchanged a look. What would I say? It had been a month since prom, since we'd last spoken.

We found them in a side room, it had pews and tissue boxes under lacquer covers. Jeremiah's head was bent, like he was praying, something I'd never known him to do. Conrad sat straight, his shoulders squared, staring into nowhere. "Hey," Steven said, clearing his throat. He moved toward them, hugging them roughly.

It occurred to me that I'd never seen Jeremiah in a suit

before. It looked a little too tight; he was uncomfortable, he kept tugging at his neck. But his shoes looked new. I wondered if my mother had helped pick them out.

When it was my turn I hurried over to Jeremiah and hugged him as hard as I could. He felt stiff in my arms. "Thanks for coming," he said, his voice oddly formal.

I had this fleeting thought that maybe he was mad at me, but I pushed it away as quickly as it had come. I felt guilty for even thinking it. This was Susannah's funeral, why would he be thinking about me?

I patted his back awkwardly, my hand moving in small circles. His eyes were impossibly blue, which was what happened when he cried.

"I'm really sorry," I said and immediately regretted saying it, because the words were so ineffectual. They didn't convey what I really meant, how I really felt. "I'm sorry" was just as pointless as rayon.

Then I looked at Conrad. He was sitting back down again, his back stiff, his white shirt one big wrinkle. "Hey," I said, sitting down next to him.

"Hey," he said. I wasn't sure if I should hug him or leave him be. So I squeezed his shoulder, and he didn't say anything. He was made of stone. I made a promise to myself: I would not leave his side all day. I would be right there, I would be a tower of strength, just like my mother.

My mother and Steven and I sat in the fourth pew, behind Conrad and Jeremiah's cousins and Mr. Fisher's

brother and his wife, who was wearing too much perfume. I thought my mother should be in the first row,
and I told her so, in a whisper. She sneezed and told me
it didn't matter. I guessed she was right. Then she took off
her suit jacket and draped it over my bare thighs.

I turned around once and saw my father in the back.
For some reason, I hadn't expected to see him there.
Which was weird, because he'd known Susannah too, so
it only made sense that he'd be at her funeral. I gave him
a little wave, and he waved back.

"Dad's here," I whispered to my mother.

"Of course he is," she said. She didn't look back.

Jeremiah and Conrad's school friends sat in a bunch
together, toward the back. They looked awkward and out
of place. The guys kept their heads down and the girls
whispered to one another nervously.

The service was long. A preacher I'd never met delivered the eulogy. He said nice things about Susannah. He
called her kind, compassionate, graceful, and she was all
of those things, but it sounded a lot like he'd never met
her. I leaned in close to my mother to tell her so, but she
was nodding along with him.

I thought I wouldn't cry again, but I did, a lot. Mr.
Fisher got up and thanked everyone for coming, told us
we were welcome to come by the house afterward for a
reception. His voice broke a few times, but he managed
to keep it together. When I last saw him, he was tan and

confident and tall. Seeing him that day, he looked like a man who was lost in a snowstorm. Shoulders hunched, face pale. I thought about how hard it must be for him to stand up there, in front of everybody who loved her. He had cheated on her, left her when she needed him most, but in the end, he had shown up. He'd held her hand those last few weeks. Maybe he'd thought there'd be more time too.

It was a closed casket. Susannah told my mother she didn't want everybody gawking at her when she didn't look her best. Dead people looked fake, she explained. Like they were made of wax. I reminded myself that the person inside the coffin wasn't Susannah, that it didn't matter what she looked like because she was already gone.

When it was over, after we'd said the Lord's Prayer, we formed our processional, everybody taking their turn to offer condolences. I felt strangely adult there, standing with my mother and my brother. Mr. Fisher leaned down and gave me a stiff hug, his eyes wet. He shook Steven's hand and when he hugged my mother, she whispered something in his ear and he nodded.

When I hugged Jeremiah, we were both crying so hard, we were holding each other up. His shoulders kept shaking.

When I hugged Conrad, I wanted to say something, to comfort him. Something better than "I'm sorry." But it was over so quick, there wasn't any time to say more than that. I had a whole line of people behind me, all waiting to pay their condolences too.

The cemetery wasn't very far. My heels kept sticking in the ground. It must have rained the day before. Before they lowered Susannah into the wet ground, Conrad and Jeremiah both put a white rose on top of the coffin, and then the rest of us added more flowers. I picked a pink peony. Someone sang a hymn. When it was over, Jeremiah didn't move. He stood right where her grave was going to be, and he cried. It was my mother who went to him. She took him by the hand, and she spoke to him softly.

Back at Susannah's house, Jeremiah and Steven and I slipped away to Jeremiah's bedroom. We sat on his bed in our fancy clothes. "Where's Conrad?" I said. I hadn't forgotten my vow to stay by his side, but he was making it hard, the way he kept disappearing.

"Let's leave him alone for a while," Jeremiah said. "Are you guys hungry?"

I was, but I didn't want to say so. "Are you?"

"Yeah, sort of. There's food downstairs." His voice lingered on the word "downstairs." I knew he didn't want to go down there and face all those people, have to see the pity in their eyes. *How sad*, they'd say, *look at those two young boys she left behind*. His friends hadn't come to the house; they'd left right after the burial. It was all adults down there.

"I'll go," I offered.

"Thanks," he said gratefully.

I got up and shut the door behind me. In the hallway I stopped to look at their family portraits. They were matted and framed in black, all the same kind of frame. In one picture, Conrad was wearing a bow tie and he was missing his front teeth. In another, Jeremiah was eight or nine and he had on the Red Sox cap he refused to take off for, like, a whole summer. He said it was a lucky hat; he wore it every day for three months. Every couple of weeks, Susannah would wash it and then put it back in his room while he slept.

Downstairs the adults were milling around, drinking coffee and talking in hushed voices. My mother stood at the buffet table, cutting cake for strangers. They were strangers to me, anyway. I wondered if she knew them, if they knew who she was to Susannah, how she was her best friend, how they'd spent every summer together for almost their whole lives.

I grabbed two plates and my mother helped me load them up. "Are you guys all right upstairs?" she asked me, putting a wedge of blue cheese on the plate.

I nodded and slid it right back off. "Jeremiah doesn't like blue cheese," I told her. Then I took a handful of water crackers and a cluster of green grapes. "Have you seen Conrad?"

"I think he's in the basement," she said. Rearranging

the cheese plate, she added, "Why don't you go check on him and bring him a plate? I'll take this one up to the boys."

"Okay." I picked up the plate and crossed the dining room just as Jeremiah and Steven came downstairs. I stood there and watched Jeremiah stop and talk to people, letting them hug him and grasp his hand. Our eyes met, and I lifted my hand and waved it just barely. He lifted his and did the same, rolling his eyes a little at the woman clutching his arm. Susannah would have been proud.

Then I headed downstairs, to the basement. The basement was carpeted and soundproofed. Susannah had it set up when Conrad took up the electric guitar.

It was dark; Conrad hadn't turned the lights on. I waited for my eyes to adjust, and then I crept down the stairs, feeling my way.

I found him soon enough. He was lying down on the couch with his head in a girl's lap. She was running her hands along the top of his head, like they belonged there. Even though summer had just barely started, she was tan. Her shoes were off, her bare legs were stretched out on top of the coffee table. And Conrad, he was stroking her leg.

Everything in me seized up, pulled in tight.

I had seen her at the funeral. I'd thought she was really pretty, and I'd wondered who she was. She looked East Asian, like she might be Indian. She had dark hair and dark eyes and she was wearing a black miniskirt and a white and black polka-dot blouse. And a headband, she was wearing a black headband.

She saw me first. "Hey," she said.

That's when Conrad looked over and saw me standing in the doorway with a plate of cheese and crackers. He sat up. "Is that food for us?" he asked, not quite looking at me.

"My mother sent it," I said, and my voice came out mumbly and quiet. I walked over and put the plate on the coffee table. I stood there for a second, unsure of what to do next.

"Thanks," the girl said, in a way that sounded more like, *You can go now.* Not in a mean way, but in a way that made it clear I was interrupting.

I backed out of the room slowly but when I got to the stairs, I started to run. I ran by all the people in the living room and I could hear Conrad coming after me.

"Wait a minute," he called out.

I'd almost made it through the foyer when he caught up to me and grabbed my arm.

"What do you want?" I said, shaking him off. "Let go of me."

"That was Aubrey," he said, letting go.

Aubrey, the girl who broke Conrad's heart. I'd pictured her differently. I'd pictured her blond. This girl was prettier than what I had pictured. I could never compete with a girl like that.

I said, "Sorry I interrupted your little moment."

"Oh, grow up," he said.

There are moments in life that you wish with all your heart you could take back. Like, just erase from existence. Like, if you could, you'd erase yourself right out of existence too, just to make that moment not exist.

What I said next was one of those moments for me.

On the day of his mother's funeral, to the boy I loved more than I had ever loved anything or anyone, I said, "Go to hell."

It was the worst thing I've ever said to anyone, ever. It wasn't that I'd never said the words before. But the look on his face. I'll never forget it. The look on his face made me want to die. It confirmed every mean and low thing I'd ever thought about myself, the stuff you hope and pray no one will ever know about you. Because if they knew, they would see the real you, and they would despise you.

Conrad said, "I should have known you'd be like this."

Miserably, I asked him, "What do you mean?"

He shrugged, his jaw tight. "Forget it."

"No, say it."

He started to turn around, to leave, but I stopped him. I stood in his way. "Tell me," I said, my voice rising.

He looked at me and said, "I knew it was a bad idea, starting something with you. You're just a kid. It was a huge mistake."

"I don't believe you," I said.

People were starting to look. My mother was standing

in the living room, talking to people I didn't recognize. She'd glanced up when I'd started speaking. I couldn't even look at her; I could feel my face burning.

I knew the right thing to do was to walk away. I knew that was what I was supposed to do. In that moment, it was like I was floating above myself and I could see me and how everybody in that room was looking at me. But when Conrad just shrugged and started to leave again, I felt so mad, and so—small. I wanted to stop myself, but I couldn't quit.

"I hate you," I said.

Conrad turned around and nodded, like he'd expected me to say exactly that. "Good," he said. The way he looked at me then, pitying and fed up and just over it. It made me feel sick.

"I never want to see you again," I said, and then I pushed past him, and I ran up the staircase so fast I tripped on the top step. I fell right onto my knees, hard. I think I heard someone gasp. I could barely see through my tears. Blindly, I got back up and ran to the guest room.

I took off my glasses and lay down on the bed and cried. It wasn't Conrad I hated. It was myself.

My father came up after a while. He knocked a few times, and when I didn't answer, he came in and sat on the edge of the bed.

"Are you all right?" he asked me. His voice was so gentle, I could feel tears leaking out of the corners of my eyes again. No one should be nice to me. I didn't deserve it.

I rolled away so my back was to him. "Is Mom mad at me?"

"No, of course not," he said. "Come back downstairs and say good-bye to everyone."

"I can't." How could I go back downstairs and face everyone after I'd made that scene? It was impossible. I was humiliated, and I had done it to myself.

"What happened with you and Conrad, Belly? Did you have a fight? Did you two break up?" It was so odd to hear the words "break up" come out of my dad's mouth. I couldn't discuss it with him. It was just too bizarre.

"Dad, I can't talk about this stuff with you. Could you just go? I want to be alone."

"All right," he said, and I could hear the hurt in his voice. "Do you want me to get your mother?"

She was the last person I wanted to see. Right away, I said, "No, please don't."

The bed creaked as my father got up and closed the door.

The only person I wanted was Susannah. She was the only one. And then I had a thought, clear as day. I would never be somebody's favorite again. I would never be a kid again, not in the same way. That was all over now. She was really gone.

I hoped Conrad listened to me. I hoped I never saw him again. If I ever had to look at him again, if he looked at me the way he did that day, it would break me.

chapter *six*
JULY 3

When the phone rang early the next morning, my first thought was, *The only kind of calls you get this early in the morning are the bad ones.* I was right, sort of.

I think I was still in a dream state when I heard his voice. For one long second, I thought it was Conrad, and for that second, I could not catch my breath. Conrad calling me again—that was enough to make me forget how to breathe. But it wasn't Conrad. It was Jeremiah.

They were brothers, after all; their voices were alike. Alike but not the same. He, Jeremiah, said, "Belly, it's Jeremiah. Conrad's gone."

"What do you mean 'gone'?" Suddenly I was wide awake and my heart was in my throat. Gone had come to mean something different, in a way that it hadn't used to. Something permanent.

"He took off from summer school a couple of days ago and he hasn't come back. Do you know where he is?"

"No." Conrad and I hadn't spoken since Susannah's funeral.

"He missed two exams. He'd never do that." Jeremiah sounded desperate, panicky even. I'd never heard him sound that way. He was always at ease, always laughing, never serious. And he was right, Conrad would never do that, he'd never just leave without telling anybody. Not the old Conrad, anyway. Not the Conrad I had loved since I was ten years old, not him.

I sat up, rubbed at my eyes. "Does your dad know?"

"Yeah. He's freaking out. He can't deal with this kind of thing." This kind of thing would be Susannah's domain, not Mr. Fisher's.

"What do you want to do, Jere?" I tried to make my voice sound the way my mother's would. Calm, reasonable. Like I wasn't scared out of my mind, the thought of Conrad gone. It wasn't so much that I thought he was in trouble. It was that if he left, really left, he might never come back. And that scared me more than I could say.

"I don't know." Jeremiah let out a big gust of air. "His phone has been off for days. Do you think you could help me find him?"

Immediately I said, "Yes. Of course. Of course I can."

Everything made sense in that moment. This was my chance to make things right with Conrad. The way I saw it, this was what I had been waiting for and I hadn't even known it. It was like the last two months I had been sleepwalking, and now here I was, finally awake. I had a goal, a purpose.

That last day I'd said horrible things. Unforgiveable things. Maybe, if I helped him in some small way, I'd be able to fix what was broken.

Even so, as scared as I was at the thought of Conrad being gone, as eager as I was to redeem myself, the thought of being near him again terrified me. No one on this earth affected me the way Conrad Fisher did.

As soon as Jeremiah and I got off the phone, I was everywhere at once, throwing underwear and T-shirts into my big overnight bag. How long would it take us to find him? Was he okay? I would have known if he wasn't okay, wouldn't I? I packed my toothbrush, a comb. Contact solution.

My mother was ironing clothes in the kitchen. She was staring off into nowhere, her forehead one big crease. "Mom?" I asked.

Startled, she looked at me. "What? What's up?"

I'd already planned what I'd say next. "Taylor's having some kind of breakdown because she and Davis broke up again. I'm gonna stay over at her place tonight, maybe tomorrow, too, depending on how she feels."

I held my breath, waiting for her to speak. My mother has a bullshit detector like no one I've ever known. It's more than a mother's intuition, it's like a homing device. But no alerts went off, no bells or whistles. Her face was perfectly blank.

"All right," she said, going back to her ironing.

And then, "Try and be home tomorrow night," she said. "I'll make halibut." She spritzed starch on khaki pants. I was home free. I should have felt relieved, but I didn't, not really.

"I'll try," I said.

For a moment, I thought about telling her the truth. Of all people, she'd understand. She'd want to help. She loved them both. It was my mother who took Conrad to the emergency room the time he broke his arm skateboarding, because Susannah was shaking so hard she couldn't drive. My mother was steady, solid. She always knew what to do.

Or at least, she used to. Now I wasn't so sure. When Susannah got sick again, my mother went on autopilot, doing what needed doing. Barely present. The other day I'd come downstairs to find her sweeping the front hallway, and her eyes were red, and I'd been afraid. She wasn't the crying kind. Seeing her like that, like an actual person and not just my mother, it almost made me not trust her.

My mother set down her iron. She picked up her purse from the counter and pulled out her wallet. "Buy Taylor some Ben & Jerry's, on me," she said, handing me a twenty.

"Thanks, Mom," I said, taking the twenty and stuffing it into my pocket. It would come in handy for gas money later.

"Have fun," she said, and she was gone again. Absent. Ironing the same pair of khaki pants she'd just gone over.

When I was in my car, driving away, I finally let myself feel it. Relief. No silent, sad mother, not today. I hated to leave her and I hated to be near her, because she made me remember what I wanted most to forget. Susannah was gone, and she wasn't coming back, and none of us would be the same ever again.

chapter *seven*

At Taylor's house, the front door was almost never locked. Her staircase, with its long banister and shiny wooden steps, was as familiar to me as my own.

After I let myself into the house, I went straight up to her room.

Taylor was lying on her stomach, flipping through gossip magazines. As soon as she saw me, she sat up and said, "Are you a masochist, or what?"

I threw my duffel bag on the floor and sat down next to her. I'd called her on the way over; I'd told her every-thing. I hadn't wanted to, but I'd done it.

"Why are you going off looking for him?" she demanded. "He's not your boyfriend anymore."

I sighed. "Like he ever really was."

"My point exactly." She thumbed through a magazine

and handed it to me. "Check it out. I could see you in this bikini. The white bandeau one. It'll look hot with your tan."

"Jeremiah's going to be here soon," I said, looking at the magazine and handing it back to her. I couldn't picture me in that bikini. But I could picture her in it.

"You *so* should have picked Jeremy," she said. "Conrad is basically a crazy person."

I'd told her and told her how it wasn't as easy as picking one or the other. Nothing ever was. It wasn't as though I'd even had a choice, not really.

"Conrad's not crazy, Taylor." She'd never forgiven Conrad for not liking her the summer I brought her to Cousins, the summer we were fourteen. Taylor was used to all the boys liking her, she was unaccustomed to being ignored. Which was exactly what Conrad had done. Not Jeremiah, though. As soon as she batted her big brown eyes at him, he was hers. Her *Jeremy*, that's what she'd called him—in that teasing kind of way, the kind that boys love. Jeremiah lapped it right up, too, until she ditched him for my brother, Steven.

Pursing her lips, Taylor said, "Fine, maybe that was a *little* harsh. Maybe he's not crazy. But, like, what? Are you always just going to be sitting around waiting for him? Whenever he wants?"

"No! But he's in some kind of trouble. He needs his friends now more than ever," I said, picking at a loose strand on the carpet. "No matter what happened between us, we'll always be friends."

She rolled her eyes. "Whatever. The only reason I'm even signing off on this is for you to get closure."

"Closure?"

"Yes. I can see now that it's the only way. You need to see Conrad face-to-face and tell him you're over him and you're not gonna play his games anymore. Then and only then can you move on from his lame ass."

"Taylor, I'm not innocent in all this either." I swallowed. "The last time I saw him, I was awful."

"Whatever. The point is, you need to move on. On to greener pastures." She eyed me. "Like Cory. Who, by the way, I doubt you even have a chance with anymore after last night."

Last night seemed like a thousand years ago. I did my best to look contrite and said, "Hey, thanks again for letting me leave my car here. If my mom calls—"

"Please, Belly. Show a little respect. I'm the queen of lying to parents, unlike you." She sniffed. "You're gonna be back in time for tomorrow night, right? We're all gonna go out on Davis's parents' boat, remember? You promised."

"That's not until eight or nine. I'm sure I'll be back by then. Besides," I pointed out, "I never *promised* you anything."

"Then promise now," she commanded. "Promise you'll be here."

I rolled my eyes. "Why do you want me back here so bad? So you can sic Cory Wheeler on me again? You don't need me. You have Davis."

"I do so need you, even if you are a terrible best friend. Boyfriends aren't the same as best friends and you know it. Pretty soon we'll be in college, you know. What if we go to different schools? What then?" Taylor glared at me, her eyes accusing.

"Okay, okay. I promise." Taylor still had her heart set on us going to the same school, the way we'd always said we would.

She held out her hand to me and we hooked pinkies.

"Is that what you're wearing?" Taylor asked me suddenly.

Looking down at my gray camisole, I said, "Well, yeah."

She shook her head so fast her blond hair swished all around. "Is that what you're wearing to see Conrad *for the first time*?"

"This isn't a date I'm going on, Taylor."

"When you see an ex, you have to look better than you've ever looked. It's, like, the first rule of breakups. You have to make him think, 'Damn, I missed out on *that*?' It's the only way."

I hadn't thought of that. "I don't care what he thinks," I told her.

She was already rifling through my overnight bag. "All you have in here is underwear and a T-shirt. And this old tank top. Ugh. I hate this tank top. It needs to be officially retired."

"Quit it," I said. "Don't go through my stuff."

Taylor leaped up, her face all glowy and excited. "Oh, please let me pack for you, Belly! Please, it would make me so happy."

"No," I said, as firmly as I could. With Taylor, you had to be firm. "I'll probably be back tomorrow. I don't need anything else."

Taylor ignored me and disappeared into her walk-in closet.

My phone rang then, and it was Jeremiah. Before I answered it, I said, "I'm serious, Tay."

"Don't worry, I've got it all covered. Just think of me as your fairy godmother," she said from inside the closet.

I popped open my phone. "Hey," I said. "Where are you?"

"I'm pretty close. About an hour away. Are you at Taylor's?"

"Yeah," I said. "Do you need me to give you the directions again?"

"No, I've got it." He paused, and for a second I thought he'd already hung up. Then he said, "Thanks for doing this."

"Come on," I said.

I thought about saying something else, like how he was one of my best friends and how part of me was almost glad to have a reason to see him again. It just wouldn't be summer without Beck's boys.

But I couldn't get the words to sound right in my head, and before I could figure them out, he hung up.

When Taylor finally emerged from the closet, she was zipping up my bag. "All set," she said, dimpling.

"Taylor—" I tried to grab the bag from her.

"No, just wait until you get wherever you're going. You'll thank me," she said. "I was *very* generous, even though you're totally deserting me."

I ignored the last bit and said, "Thanks, Tay."

"You're welcome," she said, checking out her hair in her bureau mirror. "See how much you need me?" Taylor faced me, her hands on her hips. "How are you guys even planning on finding Conrad, anyway? For all you know, he's under a bridge somewhere."

I hadn't given that part, the actual details, much thought. "I'm sure Jeremiah has some ideas," I said.

Jeremiah showed up in an hour, just like he said he would. We watched from the living room window when his car pulled into Taylor's circular driveway. "Oh my God, he looks so cute," Taylor said, running over to the dresser and putting on lip gloss. "Why didn't you tell me how cute he got?"

The last time she'd seen Jeremiah, he'd been a head shorter and scrawny. It was no wonder she'd gone after Steven instead. But he just looked like Jeremiah to me.

I picked up my bag and headed outside, with Taylor right on my heels.

When I opened the front door, Jeremiah was standing on the front steps. He was wearing his Red Sox cap, and his hair was shorter than the last time I'd seen him. It was strange to see him there, on Taylor's doorstep. Surreal.

"I was just about to call you," he said, taking off his hat. He was a boy unafraid of hat hair, of looking stupid. It was one of his most endearing qualities, one I admired because I pretty much lived in constant fear of embarrassing myself.

I wanted to hug him, but for some reason—maybe because he didn't reach for me first, maybe because I felt shy all of a sudden—I held back. Instead, I said, "You got here really fast."

"I sped like crazy," he said, and then, "Hey, Taylor."

She got on her tiptoes and hugged him and I regretted not hugging him too.

When she stepped away, Taylor surveyed him approvingly and said, "Jeremy, you look good." She smiled at him, waiting for him to tell her she looked good too. When he didn't, she said, "That was your cue to tell me how good I look. Duh."

Jeremiah laughed. "Same old Taylor. You know you look good. You don't need me to tell you."

The two of them smirked at each other.

"We'd better get going," I said.

He took my overnight bag off my shoulder and we followed him to the car. While he made room for my bag in the trunk, Taylor grabbed me by the elbow and said, "Call me when you get wherever you're going, Cinderbelly." She used to call me that when we were little, when we were obsessed with *Cinderella*. She'd sing it right along with the mice. *Cinderbelly, Cinderbelly.*

I felt a sudden rush of affection for her. Nostalgia, a shared history, counted for a lot. More than I'd realized. I'd miss her next year, when the two of us were at different colleges. "Thanks for letting me leave my car here, Tay."

She nodded. Then she mouthed the word *CLOSURE*.

"Bye, Taylor," Jeremiah said, getting into the car.

I got in too. His car was a mess, like always. There were empty water bottles all over the floor and backseat. "Bye," I called out as we began to drive away.

She stood there and waved and watched us. She called back, "Don't forget your promise, Belly!"

"What'd you promise?" Jeremiah asked me, looking in the rearview mirror.

"I promised her I'd be back in time for her boyfriend's Fourth of July party. It's going to be on a boat."

Jeremiah nodded. "You'll be back in time, don't worry. Hopefully I'll have you back by tonight."

"Oh," I said. "Okay."

I guessed I wouldn't need that overnight bag after all.

Then he said, "Taylor looks exactly the same."

"Yeah, I guess she does."

And then neither of us said anything. We were just silent.

chapter *eight*
JEREMIAH

I can pinpoint the exact moment everything changed. It was last summer. Con and I were sitting on the porch, and I was trying to talk to him about what a dick the new assistant football coach was.

"Just stick it out," he said.

Easy for him to say. He'd quit. "You don't get it, this guy's crazy," I started to tell him, but he wasn't listening anymore. Their car had just pulled into the driveway. Steven got out first, then Laurel. She asked where my mom was and gave me a big hug. She hugged Conrad next and I started to say, "Hey, where's the Belly Button?" And there she was.

Conrad saw her first. He was looking over Laurel's shoulder. At her. She walked toward us. Her hair was swinging around all over the place and her legs looked miles long. She was wearing cutoffs and dirty sneakers. Her bra strap was sticking out of her tank top. I swear I never noticed her bra strap before. She had a funny look on her face, a look I didn't recognize. Like shy and nervous, but proud at the same time.

I watched Conrad hug her, waiting my turn. I wanted to ask her what she'd been thinking about, why she had that look on her face. I didn't do it though. I stepped around Conrad and grabbed her up and said something stupid. It made her laugh, and then she was just Belly again. And that was a relief, because I didn't want her to be anything but just Belly.

I'd known her my whole life. I'd never thought of her as a girl. She was one of us. She was my friend. Seeing her in a different way, even just for a second, it shook me up.

My dad used to say that with everything in life, there's the game-changing moment. The one moment everything else hinges upon, but you hardly ever know it at the time. The three-pointer early on in the second quarter that changes up the whole tempo of the game. Wakes people up, brings them back to life. It all goes back to that one moment.

I might have forgotten about it, that moment when their car drove up and this girl walked out, a girl I barely recognized. It could have just been one of those things. You know, where a person catches your eye, like a whiff of perfume when you walk down the street. You keep walking. You forget. I might have forgotten. Things might have gone back to the way they were before.

But then came the game-changing moment.

It was nighttime, maybe a week into the summer. Belly and I were hanging out by the pool, and she was cracking up over something I said, I don't remember what. I loved that I could make her laugh. Even though she laughed a lot and it wasn't some kind of feat, it felt great. She said, "Jere, you're, like, the funniest person I know."

It was one of the best compliments of my life. But that wasn't the game-changing moment.

That happened next. I was really on a roll, doing an impersonation of Conrad when he wakes up in the mornings. A whole Frankenstein sort of thing. Then Conrad came out and sat next to her on the deck chair. He pulled on her ponytail and said, "What's so funny?"

Belly looked up at him, and she was actually blushing. Her face was all flushed, and her eyes were shining. "I don't remember," she said.

My gut just twisted. I felt like somebody had drop-kicked me in the stomach. I was jealous, crazy jealous. Of Conrad. And when she got up a little while later to get a soda, I watched him watch her walk away and I felt sick inside.

That was when I knew things would never be the same.

I wanted to tell Conrad that he had no right. That he'd ignored her all these years, that he couldn't just decide to take her just because he felt like it.

She was all of ours. My mom adored her. She called Belly her secret daughter. She looked forward to seeing her all year. Steven, even though he gave her a hard time, he was really protective of her. Everyone took care of Belly, she just didn't know it. She was too busy looking at Conrad. For as long as any of us could remember, she had loved Conrad.

All I knew was, I wanted her to look at me like that. After that day, I was done for. I liked her, as more than a friend. I maybe even loved her.

There have been other girls. But they weren't her.

I didn't want to call Belly for help. I was pissed at her. It wasn't just that she'd picked Conrad. That was old news. She was always going to pick Conrad. But we were friends too. How many times had she called me since my mom died? Twice? A few texts and emails?

But sitting in the car next to her, smelling her Belly Conklin smell (Ivory soap and coconuts and sugar), the way her nose wrinkled up as she thought, her nervous smile and chewed-up fingernails. The way she said my name.

When she leaned forward to mess with the AC vents, her hair brushed against my leg and it was really soft. It made me remember all over again. It made it hard to stay pissed and keep her at arm's length the way I'd planned. It was pretty damn near impossible. When I was near her, I just wanted to grab her and hold her and kiss the shit out of her. Maybe then she'd finally forget about my asshole of a brother.

chapter *nine*

"So where are we going?" I asked Jeremiah. I tried to catch his eye, to make him look at me, just for a second. It seemed like he hadn't looked me in the eye once since he's showed up, and it made me nervous. I needed to know that things were okay between us.

"I don't know," he said. "I haven't talked to Con in a while. I have no clue where he'd go. I was hoping you'd have some ideas."

The thing was, I didn't. Not really. Not at all, actually. I cleared my throat. "Conrad and I haven't spoken since—since May."

Jeremiah looked at me sideways, but he didn't say anything. I wondered what Conrad had told him. Probably not much.

I kept talking because he wasn't. "Have you called his roommate?"

"I don't have his number. I don't even know his name."

"His name is Eric," I said quickly. I was glad to know that at least. "It's his same roommate from the school year. They stayed in the same room for summer school. So, um, I guess that's where we'll go, then. To Brown. We'll talk to Eric, to people on his hall. You never know, he could just be hanging out on campus."

"Sounds like a plan." As he checked his rearview mirror and changed lanes, he asked me, "So you've been to visit Con at school?"

"No," I said, looking out the window. It was a pretty embarrassing thing to admit. "Have you?"

"My dad and I helped him move into the dorms." Almost reluctantly he added, "Thanks for coming."

"Sure," I said.

"So Laurel's cool with it?"

"Oh, yeah, totally," I lied. "I'm glad I could come."

I used to look forward to seeing Conrad all year. I used to wish for summer the way kids wished for Christmas. It was all I thought about. Even now, even after everything, he was still all I thought about.

Later I turned on the radio to fill the silence between Jeremiah and me.

Once I thought I heard him start to say something, and I said, "Did you just say something?"

He said, "Nope."

For a while we just drove. Jeremiah and me were two

people who never ran out of things to say to each other, but there we were, not saying a word.

Finally he said, "I saw Nona last week. I stopped by the retirement home she's been working at."

Nona was Susannah's hospice nurse. I'd met her a few times. She was funny, and strong. Nona was slight, maybe five foot two with spindly arms and legs, but I'd seen her haul up Susannah like she weighed nothing. Which, toward the end, I guess she very nearly did.

chapter *ten*

When Susannah got really sick again, no one told me right away. Not Conrad, or my mother, or Susannah herself. It all happened so fast.

I tried getting out of going to see Susannah that last time. I told my mother I had a trig exam that counted for a quarter of my grade. I would have said anything to get out of going. "I'm going to have to study all weekend. I can't come. Maybe next weekend," I said over the phone. I tried to make my voice casual and not desperate. "Okay?"

Immediately she said, "No. Not okay. You're coming up this weekend. Susannah wants to see you."

"But—"

"No buts." Her voice was razor sharp. "I already bought your train ticket. See you tomorrow."

On the train ride up, I worked hard to come up with things I could say when I saw Susannah. I would tell her about how hard trig was, how Taylor was in love, how I was thinking of running for class secretary, which was a lie. I wasn't going to run for class secretary, but I knew that Susannah would like the sound of it. I would tell her all of those things, and I would not ask about Conrad.

My mother picked me up at the train station. When I got into the car, she said, "I'm glad you came."

She went on to say, "Don't worry, Conrad's not here."

I didn't answer her, I just stared out the window. I was unjustifiably mad at her for making me come. Not that she cared. She kept right on talking. "I'm going to go ahead and warn you that she doesn't look good. She's tired. She's very tired, but she's excited to see you."

As soon as she said the words, "she doesn't look good," I closed my eyes. I hated myself for being afraid to see her, for not visiting more often. But I wasn't like my mother, as strong and durable as steel. Seeing Susannah like that, it was too hard. It felt like pieces of her, of who she used to be, crumpled away every time. Seeing her like that made it real.

When we pulled into the driveway, Nona was outside smoking a cigarette. I'd met Nona a couple of weeks before, when Susannah first moved back home. Nona had a very intimidating handshake. When we stepped out of the car, she was Purelling her hands and spraying Febreze on her uniform like she was a teenager smoking in secret, even though Susannah didn't mind it; she loved cigarettes once in a while but couldn't smoke them anymore. Just pot, just once in a while.

"Morning," Nona called out, waving to us.

"Morning," we called back.

She was sitting on the front porch. "Nice to see you," she said to me. To my mother, she said, "Susannah's all dressed and waiting for you two downstairs."

My mother sat down next to Nona. "Belly, you go on in first. I'm going to chat with Nona." And by "chat," I knew she meant she too was going to have a cigarette. She and Nona had gotten to be pretty friendly.

Nona was pragmatic and also intensely spiritual. She invited my mother to go to church with her once, and even though my mother was not religious in the least, she went. At first I thought it was just to humor Nona, but then when she started going to church alone back home, I realized it was more than that. She was looking for some kind of peace.

I said, "By myself?" and I regretted it right away. I didn't want either of them to judge me for being afraid. I was already judging myself.

"She's waiting for you," my mother said.

Which she was. She was sitting in the living room, and she was wearing actual clothes and not her pajamas. She had on makeup. Her peachy blush was bright and garish against her chalky skin. She'd made an effort, for me. So as not to scare me. So I pretended not to be scared.

"My favorite girl," she said, opening her arms for me.

I hugged her, carefully as I could, I told her she looked so much better. I lied.

She said Jeremiah wouldn't be home until later that night, that us girls had the house all to ourselves for the afternoon.

My mother came inside then, but left the two of us alone. She came into the living room to say a quick hello and then she fixed lunch while we caught up.

As soon as my mother left the room, Susannah said, "If you're worried about running into Conrad, don't be, sweetie. He won't be here this weekend."

I swallowed. "Did he tell you?"

She half laughed. "That boy doesn't tell me anything. Your mother mentioned that prom didn't go . . . as well as we'd hoped. I'm sorry, honey."

"He broke up with me," I told her. It was more complicated than that, but when you boiled it all down, that was what had happened. It had happened because he'd wanted it to. It had always been his call—his decision whether or not we were together.

Susannah took my hand and held it. "Don't hate Conrad," she said.

"I don't," I lied. I hated him more than anything. I

loved him more than anything. Because, he *was* every-thing. And I hated that, too.

"Connie's having a hard time with all of this. It's a lot." She paused and pushed my hair out of my face, her hand lingering on my forehead as if I had a fever. As if I was the one who was sick, in need of comfort. "Don't let him push you away. He needs you. He loves you, you know."

I shook my head. "No, he doesn't." In my head, I added, *The only person he loves is himself. And you.*

She acted like she hadn't heard me. "Do you love him?"

When I didn't answer, she nodded as if I had. "Will you do something for me?"

Slowly, I nodded.

"Look after him for me. Will you do that?"

"You won't need me to look after him, Susannah, you'll be here to do it," I said, and I tried not to sound desperate, but it didn't matter.

Susannah smiled and said, "You're my girl, Belly."

After lunch, Susannah took a nap. She didn't wake up until late afternoon, and when she did, she was irritable and disoriented. She snapped at my mother once, which terrified me. Susannah never snapped at anybody. Nona tried to put her to bed, and at first Susannah refused, but then she gave in. On the way to her bedroom, she gave me a little halfhearted wink.

Jeremiah came home around dinnertime. I was relieved

to see him. He made everything lighter, easier. Just seeing his face took away some of the strain of being there.

He walked into the kitchen and said, "What's that burning smell? Oh, Laurel's cooking. Hey, Laure!"

My mother swatted at him with a kitchen towel. He dodged her and started looking under pan covers playfully.

"Hey, Jere," I said to him. I was sitting on a stool, shelling beans.

He looked over at me and said, "Oh, hey. How are you?" Then he walked over to me and gave me a quick half hug. I tried to search his eyes for some clue as to how he was doing, but he didn't let me. He kept moving around, joking with Nona and my mother.

In some ways, he was the same Jeremiah, but in other ways, I could see how this had changed him. Had aged him. Everything took more effort, his jokes, his smiles. Nothing was easy anymore.

chapter *eleven*

It felt like forever before Jeremiah spoke again. I was pretending to be asleep, and he was drumming his fingers along the steering wheel. Suddenly he said, "This was my prom's theme song."

Right away I opened my eyes and asked, "How many proms have you been to?"

"Total? Five."

"What? Yeah, right. I don't believe you," I said, even though I did. Of course Jeremiah had been to five proms. He was exactly that guy, the one everyone wanted to go with. He would know how to make a girl feel like the prom queen even if she was nobody.

Jeremiah starting ticking off with his fingers. "Junior year, I went to two, mine and Flora Martinez's at Sacred

Heart. This year, I went to my prom and two others. Sophia Franklin at—"

"Okay, okay. I get it. You're in demand." I leaned forward and fiddled with the air conditioner control.

"I had to buy a tux because it was cheaper than renting over and over again," he said. Jeremiah looked straight ahead, and then he said the last thing I was expecting him to say. "You looked good at yours. I liked your dress."

I stared at him. Did Conrad show him our pictures? Had he told him anything? "How do you know?"

"My mom got one of the pictures framed."

I hadn't expected him to bring up Susannah. I'd thought prom would be a safe subject. I said, "I heard you were prom king at your prom."

"Yeah."

"I bet that was fun."

"Yeah, it was pretty fun."

I should have brought Jeremiah instead. If it had been Jeremiah, things would have been different. He would have said all the right things. It would have been Jeremiah in the center of the dance floor, doing the Typewriter and the Lawn Mower and the Toaster and all the other stupid dances he used to practice when we watched MTV. He would have remembered that daisies were my favorite flower, and he would've made friends with Taylor's boyfriend, Davis, and all the other girls would have been looking at him, wishing he was their date.

chapter *twelve*

From the start, I knew it wasn't going to be easy to get Conrad to go. He wasn't a prom kind of person. But the thing was, I didn't care. I just really wanted him to go with me, to be my date. It had been seven months since the first time we'd kissed. Two months since the last time I'd seen him. One week since the last time he'd called.

Being a person's prom date is definable; it's a real thing. And I had this fantasy of prom in my head, what it would be like. How he would look at me, how when we slow danced, he'd rest his hand on the small of my back. How we'd eat cheese fries at the diner after, and watch the sunrise from the roof of his car. I had it all planned out, how it would go.

When I called him that night, he sounded busy. But I forged ahead anyway. I asked him, "What are you doing the first weekend of April?" My voice trembled when I said the word "April." I was so nervous he'd say no. In fact, deep down I kind of expected him to.

Warily, he asked, "Why?"

"It's my prom."

He sighed. "Belly, I hate dances."

"I know that. But it's my prom, and I really want to go, and I want you to come with me." Why did he have to make everything so hard?

"I'm in college now," he reminded me. "I didn't even want to go to my own prom."

Lightly, I said, "Well, see, that's all the more reason for you to come to mine."

"Can't you just go with your friends?"

I was silent.

"I'm sorry, I just really don't feel like going. Finals are coming up, and it'll be hard for me to drive all the way down for one night."

So he couldn't do this one thing for me, to make me happy. He didn't feel like it. Fine. "That's okay," I told him. "There's plenty of other guys I can go with. No problem."

I could hear his mind working on the other end. "Never mind. I'll take you," he said at last.

"You know what? Don't even worry about it," I said. "Cory Wheeler already asked me. I can tell him I changed my mind."

"Who the hell is Corky Wheeler?"

I smiled. I had him now. Or at least I thought I did. I said, "Cory Wheeler. He plays soccer with Steven. He's a good dancer. He's taller than you."

But then Conrad said, "I guess you'll be able to wear heels, then."

"I guess I will."

I hung up. Was it so much to ask him to be my prom date for one freaking night? And I had lied about Cory Wheeler; he hadn't asked me. But I knew he would, if I let him think I wanted him to.

In bed, under my quilt, I cried a little. I had this perfect prom night in my mind, Conrad in a suit and me in the violet dress my mother bought me two summers ago, the one I had begged for. He had never seen me dressed up before, or wearing heels, for that matter. I really, really wanted him to.

Later he called and I let it go straight to voice mail. On the message, he said, "Hey. I'm sorry about before. Don't go with Cory Wheeler or any other guy. I'll come. You can still wear your heels."

I must have played that message thirty times at least. Even so, I never really listened to what he was actually saying—he didn't want me to go with some other guy, but he didn't want to go with me either.

I wore the violet dress. My mother was pleased, I

could tell. I also wore the pearl necklace Susannah gave me for my sixteenth birthday, and that pleased her too. Taylor and the other girls were all getting their hair done at a fancy salon. I decided to do mine myself. I curled my hair in loose waves and my mother helped with the back. I think the last time she did my hair was in the second grade, when I wore my hair in braids every day. She was good with a curling iron, but then, she was good with most things.

As soon as I heard his car pull into the driveway, I ran to the window. He looked beautiful in his suit. It was black; I'd never seen it before.

I launched myself down the stairs and flung the front door open before he could ring the bell. I couldn't stop smiling and I was about to throw my arms around him when he said, "You look nice."

"Thanks," I said, and my arms fell back at my sides. "So do you."

We must have taken a hundred pictures at the house. Susannah said she wanted photographic proof of Conrad in a suit and me in that dress. My mother kept her on the phone with us. She gave it to Conrad first, and whatever she said to him, he said, "I promise." I wondered what he was promising.

I also wondered if one day, Taylor and I would be like that—on the phone while our kids got ready for the prom. My mother and Susannah's friendship had spanned decades and children and husbands. I wondered if Taylor's and my friendship was made of the same stuff as theirs. Durable, impenetrable stuff. Somehow I doubted it. What they had, it was once-in-a-lifetime.

To me, Susannah said, "Did you do your hair the way we talked about?"

"Yes."

"Did Conrad tell you how pretty you look?"

"Yes," I said, even though he hadn't, not exactly.

"Tonight will be perfect," she promised me.

My mother positioned us on the front steps, on the staircase, standing next to the fireplace. Steven was there with his date, Claire Cho. They laughed the whole time, and when they took their pictures, Steven stood behind her with his arms around her waist and she leaned back into him. It was so easy. In our pictures, Conrad stood stiffly beside me, with one arm around my shoulders.

"Is everything okay?" I whispered.

"Yeah," he said. He smiled at me, but I didn't believe it. Something had changed. I just didn't know what.

I gave him an orchid boutonniere. He forgot to bring my corsage. He'd left it in his little refrigerator back at school, he said. I wasn't sad or mad. I was embarrassed. All this time, I'd made such a big deal about me and Conrad, how we were some kind of couple. But I'd had to beg him to go to the prom with me, and he hadn't even remembered to bring me flowers.

I could tell he felt awful when he realized, right at the moment Steven went to the fridge and came back with a wrist corsage, tiny pink roses to match Claire's dress. He gave her a big bouquet, too.

Claire pulled one of the roses out of her bouquet and handed it to me. "Here," she said, "we'll make you a corsage."

I smiled at her to show I was grateful. "That's okay. I don't want to poke a hole in my dress," I told her. What a crock. She didn't believe me, but she pretended to. She said, "How about we put it in your hair, then? I think it would look really pretty in your hair."

"Sure," I said. Claire Cho was nice. I hoped she and Steven never broke up. I hoped they stayed together forever.

After the thing with the corsage, Conrad tightened up even more. On the way to the car, he grabbed my wrist and said, in a quiet voice, "I'm sorry I forgot your corsage. I should have remembered."

I swallowed hard and smiled without really opening my mouth. "What kind was it?"

"A white orchid," he said. "My mom picked it out."

"Well, for my senior prom, you'll just have to get me two corsages to make up for it," I said. "I'll wear one on each wrist."

I watched him as I said it. We'd still be together in a year, wouldn't we? That was what I was asking.

His face didn't change. He took my arm and said, "Whatever you want, Belly."

In the car, Steven looked at us in the rearview mirror. "Dude, I can't believe I'm going on a double date with you and my little sister." He shook his head and laughed.

Conrad didn't say anything.

I could already feel the night slipping away from me.

The prom was a joint senior and junior prom. That was the way our school did it. In a way it was nice, because you got to go to prom twice. The seniors got to vote on the theme, and this year, the theme was Old Hollywood. It was at the Water Club, and there was a red carpet and "paparazzi."

The prom committee had ordered one of those kits, those prom packages. It cost a ton of money; they'd fundraised all spring. There were all of these old movie posters on the walls, and a big blinking Hollywood sign. The dance floor was supposed to look like a movie set, with lights and a fake camera on a tripod. There was even a director's chair off to the side.

We sat at a table with Taylor and Davis. With her four-and-a-half-inch stilettos, they were the same height.

Conrad hugged Taylor hello, but he didn't make much of an effort to talk to her or to Davis. He was uncomfortable in his suit, just sitting there. When Davis opened up his jacket and showed off his silver flask to Conrad, I cringed. Maybe Conrad *was* too old for all this.

Then I saw Cory Wheeler out on the dance floor, in the center of a circle of people, including my brother and Claire. He was break dancing.

I leaned in close to Conrad and whispered, "That's Cory."

"Who's Cory?" he said.

I couldn't believe he didn't remember. I just couldn't believe it. I stared at him for a second, searching his face, and then I moved away from him. "Nobody," I said.

After we'd been sitting there a few minutes, Taylor grabbed my hand and announced we were going to the bathroom. I was actually relieved.

In the bathroom, she reapplied her lip gloss and whispered to me, "Davis and I are going to his brother's dorm room after the after-prom."

"For what?" I said, rummaging around my little purse for my own lip gloss.

She handed me hers. "For, you know. To be *alone*." Taylor widened her eyes for emphasis.

"Really? Wow," I said slowly. "I didn't know you liked him that much."

"Well, you've been really busy with all your Conrad drama. Which, by the way, he looks hot, but why is he being so lame? Did you guys have a fight?"

"No . . ." I couldn't look her in the eyes, so I just kept applying lip gloss.

"Belly, don't take his shit. This is your prom night. I mean, he's your boyfriend, right?" She fluffed out her hair, posing in the mirror and pouting her lips. "At least make him dance with you."

When we got back to the table, Conrad and Davis were talking about the NCAA tournament, and I relaxed a little. Davis was a UConn fan, and Conrad liked UNC. Mr. Fisher's best friend had been a walk-on for the team, and Conrad and Jeremiah were both huge fans. Conrad could talk about Carolina basketball forever.

A slow song came on then, and Taylor took Davis by the hand and they headed out to the dance floor. I watched them dance, her head on his shoulder, his hands on her hips. Pretty soon, Taylor wouldn't be a virgin anymore. She always said she'd be first.

"Are you thirsty?" Conrad asked me.

"No," I said. "Do you want to dance?"

He hesitated. "Do we have to?"

I tried to smile. "Come on, you're the one who supposedly taught me how to slow dance."

Conrad stood up and offered me his hand. "So let's dance."

I gave him my hand and followed him to the middle of the dance floor. We slow danced, and I was glad the music was loud so he couldn't hear my heart beating.

"I'm glad you came," I said, looking up at him.

"What?" he asked.

Louder, I said, "I said, I'm glad you came."

"Me too." His voice sounded odd; I remember that, the way his voice caught.

Even though he was standing right in front of me, his hands around my waist, mine around his neck, he had never felt so far away.

After, we sat back down at our table. He said, "Do you want to go somewhere?"

"Well, the after-prom doesn't start till midnight," I said, fiddling with my pearl necklace. I wound it around my fingers. I couldn't look at him.

Conrad said, "No, I mean just you and me. Somewhere we can talk."

All of a sudden, I felt dizzy. If Conrad wanted to go somewhere where we could be alone, where we could talk, it meant he wanted to break up with me. I knew it.

"Let's not go anywhere, let's just stay here for a while," I said, and I tried hard not to sound desperate.

"All right," he said.

So we sat there, watching everyone around us dance, their faces shiny, makeup running. I pulled the flower out of my hair and put it in my purse.

When we had been quiet awhile, I said, "Did your mom make you come?" It broke my heart to ask, but I had to know.

"No," he said, but he waited too late to answer.

In the parking lot, it had started to drizzle. My hair, my hair that I had spent the whole afternoon curling, was already falling flat. We were walking to the car when Conrad said, "My head is killing me."

I stopped walking. "Do you want me to go back inside and see if anybody has an aspirin?"

"No, that's okay. You know what, I might head back to school. I have that exam on Monday and everything. Would it be all right if I didn't go to the after-prom? I could still drop you off." He didn't meet my eyes when he spoke.

"I thought you were spending the night."

Conrad fumbled with his car keys and mumbled, "I know, but I'm thinking now that I should get back. . . ." His voice trailed off.

"But I don't want you to leave," I said, and I hated the way I sounded like I was begging.

He jammed his hands inside his pants pockets. "I'm sorry," he said.

We stood there in the parking lot, and I thought, *If we get inside his car, it's all over. He'll drop me off and then he'll drive back to school and he'll never come back. And that'll be it.*

"What happened?" I asked him, and I could feel the panic rising up in my chest. "Did I do something wrong?"

He looked away. "No. It's not you. It has nothing to do with you."

I grabbed his arm, and he flinched. "Will you please just talk to me? Will you tell me what's going on?"

Conrad didn't say anything. He was wishing he was already in his car, driving away. From me. I wanted to hit him.

I said, "Okay, fine, then. If you won't say it, I will."

"If I won't say what?"

"That we're over. That, whatever this is, it's over. I mean, it is, right?" I was crying, and my nose was running, and it was all mixed up in the rain. I wiped my face with the back of my arm.

He hesitated. I saw him hesitate, weigh his words. "Belly—"

"Don't," I said, backing away from him. "Just don't. Don't say anything to me."

"Just wait a minute," he said. "Don't leave it like this."

"You're the one leaving it like this," I said. I started to walk away, as fast as my feet could go in those stupid heels.

"Wait!" he yelled.

I didn't turn around, I walked faster. Then I heard him slam his fist on the hood of his car. I almost stopped.

Maybe I would have if he'd followed me. But he didn't. He got in his car and he left, just like he said he would.

The next morning, Steven came to my room and sat at my desk. He'd just gotten home. He was still wearing his tux. "I'm asleep," I told him, rolling over.

"No, you're not." He paused. "Conrad's not worth it, okay?"

I knew what it cost him to say that to me, and I loved him for it. Steven was Conrad's number one fan; he always had been. When Steven got up and left, I repeated it to myself. *He's not worth it.*

When I came downstairs the next day around lunch-time, my mother said, "Are you all right?"

I sat down at the kitchen table and put my head down. The wood felt cool and smooth against my cheek. I looked up at her and said, "So I guess Steven blabbed."

Carefully, she said, "Not exactly. I did ask him why Conrad didn't stay the night like we planned."

"We broke up," I said. In a way, it was exciting to hear it said out loud, because if we were broken up, that meant that at one point, we had been together. We were real.

My mother sat down across from me. She sighed. "I was afraid this was going to happen."

"What do you mean?"

"I mean, it's more complicated than just you and Conrad. There are more people involved than just the two of you."

I wanted to scream at her, to tell her how insensitive, how cruel she was, and couldn't she see my heart was literally breaking? But when I looked up at her face, I bit back the words and swallowed them down. She was right. There was more to worry about than just my stupid heart. There was Susannah to think of. She was going to be so disappointed. I hated to disappoint her.

"Don't worry about Beck," my mother told me, her voice gentle. "I'll tell her. You want me to fix you something to eat?"

I said yes.

Later, in my room, alone again, I told myself it was better this way. That he'd been wanting to end things all along, so it was better that I said it first. I didn't believe a word of it. If he'd called and asked for me back, if he'd showed up at the house with flowers or a stereo on his shoulders playing our song—did we even have a song? I didn't know, but if he'd made even the tiniest gesture, I'd have taken him back, gladly. But Conrad didn't call.

When I found out Susannah was worse, that she wasn't going to get any better, I called, once. He didn't pick up, and I didn't leave a message. If he had picked up, if he'd called me back, I don't know what I would have said.

And that was it. We were over.

chapter *thirteen*
JEREMIAH

When my mom found out Conrad was taking Belly to prom, she freaked out. She was insanely happy. You'd have thought they were getting married or something. I hadn't seen her happy like that in a long time, and part of me was glad that he could give her that. But mostly I was just jealous. My mom kept calling him at school, reminding him of things like to make sure he rented his tux in time. She said maybe he could borrow mine, and I said I doubted it would fit. She left it at that, which I was relieved about. I ended up going to some girl from Collegiate's prom that night so he couldn't have worn it anyway. The point is, even if he could have, I wouldn't have wanted him to.

She made him promise that he'd be sweet to her, the perfect gentleman. She said, "Make it a night she'll always remember."

When I got home the afternoon after prom, Conrad's car was in the driveway, which was weird. I'd thought he was staying at Laurel's house and then going straight back to school. I stopped by his room, but he was asleep, and pretty soon after, I passed out too.

That night we ordered Chinese food that Mom said she was in the mood for, but when it came, she didn't eat any.

We ate in the TV room, on the couch, something we never did before she got sick. "So?" she asked, looking at Conrad all eagerly. It was the most energetic I'd seen her all day.

He was shoving a spring roll down his throat, like he was in some big hurry. And he'd brought all this laundry home with him, like he expected Mom to do it. "So what?" he asked.

"So you made me wait all day to hear about the prom! I want to know everything!"

"'Oh, that,'" he said. He had this embarrassed look on his face, and I knew he didn't want to talk about it. I was sure he'd done something to screw it up.

"'Oh, that,'" my mom teased. "Come on, Connie, give me some details. How did she look in her dress? Did you dance? I want to hear everything. I'm still waiting on Laurel to email me the pictures."

"It was okay," Conrad said.

"That's it?" I said. I was annoyed with him that night,

with everything about him. He'd gotten to take Belly to her prom and he acted like it was some big chore. If it had been me, I would have done it right.

Conrad ignored me. "She looked really pretty. She wore a purple dress."

My mom nodded, smiling. "I know exactly the one. How'd the corsage look?"

He shifted in his seat. "It looked nice."

"Did you end up getting the kind you pin on or the kind you wear on your wrist?"

"The kind you pin on," he said.

"And did you dance?"

"Yeah, a lot," he said. "We danced, like, every song."

"What was the theme?"

"I don't remember," Conrad said, and when my mother looked disappointed he added, "I think it was A Night on the Continent. It was, like, a tour of Europe. They had a big Eiffel Tower with Christmas tree lights on it, and a London Bridge you could walk across. And a Leaning Tower of Pisa."

I looked over at him. A Night on the Continent was our school's prom theme last year; I know because I was there.

But I guess my mother didn't remember, because she said, "Oh, that sounds so nice. I wish I could've been at Laurel's house to help Belly get ready. I'm gonna call Laure tonight and bug her to send me those pictures.

When do you think you'll get the professional pictures back? I want to get them framed."

"I'm not sure," he said.

"Ask Belly, will you?" She set her plate down on the coffee table and leaned back against the couch cushions. She looked exhausted all of a sudden.

"I will," he said.

"I think I'm going to bed now," she said. "Jere, will you get all this cleaned up?"

"Sure, Mom," I said, helping her to her feet.

She kissed us both on the cheek and went to her bedroom. We'd moved the study upstairs and put her bedroom downstairs so she didn't have to go up and down the stairs.

When she was gone, I said, sarcastically, "So you guys danced all night, huh?"

"Just leave it," Conrad said, leaning his head back against the couch.

"Did you even go to the prom? Or did you lie to Mom about that, too?"

He glared at me. "Yeah, I went."

"Well, somehow I doubt you guys danced all night," I said. I felt like a jerk but I just couldn't let it go.

"Why do you have to be such a dick? What do you care about the prom?"

I shrugged. "I just hope you didn't ruin it for her. What are you even doing here, anyway?"

I expected him to get pissed, in fact I think I hoped he would. But all he said was, "We can't all be Mr. Prom King." He started closing the takeout boxes. "Are you done eating?" he asked.

"Yeah, I'm done," I said.

chapter *fourteen*

When we drove up to campus, there were people milling around outside on the lawn. Girls were laying out in shorts and bikini tops, and a group of boys were playing Ultimate Frisbee. We found parking right in front of Conrad's dorm and then we slipped inside the building when a girl stepped out with a laundry basket full of clothes. I felt so incredibly young, and also lost—I'd never been there before. It was different than I'd pictured it. Louder. Busier.

Jeremiah knew the way and I had to hurry to keep up. He took the stairs two at a time and at the third floor, we stopped. I followed him down a brightly lit hallway. On the wall by the elevator there was a bulletin board with a poster that read, LET'S TALK ABOUT SEX, BABY. There were STD pamphlets and a breast exam how-to, and neon condoms were stapled around artfully. "Take one," some-one had written in highlighter. "Or three."

Conrad's door had his name on it, and underneath it, the name "Eric Trusky."

His roommate was a stocky, muscular guy with reddish brown hair, and he opened the door wearing gym shorts and a T-shirt. "What's up?" he asked us, his eyes falling on me. He reminded me of a wolf.

Instead of feeling flattered by a college guy check-ing me out, I just felt grossed out. I wanted to hide behind Jeremiah the way I used to hide behind my mother's skirt when I was five and really shy. I had to remind myself I was sixteen, almost seventeen. Too old to be nervous around a guy named Eric Trusky. Even if Conrad did tell me that Eric was always forwarding him freaky porno videos and stayed on his computer pretty much all day. Except for when he watched his soaps from two to four.

Jeremiah cleared his throat. "I'm Conrad's brother, and this is—our friend," he said. "Do you know where he is?"

Eric opened the door and let us in. "Dude, I have no idea. He just took off. Did Ari call you?"

"Who's Ari?" I asked Jeremiah.

"The RA," he said.

"Ari the RA," I repeated, and the corners of Jeremiah's mouth turned up.

"Who are you?" Eric asked me.

"Belly." I watched him, waiting for a glimmer of recognition, something that let me know that Conrad talked about me, had at least mentioned me. But of course there was nothing.

"Belly, huh? That's cute. I'm Eric," he said, leaning against the wall.

"Um, hi," I said.

"So—Conrad didn't say anything to you before he left?" Jeremiah interjected.

"He barely talks, period. He's like an android." Then he grinned at me. "Well, he talks to pretty girls."

I felt sick inside. What pretty girls? Jeremiah exhaled loudly and clasped his hands behind his head. Then he took out his phone and looked at it, as if there might be some answer there.

I sat down on Conrad's bed—navy sheets and navy comforter. It was unmade. Conrad always made his bed at the summer house. Hotel corners and everything.

So this was where he'd been living. This was his life now.

He didn't have a lot of things in his dorm room. No TV, no stereo, no pictures hanging up. Certainly none of me, but none even of Susannah or his dad. Just his computer, his clothes, some shoes, books.

"I was actually about to take off, dudes. Going to my parents' country house. Will you guys just make sure the door is closed when you leave? And when you find C, tell him he owes me twenty bucks for the pizza."

"No worries, man. I'll tell him." I could tell Jeremiah didn't like Eric, the way his lips almost but didn't quite form a smile when he said it. He sat down at Conrad's desk, surveying the room.

Someone knocked on the door and Eric ambled over to open it. It was a girl, wearing a long-sleeved shirt and leggings and sunglasses on the top of her head. "Have you seen my sweater?" she asked him. She peered around him like she was looking for something. Someone.

Did they date, I wondered? That was my first thought. My second thought was, *I'm prettier than her.* I was ashamed of myself for thinking it, but I couldn't help it. The truth was, it didn't matter who was prettier, her or me. He didn't want me anyway.

Jeremiah jumped up. "Are you a friend of Con's? Do you know where he went?"

She eyed us curiously. I could tell she thought Jeremiah was cute, the way she tucked her hair behind her ears and took her sunglasses off. "Um, yeah. Hi. I'm Sophie. Who are you?"

"His brother." Jeremiah walked over and shook her hand. Even though he was stressed out, he took the time to check her out and give her one of his trademark smiles, which she lapped right up.

"Oh, wow. You guys don't even look alike?" Sophie was one of those people who ended her sentences with a question mark. I could already tell that if I knew her, I would hate her.

"Yeah, we get that a lot," Jeremiah said. "Did Con say anything to you, Sophie?"

She liked the way he called her by her name. She said, "I think he said he was going to the beach, to surf or something? He's so crazy."

Jeremiah looked at me. The beach. He was at the summer house.

When Jeremiah called his dad, I sat on the edge of Conrad's bed and pretended not to listen. He told Mr. Fisher that everything was fine, that Conrad was safe in Cousins. He did not mention that I was with him.

He said, "Dad, I'll go get him, it's no big deal."

Mr. Fisher said something on his end, and Jeremiah said, "But Dad—" Then he looked over at me, and mouthed, *Be right back*.

He headed into the hallway and shut the door behind him.

After he was gone, I lay back onto Conrad's bed and stared up at the ceiling. So this was where he slept every night. I'd known him all my life, but in some ways, he was still a mystery to me. A puzzle.

I got out of bed and went over to his desk. Gingerly, I opened the drawer and found a box of pens, some books, paper. Conrad was always careful with his things. I told myself I wasn't *spying*. I was looking for proof. I was Belly Conklin, Girl Detective.

I found it in the second drawer. A robin's egg blue Tiffany box stuffed way in the back. Even as I was opening it I knew it was wrong, but I couldn't help myself. It was a little jewelry box, and there was a necklace inside, a pendant. I pulled it out and let it dangle. At first I thought it was a figure eight, and that maybe he was dating some girl who ice skated—and I decided I hated her, too. And then I took a closer look, and laid it horizontal in the palm of my hand. It wasn't an eight.

It was infinity.

Which was when I knew. It wasn't for some girl who ice skated or for Sophie down the hall. It was for me. He'd bought it for me. Here was my proof. Proof that he really did care.

Conrad was good at math. Well, he was good at everything, but he was really good at math.

A few weeks after we started talking on the phone, when it had become more routine but no less thrilling, I told him all about how much I hated trig and how badly I was doing in it already. Right away I felt guilty for bringing it up—there I was complaining about math when Susannah had cancer. My problems were so petty and juvenile, so *high school* compared to what Conrad was going through.

"Sorry," I'd said.

"For what?"

"For talking about my crappy trig grade when . . ." My voice trailed off. "When your mom's sick."

"Don't apologize. You can say whatever you want to me." He paused. "And Belly, my mom is getting better. She put on five pounds this month."

The hopefulness in his voice, it made me feel so tender toward him I could have cried. I said, "Yeah, I heard that from my mom yesterday. That's really good news."

"So, okay then. So has your teacher taught you SOH-CAH-TOA yet?"

From then on, Conrad started helping me, all over the phone. At first I didn't really pay attention, I just liked listening to his voice, listening to him explain things. But then he'd quiz me, and I hated to disappoint him. So began our tutoring sessions. The way my mother smirked at me when the phone rang at night, I knew she thought we were having some kind of romance, and I didn't correct her. It was easier that way. And it made me feel good, people thinking we were a couple. I'll admit it. I let them think it. I wanted them to. I knew that it wasn't true, not yet, but it felt like it could be. One day. In the meantime, I had my own private math tutor and I really was starting to get the hang of trig. Conrad had a way of making impossible things make sense, and I never loved him more than during those school nights he spent with me on the phone, going over the same problems over and over, until finally, I understood too.

Jeremiah came back into the room, and I closed my fist around the necklace before he could see it.

"So what's up?" I asked him. "Is your dad mad? What did he say?"

"He wanted to go to Cousins himself, but I told him I'd do it. There's no way Conrad would listen to my dad right now. If my dad came, it would only piss him off more." Jeremiah sat down on the bed. "So I guess we're going to Cousins this summer after all."

As soon as he said it, it became real. In my head, I mean. Seeing Conrad wasn't some faraway pretend thing; it was happening. Just like that I forgot all about my plans to save Conrad and I blurted out, "Maybe you should just drop me off on the way."

Jeremiah stared at me. "Are you serious? I can't deal with this by myself. You don't know how bad it's been. Ever since my mom got sick again, Conrad's been in freaking self-destruct mode. He doesn't give a shit about anything." Jeremiah stopped talking and then said, "But I know he still cares what you think about him."

I licked my lips; they felt very dry all of a sudden. "I'm not so sure about that."

"Well, I am. I know my brother. Will you please just come with me?"

When I thought about the last thing I'd said to Conrad, shame took over and it burned me up inside.

You don't say those kinds of things to a person whose mother just died. You just don't. How could I face him? I just couldn't.

Then Jeremiah said, "I'll get you back in time for your boat party, if that's what you're so worried about."

It was such an un-Jeremiah-like thing to say that it took me right out of my shame spiral and I glared at him. "You think I care about a stupid Fourth of July boat party?"

He gave me a look. "You do love fireworks."

"Shut up," I said, and he grinned. "All right," I said. "You win. I'll come."

"All right, then." He stood up. "I'm gonna go take a leak before we go. Oh, and Belly?"

"Yeah?"

Jeremiah smirked at me. "I knew you were gonna give in. You never had a chance."

I threw a pillow at him and he dodged it and did a little victory lap to the door. "Hurry up and pee, you jerk."

When he was gone, I put the necklace on, underneath my tank top. It had left a little infinity indentation in my hand, I'd been holding on to it so hard.

Why did I do it? Why did I put it on? Why didn't I just put it in my pocket, or leave it in the box? I can't even explain it. All I knew was, I just really, really wanted to wear it. It felt like it belonged to me.

chapter *fifteen*

Before we headed down to the car I grabbed Conrad's textbooks and notebooks and his laptop and stuffed as much as I could into the North Face backpack I'd found in his closet. "This way he'll be able to study for those midterms on Monday," I said, handing Jeremiah the laptop.

He winked and said, "I like the way you think, Belly Conklin."

On the way out, we stopped by Ari the RA's room. His door was open and he was sitting at his desk. Jeremiah popped his head in and said, "Hey, Ari. I'm Conrad's brother, Jeremiah. We found Conrad. Thanks for the heads-up, man."

Ari beamed at him. "No problem." Jeremiah made friends wherever he went. Everyone wanted to be Jeremiah Fisher's friend.

Then we were on our way. Headed straight to Cousins, full stop. We drove with the windows down, the radio up.

We didn't talk much, but this time I didn't mind. I think we were both too busy thinking. Me, I was thinking about the last time I headed down this road. Only, it hadn't been with Jeremiah. It had been with Conrad.

chapter *sixteen*

It was, without a doubt, one of the best nights of my life. Right up there with New Year's Eve at Disney World. My parents were still married and I was nine. We watched fireworks rocket right over Cinderella's palace, and Steven didn't even complain.

When he called, I didn't recognize his voice, partly because I wasn't expecting it and partly because I was still half-asleep. He said, "I'm in my car on my way to your house. Can I see you?"

It was twelve thirty in the morning. Boston was five and a half hours away. He had driven all night. He wanted to see me.

I told him to park down the street and I would meet him on the corner, after my mother had gone to bed. He said he'd wait.

I turned the lights off and waited by the window, watching for the taillights. As soon as I saw his car, I wanted to run outside, but I had to wait. I could hear my mother rustling around in her room, and I knew she would read in bed for at least half an hour before she fell asleep. It felt like torture, knowing he was out there waiting for me, not being able to go to him. It was a crazy idea, because it was winter, and it would be freezing cold in Cousins. But when he suggested it, it felt crazy in a good way.

In the dark I put on my scarf and hat that Granna knit me for Christmas. Then I shut my bedroom door and tiptoed down the hallway to my mother's room, pressing my ear against the door. The light was off and I could hear her snoring softly. Steven wasn't even home yet, which was lucky for me, because he's a light sleeper just like our dad.

My mother was finally asleep; the house was still and silent. Our Christmas tree was still up. We kept the lights on all night because it made it still feel like Christmas, like any minute, Santa could show up with gifts. I didn't bother leaving her a note. I would call her in the morning, when she woke up and wondered where I was.

I crept down the stairs, careful on the creaky step in the middle, but once I was out of the house, I flew down the front steps, across the frosty lawn. It crunched along the bottoms of my sneakers. I forgot to put on my coat. I remembered the scarf and hat, but no coat.

His car was on the corner, right where it was supposed to be. The car was dark, no lights, and I opened the passenger side door like I'd done it a million times before.

I poked my head inside, but I didn't go in, not yet. I wanted to look at him first. It was winter, and he was wearing a gray fleece. His cheeks were pink from the cold, his tan had faded, but he still looked the same. "Hey," I said, and then I climbed inside.

"You're not wearing a coat," he said.

"It's not that cold," I said, even though it was, even though I was shivering as I said it.

"Here," he said, shrugging out of his fleece and handing it to me.

I put it on. It was warm, and it didn't smell like cigarettes. It just smelled like him. So Conrad quit smoking after all. The thought made me smile.

He started the engine.

I said, "I can't believe you're really here."

He sounded almost shy when he said, "Me neither." And then he hesitated. "Are you still coming with me?"

I couldn't believe he even had to ask. I would go anywhere. "Yes," I told him. It felt like nothing else existed outside of that word, that moment. There was just us. Everything that had happened that summer, and every summer before it, had all led up to this. To now.

Sitting next to him in the passenger seat felt like an impossible gift. It felt like the best Christmas gift of my life. Because he was smiling at me, and he wasn't somber, or solemn, or sad, or any of the other *s*-words I had come to associate with Conrad. He was light, he was ebullient, he was all the best parts of himself.

"I think I'm going to be a doctor," he told me, looking at me sideways.

"Really? Wow."

"Medicine is pretty amazing. For a while, I thought I would want to go into the research end of it, but now I think I'd rather be working with actual people."

I hesitated, and then said, "Because of your mom?"

He nodded. "She's getting better, you know. Medicine is making that possible. She's responding really well to her new treatment. Did your mom tell you?"

"Yeah, she did," I said. Even though she had done no such thing. She probably just didn't want to get my hopes up. She probably didn't want to get her own hopes up. My mother was like that. She didn't allow herself to get excited until she knew it was a sure thing. Not me. Already I felt lighter, happier. Susannah was getting better. I was with Conrad. Everything was happening the way it was supposed to.

I leaned over and squeezed his arm. "It's the best news ever," I said, and I meant it.

He smiled at me, and it was written all over his face: hope.

When we got to the house, it was freezing cold. We cranked the heat up and Conrad started a fire. I watched him squat and tear up pieces of paper and poke at the log gently. I bet he'd been gentle with his dog, Boogie. I bet he used to let Boogie sleep in the bed with him. The thought of beds and sleep suddenly made me nervous. But I shouldn't have been, because after he lit the fire, Conrad sat on the La-Z-Boy and not on the couch next to me. The thought suddenly occurred to me: He was nervous too. Conrad, who was never nervous. Never.

"Why are you sitting all the way over there?" I asked him, and I could hear my heart pounding behind my ears. I couldn't believe I'd been brave enough to actually say what I was thinking.

Conrad looked surprised too, and he came over and sat next to me. I inched closer to him. I wanted him to put his arms around me. I wanted to do all the things I'd only seen on TV and heard Taylor talk about. Well, maybe not all, but some.

In a low voice, Conrad said, "I don't want you to be scared."

I whispered, "I'm not," even though I was. Not scared of him, but scared of everything I felt. Sometimes it was too much. What I felt for him was bigger than the world, than anything.

"Good," he breathed, and then he was kissing me.

He kissed me long and slow and even though we'd kissed once before, I never thought it could be like this. He took his time; he ran his hand along the bottom of my hair, the way you do when you walk past hanging wind chimes.

Kissing him, being with him like that . . . it was cool lemonade with a long straw, sweet and measured and pleasurable in a way that felt infinite. The thought crossed my mind that I never wanted him to stop kissing me. *I could do this forever*, I thought.

We kissed on the couch like that for what could have been hours or minutes. All we did that night was kiss. He was careful, the way he touched me, like I was a Christmas ornament he was afraid of breaking.

Once, he whispered, "Are you okay?"

Once, I put my hand up to his chest and I could feel his heart beating as fast as mine. I snuck a peek at him, and for some reason, it delighted me to see his eyes closed. His lashes were longer than mine.

He fell asleep first. I'd heard something about how you weren't supposed to sleep with a fire still burning, so I waited for it to die down. I watched Conrad sleep for a while. He looked like a little boy, the way his hair fell on his forehead and his eyelashes hit his cheek. I didn't remember him ever looking that young. When I was sure he was asleep, I leaned in, I whispered, "Conrad. There's only you. For me, there's only ever been you."

My mother freaked out when I wasn't home that morning. I missed two calls from her because I was asleep. When she called the third time, furious, I said, "Didn't you get my note?"

Then I remembered I hadn't left one.

She practically growled. "No, I did not see any note. Don't you ever leave in the middle of the night without telling me again, Belly."

"Even if I'm just going for a midnight stroll?" I joked. Me making my mother laugh was a sure thing. I would tell a joke and her anger would evaporate away. I started to sing her favorite Patsy Cline song. "I go out walkin', after midnight, out in the moonlight—"

"Not funny. Where are you?" Her voice was tight, clipped.

I hesitated. There was nothing my mother hated worse than a liar. She'd find out anyway. She was like a psychic. "Um. Cousins?"

I heard her take a breath. "With who?"

I looked over at him. He was listening intently. I wished he wasn't. "Conrad," I said, lowering my voice.

Her reaction surprised me. I heard her breathe again, but this time it was a little sigh, like a sigh of relief. "You're with Conrad?"

"Yes."

"How is he?" It was a strange question, what with her in the middle of being mad at me.

I smiled at him and fanned my face like I was relieved. He winked at me. "Great," I said, relaxing.

"Good. Good," she said, but it was like she was talking to herself. "Belly, I want you home tonight. Are we clear?"

"Yes," I said. I was grateful. I thought she'd demand that we leave right away.

"Tell Conrad to drive carefully." She paused. "And Belly?"

"Yes, Laurel?" She always smiled when I called her by her first name.

"Have fun. This will be your last fun day for a long, long time."

I groaned. "Am I grounded?" Being grounded was a novelty; my mother had never grounded me before, but I guess I had never given her a reason to.

"That is a very stupid question."

Now that she wasn't mad anymore, I couldn't resist. "I thought you said there were no stupid questions?"

She hung up the phone. But I knew I had made her smile.

I closed my phone and faced Conrad. "What do we do now?"

"Whatever we want."

"I want to go on the beach."

So that's what we did. We got bundled up and we ran on the beach in rain boots we found in the mud room.

I wore Susannah's, and they were two sizes too big, and I kept slipping in the sand. I fell on my butt twice. I was laughing the whole time, but I could barely hear it because the wind was howling so loud. When we came back inside, I put my freezing hands on his cheeks and instead of pushing them away, he said, "Ahh, feels good."

I laughed and said, "That's because you're coldhearted."

He put my hands in his coat pockets and said in a voice so soft I wondered if I heard him right, "For everyone else, maybe. But not for you." He didn't look at me when he said it, which is how I knew he meant it.

I didn't know what to say, so instead, I got on my tiptoes and kissed him on the cheek. It was cold and smooth against my lips.

Conrad smiled briefly and then started walking away. "Are you cold?" he asked, his back to me.

"Sort of," I said. I was blushing.

"I'll build another fire," he said.

While he worked on the fire, I found an old box of Swiss Miss hot chocolate in the pantry, next to the Twinings teas and my mother's Chock full o'Nuts coffee. Susannah used to make us hot chocolate on rainy nights, when there was a chill in the air. She used milk, but of course there wasn't any, so I used water.

As I sat on the couch and stirred my cup, watching the mini marshmallows disintegrate, I could feel my heart beating, like, a million times a minute. When I was with him, I couldn't seem to catch my breath.

Conrad didn't stop moving around. He was ripping up pieces of paper, he was poking at the embers, he was squatting in front of the fireplace, shifting his weight back and forth.

"Do you want your cocoa?" I asked him.

He looked back at me. "Okay, sure."

He sat next to me on the couch and drank from the *Simpsons* mug. It had always been his favorite. "This tastes—"

"Amazing?"

"Dusty."

We looked at each other and laughed. "For your information, cocoa is my specialty. And you're welcome," I said, taking my first sip. It did taste a little dusty.

He peered at me and tipped my face up. Then he reached out and rubbed my cheek with his thumb like he was wiping away soot. "Do I have cocoa powder on my face?" I asked, suddenly paranoid.

"No," he said. "Just some dirt—oops, I mean, freckles."

I laughed and slapped him on the arm, and then he grabbed my hand and pulled me closer to him. He pushed my hair out of my eyes, and I worried he could hear the way I drew my breath in when he touched me.

It was getting darker and darker outside. Conrad sighed and said, "I'd better get you back."

I looked down at my watch. It was five o'clock. "Yeah . . . I guess we'd better go."

Neither of us moved. He reached out and wound my hair around his fingers like a spool of yarn. "I love how soft your hair is," he said.

"Thanks," I whispered. I'd never thought of my hair as anything special. It was just hair. And it was brown, and brown wasn't as special as blond or black or red. But the way he looked at it . . . at me. Like it held some kind of fascination for him, like he would never get tired of touching it.

We kissed again, but it was different than the night before. There was nothing slow or lazy about it. The way he looked at me—urgent, wanting me, needing me . . . it was like a drug. It was want-want-want. But it was me who was doing the wanting most of all.

When I pulled him closer, when I put my hands underneath his shirt and up his back, he shivered for a second. "Are my hands too cold?" I asked.

"No," he said. Then he let go of me and sat up. His face was sort of red and his hair was sticking up in the back. He said, "I don't want to rush anything."

I sat up too. "But I thought you already—" I didn't know how to finish the sentence. This was so embarrassing. I'd never done this before.

Conrad turned even redder. He said, "Yeah, I mean, I have. But you haven't."

"Oh," I said, looking down at my sock. Then I looked up. "How do you know I haven't?"

Now he looked red as a beet and he stuttered, "I just

thought you hadn't—I mean, I just assumed—"

"You thought I hadn't done anything before, right?"

"Well, yeah. I mean, no."

"You shouldn't make assumptions like that," I said.

"I'm sorry," he said. He hesitated. "So—you have then?"
I just looked at him.

When he opened his mouth to speak, I stopped him.
I said, "I haven't. Not even close."

Then I leaned forward and kissed him on the cheek.
It felt like a privilege just to be able to do that, to kiss
him whenever I wanted. "You're really sweet to me," I
whispered, and I felt so glad and grateful to be there, in
that moment.

His eyes were dark and serious when he said, "I just—
want to always know that you're okay. It's important to me."

"I am okay," I said. "I'm better than okay."

Conrad nodded. "Good," he said. He stood and gave
me his hand to help me up. "Let's get you home, then."

I didn't get home that night until after midnight. We
stopped and got dinner at a diner off the highway. I
ordered pancakes and french fries, and he paid. When I got
home, my mother was so mad. But I didn't regret it. I
never regretted it, not for one second. How do you regret
one of the best nights of your entire life? You don't. You
remember every word, every look. Even when it hurts,
you still remember.

chapter *seventeen*

We drove through town, by all the old places, the mini golf course, the crab shack, and Jeremiah drove as fast he could, whistling. I wished he would slow down, make the drive last forever. But it wouldn't, of course. We were almost there.

I reached into my bag and pulled out a little pot of lip gloss. I dabbed some gloss on my lips and yanked my fingers through my hair. It was all tangled because we'd had the windows down, and it was a mess. In my peripheral vision, I could feel Jeremiah's eyes on me. He was probably shaking his head and thinking what a dumb girl I was. I wanted to tell him, I know, I am a dumb girl. I'm no better than Taylor. But I couldn't just walk in and face Conrad with ratty hair.

When I saw his car in the driveway, I could feel my

heart constrict. He was in there. Like a shot, Jeremiah was out of the car and bounding toward the house. He took the stairs two at a time, and I trailed after him.

It was strange; the house still smelled the same. For some reason, I hadn't been expecting that. Maybe with Susannah gone, I'd thought it would all feel different. But it didn't. I almost expected to see her floating around in one of her housedresses, waiting for us in the kitchen.

Conrad actually had the nerve to look annoyed when he saw us. He'd just come in from surfing; his hair was wet and he still had his suit on. I felt dazed—even though it had only been two months, it was like seeing a ghost. The ghost of first love past. His eyes flickered on me for about one second before rounding on Jeremiah. "What the hell are you doing here?" he asked him.

"I'm here to pick you up and take you back to school," Jeremiah said, and I could tell he was working hard to sound relaxed, laid-back. "You really messed up, man. Dad's going out of his mind."

Conrad waved him off. "Tell him to go screw himself. I'm staying."

"Con, you missed two classes and you've got midterms on Monday. You can't just bail. They'll kick you out of summer school."

"That's my problem. And what's she doing here?" He didn't look at me when he said it, and it was like he'd stabbed me in the chest.

I started to back away from them, toward the glass sliding doors. It was hard to breathe.

"I brought her with me to help," Jeremiah said. He looked over at me and then took a breath. "Look, we've got all your books and everything. You can study tonight and tomorrow and then we can head back to school."

"Screw it. I don't care," Conrad said, walking over to the sofa. He peeled off the top of his wetsuit. His shoulders were already getting tan. He sat down on the sofa, even though he was still wet.

"What's your problem?" Jeremiah asked him, his voice just barely even.

"Right now, this is my problem. You and her. Here." For the first time since we'd arrived, Conrad looked me in the eyes. "Why do you want to help me? Why are you even here?"

I opened my mouth to speak, but nothing came out. Just like always, he could devastate me with a look, a word.

Patiently, he waited for me to say something, and when I didn't, he did.

"I thought you never wanted to see me again. You hate me, remember?" His tone was sarcastic, belittling.

"I don't hate you," I said, and then I ran away. I pushed the sliding door open and stepped outside to the porch. I closed the door behind me and ran down the stairs, down to the beach.

I just needed to be on the beach. The beach would make me feel better. Nothing, nothing felt better than the way sand felt beneath my feet. It was both solid and shifting, constant and ever-changing. It was summer.

I sat in the sand and I watched the waves run to shore and then spread out thin like white icing on a cookie. It had been a mistake to come here. Nothing I could say or do would erase the past. The way he'd said "her," with such disdain. He didn't even call me by my name.

After a while, I headed back to the house. Jeremiah was in the kitchen by himself. Conrad was nowhere in sight.

"Well, that went well," he said.

"I never should have come."

Jeremiah ignored me. "Ten to one the only thing he has in the fridge is beer," he said. "Any takers?"

He was trying to make me laugh, but I wouldn't. I couldn't. "Only an idiot would take that bet." I bit my lip. I really, really didn't want to cry.

"Don't let him get to you," Jeremiah said. He pulled on my ponytail and wound it around his wrist like a snake.

"I can't help it." The way he'd looked at me—like I meant nothing to him, less than nothing.

"He's an idiot; he doesn't mean anything he says," Jeremiah said. He nudged me. "Are you sorry you came?"

"Yes."

Jeremiah smiled at me crookedly. "Well, I'm not. I'm glad you came. I'm glad I'm not dealing with his BS on my own."

Because he was trying, I tried too. I opened up the fridge like I was one of those women from *The Price Is Right*, the women who wore evening gowns and jeweled heels.

"Ta-da," I said. He was right, the only thing inside were two cases of Icehouse. Susannah would've flipped if she could have seen what had become of her Sub-Zero fridge. "What are we going to do?" I asked him.

He looked out the window, to the beach. "We're probably going to have to stay here tonight. I'll work on him; he'll come. I just need some time." He paused. "So how about this. Why don't you go grab some food for dinner, and I'll stay here and talk to Con."

I knew Jeremiah was trying to get rid of me, and I was glad. I needed to get out of that house, away from Conrad. "Clam rolls for dinner?" I asked him.

Jeremiah nodded and I could tell he was relieved. "Sounds good. Whatever you want." He started to pull out his wallet, but I stopped him.

"It's okay."

He shook his head. "I don't want you to use your money," he said, handing me two creased twenties and his keys. "You already came all this way to help."

"I wanted to."

"Because you're a good person and you wanted to help Con," he said.

"I wanted to help you, too," I told him. "I meant, I still do. You shouldn't have to deal with this on your own."

For one brief moment, he didn't look like himself. He looked like his father. "Who else will?" And then he smiled at me, and he was Jeremiah again. Susannah's boy, sunshine and smiles. Her little angel.

I learned to drive stick on Jeremiah's car. It felt good to be in the driver's seat again. Instead of turning on the AC, I rolled down the windows and let the salty air in. I drove into town slowly, and I parked the car by the old Baptist church.

There were kids running around in bathing suits and shorts, and also parents in khaki, and golden retrievers without leashes. It was probably the first weekend since school let out, for most of them. There was just that feeling in the air. I smiled when I saw a boy trailing after two older girls, probably his sisters. "Wait up," he yelled, his flip flops slapping along the pavement. They just walked faster, not looking back.

My first stop was the general store. I used to spend hours in there, mulling over the penny candy. Each choice seemed vitally important. The boys would dump candy in haphazardly, a scoop of this, a handful of that. But I was careful, ten big Swedish Fish, five malt balls, a medium-size scoop of pear Jelly Bellys. For old times' sake, I filled a bag. I put in Goobers for Jeremiah, a Clark Bar for Conrad, and even though he wasn't here, a Lemonhead for Steven. It was a candy memorial, a tribute to the Cousins of our childhood, when picking penny candy was the biggest and best part of our day.

I was standing in line waiting to pay when I heard someone say, "Belly?"

I turned around. It was Maureen O'Riley, who owned the fancy hat shop in town—Maureen's Millinery. She was older than my parents, in her late fifties, and she was friendly with my mother and Susannah. She took her hats very seriously.

We hugged, and she smelled the same, like Murphy Oil Soap.

"How's your mother? How's Susannah?" she asked me.

"My mother's fine," I told her. I moved up in line, away from Maureen.

She moved up with me. "And Susannah?"

I cleared my throat. "Her cancer came back, and she passed away."

Maureen's tan face wrinkled up in alarm. "I hadn't heard. I'm sorry to hear that. I was very fond of her. When?"

"Beginning of May," I said. It was almost my turn to pay, and then I could leave and this conversation would be over.

Then Maureen clasped my hand, and my first impulse was to snatch it away, even though I'd always liked Maureen. I just didn't want to stand in the general store, talking about Susannah being dead like it was town gossip. We were talking about Susannah here.

She must have sensed it, because she let go. She said, "I wish I'd known. Please send my condolences to the boys and your mother. And Belly, come by the store and see me sometime. We'll get you fitted for a hat. I think it's time you had one, something with a trim."

"I've never worn a hat," I said, fumbling for my wallet.

"It's time," Maureen said again. "Something to set you off. Come by, I'll take care of you. A present."

After, I walked through town slowly, stopping at the bookstore and the surf shop. I walked aimlessly, dipping my hand into the candy bag on occasion. I didn't want to run into anybody else but I was in no hurry to get back to the house. It was obvious Conrad didn't want me around. Was I making things worse? The way he'd looked at me . . . it was harder than I'd thought it was going to be, seeing him again. Being in that house again. A million times harder.

When I got back to the house with the rolls in a greasy paper bag, Jeremiah and Conrad were drinking beer out on the back deck. The sun was setting. It was going to be a beautiful sunset.

I threw the keys and the bag down on the table and

fell onto a lounge chair. "Pass me a beer," I said. It wasn't because I particularly liked beer. I didn't. It was because I wanted to be a part of them, the way having a few beers out back had brought them together in some small way. Just like the old days, all I wanted was to be included.

I expected Conrad to glare at me and tell me no, he would not be passing me any beer. When he didn't, I was surprised to feel disappointed. Jeremiah reached into the cooler and threw me an Icehouse. He winked at me. "Since when does our Belly Button drink?" he said.

"I'm almost seventeen," I reminded him. "Don't you think I'm too old for you to call me that?"

"I know how old you are," Jeremiah said.

Conrad reached into the paper bag and pulled out a sandwich. He bit into it hungrily, and I wondered if he had eaten anything all day.

"You're welcome," I told him. I couldn't help myself. He hadn't looked my way once since I got back. I wanted to make him acknowledge me.

He grunted thanks, and Jeremiah shot me a warning look. Like, *Don't piss him off just when things are good.*

Jeremiah's phone buzzed on the table, and he didn't move to pick it up. Conrad said, "I'm not leaving this house. Tell him that."

My head jerked up. What did that mean, he wasn't leaving? Like, ever? I stared hard at Conrad, but his face was as impassive as ever.

Jeremiah stood up, picked up the phone, and walked back into the house. He closed the sliding door behind him. For the first time, Conrad and I were left to ourselves. The air between us felt heavy, and I wondered if he was sorry for what he'd said earlier. I wondered if I should say something, try and fix things. But what would I say? I didn't know if there was anything I *could* say.

So I didn't try. Instead I let the moment pass and I just sighed and leaned back onto my chair. The sky was pinky gold. I had the feeling that there was nothing more beautiful than this, that this particular sunset matched the beauty of anything in this world, ten times over. I could feel all the tension of the day drifting away from me and out to sea. I wanted to memorize it all in case I didn't get to come back again. You never know the last time you'll see a place. A person.

chapter *eighteen*

We sat around watching TV for a while. Jeremiah didn't make any more moves to talk to Conrad, and no one mentioned school or Mr. Fisher. I wondered if Jeremiah was waiting to be alone with him again.

I forced myself to yawn. To no one in particular, I said, "I'm so tired."

As soon as I said it, I realized I really was. I was so tired. It felt like it had been the longest day ever. Even though all I really did was ride around in a car, I felt completely drained of energy.

"I'm going to sleep," I announced, yawning again, this time for real.

"Good night," Jeremiah said, and Conrad didn't say anything.

As soon as I got to my room, I opened my overnight

bag, and I was horrified when I saw what was inside. There was Taylor's brand-new gingham bikini, her prized platform sandals, an eyelet sundress, the cutoffs that her dad referred to as "denim underwear," a few silky tops, and instead of the big T-shirt I'd been looking forward to wearing to sleep, a pink pajama set with little red hearts. Little shorts and a matching tank top. I wanted to kill her. I'd assumed she was adding to what I'd already packed, not replacing it. The only thing she'd left of mine was the underwear.

The thought of prancing around the house in those pajamas, being seen on the way to brush my teeth in the morning, made me want to hit her. Hard. I knew that Taylor meant well. She thought she was doing me a favor. Giving up her platform sandals for the night was altruistic, for Taylor. But I was still mad.

It was just like the thing with Cory. Taylor did what she wanted to do, and she didn't care what I thought about it. She never cared what I thought about it. It wasn't just her fault though, because I let her.

After I brushed my teeth, I put on Taylor's pajamas and got into bed. I was deliberating over whether or not to read a book before I went to sleep, one of the old paperbacks on my shelf, when someone knocked on my door. I pulled the covers up to my neck and said, "Come in!"

It was Jeremiah. He closed the door behind him and sat at the foot of my bed. "Hey," he whispered.

I loosened the grip on my covers. It was only Jeremiah. "Hey. What's going on? Did you talk to him?"

"Not yet. I'm gonna ease up on him tonight and try again tomorrow. I'm just trying to lay down the groundwork first, plant some seeds." He gave me a conspiratorial look. "You know how he is."

I did. "Okay. That sounds good."

He held his hand out for a high five. "Don't worry. We've got this."

I high-fived him. "We've got this," I repeated. I could hear the doubt in my voice, but Jeremiah just smiled like it was already a done deal.

chapter *nineteen*
JEREMIAH

When Belly got up to go to bed, I knew she wanted me to stay and try to talk to Conrad about school. I knew it because when we were little kids, we used to practice ESP on each other. Belly was convinced I could read her mind and she could read mine. The truth was, I could just read Belly. Whenever she was about to tell a lie, her left eye squinted a little. Whenever she was nervous, she sucked in her cheeks before she spoke. She was an easy read, always had been.

I looked over at Conrad. "Wanna get up early and surf tomorrow?" I asked him.

"Sure," he said.

Tomorrow I would talk to him about school and how important it was to go back. Everything would work out.

We watched some more TV, and when Conrad fell asleep on the couch, I went upstairs to my room. Down the hall, Belly's light was still on. I went over and stood outside her door and knocked softly. I felt like such an idiot standing outside her doorway, knocking. When we were kids, we just ran in and out of each other's rooms without thinking. I wished it was still as simple as that.

"Come in," she said.

I walked in and sat at the edge of her bed. When I realized she was already in her pajamas, I almost turned right back around and left. I had to remind myself that I'd seen her in her pajamas a million times before, and what was the big deal? But she used to always wear a big T-shirt like the rest of us, and now she was wearing some skimpy pink top with little straps. I wondered if it was comfortable to sleep in.

chapter *twenty*
JULY 4

When I woke up the next morning, I didn't get out of bed right away. I just laid there and pretended like it was any other morning at the summer house. My sheets smelled the same; my stuffed bear, Junior Mint, was still sitting on the dresser. It was just like always. Susannah and my mother were taking a walk on the beach, and the boys were eating all the blueberry muffins and leaving me with my mother's Kashi cereal. There would be about an inch of milk left, and no juice, either. It used to infuriate me; now I smiled at the thought.

But it was all make-believe. I knew that. There was no mother, no brother, no Susannah here.

Even though I had gone to bed early the night before, I slept late. It was already almost eleven. I had slept for twelve hours. I hadn't slept that well in weeks.

I got out of bed and went to look out my window. Looking out my bedroom window at the summer house always made me feel better. I wished every window looked out at an ocean, nothing but miles and miles of sand and sea. Down the beach, Jeremiah and Conrad were bobbing on surfboards in black wetsuits. It was such a familiar sight. And just like that, I was hopeful. Maybe Jeremiah was right. Maybe Conrad would come back with us after all.

And then I would go back home, away from him and from everything he reminded me of. I would lay out at the neighborhood pool and I would hang by the snack bar with Taylor, and pretty soon the summer would go by. I would forget how it used to be.

This time really was the last time.

Before I did anything else, I called Taylor. I explained how we were all in Cousins, how we just needed to convince Conrad to go back to school and finish out summer session.

The first thing she said was, "Belly, what do you think you're doing?"

"What do you mean?"

"You know what I mean. This whole situation is retarded. You should be at home where you belong."

I sighed. No matter how many times I asked her not to say "retarded," she still did. She even had a little cousin with Down Syndrome. I think she did it on purpose because she knew it bothered me.

"What do you care if Conrad is a college dropout?" she said. "Let him be a loser if he wants."

Even though I knew no one could hear me, I lowered my voice. "He's going through a lot right now. He needs us."

"He needs his brother. Who, by the way, is hotter than him, hello! Conrad doesn't need you. He cheated on you, remember?"

I was whispering now. "He didn't cheat on me and you know it. We were already broken up. It's not like we were ever even a real couple in the first place." The last part was hard to say.

"Oh, right—he didn't cheat on you, he dumped you right after the prom. What an *amazing* guy. Gaylord."

I ignored her. "Will you please still cover for me if my mom calls?"

She sniffed. "Duh. I happen to be a loyal friend."

"Thank you. Oh, and thank you *so much* for taking all my clothes."

"You're welcome," she said all smug. "And Belly?"

"Yes?"

"Don't lose sight of the mission at hand."

"Well, Jeremiah's been working on him—"

"Not that, dummy. I'm talking about *the mission*. You have to get Conrad to want you back, and then you have to rebuff him. Brutally."

I was glad we were on the phone so she couldn't see me roll my eyes. But the thing was, she had a point. Taylor never got hurt because she was the one who was in charge. She called the shots. Boys wanted her, not the other way around. She was always quoting that line from *Pretty Woman*, the one about being a hooker. "I say who, I say when, I say who."

It wasn't that the idea didn't appeal to me. It was just that it would never work. Getting Conrad to notice me the first time around, however briefly, had been nearly impossible. It wouldn't work a second time.

After Taylor and I hung up, I called my mother. I told her that I was staying at Taylor's house again that night, that she was still too upset for me to leave. My mother agreed. "You're a good friend," she said. There was relief in her voice when she asked me to tell Taylor's parents hello.

She didn't even question the lie. I could hear it over the phone: All she wanted was to be left alone with her grief.

After, I took a shower and put on the clothes Taylor picked for me. A white camisole with flowers embroidered across the top and her famous cutoffs.

I went downstairs with my hair still wet, tugging on my shorts. The boys were back inside, sitting at the kitchen table and eating dirt bombs, the big sugary cinnamon muffins that Susannah used to get up early to buy.

"Look what I got," Jeremiah said. He pushed the white paper bag toward me.

I grabbed the bag and stuffed half a dirt bomb inside my mouth. It was still warm. "Yum," I said, my mouth full. "So . . . what's up?"

Jeremiah looked at Conrad hopefully. "Con?"

"You guys should head out soon, if you want to miss the Fourth of July traffic," Conrad said, and it killed me to see the look on Jeremiah's face.

"We're not leaving without you," Jeremiah told him.

Conrad exhaled. "Look, Jere, I appreciate you coming here. But as you can see, I'm fine. I've got everything under control."

"Like hell you do. Con, if you're not back on Monday for your exams, you're out. The only reason you're even taking summer school is those incompletes from last semester. If you don't go back, then what?"

"Don't worry about it. I'll figure things out."

"You keep saying that, but dude, you haven't figured out shit. All you've done so far is run away."

The way Conrad glared at him, I knew that Jeremiah had said the right thing. Conrad's old value system was still there, buried underneath the anger. The old Conrad would never give up.

It was my turn to say something. I took a breath and said, "So, how are you going to become a doctor without a college degree, Conrad?"

He did a double take, and then he stared at me. I stared right back. Yeah, I said it. I would say whatever I had to, even if it hurt him.

It was something I'd learned from watching Conrad in pretty much every game we'd ever played. At the first sign of weakness, you attack full force. You strike and you use every weapon in your arsenal, and you don't let up. No mercy.

"I never said I was going to be a doctor," he snapped. "You don't know what you're talking about."

"Then tell us," I said, and my heart was beating so fast.

No one spoke. For a minute, I thought he might really let us in.

And then finally, Conrad stood up. "There's nothing to tell. I'm gonna head back out there. Thanks for the dirt bombs, Jere." To me, he said, "You have sugar all over your face." And just like that, he was up and sliding the porch door open.

When he was gone, Jeremiah shouted, "Shit!"

I said, "I thought you were gonna work on him!" It came out sounding more accusing than I meant it.

"You can't push Conrad too hard, he just shuts down," Jeremiah said, crumbling up the paper bag.

"He's already shut down."

I looked over at Jeremiah and he looked so defeated. I felt like bad for snapping at him. So I reached out and touched his arm, and said, "Don't worry. We still have time. It's only Saturday, right?"

"Right," he said, but he didn't say it like he meant it.

Neither of us said anything more. Like always, it was Conrad who dictated the mood of the house, how everyone else felt. Nothing would feel right again until things were right with Conrad.

chapter *twenty-one*

The first time it hit me that day was when I was in the bathroom, washing the sugar off my face. There was no towel hanging up, so I opened the linen closet, and on the row below the beach towels, there was Susannah's big floppy hat. The one she wore every time she sat on the beach. She was careful with her skin. *Was*.

Not thinking about Susannah, consciously not thinking about her, made it easier. Because then she wasn't really *gone*. She was just off someplace else. That was what I'd been doing since she died. Not thinking about her. It was easier to do at home. But here, at the summer house, she was everywhere.

I picked her hat up, held it for a second, and then put it back on the shelf. I closed the door, and my chest hurt so bad I couldn't breathe. It was too hard. Being there, in this house, was too hard.

I ran up the stairs as fast as I could. I took off Conrad's necklace and I changed out of my clothes and into Taylor's bikini. I didn't care how stupid I looked in it. I just wanted to be in the water. I wanted to be where I didn't have to think about anything, where nothing else existed. I would swim, and float, and breathe in and out, and just be.

My old Ralph Lauren teddy bear towel was in the linen closet just like always. I put it around my shoulders like a blanket and headed outside. Jeremiah was eating an egg sandwich and swigging from a carton of milk. "Hey," he said.

"Hey. I'm going to swim." I didn't ask where Conrad was, and I didn't invite Jeremiah to join me. I needed a moment just by myself.

I pushed the sliding door open and closed it without waiting for him to answer me. I threw my towel onto a chair and swan-dived in. I didn't come up for air right away. I stayed down under; I held my breath until the very last second.

When I came up, I felt like I could breathe again, like my muscles were relaxing. I swam back and forth, back and forth. Here, nothing else existed. Here, I didn't have to think. Each time I went under, I held my breath for as long as I could.

Under water, I heard Jeremiah call my name. Reluctantly I came up to the surface, and he was crouching by the side of the pool. "I'm gonna go out for a while. Maybe I'll pick up a pizza at Nello's," he said, standing up.

I pushed my hair out of my eyes. "But you just ate a sandwich. And you had all those dirt bombs."

"I'm a growing boy. And that was an hour and a half ago."

An hour and a half ago? Had I been swimming for an hour and a half? It felt like minutes. "Oh," I said. I examined my fingers. They were totally pruned.

"Carry on," Jeremiah said, saluting me.

Kicking off the side of the pool, I said, "See ya." Then I swam as quick as I could to the other side and flip-turned, just in case he was still watching. He'd always admired my flip turns.

I stayed in the pool for another hour. When I came up for air after my last lap, I saw that Conrad was sitting in the chair where I'd left my towel. He held it out to me silently.

I climbed out of the pool. Suddenly I was shivering. I took the towel from him and wrapped it around my body. He did not look at me. "Do you still pretend you're at the Olympics?" he asked me.

I started, and then I shook my head and sat down next to him. "No," I said, and the word hung in the air. I hugged my knees to my chest. "Not anymore."

"When you swim," he started to say. I thought he wasn't going to continue, but then he said, "You wouldn't notice if the house was on fire. You're so into what you're doing, it's like you're someplace else."

He said it with grudging respect. Like he'd been watching me for a long time, like he'd been watching me for years. Which I guess he had.

I opened my mouth to respond, but he was already standing up, going back into the house. As he closed the sliding door, I called out, "That's why I like it."

chapter *twenty-two*

I was back in my room, about to change out of my bikini when my phone rang. It was Steven's ringtone, a Taylor Swift song he pretended to hate but secretly loved. For a second, I thought about not answering. But if I didn't pick up, he'd only call back until I did. He was annoying that way.

"Hello?" I said it like a question, like I didn't already know it was Steven.

"Hey," he said. "I don't know where you are, but I know you're not with Taylor."

"How do you know that?" I whispered.

"I just ran into her at the mall. She's worse than you at lying. Where the hell are you?"

I bit my upper lip and I said, "At the summer house. In Cousins."

"What?" he sort of yelled. "Why?"

"It's kind of a long story. Jeremiah needed my help with Conrad."

"So he called *you*?" My brother's voice was incredulous and also the tiniest bit jealous.

"Yeah." He was dying to ask me more, but I was banking on the fact that his pride wouldn't let him. Steven hated being left out. He was silent for a moment, and in those seconds, I knew he was wondering about all the summer house stuff we were doing without him.

At last he said, "Mom's gonna be so pissed."

"What do you care?"

"I don't care, but Mom will."

"Steven, chill out. I'll be home soon. We just have to do one last thing."

"What last thing?" It killed him that I knew something he didn't, that for once, he was the odd man out. I thought I'd take more pleasure in it, but I felt oddly sorry for him.

So instead of gloating the way I normally would, I said, "Conrad took off from summer school and we have to get him back in time for midterms on Monday."

That would be the last thing I would do for him. Get him to school. And then he'd be free, and so would I.

After Steven and I got off the phone, I heard a car pull up in front of the house. I looked out the window and there was a red Honda, a car I didn't recognize. We almost never had visitors at the summer house.

I dragged a comb through my hair and hurried down the stairs with my towel wrapped around me. I stopped when I saw Conrad open the door, and a woman walked in. She was petite, with bleached blond hair that was in a messy bun, and she wore black pants and a silk coral blouse. Her fingernails were painted to match. She had a big folder in her hand and a set of keys.

"Well, hello there," she said. She was surprised to see him, as if she was the one who was supposed to be there and he wasn't.

"Hello," Conrad said. "Can I help you?"

"You must be Conrad," she said. "We spoke on the phone. I'm Sandy Donatti, your dad's real estate agent."

Conrad said nothing.

She wagged her finger at him playfully. "You told me your dad changed his mind about the sale."

When Conrad still said nothing, she looked around and saw me standing at the bottom of the stairs. She frowned and said, "I'm just here to check on the house, make sure everything's coming along and getting packed up."

"Yeah, I sent the movers away," Conrad said casually.

"I really wish you hadn't done that," she said, her lips tight. When Conrad shrugged, she added, "I was told the house would be empty."

"You were given erroneous information. I'll be here for

the rest of the summer." He gestured at me. "That's Belly."

"Belly?" she repeated.

"Yup. She's my girlfriend."

I think I choked out loud.

Crossing his arms and leaning against the wall, he continued. "And you and my dad met how?"

Sandy Donatti flushed. "We met when he decided to put the house up for sale," she snapped.

"Well, the thing is, Sandy, it's not his house to sell. It's my mother's house, actually. Did my dad tell you that?"

"Yes."

"Then I guess he also told you she's dead."

Sandy hesitated. Her anger seemed to evaporate at the mention of dead mothers. She was so uncomfortable, she was shifting toward the door. "Yes, he did tell me that. I'm very sorry for your loss."

Conrad said, "Thank you, Sandy. That means a lot, coming from you."

Her eyes darted around the room one last time. "Well, I'm going to talk things over with your dad and then I'll be back."

"You do that. Make sure you let him know the house is off the market."

She pursed her lips and then opened her mouth to speak, but thought better of it. Conrad opened the door for her, and then she was gone.

I let out a big breath. A million thoughts were running through my head—I'm ashamed to say that *girl-friend* was pretty near the top of the list. Conrad didn't look at me when he said, "Don't tell Jeremiah about the house."

"Why not?" I asked. My mind was still lingering on the word "girlfriend."

He took so long to answer me that I was already walking back upstairs when he said, "I'll tell him about it. I just don't want him to know yet. About our dad."

I stopped walking. Without thinking I said, "What do you mean?"

"You know what I mean." Conrad looked at me, his eyes steady.

I suppose I did know. He wanted to protect Jeremiah from the fact that his dad was an asshole. But it wasn't like Jeremiah didn't already know who his dad was. It wasn't like Jeremiah was some dumb kid without a clue. He had a right to know if the house was for sale.

I guessed Conrad read all of this on my face, because he said in that mocking, careless way of his, "So can you do that for me, Belly? Can you keep a secret from your BFF Jeremiah? I know you two don't keep secrets from each other, but can you handle it just this once?"

When I glared at him, all ready to tell him what he could do with his secret, he said, "Please?" and his voice was pleading.

So I said, "All right. For now."

"Thank you," he said, and he brushed past me and headed upstairs. His bedroom door closed, and the air conditioning kicked on.

I stayed put.

It took a minute for everything to sink in. Conrad didn't just run away to surf. He didn't run away for the sake of running away. He came to save the house.

chapter *twenty-three*

Later that afternoon Jeremiah and Conrad went surfing again. I thought maybe Conrad wanted to tell him about the house, just the two of them. And maybe Jeremiah wanted to try and talk to Conrad about school again, just the two of them. That was fine by me. I was content just watching.

I watched them from the porch. I sat in a deck chair with my towel wrapped tight around me. There was something so comforting and right about coming out of the pool wet and your mom putting a towel around your shoulders, like a cape. Even without a mother there to do it for you, it was good, cozy. Achingly familiar in a way that made me wish I was still eight. Eight was before death or divorce or heartbreak. Eight was just eight. Hot dogs and peanut butter, mosquito bites and splinters, bikes and boogie boards. Tangled hair, sunburned shoulders, Judy Blume, in bed by nine thirty.

I sat there thinking those melancholy kinds of thoughts for a long while. Someone was barbecuing; I could smell charcoal burning. I wondered if it was the Rubensteins, or maybe it was the Tolers. I wondered if they were grilling burgers, or steak. I realized I was hungry.

I wandered into the kitchen but I couldn't find anything to eat. Just Conrad's beer. Taylor told me once that beer was just like bread, all carbohydrates. I figured that even though I hated the taste of it, I might as well drink it if it'd fill me up.

So I took one and walked back outside with it. I sat back down on my deck chair and popped the top off the can. It snapped very satisfyingly. It was strange to be in this house alone. Not a bad feeling, just a different one. I'd been coming to this house my whole life and I could count on one hand the number of times I'd been alone in it. I felt older now. Which I suppose I was, but I guess I didn't remember feeling old last summer.

I took a long sip of beer and I was glad Jeremiah and Conrad weren't there to see me, because I made a terrible face and I knew they'd give me crap for it.

I was taking another sip when I heard someone clear his throat. I looked up and I nearly choked. It was Mr. Fisher.

"Hello, Belly," he said. He was wearing a suit, like he'd

come straight from work, which he probably had, even though it was a Saturday. And somehow his suit wasn't even rumpled, even after a long drive.

"Hi, Mr. Fisher," I said, and my voice came out all nervous and shaky.

My first thought was, *We should have just forced Conrad into the car and made him go back to school and take his stupid tests.* Giving him time was a huge mistake. I could see that now. I should have pushed Jeremiah into pushing Conrad.

Mr. Fisher raised an eyebrow at my beer and I realized I was still holding it, my fingers laced around it so tight they were numb. I set the beer on the ground, and my hair fell in my face, for which I was glad. It was a moment to hide, to figure out what to say next.

I did what I always did—I deferred to the boys. "Um, so, Conrad and Jeremiah aren't here right now." My mind was racing. They would be back any minute.

Mr. Fisher didn't say anything, he just nodded and rubbed the back of his neck. Then he walked up the porch steps and sat in the chair next to mine. He picked up my beer and took a long drink. "How's Conrad?" he asked, setting the beer on his armrest.

"He's good," I said right away. And then I felt foolish, because he wasn't good at all. His mother had just died. He'd run away from school. How could he be good? How could any of us? But I guess, in a sense, he was good, because he had purpose again. He had a reason. To live.

He had a goal; he had an enemy. Those were good incentives. Even if the enemy was his father.

"I don't know what that kid is thinking," Mr. Fisher said, shaking his head.

What could I say to that? I never knew what Conrad was thinking. I was sure not many people did. Even still, I felt defensive of him. Protective.

Mr. Fisher and I sat in silence. Not companionable, easy silence, but stiff and awful. He never had anything to say to me, and I never knew what to say to him. Finally he cleared his throat and said, "How's school?"

"It's over," I said, chewing on my bottom lip and feeling twelve. "Just finished. I'll be a senior this fall."

"Do you know where you want to go to college?"

"Not really." The wrong answer, I knew, because college was one thing Mr. Fisher was interested in talking about. The right kind of college, I mean.

And then we were silent again.

This was also familiar. That feeling of dread, of impending doom. The feeling that I was In Trouble. That we all were.

chapter *twenty-four*

Milk shakes. Milk shakes were Mr. Fisher's thing. When Mr. Fisher came to the summer house, there were milk shakes all the time. He'd buy a Neapolitan carton of ice cream. Steven and Conrad were chocolate, Jeremiah was strawberry, and I liked a vanilla-chocolate mix, like those Frosties at Wendy's. But thick-thick. Mr. Fisher's milk shakes were better than Wendy's. He had a fancy blender he liked to use, that none of us kids were supposed to mess with. Not that he said so, exactly, but we knew not to. And we never did. Until Jeremiah had the idea for Kool-Aid Slurpees.

There were no 7-Elevens in Cousins, and even though we had milk shakes, we sometimes yearned for Slurpees. When it was especially hot outside, one of us would say, "Man, I want a Slurpee," and then all of us would be thinking about it all day. So when Jeremiah had this idea for Kool-Aid Slurpees, it was, like, kismet. He was nine and I was eight, and at the time it sounded like the greatest idea in the world, ever.

We eyed the blender, way up high on the top shelf. We knew we'd have to use it—in fact we *longed* to use it. But there was that unspoken rule.

No one was home but the two of us. No one would have to know.

"What flavor do you want?" he asked me at last.

So it was decided. This was happening. I felt fear and also exhilaration that we were doing this forbidden thing. I rarely broke rules, but this seemed a good one to break.

"Black Cherry," I said.

Jeremiah looked in the cabinet, but there was none. He asked, "What's your second-best flavor?"

"Grape."

Jeremiah said that grape Kool-Aid Slurpee sounded good to him, too. The more he said the words "Kool-Aid Slurpee," the more I liked the sound of it.

Jeremiah got a stool and took the blender down from the top shelf. He poured the whole packet of grape into the blender and added two big plastic cups of sugar. He let me stir. Then he emptied half the ice dispenser into the blender, until it was full to the brim, and he snapped on the top the way we'd seen Mr. Fisher do it a million times.

"Pulse? Frappe?" he asked me.

I shrugged. I never paid close enough attention when Mr. Fisher used it. "Probably frappe," I said, because I liked the sound of the word "frappe."

So Jeremiah pushed frappe, and the blender started to chop and whir. But only the bottom part was getting mixed, so Jeremiah pushed liquefy. It kept at it for a minute, but then the blender started to smell like burning rubber, and I worried it was working too hard with all that ice.

"We've got to stir it up more," I said. "Help it along."

I got the big wooden spoon and took the top off the blender and stirred it all up. "See?" I said.

I put the top back on, but I guess I didn't do it tight enough, because when Jeremiah pushed frappe, our grape Kool-Aid Slurpee went everywhere. All over us. All over the new white counters, all over the floor, all over Mr. Fisher's brown leather briefcase.

We stared at each other in horror.

"Quick, get paper towels!" Jeremiah yelled, unplugging the blender. I dove for the briefcase, mopping it up with the bottom of my T-shirt. The leather was already staining, and it was sticky.

"Oh, man," Jeremiah whispered. "He loves that briefcase."

And he did. It had his initials engraved on the brass clasp. He truly loved it, maybe even more than his blender.

I felt terrible. Tears pricked my eyelids. It was all my fault. "I'm sorry," I said.

Jeremiah was on the floor, on his hands and knees wiping. He looked up at me, grape Kool-Aid dripping down his forehead. "It's not your fault."

"Yeah, it is," I said, rubbing at the leather. My T-shirt was starting to turn brown from rubbing at the briefcase so hard.

"Well, yeah, it kinda is," Jeremiah agreed. Then he reached out and touched his finger to my cheek and licked off some of the sugar. "Tastes good, though."

We were giggling and sliding our feet along the floor with paper towels when everyone came back home. They walked in with long paper bags, the kind the lobsters come in, and Steven and Conrad had ice-cream cones.

Mr. Fisher said, "What the hell?"

Jeremiah scrambled up. "We were just—"

I handed the briefcase over to Mr. Fisher, my hand shaking. "I'm sorry," I whispered. "It was an accident."

He took it from me and looked at it, at the smeared leather. "Why were you using my blender?" Mr. Fisher demanded, but he was asking Jeremiah. His neck was bright red. "You know you're not to use my blender."

Jeremiah nodded. "I'm sorry," he said.

"It was my fault," I said in a small voice.

"Oh, Belly," my mother said, shaking her head at me. She knelt on the ground and picked up the soaked paper towels. Susannah had gone to get the mop.

Mr. Fisher exhaled loudly. "Why don't you ever listen when I tell you something? For God's sake. Did I or did I not tell you to never use this blender?"

Jeremiah bit his lip, and from the way his chin was quivering, I could tell he was really close to crying.

"Answer me when I'm talking to you."

Susannah came back in then with her mop and bucket. "Adam, it was an accident. Let it go." She put her arms around Jeremiah.

"Suze, if you baby him, he'll never learn. He'll just stay a little baby," Mr. Fisher said. "Jere, did I or did I not tell you kids never to use the blender?"

Jeremiah's eyes filled up and he blinked quickly, but a few tears escaped. And then a few more. It was awful. I felt so embarrassed for Jeremiah and also I felt guilty that it was me who had brought all this upon him. But I also felt relieved that it wasn't me who was the one getting in trouble, crying in front of everyone.

And then Conrad said, "But Dad, you never did." He had chocolate ice cream on his cheek.

Mr. Fisher turned and looked at him. "What?"

"You never said it. We knew we weren't supposed to, but you never technically said it." Conrad looked scared, but his voice was matter-of-fact.

Mr. Fisher shook his head and looked back at Jeremiah. "Go get cleaned up," he said roughly. He was embarrassed, I could tell.

Susannah glared at him and swept Jeremiah into the bathroom. My mother was wiping down the counters, her shoulders straight and stiff. "Steven, take your sister to the bathroom," she said. Her voice left no room for argument, and Steven grabbed my arm and took me upstairs.

"Do you think I'm in trouble?" I asked Steven.

He wiped my cheeks roughly with a wet piece of toilet paper. "Yes. But not as much trouble as Mr. Fisher. Mom's gonna rip him a new one."

"What does that mean?"

Steven shrugged. "Just something I heard. It means he's the one in trouble."

After my face was clean, Steven and I crept back into the hallway. My mother and Mr. Fisher were arguing. We looked at each other, our eyes huge when we heard our mother snap, "You can be such an ass-hat, Adam."

I opened my mouth, about to exclaim, when Steven clapped his hand over my mouth and dragged me to the boys' room. He shut the door behind us. His eyes were glittery from all the excitement. Our mother had cussed at Mr. Fisher.

I said, "Mom called Mr. Fisher an ass-hat." I didn't even know what an ass-hat was, but it sure sounded funny. I pictured a hat that looked like a butt sitting on top of Mr. Fisher's big head. And then I giggled.

It was all very exciting and terrible. None of us had ever really gotten in trouble at the summer house. Not big trouble anyway. It was pretty much a big trouble-free zone.

The mothers were relaxed at the summer house. Where at home, Steven would Get It if he talked back, here, my mother didn't seem to mind as much. Probably because at the Cousins house, us kids weren't the center of the world. My mother was busy doing other things, like potting plants and going to art galleries with Susannah and sketching and reading books. She was too busy to get angry or bothered. We did not have her full attention.

This was both a good and bad thing. Good, because we got away with stuff. If we played out on the beach past bedtime, if we had double dessert, no one really cared. Bad, because I had the vague sense that Steven and I weren't as important here, that there were other things that occupied my mother's mind—memories we had no part of, a life before we existed. And also, the secret life inside herself, where Steven and I didn't exist. It was like when she went on her trips without us—I knew that she did not miss us or think about us very much.

I hated that thought, but it was the truth. The mothers had a whole life separate from us. I guess us kids did too.

chapter *twenty-five*

When Jeremiah and Conrad walked up the beach with their boards under their arms, I had this crazy thought that I should try to warn them somehow. Whistle or something. But I didn't know how to whistle, and it was too late anyway.

They put the boards under the house, and then they walked up the steps and saw us sitting there. Conrad's whole body tightened up, and I saw Jeremiah mutter *"shit"* under his breath. Then Jeremiah said, "Hey, Dad." Conrad brushed right past us and into the house.

Mr. Fisher followed him in, and Jeremiah and I looked at each other for a moment. He leaned close to me and said, "How about you pull the car around while I get our stuff, and then we make a run for it?"

I giggled, and then I clapped my hand over my mouth.

I doubted Mr. Fisher would appreciate me giggling when all this serious stuff was going on. I stood up and pulled my towel closer around me, under my armpits. Then we went inside too.

Conrad and Mr. Fisher were in the kitchen. Conrad was opening up a beer, not even looking at his dad. "What the hell are you kids playing at here?" Mr. Fisher said. His voice sounded really loud and unnatural in the house. He was looking around the kitchen, the living room.

Jeremiah began, "Dad—"

Mr. Fisher looked right at Jeremiah and said, "Sandy Donatti called me this morning and told me what happened. You were supposed to get Conrad back to school, not stay and—and party and interfere with the sale."

Jeremiah blinked. "Who's Sandy Donatti?"

"She's our real estate agent," Conrad said.

I realized my mouth was open, and I snapped it shut. I wrapped my arms around myself tight, trying to turn invisible. Maybe it wasn't too late for me and Jeremiah to make a run for it. Maybe that way he'd never find out that I'd known about the house too. Would it make a difference that I'd only known about it since this afternoon? I doubted it.

Jeremiah looked over at Conrad, and then back at his dad. "I didn't know we had a real estate agent. You never told me you were selling the house."

"I told you it was a possibility."

"You never told me you were actually doing it."

Conrad broke in, speaking only to Jeremiah. "It doesn't matter. He's not selling the house." He drank his beer calmly, and we all waited to hear what he'd say next. "It's not his to sell."

"Yes, it is," Mr. Fisher said, breathing heavily. "I'm not doing this for me. The money will be for you boys."

"You think I care about the money?" Conrad finally looked at him, his eyes cold. His voice was toneless. "I'm not like you. I could give a shit about the money. I care about the house. Mom's house."

"Conrad—"

"You have no right to be here. You should leave."

Mr. Fisher swallowed and his Adam's apple bobbed up and down. "No, I won't leave."

"Tell *Sandy* not to bother coming back." Conrad said the word "Sandy" like it was an insult. Which I guess it was meant to be.

"I'm your father," Mr. Fisher said hoarsely. "And your mother left it to me to decide. This is what she would have wanted."

Conrad's smooth, hard shell cracked, and his voice was shaking when he said, "Don't talk about what she would have wanted."

"She was my wife, goddamn it. I lost her too."

That might have been true, but it was the exact wrong thing to say to Conrad at that moment. It set him off.

He punched the wall closest to him, and I flinched. I was shocked he didn't leave a hole.

He said, "You didn't lose her. You left her. You don't know the first thing about what she would have wanted. You were never there. You were a shitty dad and an even shittier husband. So don't bother trying to do the right thing now. You just fuck it all up."

Jeremiah said, "Con, shut up. Just shut up."

Conrad swung around and shouted, "You're still defending him? That's exactly why we didn't tell you!"

"We?" Jeremiah repeated. He looked at me then, and the stricken look on his face cut right through me.

I started to speak, to try to explain, but I only got as far as saying, "I just found out today, I swear," when Mr. Fisher interrupted me.

He said, "You are not the only one hurting, Conrad. You don't get to talk to me that way."

"I think I do."

The room was deadly quiet and Mr. Fisher looked like he might hit Conrad, he was so mad. They stared at each other, and I knew Conrad wouldn't be the one to back down.

It was Mr. Fisher who looked away. "The movers are coming back, Conrad. This is happening. You throwing a tantrum can't stop it."

He left soon after. He said he'd be back in the morning, and the words were ominous. He said that he was staying at the inn in town. It was clear that he couldn't wait to get out of that house.

The three of us stood around in the kitchen after he was gone, none of us saying anything. Least of all me. I wasn't even supposed to be there. For once, I wished I was at home with my mother and Steven and Taylor, away from all of this.

Jeremiah was the first to speak. "I can't believe he's really selling the house," he said, almost to himself.

"Believe it," Conrad said harshly.

"Why didn't you tell me about it?" Jeremiah demanded.

Conrad glanced at me before saying, "I didn't think you needed to know."

Jeremiah's eyes narrowed. "What the hell, Conrad? It's my house too."

"Jere, I only just found out myself." Conrad propped himself up on the kitchen counter, his head down. "I was at home picking up some clothes. That real estate agent, Sandy, called and left a message on the machine, saying movers were coming to get the stuff they packed. I went back to school and got my stuff and I came straight here."

Conrad had dropped school and everything else to come to the summer house, and here we'd just thought he was a screwup in need of saving. When in actuality, he was the one doing the saving.

I felt guilty for not giving him the benefit of the

doubt, and I knew Jeremiah did too. We exchanged a quick look and I knew we were thinking exactly the same thing. Then I guess he remembered he was pissed at me, too, and he looked away.

"So that's it, then?" Jeremiah said.

Conrad didn't answer him right away. Then he looked up and said, "Yeah, I guess it is."

"Well, great job taking care of all this, Con."

"I've been handling this on my own," Conrad snapped. "It's not like I had any help from you."

"Well, maybe if you'd told me about it—"

Conrad cut him off. "You'd have done what?"

"I would have talked to Dad."

"Yeah, exactly." Conrad could not have sounded more disdainful.

"What the hell does that mean?"

"It means that you're so busy being up his ass, you can't see him for who he is."

Jeremiah didn't say anything right away, and I was really afraid of where this was heading. Conrad was looking for a fight and the last thing we needed was for the two of them to start wrestling on the kitchen floor, breaking things and each other. This time, my mother wasn't here to stop them. There was just me, and that was hardly anything.

And then Jeremiah said, "He's our father." His voice was measured, even, and I let out a tiny breath of relief.

There wouldn't be any fight, because Jeremiah wouldn't let it happen. I admired him for that.

But Conrad just shook his head in disgust. "He's a dirtbag."

"Don't call him that."

"What kind of guy cheats on his wife and then leaves her when she has cancer? What kind of man does that? I can't even stand to look at him. He makes me sick, playing the martyr now, the grieving widower. But where was he when Mom needed him, huh, Jere?"

"I don't know, Con. Where were you?"

The room went silent, and it felt to me like the air was almost crackling. The way Conrad flinched, the way Jeremiah sucked in his breath right after he said it. He wanted to take it back, I could tell, and he was about to, when Conrad said, conversationally, "That's a low blow."

"I'm sorry," Jeremiah said.

Conrad shrugged, brushing him off like it didn't matter either way.

And then Jeremiah said, "Why can't you just let it go? Why do you have to hold on to all the shitty stuff that's ever happened to you?"

"Because I live in reality, unlike you. You'd rather live in a fantasy world than see people for who they really are." He said it in a way that made me wonder who he was really talking about.

Jeremiah bristled. He looked at me and then back at

Conrad and said, "You're just jealous. Admit it."

"Jealous?"

"You're jealous that Dad and I have an actual relationship now. It's not just all about you anymore, and that kills you."

Conrad actually laughed. It was a bitter, terrible sound. "That's such BS." He turned to me. "Belly, are you hearing this? Jeremiah thinks I'm jealous."

Jeremiah looked at me, like, *Be on my side*, and I knew that if I did, he'd forgive me for not telling him about the house. I hated Conrad for putting me in the middle, for making me choose. I didn't know whose side I was on. They were both right and they were both wrong.

I guess I took too long to answer, because Jeremiah stopped looking at me and said, "You're an asshole, Conrad. You just want everyone to be as miserable as you are." And then he walked out. The front door slammed behind him.

I felt like I should go after him. I felt like I had just let him down when he needed me most.

Then Conrad said to me, "Am I an asshole, Belly?" He popped open another beer and he was trying to sound so indifferent, but his hand was shaking.

"Yeah," I said. "You really are."

I walked over to the window and I watched Jeremiah getting into his car. It was too late to follow him; he was already pulling out of the driveway. Even though he was pissed, he had his seat belt on.

"He'll be back," Conrad said.

I hesitated and then I said, "You shouldn't have said that stuff."

"Maybe not."

"You shouldn't have asked me to keep it a secret from him."

Conrad shrugged like he was already over it, but then he looked back toward the window and I knew he was worried. He threw me a beer and I caught it. I popped the top off and took a long drink. It hardly even tasted bad. Maybe I was getting used to it. I smacked my lips loudly.

He watched me, and there was a funny look on his face. "So you like beer now, huh?"

I shrugged. "It's all right," I said, and I felt very grown-up. But then I added, "I still like Cherry Coke better though."

He almost smiled when he said, "Same old Belly. I bet if we cut your body open, white sugar would come pouring out of you."

"That's me," I said. "Sugar and spice and everything nice."

Conrad said, "I don't know about that."

And then we were both quiet. I took another sip of beer and set it down next to Conrad. "I think you really hurt Jeremiah's feelings."

He shrugged. "He needed a reality check."

"You didn't have to do it like that."

"I think you're the one who hurt Jeremiah's feelings."

I opened my mouth and then closed it. If I asked him what he meant by that, he'd tell me. And I didn't want him to. So I drank my beer and said, "What now?"

Conrad didn't let me off the hook that easy. He said, "What now with you and Jeremiah or with you and me?"

He was teasing me and I hated him for it. I could feel my cheeks burning as I said, "What now with this house, was what I meant."

He leaned back against the counter. "There's nothing to do, really. I mean, I could get a lawyer. I'm eighteen now. I could try and stall. But I doubt it would do anything. My dad's stubborn. And he's greedy."

Hesitantly, I said, "I don't know that he's doing it out of—out of greed, Conrad."

Conrad's face sort of closed off. "Trust me. He is."

I couldn't help but ask, "What about summer school?"

"I couldn't care less about school right now."

"But—"

"Just leave it, Belly." Then he walked out of the kitchen, opened the sliding door, and went outside.

Conversation over.

chapter *twenty-six*
JEREMIAH

My whole life I've looked up to Conrad. He's always been
smarter, faster—just better. The thing is, I never really
begrudged him that. He was just Conrad. He couldn't help
being good at things. He couldn't help that he never lost in
Uno or races or grades. Maybe part of me needed that, someone to look up to. My big brother, the guy who couldn't lose.

But there was this time, when I was thirteen. We were
wrestling around in the living room, had been for half
an hour. My dad was always trying to get us to wrestle.
He'd been on the wrestling team in college, and he liked
teaching us new techniques. We were wrestling, and my
mom was in the kitchen, cooking bacon-wrapped scallops because we were having people over that night and
they were my dad's favorite.

"Lock him in, Con," my dad was saying.

We were really getting into it. We'd already knocked over one of my mom's silver candlesticks. Conrad was breathing hard; he'd expected to beat me easily. But I was getting good; I wasn't giving up. He had my head locked under his arm and then I locked his knee and we were both on the ground. I could feel something shift; I almost had him. I was going to win. My dad was gonna be so proud.

When I had him pinned, my dad said, "Connie, I told you to keep your knees bent."

I looked up at my dad, and I saw the look on his face. He had that look he got sometimes when Conrad wasn't doing something right, all tight around the eyes and irritated. He never looked at me like that.

He didn't say, "Good job, Jere." He just started criticizing Conrad, telling him all the things he could've done better. And Conrad took it. He was nodding, his face red, sweat pouring down his forehead. Then he nodded at me and said, in a way that I knew he really meant it, "Good job, Jere."

That's when my dad chimed in and said, "Yeah, good job, Jere."

All of a sudden, I wanted to cry. I didn't want to beat Conrad ever again. It wasn't worth it.

After all that stuff back at the house, I got in my car and I just started driving. I didn't know where I was going and part of me didn't even want to go back. Part of me wanted to leave Conrad to deal with this shitstorm by himself, the way he'd wanted it in the first place. Let Belly deal with him. Let them have at it. I drove for half an hour.

But even as I was doing it, I knew that, eventually, I would turn back around. I couldn't just leave. That was Con's style, not mine. And it *was* low, what I said about him not being there for our mom. It wasn't like he knew she was gonna die. He was at college. It wasn't his fault. But he wasn't the one who was there when everything got bad again. It all happened so fast. He couldn't have known. If he had known, he would have stayed home. I know he would have.

Our dad was never gonna win a Father of the Year award. He was flawed, that was for sure. But when it counted, there at the end, he came home. He said all the right things. He made our mom happy. Conrad just couldn't see it. He didn't want to.

I didn't go back to the house right away.

First I stopped at the pizza place. It was dinnertime, and there wasn't any food at the house. A kid I knew, Mikey, was working the register. I ordered a large pizza with everything, and then I asked him if Ron was out on a delivery. Mikey said yeah, that Ron would be back soon, that I should wait.

Ron lived in Cousins year-round. He went to community college during the day and he delivered pizzas at night. He was an okay guy. He'd been buying underage kids beer for as long as I could remember. If you gave him a twenty, he'd hook you up.

All I knew was, if this was gonna be our last night, we couldn't go out like this.

When I got back to the house, Conrad was sitting on the front porch. I knew he was waiting for me; I knew he felt bad for what he'd said. I honked the horn, stuck my head out the window, and yelled, "Come help me with this stuff."

He came down to the car, checked out the cases of beer and the bag of liquor, and said, "Ron?"

"Yup." I hoisted up two cases of beer and handed them over. "We're having a party."

chapter *twenty-seven*

After the fight, after Mr. Fisher left, I went up to my room and stayed there. I didn't want to be around when Jeremiah got back, in case he and Conrad went for a second round. Unlike Steven and me, those two hardly ever fought. In all the time I'd known them, I'd only seen them do it, like, three times. Jeremiah looked up to Conrad and Conrad looked out for Jeremiah. It was as simple as that.

I started looking around in the drawers and closet to see if there was anything of mine left there. My mom was pretty strict about us taking all our stuff every time we left, but you never knew. I figured I might as well make sure. Mr. Fisher would probably just tell the movers to throw all the junk out.

In the bottom of the desk drawer I found an old

composition notebook from my *Harriet the Spy* days. It was colored in pink and green and yellow highlighter. I'd followed the boys around for days, taking notes in it until I drove Steven crazy and he told Mom on me.

I'd written:

> June 28. Caught Jeremiah
>
> dancing in the mirror when he
>
> thought no one was watching. Too
>
> bad I was!
>
> June 30. Conrad ate all the blue
>
> Popsicles again even though he's
>
> not supposed to. But I didn't tell.
>
> July 1. Steven kicked me for
>
> no reason.

And on and on. I'd gotten sick of it by mid-July and quit. I had been such a little tagalong then. Eight-year-old me would have loved to have been included in this last adventure, would have loved the fact that I got to hang out with the boys while Steven had to stay at home.

I found a few other things, junk like a half-used pot of cherry lip gloss, a couple of dusty hair bands. On the shelf, there were my old Judy Blumes and then my V. C. Andrews books hidden behind them. I figured I'd just leave all that stuff behind.

The one thing I had to take was Junior Mint, my old stuffed polar bear, the one Conrad had won me that time at the boardwalk a million years ago. I couldn't just let Junior Mint get thrown out like he was junk. He'd been special to me once upon a time.

I stayed upstairs for a while, just looking at my old stuff. I found one other thing worth keeping. A toy telescope. I remember the day my father bought it for me. It had been in one of the little antique stores along the boardwalk, and it was expensive but he said I should have it. There was a time when I was obsessed with stars and comets and constellations, and he thought I might grow up to be an astronomer. It turned out to be a phase, but it was fun while it lasted. I liked the way my father looked at me then, like I had taken after him, my father's daughter.

He still looked at me that way sometimes—when I asked for Tabasco sauce at restaurants, when I turned the radio station to NPR without him having to ask. Tabasco sauce I liked, but NPR not as much. I did it because I knew it made him proud.

I was glad he was my dad and not Mr. Fisher. He never would have yelled or cussed at me, or gotten mad about spilled Kool-Aid. He wasn't that kind of man. I'd never appreciated enough just what kind of man he was.

chapter *twenty-eight*

My father rarely came to the summer house, for a weekend in August maybe, but that was pretty much it. It never occurred to me to wonder why. There was this one weekend he and Mr. Fisher came up at the same time. As if they had so much in common, as if they were friends or something. They couldn't be more different. Mr. Fisher liked to talk, talk, talk, and my dad only spoke if he had something to say. Mr. Fisher was always watching SportsCenter, while my dad rarely watched TV at all—and definitely not sports.

The parents were going to a fancy restaurant in Dyerstown. A band played there on Saturday nights and they had a little dance floor. It was strange to think of my parents dancing. I'd never seen them dance before, but I was sure Susannah and Mr. Fisher danced all the time. I'd seen them once, in the living room. I remembered how Conrad had blushed and turned away.

I was lying on my stomach, on Susannah's bed, watching my mother and her get ready in the master bathroom.

Susannah had convinced my mother to wear a dress of hers; it was red and it had a deep V-neck. "What do you think, Beck?" my mother asked uncertainly. I could tell she felt funny about it. She usually wore pants.

"I think you look amazing. I think you should keep it. Red is so you, Laure." Susannah was curling her lashes and opening her eyes wide in the mirror.

When they left, I would practice using the eyelash curler. My mother didn't have one. I knew the contents of her makeup bag, one of those plastic green Clinique gift-with-purchase bags. It had a Burt's Bees chapstick and an espresso eyeliner, a pink and green tube of Maybelline mascara, and a bottle of tinted sunscreen. Boring.

Susannah's makeup case, though, was a treasure trove. It was a navy snakeskin case with a heavy gold clasp and her initials were engraved on it. Inside she had little eye pots and palettes and sable brushes and perfume samples. She never threw away anything. I liked to sort through it and organize everything in neat rows, according to color. Sometimes she gave me a lipstick or a sample eyeshadow, nothing too dark.

"Belly, you want me to do your eyes?" Susannah asked me.

I sat up. "Yeah!"

"Beck, please don't give her hooker eyes again," my mother said, running a comb through her wet hair.

Susannah made a face. "It's called a smoky eye, Laure."

"Yeah, Mom, it's a smoky eye," I piped up.

Susannah crooked her finger at me. "C'mere, Belly."

I scampered into the bathroom and propped myself up on the counter. I loved to sit on that counter with my legs dangling, listening in on everything like one of the girls.

She dipped a little brush into a pot of black eyeliner. "Close your eyes," she said.

I obeyed, and Susannah dragged the brush along my lash line, expertly blending and smudging with the ball of her thumb. Then she swept shadow across my eyelids and I wriggled in my seat excitedly. I loved it when Susannah made me up; I couldn't wait for the moment of unveiling.

"Are you and Mr. Fisher gonna dance tonight?" I asked.

Susannah laughed. "I don't know. Maybe."

"Mom, will you and Dad?"

My mother laughed too. "I don't know. Probably not. Your father doesn't like to dance."

"Dad's boring," I said, trying to twist around and get a peek at my new look. Gently, Susannah put her hands on my shoulders and sat me straight.

"He's not boring," my mother said. "He just has different interests. You like it when he teaches you the constellations, don't you?"

I shrugged. "Yeah."

"And he's very patient, and he always listens to your stories," my mother reminded me.

"True. But what does that have to do with being boring?"

"Not much, I suppose. But it has to do with being a good father, which I think he is."

"He definitely is," Susannah agreed, and she and my mother exchanged a look over my head. "Take a look at yourself."

I swiveled around and looked in the mirror. My eyes were very smoky and gray and mysterious. I felt like I should be the one going out dancing.

"See, she doesn't look like a hooker," Susannah said triumphantly.

"She looks like she has a black eye," my mother said.

"No, I don't. I look mysterious. I look like a countess." I hopped off the bathroom counter. "Thanks, Susannah."

"Anytime, sugar."

We air-kissed like two ladies who lunch. Then she took me by the hand and walked me over to her bureau. She handed me her jewelry box and said, "Belly, you have the best taste. Will you help me pick out some jewelry to wear tonight?"

I sat on her bed with the wooden box and sifted through it carefully. I found what I was looking for—her dangly opal earrings with the matching opal ring. "Wear these," I said, holding the jewelry out to her in the palm of my hand.

Susannah obeyed, and as she fastened the earrings, my mother said, "I don't know if that really goes."

In retrospect, I don't think it really did go. But I loved that opal jewelry so much. I admired it more than anything. So I said, "Mom, what do you know about style?"

Right away, I worried she'd be mad, but it had slipped out, and it was true after all. My mother knew about as much about jewelry as she did about makeup.

But Susannah laughed, and so did my mother.

"Go downstairs and tell the men we'll be ready to go in five, Countess," my mother ordered.

I jumped out of bed and curtsied dramatically. "Yes, Mum."

They both laughed. My mother said, "Go, you little imp."

I ran downstairs. When I was a kid, anytime I had to go anywhere, I ran. "They're almost ready," I yelled.

Mr. Fisher was showing my dad his new fishing rod. My dad looked relieved to see me, and he said, "Belly, what have they done to you?"

"Susannah made me up. Do you like it?"

My dad beckoned me closer, regarding me with serious eyes. "I'm not sure. You look very mature."

"I do?"

"Yes, very, very mature."

I tried to hide my delight as I made a place for myself in the crook of my dad's arm, my head right by his side. For me, there was no better compliment than being called mature.

They all left a little while later, the dads in pressed khakis and button-down shirts and the moms in their summer dresses. Mr. Fisher and my dad didn't look so different when they dressed up like that. My dad hugged me good-bye and said that if I was still awake when they got back, we'd sit on the deck awhile and look for shooting stars. My mother said they'd probably be back too late, but my dad winked at me.

On the way out, he whispered something to my mother that made her cover her mouth and laugh a low, throaty kind of laugh. I wonder what he said.

It was one of the last times I remember them being happy. I really wish I had enjoyed it more.

My parents had always been stable, as boring as two parents could be. They never fought. Taylor's parents fought all the time. I'd be over for a sleepover, and Mr. Jewel would come home late and her mom would be really pissy, stomping around in her slippers and banging pots. We'd be at the dinner table, and I would sink lower and lower into my seat, and Taylor would just go on talking about stupid stuff. Like whether or not Veronika Gerard wore the same socks two days in a row in gym or if we should volunteer to be water girls for the JV football team when we were freshmen.

When her parents got divorced, I asked Taylor if, in some little way, she was relieved. She said no. She said that even though they had fought all the time, at least they had still been a family. "Your parents never even fought," she said, and I could hear the disdain in her voice.

I knew what she meant. I wondered about it too. How could two people who had once been passionately in love not even fight? Didn't they care enough to fight it out, to fight not just with each other, but also for their marriage? Were they ever really in love? Did my mother ever feel about my dad the way I felt about Conrad— alive, crazy, drunk with tenderness? Those were the questions that haunted me.

I didn't want to make the same mistakes my parents made. I didn't want my love to fade away one day like an old scar. I wanted it to burn forever.

chapter *twenty-nine*

When I finally went back downstairs, it was dark out and Jeremiah was back. He and Conrad were sitting on the couch, watching TV like the fight had never happened. I guessed it was that way with boys. Whenever Taylor and I fought, we were mad for at least a week and there was a power struggle over who got custody of which friends. "Whose side are you on?" we'd demand of Katie or Marcy. We'd say mean things that you can't take back and then we'd cry and make up. Somehow I doubted Conrad and Jeremiah had been crying and making up while I'd been upstairs.

I wondered if I was forgiven too, for keeping a secret from Jeremiah, for not taking a side—his side. Because it was true, we'd come here together as partners, a team, and when he'd needed me, I'd let him down. I lingered there by the stairs for a second, unsure of whether or not to go over, and then Jeremiah looked up at me and I knew I was. Forgiven, that is. He smiled, a real smile, and a real Jeremiah smile was the kind that could melt ice cream. I smiled back, grateful as anything.

"I was just about to come get you," he said. "We're having a party."

There was a pizza box on the coffee table. "A pizza party?" I asked.

Susannah used to have pizza parties for us kids all the time. It was never just "pizza for dinner." It was a pizza party. Except this time, with beer. And tequila. So this was it. Our last night. It would have felt a lot more real if Steven had been there too. It would have felt complete, us four together again.

"I ran into some people in town. They're gonna come over later and bring a keg."

"A keg?" I repeated.

"Yeah. A keg, you know, of beer?"

"Oh, right," I said. "A keg."

Then I sat down on the ground and opened the pizza box. There was one slice left, and it was a small one. "You guys are such pigs," I said, stuffing it into my mouth.

"Whoops, sorry," Jeremiah said. Then he went into the kitchen, and when he came back, he had three cups. He had one balanced in the crook of his elbow. He gave that one to me. "Cheers," he said. He handed Conrad a cup too.

I sniffed it suspiciously. It was light brown with a lime wedge floating on top. "Smells strong," I said.

"That's because it's *tequila*," he sang. He lifted his cup in the air. "To the last night."

"To the last night," we repeated.

They both drank theirs in one shot. I took a teeny sip of mine, and it wasn't too bad. I'd never had tequila before. I drank the rest quickly. "This is pretty good," I said. "Not strong at all."

Jeremiah burst out laughing. "That's because yours is ninety-five percent water."

Conrad laughed too, and I glared at them both. "That's not fair," I said. "I want to drink what you guys are drinking."

"Sorry, but we don't serve minors here," Jeremiah said, falling next to me on the floor.

I punched him on the shoulder. "You're a minor too, dummy. We all are."

"Yeah, but you're really a minor," he said. "My mom would kill me."

It was the first time any of us had mentioned Susannah. My eyes darted over to Conrad, but his face was blank. I let out a breath. And then I had an idea, the best idea ever. I jumped up and opened the doors of the TV console. I ran my fingers along the drawers of DVDs and home videos, all neatly labeled in Susannah's slanted cursive handwriting. I found what I was looking for.

"What are you doing?" Jeremiah asked me.

"Just wait," I said, my back to them. I turned on the TV and popped in the video.

On the screen, there was Conrad, age twelve. With braces and bad skin. He was lying on a beach blanket, scowling. He wouldn't let anybody take a picture of him that summer.

Mr. Fisher was behind the camera, as always, saying, "Come on. Say 'Happy Fourth of July,' Connie."

Jeremiah and I looked at each other and burst out laughing. Conrad glared at us. He made a move for the remote, but Jeremiah got to it first. He held it above his head, laughing breathlessly. The two of them started wrestling around, and then they stopped.

The camera had focused in on Susannah, wearing her big beach hat and a long white shirt over her bathing suit.

"Suze, honey, how do you feel today, on our nation's birthday?"

She rolled her eyes. "Give it a rest, Adam. Go videotape the kids." And then from under her hat, she smiled—that slow, deep-down smile. It was the smile of a woman who really and truly loved the person holding the video camera.

Conrad stopped fighting for the remote and he watched for a moment, then he said, "Turn it off."

Jeremiah said, "Come on, man. Let's just watch."

Conrad didn't say anything but he didn't stop watching either.

And then the camera was on me, and Jeremiah was laughing again. Conrad too. This was what I was waiting for. I knew it would get a laugh.

Me, wearing huge glasses and a rainbow striped tankini, my round stomach popping over the bottoms like a four-year-old's. I was screaming at the top of my lungs, running away from Steven and Jeremiah. They were chasing me with what they claimed was a jellyfish, but what I later found out was a clump of seaweed.

Jeremiah's hair was white-blond in the sunlight, and he looked exactly the way I remembered.

"Bells, you look like a beach ball," he said, gasping with laughter.

I laughed too, a little. "Watch it," I said. "That summer was really great. All our summers here were really . . . great."

Great didn't even begin to describe them.

Silently, Conrad got up and then he came back with the tequila. He poured us each some, and this time mine wasn't watered down.

We all took a shot together, and when I gulped mine down it burned so bad tears streamed down my face. Conrad and Jeremiah started cracking up again. "Suck on the lime," Conrad told me, so I did.

Soon I felt warm and lazy and great. I lay down on the floor with my hair fanned out and I stared up at the ceiling and watched the fan turn round and round.

When Conrad got up and went to the bathroom,

Jeremiah rolled over to his side. "Hey, Belly," he said. "Truth or dare."

"Don't be dumb," I said.

"Oh, come on. Play with me, Bells. Please?"

I rolled my eyes and sat up. "Dare."

His eyes had that trickster's glint. I hadn't seen that look in his eyes since before Susannah got sick again. "I dare you to kiss me, old-school style. I've learned a lot since the last time."

I laughed. Whatever I had been expecting him to say, it hadn't been that.

Jeremiah tilted his face up at me and I laughed again. I leaned forward, pulled his chin toward me, and kissed him on the cheek with a loud smack.

"Aw, man!" he protested. "That's not a real kiss."

"You didn't specify," I said, and my face felt hot.

"Come on, Bells," he said. "That's not how we kissed that other time."

Conrad came back into the room then, wiping his hands on his jeans. He said, "What are you talking about, Jere? Don't you have a girlfriend?"

I looked at Jeremiah, whose cheeks were flaming. "You have a girlfriend?" I heard the accusation in my voice and I hated it. It wasn't like Jeremiah owed me anything. It wasn't like he belonged to me. But he always let me feel like he did.

All this time together, and he never once mentioned

that he had a girlfriend. I couldn't believe it. I guessed I wasn't the only one keeping secrets, and the thought made me sad.

"We broke up. She's going to school at Tulane, and I'm staying around here. We decided there's no point in staying together." He glared at Conrad and then glanced back at me. "And we've always been off and on. She's crazy."

I hated the idea of him with some crazy girl, some girl who he liked enough to go back to over and over. "Well, what's her name?" I asked.

He hesitated. "Mara," he said at last.

The alcohol in me gave me the courage to say, "Do you love her?"

This time he didn't hesitate. "No," he said.

I picked at a pizza crust and said, "Okay, my turn. Conrad, truth or dare?"

He was lying on the couch facedown. "Never said I was playing."

"Chicken," Jeremiah and I said together.

"Jinx," we said at the same time.

"You guys are two-year-olds," Conrad muttered.

Jeremiah got up and started doing his chicken dance. "Bock bock bock bock."

"Truth or dare," I repeated.

Conrad groaned. "Truth."

I was so pleased Conrad was playing with us, I couldn't think of anything good to ask. I mean, there were a million and one things I wanted to ask him. I wanted to ask him what had happened to us, if he'd ever liked me, if any of it had been real. But I couldn't ask those things. Even through my tequila haze, I knew that much.

Instead, I asked, "Remember that summer you liked that girl who worked at the boardwalk? Angie?"

"No," he said, but I knew he was lying. "What about her?"

"Did you ever hook up with her?"

Conrad finally lifted his head up from the couch. "No," he said.

"I don't believe you."

"I tried, once. But she socked me in the head and said she wasn't that kind of girl. I think she was a Jehovah's Witness or something."

Jeremiah and I busted up laughing. Jeremiah was laughing so hard, he doubled over and fell to his knees. "Oh, man," he gasped. "That's awesome."

And it was. I knew it was only because he'd had about a case of beer, but Conrad loosening up, telling us things—it felt awesome. Like a miracle.

Conrad propped himself up on his elbow. "Okay. My turn."

He was looking at me like we were the only two people in the room, and suddenly I was terrified. And elated. But then I looked over at Jeremiah, watching the two of us, and just as suddenly, I was neither.

Solemnly I said, "Nuh-uh. You can't ask me, 'cause I just asked you. It's the law."

"The law?" he repeated.

"Yeah," I said, leaning my head against the couch.

"Aren't you at least curious about what I was going to ask?"

"Nope. Not even one iota." Which was a lie. Of course I was curious. I was dying to know.

I reached over and poured some more tequila into my cup and then I stood up, my knees shaking. I felt light-headed. "To our last night!"

"We already toasted to that, remember?" Jeremiah said.

I stuck my tongue out at him. "Okay, then." The tequila made me feel brave again. This time, it let me say what I really wanted to say. What I'd been thinking all night. "Here's to . . . here's to everybody that isn't here tonight. To my mom, and to Steven, and to Susannah most of all. Okay?"

Conrad looked up at me. For a minute, I was afraid of what he would say. And then he lifted his cup too, and so did Jeremiah. We all swigged from our cups together, and it burned like liquid fire. I coughed a little.

When I sat back down I asked Jeremiah, "So, who's coming to this party?"

He shrugged. "Some kids from the country club pool from last summer. They're telling people too. Oh, and Mikey and Pete and those guys."

I wondered who "Mikey and Pete and those guys" were. I also wondered if I should clean up before people came.

"What time are people coming over?" I asked Jeremiah. He shrugged. "Ten? Eleven?"

I jumped up. "It's already almost nine! I have to get dressed."

Conrad said, "Aren't you already dressed?"

I didn't even bother to answer him. I just shot upstairs.

chapter *thirty*

I had the contents of my duffel bag dumped out on the floor when Taylor called. Which was when I remembered that it was Saturday. It felt like I'd been gone much longer. Then I remembered that it was the Fourth of July. And I was supposed to be on a boat with Taylor and Davis and everyone. *Gulp.*

"Hey, Taylor," I said.

"Hey, where are you?" Taylor didn't sound mad, which was kind of freaky.

"Um, still in Cousins. Sorry I didn't make it back in time for the boat party." From the pile of clothes, I picked out a chiffony one-shoulder blouse and tried it on. Whenever Taylor wore it, she wore her hair pulled to the side.

"It's been raining all day, so we cancelled the boat

party. Cory's having a party tonight at his brother's condo instead. What about you?"

"I think we're having a party too. Jeremiah just bought a ton of beer and tequila and stuff," I said, adjusting the blouse. I wasn't sure how much shoulder I was supposed to be showing.

"A party?" she squealed. "I wanna come!"

I tried to wiggle my foot into one of Taylor's platform sandals. I wished I hadn't mentioned the party—or the tequila. Lately, Taylor was crazy for tequila body shots. "What about Cory's party?" I said. "I heard his brother's condo has a Jacuzzi. You love Jacuzzis."

"Oh, yeah. Darn. But I want to party with you guys too! Beach parties are the funnest," she said. "Anyway, I heard from Rachel Spiro that a bunch of freshman sluts are coming now. It might not even be worth it to go. OMG, maybe I should just get in my car and drive to Cousins!"

"By the time you got here, everybody would be gone. You should probably just go to Cory's."

I heard a car pull into the driveway. People were already here. So it wasn't like I was lying to her.

I was about to tell Taylor I had to go when she said in a little voice, "Do you, like, not want me to come?"

"I didn't say that," I said.

"You basically did."

"Taylor," I began. But I didn't know what to say next. Because she was right. I didn't want her to come. If she came, it would be all about her, the way it always was. This was my last night in Cousins, in this house. I was never going to be inside this house again, ever. I wanted tonight to be about me and Conrad and Jeremiah.

Taylor waited for me to say something, to deny it at least, and when I didn't, she spat out, "I can't even believe how selfish you are, Belly."

"Me?"

"Yes, you. You keep your summer house and your summer boys all to yourself and you don't want to share anything with me. We finally get to spend a whole summer together and you don't even care! All you care about is being in Cousins, with *them*." She sounded so spiteful. But instead of feeling guilty the way I normally would, I just felt annoyed.

"Taylor," I said.

"Quit saying my name like that."

"Like how?"

"Like I'm a child."

"Well, then maybe you shouldn't act like one just because you aren't invited somewhere." As soon as I said it, I regretted it.

"Screw you, Belly! I put up with a lot. You are a really crappy best friend, you know that?"

I let out a breath. "Taylor . . . shut up."

She gasped. "Don't you dare tell me to shut up! I have been nothing but supportive of you, Belly. I listen to all your Conrad BS and I don't even complain. When you guys broke up, who was the one who spoon-fed you Chunky Monkey and got you out of bed? Me! And you don't even appreciate that. You're, like, hardly even fun anymore."

Sarcastically, I said, "Gee, Taylor, I'm so sorry I'm not fun anymore. Having someone you love die can do that."

"Don't do that. Don't just blame it on that. You've been chasing after Conrad for as long as I've known you. It's getting pathetic. Get over it! He doesn't like you. Maybe he never did."

That was maybe the meanest thing she'd ever said to me. I think she might have apologized if I hadn't come back at her with, "At least I didn't give away my virginity to a guy who shaves his legs!"

She gasped. In confidence, Taylor had once told me that Davis shaved his legs for swim team. She was silent for a moment. And then she said, "You better not wear my platforms tonight."

"Too late. I already am!" And then I hung up.

I couldn't believe her. Taylor was the crappy friend, not me. She was the selfish one. I was so angry, my hand shook when I put on my eyeliner and I had to rub it off and start over again. I wore Taylor's blouse and her shoes and I pulled my hair all to one side too. I did it because I knew it would piss her off.

And then, last of all, I put on Conrad's necklace. I tucked it underneath my shirt, and then I went downstairs.

chapter *thirty-one*

"Welcome," I said to a boy in a Led Zeppelin T-shirt.

"Nice boots," I said to a girl with cowboy boots on.

I made my way around the room, passing out drinks and throwing away empty cans. Conrad watched me with his arms crossed. "What are you doing?" he asked me.

"I'm trying to make everyone feel at home," I explained, adjusting Taylor's top. Susannah was an excellent hostess. She had a talent for making people feel welcome, wanted. Taylor's words were still hanging around in the back of my head. I wasn't selfish. I was a good friend, a good hostess. I'd show her.

When Travis from Video World put his feet up on the coffee table and almost knocked over a hurricane vase, I barked, "Careful. And take your feet off the furniture." As an afterthought, I added, "Please."

I was about to go back into the kitchen for more drinks when I saw her. The girl from last summer. Nicole, the one Conrad liked, was standing in the kitchen talking to Jeremiah. She didn't have her Red Sox hat on, but I'd recognize her perfume anywhere. It smelled like vanilla extract and decomposing roses.

Conrad must have seen her at the same time I did because he sucked in his breath and muttered, "*Shit.*"

"Did you break her heart?" I asked him. I tried to sound teasing and carefree.

I must have succeeded, because he took me by the hand and grabbed the bottle of tequila and said, "Let's get out of here."

I followed him like I was in a trance, sleepwalking. Because it was like a dream, his hand in mine. We were almost home free when Jeremiah saw us. My heart just sank. He motioned us over and called out, "Guys! Come say hi."

Conrad let go of my hand but not the tequila. "Hey, Nicole," he said, starting toward her. I grabbed a couple of beers and followed him over.

"Oh, hey, Conrad," Nicole said, all surprised, like she hadn't been watching the whole time we'd been in the kitchen. She got on her tip-toes and hugged him.

Jeremiah caught my eye and raised his eyebrows comically. He grinned at me. "Belly, you remember Nicole, right?"

I said, "Of course." I smiled at her. *Perfect hostess*, I reminded myself. *Unselfish.*

Warily, she smiled back at me. I handed her one of the beers I was holding. "Cheers," I said, opening mine.

"Cheers," she echoed. We clinked cans and drank. I drank mine fast. When I was done, I got another and I drank that, too.

Suddenly the house felt too quiet, so I turned on the stereo. I turned the music up loud and kicked off my shoes. Susannah always said it wasn't a party without dancing. I grabbed Jeremiah, threw one arm around his neck, and danced.

"Belly—," he protested.

"Just dance, Jere!" I yelled.

So he did. He was a good dancer, that Jeremiah. Other people started dancing too, even Nicole. Not Conrad though, but I didn't care. I barely even noticed.

I danced like it was 1999. I danced like my heart was breaking, which it kind of was. Mostly I just swung my hair around a lot.

I was pretty sweaty when I said, "Can we swim in the pool? One last time?"

Jeremiah said, "Screw that. Let's swim in the ocean."

"Yeah!" It sounded like a great idea to me. A perfect idea.

"No," Conrad said, coming out of nowhere. He was suddenly standing right beside me. "Belly's drunk. She shouldn't swim."

I looked at him and frowned. "But I want to," I said.

He laughed. "So what?"

"Look, I'm a really good swimmer. And I'm not even drunk." I walked in a semistraight line to prove my point.

"Sorry," he said. "But you really are."

Dumb, boring Conrad. He got so serious at the worst moments.

"You're no fun." I looked over at Jeremiah, who was sitting on the floor now. "He's no fun. And he's not the boss of us. Right, everybody?"

Before Jeremiah or anybody else could answer me, I made a run for the sliding doors, and then I stumbled down the steps and sprinted onto the beach. I felt like a flying comet, a streak in the sky, like I hadn't used my muscles in so long and it felt great to stretch my legs and *run*.

The house, all lit up with people inside, felt a million miles away. I knew he'd come after me. I didn't have to turn around to know it was him. But I did anyway.

"Come back to the house," Conrad said. He had the bottle of tequila in his hand. I grabbed it out of his hand and took a swig like I'd done it a million times before, like I was the kind of girl who could drink right from the bottle.

I was proud of myself for not spitting it back up. I took a step toward the water, smiling big at him. I was testing him.

"Belly," he warned. "I'm telling you now, I'm not

going to pull your dead body out of the ocean when you drown."

I crossed my eyes at him and then I dipped my toe in. The water was colder than I'd thought it'd be. Suddenly swimming didn't sound like such a great idea. But I hated backing down to Conrad. I hated losing to him. "Are you gonna stop me?"

He sighed and looked back toward the house.

I continued, took another glug of tequila. Anything to make him pay attention. "I mean, 'cause I am a stronger swimmer than you. I'm way, way faster. You probably couldn't catch me if you wanted to."

He was looking at me again. "I'm not coming after you."

"Really? You really aren't?" I took a big step, then another. The water was up to my knees. It was low tide, and I was shivering. It was stupid, really. I didn't even want to swim anymore. I didn't know what I was doing. Far down on the other side of the beach, somebody shot off a firecracker. It sounded like a missile. It looked like a silver weeping willow. I watched it drop down into the ocean.

And just when I started to feel disappointed, just when I'd resigned myself to the fact that he didn't care, he moved toward me. He heaved me up, over his shoulder. I dropped the bottle right into the ocean.

"Put me down!" I screamed, pounding on his back.

"Belly, you're drunk."

"Put me down right now!"

And for once, he actually listened. He dropped me, right in the sand, right on my butt. "Ow! That really hurt!"

It didn't hurt that bad, but I was mad, and more than that, I was embarrassed. I kicked sand at his back and the wind kicked it right back at me. "Jerk!" I yelled, sputtering and spitting out sand.

Conrad shook his head and turned away from me. His jeans were wet. He was leaving. He was really leaving. I'd ruined everything again.

When I stood up I felt so dizzy I almost fell right back down.

"Wait," I said, and my knees wobbled. I pushed my sandy hair out of my face and took a deep breath. I had to say it, had to tell him. My last chance.

He turned back around. His face was a closed door.

"Just wait a second, please. I need to tell you something. I'm really sorry for the way I acted that day." My voice was high and desperate, and I was crying, and I hated that I was crying, but I couldn't help it. I had to keep talking, because this was it. Last chance. "At . . . at the funeral, I was awful to you. I was horrible, and I'm so ashamed of how I acted. It wasn't how I wanted things to go, not at all. I really, really wanted to be there for you. That's why I came to find you."

Conrad blinked once and then again. "It's fine."

I wiped my cheeks and my runny nose. I said, "Do you mean it? You forgive me?"

"Yes," he said. "I forgive you. Now stop crying, all right?"

I stepped toward him, closer and closer still, and he didn't back away. We were close enough to kiss. I was holding my breath, wanting so badly for things to be like before.

I took one step closer, and that's when he said, "Let's go back, okay?"

Conrad didn't wait for me to answer him. He just started walking away, and I followed. I felt like I was going to be sick.

Just like that, the moment was over. It was an almost moment, where almost anything could have happened. But he had made it be over.

Back at the house, people were swimming in the pool in their clothes. A few girls were waving sparklers around. Clay Bertolet, our neighbor, was floating along the edge of the pool in one of his wifebeaters. He grabbed my ankles. "Come on, Belly, swim with me," he said.

"Let go," I said, kicking him off and splashing his face in the process.

I pushed my way through all the people on the deck and made my way back into the house. I accidentally stepped on some girl's foot and she screamed. "Sorry," I said, and my voice came out sounding far away. I was so dizzy. I just wanted my bed.

I crawled up the stairs with my hands, like a crab, the way I used to when I was a little kid. I fell into bed, and it was just like they say in the movies, the room was spinning. The bed was spinning, and then I remembered all the stupid stuff I said, and I started to cry.

I made a real fool of myself out on that beach. It was devastating, all of it—Susannah gone, the thought of this house not being ours anymore, me giving Conrad the chance to reject me one more time. Taylor was right: I was a masochist.

I lay on my side and hugged my knees to my chest and wept. Everything was wrong, and most of all me. Suddenly I just wanted my mother.

I reached across the bed for the phone on my nightstand. The numbers lit up in the darkness. My mother picked up on the fourth ring.

Her voice was drowsy and familiar in a way that made me cry harder. More than anything in the world, I wanted to reach inside the phone and bring her here.

"Mommy," I said. My voice came out a croak.

"Belly? What's wrong? Where are you?"

"I'm at Susannah's. At the summer house."

"What? What are you doing at the summer house?"

"Mr. Fisher's gonna sell it. He's gonna sell it and Conrad is so sad and Mr. Fisher doesn't even care. He just wants to get rid of it. He wants to get rid of her."

"Belly, slow down. I can't hear what you're saying."

"Just come, okay? Just please come and fix it."

And then I hung up, because suddenly the phone felt very heavy in my hand. I felt like I was on a merry-go-round, and not in a good way. Somebody was setting off fireworks outside, and it felt like my head was pounding right along with them. Then I closed my eyes and it was worse. But my eyelids felt heavy too and soon I was asleep.

chapter *thirty-two*
JEREMIAH

Pretty soon after Belly went up to bed, I cleared everybody out and it was just Conrad and me. He was lying facedown on the couch. He'd been lying there since he and Belly came back from the beach. They were both wet and sandy. Belly was wasted, and she'd been crying, I could tell. Her eyes were red. Conrad's fault—no doubt about that.

People had tracked sand inside and it was all over the floor. There were bottles and cans everywhere, and somebody had sat on the couch in a wet towel, and now the cushion had a big orange spot. I flipped it over. "The house is a wreck," I said, falling onto the La-Z-Boy. "Dad will freak out if he sees it like this tomorrow."

Conrad didn't open his eyes. "Whatever. We'll clean it in the morning."

I stared at him, just feeling pissed. I was sick of cleaning up his messes. "It's gonna take us hours."

Then he opened his eyes. "You're the one who invited everybody over."

He had a point. The party had been my idea. It wasn't the mess I was pissed about. It was Belly. Him and her, together. It made me sick.

"Your jeans are wet," I said. "You're getting sand all over the couch."

Conrad sat up, rubbed his eyes. "What's your problem?"

I couldn't take it anymore. I started to get up, but then I sat back down. "What the hell happened outside with you guys?"

"Nothing."

"What does that mean, nothing?"

"Nothing means nothing. Just leave it, Jere."

I hated it when he got like that, all stoic and detached, especially when I was mad. He'd always been like that, but it was more and more these days. When our mom died, he changed. Conrad didn't give two shits about anything or anyone anymore. I wondered if that included Belly.

I had to know. About him and her, how he really felt, what he was going to do about it. It was the not knowing that killed a guy.

So I asked him flat out. "Do you still like her?"

He stared at me. I'd shocked the hell out of him, I could tell. We'd never talked about her before, not like this. It was probably a good thing that I'd caught him off guard. Maybe he'd tell the truth.

If he said yes, it was over. If he said yes, I would give her up. I could live with that. If it were anyone but Conrad, I'd have tried anyway. I'd have given it one last shot.

Instead of answering the question, he said, "Do you?"

I could feel myself turn red. "I'm not the one who took her to the freaking prom."

Conrad thought that over and then said, "I only took her because she asked me to."

"Con. Do you like her or not, man?" I hesitated for about two seconds, and then I just went for it. "Because I do. I like her. I really like her. Do you?"

He didn't blink, didn't even hesitate. "No."

It really pissed me off.

He was full of shit. He liked her. He more than liked her. But he couldn't admit it, wouldn't man up. Conrad would never be that guy, the kind of guy Belly needed. Someone who would be there for her, someone she could count on. I could. If she'd let me, I could be that guy.

I was pissed at him, but I had to admit I was relieved, too. No matter how many times he hurt her, I knew that if he wanted her back, she was his. She always had been.

But maybe now that Conrad wasn't standing in the way, she'd see me there too.

chapter *thirty-three*

JULY 5

"Belly."

I tried to roll over, but then I heard it again, louder.

"Belly!" Someone was shaking me awake.

I opened my eyes. It was my mother. She had dark circles around her eyes and her mouth had all but disappeared into a thin line. She was wearing her house sweats, the ones she never left the house in, not even to go to the gym. What in the world was she doing at the summer house?

There was a beeping sound that at first I thought was the alarm clock, but then I realized that I had knocked the phone over, and it was the busy signal I was hearing. And then I remembered. I'd drunk-dialed my mother. I'd brought her here.

I sat up, my head pounding so hard it felt like my heart

was hammering inside it. So this was what a hangover felt like. I'd left my contacts in and my eyes were burning. There was sand all over the bed and some was stuck on my feet.

My mother stood up; she was one big blur. "You have five minutes to pack up your stuff."

"Wait . . . what?"

"We're leaving."

"But I can't leave yet. I still have to—"

It was like she couldn't hear me, like I was on mute. She started picking my things up off the floor, throwing Taylor's sandals and shorts into my overnight bag.

"Mom, stop! Just stop for a minute."

"We're leaving in five minutes," she repeated, looking around the room.

"Just listen to me for a second. I had to come. Jeremiah and Conrad needed me."

The look on my mother's face made me stop short. I'd never seen her angry like this before.

"And you didn't feel the need to tell me about it? Beck asked me to look after her boys. How can I do that when I don't even know they need my help? If they were in trouble, you should have told me. Instead you chose to lie to me. You *lied*."

"I didn't want to lie to you—," I started to say.

She kept on going. "You've been here doing God knows what . . ."

I stared at her. I couldn't believe she'd just said that.

"What does that mean, 'God knows what'?"

My mother whirled around, her eyes all wild. "What am I supposed to think? You snuck out here with Conrad before and you spent the night! So you tell me. What *are* you doing here with him? Because it looks to me like you lied to me so you could come here and get drunk and fool around with your boyfriend."

I hated her. I hated her so much.

"He's not my boyfriend! You don't know anything!"

The vein in my mother's forehead was pulsing. "You call me at four in the morning, drunk. I call your cell phone and it goes straight to voice mail. I call the house phone and all I get is a busy signal. I drive all night, worried out of my mind, and I get here and the house is a wreck. Beer cans everywhere, trash all over the place. What the hell do you think you're doing, Isabel? Or do you even know?"

The walls in the house were really thin. Everyone could probably hear everything.

I said, "We were going to clean it up. This was our last night here. Don't you get it? Mr. Fisher is selling the house. Don't you care?"

She shook her head, her jaw tight. "Do you really think you've helped matters by meddling? This isn't our business. How many times do I have to explain that to you?"

"It is so our business. Susannah would have wanted us to save this house!"

"Don't talk to me about what Susannah would have wanted," my mother snapped. "Now put your clothes on and get your things. We're leaving."

"No." I pulled the covers up to my shoulders.

"What?"

"I said no. I'm not going!" I stared up at my mother as defiantly as I could, but I could feel my chin trembling.

She marched over to the bed and ripped the sheets right off of me. She grabbed my arm, pulled me out of the bed and toward the door, and I twisted away from her.

"You can't make me go," I sobbed. "You can't tell me anything. You don't have the right."

My tears did not move my mother. They only made her angrier. She said, "You're acting like a spoiled brat. Can't you look beyond your own grief and think about someone else? It's not all about you. We all lost Beck. Feeling sorry for yourself isn't helping anything."

Her words stung me so badly I wanted to hurt her back a million times worse. So I said the thing I knew would hurt her most. I said, "I wish Susannah was my mother and not you."

How many times had I thought it, wished for it secretly? When I was little, Susannah was the one I ran to, not her. I used to wonder what it would be like, to have a mom like Susannah who loved me for me and wasn't disappointed in all the ways that I didn't measure up.

I was breathing hard as I waited for my mother to respond. To cry, to scream at me.

She didn't do either of those things. Instead she said, "How unfortunate for you."

Even when I tried my hardest, I couldn't get the reaction I wanted from my mother. She was impenetrable.

I said, "Susannah will never forgive you for this, you know. For losing her house. For letting down her boys."

My mother's hand reached out and struck my cheek so hard I rocked back. I didn't see it coming. I clutched my face and right away I cried, but part of me was satisfied. I finally got what I wanted. Proof that she could feel something.

Her face was white. She had never hit me before. Never ever, not in my whole life.

I waited for her to say she was sorry. To say she didn't mean to hurt me, she didn't mean the things she'd said. If she said those things, then I would say them too. Because I was sorry. I didn't mean the things I said.

When she didn't speak, I backed away from her and then around her, holding my face. Then I ran out of the room, stumbling over my feet.

Jeremiah was standing in the hallway, looking at me with his mouth open. He looked at me like he didn't recognize me, like he didn't know who this person was, this girl who screamed at her mother and said terrible things. "Wait," he said, reaching out to stop me.

I pushed past him and moved down the stairs.

In the living room, Conrad was picking up beer bottles and tossing them into a blue recycling bag. He didn't look at me. I knew he'd heard everything too.

I ran out the back door and then I almost tripped going down the stairs that headed down to the beach. I sank to the ground and sat in the sand, holding my burning cheek in the palm of my hand. And then I threw up.

I heard Jeremiah come up behind me. I knew it was him right away, because Conrad would know not to follow me.

"I just want to be alone," I said, wiping my mouth. I didn't turn around. I didn't want him to see my face.

"Belly," he started. He sat down next to me and kicked sand over my throw up.

When he didn't say anything more, I looked at him. "What?"

He bit his upper lip. Then he reached out and touched my cheek. His fingers felt warm. He looked so sad. He said, "You should just go with your mom."

Whatever I'd been expecting him to say, it hadn't been that. I'd come all this way and I'd gotten in so much trouble, just so I could help him and Conrad, and now he wanted me to leave? Tears welled up in the corners of my eyes and I wiped them away with the back of my hands. "Why?"

"Because Laurel's really upset. Everything's gone to

crap, and it's my fault. I never should have asked you to come. I'm sorry."

"I'm not leaving."

"Pretty soon we'll all have to."

"And that's it?"

He shrugged. "Yeah, I guess it is."

We sat in the sand for a while. I had never felt more lost. I cried a little more, and Jeremiah didn't say anything, which I was grateful for. There was nothing worse than your friend watching you cry after you just got in trouble with your mother. When I was done, he stood up and gave me his hand. "Come on," he said, pulling me to my feet.

We went back inside the house. Conrad was gone and the living room was clean. My mother was mopping the kitchen floor. When she saw me, she stopped. She put the mop back into the bucket and leaned it against the wall.

Right in front of Jeremiah, she said, "I'm sorry."

I looked at him, and he backed out of the kitchen and went up the stairs. I almost stopped him. I didn't want to be alone with her. I was afraid.

She continued. "You're right. I've been absent. I've been so consumed with my own grief, I haven't reached out to you. I'm sorry for that."

"Mom—," I started to say. I was about to tell her I was sorry too, for saying that thing before, that awful thing I wished I could take back. But she lifted her hand up and stopped me.

"I'm just—off balance. Ever since Beck died, I can't seem to find my equilibrium." She rested her head against the wall. "I've been coming here with Beck since I was younger than you are now. I love this house. You know that."

"I know," I said. "I didn't mean it, what I said before."

My mother nodded. "Let's sit down a minute, all right?"

She sat down at the kitchen table and I took a seat across from her.

"I shouldn't have hit you," she said, and her voice broke. "I'm sorry."

"You never did that before."

"I know."

My mother reached across the table and took my hand in hers, tight as a cocoon. At first I felt stiff, but then I let her comfort me. Because I could see it was a comfort to her, too. We sat like that for what felt like a long time.

When she let go, she said, "You lied to me, Belly. You never lie to me."

"I didn't mean to. But Conrad and Jeremiah are important to me. They needed me, so I went."

"I wish you would have told me. Beck's boys are important to me, too. If something's going on, I want to know about it. Okay?"

I nodded.

Then she said, "Are you all packed? I want to beat Sunday traffic on the way back."

I stared at her. "Mom, we can't just leave. Not with everything that's happening. You can't let Mr. Fisher sell the house. You just can't."

She sighed. "I don't know that I can say anything to change his mind, Belly. Adam and I don't see eye to eye on a lot of things. I can't stop him from selling the house if that's what he's set on."

"You can, I know you can. He'll listen to you. Conrad and Jeremiah, they need this house. They need it."

I set my head down on the table, and the wood was cool and smooth against my cheek. My mother touched the top of my head, running her hand through my tangled hair.

"I'll call him," she said at last. "Now get upstairs and take a shower." Hopefully, I looked up at her and I saw the firm set of her mouth and the narrow of her eyes. And I knew it wasn't over yet.

If anybody could make things right, it was my mother.

chapter *thirty-four*
JEREMIAH

There was this time—I think I was thirteen and Belly was eleven, about to turn twelve. She'd caught a summer cold, and she was miserable. She was camped out on the couch with balled-up tissues all around her, and she'd been wearing the same ratty pajamas for days. Because she was sick, she got to pick whatever TV show she wanted to watch. The only thing she could eat were grape Popsicles, and when I reached for one, my mother said that Belly should have it. Even though she'd already had three. I got stuck with a yellow one.

It was afternoon, and Conrad and Steven had hitch-hiked to the arcade, which I wasn't supposed to know about. The moms thought they were riding their bikes to the tackle shop for more rubber worms. I was going to go boarding with Clay, and I had my swim trunks on and a towel around my neck when I ran into my mom in the kitchen.

"What are you up to, Jere?" she asked.

I made a hang ten sign. "I'm gonna go boarding with Clay. See ya!"

I was about to push the sliding door open when she said, "Hmm. You know what?"

Suspiciously, I asked, "What?"

"It might be nice if you stayed inside today and cheered up Belly. Poor thing could use some cheering up."

"Aw, Mom—"

"Please, Jeremiah?"

I sighed. I didn't want to stay home and cheer up Belly. I wanted to go boarding with Clay.

When I didn't say anything, she added, "We can grill out tonight. I'll let you be in charge of the burgers."

I sighed again, louder this time. My mom still thought that letting me fire up the grill and flip hamburgers was a big treat for me. Not that it wasn't fun, but still. I opened my mouth to say "no thanks," but then I saw the fond, happy look on her face, the way she just knew I would say yes. So I did. "Fine," I said.

I went back upstairs and changed out of my swim trunks and then I joined Belly in the TV room. I sat as far away from her as I could. The last thing I needed was to catch her cold and be sidelined for a week.

"Why are you still here?" she asked, blowing her nose.

"It's too hot outside," I said. "Wanna watch a movie?"

"It's not that hot outside."

"How would you know if you haven't been out there?"

She narrowed her eyes. "Did your mom make you stay inside with me?"

"No," I said.

"Ha!" Belly grabbed the remote and changed the channel. "I know you're lying."

"I am not!"

Blowing her nose loudly she said, "ESP, remember?"

"That's not real. Can I have the remote?"

She shook her head and held the remote to her chest protectively. "No. My germs are all over it. Sorry. Is there any more toast bread?"

Toast bread was what we called the bread my mom bought at the farmer's market. It came sliced, and it was white and thick and a little bit sweet. I'd had the last three slices of toast bread that morning. I'd slathered it with butter and blackberry jam and I'd eaten it really fast before anyone else got up. With four kids and two adults, bread went really fast. It was every man for himself.

"No more toast bread left," I said.

"Conrad and Steven are such pigs," she said, sniffling.

Guiltily, I said, "I thought all you wanted to eat were grape Popsicles."

She shrugged. "When I woke up this morning I

wanted toast bread. I think maybe I'm getting better."

She didn't look any better to me. Her eyes were swollen and her skin looked grayish, and I don't think she'd washed her hair in days because it was all stringy and matted looking. "Maybe you should take a shower," I said. "My mom says you always feel better after you take a shower."

"Are you saying I smell?"

"Um, no." I looked out the window. It was a clear day, no clouds. I bet Clay was having a blast. I bet Steven and Conrad were too. Conrad had emptied out his old first-grade piggy bank and found a ton of quarters. I bet they'd be at the arcade all afternoon. I wondered how long Clay was gonna be outside. I might be able to catch him in a few hours; it'd still be light out.

I guess Belly caught me staring out the window, because she said, in this really snotty voice, "Just go if you want to."

"I said I didn't," I snapped. Then I took a breath. My mom wouldn't like it if I made Belly upset when she was all sick like this. And she really did look lonely. I kinda felt sorry for her, being stuck inside all day. Summer colds sucked more than anything.

So I said, "Do you want me to teach you how to play poker?"

"You don't know how to play," she scoffed. "Conrad beats you every time."

"Fine," I said. I stood up. I didn't feel *that* sorry for her.

"Never mind," she said. "You can teach me."

I sat back down. "Pass the cards," I said gruffly.

I could tell Belly felt bad because she said, "You shouldn't sit too close. You'll get sick too."

"That's okay," I said. "I never get sick."

"Neither does Conrad," she said, and I rolled my eyes. Belly worshipped Conrad, just like Steven did.

"Conrad does get sick, he gets sick all the time in the winter. He has a weak immune system," I told her, although I didn't know if that was true or not.

She shrugged, but I could tell she didn't believe me. She handed me the cards. "Just deal," she said.

We played poker all afternoon and it was actually pretty fun. I got sick two days later, but I didn't mind that much. Belly stayed home with me and we played more poker and we watched *The Simpsons* a lot.

chapter *thirty-five*
JEREMIAH

As soon as I heard Belly come up the stairs, I met her in the hallway. "So? What's going on?"

"My mom's calling your dad," she said gravely.

"She is? Wow."

"Yeah, so, don't, like, give up already. It's not over yet." Then she gave me one of her wrinkly-nose smiles.

I clapped her on the back and practically sprinted down the stairs. There was Laurel, wiping down the counter. When she saw me, she said, "Your father's coming over. For breakfast."

"Here?"

Laurel nodded. "Will you go to the store and get some things he likes? Eggs and bacon. Muffin mix. And those big grapefruit."

Laurel hated to cook. She had definitely never made

my dad a lumberjack breakfast. "Why are you cooking for him?" I asked.

"Because he's a child and children are cranky when they haven't been fed," she said in that dry way of hers.

Out of nowhere, I said, "Sometimes I hate him."

She hesitated before saying, "Sometimes I do too."

And then I waited for her to say, "But he is your father," the way my mom used to. Laurel didn't, though. Laurel was no bullshit. She didn't say things she didn't mean.

All she said was, "Now get going."

I got up and gave her a bear hug, and she was stiff in my arms. I lifted her up in the air a little, the way I used to do with my mom. "Thanks, Laure," I said. "Really, thanks."

"I'd do anything for you boys. You know that."

"How did you know to come?"

"Belly called me," she said. She narrowed her eyes at me. "Drunk."

Oh, man. "Laure—"

"Don't you 'Laure' me. How could you let her drink? I count on you, Jeremiah. You know that."

Now I felt awful too. The last thing I wanted was for Belly to get in trouble, and I really hated the thought of Laurel thinking badly of me. I'd always tried so hard to look out for Belly, unlike Conrad. If anyone had corrupted her, it was Conrad, not me. Even though I was the one who bought the tequila, not him.

I said, "I'm really sorry. It's just that with my dad's selling the house, and it being our last night, we got carried away. I swear, Laure, it'll never happen again."

She rolled her eyes. "'It'll never happen again'? Don't make promises you can't keep, hon."

"It'll never happen again on my watch," I told her.

Pursing her lips, she said, "We'll see."

I was relieved when she gave me another grimace-smile. "Hurry up and get to the store, will you?"

"Aye aye, sir." I wanted her to smile for real. I knew that if I kept trying, kept joking, she would. She was easy that way.

This time, she really did smile back at me.

chapter *thirty-six*

My mother was right. The shower helped. I tilted my face toward the shower head and let the hot water wash over me and I felt much, much better.

After my shower, I came back downstairs a new woman. My mother was wearing lipstick, and she and Conrad were talking in low voices.

They stopped talking when they saw me standing in the doorway. "Much better," my mother said.

"Where's Jeremiah?" I asked.

"Jeremiah went back to the store. He forgot the grapefruit," she said.

The timer went off and my mother took muffins out of the oven with a dish towel. She accidentally touched the muffin tin with her bare hand and she yelped and dropped the tin on the floor, muffin side down. "Damn!"

Conrad asked if she was okay before I could. "I'm fine," she said, running cold water over her hand.

Then she picked the tin back up and set it on the counter, on top of the towel. I sat down on one of the counter stools and watched my mother empty the muffin tin into a basket. "Our little secret," she said.

The muffins were supposed to cool a little while before you took them out of the tin, but I didn't tell her that. A few were smushed but they mostly looked okay.

"Have a muffin," she said.

I took one, and it was burning hot and falling apart, but it was good. I ate it quickly.

When I was done, my mother said, "You and Conrad take the recycling out."

Without a word, Conrad picked up two of the heavier bags and left me the half-empty one. I followed him outside to the trashcans at the end of the driveway.

"Did you call her?" he asked me.

"I guess I did." I waited for him to call me a baby for calling my mommy the second things got scary.

He didn't. Instead, he said, "Thanks."

I stared at him. "Sometimes you surprise me," I said.

He didn't look at me when he said, "And you hardly ever surprise me. You're still the same."

I glared at him. "Thanks a lot." I dumped my garbage bag in the bin and shut the lid a little too hard.

"No, I mean . . ."

I waited for him to say something, and it seemed like he might have, but then Jeremiah's car came down the street. We both watched Jeremiah park and then bound out of the car with a plastic grocery bag. He strode up to us, his eyes bright. "Hey," he said to me, his bag swinging.

"Hey," I said. I couldn't even look him in the eye. It had all come back to me when I was in the shower. Making Jeremiah dance with me, running away from Conrad, and him picking me up and dropping me in the sand. How humiliating. How awful that they saw me behave that way.

Then Jeremiah gave my hand a squeeze, and when I looked up at him, he said "thank you" so sweetly it hurt.

The three of us walked back to the house. The Police were singing "Message in a Bottle" and the stereo was very loud. Right away my head started pounding and all I wanted was to go back to bed.

"Can we turn down that music?" I asked, rubbing my temples.

"Nope," my mother said, taking the bag from Jeremiah. She pulled out a big grapefruit and tossed it to Conrad. "Squeeze," she said, pointing at the juicer. The juicer was Mr. Fisher's, and it was huge and complicated, one of those Jack LaLanne ones from the late night infomercials.

Conrad snorted. "For him? I'm not squeezing his grapefruit."

"Yes, you will." To me, my mother said, "Mr. Fisher's coming to breakfast."

I squealed. I ran over to her and wrapped my arms around her waist. "It's just breakfast," she warned me. "Don't go getting your hopes up."

But it was too late. I knew she'd change his mind. I knew it. And so did Jeremiah and Conrad. They believed in my mother and so did I—never more so than when Conrad started cutting the grapefruit in half. My mother nodded at him like a drill sergeant. Then she said, "Jere, you set the table, and Belly, you do the eggs."

I started cracking eggs into a bowl, and my mother fried bacon in Susannah's cast iron skillet. She left the bacon grease for me to fry the eggs in. I stirred the eggs around, and the smell of the eggs and the grease made me want to gag. I held my breath as I stirred, and my mother tried to hide a smile as she watched me. "Feeling okay, Belly?" she asked.

I nodded, my teeth clenched.

"Ever planning on drinking again?" she asked conversationally.

I shook my head as hard as I could. "Never, ever again."

When Mr. Fisher arrived half an hour later, we were ready for him. He walked in and looked at the table in amazement. "Wow," he said. "This looks great, Laure. Thank you."

He gave her a meaningful look, the adult co-conspiratorial kind of look.

My mother smiled a Mona Lisa kind of smile. Mr. Fisher wasn't gonna know what hit him. "Let's sit," she said.

We all sat down then. My mother sat next to Mr. Fisher and Jeremiah across from him. I sat next to Conrad. "Dig in," my mother said.

I watched Mr. Fisher pile a mound of eggs on his plate, and then four strips of bacon. He loved bacon, and he really loved it the way my mother made it—incinerated, almost burned to a crisp. I passed on the bacon and eggs and just took a muffin.

My mother poured Mr. Fisher a tall glass of grapefruit juice. "Fresh squeezed, courtesy of your eldest," she said. He took it, a little suspiciously. I couldn't blame him. The only person who had ever squeezed juice for Mr. Fisher was Susannah.

But Mr. Fisher rebounded quickly. He shoveled a forkful of eggs into his mouth and said, "Listen, thanks again for coming to help, Laurel. I really appreciate it." He looked at us kids, smiling. "These guys weren't too keen on listening to what I had to say. I'm glad to have a little backup."

My mother smiled back at him just as pleasantly. "Oh, I'm not here to back you up, Adam. I'm here to back up Beck's boys."

His smile faded. He put down his fork. "Laure—"

"You can't sell this house, Adam. You know that. It

means too much to the kids. It would be a mistake." My mother was calm, matter-of-fact.

Mr. Fisher looked at Conrad and Jeremiah and then back at my mother. "I've already made up my mind, Laurel. Don't make me out to be the bad guy here."

Taking a breath, my mother said, "I'm not making you out to be anything. I'm just trying help you."

Us kids sat absolutely still as we waited for Mr. Fisher to speak. He was struggling to stay calm, but his face was turning red. "I appreciate that. But I've made up my mind. The house is for sale. And frankly, Laurel, you don't get a vote in this. I'm sorry. I know Suze always made you feel like this house was part yours, but it's not."

I almost gasped. My eyes darted back to my mother, and I saw that she, too, was turning red. "Oh, I know that," she said. "This house is pure Beck. It's always been Beck. This was her favorite place. That's why the boys should have it."

Mr. Fisher stood up and pushed out his chair. "I'm not going to argue about this with you, Laurel."

"Adam, sit down," my mother said.

"No, I don't think I will."

My mother's eyes were almost glowing. "I said, sit *down*, Adam." He gaped at her—we all did. Then she said, "Kids, get out."

Conrad opened his mouth to argue but he thought better of it, especially when he saw the look on my mother's face and his dad sit back down. As for me, I couldn't get out of there fast enough. We all hustled out of the kitchen and sat at the top of the stairs, straining to hear.

We didn't have to wait long. Mr. Fisher said, "What the hell, Laurel? Did you really think you could railroad me into changing my mind?"

"Excuse me, but fuck you."

I clapped my hand over my mouth and Conrad's eyes were shining and he was shaking his head in admiration. Jeremiah, though, he looked like he might cry. I reached out and grabbed his hand and gave it a squeeze. When he tried to pull away, I held on tighter.

"This house meant everything to Beck. Can't you get past your own grief and see what it means to the boys? They need this. They *need* this. I don't want to believe that you're this cruel, Adam."

He didn't answer her.

"This house is hers. It's not yours. Don't make me stop you, Adam. Because I will. I'll do everything in my power to keep this house for Beck's boys."

Mr. Fisher said, "What will you do, Laure?" and he sounded so tired.

"I'll do what I have to do."

His voice was muffled when he said, "She's everywhere here. She's everywhere."

He might have been crying. I almost felt sorry for him. I guess my mother did too, because her voice was nearly gentle when she said, "I know. But Adam? You were a sorry excuse for a husband. But she loved you. She really did. She took you back. I tried to talk her out of it, God knows I tried. But she wouldn't listen, because when she sets her mind on someone, that's it. And she set her mind on you, Adam. Earn that. Prove me wrong."

He said something I couldn't quite hear. And then my mother said, "You do this one last thing for her. Okay?"

I looked over at Conrad, and he said in a low voice, to no one in particular, "Laurel is amazing."

I'd never heard anyone describe my mom that way, especially not Conrad. I'd never thought of her as "amazing." But in that moment, she was. She truly was. I said, "Yeah, she is. So was Susannah."

He looked at me for a minute and then he got up and went to his room without waiting to hear what else Mr. Fisher said. He didn't need to. My mother had won. She had done it.

A little while later, when it seemed safe, Jeremiah and I went back downstairs. My mother and Mr. Fisher were drinking coffee the way grown-ups do. His eyes were red-rimmed but hers were the clear eyes of a victor. When he saw us, he said, "Where's Conrad?"

How many times had I heard Mr. Fisher say, "Where's Conrad?" Hundreds. Millions.

"He's upstairs," Jeremiah said.

"Go get him, will you, Jere?"

Jeremiah hesitated and then he looked at my mother, who nodded. He bounded up the stairs and a few minutes later, Conrad was with him. Conrad's face was guarded, cautious.

"I'll make you a deal," Mr. Fisher said. This was the old Mr. Fisher, power broker, negotiator. He loved to make deals. He used to offer trades to us kids. Like, he'd drive us to the go-kart track if we swept the sand out of the garage. Or he'd take the boys fishing if they cleaned out all the tackle boxes.

Warily, Conrad said, "What do you want? My trust fund?"

Mr. Fisher's jaw tightened. "No. I want you back at school tomorrow. I want you to finish your exams. If you do that, the house is yours. Yours and Jeremiah's."

Jeremiah whooped loudly. "Yes!" he shouted. He reached over and enveloped Mr. Fisher in a guy hug, and Mr. Fisher clapped him on the back.

"What's the catch?" Conrad asked.

"No catch. But you have to make at least Cs. No Ds or Fs." Mr. Fisher had always prided himself on driving the hard bargain. "Do we have a deal?"

Conrad hesitated. I knew right away what was wrong. Conrad didn't want to owe his dad anything. Even though this was what he wanted, even though it was why he had come here. He didn't want to take anything from his dad.

"I haven't studied," he said. "I might not pass."

He was testing him. Conrad had never "not passed." He'd never gotten anything below a B, and even Bs were rare.

"Then no deal," Mr. Fisher said. "Those are the terms."

Urgently, Jeremiah said, "Con, just say yes, man. We'll help you study. Won't we, Belly?"

Conrad looked at me, and I looked at my mother. "Can I, Mom?"

My mother nodded. "You can stay, but you have to be home tomorrow."

"Take the deal," I told Conrad.

"All right," he said at last.

"Shake on it like a man, then," Mr. Fisher said, holding out his hand.

Reluctantly, Conrad extended his arm and they shook. My mother caught my eye and she mouthed, *Shake on it like a man*, and I knew she was thinking how sexist Mr. Fisher was. But it didn't matter. We had won.

"Thanks, Dad," Jeremiah said. "Really, thanks."

He hugged his dad again and Mr. Fisher hugged him back, saying, "I need to get back to the city." Then he nodded at me. "Thanks for helping Conrad, Belly."

I said, "You're welcome." But I didn't know what I was saying "you're welcome" for, because I hadn't really done anything. My mother had helped Conrad more in half an hour than I had in all my time of knowing him.

After Mr. Fisher left, my mother got up and started rinsing dishes. I joined her and loaded them into the dishwasher. I rested my head on her shoulder for a second. I said, "Thank you."

"You're welcome."

"You were a real badass, Mom."

"Don't cuss," she said, the corners of her mouth turning up.

"You're one to talk."

Then we washed the dishes in silence, and my mother had that sad look on her face and I knew she was thinking of Susannah. And I wished there was something I could say to take that look away, but sometimes there just weren't words.

The three of us walked her to the car. "You boys will get her home tomorrow?" she asked, throwing her bag onto the passenger seat.

"Definitely," Jeremiah said.

Then Conrad said, "Laurel." He hesitated. "You're coming back, aren't you?"

My mother turned to him, surprised. She was touched. "You want an old lady like me around?" she asked. "Sure, I'll be back whenever you'll have me."

"When?" he asked. He looked so young, so vulnerable my heart ached a little.

I guessed my mother was feeling the same way, because

she reached out and touched his cheek. My mother was not a cheek-touching kind of person. It just wasn't her way. But it was Susannah's. "Before the summer's over, and I'll come back to close the house up too."

My mother got into the car then. She waved at us as she backed down the driveway, her sunglasses on, the window down. "See you soon," she called out.

Jeremiah waved and Conrad said, "See you soon."

My mother told me once that when Conrad was very young, he called her "his Laura." "Where is my Laura?" he'd say, wandering around looking for her. She said he followed her everywhere; he'd even follow her into the bathroom. He called her his girlfriend and he would bring her sand crabs and seashells from the ocean and he would lay them at her feet. When she told me about it, I thought, *What I wouldn't give to have Conrad Fisher call me his girlfriend and bring me shells.*

"I'm sure he doesn't remember," she'd said, smiling faintly.

"Why don't you ask him if he does?" I'd said. I loved hearing stories about when Conrad was little. I loved to tease him, because the opportunity to tease Conrad came up so rarely.

She'd said, "No, that would embarrass him," and I'd said, "So what? Isn't that the point?"

And she'd said, "Conrad is sensitive. He has a lot of pride. Let him have that."

The way she said that, I could tell that she really got him. Understood him in a way that I didn't. I was jealous of that, of both of them.

"What was I like?" I'd asked.

"You? You were my baby."

"But what was I *like*?" I persisted.

"You used to chase after the boys. It was so cute the way you'd follow them around, trying to impress them." My mother laughed. "They used to get you to dance around and do tricks."

"Like a puppy?" I frowned at the thought.

She'd waved me off. "Oh, you were fine. You just liked to be included."

chapter *thirty-seven*
JEREMIAH

The day Laurel came, the house was a wreck and I was in my boxers ironing my white button-down. I was already late for senior banquet and I was in a foul mood. My mom had barely said two words all day and even Nona couldn't get her to talk.

I was supposed to pick up Mara, and she hated it when I was late. She'd get all pissy and she'd sit and sulk for about as long as I'd made her wait.

I had put down the iron for a second so I could turn the shirt over and I ended up burning the back of my arm. "Shit!" I yelled. It really freaking hurt.

That was when Laurel showed up. She walked through the front door and saw me standing in the living room in my boxers, holding the back of my arm.

"Run some cold water over it," she told me. I ran to

the kitchen and held my arm under the faucet for a few minutes, and when I came back, she had finished the shirt and gotten started on my khakis.

"Do you wear yours with a crease down the front?" she asked me.

"Uh, sure," I said. "What are you doing here, Laurel? It's a Tuesday." Laurel usually came on weekends and stayed in the guest room.

"I just came to check on things," she said, running the iron down the front of the pants. "I had a free afternoon."

"My mom's asleep already," I told her. "With the new medicine she's taking, she sleeps all the time."

"That's good," Laurel said. "And what about you? Why are you getting all dressed up?"

I sat down on the couch and put my socks on. "I've got senior banquet tonight," I told her.

Laurel handed me my shirt and pants. "What time does it start?"

I glanced at the grandfather clock in the foyer. "Ten minutes ago," I said, stepping into my pants.

"You'd better get going."

"Thanks for ironing my clothes," I said.

I was grabbing my keys when I heard my mom call my name from her bedroom. I turned toward her doorway, and Laurel said, "Just go to your banquet, Jere. I've got it covered."

I hesitated. "Are you sure?"

"A thousand percent. Beat it."

I sped all the way to Mara's house. She came out as soon as I pulled into her driveway. She was wearing that red dress I liked and she looked nice, and I was about to tell her so, but then she said, "You're late."

I shut my mouth. Mara didn't speak to me for the rest of the night, not even when we won Cutest Couple. She didn't feel like going to Patan's party afterward and neither did I. The whole time we were out, I was thinking about my mom and feeling guilty for being gone so long.

When we got to Mara's house, she didn't get out right away, which was her signal that she wanted to talk. I shut off the engine.

"So, what's up? Are you still mad at me for being late, Mar?"

She looked pained. "I just want to know if we're going to stay together. Can you just tell me what you want to do, and then we'll do it?"

"Honestly, I can't really think about this kind of stuff right now."

"I know. I'm sorry."

"But if I was going to have to say whether or not I think we'll be together when we're at school in the fall, long distance—" I hesitated, and then I just said it. "I would probably say no."

Mara started crying, and I felt like a real piece of shit. I should've just lied.

"That's what I thought," she said. Then she kissed me on the cheek and ran out of the car and into her house.

So that's how we broke up. If I'm going to be completely honest, I'll admit that it was a relief not to have to think about Mara anymore. The only person I had room in my head for was my mom.

When I got home, my mom and Laurel were still up playing cards and listening to music. For the first time in days, I heard my mom laugh.

Laurel didn't leave the next day. She stayed all week. At the time, I didn't wonder about her job, or all the other stuff she had going on at home. I was just grateful to have an adult around.

chapter *thirty-eight*

The three of us walked back to the house. The sun was hot on my back and I thought about how nice it would be to lay out on the beach for a while, to sleep the afternoon away and wake up tan. But there wasn't any time for that, not when we needed to get Conrad ready for his midterms by tomorrow.

When we got inside, Conrad fell onto the couch and Jeremiah sprawled out on the floor. "So tired," he moaned.

What my mother did for us, for me, was a gift. Now it was my turn to give one back. "Get up," I said.

Neither of them moved. Conrad's eyes were closed. So I threw a pillow at Conrad and jabbed Jeremiah in the stomach with my foot. "We have to start studying, you lazy bums. Now get up!"

Conrad opened his eyes. "I'm too tired to study. I need to take a power nap first."

"Me too," Jeremiah said.

Crossing my arms, I glared at them and said, "I'm tired too, you know. But look at the clock; it's already one. We're gonna have to work all night and leave really early tomorrow morning."

Shrugging, Conrad said, "I work best under pressure."

"But—"

"Seriously, Belly. I can't work like this. Just let me sleep for an hour."

Jeremiah was already falling asleep. I sighed. I couldn't fight the both of them. "Fine. One hour. But that's it."

I stalked into the kitchen and poured myself a Coke. I was tempted to take a nap too, but that would be setting the wrong example.

While they slept, I kicked the plan into gear. I got Conrad's books out of the car, brought his laptop downstairs, and set up the kitchen like a study room. I plugged in lamps, stacked books and binders according to subject, put out pens and paper. Last, I brewed a big pot of coffee, and even though I didn't drink coffee, I knew mine was good, because I brewed a pot for my mother every morning. Then I took Jeremiah's car and drove to McDonald's to pick up cheeseburgers. They loved McDonald's cheeseburgers. They used to have cheeseburger-eating contests and they'd stack them up like pancakes. Sometimes they let me play too. One time, I won. I ate nine cheeseburgers.

I let them sleep an extra half hour—but only because it took me that long to get things set up. Then I filled up Susannah's spray bottle, the one she'd used to water her more delicate plants. I sprayed Conrad first, right in the eyes.

"Hey," he said, waking up right away. He wiped his face with the bottom of his T-shirt, and I gave him another spray just because.

"Rise and shine," I sang.

Then I walked over to Jeremiah and sprayed him, too. He didn't wake up though. He had always been impossible to wake up. He could sleep through a tidal wave. I sprayed and sprayed and when he just rolled over, I unscrewed the top of the bottle and poured the water right down the back of his T-shirt.

He finally woke up and stretched his arms out, still lying down on the floor. He gave me a slow grin, like he was used to being woken up this way. "Morning," he said. Jeremiah might have been hard to wake up, but he was never a grouch when he finally did.

"It's not morning. It's almost three o'clock in the afternoon. I let you guys sleep an extra half an hour so you better be grateful," I snapped.

"I am," Jeremiah said, reaching his arm out for me to help him up. I grudgingly gave him my hand and helped heft him up. "Come on," I said.

They followed me into the kitchen.

"What the—," Conrad said, looking around the room at all his things.

Jeremiah clapped his hands together and then he held one hand up for a high five, which I gave him. "You're amazing," he said. Then he sniffed and spotted the greasy white McDonald's bag and lit up. "Yes! Mickey D's cheeseburgers! I'd know that smell anywhere."

I smacked his hand away. "Not yet. There is a reward system in place here. Conrad studies, and then he gets food."

Jeremiah frowned. "What about me?"

"Conrad studies, and you get food."

Conrad raised his eyebrows at me. "A reward system, huh? What else do I get?"

I flushed. "Just the cheeseburgers."

His eyes flickered over me appraisingly, like he was trying to decide whether or not he wanted to buy a coat. I could feel my cheeks heat up as he looked at me. "As much as I like the sound of a reward system, I'm gonna pass," he said at last.

"What are you talking about?" Jeremiah asked.

Conrad shrugged. "I study better on my own. I've got it covered. You guys can go."

Jeremiah shook his head in disgust. "Just like always. You can't handle asking for help. Well, sucks to be you, 'cause we're staying."

"What do you guys know about freshman psych?" Conrad said, crossing his arms.

Jeremiah sprang up. "We'll figure it out." He winked at me. "Bells, can we eat first? I need grease."

I felt like I had won a prize. Like I was invincible. Reaching into the bag, I said, "One each. That's it."

When Conrad's back was turned, as he was rummaging around the cupboard for Tabasco sauce, Jeremiah held his hand out for another high five. I slapped it silently and we grinned at each other. Jeremiah and I were a good team, always had been.

We ate our cheeseburgers in silence. As soon as we were done, I said, "How do you want to do this, Conrad?"

"Seeing as how I don't want to do this at all, I'll let you decide," he said. He had mustard on his lower lip.

"Okay, then." I was prepared for this. "You'll read. I'll work on note cards for psych. Jeremiah will highlight."

"Jere doesn't know how to highlight," Conrad scoffed.

"Hey!" Jeremiah said. Then, turning to me, he said, "He's right. I suck at highlighting. I just end up highlighting the whole page. I'll do note cards and you highlight, Bells."

I ripped open a pack of index cards and handed them to Jeremiah. Incredibly enough, Conrad listened. He picked his psych textbook out of the stack of books and he started to read.

Sitting at the table, studying with his forehead creased,

he looked like the old Conrad. The one who cared about things like exams and ironed shirts and being on time. The irony of all this was that Jeremiah had never been much of a student. He hated to study; he hated grades. Learning was, had always been, Conrad's thing. From the very start, he was the one with the chemistry set, thinking up experiments for us to do as his scientist's assistants. I remembered when he'd discovered the word "absurd," and he went around saying it all the time. "That's *absurd*," he'd say. Or "numbskull," his favorite insult—he said that a lot too. The summer he was ten, he tried to work his way through the *Encyclopedia Britannica*. When we came back the next summer, he was at *Q*.

I realized it suddenly. I missed him. All this time. When you got to the underneath of it, there it was. There it had always been. And even though he was sitting there only feet away, I missed him more than ever.

Underneath my lashes I watched him, and I thought, *Come back. Be the you I love and remember.*

chapter *thirty-nine*

We were done with psychology and Conrad was working on his English paper with his headphones on when my phone buzzed. It was Taylor. I wasn't sure if she was calling to apologize or to demand I bring her stuff back home immediately. Maybe a mixture of both. I turned off my phone.

With all the house drama, I hadn't thought about our fight once. I'd only been back at the summer house for a couple of days, and just like always, I'd already forgotten about Taylor and everything back home. What mattered to me was here. It had always been that way.

But those things she'd said, they hurt. Maybe they were true. But I didn't know if I could forgive her for saying them.

It was getting dark out when Jeremiah leaned over

and said in a low voice, "You know, if you wanted to, you could leave tonight. You could just take my car. I could pick it up tomorrow, after Conrad's done with his exams. We could hang out or something."

"Oh, I'm not leaving yet. I want to go with you guys tomorrow."

"Are you sure?"

"Sure, I'm sure. Don't you want me to come with you?" It was starting to hurt my feelings, the way he was acting like they were imposing on me, as if we weren't family.

"Yeah, course I do." He paused like he was going to say something else.

I poked him with my highlighter. "Are you scared that you'll get in trouble with *Mara*?" I was only halfway teasing. I still couldn't believe he hadn't told me he had a sort of girlfriend. I wasn't entirely sure why it mattered, but it did. We were supposed to be close. Or at least we used to be. I should have known if he had a girlfriend or not. And how long had they been "broken up" anyway? She hadn't been at the funeral, or at least I didn't think so. It wasn't like Jeremiah had gone around introducing her to people. What kind of girlfriend didn't go to her boyfriend's mom's funeral? Even Conrad's ex had come.

Jeremiah glanced over at Conrad and lowered his voice. "I told you, Mara and I are done."

When I didn't say anything, he said, "Come on, Belly. Don't be mad."

"I can't believe you didn't tell me about her," I said, highlighting an entire paragraph. I didn't look at him. "I can't believe you kept it a secret."

"There wasn't anything to tell, I swear."

"Ha!" I said. But I felt better. I snuck a peek at Jeremiah, and he looked back at me with anxious eyes.

"Okay?"

"Fine. It doesn't affect me one way or the other. I just thought you would have told me a thing like that."

He relaxed back into his seat. "We weren't that serious, trust me. She was just a girl. It wasn't like how it was with Conrad and—"

I started, and he broke off guiltily.

It wasn't like how it was with Conrad and Aubrey. He'd loved her. Once upon a time, he'd been crazy about her. He had never been that way with me. Never. But I had loved him. I loved him longer and truer than I had anyone in my whole life and I would probably never love anyone that way again. Which, to be honest, was almost a relief.

chapter *forty*
JULY 6

When I woke up the next morning, the first thing I did was go to my window. Who knew how many more times I would see this view? We were all growing up. I would be at college soon. But the good thing, the comforting thing, was the knowing that it would still be here. The house wasn't going away.

Looking out the window, it was impossible to see where the sky ended and the ocean began. I'd forgotten how foggy the mornings could get here. I stood there and tried to get my fill, tried to make the memory last.

Then I ran over to Jeremiah's and Conrad's rooms, banging on doors. "Wake up! Let's get this show on the road!" I yelled, starting down the hall.

I headed downstairs to get a glass of juice, and Conrad was sitting at the kitchen table, where he'd been when I went to sleep around four a.m. He was already dressed and making notes in a notebook.

I started to back out of the kitchen, but he looked up. "Nice pjs," he said.

I flushed. I was still wearing Taylor's stupid pajamas. Scowling, I said, "We're leaving in twenty minutes, so be ready."

As I headed back upstairs, I heard Conrad say, "I already am."

If he said he was ready, he was ready. He would pass those exams. He'd probably ace them. Conrad didn't fail at anything he set his mind to.

An hour later, we were almost on our way. I was locking the glass sliding door on the porch when I heard Conrad say, "Should we?"

I turned around, started to say, "Should we what?" when Jeremiah came out of nowhere.

"Yeah. For old times' sake," Jeremiah said.

Uh-oh. "No way," I said. "No freaking way."

The next thing I knew, Jeremiah was grabbing my legs and Conrad took my arms, and together they swung me back, then forth. Jeremiah yelled, "Belly Flop!" and they flung me through the air, and as I landed in the pool, I thought, *Well, there, they're finally united on something.*

When I surfaced, I yelled, "Jerks!" It only made them laugh harder.

I had to go back inside and change out of my soaked clothes, the clothes I wore the first day. I changed into Taylor's sundress and her platform sandals. As I wrung out my hair with a hand towel, it was hard to be mad. I even smiled to myself. Possibly the last Belly Flop of my life, and Steven wasn't there to partake.

It was Jeremiah's idea to take one car, so Conrad could keep studying on the way. Conrad didn't even try to take the front seat, he just went straight to the back and started flipping through his note cards.

Predictably, I cried as we drove away. I was just glad I was up front and wearing sunglasses so the boys couldn't tease me about it. But I loved that house, and I hated to say good-bye. Because, it was more than just a house. It was every summer, every boat ride, every sunset. It was Susannah.

We drove in near silence for a while, and then Britney Spears came on the radio, and I turned it up, loud. It went without saying that Conrad hated Britney Spears, but I didn't care. I started to sing along, and Jeremiah did too.

"Oh baby baby, I shouldn't have let you go," I sang, shimmying toward the dashboard.

"Show me how you want it to be," Jeremiah sang back, bouncing his shoulders.

When the song changed, it was Justin Timberlake, and Jeremiah did an amazing Justin Timberlake. He was so un-self-conscious and easy with who he was. He made me want to be like that too.

He sang to me, "And tell me how they got that pretty little face on that pretty little frame, girl." I put my hand on my heart and fake-swooned for him, like a groupie.

"Fast fast slow, whichever way you wanna run, girl."

I backed him up at the chorus. "This just can't be summer love . . ."

From the backseat, Conrad growled, "Can you guys please turn the music down? I'm trying to study here, remember?"

I turned around and said, "Oh, sorry. Is it bothering you?"

He looked at me with narrowed eyes.

Without saying a word, Jeremiah turned the music down. We drove for another hour or so and then he said, "Do you need to pee or anything? I'm gonna stop at the next exit for gas."

I shook my head. "No, but I am thirsty."

We pulled into the gas station parking lot, and while Jeremiah filled the car up and Conrad napped, I ran into the convenience store. I got Jeremiah and me both Slurpees, half Coke and half cherry, a combination I had perfected over the years.

When I got back to the car, I climbed in and handed Jeremiah his Slurpee. His whole face lit up. "Aw, thanks, Bells. What flavor did you get me?"

"Drink it and see."

He took a long sip and nodded appreciatively. "Half Coke, half cherry, your specialty. Nice."

"Hey, remember that time—," I started to say.

"Yup," he said. "My dad still doesn't want anyone touching his blender."

I put my feet up on the dashboard and leaned back, sipping on my Slurpee. I thought to myself, *Happiness is a Slurpee and a hot pink straw.*

From the back, Conrad said, irritably, "Where's mine?"

"I thought you were still asleep," I said. "And you have to drink a Slurpee right away or it'll melt, so . . . I didn't see the point."

Conrad glared at me. "Well, at least let me have a sip."

"But you hate Slurpees." Which was true. Conrad didn't like sugary drinks, he never had.

"I don't care. I'm thirsty."

I handed him my cup and turned around and watched him drink. I was expecting him to make a face or something, but he just drank and handed it back. And then he said, "I thought your specialty was cocoa."

I stared at him. Did he really just say that? Did he remember? The way he looked back at me, one eyebrow raised, I knew he did. And this time, I was the one to look away.

Because I remembered. I remembered everything.

chapter *forty-one*

When Conrad left to take his exam, Jeremiah and I bought turkey and avocado sandwiches on whole wheat bread and we ate them out on the lawn. I finished mine first; I was really hungry.

When he was done, Jeremiah balled up the foil in his hand and threw it into the trashcan. He sat back down next to me in the grass. Out of nowhere, he said to me, "Why didn't you come see me after my mom died?"

I stuttered, "I d-d-did, I came to the funeral."

Jeremiah's gaze on me was steady, unblinking. "That's not what I mean."

"I—I didn't think you'd want me there yet."

"No, it was because *you* didn't want to be there. I wanted you there."

He was right. I didn't want to be there. I didn't want to

be anywhere near her house. Thinking about her made my heart hurt; it was too much. But the thought of Jeremiah waiting for me to call him, needing someone to talk to, that hurt so bad. "You're right," I told him. "I should've come."

Jeremiah had been there for Conrad, for Susannah. For me. And who had been there for him? Nobody. I wanted him to know I was here now.

He looked up at the sky. "It's hard, you know? Because I want to talk about her. But Conrad doesn't want to, and I can't talk to my dad, and you weren't there either. We all love her, and nobody can talk about her."

"What do you want to say?"

He leaned his head back, thinking. "That I miss her. I really miss her. She's only been gone for two months, but it feels like longer. And it also feels like it just happened, like yesterday."

I nodded. That was exactly how it felt.

"Do you think she'd be glad?"

He meant glad about Conrad, the way we'd helped him. "Yeah."

"Me too." Jeremiah hesitated. "So what now?"

"What do you mean?"

"I mean, are you going to come back this summer?"

"Well, sure. When my mom comes, I'll come too."

He nodded. "Good. Because my dad was wrong, you know. It's your house too. And Laure's, and Steve's. It's all of ours."

Suddenly I was struck with the strangest sensation, of wanting, needing, to reach out and touch his cheek with the back of my hand. So he would know, so he would *feel* exactly how much those words meant to me. Because sometimes words were so pitifully inadequate, and I knew that, but I had to try anyway. I told him, "Thank you. That means—a lot."

He shrugged. "It's just the truth."

We saw him coming from far away, walking fast. We stood up and waited for him.

Jeremiah said, "Does it look like good news to you? It looks like good news to me."

It did to me, too.

Conrad strode up to us, his eyes gleaming. "I killed it," he said triumphantly. First time I'd seen him smile, really smile—joyful, carefree—since Susannah died. He and Jeremiah high-fived so hard the clap rang out in the air. And then Conrad smiled at me, and whirled me around so fast I almost tripped.

I was laughing. "See? See? I told you!"

Conrad picked me up and threw me over his shoulder like I weighed nothing, just like he had the other night. I laughed as he ran, weaving left and right like he was on a football field. "Put me down!" I shrieked, yanking at the bottom of my dress.

He did. He set me down on the ground gently. "Thanks," he said, his hand still on my waist. "For coming."

Before I could tell him you're welcome, Jeremiah walked over and said, "You still have one left, Con." His voice was strained, and I straightened my dress.

Conrad looked at his watch. "You're right. I'm gonna head over to the psychology department. This will be a quick one. I'll meet up with you guys in an hour or so."

As I watched him go, a million questions ran through my head. I felt dizzy, and not just from being spun around in the air.

Abruptly, Jeremiah said, "I'm gonna go find a bathroom. I'll meet you at the car." He fished his keys out of his pocket and threw them to me.

"Do you want me to wait?" I asked, but he was already walking away.

He didn't turn around. "No, just go ahead."

Instead of going straight to the car, I stopped at the student store. I bought a soda and a hoodie that said BROWN in block letters. Even though it wasn't cold, I put it on.

Jeremiah and I sat in the car, listening to the radio. It was starting to get dark. The windows were down and I could hear a bird calling somewhere out there. Conrad would be done with his last exam soon.

"Nice hoodie, by the way," Jeremiah said.

"Thanks. I always wanted one from Brown."

Jeremiah nodded. "I remember."

I fingered my necklace, twisting it around my pinky.

"I wonder . . ." I let my sentence trail off, waiting for Jeremiah to prod me, to ask me what it was I wondered about. But he didn't. He didn't ask me anything.

He was silent.

Sighing, I looked out the window and asked, "Does he ever talk about me? I mean, has he ever said anything?"

"Don't," he snapped.

"Don't what?" I turned toward him, confused.

"Don't ask me that. Don't ask me about him." Jeremiah spoke in a harsh, low voice, a tone he'd never used with me and one I didn't recall him using with anybody. A muscle in his jaw twitched furiously.

I recoiled and sank back into my seat. I felt as though he had slapped me. "What's the matter with you?"

He started to say something, maybe an apology and maybe not, and then he stopped, he leaned over and pulled me toward him—like by gravitational force. He kissed me, hard, and his skin was stubbly and rough against my cheek. My first thought was, *I guess he didn't have time to shave this morning,* and then—I was kissing him back, my fingers winding through his soft yellow hair and my eyes closed. He kissed like he was drowning and I was air. It was passionate, and desperate, and like nothing I had ever experienced before.

This was what people meant when they said the earth stopped turning. It felt like a world outside of that car, that moment, didn't exist. It was just us.

When he backed away, his pupils were huge and unfocused. He blinked, and then he cleared his throat. "Belly," he said, and his voice was foggy. He didn't say anything else, just my name.

"Do you still—" Care. Think about me. Want me.

Roughly, he said, "Yes. Yes, I still."

And then we were kissing again.

He must have made some noise, because we both looked up at the same time.

We sprang apart. There was Conrad, looking right at us. He had stopped short of the car. His face was white.

He said, "No, don't stop. I'm the one who's interrupting."

He turned jerkily and started off. Jeremiah and I stared at each other in silent horror. And then my hand was on the door handle and I was on my feet. I didn't look back.

I ran after him and called his name, but Conrad didn't turn around. I grabbed his arm and he finally looked at me, and there was so much hate in his eyes I winced. Even though, on some level, wasn't this what I wanted? To make his heart hurt the way he made mine? Or maybe, to make him feel something for me other than pity or indifference. To make him feel something, anything.

"So you like Jeremiah now?" He meant to sound sarcastic, cruel, and he did, but he also sounded pained. Like he cared about the answer.

Which made me feel glad. And sad.

I said, "I don't know. Does it matter to you if I do?"

He stared at me, and then he leaned forward and touched the necklace around my neck. The one I'd been hiding under my shirt all day.

"If you like Jeremiah, why are you wearing my necklace?"

I wet my lips. "I found it when we were packing up your dorm room. It doesn't mean anything."

"You know what it means."

I shook my head. "I don't." But of course I did. I remembered when he'd explained the concept of infinity to me. Immeasurable, one moment stretching out to the next. He bought me that necklace. He knew what it meant.

"Then give it back." He held his hand out, and I saw that it was shaking.

"No," I said.

"It's not yours. I never gave it to you. You just took it."

That's when I finally got it. I finally understood. It wasn't the thought that counted. It was the actual execution that mattered, the showing up for somebody. The intent behind it wasn't enough. Not for me. Not anymore. It wasn't enough to know that deep down, he loved me. You had to actually say it to somebody, show them that you cared. And he just didn't. Not enough.

I could feel him waiting for me to argue, to protest,

to plead. But I didn't do any of those things. I struggled for what felt like eternity, trying to undo the clasp on the necklace around my neck. Which was no surprise, considering the fact that my hands were shaking too. I finally got the chain free and I handed it back to him.

Surprise registered upon his face for the tiniest of moments, and then, like always, he was closed off again. Maybe I'd imagined it. That he'd cared.

He stuffed the necklace into his pocket. "Then leave," he said.

When I didn't move, he said, sharply, "Go!"

I was a tree, rooted to the spot. My feet were frozen.

"Go to Jeremiah. He's the one who wants you," Conrad said. "I don't. I never did."

And then I was stumbling, running away.

chapter *forty-two*

I didn't go back to the car right away. All I had in front of me were impossible choices. How could I face Jeremiah after what just happened? After we kissed, after I went running after Conrad? My mind was spinning in a million different directions. I kept touching my lips. Then I'd touch my collarbone, where the necklace used to be. I wandered around campus, but after a while, I headed back to the car. What choice did I have? I couldn't just leave without telling anybody. And it wasn't like I had another way home.

I guessed Conrad was thinking the same thing, because when I got back to the car, he was already there, sitting in the backseat with the window open. Jeremiah was sitting on the hood of the car. "Hi," he said.

"Hey." I hesitated, unsure of what was next. For once,

our ESP connection failed me, because I had no idea what he was thinking. His face was unreadable.

He slid off the car. "Ready to go home?"

I nodded, and he threw me the keys. "You drive," he said.

In the car, Conrad ignored me completely. I didn't exist to him anymore, and despite everything I'd said, that made me want to die. I never should have come. None of us were speaking to one another. I'd lost them both.

What would Susannah say if she saw the mess we were in now? She would have been so disappointed in me. I hadn't been a help at all. I'd only made things worse.

Just when we thought everything was going to be okay, we all fell apart.

I'd been driving for what felt like forever when it started to rain. It started out with fat little *plops* and then it came down heavy, in hard sheets.

"Can you see?" Jeremiah asked me.

"Yeah," I lied. I could barely see two feet in front of me. The windshield wipers were swishing back and forth furiously.

Traffic had been crawling along, and then it slowed almost to a stop. There were police lights way up ahead.

"There must have been an accident," Jeremiah said.

We'd been sitting in traffic for over an hour when it started to hail.

I looked at Conrad in the rearview, but his face was

impassive. He might as well have been somewhere else. "Should we pull over?"

"Yeah. Get off at the next exit and see if we can find a gas station," Jeremiah said, glancing at the clock. It was ten thirty.

The rain didn't let up. We sat in the gas station parking lot for what felt like forever. The rain was loud, but we were so quiet that when my stomach growled, I was pretty sure they both heard. I coughed to cover up the noise.

Jeremiah jumped out of the car and ran inside the gas station. When he ran back, his hair was dripping wet and matted. He tossed me a packet of peanut butter and cheese crackers without looking at me. "There's a motel a few miles down," he said, wiping his forehead with the back of his arm.

"Let's just wait it out," Conrad said. It was the first time he'd spoken since we'd left.

"Dude, the highway's pretty much shut down. There's no point. I say we just crash for a few hours and leave in the morning."

Conrad didn't say anything.

I didn't say anything because I was too busy eating the crackers. They were bright orange and salty and gritty, and I stuffed them into my mouth, one after the other. I didn't even offer one to either of them.

"Belly, what do you want to do?" Jeremiah said it very

politely, like I was his cousin from out of town. Like his mouth hadn't been on mine just hours before.

I swallowed my last cracker. "I don't care. Do whatever you want."

By the time we got to the motel, it was midnight.

I went to the bathroom to call my mother. I told her what had happened and right away she said, "I'm coming to get you."

Every part of me wanted to say *Yes, please, come right this second*, but she sounded so tired, and she'd already done so much. So instead I said, "No, it's fine, Mom."

"It's all right, Belly. It's not that far."

"It's okay, really. We'll leave early tomorrow morning."

She yawned. "Is the motel in a safe area?"

"Yes." Even though I didn't know exactly where we were or if it constituted a safe area. But it seemed safe enough.

"Just go to sleep and get up first thing. Call me when you're on the road."

After we got off the phone I leaned against the wall for a minute. How did I end up here?

I changed into Taylor's pajamas and put my new hoodie on over them.

I took my time brushing my teeth and taking out my contact lenses. I didn't care that the boys might be waiting to use the bathroom. I just wanted time alone, away from them. When I came back out, Jeremiah and Conrad were on the floor, on opposite sides of the bed. They each had a pillow and a blanket. "You guys should take the bed," I said, even though I only partly meant it. "There's two of you. I'll sleep on the floor."

Conrad was busy ignoring me, but Jeremiah said, "Nah, you take it. You're the girl."

Under ordinary circumstances, I would have argued with him just for the principle of it—what did my being a girl have to do with whether or not I slept on the floor? I was a girl, not an invalid. But I didn't argue. I was too tired. And I did want the bed.

I crawled onto the bed and got under the covers. Jeremiah set the alarm on his phone and shut off the lights. Nobody said good night or suggested we see if there was anything good on TV.

I tried to fall asleep but I couldn't. I tried to remember the last time the three of us had slept in the same room. I couldn't at first, but then I did.

We'd pitched a tent on the beach and I'd begged and begged to be included and finally my mother made them let me come. Me and Steven and Jeremiah and Conrad. We played Uno for hours and Steven high-fived me when I won twice in a row. Suddenly I missed my big brother so much I wanted to cry. Part of me thought that if Steven had been there, things wouldn't have gotten this awful. Maybe none of this would have happened, because I would still be chasing after the boys instead of being in the middle.

But now everything had changed and we could never go back to the way things used to be.

I was lying in bed thinking about all of this when I heard Jeremiah snoring, which really annoyed me. He'd always been able to fall asleep at will, as soon as his head hit the pillow. I guessed he wasn't losing any sleep over what had happened. I guessed I shouldn't either. I flipped over on my other side, facing away from Jeremiah.

And then I heard Conrad say, quietly, "Earlier, when I said I never wanted you. I didn't mean it."

My breath caught. I didn't know what to say or if I was even supposed to say anything. All I knew was, this was what I'd been waiting for. This exact moment. Exactly this.

I opened my mouth to speak, and then he said it again. "I didn't mean it."

I held my breath, waiting to hear what he'd say next.

All he said was, "Good night, Belly."

After that, of course I couldn't sleep. My head was too full of things to think about. What did he mean? That he wanted to be, like, together? Me and him, for real? It was what I'd wanted my whole life, but then there was Jeremiah's face in the car, open and wanting and needing me. In that moment, I'd wanted and needed him, too, more than I had ever known. Had it always been there? But after tonight, I didn't even know if he wanted me anymore. Maybe it was too late.

Then there was Conrad. *I didn't mean it.* I closed my eyes and heard him say those words again and again. His voice, traveling across the dark, it haunted me and it thrilled me.

So I lay there barely breathing, going over every word. The boys were asleep and every part of me was fully awake and alive. It was like a really amazing dream, and I was afraid to fall asleep because when I woke up, it would be gone.

chapter *forty-three*
JULY 7

I woke up before Jeremiah's alarm went off. I took a shower, brushed my teeth, put on the same clothes as the day before.

When I came out, Jeremiah was on the phone and Conrad was folding up his blanket. I waited for him to look at me. If he would just look at me, smile, say something, I would know what to do.

But Conrad didn't look up. He put the blankets back in the closet and then he put on his sneakers. He undid the laces and pulled them tighter. I kept waiting, but he wouldn't look at me.

"Hey," I said.

He finally raised his head. "Hey," he said. "A friend of mine is coming to get me."

"Why?" I asked.

"It's easier this way. He'll take me back to Cousins so

I can get my car, and J can take you home."

"Oh," I said. I was so surprised, it took a moment for the disappointment, the utter disbelief, to register.

We stood there, looking at each other, saying nothing. But it was the kind of nothing that meant everything. In his eyes, there was no trace of what had happened between us earlier, and I could feel something inside me break.

So that was that. We were finally, finally over.

I looked at him, and I felt so sad, because this thought occurred to me: *I will never look at you in the same way ever again. I'll never be that girl again. The girl who comes running back every time you push her away, the girl who loves you anyway.*

I couldn't even be mad at him, because this was who he was. This was who he'd always been. He'd never lied about that. He gave and then he took away. I felt it in the pit of my stomach, the familiar ache, that lost, regretful feeling only he could give me. I never wanted to feel it again. Never, ever.

Maybe this was why I came, so I could really know. So I could say good-bye.

I looked at him, and I thought, *If I was very brave or very honest, I would tell him.* I would say it, so he would know it and I would know it, and I could never take it back. But I wasn't that brave or honest, so all I did was look at him. And I think he knew anyway.

I release you. I evict you from my heart. Because if I don't do it now, I never will.

I was the one to look away first.

Jeremiah hung up the phone and asked Conrad, "Is Dan on his way to come get you?"

"Yeah. I'm just gonna hang out here and wait for him."

Jeremiah looked at me then. "What do you want to do?"

"I want to go with you," I said. I picked up my bag and Taylor's shoes.

He stood up and took my bag off my shoulder. "Then let's go." To Conrad, he said, "See you at home."

I wondered which home he meant, the summer house or their house-house. But I guessed it didn't really matter.

"Bye, Conrad," I said. I walked out the door with Taylor's shoes in my hand and I didn't bother to put them on either. I didn't look back. And right there, I felt it, the glow, the satisfaction of being the one who left first.

As we walked through the parking lot, Jeremiah said, "Maybe you should put your shoes on. You might cut your feet on something."

I shrugged. "They're Taylor's shoes," I said, as if that made sense. I added, "They're too small."

He asked, "Do you want to drive?"

I thought it over and then I said, "No, that's okay. You drive."

"But you love to drive my car," he said, coming around to the passenger side and opening my door first.

"I know. But today I just feel like riding shotgun."

"Do you want to get breakfast first?"

"No," I said. "I just want to go home."

Soon we were on the road. I opened my window all the way down. I stuck my head out and let my hair fly everywhere, just because. Steven once told me that bugs and things get caught up in girls' hair when they ride with it hanging out the window. But I didn't care. I liked the way it felt. It felt free.

Jeremiah looked over at me and said, "You remind me of our old dog, Boogie. He used to love riding around with his head out the window."

He was still using his polite voice. Distant.

I said, "You haven't said anything. About before." I glanced over at him. I could hear my heart thudding in my ears.

"What's left to say?"

"I don't know. A lot," I said.

"Belly—," he started. Then he stopped and let out a breath, shaking his head.

"What? What were you going to say?"

"Nothing," he said.

Then I reached across, and I took his hand and laced my fingers around his. It felt like the most right thing I'd done in a long time.

I worried he'd let go, but he didn't. We held hands like that the whole rest of the way home.

a couple of years later

When I used to picture forever, it was always with the same boy. In my dreams, my future was set. A sure thing.

This wasn't the way I pictured it. Me, in a white dress in the pouring rain, running for the car. Him, running ahead of me and opening the passenger door.

"Are you sure?" he asks me.

"No," I say, getting in.

The future is unclear. But it's still mine.

we'll

always

have

summer

For my two Emilys:
Emily van Beek, you are my ambassador of quan
Emily Thomas Meehan, let's stay together forever
Love, your girl

Acknowledgments

First, my sincerest thanks to Emily Meehan for seeing this book through. Many thanks also to Julia Maguire for not missing a beat, Lucy Ruth Cummins for another gorgeous cover, Justin Chanda and Anne Zafian for their steadfast support, and to the whole (frankly, amazing) S&S team. From sales to production to marketing to publicity, you guys are tops in my book. Thanks as always to Emily van Beek and Folio, to my Pippin family, and also to Siobhan Vivian, my first and finest reader.

On Wednesday nights when I was little, my mom and I would watch old musicals. It was our thing. Sometimes my dad or Steven would wander in and watch for a bit, but it was pretty much always my mother and me on the couch with a blanket and a bowl of sweet and salty popcorn, every Wednesday. We watched *The Music Man*, *West Side Story*, *Meet Me in St. Louis*, all of which I liked, *Singin' in the Rain*, which I really liked. But I loved none of them the way I loved *Bye Bye Birdie*. Of all the musicals, *Bye Bye Birdie* was my number one favorite. I watched it again and again, as many times as my mother could stand. Just like Kim MacAfee before me, I wanted to wear mascara and lipstick and heels and have that "happy grown-up female feeling," I wanted to hear boys whistle and know it was for me. I wanted to grow up and be just like Kim, because she got to have all of those things.

And after, when it was bedtime, I would sing, "We love you, Conrad, oh yes we do. We love you, Conrad, and we'll be true" into the bathroom mirror with a mouthful of toothpaste. I would sing my eight-nine-ten-year-old heart out. But I wasn't singing to Conrad Birdie. I was singing to *my* Conrad. Conrad Beck Fisher, the boy of my preteen dreams.

I've only ever loved two boys—both of them with the last name Fisher. Conrad was first, and I loved him in a way that you can really only do the first time around. It's the kind of love that doesn't know better and doesn't want to—it's dizzy and foolish and fierce. That kind of love is really a one-time-only thing.

And then there was Jeremiah. When I looked at Jeremiah, I saw past, present, and future. He didn't just know the girl I used to be. He knew the right-now me, and he loved me anyway.

My two great loves. I think I always knew I would be Belly Fisher one day. I just didn't know it was going to happen like this.

chapter *one*

When it's finals week and you've been studying for five hours straight, you need three things to get you through the night. The biggest Slurpee you can find, half cherry, half Coke. Pajama pants, the kind that have been washed so many times, they are tissue-paper thin. And finally, dance breaks. Lots of dance breaks. When your eyes start to close and all you want is your bed, dance breaks will get you through.

It was four in the morning, and I was studying for the last final of my freshman year at Finch University. I was camped out in my dorm library with my new best friend, Anika Johnson, and my old best friend, Taylor Jewel. Summer vacation was so close, I could almost taste it. Just five more days. I'd been counting down since April.

"Quiz me," Taylor commanded, her voice scratchy.

I opened my notebook to a random page. "Define *anima* versus *animus*."

Taylor chewed on her lower lip. "Give me a hint."

"Umm . . . think Latin," I said.

"I didn't take Latin! Is there going to be Latin on this exam?"

"No, I was just trying to give you a hint. Because in Latin boys' names end in *-us* and girls' names end in *-a*, and *anima* is feminine archetype and *animus* is masculine archetype. Get it?"

She let out a big sigh. "No. I'm probably going to fail."

Looking up from her notebook, Anika said, "Maybe if you stopped texting and started studying, you wouldn't."

Taylor glared at her. "I'm helping my big sister plan our end-of-year breakfast, so I have to be on call tonight."

"On call?" Anika looked amused. "Like a doctor?"

"Yes, just like a doctor," Taylor snapped.

"So, will it be pancakes or waffles?"

"French toast, thank you very much."

The three of us were all taking the same freshman psych class, and Taylor's and my exam was tomorrow, Anika's was the day after. Anika was my closest friend at school besides Taylor. Seeing as how Taylor was competitive by nature, it was a friendship that she was more than a little jealous of, not that she'd ever in a million years admit it.

My friendship with Anika was different from my

friendship with Taylor. Anika was laid-back and easy to be with. She wasn't quick to judge. More than all that, though, she gave *me* the space to be different. She hadn't known me my whole life, so she had no expectations or preconceptions. There was freedom in that. And she wasn't like any of my friends back home. She was from New York, and her father was a jazz musician and her mother was a writer.

A couple of hours later, the sun was rising and casting the room in a bluish light, and Taylor's head was down, while Anika was staring off into space like a zombie.

I rolled up two paper balls in my lap and threw them at my two friends. "Dance break," I sang out as I pressed play on my computer. I did a little shimmy in my chair.

Anika glared at me. "Why are you so chipper?"

"Because," I said, clapping my hands together, "in just a few hours, it will all be over." My exam wasn't until one in the afternoon, so my plan was to go back to my room and sleep for a couple of hours, then wake up with time to spare and study some more.

I overslept, but I still managed to get another hour of studying in. I didn't have time to go to the dining hall for breakfast, so I just drank a Cherry Coke from the vending machine.

The test was as hard as we had expected, but I was pretty sure I would get at least a B. Taylor was pretty sure she hadn't failed, which was good. Both of us were too tired to celebrate after, so we just high-fived and went our separate ways.

I headed back to my dorm room, ready to pass out until at least dinnertime, and when I opened the door, there was Jeremiah, asleep in my bed. He looked like a little boy when he slept, even with the stubble. He was stretched out on top of my comforter, his feet hanging over the edge of the bed, my stuffed polar bear hugged to his chest.

I took off my shoes and crawled into my twin, extra-long bed next to him. He stirred, opened his eyes, and said, "Hi."

"Hi," I said.

"How'd it go?"

"Pretty good."

"Good." He let go of Junior Mint and hugged me to him. "I brought you the other half of my sub from lunch."

"You're sweet," I said, burrowing my head in his shoulder.

He kissed my hair. "I can't have my girl skipping meals left and right."

"It was just breakfast," I said. As an afterthought, I added, "And lunch."

"Do you want my sub now? It's in my book bag."

Now that I thought about it, I was hungry, but I was also sleepy. "Maybe a little later," I said, closing my eyes.

Then he fell back to sleep, and I fell asleep too. When I woke up, it was dark out, Junior Mint was on the floor, and Jeremiah's arms were around me. He was still asleep.

We had started dating right before I began senior year of high school. "Dating" didn't feel like the right word for it. We were just together. It all happened so easily and so quickly that it felt like it had always been that way. One minute we were friends, then we were kissing, and then the next thing I knew, I was applying to the same college as him. I told myself and everyone else (including him, including my mother especially) that it was a good school, that it was only a few hours from home and it made sense to apply there, that I was keeping my options open. All of those things were true. But truest of all was that I just wanted to be near him. I wanted him for all seasons, not just summer.

Now here we were, lying next to each other in my dorm-room bed. He was a sophomore, and I was finishing up my freshman year. It was crazy how far we had come. We'd known each other our whole lives, and in some ways, it felt like a big surprise—in other ways it felt inevitable.

chapter *two*

Jeremiah's fraternity was throwing an end-of-year party. In less than a week we would all go home for the summer, and we wouldn't be back at Finch until the end of August. I had always loved summertime best of all, but now that I was finally going home, somehow it felt a little bittersweet. I was used to meeting Jeremiah in the dining hall for breakfast every morning and doing my laundry with him at his frat house late at night. He was good at folding my T-shirts.

This summer, he would be interning at his dad's company again, and I was going to waitress at a family restaurant called Behrs, the same as I did last summer. Our plan was to meet at the summer house in Cousins as often as we could. Last summer we hadn't made it out there once. We'd both been so busy with our jobs.

I took every shift I could to save money for school. All the while, I'd felt a little hollow inside, my first summer away from Cousins.

There were a few lightning bugs out. It was just getting dark, and it wasn't too hot of a night. I was wearing heels, which was stupid, since on a last-minute impulse I'd walked instead of taking the bus. I just figured it was the last time for a long time I'd walk across campus on a nice night like this.

I'd invited Anika and our friend Shay to come with me, but Anika had a party with her dance team, and Shay was already done with finals and had flown home to Texas. Taylor's sorority was having a mixer, so she wasn't coming either. It was just me and my sore feet.

I had texted Jeremiah to tell him I was on my way and that I was walking, so it would take me a little while. I had to keep stopping to adjust my shoes because they were cutting into the backs of my feet. Heels were dumb, I decided.

Halfway there, I saw him sitting on my favorite bench. He stood up when he saw me. "Surprise!"

"You didn't have to meet me," I said, feeling very happy he had. I sat down on the bench.

"You look hot," he said.

Even now, after being boyfriend and girlfriend for a whole two years, I still blushed a little when he said things like that. "Thanks," I said. I was wearing a sundress that

I had borrowed from Anika. It was white with little blue flowers and ruffly straps.

"That dress reminds me of *The Sound of Music*, but in a hot way."

"Thanks," I said again. *Did* the dress make me look like Fräulein Maria, I wondered? That didn't sound like a good thing. I smoothed down the straps a little.

A couple of guys I didn't recognize stopped and said hi to Jeremiah, but I stayed put on the bench so I could rest my feet.

When they were gone, he said, "Ready?"

I groaned. "My feet are killing me. Heels are dumb."

Jeremiah stooped down low and said, "Hop on, girl."

Giggling, I climbed on his back. I always giggled when he called me "girl." I couldn't help it. It was funny.

He hoisted me up and I put my arms around his neck. "Is your dad coming on Monday?" Jeremiah asked as we crossed the main lawn.

"Yeah. You're gonna help, right?"

"Come on, now. I'm carrying you across campus. I have to help you move, too?"

I swatted him on the head and he ducked. "Okay, okay," he said.

Then I blew a raspberry on his neck, and he yelped like a little girl. I laughed the whole way there.

chapter *three*

At Jeremiah's fraternity house, the doors were wide open and people were hanging out on the front lawn. Multicolored Christmas lights were haphazardly strung all over the place—on the mailbox, the front porch, even along the edge of the walkway. They had three inflatable kiddie pools set up that people were lounging in like they were in hot tubs. Guys were running around with Super Soakers and spraying beer into each other's mouths. Some of the girls were in their bikinis.

I hopped off Jeremiah's back and took my shoes off in the grass.

"The pledges did a nice job with this," Jeremiah said, nodding appreciatively at the kiddie pools. "Did you bring your suit?"

I shook my head.

"Want me to see if one of the girls has an extra?" he offered.

Quickly, I said, "No thanks."

I knew Jeremiah's fraternity brothers from hanging out at the house, but I didn't know the girls very well. Most of them were from Zeta Phi, Jeremiah's fraternity's sister sorority. That meant they had mixers and parties together, that kind of thing. Jeremiah had wanted me to rush Zeta Phi, but I'd said no. I told him it was because I couldn't afford the fees and paying extra to live in a sorority house, but it was really more that I was hoping to be friends with all kinds of girls, not just the ones I'd meet in a sorority. I wanted a broader college experience, like my mother was always saying. According to Taylor, Zeta Phi was for party girls and sluts, as opposed to her sorority, which was allegedly classier and more exclusive. And way more focused on community service, she'd added as an afterthought.

Girls kept coming up and hugging Jeremiah. They said hi to me, and I said hi back, then I went upstairs to put my bag in Jeremiah's room. On my way downstairs, I saw her.

Lacie Barone, wearing skinny jeans and a silky tank top and patent leather red heels that probably brought her up to five-four at most, talking to Jeremiah. Lacie was the social chair of Zeta Phi, and she was a junior—a year older than Jere, two years older than me. Her hair was dark brown, cut in a swishy bob, and she was petite. She was, by anybody's standards, hot. According to Taylor, she had a thing for Jeremiah. I told Taylor it didn't bother me one bit, and I meant it. Why should I care?

Of course girls would like Jeremiah. He was the kind of boy girls liked. But even a girl as pretty as Lacie didn't have anything on us. We were a couple years and years in the making. I knew him better than anyone, the same as he knew me, and I knew Jere would never look at another girl.

Jeremiah saw me then, and he waved at me to come over. I walked up to them and said, "Hey, Lacie."

"Hey," she said.

Pulling me toward him, Jeremiah said, "Lacie is gonna study abroad in Paris this fall." To Lacie, he said, "We want to go backpacking in Europe next summer."

Sipping her beer, she said, "That's cool. Which countries?"

"We're definitely going to France," Jeremiah said. "Belly speaks really fluent French."

"I actually don't," I told her, embarrassed. "I just took it in high school."

Lacie said, "Oh, I'm horrible too. I really just want to go and eat lots of cheese and chocolate."

She had a voice that was surprisingly husky for someone so small. I wondered if she smoked. She smiled at me, and I thought, Taylor was wrong about her, she was a nice girl.

When she left a few minutes later to get a drink, I said, "She's nice."

Jeremiah shrugged and said, "Yeah, she's cool. Want me to get you a drink?"

"Sure," I said.

He led me by the shoulders and planted me on the couch. "You sit right here. Don't move a muscle. I'll be right back."

I watched him make his way through the crowd, feeling proud I could call him mine. My boyfriend, my Jeremiah. The first boy I had ever fallen asleep next to. The first boy I ever told about the time I accidentally walked in on my parents doing it when I was eight. The first boy to go out and buy me Midol because my cramps were so bad, the first boy to paint my toenails, to hold my hair back when I threw up that time I got really drunk in front of all his friends, the first boy to write me a love note on the whiteboard hanging outside my dorm room.

YOU ARE THE MILK TO MY SHAKE,
forever and ever. Love, J.

He was the first boy I ever kissed. He was my best friend. More and more, I understood. This was the way it was supposed to be. He was the one. My one.

chapter *four*

It was later that night.

We were dancing. I had my arms around Jeremiah's neck, and the music was pulsing around us. I felt flushed and abuzz, from the dancing and from the alcohol. The room was packed with people, but when Jere looked at me, there was no one else. Just me and him.

He reached down and tucked a strand of hair behind my ear. He said something I couldn't hear.

"What?" I yelled.

He yelled, "Don't ever cut your hair, okay?"

"I have to! I'd look like—like a witch."

Jeremiah tapped his ear and said, "I can't hear you!"

"Witch!" I shook my hair around my face for emphasis and mimed stirring a cauldron and cackling.

"I like you witchy," he said in my ear. "How about just trims?"

I shouted, "I promise not to cut my hair short if you promise to give up your beard dream!"

He'd been talking about growing a beard ever since Thanksgiving, when some of his high school friends got a contest going to see who could grow it the longest. I'd told him no way, it reminded me too much of my dad.

"I'll consider it," he said, kissing me.

He tasted like beer, and I probably did too.

Then Jeremiah's frat brother Tom—also known as Redbird for reasons unknown to me—spotted us, and he came charging at Jeremiah like a bull. He was wearing his underwear and carrying a water bottle. And they weren't boxers, they were tighty whities. "Break it up, break it up!" he shouted.

They started messing around, and when Jeremiah got Tom in a headlock, Tom's water bottle of beer spilled all over me and Anika's dress.

"Sorry, sorry," he mumbled. When Tom was really drunk, he said everything twice.

"It's okay," I said, wringing out the skirt and trying not to look at the lower half of his body.

I left to go clean my dress in the bathroom, but there was a long line, so I went to the kitchen. People were doing body shots on the kitchen table; Jeremiah's frat brother Luke was licking salt out of a red-haired girl's belly button.

"Hey, Isabel," he said, looking up.

"Um, hey, Luke," I said. Then I spotted some girl throwing up in the sink, and I booked it out of there.

I headed to the upstairs bathroom. At the top of the staircase, I squeezed past a guy and a girl making out, and I accidentally stepped on the guy's hand. "I'm so sorry," I said, but he didn't seem to notice either way, since he had his other hand up the girl's shirt.

When I finally made it to the bathroom, I locked the door behind me and let out a little sigh of relief. This party was even wilder than usual. I guessed with the end of year upon us and finals over, everybody was letting loose. I was kind of glad Anika hadn't been able to come. It wouldn't be her scene—not that it was mine, either.

I dabbed liquid soap onto the wet marks and crossed my fingers it wouldn't stain. Someone tried to open the door, and I called out, "Just a sec."

As I stood there, dabbing at the dress, I heard girls on the other side talking. I wasn't really paying attention until I heard Lacie's voice. I heard her say, "He looks hot tonight, right?"

Another voice said, "He always looks hot."

She was slurring as she said, "Hell yeah he does."

The other girl said, "I'm so jealous you got to hook up with him."

In a singsong voice, Lacie said, "Whatever happens in Cabo stays in Cabo."

I felt dizzy all of a sudden. I leaned my back against

the bathroom door to steady myself. There was no way she was talking about Jeremiah. No way.

Someone banged on the door, and I jumped.

Without thinking, I opened it. Lacie's hand flew to her mouth when she saw me. The look on her face was like a punch in the stomach. I felt physical pain. I could hear the other girls' sharp intakes of breath, but it all felt far away. I felt like I was sleepwalking as I moved past her and the girls and down the hallway.

I couldn't believe it. It couldn't be true. Not my Jere.

I went to his room and locked the door behind me. I sat on his bed, knees curled into my chest, going over it in my head. *Whatever happens in Cabo stays in Cabo.* The look on Lacie's face, the way the other girls gasped. It played in my head like a movie, over and over. The two of them talking tonight. The way he'd shrugged when I said she was nice.

I had to know for sure. I had to hear it from Jeremiah.

I left his room and went looking for him. As I searched, I could feel the shock turning into anger. I pushed my way through the crowd. One drunk girl slurred, "Hey!" when I stepped on her foot, but I didn't stop to say "excuse me."

I finally found him standing around outside drinking beer with his frat buddies. From the open door, I said, "I need to talk to you."

"Just a sec, Bells," he said.

"No. Now."

The guys all started cracking up and going, "Oooh, somebody's in trouble." "Fisher's so whipped."

I waited.

Jeremiah must have seen something in my eyes, because he followed me inside, up the stairs, and into his bedroom. I shut the door behind me.

"What's going on?" he asked me, looking all concerned.

I practically spat the words out. "Did you hook up with Lacie Barone during spring break?"

Jeremiah's face turned white. "What?"

"Did you hook up with her?"

"Belly—"

"I knew it," I whispered. "I knew it."

Even though I didn't know it, not really. I didn't know anything.

"Hold on, just hold on."

"Hold on?" I screamed. "Oh my God, Jere. Oh my God."

I sank onto the floor. My legs couldn't even hold me up.

Jeremiah kneeled down beside me and tried to help me up, but I slapped his hands away. "Don't touch me!"

He got down on the floor next to me, his head hanging between his knees. "Belly, it was when we were on that break. When we were broken up." I stared at him.

Our so-called breakup had lasted all of a week. It wasn't even a real breakup, not for me. I always assumed we would get back together. I had cried the whole week, while he had been in Cabo kissing Lacie Barone.

"You knew we weren't really broken up! You knew it wasn't real!"

Miserably, he said, "How was I supposed to know that?"

"If I knew it, you should have known it!"

He swallowed, and his Adam's apple bobbed up and down. "Lacie kept following me around all week. She wouldn't leave me alone. I swear to you, I didn't want to hook up with her. It just happened." His voice trailed off.

I felt so dirty inside hearing him say that. Just disgusted. I didn't want to think about the two of them, didn't want to picture it. "Be quiet," I said. "I don't want to hear it."

"It was a mistake."

"A mistake? You call that a mistake? A mistake is when you left my shower shoes in the shower and they got all mildewy and I had to throw them out. That's a mistake, you jerk." I burst into tears.

He didn't say anything. He just sat there and took it, his head hanging down.

"I don't even know who you are anymore." My stomach lurched. "I think I'm going to be sick."

Jeremiah got me the wastebasket by his bed and I threw up, heaving and crying. He tried to rub my back, but I jerked away from him. "Don't touch me," I mumbled, wiping my mouth with the back of my arm.

It didn't make sense. None of it. This wasn't the

Jeremiah I knew. My Jeremiah would never hurt me like this. He would never so much as look at another girl. My Jeremiah was true and strong and steady. I didn't know who this person was.

"I'm sorry," he said. "I'm really sorry."

Jeremiah was crying now too. Good, I thought. Hurt like you've hurt me.

"I want to be totally honest with you, Belly. I don't want any more secrets." He really broke down then, crying hard.

I went totally still.

"We had sex."

Before I knew it, my hand was striking his face. I slapped him as hard as I could. I wasn't even thinking, I was just doing. My hand left a splotchy red imprint on his right cheek.

We stared at each other. I couldn't believe I had hit him, and neither could he. The shock was just beginning to register on his face, and I probably had the same look on mine. I had never hit anyone before.

Rubbing his cheek, he said, "I'm so sorry."

I cried harder. I had pictured them hooking up, making out. I hadn't even considered sex. I was so stupid.

He said, "It didn't mean anything. I swear to you, it didn't."

He tried to touch my arm, and I flinched. Wiping my cheeks, I said, "Maybe to you sex doesn't mean anything.

But it means something to me, and you knew that. You've ruined everything. I'll never trust you again."

He tried to pull me toward him, but I pushed him away. Desperately, he said, "I'm telling you, the thing with Lacie didn't mean anything."

"It means something to *me*. And it obviously meant something to her."

"I'm not in love with her!" he cried out. "I'm in love with you!"

Jeremiah crawled over to where I was. He put his arms around my knees. "Don't leave," he begged. "Please don't leave."

I tried to shake him off, but he was strong. He clung to me like I was a raft and he was at sea.

"I love you so much," he said, his whole body shaking. "It's always been you, Belly."

I wanted to keep screaming and crying and somehow find a way out of this. But I didn't see a way. Looking down at him, I felt like I was made of stone. He had never disappointed me before. For him to do it now made it that much harder, because I hadn't seen it coming. It was hard to believe that just a few short hours ago he'd carried me across campus on his back and I'd loved him more than ever.

"We can't get it back," I said, and I said it to hurt him. "What we were, it's gone. We lost it tonight."

Desperately, he said, "Yes, we can. I know we can."

I shook my head. The tears had started again, but I didn't want to cry anymore, especially not in front of him. Or with him. I didn't want to feel sad. I didn't want to feel anything. I wiped my face again and stood up, "I'm leaving."

He rose to his feet unsteadily. "Wait!"

I pushed past him and grabbed my bag from his bed. Then I was out the door, running down the stairs and outside. I ran all the way to the bus stop, my bag banging against my shoulder, my heels clacking against the pavement. I almost tripped and fell, but I made it. I caught the bus just as the last person was getting on, and we drove off. I didn't look back to see if Jeremiah had followed me.

My roommate, Jillian, had gone home for the summer earlier that day, so at least I had the room to myself and could cry alone. Jeremiah kept calling and texting, so I turned my phone off. But before I went to bed, I turned it back on again so I could see what he wrote me.

I'm so ashamed of myself.
Please talk to me.
I love you and I always will.

I cried harder.

chapter *five*

When we broke up in April, it really did come out of nowhere. Yes, we'd had little fights here and there, but you could hardly even call them fights.

Like, there was this time Shay was having a party at her godmother's country house. She invited a ton of people, and she said I could bring Jeremiah, too. We were gonna get dressed up and dance outside all night long. We'd all just crash there for the weekend, Shay said—it would be a blast. I was just happy to be included. I told Jeremiah about it, and he said he had an intramural soccer game but I should go anyway. I said, "Can't you just miss it? It's not like it's a real game." It was a bitchy thing to say, but I said it, and I meant it.

That was our first fight. Not a real fight, not like yelling or anything, but he was mad and so was I.

We always hung out with his friends. In a way it made sense. He already had them, and I was still forming mine. It took time to get close to people, and with me at his frat house all the time, the girls on my hall were bonding without me. I felt like I had given something up without even realizing it. When Shay invited me, that meant a lot, and I wanted it to mean something to Jere, too.

And there were other things, too, that annoyed me. Things I'd never known about Jeremiah, things I couldn't have known from only seeing him in the summer at the beach house. Like how obnoxious he was when he smoked weed with his suitemates and they ate pineapple-and-ham pizza and listened to "Gangsta's Paradise" by Coolio and they would laugh for, like, an hour.

Also his seasonal allergies. I'd never seen him in the springtime, so I didn't know he had them.

He called me, sneezing like crazy, all stuffed up and pitiful. "Can you come over and hang out with me?" he asked, blowing his nose. "And can you bring more Kleenex? And orange juice?"

I bit my lip to keep from saying, You have allergies, not swine flu.

I'd gone over to his frat house the day before. He and his roommate played video games while I did my home-work. Then we watched a Kung Fu movie and ordered Indian food, even though I didn't really like to eat Indian food because it gave me an upset stomach after. Jeremiah said that when his allergies got really bad, Indian food was the only thing that would make him feel better. I ate naan and rice and felt pissed while Jeremiah scarfed down chicken tikka masala and watched his movie. He could be really oblivious sometimes, and I had to wonder if it was on purpose.

"I really want to come over, but I have a paper that's due tomorrow," I said, trying to sound conflicted about it. "So I probably shouldn't. Sorry."

"Well, I guess I could go there," he said. "I'll take a ton of Benedryl and sleep while you write. Then maybe we can order Indian food again."

"Yeah," I said, sourly. "We could do that." At least I wouldn't have to take the bus. But I would have to go to the hall bathroom and get a roll of toilet paper, because Jillian would be pissed if Jeremiah used all her Kleenex again.

I didn't know then that all of that was setting the stage for our first real fight. We had one of those screaming and crying kind of fights, the kind I promised myself I would never have. I'd heard Jillian have them over the phone, girls on my hall, Taylor. I never thought it would be me. I thought Jeremiah and I understood each other too well, had known each other too long, for that kind of fight.

A fight is like a fire. You think you have it under control, you think you can stop it whenever you want, but before you know it, it's a living, breathing thing and there's no controlling it and you were a fool to think you could.

At the last minute, Jeremiah and his fraternity brothers decided to go to Cabo over spring break. They'd found some insane deal on the Internet.

I was already planning on going home over the break. My mom and I were going to go into the city and watch a ballet, and Steven would be at home too. So I wanted to be at home, I really did. But as I watched Jeremiah book his trip, I felt more and more resentful. He was supposed to be going home too. Now that Conrad was in California, Mr. Fisher was pretty much alone. Jeremiah had said he wanted to go and spend some time with him, maybe visit Susannah's grave together. We'd also talked about going to Cousins for a couple of days. Jeremiah knew how much I wanted to go to Cousins. He knew how much it meant to me. I'd done more growing up in that house than I had in my own. And with Susannah gone, it felt even more important that we kept going back.

Now he was going to Cabo. Without me.

"Do you really think you should be going to Cabo?" I asked him. He was sitting at his desk, hunched over the computer and typing away. I was sitting on his bed.

He looked up, surprised. "It's too good of a deal to pass up. Besides, all my brothers are going. I can't miss out."

"Yeah, but I thought you were gonna go home and hang out with your dad."

"I can do that over summer break."

"Summer's still months away." I crossed my arms then uncrossed them.

Jeremiah frowned. "What's this about? Are you worried about me going on spring break without you?"

I could feel my cheeks redden. "No! You can go wherever you want, I don't care. I just think that it would be nice if you spent some time with your dad. And your mom's headstone is up. I thought you wanted to go see it."

"Yeah, I do, but I can do all that after school's out. You can come with me." He peered at me. "Are you jealous?"

"No!"

He was grinning now. "Worried about all the wet T-shirt contests?"

"No!" I hated that he was making this into a joke. It was infuriating, being the only one who was mad.

"If you're so worried, then just come with us. It'll be fun."

He did not say, If you are worried, you shouldn't be. He said, *If you are worried, you should come with us.* I knew he didn't mean it that way, but it still bothered me.

"You know I can't afford it. Besides, I don't want to go to Cabo with you and your 'bros.' I'm not going to go and be the only girlfriend and drag down your party."

"You wouldn't be. Josh's girlfriend, Alison, is going to be there," Jeremiah said.

So Alison had been invited and not me? I sat up straight. "Alison's going with you guys?"

"It's not like that. Alison's going with her sorority. They're getting a bunch of rooms at the same resort as us. That's how we found out about the deal. But it's not like we'll be hanging out with them all the time. We're gonna do guy stuff, like off-road racing in the desert. Rent some ATVs, go rappelling, stuff like that."

I stared at him. "So while you race around with your buddies in the desert, you want me to hang out with a bunch of girls I don't know?"

He rolled his eyes. "You know Alison. You guys were beer-pong partners in our house tournament."

"Whatever. I'm not going to Cabo. I'm going home. My mom misses me." What I didn't say was, your dad misses you too.

When Jeremiah just shrugged, like, Have it your way, I thought, oh, what the hell, I'll say it. "Your dad misses you too."

"Oh my God. Belly, just admit that this isn't about my dad. You're paranoid about me going on spring break without you."

"Why don't you admit that you didn't want me to go in the first place, then?"

He hesitated. I saw him hesitate. "Fine. Yeah, I wouldn't mind if this was just a guys' trip."

Standing up, I said, "Well, it sounds like there will be plenty of girls there. Have fun with the Zetas."

Now his neck started to turn a dull red. "If you don't trust me by now, I don't know what to tell you. I've never done anything to make you question me. And Belly, I really don't need you guilt tripping me about my dad."

I started putting my shoes on, and I was so mad, my hands shook as I tried to lace up my sneakers. "I can't even believe how selfish you are."

"Me? I'm the selfish one now?" He shook his head, his lips tight. He opened his mouth like he was going to say something, but then he closed it.

"Yes, you are definitely the selfish one in this relationship. It's always about you, your friends, your stupid fraternity. Have I told you I think your fraternity is stupid? Because I do."

In a low voice, he said, "What's so stupid about it?"

"It's just a bunch of entitled rich guys spending their parents' money, cheating on tests with your test bank, going to class wasted."

Looking hurt, he said, "We're not all like that."

"I didn't mean you."

"Yeah, you did. What, just because I'm not pre-med, that makes me this lazy frat guy?"

"Don't put your inferiority complex on me," I said. I

said it without thinking. It was something I had thought before but never voiced. Conrad was the one who was pre-med. Conrad was the one at Stanford, working a part-time job at a lab. Jeremiah was the one who told people he majored in beerology.

He stared. "What the hell does that mean, 'inferiority complex'?"

"Forget it," I said. Too late, I could see things had gone farther than I had intended. I wanted to take it all back.

"If you think I'm so stupid and selfish and wasteful, why are you even with me?"

Before I could answer, before I could say, You're not stupid or selfish or wasteful, before I could end the fight, Jeremiah said, "Fuck it. I won't waste your time anymore. Let's end it now."

And I said, "Fine."

I grabbed my book bag, but I didn't leave right away. I was waiting for him to stop me. But he didn't.

I cried the whole way home. I couldn't believe that we had broken up. It didn't feel real. I expected Jeremiah to call me that night. It was a Friday. He left for Cabo on Sunday morning, and he didn't call then, either.

My spring break consisted of me moping around the house, eating chips, and crying. Steven said, "Chill out. The only reason he hasn't called you is that it's too expensive to make a call from Mexico. You guys will be back together by next week, guaranteed."

I was pretty sure he was right. Jeremiah just needed some space. Okay, that was fine. When he got back, I would go to him and tell him how sorry I was, and I would fix things, and it would be like it never happened.

Steven was right. We did get back together a week later. I did go to him and apologize, and he apologized too. I never asked him if anything happened in Cabo. It wouldn't even have occurred to me to wonder. This was a boy who had loved me my whole life, and I was a girl who believed in that love. In that boy.

Jere brought me back a shell bracelet. Little white puka shells. It had made me so happy. Because I knew that he had been thinking of me, that he had missed me as much as I had missed him. He knew like I knew that it wasn't over between us, that it would never be over. He spent that whole week after spring break in my room, hanging out with me and not his fraternity brothers. It drove my roommate Jillian crazy, but I didn't care. I felt closer to him than ever. I missed him even when he was in class.

But now I knew the truth. He bought me that stupid cheap bracelet because he felt guilty. And I was so desperate to make up, I hadn't seen it.

chapter *six*

When I closed my eyes, I saw the two of them, together, kissing in a hot tub. On the beach. In some club. Lacie Barone probably knew tricks and moves I'd never even heard of. But of course she did.

I was still a virgin.

I'd never had sex before, not with Jeremiah, not with anybody. When I was younger, I used to picture my first time with Conrad. It wasn't that I was still waiting for him. It wasn't that at all. I was just waiting for the perfect moment. I wanted it to feel special, to feel exactly right.

I'd pictured us finally doing it at the beach house, with the lights off and candles everywhere so I wouldn't feel shy. I'd pictured how gentle Jeremiah would be, how sweet. Lately I had been feeling more and more ready. I had thought this summer, the two of us back at Cousins—I thought that would be it.

It was humiliating thinking about it now, how naive I'd been. I'd thought he would wait as long as it took for me to be ready. I really believed that.

But how could we be together now? When I thought of him with her, Lacie, who was older and sexier and more worldly than I'd ever be, at least in my mind—it hurt so bad it was hard to breathe. The fact that she knew him in a way I didn't yet, had experienced something with him that I hadn't, that felt like the biggest betrayal of all.

A month ago, around the anniversary of his mom's death, we were lying in Jeremiah's twin bed. He rolled over and looked at me, and his eyes were so like Susannah's, I reached out my hand and covered them.

"Sometimes it hurts to look at you," I said. I loved that I could say that and he knew exactly what I meant.

"Close your eyes," he told me.

I did, and he came up close so we were face-to-face and I could feel his Crest breath warm on my cheek. We wrapped our legs around each other. I was overcome with this sudden need to keep him close to me always. "Do you think it will always be like this?" I asked him.

"How else would it be?" he asked.

We fell asleep that way. Like kids. Totally innocent.

We could never go back to that. How could we? It was all tainted now. Everything from March to now, it was tainted.

chapter *seven*

When I woke up the next morning, my eyes were so puffy, they were practically swollen shut. I splashed cold water on my face, but it didn't really help. I brushed my teeth. And then I went back to bed. I'd wake up and hear people moving out of the dorms, and then I'd just fall back to sleep. I should have been packing, but all I wanted to do was sleep. I slept all day. I woke up again when it was dark out, and I didn't turn on the lights. I just lay in bed until I fell asleep again.

It was late afternoon the next day when I finally got up. When I say "got up," I mean "sat up." I finally sat up in my bed. I was thirsty. I felt wrung dry from all the crying. This propelled me to actually get out of bed and walk the five feet over to the mini fridge and take one of the bottled waters Jillian had left behind.

Looking across the room at her empty bed and empty walls made me feel even more depressed. Last night I wanted to be alone. Today I thought I would go out of my mind if I didn't talk to another person.

I went down the hall to Anika's room. The first thing she said when she saw me was, "What's wrong?"

I sat on her bed and hugged her pillow to my chest. I had come to her wanting to talk, wanting to get it out, but now it was hard to say the words. I felt ashamed. Of him and for him. All my friends loved Jeremiah. They thought he was practically perfect. I knew that as soon as I told Anika, all of that would be gone. This would be real. For some reason, I still wanted to protect him.

"Iz, what happened?"

I'd really thought I was done crying, but a few tears leaked out anyway. I went ahead and said it. "Jeremiah cheated on me."

Anika sank onto the bed. "Shut the front door," she breathed. "When? With who?"

"With Lacey Barone, that girl in his sister sorority. During spring break. When we were broken up."

She nodded, taking this in.

"I'm so mad at him," I said. "For hooking up with another girl and then not telling me all this time. Not telling is the same as lying. I feel so stupid."

Anika handed me the box of tissues on her desk. "Girl, you let yourself feel whatever you need to feel," she said.

I blew my nose. "I feel . . . like maybe I don't know him like I thought I did. I feel like I can't trust him ever again."

"Keeping a secret like that from the person you love is probably the worst part," Anika said.

"You don't think the actual cheating is the worst part?"

"No. I mean, yeah, that is horrible. But he should have just told you. It was turning it into a secret that gave it power."

I was silent. I had a secret too. I hadn't told anyone, not even Anika or Taylor. I had told myself that it was because it wasn't important, and then I had put it out of my mind.

The past couple of years, I sometimes pulled out a memory I had of Conrad and looked at it, admired it, sort of in the same way I looked at my old shell collection. There was pleasure in just touching each shell, the ridges, the cool smoothness. Even after Jeremiah and I started dating, every once in a while, sitting in class or waiting for the bus or trying to fall asleep, I would pull out an old memory. The first time I ever beat him in a swimming race. The time he taught me how to dance. The way he used to wet down his hair in the mornings.

But there was one memory in particular, one I didn't let myself touch. It wasn't allowed.

chapter *eight*

It was the day after Christmas. My mother had gone on a weeklong trip to Turkey, a trip she'd had to postpone twice—once when Susannah's cancer came out of remission and then again after Susannah died. My father was with his girlfriend Linda's family in Washington, D.C. Steven was on a ski trip with some friends from school. Jeremiah and Mr. Fisher were visiting relatives in New York.

And me? I was at home, watching *A Christmas Story* on TV for the third time. I had on my Christmas pajamas, the ones Susannah had sent me a couple of years back—they were red flannel pjs with a jaunty mistletoe print, and they were way too long in the leg. Part of the fun of wearing them was rolling up the sleeves and ankles. I had just finished my dinner—a frozen pepperoni pizza and the rest of the sugar cookies a student had baked for my mother.

I was starting to feel like Kevin in *Home Alone*. Eight o'clock on a Saturday night, and I was dancing around the living room to "Rockin' Around the Christmas Tree," feeling sorry for myself. My fall-semester grades had been eh. My whole family was gone. I was eating frozen pizza alone. And when Steven saw me that first day back home, the first thing out of his mouth was, "Wow, freshman fifteen, huh?" I had punched him in the arm, and he said he was kidding, but he wasn't kidding. I had gained ten pounds in four months. I guessed eating hot wings and ramen and Dominos pizza at four in the morning with the boys will do that to a girl. But so what? The freshman fifteen was a rite of passage.

I went to the downstairs bathroom and slapped my cheeks like Kevin does in the movie. "So what!" I yelled.

I wasn't going to let it get me down. Suddenly I had an idea. I ran upstairs and started throwing things into my backpack—the novel my mom had bought me for Christmas, leggings, thick socks. Why should I be at home alone when I could be at my favorite place in the world?

Fifteen minutes later, after I rinsed off my dinner dishes and turned off all the lights, I was in Steven's car. His car was nicer than mine, and what he didn't know wouldn't hurt him. Besides, that was what he got for bringing up the freshman fifteen.

I was heading to Cousins, rocking out to "Please Come Home for Christmas" (the Bon Jovi version, of course) and snacking on chocolate-covered pretzels with red and green sprinkles (another gift for my mother). I knew I had made the right decision. I would be at the Cousins house in no time. I would light a fire, I would make some hot chocolate to go with my pretzels, I would wake up in the morning to a winter beach. Of course I loved the beach during the summer more, but the winter beach held its own special kind of charm for me. I decided I wouldn't tell anyone I'd gone. When everyone came back from their trips, it would be my little secret.

I did make it to Cousins in no time. The highway had been pretty much deserted, and I practically flew there. As I pulled into the driveway, I let out a big whoop. It was good to be back. This was my first time at the house in over a year.

I found the spare set of keys right where they always were—under the loose floorboard on the deck. I felt giddy as I stepped inside and turned on the lights.

The house was freezing cold, and it was a lot harder to get a fire going than I thought it would be. I gave up pretty quickly, and I made myself hot chocolate while I waited for the heat to get working. Then I brought down a bunch of blankets from the linen closet and got all cozy on the couch underneath them, with my chocolate-covered pretzels and my mug of hot chocolate. *How the Grinch Stole Christmas* was on, and I fell asleep to the sound of the Whos in Whoville singing "Welcome Christmas."

I woke up to the sound of someone breaking into the house. I heard banging on the door and then someone messing with the doorknob. At first I just lay there under my blankets, scared out of my mind and trying not to breathe too loud. I kept thinking, oh my God, oh my God, it's just like in *Home Alone*. What would Kevin do? What would Kevin do? Kevin would probably booby-trap the front hall, but there was no time for any of that.

And then the burglar called out, "Steven? Are you in there?"

I thought, oh my God, the other robber is already in the house and his name is Steven!

I hid under the blanket, and then I thought, Kevin would not hide under a blanket. He would protect his house.

I took the brass poker from the fireplace and my cell phone, and I crept over to the foyer. I was too scared to look out the window, and I didn't want him to see me, so I just pressed my body up against the door and listened hard, my finger on the number nine.

"Steve, open up. It's me."

My heart nearly stopped beating. I knew that voice. It was not the voice of a burglar. It was Conrad.

I flung the door open. It really was him. I gazed at him, and he gazed back. I didn't know it would feel that way to see him again. Heart in my throat, hard to breathe. For those couple of seconds, I forgot everything and there was just him.

He was wearing a winter coat I had never seen before, camel colored, and he was sucking on a mini candy cane. It fell out of his mouth. "What in the world?" he said, his mouth still open.

When I hugged him, he smelled like peppermint and Christmas.

His cheek was cold against mine. "Why are you holding a poker?"

I stepped back. "I thought you were a burglar."

"Of course you did."

He followed me back to the living room and sat in the chair opposite the couch. He still had that shocked look on his face. "What are you doing here?"

I shrugged and set the poker on the coffee table. My adrenaline rush was fading fast, and I was starting to feel pretty silly. "I was all alone at home, and I just felt like coming. What are *you* doing here? I didn't even know you were coming back."

Conrad was in California now. I hadn't seen him since he'd transferred the year before. He had some scruff on his face, like he hadn't shaved in a couple of days. It looked soft, though, not prickly. He looked tan, too, which I thought was weird, seeing how it was winter, and then I remembered that he went to school in California, where it was always sunny.

"My dad sent me a ticket at the last minute. It took us forever to land, because of the snow, so I got here late. Since Jere and my dad are still in New York, I figured I'd just come here." He squinted at me.

"What?" I asked, feeling self-conscious all of a sudden. I tried to smooth down the back of my hair—it was all fuzzy from being slept on. Discreetly, I touched the corners of my mouth. Had I been drooling?

"You have chocolate all over your face."

I wiped at my mouth with the back of my hand. "No, I don't," I lied. "It's probably just dirt."

Amused, he raised his eyebrows at the near-empty can of chocolate-covered pretzels. "What, did you just put your whole head in it to save time?"

"Shut it," I said, but I couldn't help smiling.

The only light in the room was from the flickering TV. It was so surreal, being with him like this. A truly random twist of what felt like fate. I shivered and drew my blankets closer to me.

Taking off his coat, he said, "Want me to start a fire?"

Right away, I said, "Yes! I couldn't get it going for some reason."

"It takes a special touch," he said in his arrogant way. I knew by now it was only posturing.

It was all so familiar. We had been here before, just like this, only two Christmases ago. So much had happened since then. He had a whole new life now, and so did I. Still, in some ways, it was like no time or distance had passed between us. In some ways, it felt the same.

Maybe he was thinking the same thing, because he said, "It might be too late for a fire. I think I'm just gonna go crash." Abruptly, he stood up and headed for the staircase. Then he turned back and asked, "Are you sleeping down here?"

"Yup," I said. "Snug as a bug in a rug."

When he reached the staircase, Conrad stopped and then said, "Merry Christmas, Belly. It's really good to see you."

"You too."

The next morning, right when I woke up, I had this funny feeling that he had already left. I don't know why. I ran over to the stairs to check, and just as I was coming around the banister, I tripped over my pajama pants and fell flat on my back, banging my head along the way.

I lay there with tears in my eyes, staring up at the ceiling. The pain was unreal. Then Conrad's head popped up above me. "Are you okay?" he asked, his mouth full of food, cereal probably. He tried to help me sit up, but I waved him off.

"Leave me alone," I mumbled, hoping that if I just blinked fast enough, my tears would dry up.

"Are you hurt? Can you move?"

"I thought you were gone," I said.

"Nope. Still here." He knelt down beside me. "Just let me try and lift you up."

I shook my head no.

Conrad got down on the floor next to me, and we both lay there on the wooden floor like we were about to start making snow angels. "How bad does it hurt, on a scale of one to ten? Does it feel like you pulled something?"

"On a scale of one to ten . . . it hurts an eleven."

"You're such a baby when it comes to pain," he said, but he sounded worried.

"I am not." I was about to prove him right. Even I could hear how teary I sounded.

"Hey, that fall you took was no joke. It was just like how animals slip and fall in cartoons, like with a banana peel."

Suddenly I didn't feel like crying anymore. "Are you calling me an animal?" I demanded, turning my head to look at him. He was trying to keep a straight face, but the corners of his mouth kept turning up. Then he turned his head to look at me, and we both started laughing. I laughed so hard my back hurt worse.

Mid-laugh, I stopped and said, "Ow."

He sat up and said, "I'm gonna pick you up and bring you over to the couch."

"No," I protested weakly. "I'm too heavy for you. I'll get up in a minute, just leave me here for now."

Conrad frowned, and I could tell he was offended. "I know I can't bench-press my body weight like Jere, but I can pick up a girl, Belly."

I blinked. "It's not that. I'm heavier than you think. You know, freshman fifteen or whatever." My face got hot, and I momentarily forgot about how badly my back hurt or how weird it was that he'd brought up Jere. I just felt embarrassed.

In a quiet voice, he said, "Well, you look the same to me." Then, very gently, he scooped me off the floor and into his arms. I held on with one arm around his neck, and said, "It was more like ten. Freshman ten."

He said, "Don't worry. I've got you."

He carried me over to the couch and set me down. "I'm gonna get you some Advil. That should help a little."

Looking up at him, I had this sudden thought.

Oh my God. I still love you.

I'd thought my feelings for Conrad were safely tucked away, like my old Rollerblades and the little gold watch my dad bought me when I first learned how to tell time.

But just because you bury something, that doesn't mean it stops existing. Those feelings, they'd been there all along. All that time. I had to just face it. He was a part of my DNA. I had brown hair and I had freckles and I would always have Conrad in my heart. He would inhabit just that tiny piece of it, the little-girl part that still believed in musicals, but that was it. That was all he got. Jeremiah would have everything else—the present me and the future me. That was what was important. Not the past.

Maybe that was how it was with all first loves. They own a little piece of your heart, always. Conrad at twelve, thirteen, fourteen, fifteen, sixteen, even seventeen years old. For the rest of my life, I would think of him fondly, the way you do your first pet, the first car you drove. Firsts were important. But I was pretty sure lasts were even more important. And Jeremiah, he was going to be my last and my every and my always.

Conrad and I spent the rest of that day together but not together. He started a fire, and then he read at the kitchen table while I watched *It's a Wonderful Life*. For lunch, we had canned tomato soup and the rest of my chocolate-covered pretzels. Then he went for a run on the beach and I settled in for *Casablanca*. I was wiping tears from the corners of my eyes with my T-shirt sleeve when he came back. "This movie makes my heart hurt," I croaked.

Taking off his fleece, Conrad said, "Why? It had a happy ending. She was better off with Laszlo."

I looked at him in surprise. "You've seen *Casablanca*?"

"Of course. It's a classic."

"Well, obviously you weren't paying that close of

attention, because Rick and Ilsa are meant for each other."

Conrad snorted. "Their little love story is nothing compared to the work Laszlo was doing for the Resistance."

Blowing my nose with a napkin, I said, "For a young guy, you're way too cynical."

He rolled his eyes. "And for a supposedly grown girl, you're way too emotional." He headed for the stairs.

"Robot!" I yelled at his back. "Tin man!"

I heard him laughing as he closed the bathroom door.

The next morning, Conrad was gone. He left just like I thought he'd leave. No good-bye, no nothing. Just gone, like a ghost. Conrad, the Ghost of Christmas Past.

Jeremiah called me when I was on the way back home from Cousins. He asked what I was doing, and I told him I was driving home, but I didn't tell him where I was driving from. It was a split-second decision. At the time I didn't know why I lied. I just knew I didn't want him to know.

I decided Conrad was right after all. Ilsa was meant to be with Laszlo. That was the way it was always supposed to end. Rick was nothing but a tiny piece of her past, a piece that she would always treasure, but that was all, because history is just that. History.

chapter *nine*

After I left Anika's room, I turned on my phone. There were texts and e-mails from Jeremiah, and they kept coming. I got under my covers and read them all, each and every one. Then I reread them, and when I was done, I finally wrote him back and said, *Give me some space.* He wrote *OK*, and that was the last text I got from him that day. I still kept checking my phone to see if there was anything from him, and when there wasn't, I was disappointed, even though I knew I didn't have a right to be. I wanted him to leave me alone, and I wanted him to keep trying to fix things. But if I didn't know what I wanted, how could he possibly?

I stayed in my room, packing up. I was hungry, and I still had meals left on my meal card, but I was afraid I might run into Lacie on campus. Or worse, Jeremiah. Still, it was good to have something to do and to be able to turn the music on loud without having to hear my roommate Jillian complain.

When I couldn't take the hunger anymore, I called Taylor and told her everything. She screamed so loud, I had to hold the phone away from my ear. She came right over with a black-bean burrito and a strawberry-banana smoothie. She kept shaking her head and saying, "That Zeta Phi slut."

"It wasn't just her, it was him, too," I said, between bites of my burrito.

"Oh, I know. Just you wait. I'm gonna drag my nails across his face when I see him. I'll leave him so scarred, no girl will ever hook up with him again." She inspected her manicured nails like they were artillery. "When I go to the salon tomorrow, I'm gonna tell Danielle to make them sharp."

My heart swelled. There are some things only a friend who's known you your whole life can say, and instantly, I felt a little better. "You don't have to scar him."

"But I want to." She hooked her pinky finger with mine. "Are you okay?"

I nodded. "Better, now that you're here."

When I was sucking down the last of my smoothie, Taylor asked me, "Do you think you'll take him back?"

I was surprised and really relieved not to hear any judgment in her voice. "What would you do?" I asked her.

"It's up to you."

"I know, but . . . would *you* take him back?"

"Under ordinary circumstances, no. If some guy cheated on me while we were on a break, if he so much as looked at another girl, no. He'd be donzo." She chewed on her straw. "But Jeremy's not some guy. You have a history together."

"What happened to all that talk about scarring him?"

"Don't get it twisted, I hate him to death right now. He effed up in a colossal way. But he'll never be just some guy, not to you. That's a fact."

I didn't say anything. But I knew she was right.

"I could still round up my sorority sisters and go slash his tires tonight." Taylor bumped my shoulder. "Hmm? Whaddyathink?"

She was trying to make me laugh. It worked. I laughed for the first time in what felt like a long time.

chapter *ten*

After our fight the summer before senior year, I really thought that Taylor and I would make up fast, the way we always did. I thought it would blow over in a week, tops. Because what were we really even mad about? Sure, we both said some hurtful things—I called her a child, she called me a crappy best friend, but it wasn't like we'd never had a fight before. Best friends fought.

When I got home from Cousins, I put Taylor's shoes and her clothes in a bag, ready to take them over to her house as soon as she gave me the signal that we were done being mad at each other. It was always Taylor who gave the signal, she was the one who initiated making up.

I waited, but it didn't come. I went to Marcy's a couple of times, hoping I'd run into her and we'd be forced to talk things out. Those times I was at Marcy's, she never came. Weeks passed. The summer was almost over.

Jeremiah kept saying the same thing he'd been saying for all of July and most of August. "Don't worry, you guys will make up. You guys always make up."

"You don't get it, this isn't like before," I told him. "She wouldn't even look at me."

"All of this over a party," he said, which pissed me off.

"It's not over a party."

"I know, I know—hold on a sec, Bells." I heard him talking to someone, and then he came back on the phone. "Our hot wings just got here. Want me to call you back after I eat? I can be quick."

"No, that's all right," I said.

"Don't be mad."

I said, "I'm not," and I wasn't. Not really. How could he understand what was going on with me and Taylor? He was a guy. He didn't get it. He didn't get how important, how really and truly vital, it was to me that Taylor and I start off our last year of high school together by each other's side.

So why couldn't I just call her, then? It was partly pride and partly something else. I was the one who had been pulling away from her this whole time, she was the one who had been holding on. Maybe I thought I was growing past her, maybe it was all for the best. We'd have to say good-bye next fall, maybe it would be easier this way. Maybe we'd been codependent, maybe more me on her than the other way around, and now I needed to stand on my own feet. This is what I told myself.

When I told this to Jeremiah the next night, he said, "Just call her."

I was pretty sure he was just sick of hearing me talk about it, so I said, "Maybe. I'll think about it."

The week before school started, the week I usually came back from Cousins, we always went back-to-school shopping together. Always. We'd been doing it since elementary school. She always knew the right kind of jeans to get. We'd go to Bath & Body Works and get those "Buy Three, Get One Free" kind of deals, and then we'd come home and split everything up so we each had a lotion, a body gel, a scrub. We'd be set until Christmas, at least.

That year, I went with my mom. My mom hated shopping. We were waiting in line to pay for jeans when Taylor and her mom walked into the store carrying a couple of shopping bags each. "Luce!" my mom called out.

Mrs. Jewel waved and came right over, with Taylor trailing behind her wearing sunglasses and cutoff shorts. My mom hugged Taylor, and Mrs. Jewel hugged me and said, "It's been a long time, honey."

To my mom, she said, "Laurel, can you believe our little girls are all grown up now? My gosh, I remember when they insisted on doing everything together. Baths, haircuts, everything."

"I remember," my mother said, smiling.

I caught Taylor's eye. Our moms kept on talking, and we just stood there looking at each other but not really.

After a minute, Taylor pulled out her cell phone. I didn't want to let this moment pass without saying something to her. I asked, "Did you get anything good?"

She nodded. Since she was wearing sunglasses, it was hard to tell what she was thinking. But I knew Taylor well. She loved to brag about her bargains.

Taylor hesitated and then said, "I got some hot boots for twenty-five percent off. And a couple of sundresses that I can winterize with tights and sweaters."

I nodded. Then it was our turn to pay, and I said, "Well, see you at school."

"See you," she said, turning away.

Without thinking, I handed the jeans to my mom and stopped Taylor. It could be the last time we ever talked to each other if I didn't say something. "Wait," I said. "Do you want to come over tonight? I bought a new skirt, but I don't know if I should tuck shirts into it or what . . ."

She pursed her lips for a second and then said, "Okay. Call me."

Taylor did come over that night. She showed me how to wear the skirt—which shoes looked best with it and which tops. Things weren't the same with us, not right away, and maybe not ever. We were growing up. We were still figuring out how to be in each other's lives without being everything to each other.

The truly ironic thing is that we ended up at the same school. Of all the schools in all the world, we ended up at each other's. It was fated. We were meant to be friends. We were meant to be in each other's lives, and you know what? I welcomed it. We weren't together all the time like we used to be—she had her sorority friends, I had my friends from my hall. But we still had each other.

chapter *eleven*

The next day, I couldn't hold out any longer. I called Jeremiah. I told him I needed to see him, that he should come over, and my voice shook as I said it. Over the phone, I could hear how grateful he was, how eager to make amends. I tried to justify calling him so fast by telling myself that I needed to see him face-to-face in order to move on. The truth was, I missed him. I, probably just as much as he did, wanted to figure out a way to forget what had happened.

But as much as I'd missed him, when I opened my door and saw his face again, all the hurt came rushing back, hard and fast. Jeremiah could see it too. At first he looked hopeful, and then he just looked devastated. When he tried to pull me to him, I wanted to hug him, but I couldn't let myself. Instead I shook my head and pushed him away from me.

We sat on my bed, our backs against the wall, our legs hanging off the edge.

I said, "How would I know that you wouldn't do it again? How would I be able to trust that?"

He got up. For a second I thought he was leaving, and my heart nearly stopped.

But then he got down on one knee, right in front of me. Very softly, he said, "You could marry me."

At first I wasn't sure I'd heard him right. But then he said it again, this time louder. "Marry me."

He reached into his jeans pocket and pulled out a ring. A silver ring with a little diamond in the center. "This would just be for starters, until I could afford to pay for a ring myself—with my money, not my dad's."

I couldn't feel my body. He was still talking, and I couldn't even hear. All I could do was stare at the ring in his hand.

"I love you so much. These past couple of days have been hell for me without you." He took a breath. "I'm so sorry for hurting you, Bells. What I did—was unforgivable. I know that I hurt us, that I'm going to have to work really hard to get you to trust me again. I'll do whatever it takes if you'll let me. Would you . . . be willing to let me try?"

"I don't know," I whispered.

He swallowed, and his Adam's apple bobbed up and down. "I'll try so hard, I swear to you. We'll get an apartment off campus, we can fix it up nice. I'll do the laundry. I'll learn how to cook stuff other than ramen and cereal."

"Putting cereal in a bowl isn't really cooking," I said, looking away from him because this picture he was putting in my head, it was too much. I could see it too. How sweet it could be. The two of us, just starting out, in our own place.

Jeremiah grabbed my hands, and I snatched them away from him. He said, "Don't you see, Belly? It's been our story all along. Yours and mine. Nobody else's."

I closed my eyes, trying to clear my head. Opening them, I said, "You just want to erase what you did by marrying me."

"No. That's not what this is. What happened the other night"—he hesitated—"it made me realize something. I don't ever want to be without you. Ever. You are the only girl for me. I've always known it. In this whole world, I will never love another girl the way I love you."

He took my hand again, and this time I didn't pull away from him. "Do you still love me?" he asked.

I swallowed. "Yeah."

"Then please, marry me."

I said, "You can't ever hurt me like that again." It was half warning, half plea.

"I won't," he said, and I knew he meant it.

He looked at me so determinedly, so earnestly. I knew his face well, maybe better than anybody now. Every line, every curve. The little bump on his nose from when he broke it surfing, the almost-faded scar on his forehead from the time he and Conrad were wrestling in the rec room and they knocked a plant over. I was there for those moments. Maybe I knew his face even better than my own—the hours I'd spent staring at it while he slept, tracing my finger along his cheekbone. Maybe he'd done the same things to me.

I didn't want to see a mark on his face one day and not know how it got there. I wanted to be with him. His was the face I loved.

Wordlessly, I slipped my left hand out of his, and Jeremiah's face slackened. Then I held out my hand for him, and his eyes lit up. The joy I felt in that moment—I couldn't even put it into words. His hand shook as he placed the ring on my finger.

He asked, "Isabel Conklin, will you marry me?" in as serious a voice as I'd ever heard him use.

"Yes, I'll marry you," I said.

He put his arms around me, and we held on to each other, clinging like we were the other's safe harbor. All I could think was, if we just get through this storm, we will make it. He'd made mistakes, I had too. But we loved each other, and that was what mattered.

We made plans all night—where we would live, how we would tell our parents. The past few days felt like another lifetime ago. That day, without another word about it, we decided to leave the past in the past. The future was where we were headed.

chapter *twelve*

That night I dreamed of Conrad. I was the same age I was now, but he was younger, ten or eleven maybe. I think he might even have been wearing overalls. We played outside my house until it got dark, just running around the yard. I said, "Susannah will be wondering where you are. You should go home." He said, "I can't. I don't know how. Will you help me?" And then I was sad, because I didn't know how either. We weren't at my house anymore, and it was so dark. We were in the woods. We were lost.

When I woke up, I was crying and Jeremiah was asleep next to me. I sat up in the bed. It was dark, the only light in the room was my alarm clock. It read 4:57. I lay back down.

I wiped my eyes, and then I breathed in Jeremiah's scent, the sweetness of his face, the way his chest rose and fell as he breathed. He was there. He was solid and real and next to me, crammed in close the way you have to be when you are sleeping in a dorm-room bed. We were that close now.

In the morning, when I woke up, I didn't remember right away. The dream was there in the back of my head, in a place I couldn't get to. It was fading fast, almost all the way, but not quite, not yet. I had to think hard and fast to piece it all together, to hold on to it.

I started to sit up, but Jeremiah pulled me back toward him and said, "Five more minutes." He was the big spoon, and I was the little spoon tucked into my spot in his arms. I closed my eyes, willing myself to remember before it was gone. Like those last few seconds before the sun sets—going, going, and then gone. Remember, remember, or the dream will slip away forever.

Jeremiah started to say something about breakfast, and I covered his mouth and said, "Shh. One sec."

And then I had it. Conrad, and how funny he looked in his denim overalls. The two of us playing outside for hours. I let out a sigh. I felt so relieved.

"What were you saying?" I asked Jeremiah.

"Breakfast," he said, planting a kiss on my palm.

Snuggling in closer to him, I said, "Five more minutes."

chapter *thirteen*

I wanted to tell everyone face-to-face, all at once. In a weird way, it would be perfect timing. Our families would be together in Cousins in a week. A battered-women's shelter that Susannah had volunteered at and fund-raised for had planted a garden in her honor, and there was going to be a little ceremony next Saturday. We were all going—me, Jere, my mom, his dad, Steven. Conrad.

I hadn't seen Conrad since Christmas. He was supposed to fly back for my mother's fiftieth birthday party, but he bailed at the last minute. "Typical Con," Jeremiah had said, shaking his head. He'd looked at me, waiting for me to agree. I didn't say anything.

My mother and Conrad had a special relationship, always had. They got each other on some level I didn't understand. After Susannah died, they became closer, maybe because they grieved for her in the same way—alone. My mom and Conrad spoke on the phone often, about what I didn't know. So when he didn't come, I could see how disappointed she was, even though she didn't say so. I wanted to tell her, Love him all you want, but don't expect anything in return. Conrad isn't someone who can be counted on.

He did send a nice bouquet of red zinnias, though. "My favorite," she'd said, beaming.

What would he say when we told him our news? I couldn't begin to guess. When it came to Conrad, I was never sure of anything.

I worried, too, about what my mother would say. Jeremiah wasn't worried, but he so rarely was. He said, "Once they know we're serious, they'll have to get on board, because they won't be able to stop us. We're adults now."

We were walking back from the dining hall. Jeremiah dropped my hand, jumped onto a bench, threw his head back, and yelled, "Hey, everybody! Belly Conklin is gonna marry me!"

A few people turned to look but then kept walking.

"Get down from there," I said, laughing and covering my face with my hoodie.

He jumped back down and ran around the bench once, his arms up and out like an airplane. He zoomed back over to me and lifted me up by the armpits. "Come on, fly," he encouraged.

I rolled my eyes and moved my arms up and down. "Happy?"

"Yes," he said, setting me back down on the ground.

I was too. *This* was the Jere I knew. This was the boy from the beach house. Getting engaged, promising to be each other's forever, it made me feel like even with all the changes over the past few years, he was still the same boy and I was still the same girl. Now nobody could take that away from us, not anymore.

chapter *fourteen*

I knew I had to talk to Taylor and Anika before my dad came and got me in the morning. I debated just telling them together, but I knew that Taylor would be hurt if I lumped her, my oldest friend, with Anika, who I had known for less than a year. I had to tell Taylor first. I owed her that much.

I knew she'd think we were crazy. Getting back together was one thing, but getting married was something else entirely. Unlike most of her sorority sisters, Taylor didn't want to get married until she was at least twenty-eight.

I called and asked her to meet me at the Drip House, the coffee shop everyone studied at. I told her I had news. She tried to get it out of me over the phone, but I resisted, saying, "It's the kind of news you have to tell in person."

Taylor was already seated with her nonfat iced latte when I got there. She had on her Ray-Bans, and she was texting. She put down her phone when she saw me.

I sat down across from her, careful to keep my hand in my lap.

Taking off her sunglasses, she said, "You're looking much better today."

"Thanks, Tay. I feel a lot better."

"So what's up?" She scrutinized me. "Did you guys get back together? Or did you break up for real?"

I held up my left hand with a flourish. She looked at it, confused. Then her eyes focused on my ring finger.

Taylor's eyes turned huge. "You're effing kidding me. You're engaged?!" she screamed. A couple of people turned around and looked at us, annoyed. I shrank down in my seat a little. Grabbing my hand, she said, "Oh my God! Let me see that thing!"

I could tell she thought it was too small, but I didn't care.

"Oh my God," she said, still staring at the ring.

"I know," I said.

"But, Belly . . . he cheated on you."

"We're starting over fresh. I really love him, Tay."

"Yeah, but the timing is kinda suspect," she said slowly. "I mean, it's really sudden."

"It is and it isn't. You said it yourself. This is Jere we're talking about. He's the love of my life."

She just stared at me, her mouth an O. She sputtered, "But—but why can't you wait at least until after you finish college?"

"We don't see the point in waiting if we're gonna get married anyways." I took a sip of Taylor's drink. "We're gonna get an apartment. You can help me pick out curtains and stuff."

"I guess," she said. "But wait, what about your mom? Did Laurel flip her shit?"

"We're telling my mom and his dad next week in Cousins. We'll tell my dad after."

She perked up. "Wait, so nobody even knows yet? Just me?"

I nodded, and I could tell Taylor was pleased. She loves being in on a secret—it's one of her top favorite things in life.

"It's gonna be an apocalypse," she said, taking her drink back. "Like, dead bodies. Like, blood in the streets. And when I say blood, I mean your blood."

"Gee, thanks a lot, Tay."

"I'm just speaking the truth. Laurel is the OG feminist. She's like Gloria freaking Steinem. She's not gonna like this one bit. She'll go all Terminator on his ass. And yours."

"My mom loves Jeremiah. She and Susannah always talked about me marrying one of her sons. It might be, like, a dream come true for her. In fact, I bet it will be." I knew that wasn't the least bit true even as I was saying it.

Taylor looked unconvinced too. "Maybe," she said. "So when is this happening?"

"This August."

"That's really, really soon. Hardly gives us any time to plan." Chewing on her straw, she cast a sneaky look my way. "What about bridesmaids? Are you going to have a maid of honor?"

"I don't know. . . . We want it to be really small. We're gonna do it at the Cousins house. Really casual, like, not a big deal."

"Not a big deal? You're getting married and you don't want it to be a big deal?"

"I didn't mean it like that. I just don't care about all that stuff. All I want is to be with Jeremiah."

"All what stuff?"

"Like, bridesmaids and wedding cake. Stuff like that."

"Liar!" She pointed her finger at me. "You wanted five bridesmaids and a four-tier carrot cake. You wanted an ice sculpture of a human heart with your initials carved into it. Which, by the way, is gross."

"Tay!"

She held up her hand to stop me. "You wanted a live band and crab cakes and a balloon drop after your first dance. What was that song you wanted to dance to?"

"'Stay' by Maurice Williams and the Zodiacs," I said automatically. "But Taylor, I was probably ten years old when I said all that stuff." I was really touched that she remembered, though. But I guessed I remembered everything Taylor wanted too. Doves, little lace gloves, hot-pink stiletto heels.

"You should have everything you want, Belly," Taylor said, her chin jutting out in her stubborn Taylor way. "You only get married once."

"I know, but we don't have the money. And anyway, I don't really care about those things anymore. That was kid stuff." But maybe I didn't have to do *all* of it, maybe just some of it. Maybe I could still have a real wedding, but simple. Because, it would be nice to wear a wedding dress and to have a father-daughter dance with my dad.

"I thought Jeremy's dad was loaded. Can't he afford to give you a real wedding?"

"There's no way my mom would let him pay for it. Besides, like I said, we don't want anything fancy."

"Okay," she conceded. "We'll forget the ice sculpture. But balloons are cheap—we can still do balloons. And the carrot cake. We could just do a regular two-layer, I guess. And I don't care what you say, you're wearing a wedding dress."

"That sounds good," I agreed, taking a sip of her drink. It felt really nice to have Taylor's blessing. It was like getting permission to be excited, something I didn't know I needed or wanted.

"And you'll still have bridesmaids. Or at least a maid of honor."

"I'll just have you."

Taylor looked pleased. "But what about Anika? You don't want Anika to be a bridesmaid?"

"Hmm, maybe," I said, and when her face fell, just slightly, I added, "But I want you to be my maid of honor. Okay?"

Tears filled her eyes. "I'm so honored."

Taylor Jewel, my oldest friend in the world. We'd been through some times together, and I knew now it was pure grace that we'd managed to come out the other side.

chapter *fifteen*

Anika was next, and I was dreading it. I respected her opinion. I didn't want her to think less of me. The prospect of being a bridesmaid wasn't going to have any sway over her. That wasn't something she would care about either way.

We had decided to room together that fall, in a suite with two of our other friends, Shay and Lynn, in the new dorm on the other side of campus. Anika and I were going to buy cute plates and cups, she was bringing her fridge, and I was bringing my TV. Everything was set.

We were hanging out in her room later that night. I was packing her books inside a big crate, and she was rolling up her posters.

The radio was on, and our campus station was playing Madonna's "The Power of Good-Bye." Maybe it was a sign.

I sat on the floor, putting away the last book, trying to

drum up the courage to tell her. Nervously, I licked my lips. "Ani, I have something I need to talk to you about," I said.

She'd been struggling with the movie poster on the back of her door. "What's up?"

There's no greater power than the power of good-bye.

I swallowed. "I feel really bad having to do this to you."

Anika turned around. "Do what?"

"I'm not going to be able to room with you next semester."

Her eyebrows were knit together. "What? Why? Did something happen?"

"Jeremiah asked me to marry him."

She did a double take. "Isabel Conklin! Shut the shit up."

Slowly, I held up my hand.

Anika whistled. "Wow. That's crazy."

"I know."

She opened her mouth, then closed it. Then she said, "Do you know what you're doing?"

"Yeah. I think so. I really, really love him."

"Where are you guys going to live?"

"In an apartment off campus." I hesitated. "I just feel bad about letting you down. Are you mad?"

Shaking her head, she said, "I'm not mad. I mean, yeah, it sucks that we won't be living together, but I'll figure something out. I could ask Trina from my dance team. Or my cousin Brandy might be transferring here. She could be our fourth."

So it wasn't such a big deal after all, my not living with them. Life goes on, I guessed. I felt a little wistful, imagining what it would be like if I was still the fourth. Shay was really good at doing hair, and Lynn loved to bake cupcakes. It would have been fun.

Anika sat down on her bed. "I'll be fine. I'm just . . . surprised."

"Me too."

When she didn't say anything else, I asked, "Do you think I'm making a huge mistake?"

In her thoughtful way, she asked, "Does it matter what I think?"

"Yes."

"It's not for me to judge, Iz."

"But you're my friend. I respect your opinion. I don't want you to think badly of me."

"You care too much about what other people think." She said it with sureness but also tenderness.

If anyone else had said it—my mother, Taylor, even Jere—I would have bristled. But not with Anika. With her, I couldn't really mind. In a way it was flattering to have her see me so clearly and still like me. Friendship in college was different that way. You spend all this time with people, sometimes every day, every meal. There was no hiding who you were in front of your friends. You were just naked. Especially in front of someone like Anika, who was so frank and open and incisive and said whatever she thought. She didn't miss a thing.

Anika said, "At least you'll never have to wear shower shoes again."

"Or have to pull other people's hair out of the drain," I added. "Jeremiah's hair is too short to get caught."

"You'll never have to hide your food." Anika's roommate, Joy, was always stealing her food, and Anika had taken to hiding granola bars in her underwear drawer.

"I might actually have to do that. Jere eats a lot," I said, twisting my ring around my finger.

I stayed a while longer, helping her take down the rest of her posters, collecting the dust bunnies under her bed with an old sock I used as a mitten. We talked about the magazine internship Anika had lined up for the summer, and me maybe going to visit her in New York for a weekend.

After, I walked down the hall back to my room. For the first time all year, it was really quiet—no hair dryers going, no one sitting in the hallway on the phone, no one microwaving popcorn in the commons area. A lot of people had already gone home for the summer. Tomorrow I would be gone too.

College life as I knew it was about to change.

chapter *sixteen*

I didn't plan to start going by Isabel. It just happened. All my life, everyone had called me Belly and I didn't really have a say in it. For the first time in a long time, I did have a say, but it didn't occur to me until we—Jeremiah, my mom, my dad, and me—were standing in front of my dorm room door on freshman move-in day. My dad and Jeremiah were lugging the TV, my mom had a suitcase, and I was carrying a laundry basket with all my toiletries and picture frames. Sweat was pouring down my dad's back, and his maroon button-down shirt had three wet spots. Jeremiah was sweating too, since he'd been trying to impress my dad all morning by insisting on bringing up the heaviest stuff. It made my dad feel awkward, I could tell.

"Hurry, Belly," my dad said, breathing hard.

"She's Isabel now," my mother said.

I remember the way I fumbled with my key and how I looked up at the door and saw it. ISABEL, it said in glue-on rhinestones. My roommate's and my door tags were made out of empty CD cases. My roommate's, Jillian Capel's, was a Mariah Carey CD, and mine was Prince.

Jillian's stuff was already unpacked, on the left side of the room, closer to the door. She had a paisley bedspread, navy and rusty orange. It looked brand new. She'd already hung up her posters—a *Trainspotting* movie poster and some band I'd never heard of called Running Water.

My dad sat down at the empty desk—my desk. He pulled out a handkerchief and wiped off his forehead. He looked really tired. "It's a good room," he said. "Good light."

Jeremiah was just hovering around, and he said, "I'll go down to the car to get that big box."

My dad started to get up. "I'll help," he said.

"I've got it," Jeremiah said, bounding out the door.

Sitting back down, my dad looked relieved. "I'll just take a break, then," he said.

Meanwhile, my mother was surveying the room, opening the closet, looking in drawers.

I sank down on the bed. So this was where I was going to live for the next year. Next door, someone was playing jazz. Down the hall, I could hear a girl arguing with her mother about where to put her laundry bin. It seemed like the elevator never stopped dinging open and closed. I didn't mind. I liked the noise. It was comforting knowing there were people all around me.

"Want me to unpack your clothes?" my mother asked.

"No, that's all right," I said. I wanted to do that myself. Then it would really feel like my room.

"At least let me make up your bed, then," she said.

When it was time to say good-bye, I wasn't ready. I thought I would be, but I wasn't. My dad stood there, his hands on his hips. His hair looked really gray in the light. He said, "Well, we should get going if we want to beat rush-hour traffic."

Irritably, my mother said, "We'll be fine."

Seeing them together like this, it was almost like they weren't divorced, like we were still a family. I was overcome with this sudden rush of thankfulness. Not all divorces were like theirs. For Steven's and my sake, they made it work and they were sincere about it. There was still genuine affection between them, but more than that: there was love for us. It was what made it possible for them to come together on days like this.

I hugged my dad, and I was surprised to see tears in his eyes. He never cried. My mother hugged me briskly, but I knew it was because she didn't want to let go. "Make sure you wash your sheets at least twice a month," she said.

"Okay," I said.

"And try making your bed in the morning. It'll make your room look nicer."

"Okay," I said again.

My mother looked over at the other side of the room. "I just wish we could have met your roommate."

Jeremiah was sitting at my desk, his head down, scrolling on his phone while we said our good-byes.

All of a sudden, my dad said, "Jeremiah, are you going to leave now too?"

Startled, Jeremiah looked up. "Oh, I was going to take Belly to dinner."

My mother shot me a look, and I knew what she was thinking. A couple of nights before, she'd given me this long speech about meeting new people and not spending all my time with Jere. Girls with boyfriends, she'd said, limit themselves to a certain kind of college experience. I'd promised her I wouldn't be one of those kind of girls.

"Just don't get her back too late," my dad said in this really meaningful kind of way.

I could feel my cheeks get red, and this time my mother gave my dad a look, which made me feel even more awkward. But Jeremiah just said, "Oh, yeah, of course," in his relaxed way.

I met my roommate, Jillian, later that night, after dinner. It was in the elevator, right after Jeremiah dropped me off in front of the dorm. I recognized her right away, from the pictures on her dresser. She had curly brown hair, and she was really little, shorter than she'd looked in the pictures.

I stood there, trying to figure out what to say. When the other girls in the elevator got off on the sixth floor, it was just the two of us. I cleared my throat and said, "Excuse me. Are you Jillian Capel?"

"Yeah," she said, and I could tell she was a little weirded out.

"I'm Isabel Conklin," I said. "Your roommate."

I wondered if I should hug her or offer her my hand to shake. I did neither, because she was staring at me.

"Oh, hi. How are you?" Without waiting for me to answer, she said, "I'm just coming back from dinner with my parents." Later, I would learn that she said "How are you" a lot, like it was more of a thing to say, not something she expected an answer to.

"I'm good," I said. "I just had dinner too."

We got off the elevator then. I felt this excited pitter-patter in my chest, like wow, this is my roommate. This was the person I was going to be living with for a whole year. I'd thought a lot about her since I got my housing letter. Jillian Capel from Washington, DC, nonsmoker. I'd imagined us talking all night, sharing secrets and shoes and microwave popcorn.

When we were in our room, Jillian sat down on her bed and said, "Do you have a boyfriend?"

"Yeah, he goes here too," I said, sitting on my hands. I was eager to get right to the girl talk and the bonding. "His name is Jeremiah. He's a sophomore."

I jumped up and grabbed a photo of us from my desk. It was from graduation, and Jeremiah was wearing a tie and he looked handsome in it. Shyly, I handed it to her.

"He's really cute," she said.

"Thanks. Do you have a boyfriend?"

She nodded. "Back home."

"Neat," I said, because it was all I could think of. "What's his name?"

"Simon."

When she didn't elaborate, I asked, "So, do people ever call you Jill? Or Jilly? Or do you just go by Jillian?"

"Jillian. Do you go to sleep early or late?"

"Late. What about you?"

"Early," she said, chewing on her lower lip. "We'll figure something out. I wake up early, too. What about you?"

"Um, sure, sometimes." I hated to wake up early, hated it more than almost anything.

"Do you like to study with music on or off?"

"Off?"

Jillian looked relieved. "Oh, good. I hate noise when I study. I need it to be really quiet." She added, "Not that I'm anal or anything."

I nodded. Her picture frames were at perfect right angles. When we walked into the room, she'd hung up her jean jacket right away. I only ever made my bed when company came over. I wondered if my sloppy tendencies would get on her nerves. I hoped not.

I was about to say so when she turned her laptop on. I guessed we were done bonding for the night. Now that my parents were gone and Jeremiah was on his way back to his frat house, I was really alone. I didn't know what to do with myself. I'd already unpacked. I'd been hoping we could explore the hall together, meet people. But she was typing away, chatting with someone. Probably her boyfriend back home.

I got my cell phone out of my purse and texted Jeremiah. *Will you come back?*

I knew he would.

For the hall icebreaker the next night, our RA, Kira, told us to bring one personal item that we felt represented us best. I settled on a pair of swim goggles. The other girls brought stuffed animals and framed photos, and one girl brought out her modeling book. Jillian brought her laptop.

We were all sitting in a circle, and Joy was sitting across from me. She was cradling a trophy in her lap. It was for a soccer state championship, which I thought was pretty impressive. I really wanted to make friends with Joy. I'd had it in my head since the night before, when we'd chatted in the hall bathroom in our pajamas, both of us with our shower caddies. Joy was short, with a sandy bob and light eyes. She didn't wear makeup. She was sturdy and sure of herself, in the way that girls who play competitive sports are.

"I'm Joy," she said. "My team won the state champion-ship. If any of you guys like soccer, hit me up and we'll get a hall league going."

When it was my turn, I said, "I'm Isabel. I like to swim," and Joy smiled at me.

I always thought that college would be It. Like, instant friends, a place to belong. I didn't think it would be this hard.

I'd thought there would be parties and mixers and midnight runs to the Waffle House. I'd been at college for four whole days, and I hadn't done any of those things. Jillian and I had eaten in the dining hall together, but that was about it. She was mostly on the phone with her boyfriend or on the computer. There had been no men-tion of clubbing or frat parties. I had a feeling Jillian was above that kind of thing.

I wasn't, and Taylor wasn't either. I'd gone to visit her dorm once already, and she and her roommate were like two peas in a trendy little color-coordinated pod. Her roommate's boyfriend was in a fraternity, and he lived off campus. Taylor said she'd call if there were any cool par-ties that weekend, but so far, she hadn't. Taylor was taking to college like a goldfish to its brand-new tank, and I just wasn't. I'd told Jeremiah I'd be busy making friends and bonding with my roommate so I probably wouldn't see him until the weekend. I didn't want to go back on that. I didn't want to be one of those girls.

Thursday night that first week, a bunch of girls were drinking in Joy's room. I could hear them down the hallway. I had been filling out my new planner, writing in all my classes and things. Jillian was at the library. We'd only had one day of classes so far, so I didn't know what she could possibly be studying. I still wished she'd asked me to go with her, though. Jeremiah had asked if I wanted him to come pick me up, but I'd said no, in the hopes that I would be invited somewhere. So far, it was just me and the planner.

But then Joy popped her head in my doorway, which I'd been keeping open the same way the other girls had. "Isabel, come and hang with us," she said.

"Sure!" I said, practically leaping out of my bed. I felt this surge of hope and excitement. Maybe these were my people.

There was Joy, her roommate Anika, Molly, who lived at the end the hall, and Shay, the girl with the modeling book. They were all sitting on the floor, a big bottle of Gatorade in the middle, only, it didn't look like Gatorade. It was light brownish yellow— Tequila, I guessed. I hadn't touched tequila since I'd gotten drunk off of it in Cousins the summer before.

"Come sit down," Joy said, patting the floor next to her. "We're playing I Never. Have you ever played before?"

"No," I said, sitting down next to her.

"Basically, when it's your turn, you say something

like, 'I never . . .'"—Anika looked around the circle—
"hooked up with someone related to me."

Everyone giggled. "And if you have, you have to
drink," Molly finished, chewing on her thumbnail.

"I'll start," said Joy, leaning forward. "I never . . .
cheated on a test."

Shay grabbed the bottle and took a swig. "What? I was
busy modeling, I didn't have time to study," she said, and
everyone laughed again.

Molly went next. "I never did it with anyone in
public!"

That time, Joy took the bottle. "It was at a park," she
explained. "It was getting dark. I doubt anyone saw us."

Shay said, "Does a restaurant bathroom count?"

I could feel my face get hot. I was dreading my turn. I
hadn't done much of anything. My I Nevers could probably last all night.

"I never hooked up with Chad from the fourth floor!"
Molly said, collapsing into a fit of giggles.

Joy threw a pillow at her. "No fair! I told you that in
secret."

"Drink! Drink!" everyone chanted.

Joy took a swig. Wiping her mouth, she said, "Your
turn, Isabel."

My mouth felt dry all of a sudden. "I never . . ." Had
sex. "I never . . . played this game before," I finished lamely.

I could feel Joy's disappointment in me. Maybe she'd

thought we could be close friends too and now she was rethinking it.

Anika chuckled just to be polite, and then they all took turns drinking before Joy started it up again with, "I never went skinny-dipping in the ocean. In a pool, though!"

Nope, never did that either. Almost, that time I was fifteen, with Cam Cameron. But almost didn't count.

I ended up taking one drink when Molly said, "I never dated two people in the same family."

"You dated brothers?" Joy asked me, looking interested all of a sudden. "Or a brother and a sister?"

Coughing a little, I said, "Brothers."

"Twins?" Shay said.

"At the same time?" Molly wanted to know.

"No, not at the same time. And they're just regular brothers," I said. "They're a year apart."

"That's kind of badass," Joy said, giving me an approving look.

And then we went on to the next thing. When Shay said she'd never stolen before and Joy took a drink, I saw the look on Anika's face, and I had to bite the insides of my cheeks to keep from laughing. She saw me, and we exchanged a secret look.

I saw Joy around after that, in the hall bathroom and in the study, and we talked, but we never became close. Jillian and I never became best buddies either, but she ended up being a pretty good roommate.

Of all those girls, Anika was the one I ended up being closest to. Even though we were the same age, she took me under her wing like a little sister, and for once I didn't mind being the little sister. Anika was too cool for me to care. She smelled the way I imagined wildflowers smelled when they grew in sand. Later, I found out it was the oil she put in her hair. Anika almost never gossiped, she didn't eat meat, and she was a dancer. I admired all of those things about her.

I was sorry we'd never be roommates. From now on, I'd only ever have one roommate again—Jeremiah, my soon-to-be husband.

chapter *seventeen*

I woke up early the next day. I showered, threw away my shower shoes, and got ready one last time in my dorm room. I didn't put my ring on, just in case. I put it in the zippered pocket in my purse. My dad wasn't the most observant guy when it came to accessories, so it wasn't likely he'd notice, but still.

My dad was at the dorm by ten o'clock to move me out. Jeremiah helped. I didn't even have to give him a wakeup call the way I'd planned; he showed up at my room at nine thirty with coffee and donuts for my dad.

I stopped in some of the girls' rooms, hugging them good-bye, wishing them good summers. Lorrie said, "See you in August," and Jules said, "We have to hang out more next year." I said good-bye to Anika last, and I teared up a little. She hugged me and said, "Chill out. I'll see you at the wedding. Tell Taylor I'll be e-mailing her about our bridesmaid dresses." I laughed out loud. Taylor was going to love that. Not.

After we were done loading up the car, my dad took us to lunch at a steak restaurant. It wasn't super fancy, but it was nice, a family place with leather booths and pickles at the table.

"Order whatever you like, guys," my dad said, sliding into the booth.

Jeremiah and I sat across from him. I looked at the menu and picked the New York strip because it was cheapest. My dad wasn't poor, but he definitely wasn't rich, either.

When the waitress came over to take our orders, my dad ordered the salmon, I got the New York strip, and Jeremiah said, "I'll have the dry-aged rib eye, medium rare."

The rib eye was the most expensive thing on the menu. It cost thirty-eight dollars. I looked at him and thought, he probably didn't even look at the price. He never had to, not when all his bills got sent to his dad. Things were gonna change when we were married, that was for sure. No more spending money on dumb stuff like vintage Air Jordans or steak.

"So, what do you have going on this summer, Jeremiah?" my dad asked.

Jeremiah looked at me and then back at my dad and

then back at me. I shook my head just slightly. I had this vision of him asking my dad for his blessing, and it was all wrong. My dad couldn't find out before my mother.

"I'm going to be interning at my dad's company again," Jeremiah said.

"Good for you," my dad said. "That'll keep you busy."

"For sure."

My dad looked at me. "What about you, Belly? Are you going to waitress again?"

I sucked soda from the bottom of my glass. "Yeah. I'm gonna go in and talk to my old manager next week. They always need help in the summer, so it should be all right."

With the wedding just a couple of months away, I would just have to work doubly—triply—hard.

When the bill came, I saw my dad squint and take a closer look. I hoped Jeremiah didn't notice, but when I realized he hadn't, I kind of wished he had.

I always felt closest to my dad when I was sitting in the passenger seat of his minivan, studying his profile, the two us listening to his Bill Evans CD. Drives with my dad were our quiet times together, when we might talk about nothing and everything.

So far the drive had been a quiet one.

He was humming along with the music when I said, "Dad?"

"Hmm?"

I wanted to tell him so badly. I wanted to share it with him, to have it happen during this perfect moment when I was still his little girl in the passenger seat and he was still the one driving the car. It would be a moment just between us. I'd stopped calling him Daddy in middle school, but it was in my heart—Daddy, I'm getting married.

"Nothing," I said at last.

I couldn't do it. I couldn't tell him before I told my mother. It wouldn't be right.

He went back to humming.

Just a little bit longer, Dad.

chapter *eighteen*

I'd thought it would take at least a little time to adjust to being at home again after being away at college, but I fell back into my old routine pretty much right away. Before the end of the first week, I was unpacked and having early-morning breakfasts with my mom and fighting with my brother Steven over the state of the bathroom we shared. I was messy, but Steven took it to a whole new level. I guessed it ran in our family. And I started working at Behrs again, taking as many shifts as they would let me, sometimes two a day.

The night before we all went to Cousins for the dedication of Susannah's garden, Jere and I were talking on the phone. We were talking about wedding stuff, and I told him some of Taylor's ideas. He loved them all but balked at the idea of a carrot cake.

"I want a chocolate cake," he said. "With raspberry filling."

"Maybe one layer can be carrot and one can be chocolate," I suggested, cradling the phone to my shoulder. "I've heard they can do that."

I was sitting on my bedroom floor, counting my tips for the night. I hadn't even changed out of my work shirt yet, even though it had grease stains all down the front, but I was too beat to bother. I just loosened the necktie.

"A chocolate-raspberry-carrot cake?"

"With cream cheese frosting for my layer," I reminded him.

"Sounds kinda complicated to me flavor profilewise, but fine. Let's do it."

I smiled to myself as I stacked my ones and fives and tens. Jeremiah was watching a lot of Food Network since he'd been home.

"Well, first we have to be able to pay for this alleged cake," I said. "I've been taking all the shifts I can, and I've only got a hundred and twenty bucks saved so far. Taylor says wedding cakes are really expensive. Maybe I should ask her mom to bake the cake instead. Mrs. Jewel's a really good baker. We probably couldn't ask for anything too fancy, though."

Jeremiah had been silent on the other line. Then he finally said, "I don't know if you should keep working at Behrs."

"What are you talking about? We need the money."

"Yeah, but I have the money my mom left me. We can use that for the wedding. I don't like you having to work so hard."

"But you're working too!"

"I'm an intern. It's a bullshit job. I'm not working half as hard as you are for this wedding. I sit around an office, and you're busting your ass working double shifts at Behrs. It doesn't feel right."

"If this is because I'm the girl and you're the guy . . . ," I began.

"That's not it, dude. I'm just saying, why should you have to work this hard when I have money in my savings account?"

"I thought we said we were going to do this on our own."

"I've been doing some Internet research, and it looks like it's going to be a lot more expensive than we thought. Even if we go really simple, we still have to pay for food and drinks and flowers. We're only getting married once, Belly."

"True."

"My mom would want to contribute. Right?"

"I guess. . . ." Susannah would want to do more than contribute. She'd want to be there every step of the way—dress shopping, deciding on the flowers and food, all of it. She'd want to do it up. I always pictured her there on my wedding day, sitting next to my mom, wearing a fancy hat. It was a really nice picture.

"So let's let her contribute. Besides, you're gonna get really busy with wedding-planning stuff with Taylor. I'll help as much as I can, but I still have to be at work from nine to five. When you call caterers and flower people or whatever, that'll have to be during the day, and I won't be able to be there."

I was really impressed that he'd thought of all this. I liked this other side of him, thinking ahead, worrying about my health. I had just been complaining about calluses on my feet too.

"Let's talk more about it after we tell our parents," I told him.

"Are you still nervous?"

I'd been trying not to think about it too much. At Behrs, I focused all my energy on delivering bread baskets and refilling drinks and cutting slices of cheesecake. In a way, I was glad to be working double shifts, because it kept me out of the house and away from my mother's watchful eye. I hadn't worn my engagement ring since I'd been home. I only pulled it out at night, in my room.

I said, "I'm scared, but I'll be relieved to finally have it out in the open. I hate keeping things from my mom."

"I know," he said.

I looked at the clock. It was twelve thirty. "We're gonna leave early tomorrow morning, so I should probably go to sleep." I hesitated before asking, "Are you driving up with just your dad? What's the deal with Conrad?"

"I have no clue. I haven't talked to him. I think he's flying in tomorrow. We'll see if he even shows."

I wasn't sure if it was disappointment I was feeling or relief. Probably both. "I doubt he'll come," I said.

"You never know with Con. He might come, he might not." He added, "Don't forget to bring your ring."

"I won't."

Then we said good night, and it was a long time before I could fall asleep. I think I was afraid. Afraid that he was coming and afraid that he wasn't.

chapter *nineteen*

I was up before the alarm; I was showered with my new dress on before Steven was even awake. I was the first one in the car.

My dress was lavender silk chiffon. It had a tight bodice and narrow straps and a floaty skirt, the kind you'd spin around in like a girl in a musical. Something Kim MacAfee might wear. I'd seen it in a store window in February, when it was still too cold to wear it without tights. Tights would ruin it. I'd used my father's for-emergencies-only card, the one I'd never used before. The dress had stayed in my closet all this time, still covered in plastic.

When my mother saw me, she burst into a smile and said, "You look beautiful. Beck would love this dress."

Steven said, "Not bad," and I gave them both a little curtsy. It was just that kind of dress.

My mother drove, and I sat in front. Steven slept in the backseat, his mouth open. He was wearing a button-down shirt and khaki pants. My mother looked nice too in her navy pantsuit and cream pumps.

"Conrad's definitely coming today, right, bean?" my mother asked me.

"You're the one who talks to him, not me," I said. I put my bare feet on the dashboard. My high heels were in a heap on the floor of the car.

Checking her rearview mirror, my mother said, "I haven't spoken to Conrad in a few weeks, but I'm sure he'll be there. He wouldn't miss something as important as this."

When I didn't say anything, she glanced at me and said, "Do you disagree?"

"Sorry, Mom, but I wouldn't get my hopes up." I didn't know why I couldn't just agree with her. I didn't know what was holding me back.

Because I really did believe he was coming. If I didn't, would I have taken extra care with my hair that morning? In the shower, would I have shaved my legs not once but twice, just to be safe? Would I have put on that new dress and worn those heels that made my feet hurt if I truly didn't believe he was coming?

No. Deep down I more than believed it. I knew it.

"Have you heard anything from Conrad, Laurel?" Mr. Fisher asked my mother. We were standing in the parking lot of the women's center—Mr. Fisher, Jere, Steven, my mother, and me. People were starting to file into the building. Mr. Fisher had already checked inside twice: Conrad wasn't there.

My mother shook her head. "I haven't heard anything new. When I spoke to him last month, he said he was coming."

"If he's late, we can just save him a seat," I offered.

"I'd better get inside," Jeremiah said. He was accepting the plaque commemorating the day on behalf of Susannah.

We watched him go because there was nothing else to do. Then Mr. Fisher said, "Maybe we should go in too," and he looked defeated. I could see where he'd cut himself shaving. His chin looked raw.

"Let's do that," my mother said, straightening up. "Belly, why don't you wait here for another minute?"

"Sure," I said. "You guys go ahead. I'll wait."

When the three of them were inside, I sat down on the curb. My feet were hurting already. I waited for another ten minutes, and when he still didn't show, I got up. So he wasn't coming after all.

chapter *twenty*
CONRAD

I saw her before she saw me. In the front row, I saw her sitting with my dad and Laurel and Steven. She had her hair pulled back, pinned up on the sides. I'd never seen her wear her hair like that before. She had on a light purple dress. She looked grown up. It occurred to me that she had grown up while I wasn't looking, that there was every likelihood she had changed and I didn't know her anymore. But when she stood up to clap, I saw the Band-Aid on her ankle and I recognized her again. She was Belly. She kept messing with the barrettes in her hair. One was coming loose.

My plane had been delayed, and even though I'd done eighty the whole way to Cousins, I was still late. Jeremiah was starting his speech just as I walked in. There was an empty seat up front next to my dad, but I just stood in the back. I saw Laurel shift in her seat, scanning the room before turning back around. She didn't see me.

A woman from the shelter got up and thanked everyone for coming. She talked about how great my mom was, how dedicated she was to the shelter, how much money she raised for it, how much awareness in the community. She said my mom was a gift. It was funny, I'd known my mom was involved with the women's shelter, but I didn't know how much she gave of herself. I felt a jolt of shame as I remembered the time she'd asked me to go help her serve breakfast one Saturday morning. I'd blown her off, told her I had stuff I needed to do.

Then Jere got up and went to the podium. "Thanks, Mona," he said. "Today means so much to my family, and I know it would have meant even more to my mom. The women's shelter was really important to her. Even when we weren't here in Cousins, she was still thinking about you guys. And she loved flowers. She used to say she needed them to breathe. She would be so honored by this garden."

It was a good speech. Our mom would have been proud to see him up there. I should have been up there with him. She would have really liked that. She would have liked the roses, too.

I watched Jere sit down in the first row in the seat next to Belly. I watched him take her hand. The muscles in my stomach clenched, and I moved behind a woman in a wide-brimmed hat.

This was a mistake. Coming back here was a mistake.

chapter *twenty-one*

The speeches were over, and everyone had gone outside and started milling around the garden.

"What kind of flowers do you want for the wedding?" Jeremiah asked me in a low voice.

I smiled and shrugged. "Pretty ones?" What did I know about flowers? What did I know about weddings, for that matter? I hadn't been to many, only my cousin Beth's that time I was a flower girl and our neighbor's. But I liked this game we were playing. It was like pretend, but real.

Then I saw him. Standing there in the back was Conrad, in a gray suit. I stared, and he lifted his hand in a wave. I lifted mine, but I didn't move. Couldn't move.

Next to me, I heard Jeremiah clear his throat. I started. I'd forgotten he was standing next to me. For those couple of seconds, I forgot everything.

Then Mr. Fisher was pushing past us, striding over to him. They embraced. My mother swept Conrad into her arms, then my brother came up from behind and pounded him on the back. Jeremiah made his way over too.

I was last. I found myself walking over to them. "Hi," I said. I didn't know what to do with my hands. I left them at my sides.

He said, "Hi." Then he opened his arms up wide and gave me a look that was a lot like a dare. Hesitantly, I stepped into them. He crushed me in a bear hug and lifted me off the ground a little. I squealed and held down my skirt. Everyone laughed. When Conrad set me back down, I moved closer to Jere. He wasn't laughing.

"Conrad's glad to have his little sister around again," Mr. Fisher said in a jovial kind of way. I wondered if he even knew that Conrad and I had once dated. Probably not. It had only been six months. It was nothing compared to the time Jeremiah and I had spent together.

"How have you been, little sis?" Conrad asked. He had that look on his face. Part mocking, part mischievous. I knew that look; I'd seen it so many times.

"Great," I said, looking at Jeremiah. "We're really great."

Jeremiah didn't look back at me. Instead he pulled his phone out of his pocket and said, "I'm starving." I could feel a little knot in my stomach. Was he mad at me?

"Let's get some pictures by the garden before we go," my mother said.

Mr. Fisher clapped his hands and rubbed them together. Putting his arms around Jeremiah and Conrad, he said, "I want a picture with the Fishermen!" which made us all laugh—this time Jeremiah, too. That was one of Mr. Fisher's oldest and corniest jokes. Whenever he and the boys would come back from fishing trips, he would yell, "The Fishermen have returned!"

By Susannah's rose garden, we took pictures of Jeremiah and Mr. Fisher and Conrad, then one with Steven, too, then one with me and my mother and Steven and Jeremiah—all sorts of combinations. Jere said, "I want one of just me and Belly," and I was relieved. We stood in front of the roses, and right before my mother snapped the picture, Jeremiah kissed me on the cheek.

"That's a nice one," my mother said. Then she said, "Let's have one of all the kids."

We stood together—Jeremiah, Conrad, me, Steven. Conrad slung his arm around Jeremiah's and my shoulders. It was all like no time had passed. The summer kids together again.

I rode with Jeremiah to the restaurant. My mother and Steven took one car, Mr. Fisher and Conrad both drove separately.

"Maybe we shouldn't tell them today," I said suddenly. "Maybe we should wait."

Jeremiah turned down the music. "What do you mean?"

"I don't know. Maybe today should just be about Susannah, and family. Maybe we should wait."

"I don't want to have to wait. You and me getting married *is* about family. It's about our two families coming together. As one." Grinning, he grabbed my hand and lifted it in the air. "I want you to be able to wear your ring, right now, loud and proud."

"I *am* loud and proud," I said.

"Then let's just do it like we planned."

"Okay."

As we pulled into the restaurant parking lot, Jeremiah said to me, "Don't have hurt feelings if—you know, if he says anything."

I blinked. "Who?"

"My dad. You know how he is. You can't take it personally, okay?"

I nodded.

We walked into the restaurant holding hands. Everyone else was already there and seated at a round table.

I sat down, Jeremiah on my left and my brother on my right. I grabbed the bread basket and took a roll. I smeared it with butter before I stuffed most of it into my mouth.

Steven shook his head at me. *Pig*, he mouthed.

Glaring at him, I said, "I didn't eat breakfast."

"I ordered a bunch of appetizers," Mr. Fisher told me.

"Thanks, Mr. Fisher," I said, my mouth partly full.

He smiled. "Belly, we're all adults here. I think you should call me Adam now. No more Mr. Fisher."

Underneath the table, Jeremiah gave my thigh a squeeze. I almost laughed out loud. Then I had another thought—like, was I going to have to call Mr. Fisher "Dad" after we were married? I would have to talk to Jeremiah about that one.

"I'll try," I said. Mr. Fisher looked at me expectantly, and I added, "Adam."

Steven asked Conrad, "So why don't you ever leave California?"

"I'm here, aren't I?"

"Yeah, for, like, the first time since you left, practically." Steven nudged him and lowered his voice. "You got a girl out there?"

"No," Conrad said. "No girl."

The champagne arrived then, and when all our glasses were full, Mr. Fisher tapped his knife to his glass. "I'd like to make a toast," he said.

My mother rolled her eyes just barely. Mr. Fisher was famous for making speeches, but today actually called for one.

"I want to thank everyone for coming together today to celebrate Susannah. It's a special day, and I'm glad we can share it together." Mr. Fisher lifted his glass. "To Suz."

Nodding, my mother said, "To Beck."

We all clinked glasses and drank, and before I could put mine down, Jeremiah gave me this look like, Get ready, it's happening.

My stomach lurched. I took another gulp of my champagne and nodded.

"I have something to say," Jeremiah announced.

While everyone was waiting to hear what it was, I snuck a look over at Conrad. He had his arm draped over the back of Steven's chair, and they'd been laughing about something. His face was easy and relaxed.

I had this wild impulse to stop Jeremiah, to clap my hand over his mouth and keep him from saying it. Everybody was so happy. This was going to wreck it.

"I'll just go ahead and warn you—it's really good news." Jeremiah flashed a smile at everyone, and I braced myself. He was being too glib, I thought. My mother wouldn't like that. "I asked Belly to marry me, and she said yes. She said yes! We're getting married this August!"

It was like the restaurant got really quiet all of a sudden, like all the noise and chatter got sucked out of the room. Everything just stopped. I looked across the table, at my mother. Her face was ashen. Steven choked on the water he was drinking. Coughing, he said, "What the?" And Conrad, his face was completely blank.

It was surreal.

The waiter came by then with the appetizers—calamari and cocktail shrimp and a tower of oysters. "Are you guys ready to order your entrees?" he asked, rearranging the table so there was room for everything.

His voice tight, Mr. Fisher said, "I think we need a few more minutes," and glanced at my mother.

She looked dazed. She opened, then closed her mouth. Then she looked right at me and asked, "Are you pregnant?"

I felt all the blood rush to my cheeks. Beside me, I could feel rather than hear Jeremiah choke.

My mother's voice shook as she said shrilly, "I don't believe this. How many times have we discussed contraception, Isabel?"

I could not have been more mortified. I looked at Mr. Fisher, who was beet red, and then I looked at the waiter, who was pouring water for the table next to ours. Our eyes met. I was pretty sure he'd been in my psychology class. "Mom, I'm not pregnant!"

Earnestly, Jeremiah said, "Laurel, I swear to you it's nothing like that."

My mother ignored him. She looked only at me. "Then what is happening here? Where is this coming from?"

My lips felt really dry all of a sudden. Fleetingly, I thought of what had led up to Jeremiah's proposal, and just as quickly the thought flitted away. None of that mattered anymore. What mattered was that we were in love. I said, "We want to get married, Mom."

"You're too young," she said in a flat voice. "You're both far too young."

Jeremiah coughed. "Laur, we love each other, and we want to be together."

"You *are* together," my mother snapped. Then she turned to Mr. Fisher, her eyes narrowed. "Did you know about this?"

"Calm down, Laurel. They're joking. You were joking, right?"

Jere and I shared a look before he said in a soft voice, "No, we're not joking."

My mother swallowed the rest of her champagne, emptying her glass. "You two are not getting married, period. You're both still in school, for God's sake. It's ridiculous."

Clearing his throat, Mr. Fisher said, "Maybe after you kids both graduate, we can discuss it again."

"A few years after you graduate," my mother put in.

"Right," Mr. Fisher said.

"Dad . . . ," Jeremiah began.

The server was back at Mr. Fisher's shoulder before Jeremiah could finish whatever it was he was going to say. He just stood there for a moment looking awkward before asking, "Do you have any questions about the menu? Or, ah, are we just doing appetizers today?"

"We'll just take the check," my mother said, tight lipped.

There was all this food on the table and no one

was touching it, no one was saying anything. I was right before. This was a mistake, a tactical error of epic proportions. We never should have told them like this. Now they were a team, united against us. We barely got a word in edgewise.

I reached into my purse, and under the tablecloth, I put my engagement ring on. It was the only thing I could think to do. When I reached for my water glass, Jeremiah saw the ring and squeezed my knee again. My mother saw too—her eyes flashed, and she looked away.

Mr. Fisher paid the bill, and for once my mother didn't argue. We all stood up. Quickly, Steven filled a cloth napkin with shrimp. And then we were leaving, me trailing my mother, Jeremiah following Mr. Fisher. Behind me, I heard Steven whispering to Conrad. "Holy shit, man. This is crazy. Did *you* know about this?"

I heard Conrad tell him no. Outside, he hugged my mother good-bye and then got in his car and drove away. He didn't look back once.

When we got to our car, I asked my mother very quietly, "Can I have the keys?"

"What for?"

I wet my lips. "I need to get my book bag out of the trunk. I'm going with Jeremiah, remember?"

I could see my mother struggle to hold her temper. She said, "No, you're not. You're coming home with us."

"But Mom—"

Before I could finish, she'd already handed the keys to Steven and climbed into the passenger seat. She closed the door.

I looked at Jeremiah helplessly. Mr. Fisher was already in his car, and Jeremiah was hanging back, waiting. More than anything, I wished I could leave with him. I was really, really scared to get into the car with my mother.

I was in trouble like I had never known.

"Get in the car, Belly," Steven said. "Don't make it worse."

"You'd better go," Jeremiah said.

I ran over to him and hugged him tight. "I'll call you tonight," he whispered into my hair.

"If I'm still alive," I whispered back.

Then I walked away from him and climbed into the backseat.

Steven started the car, his napkin a white bundle in his lap. My mother caught my eye in the rearview mirror and said, "You're returning that ring, Isabel."

If I backed down now, everything was lost. I had to be strong.

"I'm not returning it," I said.

chapter *twenty-two*

My mother and I didn't speak to each other for a week. I avoided her, and she ignored me. I worked at Behrs, mostly to get out of the house. I ate lunch and dinner there. After my shifts, I went over to Taylor's, and when I got home, I talked to Jeremiah on the phone. He begged me to at least try to talk to my mother. I knew he was worried that she hated him now, and I assured him that he wasn't the one she was mad at. That was all me.

One night after a late shift at the restaurant, I was on my way to my room when I stopped short. I heard the muffled sound of my mother crying behind her closed door. I was frozen to the spot, my heart thudding in my chest. Standing outside her door, listening to her weep, I was ready to give it all up. In that moment I would have done anything, said anything, to make her stop crying.

In that moment she had me. My hand was on the door-knob, and the words were right there, on the tip of my tongue—Okay, I won't do it.

But then it got quiet. She'd stopped crying on her own. I waited a little longer, and when I didn't hear anything more, I let go of the doorknob and went to my room. In the dark I took off my work clothes and got into bed, and I cried too.

I woke up to the smell of my father's Turkish coffee. For just those few seconds right in between sleep and wakefulness, I was ten again, and my dad still lived with us and the biggest thing I had to worry about was my math homework. I started to fall back to sleep, and then I woke up with a start.

There could only be one reason my dad was here. My mother had told him. I'd wanted to be the one to tell him, to explain. She'd beaten me to it. I was mad, but at the same time I felt glad. Her telling my father meant that she was finally taking this seriously.

After I showered, I headed downstairs. They were sitting in the living room drinking coffee. My dad had on his weekend clothes—jeans and a plaid short-sleeved shirt. And a belt, always a belt.

"Morning," I said.

"Have a seat," my mother said, setting her mug down on a coaster.

I sat. My hair was still wet, and I was trying to work my comb through the tangles.

Clearing his throat, my father said, "So, your mother told me what's going on."

"Dad, I wanted to tell you myself, I really did. Mom beat me to the punch." I threw her a pointed look, but she didn't appear the least bit bothered by it.

"I'm not in favor of this either, Belly. I think you're too young." He cleared his throat again. "We've discussed it, and if you want to live with Jeremiah in an apartment this fall, we'll allow it. You'll have to chip in if it costs more than the dorms, but we'll pay what we've been paying."

I wasn't expecting that. A compromise. I was sure it had been my dad's idea, but I couldn't take the deal.

"Dad, I don't just want to live in an apartment with Jeremiah. That's not why we're getting married."

"Then why *are* you getting married?" my mother asked me.

"We love each other. We've thought it through, we really have."

My mother gestured at my left hand. "Who paid for that ring? I know Jeremiah doesn't have a job."

I put my hand in my lap. "He used his credit card," I said.

"His credit card that Adam pays for. If Jeremiah can't afford a ring, he has no business buying one."

"It didn't cost much." I had no idea how much the ring had cost, but the diamond was so little, I figured it couldn't have been *that* expensive.

Sighing, my mother glanced over at my father and then back at me. "You might not believe me when I say this, but when your father and I got married, we were very much in love. Very, very much in love. We went into marriage with the best of intentions. But all of that just wasn't enough to sustain us."

Their love for each other, Steven and me, our family— none of it was enough to make their marriage work. I knew all of that already.

"Do you regret it?" I asked her.

"Belly, it isn't as simple as that."

I interrupted her. "Do you regret our family? Do you regret me and Steven?"

Sighing deeply, she said, "No."

"Dad, do you?"

"Belly, no. Of course not. That's not what your mother's trying to say."

"Jeremiah and I aren't you and Mom. We've known each other our whole lives." I tried to appeal to my father. "Dad, your cousin Martha got married young, and she and Bert have been married for, like, thirty years! It can work, I know it can. Jeremiah and I will make it work just like they did. We're going to be happy. We just want you guys to be happy for us. Please be happy for us."

My father rubbed his beard in a way I knew well—he was going to defer to my mother the way he always did. Any second, he would look at her with a question in his eyes. It was all up to her now. Actually, it had always been up to her.

We both looked at her. My mother was the judge. That was the way it worked in our family. She closed her eyes briefly and then said, "I can't support you in this decision, Isabel. If you go forward with this wedding, I won't support it. I won't be there."

It knocked the wind out of me. Even though I was expecting it, her continued disapproval . . . still. Still, I thought she'd come around, at least a little.

"Mom," I said, my voice breaking, "come on."

Looking pained, my father said, "Belly, let's all just think on this some more, okay? This is very sudden for us."

I ignored him and looked only at my mother. Pleadingly, I said, "Mom? I know you don't mean that."

She shook her head. "I do mean it."

"Mom, you can't not be at my wedding. That's crazy." I tried to sound calm, like I wasn't on the verge of out-and-out hysteria.

"No, what's crazy is the idea of a teenager getting married." She pressed her lips together. "I don't know what to say to get through to you. How do I get through to you, Isabel?"

"You can't," I said.

My mother leaned forward, her eyes fixed on me. "Don't do this."

"It's already decided. I'm marrying Jeremiah." I stood up jerkily. "If you can't be happy for me, then maybe—maybe it's best you don't come."

I was already at the staircase when my dad called out, "Belly, wait."

I stopped, and then I heard my mother say, "Let her go."

When I was in my room, I called Jeremiah. The first thing he said was, "Do you want me to talk to her?"

"That won't help. I'm telling you, she's made up her mind. I know her. She won't budge. At least not right now."

He was silent. "Then what do you want to do?"

"I don't know." I started to cry.

"Do you want to postpone the wedding?"

"No!"

"Then what should we do?"

Wiping my face, I said, "I guess just move ahead with the wedding. Start planning."

As soon as we got off the phone, I started seeing things more clearly. I just needed to separate emotion from reason. Refusing to go to the wedding was my mother's trump card. It was the only leg she had to stand on. And she was bluffing. She had to be bluffing. No matter how upset or disappointed she was in me, I couldn't believe that she would miss her only daughter's wedding. I just couldn't.

All there was to do now was to steamroll ahead and set this wedding in motion. With or without my mother by my side, this was happening.

chapter *twenty-three*

I was folding my laundry when Steven knocked on my door later that night. As usual he only gave me a couple of seconds before opening it; he never waited for me to say "come in." He came into the room and shut the door behind him. Steven stood in my room awkwardly, leaning against the wall, his arms folded against his chest.

"What?" I said. Although I already knew.

"Sooo . . . are you and Jere serious about this?"

I stacked some T-shirts into a pile. "Yes."

Steven crossed the room and sat at my desk, absorbing my answer for a minute. Then he faced me, straddling the chair, and said, "You realize that's insane, right? We're not living in the foothills of West Virginia. There's no reason you have to get married so young."

"What do you know about West Virginia?" I scoffed. "You've never even been there."

"That's besides the point."

"What is your point?"

"My point is, you guys are too young."

"Did Mom send you up here to talk to me?"

"No," he said, and I knew he was lying. "I'm just worried about you."

I stared him down.

"Okay, yeah, she did," he admitted. "But I would have come up anyway."

"You're not going to change my mind."

"Listen, nobody knows you two better than me." He stopped, weighing his words. "I love Jere—he's like a brother to me. But you're my little sister. You come first. This whole marriage idea—I'm sorry, but I think it's stupid. If you guys love each other that much, you can wait a couple of years to be together. And if you can't, you for sure shouldn't be getting married."

I felt both touched and annoyed. Steven never said things like "You come first." But then he called me stupid, which was more like him.

"I don't expect you to understand," I said. I folded then refolded another T-shirt. "Jeremiah wants you and Conrad to be his best men."

Steven's face broke into a smile. "He does?"

"Yeah," I said.

Steven looked really happy, but then he caught me looking at him, and he wiped his smile away. "I don't think Mom will let me be in the wedding."

"Steven, you're twenty-one years old. You can decide that for yourself."

He frowned. I could tell I'd injured his pride. He said, "Well, I still don't think it's your smartest move."

"Noted," I said. "I'm still doing it."

"Oh, man, Mom's gonna kill me. I was supposed to talk you out of getting married, not get roped into the wedding party," Steven said, getting up.

I hid my smile. That is, until Steven added, "Con and I had better start planning the bachelor party."

Quickly, I said, "Jere doesn't want any of that."

Steven puffed up his chest. "You don't get a say in it, Belly. You're a girl. This is man stuff."

"*Man* stuff?"

Grinning, he shut my door.

chapter *twenty-four*

Despite what I'd said to Steven, I still found myself waiting for my mother. Waiting for her to come around, waiting for her to give in. I didn't want to start planning the wedding until she said yes. But when days passed and she refused to discuss it, I knew I couldn't wait any longer.

Thank God for Taylor.

She brought over a big white binder with clippings from wedding magazines and checklists and all kinds of stuff. "I was saving this for my wedding, but we can use it for yours, too," she said.

All I had was one of my mother's yellow legal pads. I had written WEDDING at the top and made a list of things I needed to do. The list looked pretty skimpy, next to Taylor's binder.

We were sitting on my bed, papers and bride magazines all around us. Taylor was all business.

She said, "First things first. We have to find you a dress. August is really, really soon."

"It doesn't feel *that* soon," I said.

"Well, it is. Two months to plan a wedding is nothing. In weddingspeak that's, like, tomorrow."

"Well, I guess since the wedding is going to be simple, the dress should be too," I said.

Taylor frowned. "How simple?"

"Really simple. As simple as it gets. Nothing poofy or frou frou."

She nodded to herself. "I can picture it. It's very Cindy Crawford wedding-on-the-beach, very Carolyn Bessette."

"Yeah, sounds good," I said. I had no idea what either of their wedding dresses looked like. I didn't even know who Carolyn Bessette was. After I had the dress, it would feel more real, I would be able to visualize it happening. Right now it still felt too abstract.

"What about shoes?"

I gave her a look. "Like I'm gonna wear heels on the beach. I can barely walk in heels on level ground."

Taylor ignored me. "What about my bridesmaid dress?"

I pushed some magazines onto the carpet so I could lie down. I stretched my legs as high as I could and put my feet up on the wall. "I was thinking mustard yellow. Maybe in a satiny kind of material." Taylor hated mustard yellow.

"Mustard yellow satin," Taylor repeated, nodding and trying hard to keep the disgust off her face. I could tell she was torn between her vanity and her credo, which was, the Bride is always right. "That could maybe work with Anika's skin tone. I'm more of a spring, but if I started tanning now, it could work."

I laughed. "I'm kidding. You can wear whatever you want."

"Dork!" she said, looking relieved. She slapped my thigh. "You're so immature! I can't believe you're getting married!"

"Me neither."

"But I guess it makes sense, in a Twilight Zone kind of way. You and Jere have known each other for, like, a grillion years. It's meant to be."

"How long is a grillion years?"

"It's forever." In the air she spelled out my initials. "B.C. + J.F. forever."

"Forever," I echoed happily. Forever I could do. Me and Jere.

chapter *twenty-five*

On my way out to meet Taylor at the mall the next day, I stopped by my mother's office. "I'm going to look for a dress," I said, standing in her doorway.

She stopped typing and looked over at me. "Good luck," she said.

"Thanks." I supposed there were worse things she could have said than "good luck," but the thought didn't make me feel any better.

The formal-wear store at the mall was packed with girls looking for prom dresses with their mothers. I didn't expect to feel the pang in my chest when I saw them. Girls were supposed to go wedding dress shopping with their mothers. They were supposed to step out of the dressing room in just the right dress, and the mother would tear up and say, "That's the one." I was pretty sure that was the way it was supposed to be.

"Isn't it a little late in the year for prom?" I asked Taylor. "Wasn't ours in, like, May?"

"My sister told me they had to push back prom this year because of some scandal with the assistant principal," she explained. "All the prom money went missing or something. So now it's a grom. Graduation–prom."

I laughed. "Grom."

"Also, the private schools always have their prom later, remember? Collegiate, St. Joe's."

"I only went to one prom," I reminded her. One had been more than enough for me.

I wandered around the store and found one dress I liked—it was strapless, blinding white. I'd never known there were degrees of white before; I'd just thought white was white. When I found Taylor, she had a whole stack of dresses on her arm. We had to wait in line for a dressing room.

The girl in front of me told her mother, "I will freak out if someone wears the same dress as me."

Taylor and I rolled our eyes at each other. *I will freak out,* Taylor mouthed.

It seemed like we waited in that line forever.

"Try this one on first," Taylor ordered when it was my turn.

Dutifully, I obeyed her.

"Come out," Taylor yelled from her chair by the three-way mirror. She was camped out with the other mothers.

"I don't think I like it," I called out. "It's too sparkly. I look like Glinda the good witch or something."

"Just come out and let me see you!"

I came out, and there were already a couple of other girls at the mirror, checking themselves out from the back. I stood behind them.

Then the girl from earlier stepped out in the same dress I had on but in a champagne color. She saw me, and right away she asked, "Which prom are you going to?"

Taylor and I looked at each other in the mirror. Taylor was covering her mouth, giggling. I said, "I'm not going to prom."

Taylor said, "She's getting married!"

The girl's mouth hung open. "How old are you? You look so young."

"I'm not that young," I said. "I'm nineteen." I wouldn't be nineteen until August, but nineteen sounded a lot older than eighteen.

"Oh," she said. "I thought we were, like, the same age."

I looked at us in the mirror as we stood there in the same dress. I thought we looked the same age too. I saw her mother looking at me and whispering to the lady next to her, and I could feel myself blush.

Taylor saw too and said, loudly, "You can hardly even tell she's three months pregnant."

The woman gasped. She shook her head at me, and I gave her a little shrug. Then Taylor grabbed my hand, and we ran back to my dressing room, laughing.

"You're a good friend," I said as she unzipped me.

We looked at each other in the mirror, me in my white dress and her in her cutoffs and flip-flops. I felt like I was going to cry. But then Taylor saved it—she made me laugh instead. She crossed her eyes and stuck her tongue out sideways. It felt good to laugh again.

Three more stores later, we sat in the food court, still no dress. Taylor ate french fries, and I ate frozen yogurt with rainbow sprinkles. My feet hurt, and I was already wanting to go home. The day wasn't turning out to be as fun as I'd hoped it would be.

Taylor leaned across the table and dipped an already-ketchupped french fry into my frozen yogurt. I snatched the cup away from her.

"Taylor! That's disgusting."

She shrugged. "This coming from the girl who puts powdered sugar on Cap'n Crunch?" Handing me a fry, she said, "Just try it."

I dipped it into the cup, careful not to get any sprinkles on it, because that would just be too gross. I popped the fry into my mouth. Not bad. Swallowing, I said, "What if we can't find a dress?"

"We'll find a dress," she assured me, handing me another fry. "Don't get all Debbie Downer on me yet."

She was right. We found it at the next store. It was the last one I tried on. Everything else had been only so-so or too expensive. This dress was long and white and silky and something you could wear on the beach. It was not that expensive, which was important. But most important of all, when I looked in the mirror, I could picture myself getting married in it.

Nervously, I stepped out, smoothing the dress down on my sides. I looked up at her. "What do you think?"

Her eyes were shining. "It's perfect. Just perfect."

"You think?"

"Come look at yourself in this mirror and you tell me, beotch."

Giggling, I stepped up on the platform and stared at myself in the three-way mirror. This was it. This was the one.

chapter *twenty-six*

That night I tried on my dress again and called Jeremiah. "I found my dress," I told him. "I'm wearing it right now."

"What's it look like?"

"It's a surprise. But I promise, it's really pretty. Taylor and I found it at the fifth store we went to. It didn't even cost that much." I ran my hand along the silky fabric. "It fits me perfectly, so I won't have to get alterations or anything."

"So why do you sound so sad, then?"

I sat down on the floor, hugging my knees to my chest. "I don't know. Maybe 'cause my mom wasn't there to help me pick it out. . . . I thought buying a wedding dress was supposed to be this special thing you do with your mom, and she wasn't there. It was nice with Taylor, but I wish my mom had been there too."

Jeremiah was quiet. Then he said, "Did you ask her to go with you?"

"No, not really. But she knew I wanted her there. I just hate that she's not a part of this." I'd left my bedroom door open, hoping my mom might walk by, might see me in the dress and stop. She hadn't so far.

"She'll come around."

"I hope so. I don't know if I can picture getting married without my mom there, you know?"

I heard Jere let out a little sigh. "Yeah, me either," he said, and I knew he was thinking of Susannah.

The next morning, my mother and I were eating breakfast, my mother with her yogurt with muesli and me with my frozen waffles, when the doorbell rang.

My mother looked up from her newspaper. "Are you expecting someone?" she asked me.

I shook my head and got up to see who it was. I opened the front door, figuring it would be Taylor with more bridal magazines. Instead, it was Jeremiah. He had a bouquet of lilies, and he had on a nice shirt, white button-down with faint blue checks.

I clapped my hands over my mouth in delight. "What are you doing here?" I shrieked from behind my hands.

He hugged me to him. I could smell McDonald's coffee on his breath. He must have woken up really early to get here. Jeremiah loved McDonald's breakfasts but he could never wake up early enough to get one. He said, "Don't get too excited. These aren't for you. Is Laurel here?"

I felt swoony and dazed. "She's eating breakfast," I said. "Come on in."

I opened the door for him, and he followed me inside to the kitchen. Brightly, I said, "Mom, look who's here!"

My mother looked astonished, her spoon halfway to her mouth. "Jeremiah!"

Jeremiah walked over to her, flowers in hand. "I just had to come and greet my future mother-in-law properly," he said, grinning his impish grin. He kissed her on the cheek and set the flowers by her bowl of yogurt.

I was watching closely. If anybody could charm my mother, it was Jeremiah. Already I could feel the tension in our house being lifted.

She smiled a smile that looked brittle, but it was a smile nonetheless. She stood up. "I'm glad you came," she said. "I've been wanting to talk to the both of you."

Jeremiah rubbed his hands together. "All righty. Let's do this. Belly, get over here. Group hug first."

My mother tried not to laugh as Jeremiah gave her a bear hug. He motioned for me to join in, and I came up behind my mother and hugged her around the waist. She couldn't help it: a laugh escaped. "All right, all right. Let's go into the living room. Jere, have you eaten?"

I answered for him. "Egg McMuffin, right, Jere?"

He winked at me. "You know me so well."

My mother had already stepped into the living room, her back to us.

"I can smell McDonald's on your breath," I told him in a low voice.

He clapped his hand over his mouth, looking self-conscious, which was rare for him. "Does it smell bad?" he asked me.

I felt so much tenderness toward him in that moment. "No," I told him. "Not at all."

The three of us sat in the living room, Jeremiah and I on the couch, my mother in an armchair facing us. Everything was going so well. He had made my mother laugh. I hadn't seen her laugh or smile since we'd told her. I started to feel hopeful, like this might actually work.

The first thing she said was, "Jeremiah, you know I love you. I want nothing but the best for you. That's why I can't support what you two are doing."

Jeremiah leaned forward. "Laur—"

My mother held up her hand. "You're just too young. Both of you. You're both still gestating and becoming the people you will one day be. You're still children. You aren't ready for a commitment like this. I'm talking about a lifetime here, Jeremiah."

Eagerly, he said, "Laurel, I want to be with Belly for a lifetime. I can commit to that, easy."

My mother shook her head. "And that's how I know you're not ready, Jeremiah. You take things too lightly. This isn't the kind of thing you undertake on a whim. This is serious." The condescension in her voice really pissed me off. I was eighteen years old, not eight, and Jeremiah was nineteen. We were old enough to know that marriage was serious. We'd seen the way our parents had screwed up their own marriages. We weren't going to make the same mistakes. But I didn't say anything. I knew that if I got mad or tried to argue, it would only prove her point. So I just sat there. "I want you two to wait. I want Belly to finish school. When she graduates, if you two still feel the same way, do it then. But only after she graduates. If Beck was here, she'd agree with me."

"I think she'd be really happy for us," Jeremiah said.

Before my mother could contradict him, he added, "Belly will still finish college on time, I can promise you that. I'll take good care of her. Just give us your blessing." He reached out and touched her hand and gave it a playful shake. "Come on, Laur. You know you've always wanted me for a son-in-law."

My mother looked pained. "Not like this, hon. I'm sorry."

There was a long, awkward pause. As the three of sat there, I could feel myself start to tear up. Jeremiah put his arm around me and clasped my shoulder, then he let go.

"Does this mean you aren't coming to the wedding?" I asked her.

Shaking her head, she said, "Isabel, what wedding? You don't have the money to pay for a wedding."

"That's for us to worry about, not you," I said. "I just want to know, are you coming?"

"I already gave you my answer. No, I won't be there."

"How can you say that?" I let out a breath, trying to keep calm. "You're just mad that you don't get a say in this. You don't get a say in what happens, and it's killing you."

"Yes, it is killing me!" she snapped. "Watching you make such a stupid decision is killing me."

My mother fixed her eyes on me, and I turned my head away from her, my knees shaking. I couldn't listen to her anymore. She was poisoning our good news with all her doubts and negativity. She was twisting everything.

I stood up. "Then I'll leave. You won't have to watch anymore."

Jeremiah looked startled. "Come on, Bells, sit down."

"I can't stay here," I said.

My mother didn't say a word. She just sat there, her back ramrod straight.

I walked out of the living room and up the stairs.

In my room I packed quickly, throwing a stack of T-shirts and underwear into a suitcase. I was throwing my toiletries bag on top of the heap when Jeremiah came into my room. He closed the door behind him.

He sat down on my bed. "What just happened?" he asked, still looking dazed.

I didn't answer him, I kept packing.

"What are you doing?" he asked me.

"What does it look like?"

"Okay, but do you have a plan?"

I zipped up my suitcase. "Yes, I have a plan. I'm staying at the Cousins house until the wedding. I can't deal with her."

Jeremiah sucked in his breath. "Are you serious?"

"You heard her. She isn't changing her mind. This is the way she wants it."

He hesitated. "I don't know. . . . What about your job?"

"You're the one who told me I should quit. It's better this way. I can plan the wedding better in Cousins than I can here." I was sweating as I heaved up my suitcase. "If she can't get on board this train, then that's too bad. Because this is happening."

Jeremiah tried to take the suitcase from me, but I told him not to bother. I lugged it down the stairs and to the car without a word to or from my mother. She didn't ask where we were going, and she didn't ask when I was coming back.

On the way out of town, we stopped at Behrs. Jere waited for me in his car while I went inside. If I hadn't just had a fight with my mother, I never would have had the nerve to quit like that. Even though people came and went all the time at Behrs, especially students . . . still. I went straight back to the kitchen and found my manager, Stacey, and told her I was sorry, but as it turned out I was getting married in two months and I couldn't keep working there. Stacey eyed my stomach and then my ring finger and said, "Congratulations, Isabel. Just so you know, there's always a place for you here at Behrs."

Alone in my car again, I cried loud, ragged sobs. I cried until my throat hurt. I was mad at my mom, but bigger than that was this overwhelming, heavy sadness. I was grown up enough to do things on my own, without her. I could get married, I could quit my job. I was a big girl now. I didn't have to ask for her permission. My mother was no longer all powerful. Part of me wished she still could be.

chapter *twenty-seven*

We were half an hour from Cousins when Jeremiah called and said, "Conrad's been staying in Cousins."

My whole body went stiff. We were at a stoplight, and Jeremiah's car was in front of mine. "Since when?"

"Since last week. He just stayed after the whole thing at the restaurant. He came back once to get his stuff, but I think he's gonna spend the summer out here."

"Oh," I said. "Do you think he'll mind that I'm staying there?"

I could hear Jere hesitate. "No, I don't think he'll mind. I just wish I could be there too. If it wasn't for that stupid internship, I could be. Maybe I should just quit."

"You can't. Your dad will kill you."

"Yeah, I know." I heard him hesitate again, and then he said, "I don't feel right about the way we left things with your mom. Maybe you should go back home, Bells."

"It won't work. We'll just fight again." The light turned green. "You know, I actually think this could be for the best. It'll give us both space."

"If you say so," Jeremiah said, but I could tell he didn't completely agree.

"Let's talk more when we get to the house," I said, and we hung up.

This news that Conrad was in Cousins left me feeling uneasy. Maybe staying at the summer house wasn't the answer.

But then, when I pulled into the empty driveway, I felt such incredible relief to be back. Home, I was back home.

The house looked the same, tall and gray and white. It made me feel the same. Like I was right where I belonged. Like I could breathe again.

I was sitting in Jeremiah's lap on a lounge chair when we heard a car pull up. It was Conrad, getting out of the car with a bag of groceries. He looked taken aback to see us sitting there on the deck. I stood up and waved.

Jeremiah stretched his hands behind his head and leaned back onto his chair. "Hey, Con."

"What's up," he said, walking over to us. "What are you guys doing here?"

Conrad set down the grocery bag and took a seat next to Jeremiah's, and I just sort of hovered above them.

"Wedding stuff," Jeremiah said vaguely.

"Wedding stuff," Conrad repeated. "So you guys are really doing it?"

"Hell yeah we are." Jeremiah pulled me back onto his lap. "Right, wifey?"

"Don't call me wifey," I said, wrinkling my nose. "Gross."

Conrad ignored me. "Does that mean Laurel's changed her mind?" he asked Jere.

"Not yet, but she will," Jeremiah said, and I didn't correct him.

I sat perched there for about twenty more seconds before I twisted out of his arms and stood up again. "I'm starving," I said, leaning down and poking around Conrad's grocery bag. "Did you buy anything good?"

Conrad gave me his bemused half smile. "No Cheetos or frozen pizza for you in here. Sorry. I got stuff for dinner, though. I'll cook something for us."

He got up, took the grocery bag, and went into the house.

For dinner, Conrad made a tomato, basil, and avocado salad, and he grilled chicken breasts. We ate outside on the deck.

With a mouth full of chicken, Jeremiah said, "Wow, I'm impressed. Since when do you cook?"

"Since I've been living on my own. This is pretty much all I eat. Chicken. Every day." Conrad pushed the salad bowl toward me, not looking up. "Did you get enough?"

"Yeah. Thanks, Conrad. This is all really good."

"Really good," Jeremiah echoed.

Conrad only shrugged, but the tips of his ears turned pink, and I knew he was pleased.

I poked Jeremiah in the arm with my fork. "You could learn a thing or two."

He poked me back. "So could you." He took a big bite of salad before announcing, "Belly's gonna stay here until the wedding. Is that cool with you, Con?"

I could tell Conrad was surprised, because he didn't answer right away.

"I won't be in your way," I assured him. "I'll just be doing wedding stuff."

"It's fine. I don't care," he said.

I looked down at my plate. "Thanks," I said. So I'd been worried about nothing. Conrad didn't care if I was there or not. It wasn't like we would have to hang out with each other. He would do his own thing the way he always did, I would be busy planning the wedding, and Jeremiah would drive up every Friday to help. It would be fine.

After we finished eating dinner, Jeremiah suggested we all go get ice cream for dessert. Conrad declined, saying he would clean up. I said, "The cook shouldn't have to clean up," but he said he didn't mind.

Jere and I went into town, just the two of us. I got a scoop of cookies and cream and a scoop of cookie dough with sprinkles, in a waffle cone. Jeremiah got rainbow sherbet.

"Are you feeling better?" he asked me as we walked around the boardwalk. "About what happened with your mom?"

"Not really," I said. "I'd rather just not think about it anymore today."

Jeremiah nodded. "Whatever you want."

I changed the subject. "Did you figure out how many people you want to invite?" I asked.

"Yup." He started to tick names off on his fingers. "Josh, Redbird, Gabe, Alex, Sanchez, Peterson—"

"You can't invite everyone in your fraternity."

"They're my brothers," he said, looking wounded.

"I thought we said we were keeping it really small."

"So I'll just invite a few of them, then. Okay?"

"Okay. We still have to figure out food," I said, licking my way around the cone so it wouldn't drip.

"We could always get Con to grill some chicken," Jeremiah said with a laugh.

"He's going to be your best man. He can't be sweating over the grill."

"I was kidding."

"Did you ask him yet? To be your best man?"

"Not yet. I will, though." He leaned down and took a bite of my ice cream. He got some on his upper lip, like a milk mustache.

I bit the insides of my cheeks to keep from smiling.

"What's so funny?"

"Nothing."

When we got back to the house, Conrad was watching TV in the living room. When we sat down on the couch, he got up. "I'm gonna hit the sack," he said, stretching his arms over his head.

"It's, like, ten o'clock. Watch a movie with us," Jeremiah said.

"Nah, I'm gonna get up early tomorrow and surf. Wanna join me?"

Jeremiah glanced at me before saying, "Yeah, sounds good."

"I thought we were gonna work on the guest list in the morning," I said.

"I'll come back before you're even awake. Don't worry." To Conrad, he said, "Knock on my door when you're up."

Conrad hesitated. "I don't want to wake up Belly."

I could feel myself blush. "I don't mind," I said.

Since Jeremiah and I had become boyfriend and girlfriend, we'd only been at the summer house together once. That time, I slept in his room with him. We watched TV until he fell asleep, because he liked to sleep with the television on in the background. I couldn't fall asleep like that, so I waited until he did and then I turned it off. It felt kind of strange, sleeping in his bed when mine was just down the hall.

At college we slept in the same bed all the time, and that felt normal. But here at the summer house I just wanted to sleep in my own room, in my own bed. It was familiar to me. It made me feel like a little girl still on vacation with her whole family. My paper-thin sheets with the faded yellow rosebuds, my cherry wood dresser and vanity. I used to have two white twin beds, but Susannah got rid of them and put in what she'd called a "big girl bed." I loved that bed.

Conrad went upstairs, and I waited until I heard his bedroom door shut before I said, "Maybe I'll sleep in my room tonight."

"Why?" Jeremiah asked. "I promise I'll be quiet when I get up."

Carefully, I asked, "Aren't the bride and groom supposed to sleep in different beds before the wedding?"

"Yeah, but that's the night before the wedding. Not every night before the wedding." He looked hurt for a second, and then he said in his joking way, "Come on, you know I won't touch you."

Even though I knew he was only kidding, it still stung a little.

"It's not that. Sleeping in my own room makes me feel . . . normal. It's—it's different than at school. At school, sleeping with you next to me feels normal. But here I like remembering what it used to feel like." I searched his face to see if any of the hurt was still there. "Does that make sense at all?"

"I guess." Jeremiah looked unconvinced, and I started to wish I'd never brought it up.

I scooted closer to him, putting my feet in his lap. "You'll have me next to you every night for the rest of our lives."

"Yeah, I guess that'll be plenty," he said.

"Hey!" I said, kicking out my leg.

Jeremiah just smiled and put a pillow over my feet. Then he changed the channel and we watched TV without saying anything more about it. When it was time to go to bed, he went to his room, and I went to mine.

I slept better than I had in weeks.

chapter *twenty-eight*
CONRAD

I asked Jere if he wanted to surf because I wanted to get
him alone so I could find out what the hell was going on.
I hadn't talked to him since he made his grand announce-
ment at the restaurant. But now that we were alone, I
didn't know what to say.

We bobbed on our surfboards, waiting for the next
wave. It had been slow out there so far.

I cleared my throat. "So how pissed is Laurel?"

"*Pissed*," Jere said, grimacing. "Belly and her had a
pretty big fight yesterday."

"In front of you?"

"Yeah."

"Shit." I wasn't surprised, though. There was no way
Laurel was going to be like, sure, I'll throw my teenaged
daughter a wedding.

"Yeah, pretty much."

"What does Dad say about all this?"

He gave me a funny look. "Since when do you care what Dad says?"

I looked out toward the house. I hesitated before saying, "I don't know. If Laurel's against it and Dad's against it, maybe you shouldn't do it. I mean, you guys are still in college. You don't even have a job. When you think about it, it's kind of ridiculous." My voice trailed off. Jere was shooting daggers at me.

"Stay out of it, Conrad," he said. He was practically spitting.

"All right. Sorry. I didn't mean to . . . I'm sorry."

"I never asked for your opinion. This is between me and Belly."

I said, "You're right. Forget it."

Jeremiah didn't answer. He looked over his shoulder, and then he started to paddle away. As the wave crested, he popped up and rode it to shore.

I punched my hand through the water. I wanted to kick his ass. *This is between me and Belly.* Smug piece of shit.

He was marrying my girl, and I couldn't do anything about it. I just had to watch it happen, because he was my brother, because I promised. *Take care of him, Connie. I'm counting on you.*

chapter *twenty-nine*

When I got up the next morning, the boys were still surfing, so I took my binder and my legal pad and a glass of milk out to the deck.

According to Taylor's checklist, we had to get the guest list figured out before we could do anything else. That made sense. Otherwise, how would we know how much food we needed and everything?

So far, my list was short. Taylor, her mom, a couple of the girls we'd grown up with—Marcy and Blair and maybe Katie—Anika, my dad, Steven, and my mother. And I didn't even know if my mother was coming. My dad would—I knew he would. No matter what my mother said, he'd be there. I wanted my grandma to come too, but she'd moved out of her house in Florida and into a nursing home the year before. She'd never liked traveling, and now she couldn't. In her invitation I decided I would write a note promising to visit with Jeremiah over fall break.

That was pretty much it for me. I had a few cousins on my dad's side but none I was particularly close to.

Jeremiah had Conrad, three of his fraternity brothers like we agreed, his freshman-year roommate, and his dad. Last night Jere told me he could tell his dad was softening. He said Mr. Fisher asked about who was marrying us and how much we were planning on spending on this so-called wedding. Jere told him our budget. One thousand dollars. Mr. Fisher had snorted. To me, a thousand dollars was a lot of money. Last year, it took me the whole summer to save that much waitressing at Behrs.

Our guest list would be under twenty people. With twenty people we could have a clambake and feed everyone, easy. We could get a few kegs and some cheap champagne. Since we'd be marrying on the beach, we wouldn't even need decorations. Just some flowers for the picnic tables, or shells. Shells and flowers. I was on a roll with this wedding. Taylor was going to be proud of me.

I was writing down my ideas as Jeremiah came up the steps. The sun blazed behind him, so bright it hurt my eyes. "Morning," I said, squinting up at him. "Where's Con?"

"He's still out there." Jeremiah sat down next to me.

Grinning, he asked, "Aw, did you do all the work without me?" He was dripping wet. A drop of seawater splashed down on my notepad.

"You wish." I wiped at the water. "Hey, what do you think about a clambake?"

"I like a good clambake," he agreed.

"How many kegs do you think we'd need for twenty people?"

"If Peterson and Gomez are coming, that's two already."

I pointed my pen at his chest. "We said three brothers and that's it. Right?"

He nodded, and then he leaned forward and kissed me. His lips tasted salty, and his face was cool against my warm one.

I nuzzled his cheek before I broke away. "If you get Taylor's binder wet, she'll kill you," I warned, putting it behind me.

Jeremiah made a sad face, and then he took my arms and put them around his neck like we were slow dancing. "I can't wait to marry you," he murmured into my neck.

I giggled. I was super ticklish on my neck, and he knew it. He knew almost everything about me and he still loved me.

"And what about you?"

"What about me?"

He blew on my neck, and I burst out laughing. I tried

to wriggle away from him, but he wouldn't let me. Still giggling, I said, "Okay, I can't wait to marry you either."

Jere left later that afternoon. I walked him out to his car. Conrad's car wasn't in the driveway; I didn't know where he'd gone off to.

"Call me when you get home so I know you got there safe," I said.

He nodded. He was being quiet, which was unlike him. I guessed he was sad to be leaving so soon. I wished he could stay longer too. I really did.

I got on my tiptoes and gave him a big hug. "See you in five days," I said.

"See you in five days," he repeated.

I watched him drive off, my thumbs hooked in the belt loops of my cutoffs. When I couldn't see his car anymore, I headed back inside the house.

chapter *thirty*

That first week in Cousins, I steered clear of Conrad. I couldn't deal with one more person telling me that I was making a mistake, especially judgy Conrad. He didn't even have to say it with words; he could judge with his eyes. So I got up earlier than him and ate meals before he did. And when he watched TV in the living room, I stayed upstairs in my room addressing invitations and looking at wedding blogs that Taylor had bookmarked for me.

I doubt he even noticed. He was pretty busy too. He surfed, he hung out with friends, he worked on the house. I'd never have known he was handy if I didn't see it with my own two eyes—Conrad on a ladder checking the air-conditioning vents, Conrad repainting the mailbox. I saw it all from my bedroom window.

I was eating a strawberry Pop-Tart on the deck when

he came jogging up the steps. He'd been out all morning. His hair was sweaty, and he was wearing an old T-shirt from his high school football days and a pair of navy gym shorts.

"Hey," I said. "Where are you coming from?

"The gym," Conrad said, walking past me. Then he stopped short. "Is that what you're eating for breakfast?"

I was munching around the edge of the Pop-Tart. "Yeah, but it's my last one. Sorry."

He ignored me. "I left cereal out on the counter. There's fruit in the fruit bowl too."

I shrugged. "I thought it was yours. I didn't want to eat your stuff without asking."

Impatiently, he said, "Then why didn't you ask?"

I was taken aback. "How could I ask when I've barely even seen you?"

We scowled at each other for about three seconds before I saw a smile tugging at the corners of his mouth. "Fair enough," he said, and his trace of a smile was already gone. He started to slide the glass door open, and then he turned and said, "Whatever I buy, you can eat."

"Same here," I said.

That almost-smile again. "You can keep your Pop-Tarts and your Funyuns and your Kraft mac and cheese all to yourself."

"Hey, I eat other stuff besides just junk," I protested.

"Sure you do," he said, and he went inside.

The next morning, the cereal box was out on the counter again. This time, I helped myself to his cereal and to his skim milk, and I even cut up a banana to put on top. It wasn't half bad.

Conrad was turning out to be a pretty good housemate. He always put the seat back down on the toilet, he did his dishes right away, he even bought more paper towels when we ran out. I wouldn't have expected any less, though. Conrad had always been neat. He was the exact opposite of Jeremiah in that way. Jeremiah never changed the roll of toilet paper. It would never occur to him to buy paper towels or to soak a greasy pan in hot water and dishwashing soap.

I went to the grocery store later that day and bought stuff for dinner. Spaghetti and sauce and lettuce and tomato for a salad. I cooked it around seven, thinking, ha! This will show him how healthily I can eat. I ended up overcooking the pasta and not rinsing the lettuce thoroughly enough, but it still tasted fine.

Conrad didn't come home, though, so I ate it alone in front of the TV. I did put some leftovers on a plate for him, though, and I left it on the counter when I went up to bed.

The next morning, it was gone and the dish was washed.

chapter *thirty-one*

The next time Conrad and I spoke to each other, it was the middle of the day and I was sitting at the kitchen table with my wedding binder. Now that we had our guest list, the next thing I needed to do was mail off our invitations. It almost seemed silly to bother with invitations when we had so few guests, but a mass e-mail didn't feel quite right either. I got the invitations from David's Bridal. They were white with light turquoise shells, and all I had to do was run them through the printer. And poof, wedding invitations.

Conrad opened the sliding door and stepped into the kitchen. His gray T-shirt was soaked in sweat, so I guessed he'd gone for a run. "Good run?" I asked him.

"Yeah," he said, looking surprised. He looked at my stack of envelopes and asked, "Wedding invitations?"

"Yup. I just need to go get stamps."

Pouring himself a glass of water, he said, "I need to go into town and get a new drill at the hardware store. The post office is on the way. I can get your stamps."

It was my turn to look surprised. "Thanks," I said, "but I want to go and see what kind of love stamps they have."

He downed his water.

"Do you know what a love stamp is?" I didn't wait for him to answer. "It's a stamp that says 'love' on it. People use them for weddings. I only know because Taylor told me I had to get them."

Conrad half smiled and said, "We can take my car if you want. Save you a trip."

"Sure," I said.

"I'm gonna take a quick shower. Give me ten minutes," he said, and ran up the stairs.

Conrad was back downstairs in ten minutes, just like he said. He grabbed his keys off the counter, I slid my invitations into my purse, and then we headed out to the driveway.

"We can take my car," I offered.

"I don't mind," he said.

It felt sort of funny sitting in the passenger seat of Conrad's car again. His car was clean; it still smelled the same.

"I can't remember the last time I was in your car," I said, turning on the radio.

Without missing a beat, he said, "Your prom."

Oh, God.

Prom. The site of our breakup—us fighting in the

parking lot in the rain. It was embarrassing to think of it now. How I had cried, how I had begged him not to go. Not one of my finest moments.

There was an awkward silence between us, and I had a feeling we were both remembering the same thing. To fill the silence I said brightly, "Gosh, that was, like, a million years ago, huh?"

This time he didn't reply.

Conrad dropped me off in front of the post office and said he'd be back to pick me up in a few minutes. I hopped out of the car and ran inside.

The line moved quickly, and when it was my turn, I said, "Can I see your love stamp, please?"

The woman behind the counter rifled through her drawer and slid a sheet of stamps over to me. They had wedding bells on them and LOVE was inscribed on a ribbon tying the bells together.

I set my stack of invitations on the counter and counted them quickly. "I'll take a sheet," I said.

Eyeing me, she asked, "Are those wedding invitations?"

"Yes," I said.

"Do you want to hand cancel them?"

"Pardon?"

"Do you want to hand cancel them?" she repeated, and this time she sounded annoyed.

I panicked. What did "hand cancel" mean? I wanted to text Taylor and ask, but there was a line growing behind me, so I said hastily, "No, thank you."

After I paid for the stamps, I went outside, sat on the curb, and stamped all my invitations—one for my mother, too. Just in case. She could still change her mind. There was still a chance. Conrad drove up as I was pushing them through the mail slot outside. This was really happening. I was really getting married. No turning back now, not that I wanted to.

Climbing into the car, I asked, "Did you get your new drill?"

"Yep," he said. "Did you find your love stamps?"

"Yep," I said. "Hey, what does it mean to hand cancel mail?"

"Canceling is when the post office marks the stamp so it can't be used again. I guess hand canceling would be doing it by hand instead of machine."

"How did you know that?" I asked, impressed.

"I used to collect stamps."

That was right. He had collected stamps. I'd forgotten. He kept them in a photo album his dad gave him.

"I totally forgot about that. Holy crap, you were so serious about your stamps. You wouldn't even let us touch your book without permission. Remember how Jeremiah stole one and used it to send a postcard and you were so mad you cried?"

"Hey, that was my Abraham Lincoln stamp that my grandpa gave me," Conrad said defensively. "That was a rare stamp."

I laughed, and then he did too. It was a nice sound. When was the last time we'd laughed like this?

Shaking his head, he said, "I was such a little geek."

"No, you weren't!"

Conrad threw me a look. "Stamp collecting. Chemistry set. Encyclopedia obsession."

"Yeah, but you made all of that seem cool," I said. In my memory Conrad was no geek. He was older, smarter, interested in grown-up things.

"You were gullible," he said. And then, "When you were really little, you hated carrots. You wouldn't eat them. But then I told you that if you ate carrots, you'd get X-ray vision. And you believed me. You used to believe everything I said."

I did. I really did.

I believed him when he said that carrots could give me X-ray vision. I believed him when he told me that he'd never cared about me. And then, later that night, when he tried to take it back, I guess I believed him again. Now I didn't know what to believe. I just knew I didn't believe in him anymore.

I changed the subject. Abruptly, I asked, "Are you going to stay in California after you graduate?"

"It depends on med school," he said.

"Are you . . . do you have a girlfriend?"

I saw him start. I saw him hesitate.

"No," he said.

chapter *thirty-two*
CONRAD

Her name was Agnes. A lot of people called her Aggie, but I stuck with Agnes. She was in my chem class. On any other girl, a name like Agnes wouldn't have worked. It was an old-lady name. Agnes had short dirty-blond hair, it was wavy, and she had it cut at her chin. Sometimes she wore glasses, and her skin was as pale as milk. When we were waiting for the lab to open up one day, she asked me out. I was so surprised, I said yes.

We started hanging out a lot. I liked being around her. She was smart, and her hair carried the smell of her shampoo not just fresh out of the shower but for a whole day. We spent most of our time together studying. Sometimes we'd go get pancakes or burgers after, sometimes we'd hook up in her room during a study break when her roommate wasn't around. But it was all centered around both of us being pre-med. It wasn't like I spent the night in her room or invited her to stay over in mine. I didn't hang out with her and her friends or meet her parents, even though they lived nearby.

One day we were studying in the library. The semester was almost over. We'd been dating two, almost three, months.

Out of nowhere, she asked me, "Have you ever been in love?"

Not only was Agnes good at no chem, she was really good at catching me off guard. I looked around to see if anyone was listening. "Have you?"

"I asked you first," she said.

"Then yes."

"How many times?"

"Once."

Agnes absorbed my answer as she chewed on her pencil. "On a scale of one to ten, how in love were you?"

"You can't put being in love on a scale," I said. "Either you are or you aren't."

"But if you had to say."

I started flipping through my notes. I didn't look at her when I said, "Ten."

"Wow. What was her name?"

"Agnes, come on. We have an exam on Friday."

Agnes made a pouty face and kicked my leg under the

table. "If you don't tell me, I won't be able to concentrate. Please? Just humor me."

I let out a short breath. "Belly. I mean, Isabel. Satisfied?"

Shaking her head, she said, "Uh-uh. Now tell me how you met."

"Agnes—"

"I swear I'll stop if you just answer"—I watched her count in her head—"three more questions. Three and that's it."

I didn't say yes or no, I just looked at her, waiting.

"So, how did you meet?"

"We never really met. I just always knew her."

"When did you know you were in love?"

I didn't have an answer to that question. There hadn't been one specific moment. It was like gradually waking up. You go from being asleep to the space between dreaming and awake and then into consciousness. It's a slow process, but when you're awake, there's no mistaking it. There was no mistaking that it had been love.

But I wasn't going to say that to Agnes. "I don't know, it just happened."

She looked at me, waiting for me to go on.

"You have one more question," I said.

"Are you in love with me?"

Like I said, this girl was really good at catching me off guard. I didn't know what to say. Because the answer was no. "Um . . ."

Her face fell, and then she tried to sound upbeat as she said, "So no, huh?"

"Well, are you in love with me?"

"I could be. If I let myself, I think I could be."

"Oh." I felt like a piece of shit. "I really do like you, Agnes."

"I know. I can feel that that's true. You're an honest guy, Conrad. But you don't let people in. It's impossible to get close to you." She tried to put her hair in a ponytail, but the front pieces kept falling out because it was so short. Then she released her hair and said, "I think you still love that other girl, at least a little bit. Am I right?"

"No," I told Belly.

"I don't believe you," she said, tilting her head to one side. Teasingly, she said, "If there wasn't a girl, why would you stay away for so long? There has to be a girl."

There was.

I'd stayed away for two years. I had to. I knew I shouldn't even be at the summer house, because being there, being near her, I would just want what I couldn't have. It was dangerous. She was the one person I didn't trust myself around. The day she showed up with Jere, I called my friend Danny to see if I could crash on his couch for a while, and he'd said yes. But I couldn't bring myself to do it. I couldn't leave.

I knew I had to be careful. I had to keep my distance.

If she knew how much I still cared, it was all over. I wouldn't be able to walk away again. The first time was hard enough.

The promises you make on your mother's deathbed are promises that are absolute; they're titanium. There's no way you're breaking them. I promised my mother that I would take care of my brother. That I would look after him. I kept my word. I did it the best way I could. By leaving.

I might have been a fuckup and a failure and a disappointment, but I wasn't a liar.

I did lie to Belly, though. Just that one time in that crappy motel. I did it to protect her. That's what I kept telling myself. Still, if there was one moment in my life I could redo, one moment out of all the shitty moments, that was the one I'd pick. When I thought back to the look on her face—the way it just crumpled, how she'd sucked in her lips and wrinkled her nose to keep the hurt from showing—it killed me. God, if I could, I'd go back to that moment and say all the right things, I'd tell her I loved her, I'd make it so that she never looked that way again.

chapter *thirty-three*
CONRAD

That night in the motel, I didn't sleep. I went over and over everything that had ever happened between us. I couldn't keep doing it, going back and forth, holding her close and then pushing her away. It wasn't right.

When Belly got up to shower around dawn, Jere and I got up too. I was folding my blanket up when I said, "It's okay if you like her."

Jere stared at me, his mouth hanging open. "What are you talking about?"

I felt like I was choking as I said, "It's okay with me . . . if you want to be with her."

He looked at me like I was crazy. I felt like I'd gone crazy. I heard the water in the shower shut off, and I turned away from him and said, "Just take care of her."

And then, when she came out, dressed, her hair wet,

she looked at me with those hopeful eyes, and I looked back at her like I didn't recognize her. Completely blank. I saw her eyes dim. I saw her love for me die. I'd killed it.

When I thought about it now, that moment in the motel, I understood I was the one who'd set this thing in motion. Pushed them together. It was my doing. I was the one who was going to have to live with it. They were happy.

I'd been doing a pretty good job of making myself scarce, but I happened to be home that Friday afternoon when, out of nowhere, Belly needed me. She was sitting on the living room floor with that stupid binder, papers all around her. She looked freaked out, stressed. She had that worried grimace on her face, the look she'd get when she was working on a math problem and she couldn't figure it out.

"Jere's stuck in city traffic," she said, blowing her hair out of her face. "I told him to leave earlier. I really needed his help today."

"What did you need him to do?"

"We were gonna go to Michaels. You know, that craft store?"

Drily, I said, "I can't say I've ever been to a Michaels before." I hesitated, then added, "But if you want, I'll go with you."

"Really? Because I'm picking up some heavy stuff today. The store's all the way over in Plymouth, though."

"Sure, no problem," I said, feeling inexplicably gratified to be lifting heavy stuff.

We took her car because it was bigger. She drove. I'd only ever ridden with her a few times. This side of her was new to me. Assured, confident. She drove fast, but she was still in control. I liked it. I found myself sneaking peeks at her, and I had to force myself to cool it.

"You're not a bad driver," I said.

She grinned. "Jeremiah taught me well."

That's right. He taught her how to drive. "So what else about you has changed?"

"Hey, I was never not a good driver."

I snorted, then looked out the window. "I think Steve would disagree."

"He'll never let me live down what I did to his precious baby." She shifted gears as we came to a stoplight. "So what else?"

"You wear heels now. At the garden ceremony, you had on high heels."

There was a minute hesitation before she said, "Yeah, sometimes. I still trip in them, though." Ruefully she added, "I'm like a real lady now."

I reached out to touch her hand, but at the last second I pointed instead. "You still bite your nails."

She curled her fingers around the steering wheel. With a little smile, she said, "You don't miss a thing."

"Okay, so, what are we picking up here? Flower holders?"

Belly laughed. "Yeah. Flower holders. In other words, vases." She grabbed a cart, and I took it from her and pushed it in front of us. "I think we decided on hurricane vases."

"What's a hurricane vase? And how the hell does Jere know what one is?"

"I didn't mean Jere and I decided, I meant me and Taylor." She grabbed the cart and walked ahead of me. I followed her to aisle twelve.

"See?" Belly held up a fat glass vase.

I crossed my arms. "Very nice," I said in a bored voice.

She put down the vase and picked up a skinnier one, and she didn't look at me as she said, "I'm sorry you're the one stuck doing this with me. I know it's lame."

"It's not—that lame," I said. I started grabbing vases off the shelf. "How many do we need?"

"Wait! Should we get the big ones or the medium ones? I'm thinking maybe the medium ones," she said, lifting one up and checking the price tag. "Yeah, definitely the medium ones. I only see a few left. Can you go ask somebody who works here?"

"The big ones," I said, because I'd already stacked four of the big ones in the cart. "The big ones are much nicer. You can fit more flowers or sand or whatever."

Belly narrowed her eyes. "You're just saying that because you don't want to go find somebody."

"Okay, yeah, but seriously, I think the big ones are nicer."

She shrugged and put another big vase in the cart. "I guess we could just have one big vase on each table instead of two medium-size ones."

"Now what?" I started to push the cart again, and she took it from me.

"Candles."

I followed her down another aisle, then another. "I don't think you know where you're going," I said.

"I'm taking you on the scenic route," she said, steering the cart. "Look at all these fake flowers and garlands. Good stuff."

I stopped. "Should we get some? They might look good on the porch." I grabbed a bunch of sunflowers and added a few white roses to the bunch. "This looks kind of nice, right?"

"I was kidding," she said, sucking in her cheeks. I could tell she was trying not to smile. "But yeah, that looks all right. Not great, but all right."

I put the flowers back. "All right, I give up. From now on, I'll just do the heavy lifting."

"Nice effort, though."

Back at the house, Jeremiah's car was in the driveway.

"Jere and I can unload all of this later," I said, turning off the ignition.

"I'll help," she offered, hopping out of the car. "I'm just gonna say hi first."

I grabbed a couple of the heavier bags and followed her up the steps and into the house. Jeremiah was lying on the couch watching TV. When he saw us, he sat up. "Where have you guys been?" he asked. He said it casually, but his eyes flickered at me as he spoke.

"At Michaels," Belly said. "What time did you get here?"

"A little while ago. Why didn't you wait for me? I told you I'd be here in time." Jeremiah got up and crossed the room. He pulled Belly toward him for a hug.

"I told you, Michaels closes at nine. I doubt you would have made it in time," she said, and she sounded pissed, but she let him kiss her.

I turned away. "I'm gonna go unload the car."

"Wait, I'll help." Jeremiah released Belly and slapped his hand on my back. "Con, thanks for pinch-hitting for me today."

"No problem."

"It's after eight," Belly said. "I'm starving. Let's all go to Jimmy's for dinner."

I shook my head. "Nah, I'm not hungry. You guys go."

"But you didn't have any dinner," Belly said, frowning. "Just come with us."

"No, thanks," I said.

She started to protest again, but Jere said, "Bells, he doesn't want to. Let's just go."

"Are you sure?" she asked me.

"I'm good," I said, and it came out harsher than I meant it.

I guessed it worked though, because they left.

chapter *thirty-four*

At Jimmy's, neither of us ordered crabs. I got fried scallops and iced tea, and Jeremiah got a lobster roll and beer. The server asked for his ID and smirked when he saw it, but he still served him a beer.

I shook a few sugar packets into my iced tea, tasted it, then added two more.

"I'm wiped," Jeremiah said, leaning back into the booth and closing his eyes.

"Well, wake up. We have work to do."

He opened his eyes. "Like what?"

"What do you mean, like what? Tons of stuff. At David's Bridal they were asking me all these questions. Like, what's our color palette? And are you going to wear a suit or a tuxedo?"

Jeremiah snorted. "A tuxedo? On the beach? I probably won't even wear shoes."

"Well, yeah, I know, but you should probably figure out what you're going to wear."

"I don't know. You tell me. I'll wear whatever you and Taylor want me to wear. It's your guys's day, right?"

"Ha ha," I said. "Very funny." It wasn't like I really cared what he wore. I just wanted him to figure it out and let me know so I could check it off my list.

Drumming his fingers on the table, he said, "I was thinking white shirts and khaki shorts. Nice and simple, like we said."

"Okay."

Jeremiah gulped his beer. "Hey, can we dance to 'You Never Can Tell' at the reception?"

"I don't know that song," I said.

"Sure you do. It's from my favorite movie. Hint: we had the soundtrack on repeat in our frat house media room all semester." When I still stared at him blankly, Jeremiah sang, "It was a teenage wedding and the old folks wished them well."

"Oh, yeah. *Pulp Fiction*."

"So can we?"

"Are you serious?"

"Come on, Bells. Be a sport. We can put it on YouTube. I bet we'll get a shit ton of hits. It'll be funny!"

I gave him a look. "Funny? You want our wedding to be funny?"

"Come on. You're making all the decisions, and all I

want is this one thing," he said, pouting, and I couldn't tell if he was serious or not. Either way, it pissed me off. Plus, I was still pissed he hadn't made it in time to help me at Michaels.

The server came by with our food, and Jeremiah dug right in to his lobster roll.

"What other decisions have I made?" I asked him.

"You decided that the cake was going to be carrot," he reminded me, mayonnaise dripping down his chin. "I like chocolate cake."

"I don't want to be the one making all the decisions! I don't even know what I'm doing."

"Then I'll help more. Just tell me what to do. Hey, I've got an idea. What if the wedding was Tarantino themed?" he said.

"Yeah, what if," I said sourly. I stabbed a scallop with my fork.

"You could be the Bride like in *Kill Bill.*" He looked up from his plate. "Kidding, kidding. But this whole thing is still gonna be pretty chill, right? We said we just wanted it to be casual."

"Yeah, but people still need to, like, eat."

"Don't worry about the food and stuff. My dad will hire somebody to take care of all that."

I could feel irritation start to prickle beneath my skin like a heat rash. I let out a short breath. "It's easy for you to say don't worry. You're not the one planning our wedding."

Jeremiah put down his sandwich and sat up straight. "I told you I'd help. And like I said, my dad will take care of a lot of it."

"I don't want him to," I said. "I want us to do it together. And joking about Quent Tarantino movies doesn't really count as helping."

"It's Quent*in*," Jeremiah corrected.

I shot him a dirty look.

"I wasn't joking about the first dance," he said. "I still think it would be cool. And Bells, I have been doing stuff. I figured out what to do for music. My buddy Pete deejays on the weekends. He said he'd bring his speakers and just hook up his iPod and take care of the whole thing. He already has the *Pulp Fiction* soundtrack, by the way."

Jeremiah raised his eyebrows at me comically. I knew he was waiting for a laugh or at least a smile. And I was about to give in, just so this fight could be over and I could eat my scallops without feeling angry, when he said innocently, "Oh, wait, did you want to check with Taylor first? See if she'd be okay with it?"

I glared at him. He needed to quit with the jokes and start acting a lot more appreciative, because Taylor was the one who was actually helping, unlike him. "I don't need to check with her on this. It's a dumb idea, and it's not happening."

Jeremiah whistled under his breath. "All righty, Bridezilla."

"I'm not a Bridezilla! I don't even want to do any of this. *You* do it."

He stared at me. "What do you mean, you don't want to do any of this?"

My heart was beating really fast all of a sudden. "I mean the planning. I don't want to do any of this stupid planning. Not the actual getting married part. I still want to do that."

"Good. Me too." He reached across the table, plucked a scallop off my plate, and popped it into his mouth.

I stuffed the last scallop into my mouth before he could take that, too. Then I grabbed a bunch of fries off of his plate, even though I had fries of my own.

"Hey," he said with a frown. "You've got your own fries."

"Yours are crispier," I said, but really it was more out of spite. I wondered—the rest of our lives, was Jeremiah going to try and eat my last scallop or my last bite of steak? I liked finishing all the food on my plate—I wasn't one of those girls who left a few bites behind just to be polite.

I had a fry in my mouth when Jeremiah asked, "Has Laurel called at all?"

I swallowed. Suddenly I wasn't so hungry anymore. "No."

"She must have gotten the invite by now."

"Yeah."

"Well, hopefully she'll call this week," Jere said, stuffing the rest of his lobster roll into his mouth. "I mean, I'm sure she will."

"Hopefully," I said. I sipped on my iced tea and added, "Our first dance can be 'You Never Can Tell' if you really want."

Jere pumped his fist in the air. "See, that's why I'm marrying you!"

A smile creeped across my face. "Because I'm generous?"

"Because you're very generous, and you get me," he said, taking back a few of his fries.

When we got back to the house, Conrad's car was gone.

chapter *thirty-five*
CONRAD

I would rather have had someone shoot me in the head with a nail gun, repeatedly, than have to watch the two of them cuddling on the couch together all night. After they went to dinner, I got in my car and drove to Boston. As I drove, I thought about not going back to Cousins. Screw it. It would be easier that way. Halfway home, I made up my mind that yeah, that would be for the best. An hour from home, I decided, screw them, I had as much right to be there as they did. I still needed to clean out the gutters, and I was pretty sure I'd seen a wasp nest in the drainpipe. There was all kinds of stuff I needed to take care of. I couldn't just not go back.

Around midnight, I was sitting at the kitchen table in my boxer shorts eating cereal when my dad walked in, still wearing his work suit. I didn't even know he was home.

He didn't look surprised to see me. "Con, can I talk to you for a minute?" he asked.

"Yeah."

He sat down across from me with his glass of bourbon. In the dim light of the kitchen, my father looked like an old man. His hair was thinning on top, and he'd lost weight, too much weight. When did he get so old? In my mind he was always thirty-seven.

My dad cleared his throat. "What do you think I should do about this thing with Jeremiah? I mean, is he really set on it?"

"Yeah, I think he is."

"Laurel's really torn up about it. She's tried everything, but the kids aren't listening. Belly ran off, and now they aren't even talking to each other. You know how Laurel can get."

This was all news to me. I didn't know they weren't speaking to each other.

My dad sipped from his glass. "Do you think there's anything I can do? To put an end to it?"

For once I actually agreed with my dad. My feelings for Belly aside, I thought getting married at nineteen was dumb. What was the point? What were they trying to prove?

"You could cut Jere off," I said, and then I felt like a dick for suggesting it. I added, "But even if you did, he still has the money Mom left him."

"Most of it's in a trust."

"He's determined. He'll do it either way." I hesitated, then added, "Besides, if you pulled something like that, he'd never forgive you."

My dad got up and poured himself some more bourbon. He sipped it before he said, "I don't want to lose him the way I lost you."

I didn't know what to say. So we sat there in silence, and right when I finally opened my mouth to say, You haven't lost me, he stood up.

Sighing heavily, he emptied his glass. "Good night, son."

"Good night, Dad."

I watched my father trudge up the stairs, each step heavier than the last—like Atlas with the world on his shoulders. He'd never had to deal with this kind of thing before. He'd never had to be that kind of father. My mom was always there to take care of the hard stuff. Now that she was gone, he was all we had left, and it wasn't enough.

I had always been the favorite. I was our father's Jacob, and Jeremiah was Esau. It wasn't something I'd ever questioned; I'd always assumed it was because I was the firstborn that I came first with my dad. I just accepted it, and so did Jere. But as we got older, I saw that that wasn't it. It was that he saw himself in me. To our father, I was just a reflection of him. He thought we were so alike. Jere was like our mom, I was like our dad. So I was the one he put all the pressure on. I was the one he funneled all his energy and hope into. Football, school, all of it. I worked hard to meet those expectations, to be just like him.

The first time I realized my father wasn't perfect was when he forgot my mom's birthday. He'd been golfing all day with his friends, and he came home late. Jere and I had made a cake and bought flowers and a card. We had everything set up on the dining room table. My dad had had a few beers—I could smell it on him when he hugged me. He said, "Oh shit, I forgot. Boys, can I put my name on the card?" I was a freshman in high school. Late, I know, to figure out your dad isn't a hero. That was just the first time I remember being disappointed by something he did. After that, I found more and more reasons to be disappointed.

All of that love and pride I had in him, it turned to hate. And then I started to hate myself, who he'd made. Because I saw it too—how alike we were. That scared me. I didn't want to be the kind of man who cheated on his wife. I didn't want to be the kind of man who put work before his family, who tipped cheaply at restaurants, who never bothered to learn our housekeeper's name.

From there on I set out to destroy the picture of me he had in his head. I quit our morning runs before he left for work, I quit the fishing trips, the golf, which I'd never liked anyway. And I quit football, which I loved. He'd gone to all my games, videotaping them so we could watch later and he could point out the places where I'd messed up. Every time there was an article about me in the newspaper, he framed it and hung it in his study.

I quit it all to spite him. Anything that made him proud of me, I took away.

It took me a long time to figure it out. That I was the one who had put my dad on that pedestal. I did that, not him. And then I despised him for not being perfect. For being human.

I drove back to Cousins on Monday morning.

chapter *thirty-six*

On Monday afternoon Conrad and I were eating outside on the deck. He had grilled chicken and corn for lunch. He hadn't been kidding when he said all he ever ate was grilled chicken.

"Did Jere tell you what he wants you and Steven to wear for the wedding?" I asked him.

Conrad shook his head, looking confused. "I thought guys just wore suits for weddings."

"Well, yeah, but you guys are his best men, so you're all dressing alike. Khaki shorts and white-linen button-down shirts. He didn't tell you?"

"This is the first I'm hearing about linen shirts. Or being a best man."

I rolled my eyes. "Jeremiah needs to get on the ball. Of course you're his best man. You and Steven both are."

"How can there be two best men? 'Best' implies only one." Biting into his corn on the cob, he said, "Let Steven be it, I don't care."

"No! You're Jeremiah's brother. You have to be his best man."

My phone rang as I was explaining to him what being the best man entailed. I didn't recognize the number, but since the wedding planning had gotten under way, I'd been getting a lot of those.

"Is this Isabel?" I didn't recognize the voice. She sounded older, like someone my mother's age. Whoever she was, she had a thick Boston accent.

I said, "Um, this is she. I mean, her."

"My name is Denise Coletti, I'm calling from Adam Fisher's office."

"Oh . . . hello. It's nice to meet you."

"Yes, hello. I just need you to okay a few things for your wedding. I've selected a catering service called Elegantly Yours; they do events around the area. They're doing this very last-minute for us; this caterer books months in advance for parties. Is this all right with you?"

Faintly, I said, "Sure."

Conrad looked at me quizzically, and I mouthed, *Denise Coletti*. His eyes widened, and he gestured for me to give him the phone. I waved his hand away.

Then Denise Coletti said, "Now, how many people are you expecting?"

"Twenty, if everyone can come."

"Adam told me more like forty. I'll check with him." I could hear her typing. "So probably four to five appetizers a person. Do we want a vegetarian option for the meal?"

"I don't think Jeremiah and I have any vegetarian friends."

"All right. Are you going to want to go and do a tasting? I think you probably should."

"Uh, okay."

"Wonderful. I'll book you for next week, then. Now for seating arrangements. Do you want two or three long tables or five round tables?"

"Um . . ." I hadn't even thought of tables. And what was she talking about, forty? I was wishing I had Taylor next to me to tell me what to do. "Can I get back to you on that?"

Denise let out a little sigh, and I knew I had said the wrong thing. "Sure, but be as quick as you can so I can give them the go-ahead. That's all for now. I'll be touching base with you again later this week. Oh, and congratulations."

"Thank you very much, Denise."

Next to me, Conrad called out, "Hi, Denise!"

She said, "Is that Connie? Tell him hello from me."

"Denise says hello," I told him.

Then she said mazel tov, and we hung up.

"What's going on?" Conrad asked me. He had a corn kernel stuck on his cheek. "Why is Denise calling you?"

I put my phone down and said, "Um, apparently, your

dad's secretary is our wedding planner now. And we're inviting forty people instead of twenty."

Blandly, he said, "That's good news."

"How is that good news?"

"It means my dad is okay with you guys getting married. And he's paying for it." Conrad started to cut his chicken.

"Huh. Wow." I stood up. "I'd better call Jere. Wait, it's the middle of the day. He's still at work."

I sat back down.

I probably should have felt relieved that someone else was taking over, but instead I just felt overwhelmed. This wedding was getting a lot bigger than I had imagined it. Now we were renting tables? It was all too much, too sudden.

Across from me, Conrad was buttering another ear of corn. I looked down at my plate. I wasn't hungry anymore. I felt sick to my stomach.

"Eat," Conrad said.

I took a small bite of chicken.

I wouldn't get to talk to Jeremiah until later that evening. But the person I really wanted to talk to was my mother. She would have known how to configure the tables and where to seat everyone. Denise wasn't the one I wanted to swoop in and tell me what to do, and not Mr. Fisher either, or even Susannah. I only wanted my mother.

chapter *thirty-seven*
CONRAD

It didn't really hit me how hard of a time Belly was having until I heard her on the phone with Taylor later that week. She had her door open, and I was brushing my teeth in the hall bathroom.

I heard her say, "Taylor, I really appreciate what your mom is trying to do, but I promise you, it's okay. . . . I know, but it would just feel too weird with all the adults from the neighborhood at my wedding shower and then my mom not being there. . . ." I heard her sigh and say, "Yeah, I know. Okay. Tell your mom thanks."

She closed her door then, and I was pretty sure I heard her start to cry.

I went to my room, lay down on my bed, and stared up at the ceiling.

Belly hadn't let on to me how sad she was about her

mom. She was an upbeat kind of person, naturally cheerful, like Jere. If there was a bright side, Belly would find it. Hearing her cry, it shook me up. I knew I should stay out of it. That was the smart thing to do. She didn't need me looking out for her. She was a big girl. Besides, what could I do for her?

I was definitely staying out of it.

The next morning, I got up early to see Laurel. It was still dark out when I left. I called her on the way and asked if she could meet for breakfast. Laurel was surprised, but she didn't ask questions; she said she'd meet me at a diner off the highway.

I guess Laurel had always been special to me. Ever since I was a kid, I just liked being near her. I liked the way you could be quiet around her, and with her. She didn't talk down to kids. She treated us like equals. After my mom died and I transferred to Stanford, I started calling Laurel every once in a while. I still liked talking to her, and I liked that she reminded me of my mom without it hurting too much. It was like a link to home.

She got to the diner first—she was sitting in a booth waiting for me. "Connie," she said, standing up and opening her arms. She looked like she'd lost weight.

"Hey, Laur," I said, hugging her back. She felt gaunt in my arms, but she smelled the same. Laurel always had a clean, cinnamony smell.

I sat down across from her. After we ordered, pancakes and bacon for both of us, she said, "So how have you been?"

"I've been all right," I said, chugging down some juice.

How was I even supposed to broach this subject? This wasn't my style. It didn't come naturally to me, the way it would for Jere. I was butting in on something that wasn't my business. But I had to do it. For her.

I cleared my throat and said, "I called you because I wanted to talk about the wedding."

Her face got tight, but she didn't interrupt.

"Laur, I think you should go. I think you should be part of it. You're her mom."

Laurel stirred her coffee, and then she looked at me and said, "You think they should get married?"

"I didn't say that."

"Then, what do you think?"

"I think they love each other and they're going to do it regardless of what anyone else thinks. And . . . I think that Belly really needs her mom right now."

Drily, she said, "Isabel seems to be doing just fine without me. She never even called to let me know where she was. I had to hear it from Adam—who, by the way, is apparently paying for this wedding now. Classic Adam. And now Steven's a best man, and Belly's dad is going to give in the way he always does. It seems I'm the only holdout."

"Belly isn't fine. She's barely eating. And . . . I heard her crying last night. She was saying how Taylor's mom is throwing her a wedding shower but it won't feel right without you there."

Laurel's face softened, just a little. "Lucinda's throwing her a shower?" Then, stirring her coffee again, she said, "Jere hasn't thought this through. He isn't taking it seriously enough."

"You're right, he's not a serious guy. But believe me, he's serious about her." I took a deep breath before I said, "Laurel, if you don't go, you'll regret it."

She looked at me directly. "Are we speaking honestly with each other here?"

"Don't we always?"

Laurel nodded, taking a sip of coffee. "Yes, that we do. So tell me. What's your interest in all of this?"

I knew this was coming. This was Laurel, after all. She didn't mess around. "I want her to be happy."

"Ah," she said. "Just her?"

"Jeremiah, too."

"And that's it?" She looked at me steadily.

I just looked back at her.

I tried to pay for breakfast since I was the one who invited her out, but Laurel wouldn't let me. "Not gonna happen," she said.

On the drive back, I played back our conversation. The

knowing look on Laur's face when she asked me what my interest in this was. What was I doing? Picking out vases with Belly, trying to play peacemaker with the parents. Suddenly I was their wedding planner, and I didn't even agree with them. I needed to disengage from the situation. I was washing my hands of the whole mess.

chapter *thirty-eight*

"Where have you been?" I asked Conrad when he came back in the door. He'd been gone all morning.

He didn't answer me right away. In fact he was barely looking at me. And then he said, shortly, "Just running errands."

I gave him a weird look, but he didn't offer up any more information. So I just asked, "Wanna keep me company while I go to the florist in Dyerstown? I have to pick out flowers for the wedding."

"Isn't Jere coming today? Can't you go with him?" He sounded annoyed.

I was surprised and a little hurt. I thought we'd been getting along really well these past few weeks. "He's not going to be here until tonight," I said. Playfully, I added, "Anyway, you're the one who's the flower-arranging expert, not Jere, remember?"

Conrad stood at the sink with his back to me. He turned on the water, filling a glass. "I don't want to piss him off."

I thought I heard a trace of hurt in his voice. Hurt— and something else. Fear.

"What's wrong? Did something happen this morning?" I felt worried all of a sudden. When Conrad didn't answer me, I went up behind him and started to put my hand on his shoulder, but then he turned around and my hand fell back to my side. "Nothing happened," he said. "Let's go. I'll drive."

He was pretty quiet at the florist's. Taylor and I had decided on calla lilies, but when I looked through the book of flower arrangements, I ended up picking peonies instead. When I showed them to Conrad, he said, "Those were my mom's favorite."

"I remember," I said. I ordered five arrangements, one for each table, just like Denise Coletti told me to.

"What about bouquets?" the florist asked me.

"Can those be peonies too?" I asked.

"Sure, we can do that. I'll put together something nice for you." To Conrad, she said, "Are you and your groomsmen doing boutonnieres?"

He turned red. "I'm not the groom," he said.

"He's the brother of the groom," I said, handing her Mr. Fisher's credit card.

We left pretty soon after.

On the way back home, we passed a fruit stand on the side of the road. I wanted to stop, but I didn't say so. I guessed Conrad could tell, because he asked, "Want to go back?"

"Nah, that's okay, we already passed it," I said.

He made a U-turn on the one-way street.

The fruit stand was a couple of wooden crates of peaches and a sign that said to leave the money in the container. I put in a dollar because I didn't have change.

"Aren't you going to have one?" I asked him, wiping off my peach on my shirt.

"Nah, I'm allergic to peaches."

"Since when?" I demanded. "I've definitely seen you eat a peach before. Or peach pie, at least."

He shrugged. "Since always. I've eaten them before, but they make the inside of my mouth itch."

Before I bit into my peach, I closed my eyes and inhaled the fragrance. "Your loss."

I had never had a peach like that before. So perfectly ripe. Your fingers sank into the fruit a little just touching it. I gobbled it up, peach juice running down my chin, pulp dripping all over my hands. It was sweet and tart. A full-body experience, smell and taste and sight.

"This is a perfect peach," I said. "I almost don't want to have another one, because there's no way it can be as good."

"Let's test it out," Conrad said, and he went and

bought me another peach. I ate that one in four bites.

"Was it as good?" he asked me.

"Yeah. It was."

Conrad reached out and wiped my chin with his shirt. It was maybe the most intimate thing anyone had ever done to me.

I felt light-headed, unsteady on my feet.

It was all in the way he looked at me, just those few seconds. Then he dropped his eyes, like the sun was too bright behind me.

I sidestepped away from him and said, "I'm gonna buy some more, for Jere."

"Good idea," he said, backing away. "I'll go wait for you in the car."

I was shaking as I piled peaches into a plastic bag. Just one look, one touch from him, and I was shaking. It was madness. I was marrying his brother.

Back in the car, I didn't speak. I couldn't have even if I wanted to. I didn't have the words. In the quiet of the air-conditioned car, the silence between us felt blaringly loud. So I rolled down my window and fixed my eyes on all the moving objects on my side.

At home, Jeremiah's car was parked in the driveway. Conrad disappeared as soon as we got into the house. I found Jere napping on the couch, his sunglasses still on his head. I kissed him awake.

His eyes fluttered open. "Hey."

"Hey. Want a peach?" I asked, swinging my plastic bag like a pendulum. I felt jittery all of a sudden.

Jere hugged me and said, "You're a peach."

"Did you know Conrad's allergic to peaches?"

"Of course. Remember that time he had peach ice cream and his mouth swelled up?"

I broke away and went to wash the peaches. I told myself, there's nothing to feel guilty about, nothing happened. You didn't do anything.

I was rinsing peaches in the red plastic colander, shaking excess water off the way I'd seen Susannah do so many times. While the water was running over the peaches, Jeremiah came up behind me and grabbed one, saying, "I think they're clean now."

He lifted himself onto the kitchen counter and bit into the peach.

"Good, right?" I asked him. I held one up to my face and inhaled deeply, trying to clear my mind of all the crazy thoughts.

Jeremiah nodded. He'd already finished it and was lobbing the pit into the sink. "Really good. Did you get any strawberries? I could eat a whole box of strawberries right now."

"No, just the peaches."

I put the peaches in the silver fruit bowl, arranging them as nicely as I could. My hands were still shaking.

chapter *thirty-nine*

The apartment had wall-to-wall navy blue carpeting, and even though I had flip-flops on, I could just tell that it was moist. The kitchen was the size of an airplane bathroom, practically, and the bedroom had no windows. The place had high ceilings—that was the only nice thing about it, in my opinion.

Jeremiah and I had spent the whole day looking at apartments near our school. So far we'd seen three. This place was the worst by far.

"I like the carpet," Jeremiah said appreciatively. "It's nice to wake up in the morning and put your feet down on carpet."

I glanced toward the open door, where the landlord was waiting for us. He looked around my dad's age. He had a long white ponytail, a mustache, and a tattoo of a topless mermaid on his forearm. He caught me looking at the tattoo and grinned at me. I gave him a weak smile in return.

Then I walked back into the bedroom and motioned for Jeremiah to follow me. "It smells like cigarette smoke in here," I whispered. "It's, like, absorbed in the carpet."

"Febreeze it, baby."

"*You* Febreeze it. By yourself. I'm not living here."

"What's the problem? This place is practically on campus, it's so close. And there's outdoor space—we can grill. Think of all the parties we'll have. Come on, Belly."

"Come on nothing. Let's go back to the first place we looked at. That place had central air-conditioning." Above us, I could feel rather than hear the bass from someone's stereo pumping.

Jeremiah jammed his hands into his pockets. "That place was all old people and families. This place is for people our age. College kids like us."

I looked back at the landlord. He was looking at his cell phone, pretending not to listen to our conversation.

Lowering my voice, I said, "This place is basically a frat house. If I wanted to live in a frat house, I would bunk with you back at fraternity row."

He rolled his eyes. Loudly, he said, "I guess we're not taking the apartment." To the landlord, he shrugged, like whaddyagonnado. Like they were in on it together, just a couple of guys, partners.

"Thank you for showing us the apartment," I said.

"No problemo," the guy said, lighting a cigarette.

As we stepped out of the apartment, I shot Jeremiah a dirty look. He mouthed, *What*, in a bewildered way. I just shook my head.

"It's getting late," Jeremiah said in the car. "Let's just pick a place. I want to get this over with already."

"Okay, fine," I said, turning up the AC. "Then I pick the first place."

"Fine," he said.

"Fine," I said back.

We went back to the first apartment complex to fill out paperwork. We went straight to the management office. The building manager's name was Carolyn. She was tall and red haired and she wore a printed wrap dress. Her perfume smelled like Susannah's. I took this as a definite good omen.

"So your parents aren't renting the apartment for you?" Carolyn asked. "Most students have their parents sign the lease."

I opened my mouth to speak, but Jeremiah beat me to it.

"No, we're doing this on our own," he said. "We're engaged."

Surprise registered on her face, and I saw her glance ever so briefly at my stomach. "Oh!" she said. "Well, congratulations."

"Thank you," Jeremiah said.

I said nothing. Inside, I was thinking how sick I was of everybody thinking I was pregnant just because we were getting married.

"We'll need to do a credit check, and then I can process your application," Carolyn said. "If everything checks out, the apartment is yours."

"If you've been late on a few credit-card bills, will that, um, negatively impact a person's credit?" Jeremiah asked, leaning forward.

I could feel my eyes widen. "What are you talking about?" I whispered. "Your dad pays your credit card."

"Yeah, I know, but I started one freshman year too. To build my credit," he added, giving Carolyn a winning smile.

"I'm sure it'll be fine," she said, but her smile had faded. "Isabel, how's your credit?"

"Um, good, I think. My dad put me down on his credit card, but I never use it," I said.

"Hmm. Okay, how about any department-store cards?" she asked.

I shook my head.

"We definitely have first and last month's rent," Jeremiah put in. "And we have the security deposit, too. So it's all good."

"Great," Carolyn said, and she stood up from her chair. "I'm going to process this today, and I'll let you guys know within the next couple of days."

"I'll keep my fingers crossed," I said, trying to sound cheerful.

Jeremiah and I walked out of the building and to the parking lot. When we were standing outside the car, I said, "I really hope we get that apartment."

"If we don't, I'm sure we can get one of the other ones. I doubt Gary would even do a credit check on us."

"Who's Gary?"

Jeremiah went around to the driver's side and unlocked the door. "That guy from the last apartment we saw."

I rolled my eyes. "I'm sure Gary would still do a credit check."

"Doubt it," Jere said. "Gary was cool."

"*Gary* probably has a meth lab in the basement," I said, and this time Jeremiah rolled his eyes.

I continued. "If we lived in that apartment, we would probably wake up in the middle of the night in an ice bath without our kidneys."

"Belly, he rents apartments to lots of students. A guy from my soccer team lived there all last year, and he's fine. Still has both kidneys and everything."

We looked at each other from across the car, on opposite sides. Jere said, "Why are we still talking about this? You got your way, remember?"

He didn't finish the sentence the way I knew he

wanted to—You got your way, like you always do.

"We don't know if I got my way or not."

I didn't finish the sentence the way I wanted to—We don't know if I got my way or not, because of your bad credit.

I jerked the passenger door open and got in.

I got the call later that week. We didn't get the apartment. I didn't know if it was because of Jere's bad credit or my lack of credit, but who really cared. The point was, we didn't get it.

chapter *forty*

It was the day of Taylor's bridal shower. I kept thinking of
it as her shower because she and her mom were the ones
who were throwing it. The invitations they sent out were
nicer than my actual wedding invitations.

There were already a bunch of cars parked in front
of the house. I recognized Marcy Yoo's silver Audi and
Taylor's Aunt Mindy's blue Honda. Taylor's mailbox had
white balloons strung on it. It reminded me of every
birthday party Taylor had ever had. She always had hot
pink balloons. Always.

I was wearing a white sundress and sandals. I'd put on
mascara and blush and pink lip gloss. When I'd left the
Cousins house, Conrad said I looked nice. It was the first
time we'd spoken since the day we stopped for peaches.
He said, *You look nice*, and I said thanks. Totally normal.

I rang the doorbell, something I never did at Taylor's house. But since it was a party, I figured I should.

Taylor answered the door. She was wearing a pink dress with light green fish swimming along the hem, and she'd done her hair halfway up. She looked like she should be the bride, not me. "You look pretty," she said, hugging me.

"So do you," I said, stepping inside.

"Almost everybody's here," she said, leading me to the living room.

"I'm just gonna go pee first," I said.

"Hurry, you're the guest of honor."

I used the bathroom quickly, and after I washed my hands, I tried to brush my hair with my fingers. I put a little more lip gloss on. For some reason, I felt nervous.

Taylor had hung crepe-paper wedding bells from the ceiling, and "Going to the Chapel" was playing on the stereo.

There were our friends Marcy and Blair and Katie, Taylor's Aunt Mindy, my next door-neighbor Mrs. Evans, Taylor's mom Lucinda. And sitting next to her, on the loveseat, wearing a light blue suit, was my mother.

My eyes filled when I saw her.

We didn't run across the room to embrace, we didn't weep. I made my way around the room, hugging women and girls, and when I finally reached my mother, we hugged tightly and for a long time. We didn't have to say anything, because we both knew.

At the buffet table, Taylor squeezed my hand. "Happy?" she whispered.

"So happy," I whispered back, picking up a plate. I felt such immense relief. Everything was really working out. I had my mom back. This was really happening.

"Good," Taylor said.

"How did this even happen? Did your mom talk to my mom?"

"Mm-hmm," she said, and she blew me a little kiss. "My mom said it wasn't even hard to convince her to come."

Lucinda had set up the table with her famous white coconut cake as the centerpiece. There was sparkling lemonade, pigs in a blanket, baby carrots, and onion dip— all my favorite foods. My mom had brought her lemon squares.

I filled my plate with food and sat next to the girls. Popping a pig in a blanket in my mouth, I said, "Thank you guys so much for coming!"

"I can't believe you're getting married," Marcy said, shaking her head in awe.

"Me either," Blair said.

"Me either," I said.

Opening presents was the best part. It felt like my birthday. Cupcake tins from Marcy, drinking glasses from Blair, hand towels from Aunt Mindy, cookbooks from Lucinda, a glass pitcher from Taylor, a down comforter from my mother.

Taylor sat next to me, writing down who gave what and collecting ribbons. She poked holes into a paper plate and wove the ribbons through.

"What's that for?" I asked her.

"Your bouquet for the rehearsal, silly," Lucinda said, beaming at me. She'd been tanning that morning. I could tell because you could see the marks her goggles had left.

"Oh, we're not having a rehearsal dinner," I said. Because honestly, what was there to rehearse? We were getting married on the beach. It was going to be simple and uncomplicated, the way we both wanted it.

Taylor handed the plate to me. "Then you have to wear it like a hat."

Lucinda got up and tied the paper plate around my head like a bonnet. We all laughed as Marcy took my picture.

Taylor stood up, holding her notebook. "Okay, so get ready for what Belly's going to say on her wedding night."

I covered my face with my ribbon hat. I'd heard of this game before. The maid of honor writes down all the stuff the bride-to-be says while she's opening presents.

"'Oh, so pretty!'" Taylor exclaimed, and the room tittered.

I tried to grab the notebook from her, but she held it above my head and read, "'Jeremiah's gonna love this!'"

After the toilet-paper wedding dress competition, after we helped clean up and everyone had left, I walked my mother to her car.

I felt shy as I said, "Thank you for coming, Mom. It means a lot to me."

She brushed my hair out of my eyes. "You're my girl," she said simply.

I threw my arms around her. "I love you so, so much."

I called Jeremiah as soon as I got in my car. "We are so on!" I screamed. Not that we ever weren't. Still, planning this wedding, being away from home, being in a fight with my mom—it'd had me in knots. But with my mother by my side, I finally felt like I could breathe again. My worries were gone. I finally felt complete. I felt like I could do this.

That night, I slept at home. Steven and my mom and I watched crime TV, one of those shows where they re-create crimes. We howled like wolves at the horrible acting, and we ate Fritos and the rest of my mother's lemon squares. It was so good.

chapter *forty-one*
CONRAD

The day Belly went home, I went to visit Ernie, the old owner of the seafood restaurant I used to bus tables at. Every kid who ever went to Cousins knew who Ernie was, just like Ernie knew every kid. He never forgot a face, no matter how old he got. Ernie had to have been at least seventy years old when I worked there in high school. His nephew John was running the place now, and he was a prick. At first he demoted Ernie to bartending, but Ernie couldn't keep up, so John had him roll silverware. John ended up cutting him out of the business completely, forcing him into retirement. Sure, Ernie was old, but he was a hard worker, and everybody loved him. I used to take smoke breaks with him outside. I knew it was wrong to let him bum a cigarette, but he was an old guy, and who can really say no to an old guy?

Ernie lived in a small house off the highway, and I tried to go out and see him once a week at least. To keep him company but also to make sure he was still alive. Ernie didn't have anybody around to remind him to take his medicine, and his nephew John sure as hell wasn't coming by to visit. After John pushed him out of the business, Ernie said John wasn't his blood anymore.

So I was pretty surprised when I pulled onto Ernie's street and saw John's car on its way out. I parked in front of the house and knocked once before I let myself in.

"Did you bring me a cigarette?" Ernie asked me from the couch.

It was the same thing every time. He wasn't even allowed to smoke anymore. "No," I said. "I quit."

"Then get the hell out."

Then he laughed the way he always did, and I sat on his couch. We watched old cop shows and ate peanuts in silence. During commercial breaks, that was when we'd talk.

"Did you hear my brother's getting married next weekend?" I asked.

He snorted. "I'm not in the ground yet, boy. 'Course I heard. Everybody's heard. She's a sweet girl. Used to curtsy at me when she was little."

Grinning, I said, "That's because we told her you used to be a prince in Italy but then you became a mafioso. The Godfather of Cousins."

"Damn straight."

The show came back on, and we watched in comfortable silence. Then, at the next break, Ernie said, "So are you gonna cry about it like a punk, or are you gonna do something?"

I almost choked on my peanut. Coughing, I said, "What are you talking about?"

He made another snorty sound. "Don't be cute with me. You love her, right? She's the one?"

"Ernie, I think you forgot to take your meds today," I said. "Where's your pillbox?"

He waved me off with one bony white hand, his attention back on the TV. "Simmer down. Show's back on."

I had to wait until the next commercial until I asked him casually, "Do you really believe in that? That people are meant to be with one person?"

Shelling a nut, he said, "Sure I do. Elizabeth was my one. When she passed, I didn't figure a reason to look for another one. My girl was gone. Now I'm just biding my time. Get me a beer, will you?"

I stood up and went to his fridge. I came back with a beer and a fresh glass. Ernie had a thing about a fresh glass. "What was John doing over here?" I asked. "I saw him on my way in."

"He came to mow my lawn."

"I thought that was my job," I said, pouring the beer into his glass.

"You do a shit job of edging."

"When did you guys even start speaking again?"

Ernie shrugged and popped a peanut into his mouth. "He's probably just sniffing around here so I leave him my property when I kick it." He drank his beer and leaned back into his easy chair. "Eh, he's a good kid. My sister's only son. He's family. Family's family. Never forget that, Conrad."

"Ernie, two commercial breaks ago, you told me that if I didn't try and break up my brother's wedding, I was a punk!"

Picking at his teeth, Ernie said, "If a girl's the one, all bets are off, family or no family."

I felt lighter when I left Ernie's house a couple of hours later. I always did.

chapter *forty-two*

It was Wednesday, just a few days before the wedding. Tomorrow, Taylor and Anika were coming up to Cousins, and so were Josh, Redbird, and my brother. The boys were going to have their so-called bachelor night, and Taylor and Anika and I were just going to hang by the pool. Between Denise Coletti and Taylor, the wedding was pretty much ready to go. The food had been ordered—lobster rolls and shrimp cocktail. We had Christmas lights for the deck and yard. Conrad was going to play a song on the guitar when I walked out with my dad. I was going to wear the jewelry Susannah had left me; I was going to do my own hair and makeup.

Everything was coming together, but I still couldn't shake the feeling that there was something I'd forgotten.

I was vacuuming the living room when Conrad

pushed open the sliding door. He'd been surfing all morning. I turned off the vacuum cleaner. "What's wrong?" I asked him. He looked pale, and his hair was dripping in his eyes.

"Wipeout," he said. "I got cut by my fin."

"Bad?"

"Nah, not too bad." I watched him limp over to the bathroom, and I ran over. He was sitting on the sill of the tub, and blood was soaking through his towel and running down his leg. I felt woozy for a split second.

"It's already stopped bleeding," Conrad said, and his face was as white as the marble counter. He looked like he was going to pass out. "Looks worse than it is."

"Keep putting pressure on it," I said. "I'm gonna get some stuff to clean it."

It must have really hurt, because he obeyed me. When I came back with hydrogen peroxide and gauze and Bactine, he was still sitting there in the same position, his leg in the tub.

I sat down next to him and straddled the sill, facing him. "Let go," I told him.

"I'm fine," he said. "I'll do it."

"No, you're not fine," I said.

Then he let go of the towel, and I pressed down on it. He winced.

"Sorry," I said. I held it for a few minutes, and then I peeled the bloody towel away from his leg. The cut was a few inches long and skinny. It wasn't bleeding as heavily, so I went ahead and started to pour hydrogen peroxide on the wound.

"Ow!" he yelped.

"Don't be such a baby, it's barely a scratch," I lied. I was wondering if he was going to need stitches.

Conrad leaned in closer to me, his head just barely resting on my shoulder as I cleaned. I could feel him breathing in and out, could feel each sharp intake of breath every time I touched the cut.

When the cut was clean, it looked a lot better. I dabbed Bactine on it and then wrapped his calf in gauze. Then I patted his knee. "See? All better."

He lifted his head up and said, "Thank you."

"Sure," I said.

There was this moment between us then, of us just looking at each other, holding each other's gaze. My breath quickened. If I leaned forward just a little, we would be kissing. I knew I should move away, but I couldn't.

"Belly?" I could feel his breath on my neck.

"Yeah?"

"Will you help me stand up? I'm going to go upstairs and take a nap."

"You've lost a lot of blood," I said, and my voice vibrated off the bathroom tiles. "I don't think you're supposed to sleep."

He smiled weakly. "That's with concussions."

I scrambled up and then pulled him up next to me. "Can you walk?" I asked.

"I'll manage," he said, limping away from me, his hand on the wall.

My T-shirt was damp from his head on my shoulder. Mechanically, I started cleaning up the mess, and my heart was pounding out of my chest. What just happened? What did I almost do? This time wasn't like with the peaches. This time it was all me.

Conrad slept right through dinnertime, and I wondered if I should bring him some food but decided against it. Instead I heated up one of the frozen pizzas I'd bought, and then I spent the rest of the night cleaning the downstairs. I was relieved that everybody would be here tomorrow. It wouldn't be just me and him anymore. Once Jeremiah was here, everything would go back to normal.

chapter *forty-three*

Everything did go back to normal. I was normal, Conrad was normal: it was like nothing happened. Because nothing did happen. If he didn't have a bandage on his leg, I'd have thought I dreamed the whole thing.

The boys were all down by the beach, except for Conrad, who couldn't get water on his leg. He was in the kitchen, getting meat ready for the grill. Us girls were lying by the pool, passing a bag of kettle corn back and forth. Weatherwise, it was a perfect Cousins day. The sun was high and hot, and there were only a few clouds. No rain in the forecast for the next seven days. Our wedding was safe.

"Redbird's kind of cute, no?" Taylor said, adjusting her bikini top.

"Gross," Anika said. "Anybody with a nickname like Redbird—no thank you."

Taylor frowned at her. "Don't be so judgmental. Belly, what do you think?"

"Um . . . he's a nice guy. Jeremiah says he's very loyal."

"See?" Taylor crowed, poking Anika with her toe.

Anika gave me a look, and I smiled a sneaky smile and said, "He's very, very loyal. So what if he's, like, a smidge Cro-Magnon?"

Taylor threw a handful of popcorn at me and, giggling, I tried to catch some with my mouth.

"Are we going out with the boys tonight?" Anika asked.

"No, they're doing their own thing. They're going to some bar with half-off Irish car bombs or something."

"Eww," Taylor said.

Glancing back toward the kitchen, Anika said in a low voice, "You guys never told me how hot Conrad is."

"He's not *that* hot," Taylor said. "He just thinks he is."

"No he doesn't," I defended. To Anika, I said, "Tay's just mad because he never went for her."

"Why would he go for her when he was your man?"

I shushed her. "He was never my man," I whispered.

"He was *always* your man," Taylor said, spritzing herself with more suntan oil.

Firmly, I said, "Not anymore."

For dinner we had steaks and grilled vegetables. It was a grown-up kind of meal. Drinking red wine, sitting around a table with all my friends, I felt adult. I was sitting next to Jeremiah, and he had his arm around my chair. And yet.

All night, I talked to other people. I didn't look in his direction, but I always knew where he was. I was painfully aware of him. When he was nearby, my body hummed. When he was away, there was this dull ache. With him near, I felt everything.

He was sitting next to Anika, and he said something that made her laugh. I could feel my heart pinch. I looked away.

Tom stood up and made a toast. "To Belly and J-Fish, a really"—he belched—"amazing couple. Really freaking amazing."

I saw Anika give Taylor a look, like *you think this guy is cute?* Taylor shrugged back at her. Everyone lifted their beer cans and wine glasses, and we clinked. Jeremiah pulled me to him and kissed me on the lips, in front of everyone. I pulled away, feeling embarrassed. I saw the look on Conrad's face and wished I hadn't.

Then Steven said, "One more toast, guys." Awkwardly, he stood up. "I've known Jere my whole life. Belly too, unfortunately."

I threw my napkin at him.

"You guys are good together," Steven said, looking at me. Then he looked at Jeremiah. "Treat her right, man. She's a pain in the ass, but she's the only sister I've got."

I could feel myself tear up. I got up and hugged him. "You jerk," I said, wiping my eyes.

As I sat back down next to Jere, he said, "I guess I should say something too. First, thanks for coming, you guys. Josh, Redbird. Taylor and Anika. It means a lot to have you here with us." Jere nudged me, and I stared up at him, waiting for him to mention Conrad. I gave him a pointed look, but he didn't seem to get it. He said, "You say something too, Belly."

"Thanks for coming," I echoed. "And, Conrad, thanks for this amazing meal. Really freaking amazing."

Everyone laughed.

After dinner, I went up to Jeremiah's room and watched him get ready to go out with the boys. The girls were staying behind. I'd told Taylor she could go and get her flirt on with Redbird, but she said she'd rather stay. "He ate his steak with his hands," she'd said, looking sick.

Jere was putting on deodorant, and I was sitting on his unmade bed. "You sure you don't want to come with us?" he asked.

"I'm sure." Suddenly, I said, "Hey, remember that time when you found that dog on the beach? And we named her Rosie until we realized she was a boy, and then we still kept calling her Rosie anyway?"

He looked at me, frowning slightly, remembering. "It wasn't me who found her, it was Conrad."

"No, it wasn't. It was you. And you cried when her owners came and got her."

"No, that was Conrad." His voice was hard all of a sudden.

"I don't think so," I said.

"It definitely was."

"Are you sure?" I asked him.

"I'm positive. Steve and I gave him so much shit for crying."

Had it really been Conrad? I'd been so sure of that memory.

We had Rosie for three glorious days before someone claimed her. Rosie was sweet. She was yellow and she had soft fur and we fought over whose bed she would sleep in at night. We decided to take turns, and my turn was last because I was the youngest, so I never got to keep her in my bed.

What else had I remembered wrong? I was a person who loved to play Remember When in my head. I'd always prided myself on how I remembered every detail. It scared me to think that my memories could be just ever-so-slightly wrong.

chapter *forty-four*

After the boys left, we went up to my room to do nails and practice makeup for the wedding. "I still think you should get your makeup done," Taylor said from my bed. She was doing her toes a pale, chalky pink.

"I don't want to spend any more of Mr. Fisher's money. He's spending enough as it is," I said. "Besides, I hate wearing a lot of makeup. I never look like me."

"They're professionals—they know what they're doing."

"That time you took me to the MAC counter, they made me look like a drag queen," I said.

"That's their aesthetic," Taylor said. "At least let me put false eyelashes on you. I'm wearing them. So is Anika."

I looked at Anika, who was lying on the floor with a cucumber face mask on. "Your eyelashes are already long," I said.

"She's making me," Anika said through gritted teeth, trying not to crack her mask.

"Well, I'm not wearing them," I said. "Jere knows what my real eyelashes look like, and he doesn't care. Besides, they make my eyes itch. Remember, Tay? You put them on me for Halloween, and I took them off as soon as you had your back turned."

"A waste of fifteen dollars," Taylor sniffed. She slid off the bed and sat next to me on the floor. I was trying on the different lipsticks Taylor had brought with her. So far it was between a rosy pink lip gloss and an apricot lipstick.

"Which do you like better?" I asked her. I had the gloss on my top lip and the lipstick on my bottom lip.

"The lipstick," Taylor said. "It'll pop better in pictures."

At first we were just going to have Josh take pictures—he'd taken a couple of photography classes at Finch, and he was the official frat photographer for all their parties. But now that Mr. Fisher and Denise Coletti were involved, we'd hired an actual photographer, someone Denise knew.

"I might still get my hair done," Taylor said.

"Go for it," I told her.

We all changed into our pajamas, and Taylor and Anika presented me with a wedding gift—a lacy white babydoll nightie with matching panties.

"For the wedding night," Taylor said meaningfully.

"Uh, yeah, I got that," I said, holding up the under-wear. I hoped I wasn't blushing too red. "Thanks, guys."

"Do you have any questions for us?" Taylor asked, perching on my bed.

"Taylor! I, like, live in the world. I'm not an idiot."

"I'm just saying . . ." She paused. "You probably won't like it that much the first couple of times. I mean, I'm super tiny, which means I'm really little down there, so it hurt a lot. It might not hurt as bad for you. Tell her, Anika."

Anika rolled her eyes. "It didn't hurt me at all, Iz."

"Well, you probably have a large vagina," Taylor said.

Anika thumped Taylor on the head with a pillow, and we all started giggling and couldn't stop. Then I said, "Wait, exactly how bad did it hurt, Tay? Did it hurt the way a punch in the stomach hurts?"

"Who's ever punched you in the stomach?" Anika asked me.

"I have an older brother," I reminded her.

"It's a different kind of pain," Taylor said.

"Did it hurt worse than period cramps?"

"Yes. But I would say it's more comparable to getting a shot of Novocain in your gums."

"Great, now she's comparing losing your virginity to getting a cavity filled," Anika said, getting up. "Iz, quit listening to her. I promise you it's more fun than going to the dentist. It would be one thing if you were both virgins, but Jeremiah knows what's up. He'll take care of you."

Taylor collapsed into another fit of giggles. "He'll take *care* of her!"

I tried to smile, but my face felt frozen. Jeremiah had been with two other girls. His high school girlfriend, Mara, and now Lacie Barone. So yeah, I was pretty sure he'd know what to do. I just wished he didn't.

We were all lying in my bed, side by side by side. We were just talking with the lights off, and Anika fell asleep first. I'd been going over and over it, whether or not I should confide in Taylor, tell her about Conrad, how mixed up I'd been feeling. I wanted to tell her, but I was also afraid.

"Tay?" I whispered. She was lying next to me, and I was on the edge of the bed because I was going to leave and sleep in Jere's room when the boys came back.

"What?" Her voice was sleepy.

"Something weird happened."

"What?" She was alert now.

"Yesterday, Conrad cut his leg up surfing, and I helped him, and there was this weird moment between us."

"Did you kiss?" she hissed.

"No!" But then I whispered, "But I wanted to. I was—I was tempted to."

"Whoa," she said with a little sigh. "But nothing *happened*, right?"

"Nothing happened. I just feel . . . freaked out because I kind of wanted it to. Just for a second." I let out a big breath. "I'm getting married in a couple of days. I shouldn't be thinking about kissing other boys."

Softly, she said, "Conrad's not other boys. He's your first love. Your first great love."

"You're right!" I said, relieved. I felt lighter already. "It's nostalgia. That's all this is."

Taylor hesitated and then said, "There's something I haven't told you. Conrad went to see your mom."

My breath caught. "When?"

"A couple of weeks ago. He convinced her to come to the bridal shower. She told my mom, and my mom told me. . . ."

I was silent. He did that for me?

"I didn't tell you, because I didn't want it to get you all mixed up again. Because you love Jere, right? You want to marry him?"

"Uh-huh."

"Are you sure? Because it's not too late, you know. You could still call the whole thing off—you don't have to do this this weekend. You could take some more time. . . ."

"I don't need more time," I said.

"Okay."

I rolled over. "Good night, Tay."

"Good night."

It took a while before her breathing turned heavy and regular, and I just lay there next to her, thinking.

Conrad was still looking out for me. Silently, I got out of bed, crossed the room, and felt my way around my bureau until I found it. My glass unicorn.

chapter *forty-five*

When Susannah would drop us off at the mall or the Putt Putt, she would put Conrad in charge every time. She'd say, "Take care of them, Connie. I'm counting on you."

There was this time we split up at the mall, because the boys wanted to go to the arcade and I didn't. I was eight. I said I'd meet them in the food court in one hour. I went straight to the glass-blower shop. The boys never wanted to go in the glass-blower shop, but I loved it. I'd wander from counter to counter. I especially liked looking at the glass unicorns. I wanted to buy one, just a little one, but they were twelve dollars. I only had ten. I couldn't stop looking at the unicorn. I'd pick it up then put it down again then pick it up again. Before I knew it, more than an hour had passed, almost two. I ran back to the food court as fast as I could. I worried the boys had left without me.

When I showed up, Conrad wasn't there. Jeremiah and Steven were sitting in the Taco Bell section counting their arcade tickets. "Where have you been?" Steven said, looking annoyed.

I ignored him. "Where's Conrad?" I asked Jeremiah, panting.

"He went off looking for you," Jeremiah said. To Steven, he said, "Do you want to use our tickets to buy something now or save up a ton for next time?"

"Let's wait," Steven said. "The guy told me they're getting more prizes next week."

When Conrad came back a little while later to find me sitting with Jeremiah and Steven and eating an ice cream cone, he looked so mad. "Where were you?" he yelled. "You were supposed to be back here at three!"

I could feel a lump in my throat, and I knew I was about to cry. "At the glass-blower shop," I whispered, my Moose Tracks ice cream dripping in my hand.

"If something happened to you, my mom would have killed me! I'm the one she left in charge."

"There was this unicorn . . ."

"Forget it. You're not coming anywhere with us anymore."

"No, Conrad! Come on," I cried, brushing my tears away with my sticky hand. "I'm sorry."

He felt bad for yelling, I could tell. He sat down next to me and said, "Don't ever do that again, Belly. From now on, we stick together. Okay?"

"Okay," I said, sniffling.

For my birthday that August, Conrad gave me a glass unicorn. Not the small one, but the big one that cost twenty dollars. Its horn broke off during one of Jeremiah and Steven's wrestling matches, but I kept it. I kept it right on top of my bureau. How could I have thrown such a gift away?

chapter *forty-six*
CONRAD

I volunteered to be the DD. By the time we left the house, everyone was already pretty sloppy from the wine and beer.

We took that kid Tom or Redbird or whatever-his-name-is's car because it was the biggest. It was practically a Hummer. Jere sat in the passenger seat next to me, and the other guys sat in the back.

Tom reached up between us and turned the radio on. He started to rap with the music, off beat and wrong lyrics. Josh joined him, and Steven opened up the sunroof and stuck his head out.

With a sidelong glance at Jere, I said, "These are your friends?"

He laughed and started rapping too.

The bar was packed. Girls everywhere in high heels

and glossy lipstick, with their hair shiny and straight. Right away, Redbird started trying to dance on every girl that walked by. Shot down each and every time.

I went to the bar to get the first round, and Steven followed me. We were waiting to get the bartender's attention when he clapped his hand on my shoulder and said, "So how are you doing with this whole thing?"

"What? The wedding?"

"Yeah."

I turned away from him. "It is what it is."

"Do you think it's a mistake?"

I didn't have to answer him, because the bartender finally looked our way. "Five double shots of tequila and a Newcastle," I said.

Steven said, "You're not going to take a shot with us?"

"I've got to take care of you numskulls, remember?"

We carried the shots back to the table where the other guys were sitting. All five guys pounded them back, and then Redbird got up and started beating his chest and yelling like Tarzan. The guys busted up laughing and started egging him on to go talk to a couple of girls on the dance floor. He and Steven went over to them, and we all sat back and watched. Steven was having better luck than Redbird. He and the red-haired girl started dancing, and Redbird came back to our table, dejected.

"I'll get us another round," I said. I figured it was my duty as best man to get them all wasted.

I came back with five more shots of tequila, and since Steven was still out on the dance floor, Jere downed his shot.

I was nursing my beer when I heard that guy Josh say to Jeremiah, "Dude, you're finally gonna get to close with Belly."

My head snapped up. Jeremiah had his arm slung around Josh while he sang, "It's a nice day for a white wedding."

They hadn't had sex yet?

Then I heard Josh say, "Yo, you're, like, a virgin now too. You haven't gotten any since Lacie in Cabo."

Cabo? Jeremiah had gone to Cabo this past spring break. When he and Belly were a couple.

Jeremiah started to sing, off-key, "Like a virgin, touched for the very first time." Then he stood up. "I gotta piss."

I watched him stumble off to the bathroom, and Josh said, "Fisher's a lucky bastard. Lacie is smokin'."

Tom elbowed him and said, loudly, "Shit, remember how they locked us out of the hotel room?" To me, he said, "This is hilarious, man. Hilarious. They locked us out, and they were so into it, they didn't even hear us knocking. We had to sleep in the friggin' hallway that night."

Laughing, Josh said, "That girl was hella loud, too. Oh, Jere-uhhh-mi-uhhh…"

I saw red. Under the tables, I clenched my fists. I wanted to hit something. First I wanted to hit these two guys, and then I wanted to go find my brother and beat the shit out of him.

I jumped up from the table and made my way across the club, shouldering and pushing my way through the crowd until I got to the bathroom.

I banged on the door.

"Somebody's in here," Jeremiah slurred from inside. Then I heard him retch into the toilet.

I stood there another few seconds, and then I walked away, past our table and out to the parking lot.

chapter *forty-seven*

An hour later, the boys came back, drunk as skunks. I'd seen Jere drunk before, but not like this. He was so wasted, the boys practically had to carry him upstairs. He could barely open his eyes. "Bellllly," he called out. "I'm gonna marry you, girl."

From the bottom of the staircase, I yelled back, "Go to sleep!"

Conrad wasn't with them. I asked Tom, "Where's Conrad? I thought he was your designated driver."

Tom was swaying upstairs. "I dunno. He was with us."

I went out to the car, thinking maybe he'd passed out in the backseat. But he wasn't there. I was starting to get worried, but just then I caught a glimpse of him way down the beach, sitting in the lifeguard stand. I took off my shoes and made my way over to him.

"Come down," I called up. "Don't fall asleep up there."

"Come up," he said. "Just for a minute."

I thought about it for a second. He didn't sound drunk; he sounded fine. I climbed up the side of the chair and sat next to him. "Did you guys have fun?" I asked him.

He didn't answer me.

I watched the water lap along the shore. There was a crescent moon. I said, "I love it here at night."

And then, suddenly, he said, "I have to tell you something."

Something in his voice scared me. "What?"

Looking out at the ocean, he said, "Jere cheated on you when he was in Cabo."

That wasn't what I expected him to say. It was maybe the last thing I expected him to say. His jaw was clenched, and he looked angry. "Tonight at the club, one of his dumbass friends said something." He finally looked at me. "I'm sorry you had to hear it from me. I thought you had a right to know."

I didn't know how to answer him. I finally said, "I already knew about it."

His head jerked back. "You knew?"

"Yeah."

"And you're still marrying him?"

My cheeks felt hot. "He made a mistake," I said softly. "He hates himself for what he did. I forgave him. Everything's fine now. Everything's really great."

Conrad's mouth curled in disgust. "Are you kidding me? He spent the night in a hotel room with some girl and you're defending him?"

"Who are you to judge us? It's none of your business."

"None of my business? That shithead is my brother, and you're . . ." He didn't finish his sentence. Instead he said, "I never thought you'd be the kind of girl who would put up with that from a guy."

"I put up with a lot worse from you." I said it automatically. I said it without thinking.

Eyes flashing, he said, "I never once cheated on you. I never even looked at another girl when we were together."

I slid away from him and started to climb down. "I don't want to talk about this anymore." I didn't know why he was bringing any of this up now. I just wanted it all to go away.

"I thought I knew you," he said.

"I guess you thought wrong," I said. Then I jumped the rest of the way down.

I heard him jump down behind me, and I started to walk away. I could feel tears coming, and I didn't want him to see.

Conrad ran up behind me and grabbed my arm. I tried to turn my head away from him, but he saw, and his face changed. He felt sorry for me. That only made me feel worse. "I'm sorry," he said. "I shouldn't have said anything. You're right. It's not my business."

I spun away from him. I didn't need his pity.

I started walking in the opposite direction of the house. I didn't know where I was going, I just wanted to get away from him.

He called out, "I still love you."

I froze. And then slowly, I turned around to look at him. "Don't say that."

He took a step closer. "I don't know if I'll ever get you out of my system, not completely. I have . . . this feeling. That you'll always be there. Here." Conrad clawed at his heart and then dropped his hand.

"It's only because I'm marrying Jeremiah." I hated the way my voice sounded—shaky and small. Weak. "That's why you're saying all this all of a sudden."

"It's not all of a sudden," he said, his eyes locked on mine. "It's always."

"It doesn't matter. It's too late." I turned away from him.

"Wait," he said. He grabbed my arm again.

"Let go of me," I said, and my voice was so cold, I wouldn't have recognized it. It surprised him, too.

He flinched, and his hand dropped. "Just tell me one thing. Why get married now?" he said. "Why not just live together?"

I had asked myself the same question. I still hadn't come up with a good answer.

I started to walk away, but he followed me. He wrapped his arms around me, over my shoulders.

"Let go." I struggled, but he held on.

"Wait. Wait."

My heart was racing. What if someone saw us? What if someone heard? "If you don't let go of me, I'm going to scream."

"Hear me out, just for a minute. Please. I'm begging you." He sounded strangled and hoarse.

I let out a breath. In my head I started to count backward. Sixty seconds was all he would get from me. I would let him talk for sixty seconds, and then I would go and not look back. Two years ago, this was all I wanted to hear from him. But it was too late now.

Quietly, he said, "Two years ago, I fucked up. But not in the way you think. That night—do you remember that night? The night we were driving back from school and it was raining so hard, we had to stop at that motel. Do you remember?"

I remembered that night. Of course I did.

"That night, I didn't sleep at all. I stayed up, thinking about what to do. What was the right thing to do? Because I knew I loved you. But I knew I shouldn't. I didn't have the right to love anybody then. After my mom died, I was so pissed off. I had this anger in me all the time. I felt like I was going to erupt any minute."

He drew his breath in. "I didn't have it in me to love you the way you deserved. But I knew who did. Jere. He loved you. If I kept you with me, I was going to hurt you somehow. I knew it. I couldn't have it. So I let you go."

I'd stopped counting by then. I just concentrated on breathing. In and out.

"But this summer . . . God, this summer. Being near you again, talking the way we used to talk. You looking at me the way you used to."

I closed my eyes. It didn't matter what he said now. That was what I told myself.

"I see you again, and everything I planned goes to shit. It's impossible. . . . I love Jere more than anybody. He's my brother, my family. I hate myself for doing this. But when I see you two together, I hate him too." His voice broke. "Don't marry him. Don't be with him. Be with me."

His shoulders shook. He was crying. Hearing him beg like this, seeing him exposed and vulnerable, it felt like my heart was breaking. There were so many things I wanted to say to him. But I couldn't. With Conrad, once I started, I couldn't stop.

I broke away from him roughly. "Conrad—"

He grabbed me. "Just tell me. Do you still feel any-thing for me?"

I pushed him away. "No! Don't you get it? You will never be what Jere is to me. He's my best friend. He loves me no matter what. He doesn't take it away whenever he feels like it. Nobody has ever treated me the way he does. Nobody. Least of all you.

"You and I," I said, and then I stopped. I had to get this

right. I had to make it so that he let me go forever. "You and I were never anything."

His face went slack. I saw the light die out in his eyes. I couldn't look at him anymore.

I started walking again, and this time he didn't follow me. I didn't look back. Couldn't look back. If I saw his face again, I might not be able to leave.

As I walked, I told myself, Hold it, hold it, just a little longer. Only when I was sure he couldn't see me, only when the house was in sight again, that was when I let myself cry. I dropped down in the sand and cried for Conrad and then for me. I cried for what was never going to be.

It's a known fact that in life, you can't have everything. In my heart I knew I loved them both, as much as it is possible to love two people at the same time. Conrad and I were linked, we would always be linked. That wasn't something I could do away with. I knew that now—that love wasn't something you could erase, no matter how hard you tried.

I got up, I brushed the sand from my body, and I went inside the house. I climbed into Jeremiah's bed, next to him. He was passed out, snoring loudly the way he did when he drank too much.

"I love you," I said to his back.

chapter *forty-eight*

Late the next morning, Taylor and Anika went into town to pick up some last-minute things. I stayed behind to clean the bathrooms, since the parents were arriving later that day. The boys were all still asleep, which was a good thing. I didn't know what I would or wouldn't say to Jeremiah. The worry was eating me up inside. Would it be selfish or would it be merciful not to say anything?

I ran into Conrad on my way out of the shower, and I couldn't even look him in the eye. I heard his car leave soon after. I didn't know where he'd gone, but I hoped he'd stay far away from me. It felt too raw, too soon. I found myself wishing that either he or I wasn't there. I couldn't leave—I was the one getting married—but I wished he would. It would make things easier. It was a selfish thought, I knew. It was half Conrad's house, after all.

After I'd made the beds and straightened up the guest bathroom, I went down to the kitchen to make myself a sandwich. I thought I was safe, I thought he was still out. But there he was, eating a sandwich himself.

As soon as he saw me, Conrad put down his sandwich. Roast beef, it looked like. "Can I talk to you for a sec?"

"I'm about to go into town to run some errands," I said, looking somewhere in the vicinity of over his shoulder, anywhere but at him. "Wedding stuff."

I started to walk away, but he followed me out to the porch.

"Listen, I'm sorry about last night."

I didn't say anything.

"Will you do me a favor? Will you just forget everything I said?" He flashed a slight, ironic kind of smile. I wanted to smack the smile off his face. "I was out of my mind last night, drunk off my ass. Being here again, it just brought back a lot of stuff. But it's all ancient history, I know that. Honestly, I can barely remember what I said, but I'm sure that whatever it was, it was out of line. I'm really sorry."

For a moment I felt such rage, I think I forgot how to speak. I found it was hard to catch my breath. I felt like a flopping goldfish, opening and closing my mouth, sucking in pockets of air. I hadn't even slept the night before; instead, I'd agonized over every word he said to me. I felt so stupid. And to think, just for a second, just for a moment, I had wavered. I had pictured it, what it would be like, if I was marrying *him* and not Jeremiah. I hated him for that.

"You weren't drunk," I said.

"Yeah, I really was." This time he gave me an apologetic smile.

I ignored it. "You brought up all that the weekend of my wedding, and now you want me to just 'forget it'? You're sick. Don't you get that you can't play with people like that?"

Conrad's smile faded. "Hold on a second. Belly—"

"Don't say my name." I backed away from him. "Don't even think it. In fact, don't ever speak to me again."

Again with the ironic half smile, he said, "Well, that would be kind of hard, considering the fact that you're marrying my brother. Come on, Belly."

I didn't think I could be angrier, and now I was. I was so mad, I practically spat as I said, "I want you to leave. Make up one of your bullshit excuses and just go. Go back to Boston or California. I don't care where. I just want you gone."

His eye twitched. "I'm not leaving."

"Go," I said, shoving him, hard. "Just go."

That's when I saw the first cracks in his armor.

His voice cracking, he said, "What did you expect me to say to you, Belly?"

"Stop saying my name!" I screamed.

"What do you want from me?" he yelled back. "I laid myself fucking bare last night! I put it all out there, and you shut me down. Rightfully so. I get that I shouldn't have said any of that stuff to you. But now here I am trying to find a way to come out of this with just a little fragment of pride so I can look you in the eye when this is all over, and you won't even let me have that. You broke my heart last night, all right? Is that what you want to hear?"

Again, I was at a loss for words. And then I found them. I said, "You really are heartless."

"No, I think you might actually be the heartless one," he said.

He was already walking away as I called out, "What is that supposed to mean?" I walked up right behind and twisted his arm toward me so we were facing each other. "Tell me what you meant by that."

"You know what it means." Conrad jerked away from me. "I still love you. I never stopped. I think you know it. I think you've known it all along."

I pressed my lips together, shaking my head. "That's not true."

"Don't lie."

I shook my head again.

"Have it your way. But I'm not going to pretend for you anymore." With that, he walked down the steps and to his car.

I sank onto the deck. My heart was pounding a million trillion times a minute. I never felt more alive. Anger, sadness, joy. He made me feel it all. No one else had that kind of effect on me. No one.

Suddenly I had this feeling, this absolute certainty, that I was never going to be able to let him go. It was as simple and as hard as that. I had clung to him like a barnacle all these years, and now I couldn't cut away. It was my own fault, really. I couldn't let go of Conrad, and I couldn't walk away from Jeremiah.

Where did that leave me?

I was getting married tomorrow.

If I did it, if I chose Conrad, I could never go back. I would never cup the back of Jere's neck in my hand again, feel its downy softness. Like feathers. Jere would never look at me the way he did now. He looked at me like I was his girl. Which I was, and it felt like it had always been that way. That would all be lost. Over. Some things you can't take back. How was I supposed to say good-bye to all of those things? I couldn't. And what about our families? What would it do to my mother, his father? It would destroy us. I couldn't do that. Especially—especially with everything so fragile now that Susannah was gone. We were still figuring out how to all be together without her, how to still be that summer family.

I couldn't give all that up, just for this. Just for Conrad.

Conrad, who told me he loved me. At last, he said the words.

When Conrad Fisher told a girl he loved her, he meant it. A girl could believe in that. A girl could maybe even bet her whole life on it.

That was what I would be doing. I would be betting my whole life on him. And I couldn't do it. I wouldn't.

chapter *forty-nine*
CONRAD

I was in my car, driving away, my adrenaline pumping hard.

I finally said it. The actual words, out loud, to her face. It was a relief, not carrying it around anymore, and it was a rush, actually telling her. I was in an elated sort of daze, on a high. She loved me. I didn't need to hear her say it out loud, I knew it innately in the way she looked at me just then.

But now what? If she loved me and I loved her, what did we do now, when there were so many people in between us? How could I ever get to her? Did I have it in me to just grab her hand and run away? I believed she'd come with me. If I asked her, I believed she really might come. But where would we even go? Would they forgive us? Jere, Laurel, my dad. And if I really did take her away, where would I be leading her?

Beyond that, the questions and the doubts, in the pit of my stomach, there was all this regret. If I had told her a year ago, a month ago, even a week ago, would things be different now? It was the day before her wedding. In twenty-four hours, she would be married to my brother. Why did I wait so long?

I drove around for a while, into town and then along the water, then I went back to the house. None of the cars were parked in the driveway, so I thought I was home free for a while—but then there was Taylor sitting on the front porch.

"Where is everybody?" I asked her.

"Well hello to you, too." She pushed her sunglasses to the top of her head. "They went sailing."

"Why didn't you go with them?"

"I get seasick." Taylor eyed me. "I need to talk to you."

Warily, I eyed her back. "About what?"

She pointed at the chair next to hers. "Come sit down first."

I sat.

"What did you say to Belly last night?"

Averting my eyes, I said, "What did she tell you?"

"Nothing. But I can tell something's wrong. I know she was crying last night. Her eyes were completely swollen this morning. I would be willing to bet money that she was crying because of you. Again. Nice one, Conrad."

I could feel my chest tighten. "It's none of your business."

Taylor glared at me. "Belly is my oldest friend in the world. Of course it's my business. I'm warning you, Conrad. Leave her alone. You're confusing her. Again."

I started to stand up. "Are we done?"

"No. Sit your ass back down."

I sat down again.

"Do you have any idea how badly you've hurt her, over and over again? You treat her like a toy that you just pick up and play with whenever you feel like it. You're like a little boy. Someone else took what was yours, and you don't like that one bit, so you swoop in and shit all over everything just because you can."

I exhaled. "That's not what I'm trying to do."

She bit her lip. "Belly told me that a part of her will always love you. Are you still trying to tell me you don't care?"

She said that? "I never said I didn't care."

"You're probably the only one who could stop her from going though with this wedding. But you'd better be damn sure you still want her, because if you don't, you're just effing up their lives for no reason." She put her sunglasses back on. "Don't eff up my best friend's life, Conrad. Don't be a selfish bastard like usual. Be the good guy she says you are. Let her go."

Be the good guy she says you are.

I thought I could do it, fight for her till the end, not think about anyone else. Just grab her hand and run. But if I did that, wouldn't I be proving Belly wrong? I wasn't a good guy. I would be a selfish bastard just like Taylor said. But I would have Belly next to me.

chapter *fifty*

That night, we all had dinner at a newish restaurant in town—my parents, Mr. Fisher, all of us kids. I wasn't hungry, but I ordered a lobster roll and I ate every bite of it, because my dad was paying. He insisted. My dad, who wore the same white dress shirt with gray stripes for every "fancy" occasion. He was wearing it that night, sitting next to my mother in her navy shirtdress, and my heart just swelled with love every time I looked at the two of them.

And there was Taylor, pretending to be interested as my dad went on about a lobster's nervous system. Sitting next to Anika, who actually did look interested. Next to Anika was my brother, who was rolling his eyes.

Conrad sat at the far end of the table, with Jere's friends. I made a conscious effort not to look in his direction, to just keep focused on my plate, on Jeremiah next to me. I didn't have to bother, because Conrad wasn't looking at me either. He was talking to the guys, to Steven, to my mother. To everyone but me. This is what you wanted, I reminded myself. You told him to leave you alone. You asked for this.

You can't have it both ways.

"Are you okay?" Jeremiah whispered.

I lifted my head and smiled at him. "Yeah! Of course. I'm just full."

Jeremiah took one of my fries and said, "Save room for dessert."

I nodded. Then he leaned over and kissed me, and I kissed him back. After, I saw his eyes flicker over to the end of the table, so quick I could have imagined it.

chapter *fifty-one*
CONRAD

I felt like I was going out of my mind that night. Sitting there at the table with everyone, cheersing when my dad made a toast, trying not to watch when Jere kissed her in front of all of us.

After dinner was over, Jere and Belly and all their friends went to the boardwalk for ice cream. My dad and Belly's dad went to their hotel. It was just Laur and me back at the house. I was on my way up to my room, but Laurel stopped me and said, "Hey, let's have a beer, Connie. I think we deserve it, don't you?"

We sat at the kitchen table with our beers. She clinked my bottle and said, "To . . . what should we toast to?"

"What else? To the happy couple."

Without looking at me, Laurel said, "How are you doing?"

"Good," I said. "Great."

"Come on. This is your Laura you're talking to. Tell me. How are you feeling?"

"Honestly?" I swigged my beer. "It's pretty much killing me."

Laurel looked back at me, her face tender. "I'm sorry. I know you love her a lot, kid. This must be really hard on you."

I could feel my throat starting to close up. I tried to clear it, unsuccessfully. I could feel it coming up in my chest, behind my eyes. I was going to cry in front of her. It was the way she said it, it was like my mom was right there, knowing without me having to tell her.

Laurel took my hand and clasped it in hers. I tried to pull it away, but she held on tighter. "We'll get through it tomorrow, I promise. It'll be you and me, kid." Squeezing my hand, she said, "God, I miss your mom."

"Me too."

"We really need her right now, don't we?"

I bowed my head and started to cry.

chapter *fifty-two*

I wanted to sleep in Jeremiah's room that night, but when I started to follow him upstairs, Taylor wagged her finger at me. "Uh-uh. It's bad luck."

So I'd gone to my room, and he'd gone to his.

It was too hot. I couldn't sleep. I'd kick the covers off and flip my pillow over to cool off, but it didn't help. I kept looking at the alarm clock. One o'clock, two o'clock.

When I couldn't stand it anymore, I threw off my sheets and put on my bathing suit. I didn't turn on any lights, I just found my way downstairs in the darkness. The moonlight was enough to guide me. Everyone else was asleep.

I made my way outside, down to the pool. I dove in, held my breath for as long as I could. I could already feel my bones start to relax. When I came back up for air, I floated on my back and looked up at the sky. The stars were out. I loved how quiet it was, how still. The only thing I could hear was the ocean lapping against the sand.

Tomorrow I would become Isabel Fisher. It was what I always wanted, my girlhood dream come true a thousand times over. And I'd wrecked it. Or rather, I was about to wreck it. I had to tell the truth. I couldn't marry Jeremiah tomorrow like this, not with a secret that big between us.

I climbed out of the pool, put the towel around me, and went inside the house, up to Jeremiah's room. He was asleep, but I shook him awake. "I need to talk to you," I said. Water from my hair dripped onto his pillow, onto his face.

Groggily, he said, "Isn't it bad luck?"

"I don't care."

Jeremiah sat up, wiping his cheeks. "What's up?"

"Let's talk outside," I said.

We went down to the porch and sat on a lounge chair.

Without preamble, I said, quietly, "Last night Conrad told me he still has feelings for me."

I could feel Jeremiah's body go rigid beside me. I waited for him to speak, and when he didn't, I went on. "Of course I told him I didn't feel the same way. I wanted to tell you sooner, but then I thought it would be a mistake, that I should keep it to myself—"

"I'm going to kill him," he said, and hearing those

words coming out of his mouth shocked me. He stood up.

I tried to pull him back down next to me, but he resisted. I pleaded, "Jere, no. Don't. Please just sit here and talk to me."

"Why are you protecting him?"

"I'm—I'm not. I'm not."

He looked down at me. "Are you marrying me to erase him?"

"No," I said, and it came out more like a gasp. "No."

"The thing is, Bells, I don't believe you," Jeremiah said, and his voice was strangely flat. "I see the way you look at him. I don't think you've ever looked at me like that. Not even once."

I jumped up and grabbed at his hands desperately, but he pulled away. I was breathing hard when I said, "That's not true, Jere. It's not true at all. What I feel for him is all memories. That's it. It has nothing to do with us. All that's in the past. Can't we just forget the past and make our own future? Just the two of us?"

Levelly, he said, "Is it the past? I know you saw him over Christmas. I know you guys were together here."

I opened my mouth, but no words came out.

"Say something. Go ahead, try to deny it."

"Nothing happened between us, Jere. I promise you. I didn't even know he was gonna be here. The only reason I didn't tell you was—" What was it? Why didn't I tell him? Why couldn't I think of a reason? "I didn't want you to be upset over nothing."

"If it was nothing, you would have told me about it. Instead you kept it a secret. After all that stuff you said to me about trust, you kept that to yourself. I felt like shit for what I did with Lacie, and you and I weren't even together when it happened."

I felt sick inside. "How long have you known?"

"Does it matter?" he snapped.

"Yes, to me it does."

Jeremiah started to back away from me. "I've known since it happened. Conrad mentioned he saw you, he thought I already knew. So of course I had to play it off like I did. Do you know how stupid I felt?"

"I can imagine," I whispered. "Why didn't you say something?" We were standing only five or six feet away from each other, but it felt like miles. It was his eyes. They were so distant.

"I was waiting for you to tell me. And you never did."

"I'm sorry. I'm so sorry. I should have told you. I was wrong." It was stupid. My heart was beating so fast. "I love you. We're getting married tomorrow. Me and you, right?"

When he didn't answer me, I asked again. "Aren't we?"

"I've got to get out of here," he said at last. "I need to think."

"Can I come with you?"

This time the answer came swiftly, and it was devastating. "No," he said.

He left, and I didn't try to follow him. I just sank onto the steps. I couldn't feel my legs. I couldn't feel my body. Was this happening? Was this real? It didn't feel real.

chapter *fifty-three*

Somewhere outside, a goldfinch was singing. Or maybe it was a song sparrow. My dad had tried to teach me the different kinds of bird songs, but I couldn't quite remember.

The sky was gray. It wasn't raining yet. But any minute now, it was going to pour. It was like any other morning in Cousins Beach. Except it wasn't, because I was getting married.

I was reasonably sure I was getting married. The only thing was, I had no idea where Jeremiah had gone or if he was even coming back.

I was sitting at the vanity mirror in my pink bathrobe, trying to curl my hair. Taylor was at the beauty salon, and she'd tried to persuade me to get mine done there too, but I'd said no. The only time I ever got my hair done, I hated the way it looked. Like a beauty pageant contestant, stiff and high. I didn't look like me. I thought that today of all days, I should look like me.

There was a knock at the door.

"Come in," I said, trying to fix a curl that had already gone limp.

The door opened. It was my mother. She was already dressed. She was wearing a suit jacket and linen pants and was carrying a lemon yellow envelope. I recognized it right away: Susannah's personal stationery. It was so like her. I wished I was worthy of it. It hurt to think that I had let her down like this. What would she say if she knew?

My mother closed the door behind her. "Do you want me to help?" she asked.

I handed her the curling iron. She set down the letter on my dresser. She stood behind me, sectioning my hair off into thirds. "Did Taylor do your makeup? It looks nice."

"Yeah, she did. Thanks. You look really nice too."

"I'm not ready for this," she said.

I looked at her in the mirror, winding my hair around the barrel, her head down. My mother was beautiful to me in that moment.

She put her hands on my shoulders and looked at me in the mirror. "This isn't what I wanted for you. But I'm here. This is your wedding day. My only daughter."

I reached over my shoulder and took her hand. She

squeezed my hand tight, so tight it hurt. I wanted to confide in her, to confess that things were a mess, that I didn't even know where Jeremiah was or if I would be getting married after all. But it had taken her so long to get here, and if I raised one single doubt now, that would be more than enough for her to put an end to it. She would throw me over her shoulder and carry me away from this whole wedding.

So all that came out was, "Thank you, Mommy."

"You're welcome," she said. She looked over toward my window. "Do you think the weather will hold?"

"I don't know. I hope so."

"Well, if worst comes to worst, we'll move the wedding inside. No big shakes." Then she handed me the letter. "Susannah wanted you to have this on your wedding day."

My mother kissed me on the top of my head and walked out of the room.

I picked up the letter, ran my fingers along my name, written in Susannah's smooth cursive. Then I put it back down on the dresser. Not yet.

There was a knock at the door. "Who is it?" I asked.

"Steven."

"Come in."

The door opened, and Steven came in, closing it behind him. He was wearing the white linen shirt and khaki shorts all the groomsmen were wearing. "Hey," he said, sitting down on my bed. "Your hair looks nice."

"Is he back?"

Steven hesitated.

"Just tell me, Steven."

"No. He's not back. Conrad went off to find him. He thinks he knows where Jere went."

I let out a breath. I was relieved, but at the same time—what would Jeremiah do when he saw Conrad? What if it only made things worse?

"He's going to call as soon as he finds him."

I nodded, then picked up the curling iron again. My fingers trembled, and I had to steady my hand so I wouldn't burn my cheek.

"Did you tell Mom anything?" Steven asked.

"No. I haven't told anybody. So far there's nothing to tell." I wound a piece of hair around the barrel. "He'll be here. I know he will." And I mostly believed it.

"Yeah," Steven said. "Yeah, I'm sure you're right. Do you want me to stay with you?"

I shook my head. "I need to get ready."

"You sure?"

"Yeah. Just let me know as soon as you hear something."

Steven stood up. "I will." Then he came over and patted my shoulder awkwardly. "Everything's going to work out, Belly."

"Yup, I know it will. Don't worry about me. Just find Jere."

As soon as he was gone, I set the curling iron down again. My hand was shaking. I would probably burn myself if I didn't give it a rest. My hair was curled enough anyway.

He was coming back. He was coming back. I knew he was.

And then, because there was nothing left to do, I put on my wedding dress.

I was sitting at the window, watching my dad string Christmas lights on the back porch, when Taylor burst into the room.

Her hair was in an updo, and it looked tight around her forehead. She was carrying a brown paper bag and an ice coffee. "Okay, so, I brought lunch, Anika's helping your mom set the tables up, and this weather isn't doing my hair any favors," Taylor announced, all in one breath. "And I don't know how to tell you this, but I'm pretty sure I felt a raindrop on the way inside." Then she said, "Why are you already in your dress? There's still loads of time before the wedding. Take it off. It's going to get all wrinkly."

When I didn't answer her, she asked, "What's wrong?"

"Jeremiah isn't here," I said.

"Well, of course he isn't here, dummy. It's bad luck to see the bride before the ceremony."

"He's not at home. He left last night, and he hasn't come back." My voice was surprisingly calm. "I told him everything."

Her eyes bulged. "What do you mean, everything?"

"The other day, Conrad told me he still has feelings for me. And last night, I told Jeremiah." I let out a breath that was more like a gasp. These past couple of days had felt like weeks. I didn't even know when or how it all happened. How things got so confused. It was jumbling up in my mind, my heart.

"Oh my God," Taylor said, covering her mouth with her hands. She sank down onto the bed. "What are we going to do?"

"Conrad went looking for him." I was looking out the window again. My dad was finished with the porch, and he'd moved on to the bushes. I came away from the window and started unzipping my dress.

Startled, she said, "What are you doing?"

"You said it's going to wrinkle, remember?" I stepped out of the dress, and it slipped to the floor, a silky white puddle. And then I picked it up and put it on a hanger.

Taylor put my robe over my shoulders, and then she turned me around and tied the sash for me like I was a little girl. "It's going to be okay, Belly."

Someone knocked on the door, and both our eyes flew over to it. "It's Steven," my brother said, opening it. He came in and shut the door behind him. "Conrad got him back."

I sank onto the floor and let out a big gust of air. "He's back," I repeated.

Steven said, "He's showering, and then he'll be dressed and ready to go. Go get married, I mean. Not leave again."

Taylor knelt down next to me. Perched on her knees, she grabbed my hand and entwined my fingers with hers. "Your hand is cold," she said, warming it with her other hand. Then she said, "Do you still want to do this? You don't have to do this if you don't want to."

I squeezed my eyes shut. I had been so scared he wasn't going to go come back. Now that he was here, all the fear and panic were rising up to the surface.

Steven sat next to me and Taylor on the floor. He put his arm around me, and he said, "Belly. Take this however you want to take it, okay? I have five words for you. Are you ready?"

I opened my eyes and nodded.

Very solemnly he said, "Go big or go home."

"What the hell does that even mean, Steven?" Taylor snapped.

A laugh escaped from deep down in my chest. "Go big or go home? Go big or go home." I was laughing so hard, tears were running down my cheeks.

Taylor jumped up. "Your makeup!"

She grabbed the box of tissues on the dresser and wiped my face delicately. I was still laughing. "Snap out of it, Conklin," Taylor said, shooting a worried look at my brother. The flower in her hair was askew. She was right: the humidity wasn't doing her hair any favors.

Steven said, "Aw, she's fine. She's just having a laugh. Right, Belly?"

"Go big or go home," I repeated, giggling.

"I think she's hysterical or something. Should I slap her?" Taylor asked my brother.

"No, I'll do it," he said, advancing toward me.

I stopped laughing. I wasn't hysterical. Or maybe I was, a little bit. "I'm fine, you guys! Nobody gets to slap me. Geez." I stood up. "What time is it?"

Steven pulled his cell phone out of his pocket. "It's two o'clock. We still have a couple of hours before people get here."

Taking a deep breath, I said, "Okay. Steven, will you go tell Mom I think we should move the wedding inside? If we push the couches to the side, we can probably fit a couple of the tables in the living room."

"I'll get the other guys on it," he said.

"Thanks, Stevie. And Taylor, will you—"

Hopefully, she asked, "Stay and fix your makeup?"

"No. I was going to ask if you could get out too. I need to think."

Exchanging looks, the two of them shuffled out of my room, and I shut the door behind them.

As soon as I saw him, everything would make sense again. It had to.

chapter *fifty-four*
CONRAD

I woke up that morning to Steven shaking my bed. "Have you seen Jere?" he demanded.

"I was asleep until three seconds ago," I muttered, my eyes still closed. "How could I have seen him?"

Steven stopped shaking the bed and sat down on the edge. "He's gone, man. I can't find him anywhere, and he left his phone. What the hell happened last night?"

I sat up. Belly must have told him. Shit. "I don't know," I said, rubbing my eyes.

"What are we gonna do?"

This was all my fault.

I got out of bed and said, "Go ahead and get dressed. I'll look for him. Don't tell Belly anything."

Looking relieved, he said, "Sounds good. But shouldn't Belly know? We don't have a ton of time before the wedding. I don't want her to get ready and everything if he's not coming."

"If I'm not back in an hour, you can tell her then." I threw off my T-shirt and put on the white linen shirt Jere had made us all buy.

"Where are you gonna go?" Steven asked me. "Maybe I should go with you."

"No, you stay here and take care of her. I'll find him."

"So you know where he is, then?"

"Yeah, I think so," I said. I didn't have a clue where that bastard was. I just knew I had to fix this.

On my way out, Laurel stopped me and said, "Have you seen Jere? I need to give him something."

"He went out to get something for the wedding," I said. "I'm going to meet him now. I'll give it to him."

She handed me an envelope. I recognized the paper right away. It was my mom's stationery. Jere's name was written on the front in her handwriting. Smiling, Laurel said, "You know, I think it might be nicer this way, coming from you. Beck would like that, don't you think?"

I nodded. "Yeah, I think she would." There was no way I was coming back without Jere.

As soon as I was outside, I sprinted to my car and just gunned it out of there.

I went to the boardwalk first, then the skate park we used to hang out at as kids, then the gym, then a diner we'd stop at on the way into town. He'd always liked their strawberry milk shakes. But he wasn't there. I drove around the mall parking lot. No car and no Jere. I couldn't find him anywhere, and my hour was almost up. I was screwed. Steven was going to tell Belly, and then this would be just one more, epic time I messed up her life. What if Jere had left Cousins completely? He could be back in Boston for all I knew.

It would have been great if I had some sudden epiphany, some insight into where he was, seeing as how we were brothers. But all I could do was run down the list, every place we ever went. Where would Jeremiah go if he was upset? He'd go to my mom. But her grave wasn't here, it was in Boston.

In Cousins she was everywhere. Then it came to me—the garden. Maybe Jere had gone to the garden at the shelter. It was worth a shot. I called Steven on the way over. "I think I know where he is. Don't tell Belly anything yet."

"All right. But if I don't hear from you in half an hour, I'm telling her. Either way, I'm kicking his ass for this."

We hung up as I pulled into the women's shelter parking lot. I saw his car right away. I felt a mixture of profound relief and dread. What right did I have to say anything to him? I was the one who was responsible for this mess.

Jere was sitting on a bench by the garden, his head

in his hands. He was still in last night's clothes. His head snapped up when he heard me coming. "I'm warning you, man. Don't come near me right now."

I kept walking. When I was standing right in front of him, I said, "Come back to the house with me."

He glowered at me. "Fuck you."

"You're supposed to be getting married in a couple of hours. We don't have time to do this right now. Just hit me. It'll make you feel better." I tried to pick up his arm, and he shoved me off.

"No, it'll make *you* feel better. You don't deserve to feel better. But after the shady shit you pulled, I should beat the crap out of you."

"Then do it," I said. "And then let's go. Belly's waiting for you. Don't make her wait on her wedding day."

"Shut up!" he yelled, lunging at me. "You don't get to talk to me about her."

"Come on, man. Please. I'm begging you."

"Why? Because you still love her, right?" He didn't wait for me to answer. "What I want to know is, if you still had feelings for her, why did you give me the go-ahead, huh? I did the right thing. I didn't go behind your back. I asked you, straight up. You told me you were over her."

"You weren't exactly asking for my permission when I walked in on you kissing her in your car. Yeah, I still gave you the go-ahead, because I trusted you to take care of her and treat her right. Then you go and cheat on her in

Cabo during spring break. So maybe I should be the one asking if you love her or not." As soon as I got the last word out, Jere's fist was connecting with my face, hard. It was like getting hit with a ten-foot wave—all I could hear was the ringing in my ears. I staggered backward. "Good." I gasped. "Can we get out of here now?"

He punched me again. This time I fell to the ground.

"Shut up!" he yelled. "Don't talk to me about who loves Belly more. I've always loved her. Not you. You treated her like garbage. You left her so many times, man. You're a coward. Even now, you can't admit it to my face."

Breathing hard, I spat out a mouthful of blood and said, "Fine. I love her. I admit it. Sometimes—sometimes I think she's the only girl I could ever be with. But Jere, she picked you. You're the one she wants to marry. Not me." I pulled the envelope out of my pocket, stumbled up, and pushed it at his chest. "Read this. It's for you, from Mom. For your wedding day."

Swallowing, he tore the envelope open. I watched him as he read, hoping, knowing, my mom would have the right words. She always knew what to say to Jeremiah.

Jere started to cry as he read, and I turned my head away.

"I'm going back," he finally said. "But not with you. You're not my brother anymore. You're dead to me. I don't want you at my wedding. I don't want you in my life. I want you gone."

"Jere—"

"I hope you said everything you needed to say to her. Because after this, you're never seeing her again. Or me. It's over. You and I are done." He handed me the letter. "This is yours, not mine."

Then he left.

I sat on the bench and opened the paper up. It said, Dear Conrad.

And then I started to cry too.

chapter *fifty-five*

Outside my window, far down the beach, I could see a group of little kids with plastic pails and shovels, digging for sand crabs.

Jere and I used to do that. There was this one time, I think I was eight, which meant Jeremiah must have been nine. We'd searched for sand crabs all afternoon, and even when Conrad and Steven came looking for him, he didn't leave. They said, "We're going to ride our bikes into town and rent a video game, and if you don't come with us, you can't play tonight."

"You can go if you want," I'd said, feeling wretched because I knew he'd choose to go. Who would choose sandy old sand crabs over a new video game?

He hesitated, and then said, "I don't care." And then he stayed.

I felt guilty but also triumphant, because Jeremiah had chosen me. I was worthy of being chosen over someone else.

We played outside until it got dark. We collected our sand crabs in a plastic cup, and then we set them free. We watched them wriggle back into the sand. They all seemed to know exactly where they were going. Some clear destination in mind. Home.

That night, Conrad and Steven played their new game. Jeremiah watched them. He didn't ask if he could play, and I could see how much he wanted to.

In my memory he would always be golden.

Someone knocked on the door. "Taylor, I need a minute by myself," I said, turning around.

It wasn't Taylor. It was Conrad. He looked worn down, exhausted. His white linen shirt was wrinkled. So were his shorts. When I looked closer, I saw that his eyes were bloodshot, and I could see a bruise forming on his cheek.

I ran over to him. "What happened? Did you guys get into a fight?"

He shook his head.

"You shouldn't be in here," I said, backing away. "Jeremiah's coming up any minute."

"I know, I just need to say something to you."

I moved back to the window, turning my back on him. "You've said plenty. Just go."

I heard him turn the doorknob, and then I heard him close the door again. I thought he'd gone, until I heard him say, "Do you remember infinity?"

Slowly, I turned around. "What about it?"

Tossing something toward me, he said, "Catch."

I reached out and caught it in the air. A silver necklace. I held it up and examined it. The infinity necklace. It didn't shine the way it used to; it looked a bit coppery now. But I recognized it. Of course I recognized it.

"What is this?" I asked.

"You know what it is," he said.

I shrugged. "Nope, sorry."

I could see that he was both hurt and angry. "Okay, then. You don't remember it. I'll remind you. I bought you that necklace for your birthday."

My birthday.

It had to have been for my sixteenth birthday. It was the only year he ever forgot to buy me a birthday present—the last summer we'd all been together at the beach house, when Susannah was still alive. The next year, when Conrad took off and Jeremiah and I went looking for him, I found it in his desk. And I took it, because I knew it was mine. He took it back later. I never knew when he had bought it or why, I just knew it was mine. Hearing him say it now, that it was my birthday present, touched me in the last place I wanted him to touch me. My heart.

I took his hand and put the necklace in his palm. "I'm sorry."

Conrad held the necklace out to me. Softly, he said, "It belongs to you, always has. I was too afraid to give it to you then. Consider it an early birthday gift. Or a belated one. You can do whatever you want with it. I just—can't keep it anymore."

I was nodding. I took the necklace from him.

"I'm sorry for screwing everything up. I hurt you again, and for that I'm sorry. I'm so sorry. I don't want to do that anymore. So . . . I'm not going to stay for the wedding. I'm just going to take off now. I won't see you again, not for a long time. Probably for the best. Being near you like this, it hurts. And Jere"—Conrad cleared his throat and stepped backward, making space between us—"he's the one who needs you."

I bit my lip to keep from crying.

Hoarsely, he said, "I need you to know that no matter what happens, it was worth it to me. Being with you, loving you. It was all worth it." Then he said, "I wish you both the best. Take good care of each other."

I had to fight every instinct in me not to reach out, not to touch the bruise that was blooming on his left cheekbone. Conrad wouldn't want me to. I knew him well enough to know that.

He came up and kissed me on my forehead, and before he stepped away, I closed my eyes and tried hard to memorize this moment. I wanted to remember him exactly as he was right then, how his arms looked brown against his white shirt, the way his hair was cut a little too short in the front. Even the bruise, there because of me.

Then he was gone.

Just for that moment, the thought that I might never see him again . . . it felt worse than death. I wanted to run after him. Tell him anything, everything. Just don't go. Please just never go. Please just always be near me, so I can at least see you.

Because it felt final. I always believed that we would find our way back to each other every time. That no matter what, we would be connected—by our history, by this house. But this time, this last time, it felt final. Like I would never see him again, or that when I did, it would be different, there would be a mountain between us.

I knew it in my bones. That this time was it. I had finally made my choice, and so had he. He let me go. I was relieved, which I expected. What I didn't expect was to feel so much grief.

Bye bye, Birdie.

chapter *fifty-six*

It was Valentine's Day. I was sixteen, and he was eighteen. It fell on a Thursday that year, and Conrad had classes until seven on Thursdays, so I knew we wouldn't be going on a date or anything. We'd talked about hanging out on Saturday, maybe watching a movie, but neither of us mentioned Valentine's Day. He just wasn't a flowers and candy hearts kind of guy. No big deal. I'd never been that kind of girl either, not like Taylor was.

At school the drama club delivered roses during fourth period. People had been buying them all week during lunch. You could have them sent to whoever you wanted. Freshman year, neither of us had boyfriends, and Taylor and I secretly sent each other one. That year, her boyfriend, Davis, sent her a dozen pink ones, and he bought her a red headband she'd been eyeing at the mall. She wore the headband all day.

I was up in my room that night, doing homework, when I got a text from Conrad. It said, LOOK OUT YOUR WINDOW. I'd gone to look, thinking there might be a meteor shower that night. Conrad kept track of that kind of thing.

But what I saw was Conrad, waving at me from a plaid blanket in my front yard. I clapped my hand to my mouth and let out a shriek. I couldn't believe it. Then I jammed my feet into my sneakers, put my puffy coat over my flannel pajamas, and ran down the stairs so fast I almost tripped. I made a running leap off the front porch and into his arms.

"I can't believe you're here!" I couldn't stop hugging him.

"I came right after class. Surprised?"

"So surprised! I didn't think you even knew it was Valentine's Day!"

He laughed. "Come on," he said, leading me by my shoulders over to the blanket. There was a thermos and a box of Twinkies.

"Lie down," Conrad said, stretching out his legs on the blanket. "It's a full moon."

So I lay down next to him and looked up at the inky black sky and at that shining white moon, and I shivered. Not because I was cold, but because I was happy.

He wrapped the edge of the blanket around me. "Too cold?" he asked, looking concerned.

I shook my head.

Conrad unscrewed the thermos and poured liquid into the lid. He passed it to me and said, "It's not that hot anymore, but it might still help."

I got up on my elbows and sipped. It was cocoa. Lukewarm.

"Is it cold?" Conrad asked.

"No, it's good," I said.

Then we both lay down flat on our backs and stared up at the sky together. So many stars. It was freezing cold, but I didn't care. Conrad took my hand, and he used it to point out constellations and connect the dots. He told me the stories behind Orion's belt and Cassiopeia. I didn't have the heart to tell him I already knew; my dad had taught me those constellations when I was a kid. I just loved listening to Conrad talk. He had the same wonder in his voice, the same reverence he always had when he talked about nature and science.

"Wanna go back in?" he asked, sometime later. He warmed my hand with his.

"I'm not going in until we see a shooting star," I answered him.

"We might not," he said.

I wriggled next to him happily. "It's okay if we don't. I just want to try."

Smiling, he said, "Did you know that astronomers call them interplanetary dust?"

"Interplanetary dust," I repeated, liking the feel of the words on my tongue. "Sounds like a band."

Conrad breathed hot air on my hand, and then he put it in his coat pocket. "Yeah, it kinda does."

"Tonight, it's—the sky is like—" I searched for the right word to encapsulate how it made me feel, how beautiful it was. "Lying here and looking up at the stars like this, it makes me feel like I'm lying on a *planet*. It's so wide. So infinite."

"I knew you'd get it," he said.

I smiled. His face was close to mine, and I could feel the heat from his body. If I turned my head, we'd be kissing. I didn't, though. Being close to him was enough.

"Sometimes I think I'll never trust another girl the way I trust you," he said then.

I looked over at him, surprised. He wasn't looking at me, he was still looking up at the sky, still focused.

We never did see a shooting star, but it didn't matter to me one bit. Before the night was over, I said, "This is one of my top moments."

He said, "Mine too."

We didn't know what was ahead of us then. We were just two teenagers, looking up at the sky on a cold February night. So no, he didn't give me flowers or candy. He gave me the moon and the stars. Infinity.

chapter *fifty-seven*

He knocked on the door once. "It's me," he said.

"Come in." I was sitting on the bed. I had changed back into my dress. People would be arriving soon.

Jeremiah opened the door. He was in his linen shirt and khaki shorts. He hadn't shaved yet. But he was dressed, and his face was unmarked, no bruises. I took that as a good sign.

He sat down on the bed next to me. "Isn't it bad luck for us to see each other before the wedding?" he asked.

Relief washed over me. "So there's going to be a wedding, then?"

"Well, I'm all dressed up and so are you." He kissed me on the cheek. "You look great, by the way."

"Where did you go?"

Shifting, he said, "I just needed some time to think.

I'm ready now." Leaning toward me, he kissed me again, this time on the lips.

I drew back. "What's the matter with you?"

"I told you, it's all good. We're getting married, right? You still want to get married?" He said it lightly, but I could hear an edge in his voice I'd never heard before.

"Can't we at least talk about what happened?"

"I don't want to talk about it," Jeremiah snapped. "I don't even want to think about it again."

"Well, I do want to talk about it. I need to. I'm freaked out, Jere. You just left. I didn't even know if you were coming back."

"I'm here, aren't I? I'm always here for you." He tried to kiss me again, and this time I pushed him off.

He rubbed his jawline roughly. Then he stood up and started pacing around the room. "I want all of you. I want every part. But you're still holding back from me."

"What are we talking about here?" I asked, my voice shrill. "Sex?"

"That's part of it. But it's more than that. I don't have your whole heart. Be honest. I'm right, aren't I?"

"No!"

"How do you think it makes me feel, knowing I'm second choice? Knowing it was always supposed to be you two?"

"You're not my second choice! You're first!"

Jeremiah shook his head. "No, I'll never be first. That'll

always be Con." He hit his palm against the wall. "I thought I could do this, but I can't."

"You can't what? You can't marry me?" My mind was spinning like a top, and then I started talking, fast. "Okay, maybe you're right. It's all too crazy right now. We won't get married today. We'll just move in to that apartment. Gary's apartment, the one you wanted. I'm fine with it. We can move second semester. Okay?"

He didn't say anything, and so I said it again, this time more panicked. "Okay, Jere?"

"I can't. Not unless you can look at me right now—look me in the eyes and tell me you don't still love Con."

"Jere, I love *you*."

"That's not what I'm asking. I know you love me. What I'm asking is, do you love him too?"

I wanted to tell him no. I opened my mouth. Why wouldn't the words come out? Why couldn't I say what he needed to hear? It would be so easy to just say it. One word and this would all go away. He wanted to forgive and forget it all. I could see it in his face: all he needed was for me to tell him no. He would still marry me. If I would just say the word. One word.

"Yes."

Jere inhaled sharply. We stared at each other for a long moment, and then he inclined his head.

I stepped toward him and filled the space between us. "I think—I think I'll always love him a little bit. I'll always have him in my heart. But he's not the one I choose. I choose you, Jeremiah."

All my life, I never felt like I had a choice when it came to Conrad. Now I knew it wasn't true. I did have a choice. I chose to walk away, then and now. I chose Jeremiah. I chose the boy who would never walk away from me.

His head was still bowed. I willed him to look at me, to believe me just one more time. Then he lifted his head and said, "That's not enough. I don't just want a part of you. I want all of you."

My eyes filled.

He walked over to my dresser and picked up the letter from Susannah. "You haven't read yours yet."

"I didn't even know if you were coming back!"

He ran his finger along the edges, staring down at it. "I got one too. But it wasn't for me. It was Con's. My mom must have mixed up the envelopes. In the letter she said— she said she only ever got to see him in love once. That was with you." He looked at me then. "I won't be the reason you don't go to him. I won't be your excuse. You've got to see for yourself, or you'll never be able to let him go."

"I already have," I whispered.

Jeremiah shook his head. "No, you haven't. The worst part is, I knew you hadn't and I still asked you to marry me. So I guess I'm partly to blame too, huh?"

"No."

He acted like he didn't hear me. "He will let you down, because that's what he does. That's who he is."

For the rest of my life, I was going to remember those words. Everything Jeremiah said to me that day, our wedding day, I would remember. I would remember the words Jeremiah said and the way he looked at me when he said them. With pity, and with bitterness. I hated myself for being the one who made him bitter, because that was one thing he'd never been.

I reached up and laid my palm on his cheek. He could have pushed my hand away, he could have recoiled at my touch. He didn't. Just that one tiny thing told me what I needed to know—that Jere was still Jere and nothing could ever change that.

"I still love you," he said, and the way he said it, I knew that if I wanted him to, he would still marry me. Even after everything that had happened.

There are moments in every girl's life that are bigger than we know at the time. When you look back, you say, That was one of those life-changing, fork-in-the-road moments and I didn't even see it coming. I had no idea. And then there are the moments that you know are big. That whatever you do next, there will be an impact. Your life could go in one of two directions. Do or die.

This was one of those moments. Big. They didn't get much bigger than this.

It ended up not raining that day. Jeremiah's frat brothers and my actual brother moved the tables and chairs and hurricane vases in for nothing.

Another thing that didn't happen that day: Jeremiah and I didn't get married. It wouldn't have been right. Not for either of us. Sometimes I wondered if we had rushed into getting married because we were both trying to prove something to the other and maybe even to ourselves. But then I think no, we truly did love each other. We truly did have the best of intentions. It, we, just weren't meant to be.

a couple of years later

Dearest Belly,

Right now I am picturing you today, on your
wedding day, looking radiant and lovely, the
prettiest bride there ever was. I picture you about
thirty or so, a woman who's had lots and lots of
adventures and romances. I picture you marrying
a man who is solid and steady and strong, a man
with kind eyes. I am sure your young man is
completely wonderful, even if he doesn't have the
last name Fisher! Ha.

You know that I could not love you more if you
were my own daughter. My Belly, my special girl.
Watching you grow up was one of the great joys of
my life.

My girl who ached and yearned for so many things . . . a kitten you could name Margaret, rainbow roller skates, edible bubble bath! A boy who would kiss you the way Rhett kissed Scarlett. I hope you've found him, darling.

Be happy. Be good to each other.

All of my love always, Susannah

Oh, Susannah. If you could see us now.

You were wrong about a couple of things. I'm not thirty yet. I'm twenty-three, almost twenty-four. After Jeremiah and I broke up, he went back to live in the fraternity house, and I ended up living with Anika after all. Junior year, I studied abroad. I went to Spain, where I did have lots and lots of adventures.

Spain is where I got my first letter from him. Real letters, written by his hand, not e-mails. I didn't write him back, not at first, but they still came, once a month, every month. The first time I saw him again, it was another year, at my college graduation. And I just knew.

My young man is kind and good and strong, just like you said. But he doesn't kiss me like Rhett kissed Scarlett. He kisses me even better. And there's one other thing you were right about. He does have the last name Fisher.

I am wearing the dress my mother and I picked out together—creamy white with lace cap sleeves and a low back. My hair, my hair that we spent an hour pinning up, is falling out of the side bun, and long wet strands of hair are flying around my face as we run for the car in the pouring rain. Balloons are everywhere. My shoes are off, I am barefoot, holding his gray suit jacket over my head. He's got one high-but-not-too-high heel in each hand. He runs ahead of me and opens the car door.

We are just married.

"Are you sure?" he asks me.

"No," I say, getting in. Everyone will be expecting us at the reception hall. We shouldn't keep them waiting. But then again, it's not like they can get started without us. We have to dance the first dance. "Stay," by Maurice Williams and the Zodiacs.

I look out the window, and there is Jere across the lawn. He has his arm around his date, and our eyes meet. He gives me a small wave. I wave back and blow him a kiss. He smiles and turns back to his date.

Conrad opens the car door and slides into the driver's seat. His white shirt is soaked through—I can see his skin. He is shivering. He grabs my hand, locks my fingers into his, and brings it to his lips. "Then let's do it. We're both wet already."

He turns on the ignition, and then we're off. We head for the ocean. We hold hands the whole way. When we get there, it is empty, so we park right on the sand. It's still raining out.

I jump out of the car, hitch up my skirt, and call out, "Ready?"

He rolls up his pant legs, and then he grabs my hand. "Ready."

We run toward the water, tripping in the sand, screaming and laughing like little kids. At the last second he picks me up like he is carrying me across a threshold. "If you dare try and Belly Flop me right now, you're going down with me," I warn, my arms tight around his neck.

"I go wherever you go," he says, launching us into the water.

This is our start. This is the moment it becomes real. We are married. We are infinite. Me and Conrad. The first boy I ever slow danced with, ever cried over. Ever loved.

Turn the page to read the letters
Conrad sent to Belly!

Even now, all these years later, I still read them—Conrad's letter to me when I was studying abroad in Spain. Just every once in while, I pull them all out and sit down and read each one. I know them all by heart, but they still touch me, they still make me feel it all over again. . . . To think that once we were both very young and very far apart, and still finding our way back to each other.

Dear Belly,

Firstly—I don't even know if I should be writing you, if this is allowed. I hope it's allowed. I hope you don't throw this away without even opening the box—because if you do, you'll miss out on something very important. Okay, fine, something that was once very important. To you.

I went over to your house to fix your mom's computer. I went into your room to use the printer and I saw Junior Mint sitting on the bookshelf, looking incredibly pathetic. Remember him? Polar bear, wears glasses and a very stylish scarf? I won him for you at the ring toss? Do you remember how you used to go over to the ring toss and just stare at the polar bears because you wanted one so bad? I probably spent thirty or forty bucks trying to win you that damn bear.

Apparently, he misses you irrespective of that fact that you left him behind. He feels lost without you. I'm serious, that's what he told me. Pathetic, right?

So here he is. Be nice to him, will you?

Conrad

Dear Belly,

This is weird, writing you like this. I think the last time I wrote someone an actual letter was a thank-you card to my grandma. For graduation money, I think. My mom was big on thank-you cards. Oh, by the way, you're welcome for Junior Mint. Laur told me you said thanks. Geez, I was hoping for a thank-you card, but I guess we can't all be as polite as me. Haha.

I should be working on biochem, but I'd rather be talking to you. Laurel says your spanish is getting better. She told me you got lost the other day trying to hunt down a pack of Sour Patch Kids. Sour Patch Kids? Really? You're too grown-up for Junior Mint but not for Sour Patch Kids, huh?

Here's the biggest bag I could find. It's economy sized. The next time I see you, I'm sure you'll be toothless. But happy. I really do hope you're happy.

Conrad

Dear Belly,

So far I've written you two letters and you've written me-well, none. . . . Which is fine. Go ahead and feel free not to write me back. Seriously, don't feel obligated or anything. Even though I've sent you two handwritten letters and two gifts. . . . But seriously, don't write back. I'm serious. It's better this way. I like hearing my news secondhand, from Laur.

Speaking of news, she told me you met some Spanish guy named Benito, and he rides around on a scooter. Really, Belly? A guy named Benito with a scooter? He probably wears leather pants and has a long stringy ponytail. I don't even want to know. Don't tell me. He probably looks like a model and weighs 100 pounds and writes you poetry in Spanish. I don't know what you see in a guy like that, but I don't know what you ever saw in me either, so I guess there's no accounting for taste, right?

Don't forget-don't write back.

Conrad

Dear Belly,

You didn't write back. I thought for sure
you would, you used to be so bad at following
directions, now look at you. . . . Kidding.
Actually I'm not-remember that time you tried
to make box potatoes au gratin and you forgot
to put in the cheese?

Speaking of potatoes au gratin, your mom
made some for Thanksgiving. Laurel invited us
to dinner-my dad and Jere and me. I wasn't
sure if Jere would come, but he did. It
was awkward as hell. But then Steven put on
football and we all just sat and watched and it
was better. During the half, Jere asked if I'd
heard from you, and I said no. He said you'd
been chatting online. He said you cut your hair
shorter, that it makes you look older, more
mature. Then Laur showed us pictures of when
she came to visit you. I want to go there
some day. I heard you aren't hanging out with
that guy Benito anymore. Don't say I didn't
warn you. . . .

By the way, it looks good. Your hair. I don't
think it makes you look older, though. Younger,
if anything.

I might as well be completely honest here,
because who even knows if you're reading this
. . . you might have thrown it out without
opening it, which is your right. But I'll go
ahead and say it-it killed me a little that
Jere's seen you, talked to you.

But I don't think he hates me anymore, which
is the important thing.

Also-in case I haven't made it clear . . . I
think about you a lot. You're pretty much all I
think about. Just so we're clear.

Conrad

Dear Belly,

It's Christmas here. I guess it's Christmas where you are too. I went to the summerhouse for a few days. I kept thinking I'd turn around and see you-stuffing your face with chocolate pretzels, or sliding around the downstairs living room in those god-awful mistletoe pajama pants. I bet my mom bought them for you. She used to buy Jere and me matching Christmas sweaters. There's one horrible family portrait of all of us in red button-downs and reindeer bowties. It's basically a blight on humanity. I hid it in the attic one night and no one's seen it since. If you've been a very good girl this year, maybe I'll show you when you come back. My gift to you.

You know what you could give me? A letter back. Hell, I'll even take a postcard. Or an e-mail. Anything. I just want to hear from you. I want to know how you're doing. By the time you get this, Christmas will have passed-I hope it was a nice one.

Merry Christmas, Belly. Remember last year? Me and you at the summerhouse? Best Christmas of my life.

Love,

Conrad

Dear Conrad,

When I come home next spring, you'd better show me that family portrait. Don't you dare try to get out of it. Oh, and I'll be taking it with me, since it's my gift and all.

And yes. I do remember. Of course I remember. It was my best Christmas, too.

Write back soon,

Belly

For years he kept it in his wallet, soft and creased into a million little folds. He said it kept him going. Kept him hoping. He said he wanted to keep it with him always, but I said we should keep the letters together, where they belong. And he did show me the family photo. It's hanging up in our living room.

Check out the
first chapters of

BURN
FOR
BURN

The first in an incendiary series by
Jenny Han and Siobhan Vivian!

KAT

The clock on my dashboard reads a quarter to two in the morning.

I check my cell phone one last time before chucking it on the backseat. No calls, no texts. Nothing. She's not coming.

Why am I such an idiot?

I should have kept this whole revenge idea to myself. Revenge is supposed to be a solitary thing, I think I heard that somewhere. And I don't know what help I thought Lillia could give me. Her mind can't go to the dark places mine does. She's way too pure for that. And even with whatever's going on between Lillia and Rennie, there's no way Lillia would ever betray her best friend. Actually, knowing Lillia, she's probably holding up her phone so she and Rennie can laugh at me. I got too excited, and now look. I'm going to be done before I even get started.

I'm just gonna go home and work on my early decision app to Oberlin. That's the only thing that will get me through this year—the thought of finally leaving this island for good.

I pull into the ferry parking lot to turn around. The lights are off, the place is cleared out, except for one girl sitting on the curb.

She's got her elbows on her knees, her head in her hands, and her blond hair over one shoulder.

I think about just cruising right past, but something makes me drive over. As I get close, I see that it's the girl from the bathroom.

"Bathroom girl," I say, pulling to a stop.

"My name's Mary," she says. She's chewing on a piece of hair.

"I know," I lie. "I was being funny." I shake my head and start over. "What the hell are you doing out so late?"

Her eyes are wide and frantic. "I have to get out off the island."

"Well, you know it's almost two in the morning, right? There's not going to be another ferry until tomorrow. You missed the last one by, like, three hours."

Mary doesn't say anything. She just stares off toward the piers. You can hardly tell water from the sky. Everything's black. "I think I'm losing my mind."

She says it, and honestly, I believe her. This girl is totally weird. Anyway, I should get down to the Yacht Club. On the miniscule chance that Lillia does show up, I want to be there. "Do you want a ride home or something?" I ask Mary, hoping her answer is no.

"I'm just going to wait. Maybe I'll get up the guts to leave by the morning."

"You're going to sit here all night?"

"It's just a few more hours."

"Where's all your clothes and stuff? Didn't you move back here with anything?"

"I—I'll get it some other time."

This is crazy. Girlfriend is full-on freaking out. "Is this about Reeve?"

Mary lowers her eyes. "It's always been about Reeve."

I'm about to say *Screw him*—but before I can, I see Lillia's silver Audi fly down the road and take the first right into the Yacht Club parking lot. I can't believe it. She showed. She actually showed.

"Get in," I tell Mary, because I can't leave her here alone in the dark.

"I—"

"Hurry up!"

For a second, Mary looks like she's going to argue with me. If she does, I'm out of here. I don't have time to baby her. Lillia might not even get out of the car if she doesn't see me waiting there. Mary hesitates and then she tries to open the door, but it's stuck. "It's locked."

"Let go of the handle," I say, and push the unlock button, but when Mary tries the door, it still won't open. God. "Just hop in, all right!"

"Who are you chasing?" she asks, as I gun it to close the distance between us and Lillia's taillights.

I don't answer her. I just drive.

When we get into the parking lot, Lillia's standing by her car. She's got on a tight hooded sweatshirt, rolled-up pajama shorts with pink and red hearts on them, and flip-flops. Her hair is pulled up into a long ponytail. I think, from the way the moon hits it, that it's wet. She must have just taken her bath. That's a weird thing about Lillia, she always took a bath every night like a kid. I guess some things don't change.

"You're late, Kat," she says. Then she notices Mary with me, and her grip tightens around her car keys.

I hurry out of the car and walk over. I'm excited and relieved Lillia's here but trying to hide it. "She needed a ride," I whisper. "Don't worry. It's cool."

"Kat—" Lillia's giving me a death glare. "I'm not saying anything in front of her!"

I guess Mary can hear us, because she calls out, "It's fine, I can leave." She climbs out of the car.

I hold up my hand for Lillia to give me a second and look back at Mary. I say, "Leave Jar Island tomorrow morning like a scared little baby?"

"I *am* scared. I'm scared out of my mind."

"Of Reeve Tabatsky?" I'm actually pissed now. This girl needs to get a backbone, stat. "I won't let him touch you."

"That's not what I'm worried about." Mary covers her face with her hands. "It's me. I'm the problem. I—I just can't get over it. I can't move on."

"Well, yeah. Because you don't have any closure. The wrong hasn't been made right. Reeve's never gotten what's coming to him."

Lillia shakes her head. "Forget this. I'm out." She clicks her car alarm. The headlights flash on and off like a lighthouse and the doors unlock.

I sidle up to her car cover the door handle with my back so she can't open it. "Don't leave now. You wouldn't have come here if you didn't want to get back at Alex as badly as I want to get Rennie."

Mary slowly approaches us. "What did Alex do to you?"

Lillia hesitates before saying, "He didn't do anything to me. He did something to my sister."

Yeah, Nadia and me both. Not that I'm not scarred or anything. It was just a stupid hookup. I'm over it. Almost.

Mary says, "I'm sorry. I really didn't mean to intrude. I'm going to go. And listen, I promise I won't tell a soul. You can trust me. know more than maybe anyone else on the island how this kind of thing can weigh you down. I just . . . I think it's really cool you both are going to do something about it." She turns around, and starts walking away, back toward the ferry. "Good luck."

Lillia and I look at each other. "Wait!" I call out. Mary turns around. "You want in on this, Mary? Help us . . . and we'll help you take down Reeve." I'm afraid to look at Lillia, because I know she's probably pissed at me right now. But she doesn't say anything. And she doesn't leave, either.

"Why would you do that? You don't even know me."

Mary's staring at me all intense and unblinking, and it throws me off. It takes me a sec to recover. I say, "I don't have to know you to see that you're a total effing mess over whatever happened, like, years ago. And hey, it wouldn't be a free ride. You'd have to get your hands dirty too. But we'd be in it together. The three of us."

Mary looks at me and Lillia for a long moment. So long I start to get antsy. At last she says, "If you help me get Reeve, I'll do whatever it is that you want."

Lillia's doesn't move. Her lips are tight and she's shaking her head. "I don't know."

"Think about it," I tell her. I'm so psyched, I'm practically bouncing on my toes. "Mary's new. No one even knows her, much less suspects her. Plus, with one other person, it'll be easier on both of us." She doesn't look convinced. I throw my hands in the air and say, "You trusted me enough to come here, didn't you? All you need to do is trust me just a little bit more. I've got a good feeling about this."

Biting her lip, Lillia says, "So we're going to get revenge on Rennie, Alex, and now Reeve? You're basically asking me to take down everyone in my group."

She has a point. *Maybe you shouldn't be friends with such jerks* is right there on the tip of my tongue. But I swallow that down and go with diplomacy. "I hear you," I say, nodding. "You've got the most to lose, I get that. So we'll take care of Alex first." Pointing, I say, "Let's go scheme where we're not out in the open. My boat's parked down that way."

I lead the way along the dock with the moon at my back. Mary's next to me, and Lillia a few steps behind.

As we walk, my mind is racing with possibilities. How we can do this, what will be the best way to get started. I've already given it some thought, just in case Lillia did show up tonight. But now that Mary's in the mix too, I've got to make a few quick adjustments. All I know is that I have to seem prepared, for Lillia's sake, to put her mind at ease. That girl is as skittish as a cat in a thunderstorm. One hiccup and she'll bolt.

When Mary asks me if I own one of these boats, pointing at the souped up yachts, I barely hear her. She has to ask me again. Shaking my head, I say, "Not exactly."

Because I work at the club, I get to park my boat for free. But not here with these boats, obviously. Mine's tied up back behind the gas pumps on an older stretch of dock where my boss keeps his junkers, the broken old boats he's bought cheap to strip for parts.

"Be careful," I tell them. "The planks along this dock are half rotted and there're lots of rusted nail heads poking up through the cracks. I think I still have a splinter stuck in my heel. This jerk pulled his yacht in too fast and made a wake so big that it rocked me right off my boat."

"That sucks," Mary says.

I nod. "And he barely even said sorry. Rich people never say sorry."

Lillia rolls her eyes but keeps her mouth shut.

I take the tarp off my Catalina Daysailer, fold it up, and put it in the hatch. It's been a while since I've had it out on the water. Maybe not even since June, which is crazy. But the thing is, Alex and I would always hang out on his boat, because it had a fridge to keep our drinks cool and leather bucket seats that reclined, and an amazing stereo system. For some weird reason, I feel guilty about this. About forgetting who I was before I met him. The things that used to be important to me. Fixing up my boat, hanging out with my real friends. I never thought I'd be one of those girls, those girls that compromise who they are just for a guy. Especially some two-timing wanna-be player like Alex Lind.

"Get in," I say, hooking my floodlight up to the battery. It sends a bright beam out through the night, lighting up the caps of the waves. Perfect.

Lillia takes one step on board and freezes as the boat sways. Then she hops off like a scared bunny rabbit. She backs right into Mary, who looks nervous too. Crossing her arms, Lillia says, "Let's just talk out here."

Laughing, I say, "I've been sailing ever since I was old enough o turn the steering wheel on my own, for God's sakes! I feel safer driving this thing than a car."

"I said I'm not getting on that thing," Lillia snaps. "Either we walk out here, or I leave."

Under my breath, I mutter, "Diva," unhook my floodlight, and then join them on the dock.

The three of us sit in a semicircle.

It hits me right then that I've already won. Because Rennie's best friend is sitting here right now, pledging to help me take her down. And Alex is going to get his, too. I could give two shits about Reeve, but it'll be nice to see him get what's coming to him. It's like a freaking three-for-one deal.

I stretch my legs out in front of me. "We've got to set some ground rules. First off, I think each of us has to participate in all three acts of revenge. That way, no one can back out or blame someone else."

"Obviously," Lillia says.

I shoot her a look, but keep going. "Secondly, we can't be seen talking to each other in public. Ever. Not that we would . . ."

Mary nods. "Yeah. I guess that makes sense."

I continue, "In fact, I even think texting each other is too risky. Lillia, what if Rennie picked up your phone and saw my number?"

Lillia looks down at her lap. "Not that Rennie's like, snooping around on my phone, but yeah, I guess you have a point. We're going to have to be careful."

"We have to be more than careful," I say. "No one can ever know what we're up to. What we do together lives and dies with us." Then I clear my throat, because this is the most important part. "And if we're really going to do this, no one can bail halfway through. If you're in, you need to be in until the very end. Until we all get what we want. If not, well . . . consider yourself fair game. It'll be open season, and we'll have a hell of a lot of ammo to use against you. If you can't swear to that, we might as well just pretend like tonight never happened."

Mary nods first, then Lillia. I smile, because, hot damn, we're really doing this.

There is still more Jenny Han to enjoy!
Don't miss an excerpt from Jenny's latest novel

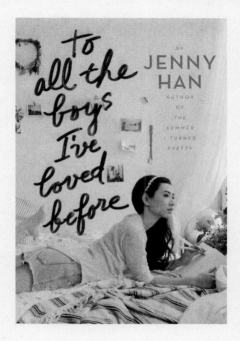

I like to save things. Not important things like whales or people or the environment. Silly things. Porcelain bells, the kind you get at souvenir shops. Cookie cutters you'll never use, because who needs a cookie in the shape of a foot? Ribbons for my hair. Love letters. Of all the things I save, I guess you could say my love letters are my most prized possession.

I keep my letters in a teal hatbox my mom bought me from a vintage store downtown. They aren't love letters that someone else wrote for me; I don't have any of those. These are ones I've written. There's one for every boy I've ever loved—five in all.

When I write, I hold nothing back. I write like he'll never read it. Because he never will. Every secret thought, every careful observation, everything I've saved up inside me, I put it all in the letter. When I'm done, I seal it, I address it, and then I put it in my teal hatbox.

They're not love letters in the strictest sense of the word. My letters are for when I don't want to be in love anymore. They're for good-bye. Because after I write my letter, I'm no longer consumed by my all-consuming love. I can eat my cereal and not wonder if he likes bananas over his Cheerios too; I can sing along to love songs and not be singing them to him. If love is like a possession, maybe my letters are like my exorcisms. My letters set me free. Or at least they're supposed to.

JOSH IS MARGOT'S BOYFRIEND, BUT I GUESS
you could say my whole family is a little in love with him.
It's hard to say who most of all. Before he was Margot's boyfriend, he was just Josh. He was always there. I say always, but
I guess that's not true. He moved next door five years ago
but it feels like always.

My dad loves Josh because he's a boy and my dad is surrounded by girls. I mean it: all day long he is surrounded
by females. My dad is an ob-gyn, and he also happens to be
the father of three daughters, so it's like girls, girls, girls all
day. He also likes Josh because Josh likes comics and he'll go
fishing with him. My dad tried to take us fishing once, and
I cried when my shoes got mud on them, and Margot cried
when her book got wet, and Kitty cried because Kitty was
still practically a baby.

Kitty loves Josh because he'll play cards with her and not
get bored. Or at least pretend to not get bored. They make
deals with each other—if I win this next hand, you have
to make me a toasted crunchy-peanut-butter-sandwich, no
crusts. That's Kitty. Inevitably there won't be crunchy peanut
butter and Josh will say too bad, pick something else. But
then Kitty will wear him down and he'll run out and buy
some, because that's Josh.

If I had to say why Margot loves him, I think maybe I would say it's because we all do.

We are in the living room, Kitty is pasting pictures of dogs to a giant piece of cardboard. There's paper and scraps all around her. Humming to herself, she says, "When Daddy asks me what I want for Christmas, I am just going to say, 'Pick any one of these breeds and we'll be good.'"

Margot and Josh are on the couch; I'm lying on the floor, watching TV. Josh popped a big bowl of popcorn, and I devote myself to it, handfuls and handfuls of it.

A commercial comes on for perfume: a girl is running around the streets of Paris in an orchid-colored halter dress that is thin as tissue paper. What I wouldn't give to be that girl in that tissue-paper dress running around Paris in springtime! I sit up so suddenly I choke on a kernel of popcorn. Between coughs I say, "Margot, let's meet in Paris for my spring break!" I'm already picturing myself twirling with a pistachio macaron in one hand and a raspberry one in the other.

Margot's eyes light up. "Do you think Daddy will let you?"

"Sure, it's culture. He'll have to let me." But it's true that I've never flown by myself before. And also I've never even left the country before. Would Margot meet me at the airport, or would I have to find my own way to the hostel?

Josh must see the sudden worry on my face because he says, "Don't worry. Your dad will definitely let you go if I'm with you."

I brighten. "Yeah! We can stay at hostels and just eat pastries and cheese for all our meals."

"We can go to Jim Morrison's grave!" Josh throws in.

"We can go to a *parfumerie* and get our personal scents done!" I cheer, and Josh snorts.

"Um, I'm pretty sure 'getting our scents done' at a *parfumerie* would cost the same as a week's stay at the hostel," he says. He nudges Margot. "Your sister suffers from delusions of grandeur."

"She is the fanciest of the three of us," Margot agrees.

"What about me?" Kitty whimpers.

"You?" I scoff. "You're the *least* fancy Song girl. I have to beg you to wash your feet at night, much less take a shower."

Kitty's face gets pinched and red. "I wasn't talking about that, you dodo bird. I was *talking* about Paris."

Airily, I wave her off. "You're too little to stay at a hostel."

She crawls over to Margot and climbs in her lap, even though she's nine and nine is too big to sit in people's laps. "Margot, you'll let me go, won't you?"

"Maybe it could be a family vacation," Margot says, kissing her cheek. "You and Lara Jean and Daddy could all come."

I frown. That's not at all the Paris trip I was imagining. Over Kitty's head Josh mouths to me, *We'll talk later,* and I give him a discreet thumbs-up.

It's later that night; Josh is long gone. Kitty and our dad are asleep. We are in the kitchen. Margot is at the table on her computer; I am sitting next to her, rolling cookie dough into balls and dropping them in cinnamon and sugar. Snickerdoodles to get back in Kitty's good graces. Earlier, when I went in to say good night, Kitty rolled over and wouldn't speak to me because she's still convinced I'm going to try to cut her out of the Paris trip. My plan is to put the snickerdoodles on a plate right next to her pillow so she wakes up to the smell of fresh-baked cookies.

Margot's being extra quiet, and then, out of nowhere, she looks up from her computer and says, "I broke up with Josh tonight. After dinner."

My cookie-dough ball falls out of my fingers and into the sugar bowl.

"I mean, it was time," she says. Her eyes aren't red-rimmed; she hasn't been crying, I don't think. Her voice is calm and even. Anyone looking at her would think she was fine. Because Margot is always fine, even when she's not.

"I don't see why you had to break up," I say. "Just 'cause you're going to college doesn't mean you have to break up."

"Lara Jean, I'm going to Scotland, not UVA. Saint Andrews is nearly four thousand miles away." She pushes up her glasses. "What would be the point?"

I can't even believe she would say that. "The point is, it's Josh. Josh who loves you more than any boy has ever loved a girl!"

Margot rolls her eyes at this. She thinks I'm being dramatic, but I'm not. It's true—that's how much Josh loves Margot. He would never so much as look at another girl.

Suddenly she says, "Do you know what Mommy told me once?"

"What?" For a moment I forget all about Josh. Because

no matter what I am doing in life, if Margot and I are in the middle of an argument, if I am about to get hit by a car, I will always stop and listen to a story about Mommy. Any detail, any remembrance that Margot has, I want to have it too. I'm better off than Kitty, though. Kitty doesn't have one memory of Mommy that we haven't given her. We've told her so many stories so many times that they're hers now. "Remember that time . . . ," she'll say. And then she'll tell the story like she was there and not just a little baby.

"She told me to try not to go to college with a boyfriend. She said she didn't want me to be the girl crying on the phone with her boyfriend and saying no to things instead of yes."

Scotland is Margot's yes, I guess. Absently, I scoop up a mound of cookie dough and pop it in my mouth.

"You shouldn't eat raw cookie dough," Margot says.

I ignore her. "Josh would never hold you back from anything. He's not like that. Remember how when you decided to run for student-body president, he was your campaign manager? He's your biggest fan!"

At this, the corners of Margot's mouth turn down, and I get up and fling my arms around her neck. She leans her head back and smiles up at me. "I'm okay," she says, but she isn't, I know she isn't.

"It's not too late, you know. You can go over there right now and tell him you changed your mind."

Margot shakes her head. "It's done, Lara Jean." I release her and she closes her laptop. "When will the first batch be ready? I'm hungry."

I look at the magnetic egg timer on the fridge. "Four more minutes." I sit back down and say, "I don't care what you say, Margot. You guys aren't done. You love him too much."

She shakes her head. "Lara Jean," she begins, in her patient Margot voice, like I am a child and she is a wise old woman of forty-two.

I wave a spoonful of cookie dough under Margot's nose, and she hesitates and then opens her mouth. I feed it to her like a baby. "Wait and see, you and Josh will be back together in a day, maybe two." But even as I'm saying it, I know it's not true. Margot's not the kind of girl to break up and get back together on a whim; once she's decided something, that's it. There's no waffling, no regrets. It's like she said: when she's done, she's just done.

I wish (and this is a thought I've had many, many times, too many times to count) I was more like Margot. Because sometimes it feels like I'll never be done.

Later, after I've washed the dishes and plated the cookies and set them on Kitty's pillow, I go to my room. I don't turn the light on. I go to my window. Josh's light is still on.

THE NEXT MORNING, MARGOT IS MAKING coffee and I am pouring cereal in bowls, and I say the thing I've been thinking all morning. "Just so you know, Daddy and Kitty are going to be really upset." When Kitty and I were brushing our teeth just now, I was tempted to go ahead and spill the beans, but Kitty was still mad at me from yesterday, so I kept quiet. She didn't even acknowledge my cookies, though I know she ate them because all that was left on the plate were crumbs.

Margot lets out a heavy sigh. "So I'm supposed to stay with Josh because of you and Daddy and Kitty?"

"No, I'm just telling you."

"It's not like he would come over here that much once I was gone, anyway."

I frown. This didn't occur to me, that Josh would stop coming over because Margot was gone. He was coming over long before they were ever a couple, so I don't see why he should stop. "He might," I say. "He really loves Kitty."

She pushes the start button on the coffee machine. I'm watching her super carefully because Margot's always been the one to make the coffee and I never have, and now that she's leaving (only six more days), I'd better know how. With her back to me she says, "Maybe I won't even mention it to them."

"Um, I think they'll figure it out when he's not at the airport, Gogo." Gogo is my nickname for Margot. As in go-go boots. "How many cups of water did you put in there? And how many spoons of coffee beans?"

"I'll write it all down for you," Margot assures me. "In the notebook."

We keep a house notebook by the fridge. Margot's idea, of course. It has all the important numbers and Daddy's schedule and Kitty's carpool. "Make sure you put in the number for the new dry cleaners," I say.

"Already done." Margot slices a banana for her cereal: each slice is perfectly thin. "And also, Josh wouldn't have come to the airport with us anyway. You know how I feel about sad good-byes." Margot makes a face, like *Ugh, emotions.*

I do know.

When Margot decided to go to college in Scotland, it felt like a betrayal. Even though I knew it was coming, because of course she was going to go to college somewhere far away. And of course she was going to go to college in Scotland and study anthropology, because she is Margot, the girl with the maps and the travel books and the plans. Of course she would leave us one day.

I'm still mad at her, just a little. Just a teeny-tiny bit. Obviously I know it's not her fault. But she's going so far away, and we always said we'd be the Song girls forever. Margot first, me in the middle, and my sister Kitty last. On her birth certificate she is Katherine; to us she is Kitty.

Occasionally we call her Kitten, because that's what I called her when she was born: she looked like a scrawny, hairless kitten.

We are the three Song girls. There used to be four. My mom, Eve Song. Evie to my dad, Mommy to us, Eve to everyone else. Song is, was, my mom's last name. Our last name is Covey—Covey like lovey, not like cove. But the reason we are the Song girls and not the Covey girls is my mom used to say that she was a Song girl for life, and Margot said then we should be too. We all have Song for our middle name, and we look more Song than Covey anyway, more Korean than white. At least Margot and I do; Kitty looks most like Daddy: her hair is light brown like his. People say I look the most like Mommy, but I think Margot does, with her high cheekbones and dark eyes. It's been almost six years now, and sometimes it feels like just yesterday she was here, and sometimes it feels like she never was, only in dreams.

She'd mopped the floors that morning; they were shiny and everything smelled like lemons and clean house. The phone was ringing in the kitchen, she came running in to answer it, and she slipped. She hit her head on the floor, and she was unconscious, but then she woke up and she was fine. That was her lucid interval. That's what they call it. A little while later she said she had a headache, she went to lie down on the couch, and then she didn't wake up.

Margot was the one who found her. She was twelve. She took care of everything: she called 911; she called Daddy; she told me to watch over Kitty, who was only three. I turned on the TV for Kitty in the playroom and I sat with her. That's all I did. I don't know what I would have done if Margot hadn't been there. Even though Margot is only two years older than me, I look up to her more than anybody.

When other adults find out that my dad is a single father of three girls, they shake their heads in admiration, like *How does he do it? How does he ever manage that all by himself?* The answer is Margot. She's been an organizer from the start, everything labeled and scheduled and arranged in neat, even rows.

Margot is a good girl, and I guess Kitty and I have followed her lead. I've never cheated or gotten drunk or smoked a cigarette or even had a boyfriend. We tease Daddy and say how lucky he is that we're all so good, but the truth is, we're the lucky ones. He's a really good dad. And he tries hard. He doesn't always understand us, but he tries, and that's the important thing. We three Song girls have an unspoken pact: to make life as easy as possible for Daddy. But then again, maybe it's not so unspoken, because how many times have I heard Margot say, "Shh, be quiet, Daddy's taking a nap before he has to go back to the hospital," or "Don't bother Daddy with that; do it yourself"?

I've asked Margot what she thinks it would have been like if Mommy hadn't died. Like would we spend more time with our Korean side of the family and not just on Thanksgiving and New Year's Day? Or—

Margot doesn't see the point in wondering. This is our life; there's no use in asking what if. No one could ever give you the answers. I try, I really do, but it's hard for me to accept this way of thinking. I'm always wondering about the what-ifs, about the road not taken.

Daddy and Kitty come downstairs at the same time. Margot pours Daddy a cup of coffee, black, and I pour milk in Kitty's cereal bowl. I push it in front of her, and she turns her head away from me and gets a yogurt out of the fridge. She takes it into the living room to eat in front of the TV. So she's still mad.

"I'm going to go to Costco later today, so you girls make a list for whatever you need," Daddy asks, taking a big sip of coffee. "I think I'll pick up some New York strips for dinner. We can grill out. Should I get one for Josh, too?"

My head whips in Margot's direction. She opens her mouth and closes it. Then she says, "No, just get enough for the four of us, Daddy."

I give her a reproving look, and she ignores me. I've never known Margot to chicken out before, but I suppose in matters of the heart, there's no predicting how a person will or won't behave.

SO NOW IT'S THE LAST DAYS OF SUMMER and our last days with Margot. Maybe it's not altogether such a bad thing that she broke up with Josh; this way we have more time with just us sisters. I'm sure she must have thought of that. I'm sure it was part of the plan.

We're driving out of our neighborhood when we see Josh run past. He joined track last year, so now he's always running. Kitty yells his name, but the windows are up, and it's no use anyway—he pretends not to hear. "Turn around," Kitty urges Margot. "Maybe he wants to come with us."

"This is a Song-girls-only day," I tell her.

We spend the rest of the morning at Target, picking up last minute things like Honey Nut Chex mix for the flight and deodorant and hair ties. We let Kitty push the cart so she can do that thing where she gets a running start and then rides the cart like she's pushing a chariot. Margot only lets her do it a couple of times before she makes her stop, though, so as not to annoy other customers.

Next we go back home and make chicken salad with green grapes for lunch and then it's nearly time for Kitty's swim meet. We pack a picnic dinner of ham-and-cheese sandwiches and fruit salad and bring Margot's laptop to watch movies on, because swim meets can go long into the night. We make a sign, too, that says *Go Kitty Go!* I draw a dog on it. Daddy ends up missing the swim meet because he is delivering a baby, and as far as excuses go, it's a pretty good one. (It was a girl, and they named her Patricia Rose after her two grandmothers. Daddy always finds out the first and middle name for me. It's the first thing I ask when he gets home from a delivery.)

Kitty's so excited about winning two first-place ribbons and one second place that she forgets to ask where Josh is until we're in the car driving back home. She's in the back-seat and she's got her towel wrapped around her head like a turban and her ribbons dangling from her ears like earrings. She leans forward and says, "Hey! Why didn't Josh come to my meet?"

I can see Margot hesitate, so I answer before she can. Maybe the only thing I'm better at than Margot is lying. "He had to work at the bookstore tonight. He really wanted to make it, though." Margot reaches across the console and gives my hand a grateful squeeze.

Sticking out her lower lip, Kitty says, "That was the last regular meet! He promised he'd come watch me swim."

"It was a last-minute thing," I say. "He couldn't get out of working the shift because one of his coworkers had an emergency."

Kitty nods begrudgingly. Little as she is, she understands emergency shifts.

"Let's get frozen custards," Margot says suddenly.

Kitty lights up, and Josh and his imaginary emergency

shift is forgotten. "Yeah! I want a waffle cone! Can I get a waffle cone with two scoops? I want mint chip and peanut brittle. No, rainbow sherbet and double fudge. No, wait—"

I twist around in my seat. "You can't finish two scoops and a waffle cone," I tell her. "Maybe you could finish two scoops in a cup, but not in a cone."

"Yes, I can. Tonight I can. I'm *starving*."

"Fine, but you better finish the whole thing." I shake my finger at her and say it like a threat, which makes her roll her eyes and giggle. As for me, I'll get what I always get—the cherry chocolate-chunk custard in a sugar cone.

Margot pulls into the drive-thru, and as we wait our turn, I say, "I bet they don't have frozen custard in Scotland."

"Probably not," she says.

"You won't have another one of these until Thanksgiving," I say.

Margot looks straight ahead. "Christmas," she says, correcting me. "Thanksgiving's too short to fly all that way, remember?"

"Thanksgiving's gonna suck." Kitty pouts.

I'm silent. We've never had a Thanksgiving without Margot. She always does the turkey and the broccoli casserole and the creamed onions. I do the pies (pumpkin and pecan) and the mashed potatoes. Kitty is the taste tester and the table setter. I don't know how to roast a turkey. And both of our grandmothers will be there, and Nana, Daddy's mother, likes Margot best of all of us. She says Kitty drains her and I'm too dreamy-eyed.

All of a sudden I feel panicky and it's hard to breathe and I couldn't care less about cherry chocolate-chunk custard. I can't picture Thanksgiving without Margot. I can't even picture next Monday without her. I know most sisters don't get along, but I'm closer to Margot than I am to anybody in the world. How can we be the Song girls without Margot?

MY OLDEST FRIEND CHRIS SMOKES, SHE hooks up with boys she doesn't know hardly at all, and she's been suspended twice. One time she had to go before the court for truancy. I never knew what truancy was before I met Chris. FYI, it's when you skip so much school you're in trouble with the law.

I'm pretty sure that if Chris and I met each other now, we wouldn't be friends. We're as different as different can be. But it wasn't always this way. In sixth grade Chris liked stationery and sleepovers and staying up all night watching John Hughes movies, just like me. But by eighth grade she was sneaking out after my dad fell asleep to meet boys she met at the mall. They'd drop her back off before it got light outside. I'd stay up until she came back, terrified she wouldn't make it home before my dad woke up. She always made it back in time though.

Chris isn't the kind of friend you call every night or have lunch with every day. She is like a street cat, she comes and goes as she pleases. She can't be tied down to a place or a person. Sometimes I won't see Chris for days and then in the middle of the night there will be a knock at my bedroom window and it'll be Chris, crouched in the magnolia tree. I keep my window unlocked for her in case. Chris and Margot can't stand each other. Chris thinks Margot is uptight, and Margot thinks Chris is bipolar. She thinks Chris uses me; Chris thinks Margot controls me. I think maybe they're both a little bit right. But the important thing, the real thing, is Chris and I understand each other, which I think counts for a lot more than people realize.

Chris calls me on the way over to our house; she says her mom's being a beotch and she's coming over for a couple hours and do we have any food?

Chris and I are sharing a bowl of leftover gnocchi in the living room when Margot comes home from dropping Kitty off at her swim team's end-of-season barbecue. "Oh, hey," she says. Then she spots Chris's glass of Diet Coke on the coffee table, sans coaster. "Can you please use a coaster?"

As soon as Margot's up the stairs, Chris says, "Gawd! Why is your sister such a beotch?"

I slide a coaster under her glass. "You think everyone's a beotch today."

"That's because everyone is." Chris rolls her eyes toward the ceiling. Loudly, she says, "She needs to pull that stick out of her ass."

From her room Margot yells, "I heard that!"

"I meant for you to!" Chris yells back, scraping up the last piece of gnocchi for herself.

I sigh. "She's leaving so soon."

Snickering, Chris says, "So is Joshy, like, going to light a candle for her every night until she comes back home?"

I hesitate. While I'm not sure if it's still supposed to be a secret, I *am* sure that Margot wouldn't want Chris knowing any of her personal business. All I say is, "I'm not sure."

"Wait a minute. Did she dump him?" Chris demands.

Reluctantly I nod. "Don't say anything to her, though," I warn. "She's still really sad about it."

"Margot? Sad?" Chris picks at her nails. "Margot doesn't have normal human emotions like the rest of us."

"You just don't know her," I say. "Besides, we can't all be like you."

She grins a toothy grin. She has sharp incisors, which make her look always a little bit hungry. "True."

Chris is pure emotion. She screams at the drop of a hat. She says sometimes you have to scream out emotions; if you don't, they'll fester. The other day she screamed at a lady at the grocery store for accidentally stepping on her toes. I don't think she's in any danger of her emotions festering.

"I just can't believe that in a few days she'll be gone," I say, feeling sniffly all of a sudden.

"She's not *dying*, Lara Jean. There's nothing to get all boo-hoo about." Chris pulls at a loose string on her red shorts. They're so short that when she's sitting, you can see her underwear. Which are red to match her shorts. "In fact, I think this is good for you. It's about time you did your own thing and stopped just listening to whatever Queen Margot says. This is your junior year, beotch. This is when it's supposed to get good. French some guys, live a little, you know?"

"I live plenty," I say.

"Yeah, at the nursing home." Chris snickers and I glare at her.

Margot started volunteering at the Belleview Retirement Community when she got her driver's license; it was her job to help host cocktail hour for the residents. I'd help sometimes. We'd set out peanuts and pour drinks and sometimes Margot would play the piano, but usually Stormy hogged that. Stormy is the Belleview diva. She rules the roost. I like listening to her stories. And Miss Mary, she might not be so good at conversation due to her dementia, but she taught me how to knit.

They have a new volunteer there now, but I know that at Belleview it really is the more the merrier, because most of the residents get so few visitors. I should go back soon; I miss going there. And I for sure don't appreciate Chris making fun of it.

"Those people at Belleview have lived more life than everyone we know combined," I tell her. "There's this one lady, Stormy, she was a USO girl! She used to get a hundred letters a day from soldiers who were in love with her. And there was this one veteran who lost his leg—he sent her a diamond ring!"

Chris looks interested all of a sudden. "Did she keep it?"

"She did," I admit. I think it was wrong of her to keep the ring since she had no intention of marrying him, but she showed it to me, and it was beautiful. It was a pink diamond, very rare. I bet it's worth so much money now.

"I guess Stormy sounds kind of like a badass," Chris says begrudgingly.

"Maybe you could come with me to Belleview sometime," I suggest. "We could go to their cocktail hour. Mr. Perelli loves to dance with new girls. He'll teach you how to fox-trot."

Chris makes a horrible face like I suggested we go hang out at the town dump. "No, thanks. How about I take *you* dancing?" She nudges her chin toward upstairs. "Now that your sister's leaving, we can have some real fun. You know I always have fun."

It's true, Chris does always have fun. Sometimes a little too much fun, but fun nonetheless.

THE NIGHT BEFORE MARGOT LEAVES, ALL three of us are in her room helping pack up the last little things. Kitty is organizing Margot's bath stuff, packing it nice and neat in the clear shower caddy. Margot is trying to decide which coat to bring.

"Should I bring my peacoat and my puffy coat or just my peacoat?" she asks me.

"Just the peacoat," I say. "You can dress that up or down." I'm lying on her bed directing the packing process. "Kitty, make sure the lotion cap is on tight."

"It's brand-new—course it's on tight!" Kitty growls, but she double-checks.

"It gets cold in Scotland sooner than it does here," Margot said, folding the coat and setting it on top of her suitcase. "I think I'll just bring both."

"I don't know why you asked if you already knew what you were going to do," I say. "Also, I thought you said you were coming home for Christmas. You're still coming home for Christmas, right?"

"Yes, if you'll stop being a brat," Margot says.

Honestly, Margot isn't even packing that much. She doesn't need a lot. If it was me, I'd have packed up my whole room, but not Margot. Her room looks the same, almost.

Margot sits down next to me, and Kitty climbs up and sits at the foot of the bed. "Everything's changing," I say, sighing.

Margot makes a face and puts her arm around me. "Nothing's changing, not really. We're the Song girls forever, remember?"

Our father stands in the doorway. He knocks, even though the door is open and we can clearly see it is him. "I'm going to start packing up the car now," he announces. We watch from the bed as he lugs one of the suitcases downstairs, and then he comes up for the other one. Drily he says, "Oh no, don't get up. Don't trouble yourselves."

"Don't worry, we won't," we sing out.

For the past week our father has been in spring-cleaning mode, even though it isn't spring. He's getting rid of everything—the bread machine we never used, CDs, old blankets, our mother's old typewriter. It's all going to Goodwill. A psychiatrist or someone could probably connect it to Margot's leaving for college, but I can't explain the exact significance of it. Whatever it is, it's annoying. I had to shoo him away from my glass-unicorn collection twice.

I lay down my head in Margot's lap. "So you really are coming home for Christmas, right?"

"Right."

"I wish I could come with you." Kitty pouts. "You're nicer than Lara Jean."

I give her a pinch.

"See?" she crows.

"Lara Jean will be nice," Margot says, "as long as you

behave. And you both have to take care of Daddy. Make sure he doesn't work too many Saturdays. Make sure he takes the car in for inspection next month. And make sure you buy coffee filters—you're always forgetting to buy coffee filters."

"Yes, drill sergeant," Kitty and I chorus. I search Margot's face for sadness or fear or worry, for some sign that she is scared to go so far away, that she will miss us as much as we will miss her. I don't see it, though.

The three of us sleep in Margot's room that night.

Kitty falls asleep first, as always. I lie in the dark beside her with my eyes open. I can't sleep. The thought that tomorrow night Margot won't be in this room—it makes me so sad I can hardly bear it. I hate change more than almost anything.

In the dark next to me Margot asks, "Lara Jean . . . do you think you've ever been in love before? Real love?"

She catches me off guard; I don't have an answer ready for her. I'm trying to think of one, but she's already talking again.

Wistfully, she says, "I wish I'd been in love more than once. I think you should fall in love at least twice in high school." Then she lets out a little sigh and falls asleep. Margot falls asleep like that—one dreamy sigh and she's off to never-never land, just like that.

I wake up in the middle of the night and Margot's not there. Kitty's curled up on her side next to me, but no Margot. It's pitch dark; only the moonlight filters through the curtains. I crawl out of bed and move to the window. My breath catches. There they are: Josh and Margot standing in the driveway. Margot's face is turned away from him, toward the moon. Josh is crying. They aren't touching. There's enough space between them for me to know that Margot hasn't changed her mind.

I drop the curtain and find my way back to the bed, where Kitty has rolled farther into the center. I push her back a few inches so there will be room for Margot. I wish I hadn't seen that. It was too personal. Too real. It was supposed to be just for them. If there was a way for me to unsee it, I would.

I turn on my side and close my eyes. What must it be like, to have a boy like you so much he cries for you? And not just any boy. Josh. Our Josh.

To answer her question: yes, I think I have been in real love. Just once, though. With Josh. Our Josh.

THIS IS HOW MARGOT AND JOSH GOT together. In a way I heard about it from Josh first.

It was two years ago. We were sitting in the library during our free. I was doing math homework; Josh was helping because he's good at math. We had our heads bent over my page, so close I could smell the soap he'd used that morning. Irish Spring.

And then he said, "I need your advice on something. I like someone."

For a split second I thought it was me. I thought he was going to say me. I hoped. It was the start of the school year. We'd hung out nearly every day that August, sometimes with Margot but mostly just by ourselves, because Margot had her internship at the Montpelier plantation three days a week. We swam a lot. I had a great tan from all the swimming. So for that split second I thought he was going to say my name.

But then I saw the way he blushed, the way he looked off into space, and I knew it wasn't for me.

Mentally, I ran through the list of girls it could be. It was a short list. Josh didn't hang out with a ton of girls; he had his best friend Jersey Mike, who had moved from New Jersey in middle school, and his other best friend, Ben, and that was it.

It could have been Ashley, a junior on the volleyball team. He'd once pointed her out as the cutest of all the junior girls. In Josh's defense, I'd made him do it: I asked him who was the prettiest girl in each grade. For prettiest freshman, my grade, he said Genevieve. Not that I was surprised, but it still gave me a little pinch in my heart.

It could have been Jodie, the college girl from the bookstore. Josh often talked about how smart Jodie was, how she was so cultured because she'd studied abroad in India and was now Buddhist. Ha! I was the one who was half-Korean; I was the one who'd taught Josh how to eat with chopsticks. He'd had kimchi for the first time at *my* house.

I was about to ask him who when the librarian came over to shush us, and then we went back to doing work and Josh didn't bring it up again and I didn't ask. Honestly, I didn't want to know. It wasn't me, and that was all I cared about.

I didn't think for one second that the girl he liked was Margot. Not that I didn't see her as a girl who could be liked. She'd been asked out before, by a certain type of guy. Smart guys who would partner up with her in chemistry and run against her for student government. In retrospect, it wasn't so surprising that Josh would like Margot, since he's that kind of guy too.

If someone were to ask me what Josh looks like, I would say he's just ordinary. He looks like the kind of guy you'd expect would be good at computers, the kind of guy who calls comic books graphic novels. Brown hair. Not a special brown, just regular brown. Green eyes that go muddy in the center. He's on the skinny side, but he's strong. I know because I sprained my ankle once by the old baseball field and he piggybacked me all the way home. He has freckles, which make him look younger than his age. And a dimple on his left check. I've always liked that dimple. He has such a serious face otherwise.

What was surprising, what was shocking, was that Margot would like him back. Not because of who Josh was, but because of who Margot was. I'd never heard her talk about liking a boy before, not even once. I was the flighty one, the flibbertigibbet, as my white grandma would say. Not Margot. Margot was above all that. She existed on some higher plane where those things—boys, makeup, clothes—didn't really matter.

The way it happened was sudden. Margot came home from school late that day in October; her cheeks were pink from the cold mountainy air and she had her hair in a braid and a scarf around her neck. She'd been working on a project at school, it was dinnertime, and I'd cooked chicken parmesan with thin spaghetti in watery tomato sauce.

She came into the kitchen and announced, "I have something to tell you." Her eyes were very bright; I remember she was unspooling the scarf from around her neck.

Kitty was doing her homework at the kitchen table, Daddy was on his way home, and I was stirring the watery sauce. "What?" Kitty and I asked.

"Josh likes me." Margot gave a pleased kind of shrug; her shoulders nearly went up to her ears.

I went very still. Then I dropped my wooden spoon into the sauce. "*Josh* Josh? Our Josh?" I couldn't even look at her. I was afraid that she would see.

"Yes. He waited for me after school today so he could tell me. He said—" Margot grinned ruefully. "He said I'm his dream girl. Can you believe that?"

"Wow," I said, and I tried to communicate happiness in that word, but I don't know if it came out that way. All I was feeling was despair. And envy. Envy so thick and so black I felt like I was choking on it. So I tried again, this time with a smile. "Wow, Margot."

"Wow," Kitty echoed. "So are you boyfriend and girl-friend now?"

I held my breath, waiting for her to answer.

Margot took a pinch of parmesan between her fingers and dropped it in her mouth. "Yeah, I think so." And then she smiled, and her eyes went all soft and liquid. I understood then that she liked him too. So much.

That night I wrote my letter to Josh.

Dear Josh . . .

I cried a lot. Just like that, it was over. It was over before I even had a chance. The important thing wasn't that Josh had chosen Margot. It was that Margot had chosen him.

So that was that. I cried my eyes out; I wrote my letter; I put the whole thing to rest. I haven't thought of him that way since. He and Margot are meant to be. They're MFEO. Made for each other.

I'm still awake when Margot comes back to bed, but I quickly shut my eyes and pretend to be asleep. Kitty's cuddled up next to me.

I hear a snuffly sound and I peek out of one eye to look at Margot. Her back is to us; her shoulders are shaking. She's crying.

Margot never cries.

Now that I've seen Margot cry over him, I believe it more than ever—they're not over.